Wilt in Triplicate

TOM SHARPE

Wilt in Triplicate

WILT

THE WILT ALTERNATIVE

WILT ON HIGH

Secker & Warburg
London

Wilt first published England 1976
The Wilt Alternative first published in England 1979
Wilt on High first published in England 1984

This collection first published in England 1996
by Martin Secker & Warburg Limited,
an imprint of Reed International Books Limited,
Michelin House, 81 Fulham Road, London SW3 6RB
and Auckland, Melbourne, Singapore and Toronto

A CIP catalogue record for this book
is available from the British Library

ISBN 0 436 20415 0

www.secker.com

Printed and bound in Great Britain
Clays Ltd, St. Ives PLC

Contents

Wilt

For Meat One

Chapter 1

Whenever Henry Wilt took the dog for a walk, or, to be more accurate, when the dog took him, or, to be exact, when Mrs Wilt told them both to go and take themselves out of the house so that she could do her yoga exercises, he always took the same route. In fact the dog followed the route and Wilt followed the dog. They went down past the Post Office, across the playground, under the railway bridge and out onto the footpath by the river. A mile along the river and then under the railway line again and back through streets where the houses were bigger than Wilt's semi and where there were large trees and gardens and the cars were all Rovers and Mercedes. It was here that Clem, a pedigree Labrador, evidently feeling more at home, did his business while Wilt stood looking around rather uneasily, conscious that this was not his sort of neighbourhood and wishing it was. It was about the only time during their walk that he was at all aware of his surroundings. For the rest of the way Wilt's walk was an interior one and followed an itinerary completely at variance with his own appearance and that of his route. It was in fact a journey of wishful thinking, a pilgrimage along trails of remote possibility involving the irrevocable disappearance of Mrs Wilt, the sudden acquisition of wealth, power, what he would do if he was appointed Minister of Education or, better still, Prime Minister. It was partly concocted of a series of desperate expedients and partly in an unspoken dialogue so that anyone noticing Wilt (and most people didn't) might have seen his lips move occasionally and his mouth curl into what he fondly imagined was a sardonic smile as he dealt with questions or parried arguments with devastating repartee. It was on one of these walks taken in the rain after a particularly trying day at the Tech that Wilt first conceived the notion that he would only be able to fulfil his latent promise and call his life his own if some not entirely fortuitous disaster overtook his wife.

Like everything else in Henry Wilt's life it was not a sudden

3

decision. He was not a decisive man. Ten years as an Assistant Lecturer (Grade Two) at the Fenland College of Arts and Technology was proof of that. For ten years he had remained in the Liberal Studies department teaching classes of Gasfitters, Plasterers, Bricklayers and Plumbers. Or keeping them quiet. And for ten long years he had spent his days going from classroom to classroom with two dozen copies of *Sons and Lovers* or Orwell's *Essays* or *Candide* or *The Lord of the Flies* and had done his damnedest to extend the sensibilities of Day-Release Apprentices with notable lack of success.

'Exposure to Culture,' Mr Morris, the Head of Liberal Studies, called it but from Wilt's point of view it looked more like his own exposure to barbarism, and certainly the experience had underminded the ideals and illusions which had sustained him in his younger days. So had twelve years of marriage to Eva.

If Gasfitters could go through life wholly impervious to the emotional significance of the interpersonal relationships portrayed in *Sons and Lovers*, and coarsely amused by D. H. Lawrence's profound insight into the sexual nature of existence, Eva Wilt was incapable of such detachment. She hurled herself into cultural activities and self-improvement with an enthusiasm that tormented Wilt. Worse still, her notion of culture varied from week to week, sometimes embracing Barbara Cartland and Anya Seton, sometimes Ouspensky, sometimes Kenneth Clark, but more often the instructor at the Pottery Class on Tuesdays or the lecturer on Transcendental Meditation on Thursdays, so that Wilt never knew what he was coming home to except a hastily cooked supper, some forcibly expressed opinions about his lack of ambition, and a half-baked intellectual eclecticism that left him disoriented.

To escape from the memory of Gasfitters as putative human beings and of Eva in the lotus position, Wilt walked by the river thinking dark thoughts, made darker still by the knowledge that for the fifth year running his application to be promoted to Senior Lecturer was almost certain to be turned down and that unless he did something soon he would be doomed to Gasfitters Three and Plasterers Two—and to Eva—for the rest of his life. It was not a prospect to be borne. He would act decisively. Above his head a train thundered by. Wilt stood

4

watching its dwindling lights and thought about accidents involving level crossings.

'He's in such a funny state these days,' said Eva Wilt, 'I don't know what to make of him.'

'I've given up trying with Patrick,' said Mavis Mottram studying Eva's vase critically. 'I think I'll put the lupin just a fraction of an inch to the left. Then it will help to emphasize the oratorical qualities of the rose. Now the iris over here. One must try to achieve an almost *audible* effect of contrasting colours. Contrapuntal, one might say.'

Eva nodded and sighed. 'He used to be so energetic,' she said, 'but now he just sits about the house watching telly. It's as much as I can do to get him to take the dog for a walk.'

'He probably misses the children,' said Mavis. 'I know Patrick does.'

'That's because he has some to miss,' said Eva Wilt bitterly. 'Henry can't even whip up the energy to have any.'

'I'm so sorry, Eva. I forgot,' said Mavis, adjusting the lupin so that it clashed more significantly with a geranium.

'There's no need to be sorry,' said Eva, who didn't number self-pity among her failings, 'I suppose I should be grateful. I mean, imagine having children like Henry. He's so uncreative, and besides children are so tiresome. They take up all one's creative energy.'

Mavis Mottram moved away to help someone else to achieve a contrapuntal effect, this time with nasturtiums and hollyhocks in a cerise bowl. Eva fiddled with her rose. Mavis was so lucky. She had Patrick, and Patrick Mottram was such an energetic man. Eva, in spite of her size, placed great emphasis on energy, energy and creativity, so that even quite sensible people who were not unduly impressionable found themselves exhausted after ten minutes in her company. In the lotus position at her yoga class she managed to exude energy, and her attempts at Transcendental Meditation had been likened to a pressure-cooker on simmer. And with creative energy there came enthusiasm, the febrile enthusiasms of the evidently unfulfilled woman for whom each new idea heralds the dawn of a new day and vice versa. Since the ideas she espoused were either trite or incomprehensible to her, her attachment to them was correspondingly brief and did nothing to fill the gap left in her life by Henry Wilt's lack of attainment. While he lived a violent life in his imagination, Eva, lacking any imagination at all, lived violently in fact. She threw herself into things, situations, new friends, groups and happenings with a reckless abandon that concealed the fact that she lacked the emotional stamina to stay for more than a moment. Now, as she backed away from her vase, she bumped into someone behind her.

'I beg your pardon,' she said and turned to find herself looking into a pair of dark eyes.

'No need to apologize,' said the woman in an American accent. She was slight and dressed with a simple scruffiness that was beyond Eva Wilt's moderate income.

'I'm Eva Wilt,' said Eva, who had once attended a class on Getting to Know People at the Oakrington Village College. 'My husband lectures at the Tech and we live at 34 Parkview Avenue.'

'Sally Pringsheim,' said the woman with a smile. 'We're in Rossiter Grove. We're over on a sabbatical. Gaskell's a biochemist.'

Eva Wilt accepted the distinctions and congratulated herself on her perspicacity about the blue jeans and the sweater. People who lived in Rossiter Grove were a cut above Parkview Avenue and husbands who were biochemists on sabbatical were also in the University. Eva Wilt's world was made up of such nuances.

'You know, I'm not all that sure I could live with an oratorical rose,' said Sally Pringsheim. 'Symphonies are OK in auditoriums but I can do without them in vases.'

Eva stared at her with a mixture of astonishment and admiration. To be openly critical of Mavis Mottram's flower arrangements was to utter blasphemy in Parkview Avenue. 'You know, I've always wanted to say that,' she said with a sudden surge of warmth, 'but I've never had the courage.'

Sally Pringsheim smiled. 'I think one should always say what one thinks. Truth is so essential in any really meaningful relationship. I always tell G baby exactly what I'm thinking.'

'Gee baby?' said Eva Wilt.

'Gaskell's my husband,' said Sally. 'Not that he's really a husband. It's just that we've got this open-ended arrangement

6

for living together. Sure, we're legal and all that, but I think it's important sexually to keep one's options open, don't you?'

By the time Eva got home her vocabulary had come to include several new words. She found Wilt in bed pretending to be asleep and woke him up and told him about Sally Pringsheim. Wilt turned over and tried to go back to sleep wishing to God she had stuck to contrapuntal flower arrangements. Sexually open-ended freewheeling options were the last thing he wanted just now, and, coming from the wife of a biochemist who could afford to live in Rossiter Grove, didn't augur well for the future. Eva Wilt was too easily influenced by wealth, intellectual status and new acquaintances to be allowed out with a woman who believed that clitoral stimulation oralwise was a concomitant part of a fully emancipated relationship and that unisex was here to stay. Wilt had enough troubles with his own virility without having Eva demand that her conjugal rights be supplemented oralwise. He spent a restless night thinking dark thoughts about accidental deaths involving fast trains, level crossings, their Ford Escort and Eva's seat belt, and got up early and made himself breakfast. He was just going off to a nine o'clock lecture to Motor Mechanics Three when Eva came downstairs with a dreamy look on her face.

'I've just remembered something I wanted to ask you last night,' she said. 'What does "transexual diversification" mean?'

'Writing poems about queers,' said Wilt hastily and went out to the car. He drove down Parkview Avenue and got stuck in a traffic jam at the roundabout. He sat and cursed silently. He was thirty-four and his talents were being dissipated on MM 3 and a woman who was clearly educationally subnormal. Worst of all, he had to recognize the truth of Eva's constant criticism that he wasn't a man. 'If you were a proper man,' she was always saying, 'you would show more initiative. You've got to assert yourself.'

Wilt asserted himself at the roundabout and got into an altercation with a man in a mini-bus. As usual, he came off second best.

'The problem with Wilt as I see it is that he lacks drive,' said the Head of English, himself a nerveless man with a tendency

7

to see and solve problems with a degree of equivocation that made good his natural lack of authority.

The Promotions Committee nodded its joint head for the fifth year running.

'He may lack drive but he *is* committed,' said Mr Morris, fighting his annual rearguard on Wilf's behalf.

'Committed?' said the Head of Catering with a snort. 'Committed to what? Abortion, Marxism or promiscuity? It's bound to be one of the three. I've yet to come across a Liberal Studies lecturer who wasn't a crank, a pervert or a red-hot revolutionary and a good many have been all three.'

'Hear, hear,' said the Head of Mechanical Engineering, on whose lathes a demented student had once turned out several pipe bombs.

Mr Morris bristled. 'I grant you that one or two lecturers have been . . . er . . . a little overzealous politically but I resent the imputation that . . .'

'Let's leave generalities aside and get back to Wilt,' said the Vice-Principal. 'You were saying that he is committed.'

'He needs encouragement,' said Mr Morris. 'Damn it, the man has been with us ten years and he's still only Grade Two.'

'That's precisely what I mean about his lacking drive,' said the Head of English. 'If he had been worth promoting he'd have been a Senior Lecturer by now.'

'I must say I agree,' said the Head of Geography. 'Any man who is content to spend ten years taking Gasfitters and Plumbers is clearly unfit to hold an administrative post.'

'Do we always have to promote solely for administrative reasons?' Mr Morris asked wearily. 'Wilt happens to be a good teacher.'

'If I may just make a point,' said Dr Mayfield, the Head of Sociology, 'at this moment in time it is vital we bear in mind that, in the light of the forthcoming introduction of the Joint Honours degree in Urban Studies and Medieval Poetry, provisional approval for which degree by the Council of National Academic Awards I am happy to announce at least in principle, that we maintain a viable staff position in regard to Senior Lectureships by allocating places for candidates with specialist knowledge in particular spheres of academic achievement rather than—'

8

'If I may just interrupt for a moment, in or out of time,' said Dr Board, Head of Modern Languages, 'are you saying we should save Senior Lectureships for highly qualified specialists who can't teach rather than promote Assistant Lecturers without doctorates who can?'

'If Dr Board had allowed me to continue,' said Dr Mayfield, 'he would have understood that I was saying . . .'

'I doubt it,' said Dr Board, 'quite apart from your syntax . . .'

And so for the fifth year running Wilt's promotion was forgotten. The Fenland College of Arts and Technology was expanding. New degree courses proliferated and more students with fewer qualifications poured in to be taught by more staff with higher qualifications until one day the Tech would cease to be a mere Tech and rise in status to become a Poly. It was the dream of every Head of Department and in the process Wilt's self-esteem and the hopes of Eva Wilt were ignored.

Wilt heard the news before lunch in the canteen.

'I'm sorry, Henry,' said Mr Morris as they lined up with their trays, 'it's this wretched economic squeeze. Even Modern Languages had to take a cut. They only got two promotions through.'

Wilt nodded. It was what he had come to expect. He was in the wrong department, in the wrong marriage and in the wrong life. He took his fish fingers across to a table in the corner and ate by himself. Around him other members of staff sat discussing A-level prospects and who was going to sit on the course board next term. They taught Maths or Economics or English, subjects that counted and where promotion was easy. Liberal Studies didn't count and promotion was out of the question. It was as simple as that. Wilt finished his lunch and went up to the reference library to look up Insulin in the Pharmacopoeia. He had an idea it was the one untraceable poison.

At five to two, none the wiser, he went down to Room 752 to extend the sensibilities of fifteen apprentice butchers, designated on the timetable as Meat One. As usual they were late and drunk.

'We've been drinking Bill's health,' they told him when they drifted in at ten past two.

'Really?' said Wilt, handing out copies of *The Lord of the Flies*. 'And how is he?'

'Bloody awful,' said a large youth with 'Stuff Off' painted across the back of his leather jacket. 'He's puking his guts out. It's his birthday and he had four vodkas and a Babycham . . .'

'We'd got to the part where Piggy is in the forest,' said Wilt, heading them off a discussion of what Bill had drunk for his birthday. He reached for a board duster and rubbed a drawing of a Dutch Cap off the blackboard.

'That's Mr Sedgwick's trademark,' said one of the butchers, 'he's always going on about contraceptives and things. He's got a thing about them.'

'A thing about them?' said Wilt loyally.

'You know, birth control. Well, he used to be a Catholic, didn't he? And now he's not, he's making up for lost time,' said a small pale-faced youth unwrapping a Mars Bar.

'Someone should tell him about the pill,' said another youth lifting his head somnolently from the desk. 'You can't feel a thing with a Frenchie. You get more thrill with the pill.'

'I suppose you do,' said Wilt, 'but I understood there were side-effects.'

'Depends which side you want it,' said a lad with sideburns.

Wilt turned back to *The Lord of the Flies* reluctantly. He had read the thing two hundred times already.

'Now Piggy goes into the forest . . .' he began, only to be stopped by another butcher, who evidently shared his distaste for the misfortunes of Piggy.

'You only get bad effects with the pill if you use ones that are high in oestrogen.'

'That's very interesting,' said Wilt. 'Oestrogen? You seem to know a lot about it.'

'Old girl down our street got a bloodclot in her leg . . .'

'Silly old clot,' said the Mars Bar.

'Listen,' said Wilt. 'Either we hear what Peter has to tell us about the effects of the pill or we get on and read about Piggy.'

'Fuck Piggy,' said the sideburns.

'Right,' said Wilt heartily, 'then keep quiet.'

'Well,' said Peter, 'this old girl, well she wasn't all that old, maybe thirty, she was on the pill and she got this bloodclot and the doctor told my auntie it was the oestrogen and she'd better take a different sort of pill just in case and the old girl down the street, her old man had to go and have a vasectomy so's she wouldn't have another bloodclot.'

'Buggered if anyone's going to get me to have a vasectomy,' said the Mars Bar, 'I want to know I'm all there.'

'We all have ambitions,' said Wilt.

'Nobody's going to hack away at my knackers with a bloody great knive,' said the sideburns.

'Nobody'd want to,' said someone else.

'What about the bloke whose missus you banged,' said the Mars Bar. 'I bet he wouldn't mind having a go.'

Wilt applied the sanction of Piggy again and got them back onto vasectomy.

'Anyway, it's not irreversible any more,' said Peter. 'They can put a tiny little gold tap in and you can turn it on when you want a nipper.'

'Go on! That's not true.'

'Well, not on the National Health you can't, but if you pay they can. I read about it in a magazine. They've been doing experiments in America.'

'What happens if the washer goes wrong?' asked the Mars Bar.

'I suppose they call a plumber in.'

Wilt sat and listened while Meat One ranged far and wide about vasectomy and the coil and Indians getting free transistors and the plane that landed at Audley End with a lot of illegal immigrants and what somebody's brother who was a policeman in Brixton said about blacks and how the Irish were just as bad and bombs and back to Catholics and birth control and who'd want to live in Ireland where you couldn't even buy French letters and so back to the Pill. And all the time his mind filled itself obsessively with ways and means of getting rid of Eva. A diet of birth-control pills high on oestrogen? If he ground them up and mixed them with the Ovaltine she took at bedtime there was a chance she'd develop bloodclots all over the place in no time at all. Wilt put the notion out of his head. Eva with bloodclots was too awful to stomach, and anyway it might not work. No, it would have to be something quick, certain and painless. Preferably an accident.

At the end of the hour Wilt collected the books and made his way back to the Staff Room. He had a free period. On the way he passed the site of the new Administration block. The ground had been cleared and the builders had moved in and were boring pile holes for the foundations. Wilt stopped and watched as the drilling machine wound slowly down into the ground. They were making wide holes. Very wide. Big enough for a body.

'How deep are you going?' he asked one of the workmen.

'Thirty feet.'

'Thirty feet?' said Wilt. 'When's the concrete going in?'

'Monday, with any luck,' said the man.

Wilt passed on. A new and quite horrible idea had just occurred to him.

Chapter 2

It was one of Eva Wilt's better days. She had days, better days, and one of those days. Days were just days when nothing went wrong and she got the washing-up done and the front room vacuumed and the windows washed and the beds made and the bath Vimmed and the lavatory pan Harpicked and went round to the Harmony Community Centre and helped with Xeroxing or sorted old clothes for the Jumble Sale and generally made herself useful and came home for lunch and went to the library and had tea with Mavis or Susan or Jean and talked about life and how seldom Henry made love to her even perfunctorily nowadays and how she had missed her opportunity by refusing a bank clerk who was a manager now and came home and made Henry's supper and went out to Yoga or Flower Arrangement or Meditation or Pottery and finally climbed into bed with the feeling that she had got something done.

On one of those days nothing went right. The activities were exactly the same but each episode was tainted with some minor disaster like the fuse blowing on the vacuum-cleaner or the drain in the sink getting blocked with a piece of carrot so that by the time Henry came home he was either greeted by silence or subjected to a quite unwarranted exposé of all his faults and shortcomings. On one of those days Wilt usually took the dog for an extended walk via the Ferry Path Inn and spent a restless night getting up and going to the bathroom, thus nullifying the cleansing qualities of the Harpic Eva had puffed round the pan and providing her with a good excuse to point out his faults once again in the morning.

'What the hell am I supposed to do?' he had asked after one of those nights. 'If I pull the chain you grumble because I've woken you up and if I don't you say it looks nasty in the morning.'

'Well, it does, and in any case you don't have to wash all the Harpic off the sides. And don't say you don't. I've seen you. You aim it all the way round so that it all gets taken off. You do it quite deliberately.'

'If I pulled the chain it would all get flushed off anyway and you'd get woken up into the bargain,' Wilt told her, conscious that he did make a habit of aiming at the Harpic. He had a grudge against the stuff.

'Why can't you just wait until the morning? And anyway it serves you right,' she continued, forestalling his obvious answer, 'for drinking all that beer. You're supposed to be taking Clem for a walk, not swilling ale in that horrid pub.'

'To pee or not to pee, that is the question,' said Wilt helping himself to All-Bran. 'What do you expect me to do? Tie a knot in the damned thing?'

'It wouldn't make any difference to me if you did,' said Eva bitterly.

'It would make a hell of a lot of difference to me, thank you very much.'

'I was talking about our sex life and you know it.'

'Oh, that,' said Wilt.

But that was on one of those days.

On one of her better days something unexpected happened to inject the daily round with a new meaning and to awake in her those dormant expectations that somehow everything would suddenly change for the better and stay that way. It was on such expectations that her faith in life was based. They were the spiritual equivalent of the trivial activities that kept her busy and Henry subdued. On one of her better days the sun shone brighter, the floor in the hall gleamed brighter and Eva Wilt was brighter herself and hummed 'Some day my prince will come' while Hoovering the stairs. On one of her better days Eva went forth to meet the world with a disarming goodheartedness and awoke in others the very same expectations that so thrilled her in herself. And on one of her better days Henry had to get his own supper and if he was wise kept out of the house as long as possible. Eva Wilt's expectations demanded something a sight more invigorating than Henry Wilt after a day at the Tech. It was on the evenings of such days that he came nearest to genuinely deciding to murder her and to hell with the consequences.

On this particular day she was on her way to the Community Centre when she ran into Sally Pringsheim. It was one of those

14

entirely fortuitous meetings that resulted from Eva making her way on foot instead of by bicycle and going through Rossiter Grove instead of straight down Parkview Avenue which was half a mile shorter. Sally was just driving out of the gate in a Mercedes with a P registration which meant it was brand new. Eva noted the fact and smiled accordingly.

'How funny me running into you like this,' she said brightly as Sally stopped the car and unlocked the door.

'Can I give you a lift? I'm going into town to look for something casual to wear tonight. Gaskell's got some Swedish professor coming over from Heidelberg and we're taking him to Ma Tante's.'

Eva Wilt climbed in happily, her mind computing the cost of the car and the house and the significance of wearing something casual at Ma Tante's (where she had heard that starters like Prawn Cocktails cost 95p) and the fact that Dr Pringsheim entertained Swedish professors when they came to Ipford.

'I was going to walk to town,' she lied. 'Henry's taken the car and it's such a lovely day.'

'Gaskell's bought a bicycle. He says it's quicker and it keeps him fit,' said Sally, thus condemning Henry Wilt to yet another misfortune. Eva made a note to see that he bought a bike at the police auction and cycled to work in rain or snow. 'I was thinking of trying Felicity Fashions for a shantung poncho. I don't know what they're like but I've been told they're good. Professor Grant's wife goes there and she says they have the best selection.'

'I'm sure they must have,' said Eva Wilt, whose patronage of Felicity Fashions had consisted of looking in the window and wondering who on earth could afford dresses at forty pounds. Now she knew. They drove into town and parked in the multi-storey car park. By that time Eva had stored a lot more information about the Pringsheims in her memory. They came from California. Sally had met Gaskell while hitch-hiking through Arizona. She had been to Kansas State but had dropped out to live on a commune. There had been other men in her life. Gaskell loathed cats. They gave him hay fever. Women's Lib meant more than burning your bra. It meant total commitment to the programme of women's superiority over men. Love was great if you didn't let it get to you. Compost was in and colour TV out. Gaskell's father had owned a chain of stores which

15

was sordid. Money was handy and Rossiter Grove was a bore. Above all, fucking had to be, just *had* to be fun whichever way you looked at it.

Eva Wilt received this information with a jolt. In her circle 'fuck' was a word husbands used when they hit their thumbs with hammers. When Eva used it she did so in the isolation of the bathroom and with a wistfulness that robbed it of its crudity and imbued it with a splendid virility so that a good fuck became the most distant and abstract of all her expectations and quite removed from Henry's occasional early morning fumblings. And if 'fuck' was reserved for the bathroom, fucking was even more remote. It suggested an almost continuous activity, a familiar occurrence that was both casual and satisfying and added a new dimension to life. Eva Wilt stumbled out of the car and followed Sally to Felicity Fashions in a state of shock.

If fucking was fun, shopping with Sally Pringsheim was a revelation. It was marked by a decisiveness that was truly breathtaking. Where Eva would have hummed and haaed, Sally selected and having selected moved on down the racks, discarded things she didn't like leaving them hanging over chairs, seized others, glanced at them and said she supposed they would do with a bored acceptance that was infectious, and left the shop with a pile of boxes containing two hundred pounds' worth of shantung ponchos, silk summer coats, scarves and blouses. Eva Wilt had spent seventy on a pair of yellow lounging pyjamas and a raincoat with lapels and a belt that Sally said was pure Gatsby.

'Now all you need is the hat and you'll be it,' she said as they loaded the boxes into the car. They bought the hat, a trilby, and then had coffee at the Mombasa Coffee House where Sally leant across the table intensely, smoking a long thin cigar, and talking about body contact in a loud voice so that Eva was conscious that the women at several nearby tables had stopped talking and were listening rather disapprovingly.

'Gaskell's nipples drive me wild,' Sally said. 'They drive him wild too when I suck them.'

Eva drank her coffee and wondered what Henry would do if she took it into her head to suck his nipples. Drive him wild was hardly the word and besides she was beginning to regret having spent seventy pounds. That would drive him wild too.

16

Henry didn't approve of credit cards. But she was enjoying herself too much to let the thought of his reaction spoil her day.

'I think teats are so important,' Sally went on. Two women at the next table paid their bill and walked out.

'I suppose they must be,' said Eva Wilt uneasily. 'I've never had much use for mine.'

'Haven't you?' said Sally. 'We'll have to do something about that.'

'I don't see that there is much anyone can do about it,' said Eva. 'Henry never even takes his pyjamas off and my nightie gets in the way.'

'Don't tell me you wear things in bed. Oh you poor thing. And nighties, God, how humiliating for you! I mean it's typical of a male-dominated society, all this costume differentiation. You must be suffering from touch deprivation. Gaskell says it's as bad as vitamin deficiency.'

'Well, Henry is always tired when he gets home,' Eva told her. 'And I go out a lot.'

'I'm not surprised,' said Sally, 'Gaskell says male fatigue is a symptom of penile insecurity. Is Henry's big or small?'

'Well it depends,' said Eva hoarsely. 'Sometimes it's big and sometimes it isn't.'

'I much prefer men with small ones,' said Sally, 'they try so much harder.'

They finished their coffee and went back to the car discussing Gaskell's penis and his theory that in a sexually undifferentiated society nipple stimulation would play an increasingly important role in developing the husband's sense of his hermaphroditic nature.

'He's written an article on it,' Sally said as they drove home. 'It's called "The Man As Mother." It was published in *Suck* last year.'

'Suck?' said Eva.

'Yes, it's a journal published by the Society for Undifferentiated Sexual Studies in Kansas. G's done a lot of work for them on animal behaviour. He did his thesis on Role Play in Rats there.'

'That sounds very interesting,' said Eva uncertainly. Roll or role? Whichever it was it was impressive and certainly Henry's occasional pieces on Day Release Apprentices and Literature in

17

the *Liberal Studies Quarterly* hardly measured up to Dr Pringsheim's monographs.

'Oh I don't know. It's all so obvious really. If you put two male rats together in a cage long enough one of them is simply bound to develop active tendencies and the other passive ones,' said Sally wearily. 'But Gaskell was absolutely furious. He thought they ought to alternate. That's G all over. I told him how silly he was being. I said, "G honey, rats are practically undifferentiated anyway. I mean how can you expect them to be able to make an existential choice?" and you know what he said? He said, "Pubic baby, rats are the paradigm. Just remember that and you won't go far wrong. Rats are the paradigm." What do you think of that?'

'I think rats are rather horrid,' said Eva without thinking. Sally laughed and put her hand on her knee.

'Oh Eva, darling,' she murmured, 'you're so adorably down to earth. No, I'm not taking you back to Parkview Avenue. You're coming home with me for a drink and lunch. I'm simply dying to see you in those lemon loungers.'

They turned into Rossiter Grove.

If rats were a paradigm for Dr Pringsheim, Printers Three were a paradigm for Henry Wilt, though of a rather different sort. They represented all that was most difficult, insensitive and downright bloodyminded about Day Release classes and to make matters worse the sods thought they were literate because they could actually read and Voltaire was an idiot because he made everything go wrong for Candide. Coming after Nursery Nurses and during his Stand-In period, Printers Three brought out the worst in him. They had obviously brought out the worst in Cecil Williams who should have been taking them.

'It's the second week he's been off sick,' they told Wilt.

'I'm not at all surprised,' said Wilt. 'You lot are enough to make anyone sick.'

'We had one bloke went and gassed himself. Pinkerton his name was. He took us for a term and made us read this book *Jude the Obscure*. That wasn't half a depressing book. All about this twit Jude.'

'I had an idea it was,' said Wilt.

'Next term old Pinky didn't come back. He went down by

18

the river and stuck a pipe up the exhaust and gassed himself.'

'I can't say I blame him,' said Wilt.

'Well I like that. He was supposed to set us an example.'

Wilt looked at the class grimly.

'I'm sure he had that in mind when he gassed himself,' he said. 'And now if you'll just get on and read quietly, eat quietly and smoke so that no one can see you from the Admin block, I've got work to do.'

'Work? You lot don't know what work is. All you do is sit at a desk all day and read. Call that work? Buggered if I do and they pay you to do it . . .'

'Shut up,' said Wilt with startling violence. 'Shut your stupid trap.'

'Who's going to make me?' said the Printer.

Wilt tried to control his temper and for once found it impossible. There was something incredibly arrogant about Printers Three.

'I am,' he shouted.

'You and who else? You couldn't make a mouse shut its trap, not if you tried all day.'

Wilt stood up. 'You fucking little shit,' he shouted. 'You dirty snivelling . . .'

'I must say, Henry, I'd have expected you to show more restraint,' said the Head of Liberal Studies an hour later when Wilt's nose had stopped bleeding and the Tech Sister had put a Band-Aid on his eyebrow.

'Well it wasn't my class and they got my goat by gloating about Pinkerton's suicide. If Williams hadn't been off sick it wouldn't have happened,' Wilt explained. 'He's always sick when he has to take Printers Three.'

Mr Morris shook his head dispiritedly. 'I don't care who they were. You simply can't go around assaulting students . . .'

'Assaulting students? I never touched . . .'

'All right, but you did use offensive language. Bob Fenwick was in the next classroom and he heard you call this Allison fellow a fucking little shit and an evil-minded moron. Now, is it any wonder he took a poke at you?'

'I suppose not,' said Wilt. 'I shouldn't have lost my temper. I'm sorry.'

'In that case we'll just forget it happened,' said Mr Morris. 'But just remember if I'm to get you a Senior Lectureship I can't have you blotting your copybook having punch-ups with students.'

'I didn't have a punch-up,' said Wilt, 'he punched me.'

'Well, let's just hope he doesn't go to the police and charge you with assault. That's the last sort of publicity we want.'

'Just take me off Printers Three,' said Wilt, 'I've had my fill of the brutes.'

He went down the corridor and collected his coat and brief-case from the Staff Room. His nose felt twice its normal size and his eyebrow hurt abominably. On his way out to the car park he passed several other members of staff but no one stopped to ask him what had happened. Henry Wilt passed unnoticed out of the Tech and got into his car. He shut the door and sat for several minutes watching the piledrivers at work on the new block. Up, down, up, down. Nails in a coffin. And one day, one inevitable day he would be in his coffin, still unnoticed, still an Assistant Lecturer (Grade Two) and quite forgotten by everyone except some lout in Printers Three who would always remember the day he had punched a Liberal Studies lecturer on the nose and got away with it. He'd probably boast about it to his grandchildren.

Wilt started the car and drove out onto the main road filled with loathing for Printers Three, the Tech, life in general and himself in particular. He understood now why terrorists were prepared to sacrifice themselves for the good of some cause. Given a bomb and a cause he would cheerfully have blown himself and any innocent bystanders to Kingdom Come just to prove for one glorious if brief moment that he was an effective force. But he had neither bomb nor cause. Instead he drove home recklessly and parked outside 34 Parkview Avenue. Then he unlocked the front door and went inside.

There was a strange smell in the hall. Some sort of perfume. Musky and sweet. He put his brief-case down and looked into the living-room. Eva was evidently out. He went into the kitchen and put the kettle on and felt his nose. He would have a good look at it in the bathroom mirror. He was halfway upstairs and conscious that there was a positively miasmic quality about the

20

perfume when he was brought to a halt. Eva Wilt stood in the bedroom doorway in a pair of astonishingly yellow pyjamas with enormously flared trousers. She looked quite hideous, and to make matters worse she was smoking a long thin cigarette in a long thin holder and her mouth was a brilliant red.

'Penis baby,' she murmured hoarsely and swayed. 'Come in here. I'm going to suck your nipples till you come me oral-wise.'

Wilt turned and fled downstairs. The bitch was drunk. It was one of her better days. Without waiting to turn the kettle off, Henry Wilt went out of the front door and got back into the car. He wasn't staying around to have her suck his nipples. He'd had all he could take for one day.

Chapter 3

Eva Wilt went downstairs and looked for penis baby half-heartedly. For one thing she didn't want to find him and for another she didn't feel like sucking his nipples and for a third she knew she shouldn't have spent seventy pounds on a raincoat and a pair of beach pyjamas she could have got for thirty at Blowdens. She didn't need them and she couldn't see herself walking down Parkview Avenue looking like The Great Gatsby. Besides, she felt a bit sick.

Still, he had left the kettle on so he must be somewhere. It wasn't like Henry to go out and leave the kettle on. She looked in the lounge. It had been the sitting-room until lunchtime when Sally called her sitting-room a lounge. She looked in the dining-room, now the diner, and even in the garden but Henry had vanished, taking with him the car and her hopes that nipple-sucking would bring new meaning to their marriage and put an end to her body contact deprivation. Finally she gave up the search and made herself a nice pot of tea and sat in the kitchen wondering what on earth had induced her to marry a male chauvinist pig like Henry Wilt who wouldn't have known a good fuck if he had been handed one on a plate and whose idea of a sophisticated evening was a boneless chicken curry at the New Delhi and a performance of *King Lear* at the Guildhall. Why couldn't she have married someone like Gaskell Pringsheim who entertained Swedish professors at Ma Tante and who understood the importance of clitoral stimulation as a necessary con-something-or-other of a truly satisfying interpersonal penetration? Other people still found her attractive. Patrick Mottram did and so did John Frost who taught her pottery, and Sally had said she was lovely. Eva sat staring into space, the space between the washing-up rack and the Kenwood mixer Henry had given her for Christmas, and thought about Sally and how she had looked at her so strangely when she was changing into her lemon loungers. Sally had stood in the doorway of the Pringsheims' bedroom, smoking a cigar and watching her

22

movements with a sensual calculation that had made Eva blush.

'Darling, you have such a lovely body,' she had said as Eva turned hurriedly and scrambled into the trousers to avoid revealing the hole in her panties. 'You mustn't let it go to waste.'

'Do you really think they suit me?'

But Sally had been staring at her breasts intently. 'Booby baby,' she murmured. Eva Wilt's breasts were prominent and Henry, in one of his many off moments, had once said something about the dugs of hell going dingalingaling for you but not for me. Sally was more appreciative, and had insisted that Eva remove her bra and burn it. They had gone down to the kitchen and had drunk Tequila and had put the bra on a dish with a sprig of holly on it and Sally had poured brandy over it and had set it alight. They had had to carry the dish out into the garden because it smelt so horrible and smoked so much and they had lain on the grass laughing as it smouldered. Looking back on the episode Eva regretted her action. It had been a good bra with double-stretch panels designed to give confidence where a woman needs it, as the TV adverts put it. Still, Sally had said she owed it to herself as a free woman and with two drinks inside her Eva was in no mood to argue.

'You've got to feel free,' Sally had said. 'Free to be. Free to be.'

'Free to be what?' said Eva.

'Yourself, darling,' Sally whispered, 'your secret self,' and had touched her tenderly where Eva Wilt, had she been sober and less elated, would staunchly have denied having a self. They had gone back into the house and had lunch, a mixture of more Tequila, salad and Ryvita and cottage cheese which Eva, whose appetite for food was almost as omnivorous as her enthusiasm for new experiences, found unsatisfying. She had hinted as much but Sally had poohpoohed the idea of three good meals a day.

'It's not good caloriewise to have a high starch intake,' she said, 'and besides it's not how much you put into yourself but what. Sex and food, honey, are much the same. A little a lot is better than a lot a little.' She had poured Eva another Tequila, insisted she take a bite of lemon before knocking it back and had helped her upstairs to the big bedroom with the big bed and the big mirror in the ceiling.

'It's time for TT,' she said adjusting the slats of the Venetian blinds.

'Tea tea,' Eva mumbled, 'but we've just had din din.'

'Touch Therapy, darling,' said Sally and pushed her gently back onto the bed. Eva Wilt stared up at her reflection in the mirror; a large woman, two large women in yellow pyjamas lying on a large bed, a large crimson bed; two large women without yellow pyjamas on a large crimson bed; four women naked on a large crimson bed.

'Oh Sally, no Sally.'

'Darling,' said Sally and silenced her protests oralwise. It had been a startlingly new experience though only partly remembered. Eva had fallen asleep before the Touch Therapy had got well under way and had woken an hour later to find Sally fully dressed standing by the bed with a cup of black coffee.

'Oh I do feel bad,' Eva said, referring as much to her moral condition as to her physical.

'Drink this and you'll feel better.'

Eva had drunk the coffee and got dressed while Sally explained that post-contact inhibitory depression was a perfectly natural reaction to Touch Therapy at first.

'You'll find it comes naturally after the first few sessions. You'll probably break down and cry and scream and then feel tremendously liberated and relieved.'

'Do you think so? I'm sure I don't know.'

Sally had driven her home. 'You and Henry must come to our barbecue Thursday night,' she said. 'I know G baby will want to meet you. You'll like him. He's a breast baby. He'll go crazy about you.'

'I tell you she was pissed,' said Wilt as he sat in the Braintrees' kitchen while Peter Braintree opened a bottle of beer for him. 'Pissed and wearing some Godawful yellow pyjamas and smoking a cigarette in a long bloody holder.'

'What did she say?'

'Well if you must know, she said, "Come here . . ." No, it's too much. I have a perfectly foul day at the Tech. Morris tells me I haven't got my senior lectureship. Williams is off sick again so I lose a free period. I get punched in the face by a great

24

lout in Printers Three and I come home to a drunk wife who calls me penis baby.'

'She called you what?' said Peter Braintree, staring at him.

'You heard me.'

'Eva called you penis baby? I don't believe it.'

'Well you go round there and see what she calls you,' said Wilt bitterly, 'and don't blame me if she sucks your nipples off oralwise while she's about it.'

'Good Lord. Is that what she threatened to do?'

'That and more,' said Wilt.

'It doesn't sound like Eva. It really doesn't.'

'It didn't fucking look like her either, come to that. She was all dolled up in yellow beach pyjamas. You should have seen the colour. It would have made a buttercup look drab. And she'd got some ghastly scarlet lipstick smeared round her mouth and she was smoking . . . She hasn't smoked for six years and then all this penis baby nipple-sucking stuff. And oralwise.'

Peter Braintree shook his head. 'That's a filthy word,' he said.

'It's a perfectly filthy act too, if you ask me,' said Wilt.

'Well, I must say it all sounds pretty peculiar,' said Braintree, 'God knows what I'd do if Susan came home and started insisting on sucking my teats.'

'Do what I did. Get out of the house,' said Wilt. 'And anyway it isn't just nipples either. Damn it, we've been married twelve long years. It's a bit late in the day to start arsing about oralwise. The thing is she's on this sexual liberation kick. She came home last night from Mavis Mottram's flower arrangement do jabbering about clitoral stimulation and open-ended freewheeling sexual options.'

'Freewheeling what?'

'Sexual options. Perhaps I've got it wrong. I know sexual options came into it somewhere. I was half asleep at the time.'

'Where the hell did she get all this from?' asked Braintree.

'Some bloody Yank called Sally Pringsheim,' said Wilt. 'You know what Eva's like. I mean she can smell intellectual claptrap a mile off and homes in on it like a bloody dung-beetle heading for an open sewer. You've no idea how many phoney "latest ideas" I've had to put up with. Well, most of them I can manage to live with. I just let her get on with it and go my

25

own quiet way, but when it comes to participating oralwise while she blathers on about Women's Lib, well you can count me out.'

'What I don't understand about Sexual Freedom and Women's Lib is why you have to go back to the nursery to be liberated,' said Braintree. 'There seems to be this loony idea that you have to be passionately in love all the time.'

'Apes,' said Wilt morosely.

'Apes? What about apes?'

'It's all this business about the animal model. If animals do it then humans must. Territorial Imperative and the Naked Ape. You stand everything on its head and instead of aspiring you retrogress a million years. Hitch your wagon to an orang-outang. The egalitarianism of the lowest common denominator.'

'I don't quite see what that has to do with sex,' said Braintree.

'Nor do I,' said Wilt. They went down to the Pig In A Poke and got drunk.

It was midnight before Wilt got home and Eva was asleep. Wilt climbed surreptitiously into bed and lay in the darkness thinking about high levels of oestrogen.

In Rossiter Grove the Pringsheims came back from Ma Tante's tired and bored.

'Swedes are the bottom,' said Sally as she undressed.

Gaskell sat down and took off his shoes. 'Ungstrom's all right. His wife has just left him for a low-temperature physicist at Cambridge. He's not usually so depressed.'

'You could have fooled me. And talking about wives, I've met the most unliberated woman you've ever set eyes on. Name of Eva Wilt. She's got boobs like cantaloupes.'

'Don't,' said Dr Pringsheim, 'if there's one thing I don't need right now it's unliberated wives with breasts.' He climbed into bed and took his glasses off.

'I had her round here today.'

'Had her?'

Sally smiled, 'Gaskell, honey, you've got a toadsome mind.'

Gaskell Pringsheim smiled myopically at himself in the mirror above. He was proud of his mind. 'I just know you, lover,' he said, 'I know your funny little habits. And while we're on the subject of habits what are all those boxes in the guest room?

26

You haven't been spending money again? You know our budget this month . . .'

Sally flounced into bed. 'Budget fudget,' she said, 'I'm sending them all back tomorrow.'

'All?'

'Well, not all, but most. I had to impress booby baby somehow.'

'You didn't have to buy half a shop just to . . .'

'Gaskell, honey, if you would just let me finish,' said Sally, 'she's a manic, a lovely, beautiful, obsessive compulsive manic. She can't sit still for half a minute without tidying and cleaning and polishing and washing up.'

'That's all we need, a manic compulsive woman around the house all the time. Who needs two?'

'Two? I'm not manic.'

'You're manic enough for me,' said Gaskell.

'But this one's got boobs, baby, boobs. Anyway I've invited them over on Thursday for the barbecue.'

'What the hell for?'

'Well, if you won't buy me a dishwasher like I've asked you a hundred times, I'm going out to get me one. A nice manic compulsive dishwasher with boobs on.'

'Jesus,' sighed Gaskell, 'are you a bitch.'

'Henry Wilt, you are a sod,' Eva said next morning. Wilt sat up in bed. He felt terrible. His nose was even more painful than the day before, his head ached and he had spent much of the night expunging the Harpic from the bowl in the bathroom. He was in no mood to be woken and told he was a sod. He looked at the clock. It was eight o'clock and he had Bricklayers Two at nine. He got out of bed and made for the bathroom.

'Did you hear what I said?' Eva demanded, getting out of bed herself.

'I heard,' said Wilt, and saw that she was naked. Eva Wilt naked at eight o'clock in the morning was almost as startling a sight as Eva Wilt drunk, smoking and dressed in lemon yellow pyjamas at six o'clock at night. And even less enticing. 'What the hell are you going about like that for?'

'If it comes to that, what's wrong with your nose? I suppose you got drunk and fell down. It looks all red and swollen.'

27

'It *is* all red and swollen. And if you must know I didn't fall down. Now for goodness sake get out of the way. I've got a lecture at nine.'

He pushed past her and went into the bathroom and looked at his nose. It looked awful. Eva followed him in. 'If you didn't fall on it what did happen?' she demanded.

Wilt squeezed foam from an aerosol and patted it gingerly on his chin.

'Well?' said Eva.

Wilt picked up his razor and put it under the hot tap. 'I had an accident,' he muttered.

'With a lamp-post, I suppose. I knew you'd been drinking.'

'With a Printer,' said Wilt indistinctly and started to shave.

'With a Printer?'

'To be precise, I got punched in the face by a particularly pugnacious apprentice printer.'

Eva stared at him in the mirror. 'You mean to say a student hit you in the classroom?'

Wilt nodded.

'I hope you hit him back.'

Wilt cut himself.

'No I bloody didn't,' he said, dabbing his chin with a finger. 'Now look what you've made me do.'

Eva ignored his complaint. 'Well you should have. You're not a man. You should have hit him back.'

Wilt put down the razor. 'And got the sack. Got hauled up in court for assaulting a student. Now that's what I call a brilliant idea.' He reached for the sponge and washed his face.

Eva retreated to the bedroom satisfied. There would be no mention of her lemon loungers now. She had taken his mind off her own little extravagance and given him a sense of grievance that would keep him occupied for the time being. By the time she had finished dressing, Wilt had eaten a bowl of All-Bran, drunk half a cup of coffee and was snarled up in a traffic jam at the roundabout. Eva went downstairs and had her own breakfast and began the daily round of washing up and Hoovering and cleaning the bath and . . .

'Commitment,' said Dr Mayfield, 'to an integrated approach is an essential element in . . .'

The Joint Committee for the Further Development of Liberal Studies was in session. Wilt squirmed in his chair and wished to hell it wasn't. Dr Mayfield's paper 'Cerebral Content and the Non-Academic Syllabus' held no interest for him, and besides, it was delivered in such convoluted sentences and with so much monotonous fervour that Wilt found it difficult to stay awake. He stared out of the window at the machines boring away on the site of the new Admin block. There was a reality about the work going on down there that was in marked contrast to the impractical theories Dr Mayfield was expounding. If the man really thought he could instil Cerebral Content, whatever that was, into Gasfitters Three he was out of his mind. Worse still, his blasted paper was bound to provoke an argument at question time. Wilt looked round the room. The various factions were all there, the New Left, the Left, the Old Left, the Indifferent Centre, the Cultural Right and the Reactionary Right.

Wilt classed himself with the Indifferents. In earlier years he had belonged to the Left politically and to the Right culturally. In other words he had banned the bomb, supported abortion and the abolition of private education and had been against capital punishment, thus earning himself something of a reputation as a radical while at the same time advocating a return to the craft of the wheelwright, the blacksmith and the handloom weaver which had done much to undermine the efforts of the Technical staff to instil in their students an appreciation of the opportunities provided by modern technology. Time and the intransigent coarseness of Plasterers had changed all that. Wilt's ideals had vanished, to be replaced by the conviction that the man who said the pen was mightier than the sword ought to have tried reading *The Mill on the Floss* to Motor Mechanics Three before he opened his big mouth. In Wilt's view, the sword had much to recommend it.

As Dr Mayfield droned on, as question time with its ideological arguments followed, Wilt studied the pile hole on the building site. It would make an ideal depository for a body and there would be something immensely satisfying in knowing that Eva, who in her lifetime had been so unbearable, was in death supporting the weight of a multi-storey concrete building. Besides it would make her discovery an extremely remote possibility and her identification out of the question. Not even

29

Eva, who boasted a strong constitution and a stronger will, could maintain an identity at the bottom of a pile shaft. The difficulty would be in getting her to go down the hole in the first place. Sleeping pills seemed a sensible preliminary but Eva was a sound sleeper and didn't believe in pills of any sort. 'I can't imagine why not,' Wilt thought grimly, 'she's prepared to believe in just about everything else.'

His reverie was interrupted by Mr Morris who was bringing the meeting to a close. 'Before you all go,' he said, 'there is one more subject I want to mention. We have been asked by the Head of Engineering to conduct a series of one-hour lectures to Sandwich-Course Trainee Firemen. The theme this year will be Problems of Contemporary Society. I have drawn up a list of topics and the lecturers who will give them.'

Mr Morris handed out subjects at random. Major Millfield got Media, Communications and Participatory Democracy about which he knew nothing and cared less. Peter Braintree was given The New Brutalism in Architecture, Its Origins and Social Attributes, and Wilt ended up with Violence and the Break-Up of Family Life. On the whole he thought he had done rather well. The subject fitted in with his present preoccupations. Mr Morris evidently agreed.

'I thought you might like to have a go at it after yesterday's little episode with Printers Three,' he said, as they went out. Wilt smiled wanly and went off to take Fitters and Turners Two. He gave them *Shane* to read and spent the hour jotting down notes for his lecture. In the distance he could hear the pile-boring machines grinding away. Wilt could imagine Eva lying at the bottom as they poured the concrete in. In her lemon pyjamas. It was a nice thought, and helped him with his notes. He wrote down a heading, Crime in the family, subheading (A) Murder of Spouse, decline in since divorce laws.

Yes, he should be able to talk about that to Trainee Firemen.

Chapter 4

'I loathe parties,' said Wilt on Thursday night, 'and if there's one thing worse than parties it's university parties and bottle parties are worst of all. You take along a bottle of decent burgundy and end up drinking someone else's rotgut.'

'It isn't a party,' said Eva, 'it's a barbecue.'

'It says here "Come and Touch and Come with Sally and Gaskell 9PM Thursday. Bring your own ambrosia or take pot luck with the Pringsheim punch." If ambrosia doesn't mean Algerian bilgewater I'd like to know what it does mean.'

'I thought it was that stuff people take to get a hard-on,' said Eva.

Wilt looked at her with disgust. 'You've picked up some choice phrases since you've met these bloody people. A hard-on. I don't know what's got into you.'

'You haven't. That's for sure,' said Eva, and went through to the bathroom. Wilt sat on the bed and looked at the card. The beastly thing was shaped like a . . . What the hell was it shaped like? Anyway it was pink and opened out and inside were all these ambiguous words. Come and Touch and Come. Anyone touched him and they'd get an earful. And what about pot luck? A lot of trendy dons smoking joints and talking about set-theoretic data-manipulation systems or the significance of pre-Popper Hegelianism in the contemporary dialectical scene, or something equally unintelligible, and using fuck and cunt every now and then to show that they were still human.

'And what do you do?' they would ask him.

'Well, actually I teach at the Tech.'

'At the Tech? How frightfully interesting,' looking over his shoulder towards more stimulating horizons, and he would end the evening with some ghastly woman who felt strongly that Techs fulfilled a real function and that intellectual achievement was vastly overrated and that people should be oriented in a way that would make them community coordinated and that's what Techs were doing, weren't they? Wilt knew what Techs were doing. Paying people like him £3500 a year to keep Gasfitters quiet for an hour.

And Pringsheim Punch. Planters Punch. Printers Punch. He'd had enough punches recently.

'What the hell am I to wear?' he asked.

'There's that Mexican shirt you bought on the Costa del Sol last year,' Eva called from the bathroom. 'You haven't had a chance to wear it since.'

'And I don't intend to now,' muttered Wilt, rummaging through a drawer in search of something nondescript that would demonstrate his independence. In the end he put on a striped shirt with blue jeans.

'You're surely not going like that?' Eva told him emerging from the bathroom largely naked. Her face was plastered with white powder and her lips were carmine.

'Jesus wept,' said Wilt, 'Mardi Gras with pernicious anaemia.'

Eva pushed past him. 'I'm going as The Great Gatsby,' she announced, 'and if you had any imagination you'd think of something better than a business shirt with blue jeans.'

'The Great Gatsby happened to be a man,' said Wilt.

'Bully for him,' said Eva, and put on her lemon loungers.

Wilt shut his eyes and took off his shirt. By the time they left the house he was wearing a red shirt with jeans while Eva, in spite of the hot night, insisted on putting on her new raincoat and trilby.

'We might as well walk,' said Wilt.

They took the car. Eva wasn't yet prepared to walk down Parkview Avenue in a trilby, a belted raincoat and lemon loungers. On the way they stopped at an off-licence where Wilt bought a bottle of Cyprus red.

'Don't think I'm going to touch the muck,' he said, 'and you had better take the car keys now. If it's as bad as I think it will be, I'm walking home early.'

It was. Worse. In his red shirt and blue jeans Wilt looked out of place.

'Darling Eva,' said Sally, when they finally found her talking to a man in a loincloth made out of a kitchen towel advertising Irish cheeses, 'you look great. The twenties suit you. And so

32

this is Henry.' Henry didn't feel Henry at all. 'In period costume too. Henry meet Raphael.'

The man in the loincloth studied Wilt's jeans. 'The fifties are back,' he said languidly, 'I suppose it was bound to happen.'

Wilt looked pointedly at a Connemara Cheddar and tried to smile.

'Help yourself, Henry,' said Sally, and took Eva off to meet the freest but the most liberated woman who was simply dying to meet booby baby. Wilt went into the garden and put his bottle on the table and looked for a corkscrew. There wasn't one. In the end he looked into a large bucket with a ladle in it. Half an orange and segments of bruised peach floated in a purple liquid. He poured himself a paper cup and tried it. As he had anticipated, it tasted like cider with wood alcohol and orange squash. Wilt looked round the garden. In one corner a man in a chef's hat and a jockstrap was cooking, was *burning* sausages over a charcoal grill. In another corner a dozen people were lying in a circle listening to the Watergate tapes. There was a sprinkling of couples talking earnestly and a number of individuals standing by themselves looking supercilious and remote. Wilt recognized himself among them and selected the least attractive girl on the theory that he might just as well jump in the deep end and get it over with. He'd end up with her anyway.

'Hi,' he said, conscious that already he was slipping into the Americanese that Eva had succumbed to. The girl looked at him blankly and moved away.

'Charming,' said Wilt, and finished his drink. Ten minutes and two drinks later he was discussing Rapid Reading with a small round man who seemed deeply interested in the subject.

In the kitchen Eva was cutting up French bread while Sally stood with a drink and talked about Lévi-Strauss with an Ethiopian who had just got back from New Guinea.

'I've always felt that L-S was all wrong on the woman's front,' she said, languidly studying Eva's rear, 'I mean he disregards the essential similarity . . .' She stopped and stared out of the window. 'Excuse me a moment,' she said, and went out to rescue Dr Scheimacher from the clutches of Henry Wilt.

'Ernst is such a sweetie,' she said, when she came back, 'you'd never guess he got the Nobel prize for spermatology.'

Wilt stood in the middle of the garden and finished his third drink. He poured himself a fourth and went to listen to the Watergate tapes. He got there in time to hear the end.

'You get a much clearer insight into Tricky Dick's character quadraphonically,' someone said as the group broke up.

'With the highly gifted child one has to develop a special relationship. Roger and I find that Tonio responds best to a constructional approach.'

'It's a load of bull. Take what he says about quasars for example . . .'

'I can't honestly see what's wrong with buggery . . .'

'I don't care what Marcuse thinks about tolerance. What I'm saying is . . .'

'At minus two-fifty nitrogen . . .'

'Bach does have his moments I suppose but he has his limitations . . .'

'We've got this place at St Trop . . .'

'I still think Kaldor had the answer . . .'

Wilt finished his fourth drink and went to look for Eva. He'd had enough. He was halted by a yell from the man in the chef's hat.

'Burgers up. Come and get it.'

Wilt staggered off and got it. Two sausages, a burnt beef-burger and a slosh of coleslaw on a paper plate. There didn't seem to be any knives or forks.

'Poor Henry's looking so forlorn,' said Sally, 'I'll go and transfuse him.'

She went out and took Wilt's arm.

'You're so lucky to have Eva. She's the babiest baby.'

'She's thirty-five,' said Wilt drunkenly, 'thirty-five if she's a day.'

'It's marvellous to meet a man who says what he means,' said Sally, and took a piece of beefburger from his plate. 'Gaskell just never says anything straightforwardly. I love down-to-earth people.' She sat down on the grass and pulled Wilt down with her. 'I think it's terribly important for two people to tell one another the truth,' she went on, breaking off another piece of beefburger and popping it into Wilt's mouth.

34

She licked her fingers slowly and looked at him with wide eyes. Wilt chewed the bit uneasily and finally swallowed it. It tasted like burnt mincemeat with a soupçon of Lancôme. Or a bouquet.

'Why two?' he asked, rinsing his mouth out with coleslaw.

'Why two what?'

'Why two people,' said Wilt. 'Why is it so important for two people to tell the truth?'

'Well, I mean . . .'

'Why not three? Or four? Or a hundred?'

'A hundred people can't have a relationship. Not an intimate one,' said Sally, 'not a meaningful one.'

'I don't know many twos who can either,' said Wilt. Sally dabbed her finger in his coleslaw.

'Oh but you do. You and Eva have this real thing going between you.'

'Not very often,' said Wilt. Sally laughed.

'Oh baby, you're a truth baby,' she said, and got up and fetched two more drinks. Wilt looked down into his paper cup doubtfully. He was getting very drunk.

'If I'm a truth baby, what sort of baby are you, baby?' he asked, endeavouring to instil the last baby with more than a soupçon of contempt. Sally snuggled up to him and whispered in his ear.

'I'm a body baby,' she said.

'I can see that,' said Wilt. 'You've got a very nice body.'

'That's the nicest thing anybody has ever said to me,' said Sally.

'In that case,' said Wilt, picking up a blackened sausage, 'you must have had a deprived childhood.'

'As a matter of fact I did,' Sally said and plucked the sausage from his fingers. 'That's why I need so much loving now.' She put most of the sausage in her mouth, drew it slowly out and nibbled the end. Wilt finished off the coleslaw and washed it down with Pringsheim Punch.

'Aren't they all awful?' said Sally, as shouts and laughter came from the corner of the garden by the grill.

Wilt looked up.

'As a matter of fact they are,' he said, 'who's the clown in the jockstrap?'

'That's Gaskell. He's so arrested. He loves playing at things.

35

In the States he just loves to ride footplate on a locomotive and he goes to rodeos and last Christmas he insisted on dressing up as Santa Claus and going down to Watts and giving out presents to the black kids at an orphanage. Of course they wouldn't let him.'

'If he went in a jockstrap I'm not in the least surprised,' said Wilt. Sally laughed.

'You must be an Aries,' she said, 'you don't mind what you say.' She got to her feet and pulled Wilt up. 'I'm going to show you his toy room. It's ever so droll.'

Wilt put his plate down and they went into the house. In the kitchen Eva was peeling oranges for a fruit salad and talking about circumcision rites with the Ethiopian, who was slicing bananas for her. In the lounge several couples were dancing back to back very vigorously to an LP of Beethoven's Fifth played at 78.

'Christ,' said Wilt, as Sally collected a bottle of Vodka from a cupboard. They went upstairs and down a passage to a small bedroom filled with toys. There was a model train set on the floor, a punchbag, an enormous Teddy Bear, a rocking horse, a fireman's helmet and a lifesize inflated doll that looked like a real woman.

'That's Judy,' said Sally, 'she's got a real cunt. Gaskell is a plastic freak.' Wilt winced. 'And here are Gaskell's toys. Puberty baby.'

Wilt looked round the room at the mess and shook his head. 'Looks as though he's making up for a lost childhood,' he said.

'Oh, Henry, you're so perceptive,' said Sally, and unscrewed the top of the Vodka bottle.

'I'm not. It's just bloody obvious.'

'Oh you are. You're just terribly modest, is all. Modest and shy and manly.' She swigged from the bottle and gave it to Wilt. He took a mouthful inadvisedly and had trouble swallowing it. Sally locked the door and sat down on the bed. She reached up a hand and pulled Wilt towards her.

'Screw me, Henry baby,' she said and lifted her skirt, 'fuck me, honey. Screw the pants off me.'

'That,' said Wilt, 'would be a bit difficult.'

'Oh. Why?'

36

'Well for one thing you don't appear to be wearing any and anyway why should I?'

'You want a reason? A reason for screwing?'

'Yes,' said Wilt. 'Yes I do.'

'Reason's treason. Feel free.' She pulled him down and kissed him. Wilt didn't feel at all free. 'Don't be shy, baby.'

'Shy?' said Wilt lurching to one side. 'Me shy?'

'Sure you're shy. OK, you're small. Eva told me . . .'

'Small? What do you mean I'm small?' shouted Wilt furiously.

Sally smiled up at him. 'It doesn't matter. It doesn't matter. Nothing matters. Just you and me and . . .'

'It bloody well does matter,' snarled Wilt. 'My wife said I was small. I'll soon show the silly bitch who's small. I'll show . . .'

'Show me, Henry baby, show me. I like them small. Prick me to the quick.'

'It's not true,' Wilt mumbled.

'Prove it, lover,' said Sally squirming against him.

'I won't,' said Wilt, and stood up.

Sally stopped squirming and looked at him. 'You're just afraid,' she said. 'You're afraid to be free.'

'Free? Free?' shouted Wilt, trying to open the door. 'Locked in a room with another man's wife is freedom? You've got to be joking.'

Sally pulled down her skirt and sat up.

'You won't?'

'No,' said Wilt.

'Are you a bondage baby? You can tell me. I'm used to bondage babies. Gaskell is real . . .'

'Certainly not,' said Wilt. 'I don't care what Gaskell is.'

'You want a blow job, is that it? You want for me to give you a blow job?' She got off the bed and came towards him. Wilt looked at her wildly.

'Don't you touch me,' he shouted, his mind alive with images of burning paint. 'I don't want anything from you.'

Sally stopped and stared at him. She wasn't smiling any more.

'Why not? Because you're small? Is that why?'

Wilt backed against the door.

'No, it isn't.'

'Because you haven't the courage of your instincts? Because you're a psychic virgin? Because you're not a man? Because you can't take a woman who thinks?'

'Thinks?' yelled Wilt, stung into action by the accusation that he wasn't a man. 'Thinks? You think? You know something? I'd rather have it off with that plastic mechanical doll than you. It's got more sex appeal in its little finger than you have in your whole rotten body. When I want a whore I'll buy one.'

'Why you little shit,' said Sally, and lunged at him. Wilt scuttled sideways and collided with the punchbag. The next moment he had stepped on a model engine and was hurtling across the room. As he slumped down the wall onto the floor Sally picked up the doll and leant over him.

In the kitchen Eva had finished the fruit salad and had made coffee. It was a lovely party. Mr Osewa had told her all about his job as underdevelopment officer in Cultural Affairs to UNESCO and how rewarding he found it. She had been kissed twice on the back of the neck by Dr Scheimacher in passing and the man in the Irish Cheese loincloth had pressed himself against her rather more firmly than was absolutely necessary to reach the tomato ketchup. And all around her terribly clever people were being so outspoken. It was all so sophisticated. She helped herself to another drink and looked around for Henry. He was nowhere to be seen.

'Have you seen Henry?' she asked when Sally came into the kitchen holding a bottle of Vodka and looking rather flushed.

'The last I saw of him he was sitting with some dolly bird,' said Sally, helping herself to a spoonful of fruit salad. 'Oh, Eva darling, you're absolutely Cordon Bleu baby.' Eva blushed.

'I do hope he's enjoying himself. Henry's not awfully good at parties.'

'Eva baby, be honest. Henry's not awfully good period.'

'It's just that he . . .' Eva began but Sally kissed her.

'You're far too good for him,' she said, 'we've got to find you someone really beautiful.' While Eva sipped her drink, Sally found a young man with a frond of hair falling across his forehead who was lying on a couch with a girl, smoking and staring at the ceiling.

'Christopher precious,' she said, 'I'm going to steal you for a moment. I want you to do someone for me. Go into the kitchen and sweeten the woman with the boobies and the awful yellow pyjamas.'

'Oh God. Why me?'

'My sweet, you know you're utterly irresistible. But the sexiest. For me, baby, for me.'

Christopher got off the couch and went into the kitchen and Sally stretched out beside the girl.

'Christopher is a dreamboy,' she said.

'He's a gigolo,' said the girl. 'A male prostitute.'

'Darling,' said Sally, 'it's about time we women had them.'

In the kitchen Eva stopped pouring coffee. She was feeling delightfully tipsy.

'You mustn't,' she said hastily.

'Why not?'

'I'm married.'

'I like it. I like it.'

'Yes but . . .'

'No buts, lover.'

'Oh.'

Upstairs in the toyroom Wilt, recovering slowly from the combined assaults on his system of Pringsheim punch, Vodka, his nymphomaniac hostess and the corner of the cupboard against which he had fallen, had the feeling that something was terribly wrong. It wasn't simply that the room was oscillating, that he had a lump on the back of his head or that he was naked. It was rather the sensation that something with all the less attractive qualities of a mousetrap, or a vice, or a starving clam, had attached itself implacably to what he had up till now always considered to be the most private of his parts. Wilt opened his eyes and found himself staring into a smiling if slightly swollen face. He shut his eyes again, hoped against hope, opened them again, found the face still there and made an effort to sit np.

It was an uuwise move. Judy, the plastic doll, inflated beyond her normal pressure, resisted. With a squawk Wilt fell back onto the floor. Judy followed. Her nose bounced on his face

39

and her breasts on his chest. With a curse Wilt rolled onto his side and considered the problem. Sitting up was out of the question. That way led to castration. He would have to try something else. He rolled the doll over further and climbed on top only to decide that his weight on it was increasing the pressure on what remained of his penis and that if he wanted to get gangrene that was the way to go about getting it. Wilt rolled off precipitately and groped for a valve. There must be one somewhere if he could only find it. But if there was a valve it was well hidden and by the feel of things he hadn't got time to waste finding it. He felt round on the floor for something to use as a dagger, something sharp, and finally broke off a piece of railway track and plunged it into his assailant's back. There was a squeak of plastic but Judy's swollen smile remained unchanged and her unwanted attentions as implacable as ever. Again and again he stabbed her but to no avail. Wilt dropped his makeshift dagger and considered other means. He was getting frantic, conscious of a new threat. It was no longer that he was the subject of her high airpressure. His own internal pressures were mounting. The Pringsheim Punch and the Vodka were making their presence felt. With a desperate thought that if he didn't get out of her soon he would burst, Wilt seized Judy's head, bent it sideways and sank his teeth into her neck. Or would have had her pounds per square inch permitted. Instead he bounced off and spent the next two minutes trying to find his false tooth which had been dislodged in the exchange.

By the time he had got it back in place, panic had set in. He had to get out of the doll. He just had to. There would be a razor in the bathroom or a pair of scissors. But where on earth was the bathroom? Never mind about that. He'd find the damned thing. Carefully, very carefully he rolled the doll onto her back and followed her over. Then he inched his knees up until he was straddling the thing. All he needed now was something to hold on to while he got to his feet. Wilt leant over and grasped the edge of a chair with one hand while lifting Judy's head off the floor with the other. A moment later he was on his feet. Holding the doll to him he shuffled towards the door and opened it. He peered out into the passage. What if someone saw him? To hell with that. Wilt no longer cared what people thought about him. But which way was the bathroom? Wilt

40

turned right, and peering frantically over Judy's shoulder, shuffled off down the passage.

Downstairs, Eva was having a wonderful time. First Christopher, then the man in the Irish Cheese loincloth and finally Dr Scheimacher, had all made advances to her and been rebuffed. It was such a change from Henry's lack of interest. It showed she was still attractive. Dr Scheimacher had said that she was an interesting example of latent steatopygia, Christopher tried to kiss her breasts and the man in the loincloth had made the most extraordinary suggestion to her. And through it all, Eva had remained entirely virtuous. Her massive skittishness, her insistence on dancing and, most effective of all, her habit of saying in a loud and not wholly cultivated voice, 'Oh, you are awful' at moments of their greatest ardour, had had a markedly deterrent effect. Now she sat on the floor in the living-room, while Sally and Gaskell and the bearded man from the Institute of Ecological Research argued about sexually interchangeable role-playing in a population-restrictive society. She felt strangely elated. Parkview Avenue and Mavis Mottram and her work at the Harmony Community Centre seemed to belong to another world. She had been accepted by people who flew to California or Tokyo to conferences and Think Tanks as casually as she took the bus to town. Dr Scheimacher had mentioned that he was flying to New Delhi in the morning, and Christopher had just come back from a photographic assignment in Trinidad. Above all, there was an aura of importance about what they were doing, a glamour that was wholly lacking in Henry's job at the Tech. If only she could get him to do something interesting and adventurous. But Henry was such a stick-in-the-mud. She had made a mistake in marrying him. She really had. All he was interested in was books, but life wasn't to be found in books. Like Sally said, life was for living. Life was people and experiences and fun. Henry would never see that.

In the bathroom Wilt could see very little. He certainly couldn't see any way of getting out of the doll. His attempt to slit the beastly thing's throat with a razor had failed, thanks largely to the fact that the razor in question was a Wilkinson bonded blade. Having failed with the razor he had tried shampoo as a lubricant but apart from working up a lather which even to his jaundiced eye looked as though he had aroused the doll to positively frenzied heights of sexual expectation the shampoo had achieved nothing. Finally he had reverted to a quest for the valve. The damned thing had one somewhere if only he could find it. In this endeavour he peered into the mirror on the door of the medicine cabinet but the mirror was too small. There was a large one over the washbasin. Wilt pulled down the lid of the toilet and climbed onto it. This way he would be able to get a clear view of the doll's back. He was just inching his way round when there were footsteps in the passage. Wilt stopped inching and stood rigid on the toilet lid. Someone tried the door and found it locked. The footsteps retreated and Wilt breathed a sigh of relief. Now then, just let him find that valve.

And at that moment disaster struck. Wilt's left foot stepped in the shampoo that had dripped onto the toilet seat, slid sideways off the edge and Wilt, the doll and the door of the medicine cabinet with which he had attempted to save himself were momentarily airborne. As they hurtled into the bath, as the shower curtain and fitting followed, as the contents of the medicine cabinet cascaded onto the washbasin, Wilt gave a last despairing scream. There was a pop reminiscent of champagne corks and Judy, finally responding to the pressure of Wilt's eleven stone dropping from several feet into the bath, ejected him. But Wilt no longer cared. He had in every sense passed out. He was only dimly aware of shouts in the corridor, of someone breaking the door down, of faces peering at him and of hysterical laughter. When he came to he was lying on the bed in the toy room. He got up and put on his clothes and crept downstairs and out of the front door. It was 3AM.

Chapter 5

Eva sat on the edge of the bed crying.

'How could he? How could he do a thing like that?' she said, 'in front of all these people.'

'Eva baby, men are like that. Believe me,' said Sally.

'But with a doll. . . .'

'That's symbolic of the male chauvinist pig attitude to women. We're just fuck artefacts to them. Objectification. So now you know how Henry feels about you.'

'It's horrible,' said Eva.

'Sure it's horrible. Male domination debases us to the level of objects.'

'But Henry's never done anything like that before,' Eva wailed.

'Well, he's done it now.'

'I'm not going back to him. I couldn't face it. I feel so ashamed.'

'Honey, you just forget about it. You don't have to go anywhere. Sally will look after you. You just lie down and get some sleep.'

Eva lay back, but sleep was impossible. The image of Henry lying naked in the bath on top of that horrible doll was fixed in her mind. They had had to break the door down and Dr Scheimacher had cut his hand on a broken bottle trying to get Henry out of the bath . . . Oh, it was all too awful. She would never be able to look people in the face again. The story was bound to get about and she would be known as the woman whose husband went around . . . With a fresh paroxysm of embarrassment Eva buried her head in the pillow and wept.

'Well that sure made the party go with a bang,' said Gaskell. 'Guy screws a doll in the bathroom and everyone goes berserk.' He looked round the living-room at the mess. 'If anyone thinks I'm going to start clearing this lot up now they'd better think again. I'm going to bed.'

'Just don't wake Eva up. She's hysterical,' said Sally.

'Oh great. Now we've got a manic obsessive compulsive woman with hysteria in the house.'

'And tomorrow she's coming with us on the boat.'

'She's what?'

'You heard me. She's coming with us on the boat.'

'Now wait a bit . . .'

'I'm not arguing with you, G. I'm telling you. She's coming with us.'

'Why, for Chrissake?'

'Because I'm not having her go back to that creep of a husband of hers. Because you won't get me a cleaning-woman and because I like her.'

'Because I won't get you a cleaning-woman. Now I've heard it all.'

'Oh no you haven't,' said Sally, 'you haven't heard the half of it. You may not know it but you married a liberated woman. No male pig is going to put one over on me . . .'

'I'm not trying to put one over on you,' said Gaskell. 'All I'm saying is that I don't want to have to . . .'

'I'm not talking about you. I'm talking about that creep Wilt. You think he got into that doll by himself? Think again, G baby, think again.'

Gaskell sat down on the sofa and stared at her.

'You must be out of your mind. What the hell did you want to do a thing like that for?'

'Because when I liberate someone I liberate them. No mistake.'

'Liberate someone by . . .' he shook his head. 'It doesn't make sense.'

Sally poured herself a drink. 'The trouble with you, G, is that you talk big but you don't do. It's yakkity yak with you. "My wife is a liberated woman. My wife's free." Nice-sounding talk but come the time your liberated wife takes it into her head to do something, you don't want to know.'

'Yeah, and when you take it into your goddam head to do something who takes the can back? I do. Where's petticoats then? Who got you out of that mess in Omaha? Who paid the fuzz in Houston that time . . .'

'So you did. So why did you marry me? Just why?'

Gaskell polished his glasses with the edge of the chef's hat. 'I don't know,' he said, 'so help me I don't know.'

'For kicks, baby, for kicks. Without me you'd have died of boredom. With me you get excitement. With me you get kicks.'

'In the teeth.'

Gaskell got up wearily and headed for the stairs. It was at times like these that he wondered what he had married.

Wilt walked home in agony. His pain was no longer physical. It was the agony of humiliation, hatred and self-contempt. He had been made to look a fool, a pervert and an idiot in front of people he despised. The Pringsheims and their set were everything he loathed, false, phoney, pretentious, a circus of intellectual clowns whose antics had not even the merit of his own, which had at least been real. Theirs were merely a parody of enjoyment. They laughed to hear themselves laughing and paraded a sensuality that had nothing to do with feelings or even instincts but was dredged up from shallow imaginations to mimic lust. *Copulo ergo sum.* And that bitch, Sally, had taunted him with not having the courage of his instincts as if instinct consisted of ejaculating into the chemically sterilized body of a woman he had first met twenty minutes before. And Wilt had reacted instinctively, shying away from a concupiscence that had to do with power and arrogance and an intolerable contempt for him which presupposed that what he was, what little he was, was a mere extension of his penis and that the ultimate expression of his thoughts, feelings, hopes and ambitions was to be attained between the legs of a trendy slut. And *that* was being liberated.

'Feel free,' she had said and had knotted him into that fucking doll. Wilt ground his teeth underneath a streetlamp.

And what about Eva? What sort of hell was she going to make for him now? If life had been intolerable with her before this, it was going to be unadulterated misery now. She wouldn't believe that he hadn't been screwing that doll, that he hadn't got into it of his own accord, that he had been put into it by Sally. Not in a month of Sundays. And even if by some miracle she accepted his story, a fat lot of difference that would make.

'What sort of man do you think you are, letting a woman do a thing like that to you?' she would ask. There was absolutely no reply to the question. What sort of man was he? Wilt had no idea. An insignificant little man to whom things happened and for whom life was a chapter of indignities. Printers punched him in the face and he was blamed for it. His wife bullied him and other people's wives made a laughing-stock out of him. Wilt wandered on along suburban streets past semi-detached houses and little gardens with a mounting sense of determination. He had had enough of being the butt of circumstance. From now on things would happen because he wanted them to. He would change from being the recipient of misfortune. He would be the instigator. Just let Eva try anything now. He would knock the bitch down.

Wilt stopped. It was all very well to talk. The bloody woman had a weapon she wouldn't hesitate to use. Knock her down, my eye. If anyone went down it would be Wilt, and in addition she would parade his affair with the doll to everyone they knew. It wouldn't be long before the story reached the Tech. In the darkness of Parkview Avenue Wilt shuddered at the thought. It would be the end of his career. He went through the gate of Number 34 and unlocked the front door with the feeling that unless he took some drastic action in the immediate future he was doomed.

In bed an hour later he was still awake, wide awake and wrestling with the problem of Eva, his own character and how to change it into something he could respect. And what did he respect? Under the blankets Wilt clenched his fist.

'Decisiveness,' he murmured. 'The ability to act without hesitation. Courage.' A strange litany of ancient virtues. But how to acquire them now? How had they turned men like him into Commandos and professional killers during the war? By training them. Wilt lay in the darkness and considered ways in which he could train himself to become what he was clearly not. By the time he fell asleep he had determined to attempt the impossible.

At seven the alarm went. Wilt got up and went into the bathroom and stared at himself in the mirror. He was a hard man, a man without feelings. Hard, methodical, cold-blooded and logical. A man who made no mistakes. He went downstairs and ate his All-Bran and drank his cup of coffee. So Eva wasn't

46

home. She had stayed the night at the Pringsheims. Well that was something. It made things easier for him. Except that she still had the car and the keys. He certainly wasn't going to go round and get the car. He walked down to the roundabout and caught the bus to the Tech. He had Bricklayers One in Room 456. When he arrived they were talking about gradbashing.

'There was this student all dressed up like a waiter see. "Do you mind?" he says, "Do you mind getting out of my way." Just like that and all I was doing was looking in the window at the books . . .'

'At the books?' said Wilt sceptically. 'At eleven o'clock at night you were looking at books? I don't believe it.'

'Magazines and cowboy books,' said the bricklayer. 'They're in a junk shop in Finch Street.'

'They've got girlie mags,' someone else explained. Wilt nodded. That sounded more like it.

'So I says "Mind what?" ' continued the bricklayer, 'and he says, "Mind out of my way." His way. Like he owned the bloody street.'

'So what did you say?' asked Wilt.

'Say? I didn't say anything. I wasn't wasting words on him.'

'What did you do then?'

'Well, I put the boot in and duffed him up. Gave him a good going-over and no mistake. Then I pushed off. There's one bloody grad who won't be telling people to get out of his way for a bit.'

The class nodded approvingly.

'They're all the bloody same, students,' said another bricklayer. 'Think because they've got money and go to college they can order you about. They could all do with a going-over. Do them a power of good.'

Wilt considered the implications of mugging as part of an intellectual's education. After his experience the previous night he was inclined to think there was something to be said for it. He would have liked to have duffed up half the people at the Pringsheims' party.

'So none of you feel there's anything wrong with beating a student up if he gets in your way?' he asked.

'Wrong?' said the bricklayers in unison. 'What's wrong with

47

a good punch-up? It's not as if a grad is an old woman or something. He can always hit back, can't he?'

They spent the rest of the hour discussing violence in the modern world. On the whole, the bricklayers seemed to think it was a good thing.

'I mean what's the point of going out on a Saturday night and getting pissed if you can't have a bit of a barney at the same time? Got to get rid of your aggression somehow,' said an unusually articulate bricklayer, 'I mean it's natural isn't it?'

'So you think man is a naturally aggressive animal,' said Wilt.

'Course he is. That's history for you, all them wars and things. It's only bloody poofters don't like violence.'

Wilt took this view of things along to the Staff Room for his free period and collected a cup of coffee from the vending machine. He was joined by Peter Braintree.

'How did the party go?' Braintree asked.

'It didn't,' said Wilt morosely.

'Eva enjoy it?'

'I wouldn't know. She hadn't come home by the time I got up this morning.'

'Hadn't come home?'

'That's what I said,' said Wilt.

'Well did you ring up and find out what had happened to her?'

'No,' said Wilt.

'Why not?'

'Because I'd look a bit of a twit ringing up and being told she was shacked up with the Abyssinian ambassador, wouldn't I?'

'The Abyssinian ambassador? Was he there?'

'I don't know and I don't want to know. The last I saw of her she was being chatted up by this big black bloke from Ethiopia. Something to do with the United Nations. She was making fruit salad and he was chopping bananas for her.'

'Doesn't sound a very compromising sort of activity to me,' said Braintree.

'No, I daresay it doesn't. Only you weren't there and don't know what sort of party it was,' said Wilt rapidly coming to the conclusion that an edited version of the night's events was called for. 'A whole lot of middle-aged with-it kids doing their withered thing.'

'It sounds bloody awful. And you think Eva . . .'

'I think Eva got pissed and somebody gave her a joint and she passed out,' said Wilt, 'that's what I think. She's probably sleeping it off in the downstairs loo.'

'Doesn't sound like Eva to me,' said Braintree. Wilt drank his coffee and considered his strategy. If the story of his involvement with that fucking doll was going to come out, perhaps it would be better if he told it his way first. On the other hand . . .

'What were you doing while all this was going on?' Braintree asked.

'Well,' said Wilt, 'as a matter of fact . . .' He hesitated. On second thoughts it might be better not to mention the doll at all. If Eva kept her trap shut . . . 'I got a bit slewed myself.'

'That sounds more like it,' said Braintree, 'I suppose you made a pass at another woman too.'

'If you must know,' said Wilt, 'another woman made a pass at me. Mrs Pringsheim.'

'Mrs Pringsheim made a pass at you?'

'Well, we went upstairs to look at her husband's toys. . . .'

'His toys? I thought you told me he was a biochemist.'

'He is a biochemist. He just happens to like playing with toys. Model trains and Teddy Bears and things. She says he's a case of arrested development. She would, though. She's that sort of loyal wife.'

'What happened then?'

'Apart from her locking the door and lying on the bed with her legs wide open and asking me to screw her and threatening me with a blow job, nothing happened,' said Wilt.

Peter Braintree looked at him sceptically. 'Nothing?' he said finally. 'Nothing? I mean what did you do?'

'Equivocated,' said Wilt.

'That's a new word for it,' said Braintree. 'You go upstairs with Mrs Pringsheim and equivocate while she lies on a bed with her legs open and you want to know why Eva hasn't come home? She's probably round at some lawyer's office filing a petition for divorce right now.'

'But I tell you I didn't screw the bitch,' said Wilt, 'I told her to hawk her pearly somewhere else.'

'And you call that equivocating? Hawk her pearly? Where the hell did you get that expression from?'

'Meat One,' said Wilt and got up and fetched himself another cup of coffee.

By the time he came back to his seat he had decided on his version.

'I don't know what happened after that,' he said when Braintree insisted on hearing the next episode. 'I passed out. It must have been the vodka.'

'You just passed out in a locked room with a naked woman? Is that what happened?' said Braintree. He didn't sound as if he believed a word of the story.

'Precisely,' said Wilt.

'And when you came to?'

'I was walking home,' said Wilt. 'I've no idea what happened in between.'

'Oh well, I daresay we'll hear about that from Eva,' said Braintree. 'She's bound to know.'

He got up and went off and Wilt was left alone to consider his next move. The first thing to do was to make sure that Eva didn't say anything. He went through to the telephone in the corridor and dialled his home number. There was no reply. Wilt went along to Room 187 and spent an hour with Turners and Fitters. Several times during the day he tried to telephone Eva but there was no answer.

'She's probably spent the day round at Mavis Mottram's weeping on her shoulder and telling all and sundry what a pig I am,' he thought. 'She's bound to be waiting for me when I get home tonight.'

But she wasn't. Instead there was a note on the kitchen table and a package. Wilt opened the note.

'I'm going away with Sally and Gaskell to think things over. What you did last night was horrible. I won't ever forgive you. Don't forget to buy some dogfood. Eva. P.S. Sally says next time you want a blow job get Judy to give you one.'

Wilt looked at the package. He knew without opening it what it contained. That infernal doll. In a sudden paroxysm of rage Wilt picked it up and hurled it across the kitchen at the sink. Two plates and a saucer bounced off the washing-up rack and broke on the floor.

50

'Bugger the bitch,' said Wilt inclusively, Eva, Judy and Sally Pringsheim all coming within the ambit of his fury. Then he sat down at the table and looked at the note again. 'Going away to think things over.' Like hell she was. Think? The stupid cow wasn't capable of thought. She'd emote, drool over his deficiencies and work herself into an ecstasy of self-pity. Wilt could hear her now blathering on about that blasted bank manager and how she should have married him instead of saddling herself with a man who couldn't even get promotion at the Tech and who went around fucking inflatable dolls in other people's bathrooms. And there was that filthy slut, Sally Pringsheim, egging her on. Wilt looked at the postscript. 'Sally says next time you want a blow job . . .' Christ. As if he'd wanted a blow job the last time. But there it was, a new myth in the making, like the business of his being in love with Betty Crabtree when all he had done was give her a lift home one night after an Evening Class. Wilt's home life was punctuated by such myths, weapons in Eva's armoury to be brought out when the occasion demanded and brandished above his head. And now Eva had the ultimate deterrent at her disposal, the doll and Sally Pringsheim and a blow job. The balance of recrimination which had been the sustaining factor in their relationship had shifted dramatically. It would take an act of desperate invention on Wilt's part to restore it.

'Don't forget to buy some dogfood.' Well at least she had left him the car. It was standing in the carport. Wilt went out and drove round to the supermarket and bought three tins of dogfood, a boil-in-the-bag curry and a bottle of gin. He was going to get pissed. Then he went home and sat in the kitchen watching Clem gulp his Bonzo while the bag boiled. He poured himself a stiff gin, topped it up with lime and wandered about. And all the time he was conscious of the package lying there on the draining board waiting for him to open it. And inevitably he would open it. Out of sheer curiosity. He knew it and they knew it wherever they were, and on Sunday night Eva would come home and the first thing she would do would be to ask about the doll and if he had had a nice time with it. Wilt helped himself to some more gin and considered the doll's utility. There must be some way of using the thing to turn the tables on Eva.

By the time he had finished his second gin he had begun to formulate a plan. It involved the doll, a pile hole and a nice test of his own strength of character. It was one thing to have fantasies about murdering your wife. It was quite another to put them into effect and between the two there lay an area of uncertainty. By the end of his third gin Wilt was determined to put the plan into effect. If it did nothing else it would prove he was capable of executing a murder.

Wilt got up and unwrapped the doll. In his interior dialogue Eva was telling him what would happen if Mavis Mottram got to hear about his disgusting behaviour at the Pringsheim's. 'You'd be the laughing stock of the neighbourhood,' she said, 'you'd never live it down.'

Wouldn't he though? Wilt smiled drunkenly to himself and went upstairs. For once Eva was mistaken. He might not live it down but Mrs Eva Wilt wouldn't be around to gloat. She wouldn't live at all.

Upstairs in the bedroom he closed the curtains and laid the doll on the bed and looked for the valve which had eluded him the previous night. He found it and fetched a footpump from the garage. Five minutes later Judy was in good shape. She lay on the bed and smiled up at him. Wilt half closed his eyes and squinted at her. In the half darkness he had to admit that she was hideously lifelike. Plastic Eva with the mastic boobs. All that remained was to dress it up. He rummaged around in several drawers in search of a bra and blouse, decided she didn't need a bra, and picked out an old skirt and a pair of tights. In a cardboard box in the wardrobe he found one of Eva's wigs. She had had a phase of wigs. Finally a pair of shoes. By the time he had finished, Eva Wilt's replica lay on the bed smiling fixedly at the ceiling.

'That's my girl,' said Wilt and went down to the kitchen to see how the boil-in-the-bag was coming along. It was burnt-in-the-bag. Wilt turned the stove off and went into the lavatory under the stairs and sat thinking about his next move. He would use the doll for dummy runs so that if and when it came to the day he would be accustomed to the whole process of murder and would act without feeling like an automaton. Killing by conditioned reflex. Murder by habit. Then again he would know how to time the whole affair. And Eva's going off with the

Pringsheims for the weekend would help too. It would establish a pattern of sudden disappearances. He would provoke her somehow to do it again and again and again. And then the visit to the doctor.

'It's just that I can't sleep, doctor. My wife keeps on going off and leaving me and I just can't get used to sleeping on my own.' A prescription for sleeping tablets. Then on the night. 'I'll make the Ovaltine tonight, dear. You're looking tired. I'll bring it up to you in bed.' Gratitude followed by snores. Down to the car . . . fairly early would be best . . . around ten thirty . . . over to the Tech and down the hole. Perhaps inside a plastic bag . . . no, not a plastic bag. 'I understand you bought a large plastic bag recently, sir. I wonder if you would mind showing it to us.' No, better just to leave her down the hole they were going to fill with concrete next morning. And finally a bewildered Wilt. He would go round to the Pringsheims'. 'Where's Eva? Yes, you do.' 'No, we don't.' 'Don't lie to me. She's always coming round here.' 'We're not lying. We haven't seen her.' After that he would go to the police.

Motiveless, clueless and indiscoverable. And proof that he was a man who could act. Or wasn't. What if he broke down under the strain and confessed? That would be some sort of vindication too. He would know what sort of man he was one way or another and at least he would have acted for once in his life. And fifteen years in prison would be almost identical to fifteen, more, twenty years at the Tech confronting louts who despised him and talking about Piggy and the Lord of the Flies. Besides he could always plead the book as a mitigating circumstance at his trial.

'Me lud, members of the Jury, I ask you to put yourself in the defendant's place. For twelve years he has been confronted by the appalling prospect of reading this dreadful book to classes of bored and hostile youths. He has had to endure agonies of repetition, of nausea and disgust at Mr Golding's revoltingly romantic view of human nature. Ah, but I hear you say that Mr Golding is not a romantic, that his view of human nature as expressed in his portrait of a group of young boys marooned on a desert island is the very opposite of romanticism and that the sentimentality of which I accuse him and to which my client's appearance in this court attests is to be found not in

The Lord of the Flies but in its predecessor, *Coral Island*. But me lud, gentlemen of the Jury, there is such a thing as inverted romanticism, the romanticism of disillusionment, of pessimism and of nihilism. Let us suppose for one moment that my client had spent twelve years reading not Mr Golding's work but *Coral Island* to groups of apprentices; is it reasonable to imagine that he would have been driven to the desperate remedy of murdering his wife? No. A hundred times no. Mr Ballantyne's book would have given him the inspiration, the self-discipline, the optimism and the belief in man's ability to rescue himself from the most desperate situation by his own ingenuity . . .'

It might not be such a good idea to pursue that line of argument too far. The defendant Wilt had after all exercised a good deal of ingenuity in rescuing himself from a desperate situation. Still, it was a nice thought. Wilt finished his business in the lavatory and looked around for the toilet paper. There wasn't any. The bloody roll had run out. He reached in his pocket and found Eva's note and put it to good use. Then he flushed it down the U-bend, puffed some Harpic after it to express his opinion of it and her and went out to the kitchen and helped himself to another gin.

He spent the rest of the evening sitting in front of the TV with a piece of bread and cheese and a tin of peaches until it was time to try his first dummy run. He went out to the front door and looked up and down the street. It was almost dark now and there was no one in sight. Leaving the front door open he went upstairs and fetched the doll and put it in the back seat of the car. He had to push and squeeze a bit to get it in but finally the door shut. Wilt climbed in and backed the car out into Parkview Avenue and drove down to the roundabout. By the time he reached the car park at the back of the Tech it was half past ten exactly. He stopped and sat in the car looking around. Not a soul in sight and no lights on. There wouldn't be. The Tech closed at nine.

Chapter 6

Sally lay naked on the deck of the cabin cruiser, her tight breasts pointing to the sky and her legs apart. Beside her Eva lay on her stomach and looked downriver.

'Oh God, this is divine,' Sally murmured, 'I have this deep thing about the countryside.'

'You've got this deep thing period,' said Gaskell steering the cruiser erratically towards a lock. He was wearing a Captain's cap and sunglasses.

'Cliché baby,' said Sally.

'We're coming to a lock,' said Eva anxiously. 'There are some men there.'

'Men? Forget men, darling. There's just you and me and G and G's not a man, are you G baby?'

'I have my moments,' said Gaskell.

'But so seldom, so awfully seldom,' Sally said. 'Anyway what does it matter? We're here idyllicstyle, cruising down the river in the good old summertime.'

'Shouldn't we have cleared the house up before we left?' Eva asked.

'The secret of parties is not to clear up afterward but to clear off. We can do all that when we get back.'

Eva got up and went below. They were quite near the lock and she wasn't going to be stared at in the nude by the two old men sitting on the bench beside it.

'Jesus, Sally, can't you do something about soulmate? She's getting on my teats,' said Gaskell.

'Oh G baby, she's never. If she did you'd Cheshire cat.'

'Cheshire cat?'

'Disappear with a smile, honey chil', foetus first. She's but positively gargantuanly uterine.'

'She's but positively gargantuanly boring.'

'Time, lover, time. You've got to accentuate the liberated, eliminate the negative and not mess with Mister-in-between.'

'Not mess with Missus-in-between. Operative word missus,' said Gaskell bumping the boat into the lock.

'But that's the whole point.'

'What is?' said Gaskell.

'Messing with Missus-in-between. I mean it's all ways with Eva and us. She does the housework. Gaskell baby can play ship's captain and teatfeast on boobs and Sally sweetie can minotaur her labyrinthine mind.'

'Mind?' said Gaskell. 'Polyunsaturated hasn't got a mind. And talking of cretins, what about Mister-in-between?'

'He's got Judy to mess with. He's probably screwing her now and tomorrow night he'll sit up and watch *Kojak* with her. Who knows, he may even send her off to Mavis Contracuntal Mottram's Flower Arrangement evening. I mean they're suited. You can't say he wasn't hooked on her last night.'

'You can say that again,' said Gaskell and closed the lock gates.

As the cruiser floated downwards the two old men sitting on the bench stared at Sally. She took off her sunglasses and glared at them.

'Don't blow your prostates, senior citizens,' she said rudely. 'Haven't you seen a fanny before?'

'You talking to me?' said one of the men.

'I wouldn't be talking to myself.'

'Then I'll tell you,' said the man, 'I've seen one like yours before. Once.'

'Once is about right,' said Sally. 'Where?'

'On an old cow as had just dropped her calf,' said the man and spat into a neat bed of geraniums.

In the cabin Eva sat and wondered what they were talking about. She listened to the lapping of the water and the throb of the engine and thought about Henry. It wasn't like him to do a thing like that. It really wasn't. And in front of all those people. He must have been drunk. It was so humiliating. Well, he could suffer. Sally said men ought to be made to suffer. It was part of the process of liberating yourself from them. You had to show them that you didn't need them and violence was the only thing the male psyche understood. That was why she was so harsh with Gaskell. Men were like animals. You had to show them who was master.

56

Eva went through to the galley and polished the stainless-steel sink. Henry would have to learn how important she was by missing her and doing the housework and cooking for himself and when she got back she would give him such a telling-off about that doll. I mean, it wasn't natural. Perhaps Henry ought to go and see a psychiatrist. Sally said that he had made the most horrible suggestion to her too. It only went to show that you couldn't trust anyone. And Henry of all people. She would never have imagined Henry would think of doing anything like that. But Sally had been so sweet and understanding. She knew how women felt and she hadn't even been angry with Henry.

'It's just that he's a sphincter baby,' she had said, 'it's symptomatic of a male-dominated chauvinist pig society. I've never known an MCP who didn't say "Bugger you" and mean it.'

'Henry's always saying "Bugger",' Eva had admitted. 'It's bugger this, and bugger that.'

'There you are, Eva baby. What did I tell you? It's semantic degradation analwise.'

'It's bloody disgusting,' said Eva, and so it was.

She went on polishing and cleaning until they were clear of the lock and steering downriver towards the open water of the Broads. Then she went up on deck and sat looking out over the flat empty landscape at the sunset. It was all so romantic and exciting, so different from everything she had known before. This was life as she had always dreamt it might be, rich and gay and fulfilling. Eva Wilt sighed. In spite of everything she was at peace with the world.

In the car park at the back of the Tech Henry Wilt wasn't at peace with anything. On the contrary, he was at war with Eva's replica. As he stumbled drunkenly round the car and struggled with Judy he was conscious that even an inflatable doll had a will of its own when it came to being dragged out of small cars. Judy's arms and legs got caught in things. If Eva behaved in the same way on the night of her disposal he would have the devil's own job getting her out of the car. He would have to tie her up in a neat bundle. That would be the best thing to do. Finally, by tugging at the doll's legs, he hauled her out and laid her on the ground. Then he got back into the car to look for her wig. He found it under the seat and after rearranging Judy's skirt so that it wasn't quite so revealing, he put the wig on her head. He looked round the car park at the terrapin huts and the main building but there was no one to be seen. All clear. He picked the doll up and carrying it under his arm set off towards the building site. Halfway there he realized that he wasn't doing it properly. Eva drugged and sleeping would be far too heavy to carry under his arm. He would have to use a fireman's lift. Wilt stopped and hoisted the doll onto his back, and set off again weaving erratically, partly because, thanks to the gin, he couldn't help it, and partly because it added verisimilitude to the undertaking. With Eva over his shoulder he would be bound to weave a bit. He reached the fence and dropped the doll over. In the process the wig fell off again. Wilt groped around in the mud and found it. Then he went round to the gate. It was locked. It would be. He would have to remember that. Details like that were important. He tried to climb over but couldn't. He needed something to give him a leg up. A bicycle. There were usually some in the racks by the main gate. Stuffing the wig into his pocket Wilt made his way round the terrapin huts and past the canteen and was just crossing the grass by the Language Lab when a figure appeared out of the darkness and a torch shone in his face. It was the caretaker.

'Here, where do you think you're going?' the caretaker asked. Wilt halted.

'I've . . . I've just come back to get some notes from the Staff Room.'

'Oh it's you, Mr Wilt,' said the caretaker. 'You should know by now that you can't get in at this time of night. We lock up at nine thirty.'

'I'm sorry. I forgot,' said Wilt.

The caretaker sighed. 'Well, since it's you and it's just this once . . .' he said, and unlocked the door to the General Studies building. 'You'll have to walk up. The lifts don't work at this time of night. I'll wait for you down here.'

Wilt staggered slowly up five flights of stairs to the Staff Room and went to his locker. He took out a handful of papers and a copy of *Bleak House* he'd been meaning to take home for some months and hadn't. He stuffed the notes into his pocket and found the wig. While he was about it he might as well pick up an elastic band. That would keep the wig on Judy's head. He found some in a box in the stationery cupboard, stuffed the notes into his other pocket and went downstairs.

'Thanks very much,' he told the caretaker, 'sorry to have bothered you.' He wove off round the corner to the bike sheds.

'Pissed as a newt,' said the caretaker, and went back into his office.

Wilt watched him light his pipe and then turned his attention to the bicycles. The bloody things were all locked. He would just have to carry one round. He put *Bleak House* in the basket, picked the bike up and carried it all the way round to the fence. Then he climbed up and over and groped around in the darkness for the doll. In the end he found it and spent five minutes trying to keep the wig on while he fastened the elastic band under her chin. It kept on jumping off. 'Well, at least that's one problem I won't have with Eva,' he muttered to himself when the wig was secured. Having satisfied himself that it wouldn't come off he moved cautiously forward skirting mounds of gravel, machines, sacks and reinforcing rods when it suddenly occurred to him that he was running considerable risk of disappearing down one of the pile holes himself. He put the doll down and fumbled in his pocket for the torch and shone it on the ground. Some yards ahead there was a large square of thick plywood. Wilt moved forward and lifted it. Underneath was the hole, a nice big hole. Just the right size. She would fit in there perfectly. He shone the torch down. Must be thirty feet deep. He pushed the plywood to one side and went back for the doll. The wig had fallen off again.

'Fuck,' said Wilt, and reached in his pocket for another elastic band. Five minutes later Judy's wig was firmly in place with four elastic bands fastened under her chin. That should do it. Now all he had to do was to drag the replica to the hole and make sure it fitted. At this point Wilt hesitated. He was beginning to have doubts about the soundness of the scheme. Too many unexpected contingencies had arisen for his liking. On the other hand there was a sense of exhilaration about being alone on the building site in the middle of the night. Perhaps it would be better if he went home now. No, he had to see the thing through. He would put the doll into the hole to make quite sure that it fitted. Then he would deflate it and go home and repeat the process until he had trained himself to kill by proxy. He would keep the doll in the boot of the car. Eva never looked there. And in future he would only blow her up when he reached the car park. That way Eva would have no idea what was going on. Definitely not. Wilt smiled to himself at the simplicity of the scheme. Then he picked Judy up and pushed her towards the hole feet first. She slid in easily while Wilt leant forward. Perfect. And at that moment he slipped on the muddy ground. With a desperate effort which necessitated letting go of the doll he hurled himself to one side and grabbed at the plywood. He got to his feet cautiously and cursed. His trousers were covered with mud and his hands were shaking.

'Damned near went down myself,' he muttered, and looked around for Judy. But Judy had disappeared. Wilt reached for his torch and shone it down the hole. Halfway down the doll was wedged lightly against the sides and for once the wig was still on. Wilt stared desperately down at the thing and wondered what the hell to do. It—or she—must be at least twenty feet down. Fifteen. Anyway a long way down and certainly too far for him to reach. But still too near the top not to be clearly visible to the workmen in the morning. Wilt switched off the torch and pulled the plywood square so that it covered half the hole. That way he wouldn't be in danger of joining the doll. Then he stood up and tried to think of ways of getting it out.

Rope with a hook on the end of it? He hadn't a rope or a hook. He might be able to find a rope but hooks were another matter. Get a rope and tie it to something and climb down it and bring the doll up? Certainly not. It would be bad enough climbing down the rope with two hands but to think of climbing back up with one hand holding the doll in the other was sheer lunacy. That way he would end up at the bottom of the hole himself and if one thing was clear in his mind it was that he didn't intend to be discovered at the bottom of a thirty-foot pile hole on Monday morning clutching a plastic fucking doll with a cunt dressed in his wife's clothes. That way lay disaster. Wilt visualized the scene in the Principal's office as he tried to explain how he came to be . . . And anyway they might not find him or hear his yells. Those damned cement lorries made a hell of a din and he bloody well wasn't going to risk being buried under . . . Shit. Talk about poetic justice. No the only thing to do

60

was to get that fucking doll down to the bottom of the hole and hope to hell that no one spotted it before they poured the concrete in. Well, at least that way he would learn if it was a sensible method of getting rid of Eva. There was that to be said for it. Every cloud had . . .

Wilt left the hole and looked around for something to move Judy down to the bottom. He tried a handful of gravel but she merely wobbled a bit and stayed put. Something weightier was needed. He went across to a pile of sand and scooped some into a plastic sack and poured it down the hole, but apart from adding an extra dimension of macabre realism to Mrs Wilt's wig the sand did nothing. Perhaps if he dropped a brick on the doll it would burst. Wilt looked around for a brick and ended up with a large lump of clay. That would have to do. He dropped it down the hole. There was a thump, a rattle of gravel and another thump. Wilt shone his torch down. Judy had reached the bottom of the hole and had settled into a grotesque position with her legs crumpled up in front of her and one arm outstretched towards him as if in supplication. Wilt fetched another lump of clay and hurled it down. This time the wig slid sideways and her head lolled. Wilt gave up. There was nothing more he could do. He pulled the plywood back over the hole and went back to the fence.

Here he ran into more trouble. The bicycle was on the other side. He fetched a plank, leant it against the fence and climbed over. Now to carry the bike back to the shed. Oh bugger the bicycle. It could stay where it was. He was fed up with the whole business. He couldn't even dispose of a plastic doll properly. It was ludicrous to think that he could plan, commit and carry through a real murder with any hope of success. He must have been mad to think of it. It was all that blasted gin.

'That's right, blame the gin,' Wilt muttered to himself, as he trudged back to his car. 'You had this idea months ago.' He climbed into the car and sat there in the darkness wondering what on earth had ever possessed him to have fantasies of murdering Eva. It was insane, utterly insane, and just as mad as to imagine that he could train himself to become a cold-blooded killer. Where had the idea originated from? What was it all about? All right, Eva was a stupid cow who made his life a misery by nagging at him and by indulging a taste for Eastern

61

mysticism with a frenetic enthusiasm calculated to derange the soberest of husbands, but why his obsession with murder? Why the need to prove his manliness by violence? Where had he got that from? In the middle of the car park, Henry Wilt, suddenly sober and clear-headed, realized the extraordinary effect that ten years of Liberal Studies had had upon him. For ten long years Plasterers Two and Meat One had been exposed to culture in the shape of Wilt and *The Lord of the Flies*, and for as many years Wilt himself had been exposed to the barbarity, the unhesitating readiness to commit violence of Plasterers Two and Meat One. That was the genesis of it all. That and the unreality of the literature he had been forced to absorb. For ten years Wilt had been the duct along which travelled creatures of imagination, Nostromo, Jack and Piggy, Shane, creatures who acted and whose actions effected something. And all the time he saw himself, mirrored in their eyes, an ineffectual passive person responding solely to the dictates of circumstance. Wilt shook his head. And out of all that and the traumas of the past two days had been born this *acte gratuit*, this semi-crime, the symbolic murder of Eva Wilt.

He started the car and drove out of the car park. He would go and see the Braintrees. They would still be up and glad to see him and besides he needed to talk to someone. Behind him on the building site his notes on Violence and the Break-Up of Family Life drifted about in the night wind and stuck in the mud.

Chapter 7

'Nature is so libidinous,' said Sally, shining a torch through the porthole at the reeds. 'I mean take bullrushes. I mean they're positively archetypally phallus. Don't you think so, G?'

'Bullrushes?' said Gaskell, gazing helplessly at a chart. 'Bullrushes do nothing for me.'

'Maps neither, by the look of it.'

'Charts, baby, charts.'

'What's in a name?'

'Right now, a hell of a lot. We're either in Frogwater Reach or Fen Broad. No telling which.'

'Give me Fen Broad every time. I just adore broads. Eva sweetheart, how's about another pot of coffee? I want to stay awake all night and watch the dawn come up over the bullrushes.'

'Yes, well I don't,' said Gaskell. 'Last night was enough for me. That crazy guy with the doll in the bath and Schei cutting himself. That's enough for one day. I'm going to hit the sack.'

'The deck,' said Sally, 'hit the deck, G. Eva and I are sleeping down here. Three's a crowd.'

'Three? With boobs around it's five at the least. OK, so I sleep on deck. We've got to be up early if we're to get off this damned sandbank.'

'Has Captain Pringsheim stranded us, baby?'

'It's these charts. If only they would give an exact indication of depth.'

'If you knew where we were, you'd probably find they do. It's no use knowing it's three feet—'

'Fathoms, honey, fathoms.'

'Three fathoms in Frogwater Reach if we're really in Fen Broad.'

'Well, wherever we are, you'd better start hoping there's a tide that will rise and float us off,' said Gaskell.

'And if there isn't?'

'Then we'll have to think of something else. Maybe someone will come along and tow us off.'

'Oh God, G, you're the skilfullest,' said Sally. 'I mean why couldn't we have just stayed out in the middle? But no, you had to come steaming up this creek wham into a mudbank and all because of what? Ducks, goddamned ducks.'

'Waders, baby, waders. Not just ducks.'

'OK, so they're waders. You want to photograph them so now we're stuck where no one in their right minds would come in a boat. Who do you think is going to come up here? Jonathan Seagull?'

In the galley Eva made coffee. She was wearing the bright red plastic bikini Sally had lent her. It was rather too small for her so that she bulged round it uncomfortably and it was revealingly tight but at least it was better than going around naked even though Sally said nudity was being liberated and look at the Amazonian Indians. She should have brought her own things but Sally had insisted on hurrying and now all she had were the lemon loungers and the bikini. Honestly Sally was so authora . . . authorasomething . . . well, bossy then.

'Dual-purpose plastic, baby, apronwise,' she had said, 'and G has this thing about plastic, haven't you, G?'

'Bio-degradably yes.'

'Bio-degradably?' asked Eva, hoping to be initiated into some new aspect of women's liberation.

'Plastic bottles that disintegrate instead of lying around making an ecological swamp,' said Sally, opening a porthole and dropping an empty cigar packet over the side, 'that's G's lifework. That and recyclability. Infinite recyclability.'

'Right,' said Gaskell. 'We've got in-built obsolescence in the automotive field where it's outmoded. So what we need now is in-built bio-degradable deliquescence in ephemera.'

Eva listened incomprehendingly but with the feeling that she was somehow at the centre of an intellectual world far surpassing that of Henry and his friends who talked about new degree courses and their students so boringly.

'We've got a compost heap at the bottom of the garden,' she said when she finally understood what they were talking about. 'I put the potato peelings and odds and ends on it.'

64

Gaskell raised his eyes to the cabin roof. Correction. Deck-head.

'Talking of odds and ends,' said Sally, running a fond hand over Eva's bottom, 'I wonder how Henry is getting along with Judy.'

Eva shuddered. The thought of Henry and the doll lying in the bath still haunted her.

'I can't think what had got into him,' she said, and looked disapprovingly at Gaskell when he sniggered. 'I mean it's not as if he has ever been unfaithful or anything like that. And lots of husbands are. Patrick Mottram is always going off and having affairs with other women but Henry's been very good in that respect. He may be quiet and not very pushing but no one could call him a gadabout.'

'Oh sure,' said Gaskell, 'so he's got a hang-up about sex. My heart bleeds for him.'

'I don't see why you should say he's got something wrong with him because he's faithful,' said Eva.

'G didn't mean that, did you, G?' said Sally. 'He meant that there has to be true freedom in a marriage. No dominance, no jealousy, no possession. Right, G?'

'Right,' said Gaskell.

'The test of true love is when you can watch your wife having it off with someone else and still love her,' Sally went on.

'I could never watch Henry . . .' said Eva. 'Never.'

'So you don't love him. You're insecure. You don't trust him.'

'Trust him?' said Eva. 'If Henry went to bed with another woman I don't see how I could trust him. I mean if that's what he wants to do why did he marry me?'

'That,' said Gaskell, 'is the sixty-four-thousand dollar question.' He picked up his sleeping bag and went out on deck. Behind him Eva had begun to cry.

'There, there,' said Sally, putting her arm round her. 'G was just kidding. He didn't mean anything.'

'It's not that,' said Eva, 'it's just that I don't understand anything any more. It's all so complicated.'

'Christ, you look bloody awful,' said Peter Braintree as Wilt stood on the doorstep.

'I feel bloody awful,' said Wilt. 'It's all this gin.'

'You mean Eva's not back?' said Braintree, leading the way down the passage to the kitchen.

'She wasn't there when I got home. Just a note saying she was going away with the Pringsheims to think things over.'

'To think things over? Eva? What things?'

'Well . . .' Wilt began and thought better of it, 'that business with Sally I suppose. She says she won't ever forgive me.'

'But you didn't do anything with Sally. That's what you told me.'

'I know I didn't. That's the whole point. If I had done what that nymphomaniac bitch wanted there wouldn't have been all this bloody trouble.'

'I don't see that, Henry. I mean if you had done what she wanted Eva would have had something to grumble about. I don't see why she should be up in the air because you didn't.'

'Sally must have told her that I did do something,' said Wilt, determined not to mention the incident in the bathroom with the doll.

'You mean the blow job?'

'I don't know what I mean. What is a blow job anyway?'

Peter Braintree looked puzzled.

'I'm not too sure,' he said, 'but it's obviously something you don't want your husband to do. If I came home and told Betty I'd done a blow job she'd think I'd been robbing a bank.'

'I wasn't going to do it anyway,' said Wilt. 'She was going to do it to me.'

'Perhaps it's a suck off,' said Braintree, putting a kettle on the stove. 'That's what it sounds like to me.'

'Well it didn't sound like that to me,' said Wilt with a shudder. 'She made it sound like a paint-peeling exercise with a blow lamp. You should have seen the look on her face.'

He sat down at the kitchen table despondently.

Braintree eyed him curiously. 'You certainly seem to have been in the wars,' he said.

Wilt looked down at his trousers. They were covered with mud and there were round patches caked to his knees. 'Yes . . . well . . . well I had a puncture on the way here,' he explained with lack of conviction, 'I had to change a tyre and I knelt down. I was a bit pissed.'

Peter Braintree grunted doubtfully. It didn't sound very convincing to him. Poor old Henry was obviously a bit under the weather. 'You can wash up in the sink,' he said.

Presently Betty Braintree came downstairs. 'I couldn't help hearing what you said about Eva,' she said, 'I'm so sorry, Henry. I wouldn't worry. She's bound to come back.'

'I wouldn't be too sure,' said Wilt, gloomily, 'and anyway I'm not so sure I want her back.'

'Oh, Eva's all right,' Betty said. 'She gets these sudden urges and enthusiasms but they don't last long. It's just the way she's made. It's easy come and easy go with Eva.'

'I think that's what's worrying Henry,' said Braintree, 'the easy come bit.'

'Oh surely not. Eva isn't that sort at all.'

Wilt sat at the kitchen table and sipped his coffee. 'I wouldn't put anything past her in the company she's keeping now,' he muttered lugubriously. 'Remember what happened when she went through that macrobiotic diet phase? Dr Mannix told me I was the nearest thing to a case of scurvy he'd seen since the Burma railway. And then there was that episode with the trampoline. She went to a Keep Fit Class at Bulham Village College and bought herself a fucking trampoline. You know she put old Mrs Portway in hospital with that contraption.'

'I knew there was some sort of accident but Eva never told me what actually happened,' said Betty.

'She wouldn't. It was a ruddy miracle we didn't get sued,' said Wilt. 'It threw Mrs Portway clean through the greenhouse roof. There was glass all over the lawn and it wasn't even as though Mrs Portway was a healthy woman at the best of times.'

'Wasn't she the woman with the rheumatoid arthritis?'

Wilt nodded dismally. 'And the duelling scars on her face,' he said, 'that was our greenhouse, that was.'

'I must say I can think of better places for trampolines than greenhouses,' said Braintree. 'It wasn't a very big greenhouse was it?'

'It wasn't a very big trampoline either, thank God,' said Wilt, 'she'd have been in orbit otherwise.'

'Well it all goes to prove one thing,' said Betty, looking on the bright side, 'Eva may do crazy things but she soon gets over them.'

'Mrs Portway didn't,' said Wilt, not to be comforted, 'she was in hospital for six weeks and the skin grafts didn't take. She hasn't been near our house since.'

'You'll see. Eva will get fed up with these Pringsheim people in a week or two. They're just another fad.'

'A fad with a lot of advantages if you ask me,' said Wilt. 'Money, status and sexual promiscuity. All the things I couldn't give her and all dressed up in a lot of intellectual claptrap about Women's Lib and violence and the intolerance of tolerance and the revolution of the sexes and you're not fully mature unless you're ambisextrous. It's enough to make you vomit and it's just the sort of crap Eva would fall for. I mean she'd buy rotten herrings if some clown up the social scale told her they were the sophisticated things to eat. Talk about being gullible!'

'The thing is that Eva's got too much energy,' said Betty. 'You should try and persuade her to get a full-time job.'

'Full-time job?' said Wilt. 'She's had more full-time jobs than I've had hot dinners. Mind you, that's not saying much these days. All I ever get is a cold supper and a note saying she's gone to Pottery or Transcendental Meditation or something equally half-baked. And anyway Eva's idea of a job is to take over the factory. Remember Potters, that engineering firm that went broke after a strike a couple of years ago? Well, if you ask me that was Eva's fault. She got this job with a consultancy firm doing time and motion study and they sent her out to the factory and the next thing anyone knew they had a strike on their hands . . .'

They went on talking for another hour until the Braintrees asked him to stay the night. But Wilt wouldn't. 'I've got things to do tomorrow.'

'Such as?'

'Feed the dog for one thing.'

'You can always drive over and do that. Clem won't starve overnight.'

But Wilt was too immersed in self-pity to be persuaded and besides he was still worried about that doll. He might have another go at getting the thing out of that hole. He drove home and went to bed in a tangle of sheets and blankets. He hadn't made it in the morning.

'Poor old Henry,' said Betty as she and Peter went upstairs. 'He did look pretty awful.'

'He said he'd had a puncture and had to change the wheel.'

'I wasn't thinking of his clothes. It was the look on his face that worried me. You don't think he's on the verge of a break-down?'

Peter Braintree shook his head. 'You'd look like that if you had Gasfitters Three and Plasterers Two every day of your life for ten years and then your wife ran away,' he told her.

'Why don't they give him something better to teach?'

'Why? Because the Tech wants to become a Poly and they keep starting new degree courses and hiring people with PhDs to teach them and then the students don't enrol and they're lumbered with specialists like Dr Fitzpatrick who knows all there is to know about child labour in four cotton mills in Manchester in 1837 and damn all about anything else. Put him in front of a class of Day Release Apprentices and all hell would break loose. As it is I have to go into his A-level classes once a week and tell them to shut up. On the other hand Henry looks meek but he can cope with rowdies. He's too good at his job. That's his trouble and besides he's not a bumsucker and that's the kiss of death at the Tech. If you don't lick arses you get nowhere.'

'You know,' said Betty, 'teaching at that place has done horrible things to your language.'

'It's done horrible things to my outlook on life, never mind my language,' said Braintree. 'It's enough to drive a man to drink.'

'It certainly seems to have done that to Henry. His breath reeked of gin.'

'He'll get over it.'

But Wilt didn't. He woke in the morning with the feeling that something was missing quite apart from Eva. That bloody doll. He lay in bed trying to think of some way of retrieving the thing before the workmen arrived on the site on Monday morning but apart from pouring a can of petrol down the hole and lighting it, which seemed on reflection the best way of drawing attention to the fact that he had stuffed a plastic doll dressed in his wife's clothes down there, he could think of nothing prac-tical. He would just have to trust to luck.

When the Sunday papers came he got out of bed and went down to read them over his All-Bran. Then he fed the dog and mooched about the house in his pyjamas, walked down to the Ferry Path Inn for lunch, slept in the afternoon and watched the box all evening. Then he made the bed and got into it and spent a restless night wondering where Eva was, what she was doing, and why, since he had occupied so many fruitless hours speculating on ways of getting rid of her homicidally, he should be in the least concerned now that she had gone of her own accord.

'I mean if I didn't want this to happen why did I keep thinking up ways of killing her,' he thought at two o'clock. 'Sane people don't go for walks with a Labrador and devise schemes for murdering their wives when they can just as easily divorce them.' There was probably some foul psychological reason for it. Wilt could think of several himself, rather too many in fact to be able to decide which was the most likely one. In any case a psychological explanation demanded a degree of self-knowledge which Wilt, who wasn't at all sure he had a self to know, felt was denied him. Ten years of Plasterers Two and Exposure to Barbarism had at least given him the insight to know that there was an answer for every question and it didn't much matter what answer you gave so long as you gave it convincingly. In the 14th century they would have said the devil put such thoughts into his head, now in a post-Freudian world it had to be a complex or, to be really up-to-date, a chemical imbalance. In a hundred years they would have come up with some completely different explanation. With the comforting thought that the truths of one age were the absurdities of another and that it didn't much matter what you thought so long as you did the right thing, and in his view he did, Wilt finally fell asleep.

At seven he was woken by the alarm clock and by half past eight had parked his car in the parking lot behind the Tech. He walked past the building site where the workmen were already at work. Then he went up to the Staff Room and looked out of the window. The square of plywood was still in place covering the hole but the pile-boring machine had been backed away. They had evidently finished with it.

At five to nine he collected twenty-five copies of *Shane* from the cupboard and took them across to Motor Mechanics Three. *Shane* was the ideal soporific. It would keep the brutes quiet while he sat and watched what happened down below. Room 593 in the Engineering block gave him a grandstand view. Wilt filled in the register and handed out copies of *Shane* and told the class to get on with it. He said it with a good deal more vigour than was usual even for a Monday morning and the class settled down to consider the plight of the homesteaders while Wilt stared out of the window, absorbed in a more immediate drama.

A lorry with a revolving drum filled with liquid concrete had arrived on the site and was backing slowly towards the plywood square. It stopped and there was an agonizing wait while the driver climbed down from the cab and lit a cigarette. Another man, evidently the foreman, came out of a wooden hut and wandered across to the lorry and presently a little group was gathered round the hole. Wilt got up from his desk and went over to the window. Why the hell didn't they get a move on? Finally the driver got back into his cab and two men removed the plywood. The foreman signalled to the driver. The chute for the concrete was swung into position. Another signal. The drum began to tilt. The concrete was coming. Wilt watched as it began to pour down the chute and just at that moment the foreman looked down the hole. So did one of the workmen. The next instant all hell had broken loose. There were frantic signals and shouts from the foreman. Through the window Wilt watched the open mouths and the gesticulations but still the concrete came. Wilt shut his eyes and shuddered. They had found that fucking doll.

Outside on the building site the air was thick with misunderstanding.

'What's that? I'm pouring as fast as I can,' shouted the driver, misconstruing the frenzied signals of the foreman. He pulled the lever still further and the concrete flood increased. The next moment he was aware that he had made some sort of mistake. The foreman was wrenching at the door of the cab and screaming blue murder.

'Stop, for God's sake stop,' he shouted. 'There's a woman down that hole!'

'A what?' said the driver, and switched off the engine.

'A fucking woman and look what you've been and fucking done. I told you to stop. I told you to stop pouring and you went on. You've been and poured twenty tons of liquid concrete on her.'

The driver climbed down from his cab and went round to the chute where the last trickles of cement were still sliding hesitantly into the hole.

'A woman?' he said. 'What? Down that hole? What's she doing down there?'

The foreman stared at him demonically. 'Doing?' he bellowed, 'what do you think she's doing? What would you be doing if you'd just had twenty tons of liquid concrete dumped on top of you? Fucking drowning, that's what.'

The driver scratched his head. 'Well I didn't know she was down there. How was I to know? You should have told me.'

'Told you?' shrieked the foreman. 'I told you. I told you to stop. You weren't listening.'

'I thought you wanted me to pour faster. I couldn't hear what you were saying.'

'Well, every other bugger could,' yelled the foreman. Certainly Wilt in Room 593 could. He stared wild-eyed out of the window as the panic spread. Beside him Motor Mechanics Three had lost all interest in *Shane*. They clustered at the window and watched.

'Are you quite sure?' asked the driver.

'Sure? Course I'm sure,' yelled the foreman. 'Ask Barney.'

The other workman, evidently Barney, nodded. 'She was down there all right. I'll vouch for that. All crumpled up she was. She had one hand up in the air and her legs was . . .'

'Jesus,' said the driver, visibly shaken. 'What the hell are we going to do now?'

It was a question that had been bothering Wilt. Call the police, presumably. The foreman confirmed his opinion. 'Get the cops. Get an ambulance. Get the Fire Brigade and get a pump. For God's sake get a pump.'

'Pump's no good,' said the driver, 'you'll never pump that concrete out of there, not in a month of Sundays. Anyway it wouldn't do any good. She'll be dead by now. Crushed to death.

Wouldn't drown with twenty tons on her. Why didn't she say something?'

'Would it have made any difference if she had?' asked the foreman hoarsely. 'You'd have still gone on pouring.'

'Well, how did she get down there in the first place?' said the driver, to change the subject.

'How the fuck would I know. She must have fallen . . .'

'And pulled that plywood sheet over her, I suppose,' said Barney, who clearly had a practical turn of mind. 'She was bloody murdered.'

'We all know that,' squawked the foreman. 'By Chris here. I told him to stop pouring. You heard me. Everyone for half a mile must have heard me but not Chris. Oh, no, he has to go on—'

'She was murdered before she was put down the hole,' said Barney. 'That wooden cover wouldn't have been there if she had fallen down herself.'

The foreman wiped his face with a handkerchief and looked at the square of plywood. 'There is that to it,' he muttered. 'No one can say we didn't take proper safety precautions. You're right. She must have been murdered. Oh, my God!'

'Sex crime, like as not,' said Barney. 'Raped and strangled her. That or someone's missus. You mark my words. She was all crumpled up and that hand . . . I'll never forget that hand, not if I live to be a hundred.'

The foreman stared at him lividly. He seemed incapable of expressing his feelings. So was Wilt. He went back to his desk and sat with his head in his hands while the class gaped out of the window and tried to catch what was being said. Presently sirens sounded in the distance and grew louder. A police car arrived, four fire engines hurtled into the car park and an ambulance followed. As more and more uniformed men gathered around what had once been a hole in the ground it became apparent that getting the doll down there had been a damned sight easier than getting it out.

'That concrete starts setting in twenty minutes,' the driver explained when a pump was suggested for the umpteenth time. An Inspector of Police and the Fire Chief stared down at the hole.

'Are you sure you saw a woman's body down there?' the Inspector asked. 'You're positive about it?'

73

'Positive?' squeaked the foreman, 'course I'm positive. You don't think . . . Tell them, Barney. He saw her too.'

Barney told the Inspector even more graphically than before. 'She had this hair see and her hand was reaching up like it was asking for help and there were these fingers . . . I tell you it was horrible. It didn't look natural.'

'No, well, it wouldn't,' said the Inspector sympathetically. 'And you say there was a board on top of the hole when you arrived this morning.'

The foreman gesticulated silently and Barney showed them the board. 'I was standing on it at one time,' he said. 'It was here all right so help me God.'

'The thing is, how are we to get her out?' said the Fire Chief. It was a point that was put to the manager of the construction company when he finally arrived on the scene. 'God alone knows,' he said. 'There's no easy way of getting that concrete out now. We'd have to use drills to get down thirty feet.'

At the end of the hour they were no nearer a solution to the problem. As the Motor Mechanics dragged themselves away from this fascinating situation to go to Technical Drawing, Wilt collected the unread copies of *Shane* and walked across to the Staff Room in a state of shock. The only consolation he could think of was that it would take them at least two or three days to dig down and discover that what had all the appearances of being the body of a murdered woman was in fact an inflatable doll. Or had been once. Wilt rather doubted if it would be inflated now. There had been something horribly intractable about that liquid concrete.

Chapter 8

There was something horribly intractable about the mudbank on which the cabin cruiser had grounded. To add to their troubles the engine had gone wrong. Gaskell said it was a broken con rod.

'Is that serious?' asked Sally.

'It just means we'll have to be towed to a boatyard.'

'By what?'

'By a passing cruiser I guess,' said Gaskell.

Sally looked over the side at the bullrushes.

'Passing?' she said. 'We've been here all night and half the morning and nothing has passed so far and if it did we wouldn't be able to see it for all these fucking bullrushes.'

'I thought bullrushes did something for you.'

'That was yesterday,' snapped Sally, 'today they just mean we're invisible to anyone more than fifty feet away. And now you've screwed the motor. I told you not to rev it like that.'

'So how was I to know it would bust a con rod,' said Gaskell. 'I was just trying to get us off this mudbank. You just tell me how I'm supposed to do it without revving the goddamned motor.'

'You could get out and push.'

Gaskell peered over the side. 'I could get out and drown,' he said.

'So the boat would be lighter,' said Sally. 'We've all got to make sacrifices and you said the tide would float us off.'

'Well I was mistaken. That's fresh water down there and means the tide doesn't reach this far.'

'Now he tells me. First we're in Frogwater Beach . . .'

'Reach,' said Gaskell.

'Frogwater wherever. Then we're in Fen Broad. Now where are we for God's sake?'

'On a mudbank,' said Gaskell.

In the cabin Eva bustled about. There wasn't much space for bustling but what there was she put to good use. She made the bunks and put the bedding away in the lockers underneath and she plumped the cushions and emptied the ashtrays. She swept the floor and polished the table and wiped the windows and dusted the shelves and generally made everything as neat and tidy as it was possible to make it. And all the time her thoughts got untidier and more muddled so that by the time she was finished and every object in sight was in its right place and the whole cabin properly arranged she was quite confused and in two minds about nearly every thing.

The Pringsheims were ever so sophisticated and rich and intellectual and said clever things all the time but they were always quarrelling and getting at one another about something and to be honest they were quite impractical and didn't know the first thing about hygiene. Gaskell went to the lavatory and didn't wash his hands afterwards and goodness only knew when he had last had a shave. And look at the way they had walked out of the house in Rossiter Grove without clearing up after the party and the living-room all over cups and things. Eva had been quite shocked. She would never have left her house in that sort of mess. She had said as much to Sally but Sally had said how nonspontaneous could you get and anyway they were only renting the house for the summer and that it was typical of a male-oriented social system to expect a woman to enter a contractual relationship based upon female domestic servitude. Eva tried to follow her and was left feeling guilty because she couldn't and because it was evidently infra dig to be houseproud and she was.

And then there was what Henry had been doing with that doll. It was so unlike Henry to do anything like that and the more she thought about it the more unlike Henry it became. He must have been drunk but even so . . . without his clothes on? And where had he found the doll? She had asked Sally and had been horrified to learn that Gaskell was mad about plastic and just adored playing games with Judy and men were like that and so to the only meaningful relationships being between women because women didn't need to prove their virility by any overt act of extrasexual violence did they? By which time Eva was lost in a maze of words she didn't understand but which sounded important and they had had another session of Touch Therapy.

And that was another thing she was in two minds about.

Touch Therapy. Sally had said she was still inhibited and being inhibited was a sign of emotional and sensational immaturity. Eva battled with her mixed feelings about the matter. On the one hand she didn't want to be emotionally and sensationally immature and if the revulsion she felt lying naked in the arms of another woman was anything to go by and in Eva's view the nastier a medicine tasted the more likely it was to do you good, then she was certainly improving her psycho-sexual behaviour pattern by leaps and bounds. On the other hand she wasn't altogether convinced that Touch Therapy was quite nice. It was only by the application of considerable will-power that she overcame her objections to it and even so there was an undertow of doubt about the propriety of being touched quite so sensationally. It was all very puzzling and to cap it all she was on The Pill. Eva had objected very strongly and had pointed out that Henry and she had always wanted babies and she'd never had any but Sally had insisted.

'Eva baby,' she had said, 'with Gaskell one just never knows. Sometimes he goes for months without so much as a twitch and then, bam, he comes all over the place. He's totally un-discriminating.'

'But I thought you said you had this big thing between you,' Eva said.

'Oh, sure. In a blue moon. Scientists sublimate and G just lives for plastic. And we wouldn't want you to go back to Henry with G's genes in your ovum, now would we?'

'Certainly not,' said Eva horrified at the thought and had taken the pill after breakfast before going through to the tiny galley to wash up. It was all so different from Transcendental Meditation and Pottery.

On deck Sally and Gaskell were still wrangling.

'What the hell are you giving brainless boobs?' Gaskell asked.

'TT, Body Contact, Tactile Liberation,' said Sally. 'She's sensually deprived.'

'She's mentally deprived too. I've met some dummies in my time but this one is the dimwittiest. Anyway, I meant those pills she takes at breakfast.'

Sally smiled. 'Oh those,' she said.

'Yes those. You blowing what little mind she's got or something?' said Gaskell. 'We've got enough troubles without Moby Dick taking a trip.'

'Oral contraceptives, baby, just the plain old Pill.'

'Oral contraceptives? What the hell for? I wouldn't touch her with a sterilized stirring rod.'

'Gaskell, honey, you're so naïve. For authenticity, pure authenticity. It makes my relationship with her so much more real, don't you think. Like wearing a rubber on a dildo.'

Gaskell gaped at her. 'Jesus, you don't mean you've . . .'

'Not yet. Long John Silver is still in his bag but one of these days when she's a little more emancipated. . . .' She smiled wistfully over the bullrushes. 'Perhaps it doesn't matter all that much us being stuck here. It gives us time, so much lovely time and you can look at your ducks . . .'

'Waders,' said Gaskell, 'and we're going to run up one hell of a bill at the Marina if we don't get this boat back in time.'

'Bill?' said Sally. 'You're crazy. You don't think we're paying for this hulk?'

'But you hired her from the boatyard. I mean you're not going to tell me you just took the boat,' said Gaskell. 'For Chrissake, that's theft!'

Sally laughed. 'Honestly, G, you're so moral. I mean you're inconsistent, You steal books from the library and chemicals from the lab but when it comes to boats you're all up in the air.'

'Books are different,' said Gaskell hotly.

'Yes,' said Sally, 'books you don't go to jail for. That's what's different. So you want to think I stole the boat, you go on thinking that.'

Gaskell took out a handkerchief and wiped his glasses. 'Are you telling me you didn't?' he asked finally.

'I borrowed it.'

'Borrowed it? Who from?'

'Schei.'

'Scheimacher?'

'That's right. He said we could have it whenever we wanted it so we've got it.'

'Does he know we've got it?'

Sally sighed. 'Look, he's in India isn't he, currying sperm? So what does it matter what he knows? By the time he gets back we'll be in the Land of the Free.'

78

'Shit,' said Gaskell wearily, 'one of these days you're going to land us in it up to the eyeballs.'

'Gaskell honey, sometimes you bore me with your worrying so.'

'Let me tell you something. You worry me with your god-damned attitude to other people's property.'

'Property is theft.'

'Oh sure. You just get the cops to see it that way when they catch up with you. The fuzz don't go a ball on stealing in this country.'

The fuzz weren't going much of a ball on the well-nourished body of a woman apparently murdered and buried under thirty feet and twenty tons of rapidly setting concrete. Barney had supplied the well-nourished bit. 'She had big breasts too,' he explained, in the seventh version of what he had seen. 'And this hand reaching up—'

'Yes, well we know all about the hand,' said Inspector Flint. 'We've been into all that before but this is the first time you've mentioned breasts.'

'It was the hand that got me,' said Barney. 'I mean you don't think of breasts in a situation like that.'

The Inspector turned to the foreman. 'Did you notice the deceased's breasts?' he enquired. But the foreman just shook his head. He was past speech.

'So we've got a well-nourished woman . . . What age would you say?'

Barney scratched his chin reflectively. 'Not old,' he said finally. 'Definitely not old.'

'In her twenties?'

'Could have been.'

'In her thirties?'

Barney shrugged. There was something he was trying to recall. Something that had seemed odd at the time.

'But definitely not in her forties?'

'No,' said Barney. 'Younger than that.' He said it rather hesitantly.

'You're not being very specific,' said Inspector Flint.

'I can't help it,' said Barney plaintively. 'You see a woman down a dirty great hole with concrete sloshing down on top of her you don't ask her her age.'

79

'Quite. I realize that but if you could just think. Was there anything peculiar about her . . .'

'Peculiar? Well, there was this hand see . . .'

Inspector Flint sighed. 'I mean anything out of the ordinary about her appearance. Her hair for instance. What colour was it?'

Barney got it. 'I knew there was something,' he said, triumphantly. 'Her hair. It was crooked.'

'Well, it would be, wouldn't it. You don't dump a woman down a thirty-foot pile shaft without mussing up her hair in the process.'

'No, it wasn't like that. It was on sideways and flattened. Like she'd been hit.'

'She probably had been hit. If what you say about the wooden cover being in place is true, she didn't go down there of her own volition. But you still can't give any precise indication of her age?'

'Well,' said Barney, 'bits of her looked young and bits didn't. That's all I know.'

'Which bits?' asked the Inspector, hoping to hell Barney wasn't going to start on that hand again.

'Well, her legs didn't look right for her teats if you see what I mean.' Inspector Flint didn't. 'They were all thin and crumpled-up like.'

'Which were? Her legs or her teats?'

'Her legs, of course,' said Barney. 'I've told you she had these lovely great . . .'

'We're treating this as a case of murder,' Inspector Flint told the Principal ten minutes later. The Principal sat behind his desk and thought despairingly about adverse publicity.

'You're quite convinced it couldn't have been an accident?'

'The evidence to date certainly doesn't suggest accidental death,' said the Inspector, 'however, we'll only be absolutely certain on that point when we manage to reach the body and I'm afraid that is going to take some time.'

'Time?' said the Principal. 'Do you mean to say you can't get her out this morning?'

Inspector Flint shook his head. 'Out of the question, sir,' he said. 'We are considering two methods of reaching the body and they'll both take several days. One is to drill down through

80

the concrete and the other is to sink another shaft next to the original hole and try and get at her from the side.'

'Good Lord,' said the Principal, looking at his calendar, 'but that means you're going to be digging away out there for several days.'

'I'm afraid it can't be helped. Whoever put her down there made a good job of it. Still, we'll try to be as unobtrusive as possible.'

Out of the window the Principal could see four police cars, a fire engine and a big blue van. 'This is really most unfortunate,' he murmured.

'Murder always is,' said the Inspector, and got to his feet. 'It's in the nature of the thing. In the meantime we are sealing off the site and we'd be grateful for your cooperation.'

'Anything you require,' said the Principal, with a sigh.

In the Staff Room the presence of so many uniformed men peering down a pile hole provoked mixed reactions. So did the dozen policemen scouring the building site, stopping now and then to put things carefully into envelopes, but it was the arrival of the dark blue caravan that finally clinched matters.

'That's a Mobile Murder Headquarters,' Peter Fenwick explained. 'Apparently some maniac has buried a woman at the bottom of one of the piles.'

The New Left, who had been clustered in a corner discussing the likely implications of so many paramilitary Fascist pigs, heaved a sigh of unmartyred regret but continued to express doubts.

'No, seriously,' said Fenwick, 'I asked one of them what they were doing. I thought it was some sort of bomb scare.'

Dr Cox, Head of Science, confirmed it. His office looked directly onto the hole. 'It's too dreadful to contemplate,' he murmured, 'every time I look up I think what she must have suffered.'

'What do you suppose they are putting into those envelopes,' asked Dr Mayfield.

'Clues,' said Dr Board, with evident satisfaction. 'Hairs. Bits of skin and bloodstains. The usual trivial detritus of violent crime.'

Dr Cox hurried from the room and Dr Mayfield looked

disgusted. 'How revolting,' he said, 'isn't it possible that there has been some mistake? I mean why should anyone want to murder a woman here?'

Dr Board sipped his coffee and looked wistfully at him. 'I can think of any number of reasons,' he said happily. 'There are at least a dozen women in my evening class whom I would cheerfully beat to death and drop down holes. Sylvia Swansbeck for one.'

'Whoever did it must have known they were going to pour concrete down today,' said Fenwick. 'It looks like an inside job to me.'

'One of our less community-conscious students perhaps,' suggested Dr Board, 'I don't suppose they've had time to check if any of the staff are missing.'

'You'll probably find it had nothing to do with the Tech,' said Dr Mayfield. 'Some maniac . . .'

'Come now, give credit where credit is due,' interrupted Dr Board. 'There was obviously an element of premeditation involved. Whoever the murderer was . . . is, he planned it pretty carefully. What puzzles me is why he didn't shovel earth down on top of the wretched woman so that she couldn't be seen. Probably intended to but was disturbed before he could get around to it. One of those little accidents of fate.'

In the corner of the Staff Room Wilt sat and drank his coffee, conscious that he was the only person not staring out of the window. What the hell was he to do? The sensible thing would be to go to the police and explain that he had been trying to get rid of an inflatable doll that someone had given him. But would they believe him? If that was all that had happened why had he dressed it up in a wig and clothes? And why had he left it inflated? Why hadn't he just thrown the thing away? He was just rehearsing the pros and cons of the argument when the Head of Engineering came in and announced that the police intended boring another hole next to the first one instead of digging down through the concrete.

'They'll probably be able to see bits of her sticking out the side,' he explained. 'Apparently she had one arm up in the air and with all that concrete coming down on top of her there's a chance that arm will have been pressed against the side of the hole. Much quicker that way.'

82

'I must say I can't see the need for haste,' said Dr Board, 'I should have thought she'd be pretty well preserved in all that concrete. Mummified I daresay.'

In his corner Wilt rather doubted it. With twenty tons of concrete on top of her even Judy who had been an extremely resilient doll was hardly likely to have withstood the pressure. She would have burst as sure as eggs were eggs in which case all the police would find was the empty plastic arm of a doll. They would hardly bother to dig a burst plastic doll out.

'And another thing,' continued the Head of Engineering, 'if the arm is sticking out they'll be able to take fingerprints straight away.'

Wilt smiled to himself. That was one thing they weren't going to find on Judy, fingerprints. He finished his coffee more cheerfully and went off to a class of Senior Secretaries. He found them agog with news of the murder.

'Do you think it was a sex killing?' a small blonde girl in the front row asked as Wilt handed out copies of *This Island Now*. He had always found the chapter on the Vicissitudes of Adolescence appealed to Senior Secs. It dealt with sex and violence and was twelve years out of date but then so were the Senior Secretaries. Today there was no need for the book.

'I don't think it was any sort of killing,' said Wilt taking his place behind the desk.

'Oh but it was. They saw a woman's body down there,' the small blonde insisted.

'They thought they saw something down there that looked like a body,' said Wilt, 'that doesn't mean it was one. People's imaginations play tricks with them.'

'The police don't think so,' said a large girl whose father was something in the City. 'They must be certain to go to all that trouble. We had a murder on our golf course and all they found were bits of body cut up and put in the water hazard on the fifteenth. They'd been there six months. Someone sliced a ball on the dogleg twelfth and it went into the pond. They fished out a foot first. It was all puffy and green and . . .' A pale girl from Wilstanton fainted in the third row. By the time Wilt had revived her and taken her to the Sick Room, the class had got onto Crippen, Haigh and Christie. Wilt returned to find them discussing acid baths.

'. . . and all they found were her false teeth and gallstones.'

'You seem to know a lot about murder,' Wilt said to the large girl.

'Daddy plays bridge with the Chief Constable,' she explained. 'He comes to dinner and tells super stories. He says they ought to bring back hanging.'

'I'm sure he does,' said Wilt grimly. It was typical of Senior Secs that they knew Chief Constables who wanted to bring back hanging. It was all mummy and daddy and horses with Senior Secretaries.

'Anyway, hanging doesn't hurt,' said the large girl. 'Sir Frank says a good hangman can have a man out of the condemned cell and onto the trap with a noose around his neck and pull the lever in twenty seconds.'

'Why confine the privilege to men?' asked Wilt bitterly. The class looked at him with reproachful eyes.

'The last woman they hanged was Ruth Ellis,' said the blonde in the front row.

'Anyway with women it's different,' said the large girl.

'Why?' said Wilt inadvisedly.

'Well it's slower.'

'Slower?'

'They had to tie Mrs Thomson to a chair,' volunteered the blonde. 'She behaved disgracefully.'

'I must say I find your judgements peculiar,' said Wilt. 'A woman murdering her husband is doubtless disgraceful. The fact that she puts up a fight when they come to execute her doesn't strike me as disgraceful at all. I find that . . .'

'It's not just that,' interrupted the large girl, who wasn't to be diverted.

'What isn't?' said Wilt.

'It's being slower with women. They have to make them wear waterproof pants.'

Wilt gaped at her in disgust. 'Waterproof what?' he asked without thinking.

'Waterproof pants,' said the large girl.

'Dear God,' said Wilt.

'You see, when they get to the bottom of the rope their insides drop out,' continued the large girl, administering the *coup de grâce*. Wilt stared at her wildly and stumbled from the room.

'What's the matter with him?' said the girl. 'Anyone would think I had said something beastly.'

In the corridor Wilt leant against the wall and felt sick. Those fucking girls were worse than Gasfitters. At least Gasfitters didn't go in for such disgusting anatomical details and besides Senior Secs all came from so-called respectable families. By the time he felt strong enough to face them again the hour had ended. Wilt went back into the classroom sheepishly and collected the books.

'Name of Wilt mean anything to you? Henry Wilt?' asked the Inspector.

'Wilt?' said the Vice-Principal, who had been left to cope with the police while the Principal spent his time more profitably trying to offset the adverse publicity caused by the whole appalling business. 'Well, yes it does. He's one of our Liberal Studies lecturers. Why? Is there . . .'

'If you don't mind, sir, I'd just like a word with him. In private.'

'But Wilt's a most inoffensive man,' said the Vice-Principal, 'I'm sure he couldn't help you at all.'

'Possibly not but all the same . . .'

'You're not suggesting for one moment that Henry Wilt had anything to do with . . .' the Vice-Principal stopped and studied the expression on the Inspector's face. It was ominously neutral.

'I'd rather not go into details,' said Inspector Flint, 'and it's best if we don't jump to conclusions.'

The Vice-Principal picked up the phone. 'Do you want him to come across to that . . . er . . . caravan?' he asked.

Inspector Flint shook his head. 'We like to be as inconspicuous as possible. If I could just have the use of an empty office.'

'There's an office next door. You can use that.'

Wilt was in the canteen having lunch with Peter Braintree when the Vice-Principal's secretary came down with a message.

'Can't it wait?' asked Wilt.

'He said it was most urgent.'

'It's probably your senior lectureship come through at last,'

85

said Braintree brightly. Wilt swallowed the rest of his Scotch egg and got up.

'I doubt that,' he said and went wanly out of the canteen and up the stairs. He had a horrid suspicion that promotion was the last thing the Vice-Principal wanted to see him about.

'Now, sir,' said the Inspector when they were seated in the office, 'my name is Flint, Inspector Flint, CID, and you're Mr Wilt? Mr Henry Wilt?'

'Yes,' said Wilt.

'Now, Mr Wilt, as you may have gathered we are investigating the suspected murder of a woman whose body is believed to have been deposited at the bottom of one of the foundation holes for the new building. I daresay you know about it.' Wilt nodded. 'And naturally we are interested in anything that might be of assistance. I wonder if you would mind having a look at these notes.'

He handed Wilt a piece of paper. It was headed 'Notes on Violence and the Break-Up of Family Life', and underneath were a number of sub-headings.

1. Increasing use of violence in public life to attain political ends. A) Bombings. B) Hijacking. C) Kidnapping. D) Assassination.
2. Ineffectuality of Police Methods in combating Violence.
   A) Negative approach. Police able only to react to crime after it has taken place.
   B) Use of violence by police themselves.
   C) Low level of intelligence of average policeman.
   D) Increasing use of sophisticated methods such as diversionary tactics by criminals.
3. Influence of media. TV brings crime techniques into the home.

There was more. Much more. Wilt looked down the list with a sense of doom.

'You recognize the handwriting?' asked the Inspector.

'I do,' said Wilt, adopting rather prematurely the elliptical language of the witness box.

'You admit that you wrote those notes?' The Inspector reached out a hand and took the notes back.

'Yes.'

'They express your opinion of police methods?'

Wilt pulled himself together. 'They were jottings I was making for a lecture to Sandwich-Course Trainee Firemen,' he explained. 'They were simply rough ideas. They need amplifying of course . . .'

'But you don't deny you wrote them?'

'Of course I don't. I've just said I did, haven't I?'

The Inspector nodded and picked up a book. 'And this is yours too?'

Wilt looked at *Bleak House*. 'It says so, doesn't it?'

Inspector Flint opened the cover. 'So it does,' he said with a show of astonishment, 'so it does.'

Wilt stared at him. There was no point in maintaining the pretence any longer. The best thing to do was to get it over quickly. They had found that bloody book in the basket of the bicycle and the notes must have fallen out of his pocket on the building site.

'Look, Inspector,' he said, 'I can explain everything. It's really quite simple. I did go into that building site . . .'

The Inspector stood up. 'Mr Wilt, if you're prepared to make a statement I think I should warn you . . .'

Wilt went down to the Murder Headquarters and made a statement in the presence of a police stenographer. His progress to the blue caravan and his failure to come out again were noted with interest by members of the staff teaching in the Science block, by students in the canteen and by twenty-five fellow lecturers gaping through the windows of the Staff Room.

Chapter 9

'Goddamn the thing,' said Gaskell as he knelt greasily beside the engine of the cruiser, 'you'd think that even in this pre-technological monarchy they'd fit a decent motor. This contraption must have been made for the Ark.'

'Ark Ark the Lark,' said Sally, 'and cut the crowned heads foolery. Eva's a reginaphile.'

'A what?'

'Reginaphile. Monarchist. Get it. She's the Queen's Bee so don't be anti-British. We don't want her to stop working as well as the motor. Maybe it isn't the con rod.'

'If I could only get the head off I could tell,' said Gaskell.

'And what good would that do? Buy you another?' said Sally and went into the cabin where Eva was wondering what they were going to have for supper. 'Tarbaby is still tinkering with the motor. He says it's the con rod.'

'Con rod?' said Eva.

'Only connect, baby, only connect.'

'With what?'

'The thigh bone's connected to the knee bone. The con rod's connected to the piston and as everyone knows pistons are penis symbols. The mechanized male's substitute for sex. The Outboard Motor Syndrome. Only this happens to be inboard like his balls never dropped. Honestly, Gaskell is so regressive.'

'I'm sure I don't know,' said Eva.

Sally lay back on the bunk and lit a cigar. 'That's what I love about you, Eva. You don't know. Ignorance is blissful, baby. I lost mine when I was fourteen.'

Eva shook her head. 'Men,' she said disapprovingly.

'He was old enough to be my grandfather,' said Sally. 'He *was* my grandfather.'

'Oh no. How awful.'

'Not really,' said Sally laughing, 'he was an artist. With a beard. And the smell of paint on his smock and there was this studio and he wanted to paint me in the nude. I was so pure in

88

those days. He made me lie on this couch and he arranged my legs. He was always arranging my legs and then standing back to look at me and painting. And then one day when I was lying there he came over and bent my legs back and kissed me and then he was on top of me and his smock was up and . . .'

Eva sat and listened, fascinated. She could visualize it all so clearly, even the smell of the paint in the studio and the brushes. Sally had had such an exciting life, so full of incident and so romantic in a dreadful sort of way. Eva tried to remember what she had been like at fourteen and not even going out with boys and there was Sally lying on a couch with a famous artist in his studio.

'But he raped you,' she said finally. 'Why didn't you tell the police?'

'The police? You don't understand. I was at this terribly exclusive school. They would have sent me home. It was progressive and all that but I shouldn't have been out being painted by this artist and my parents would never have forgiven me. They were so strict.' Sally sighed, overcome by the rigours of her wholly fictitious childhood. 'And now you can see why I'm so afraid of being hurt by men. When you've been raped you know what penile aggression means.'

'I suppose you do,' said Eva, in some doubt as to what penile aggression was.

'You see the world differently too. Like G says, nothing's good and nothing's bad. It just is.'

'I went to a lecture on Buddhism once,' said Eva, 'and that's what Mr Podgett said. He said—'

'Zen's all wrong. Like you just sit around waiting. That's passive. You've got to make things happen. You sit around waiting long enough, you're dead. Someone's trampled all over you. You've got to see things happen your way and no one else's.'

'That doesn't sound very sociable,' said Eva. 'I mean if we all did just what we wanted all the time it wouldn't be very nice for other people.'

'Other people are hell,' said Sally. 'That's Sartre and he should know. You do what you want is good and no moral kickback. Like G says, rats are the paradigm. You think rats go around thinking what's good for other people?'

'Well no, I don't suppose they do,' said Eva.

'Right. Rats aren't ethical. No way. They just do. They don't get screwed up thinking.'

'Do you think rats can think?' asked Eva, now thoroughly engaged in the problems of rodent psychology.

'Of course they can't. Rats just are. No *Schadenfreude* with rats.'

'What's *Schadenfreude*?'

'Second cousin to *Weltschmerz*,' said Sally, stubbing her cigar out in the ashtray. 'So we can all do what we want whenever we want to. That's the message. It's only people like G who've got the know bug who get balled up.'

'No bug?' said Eva.

'They've got to know how everything works. Scientists. Lawrence was right. It's all head and no body with G.'

'Henry's a bit like that,' said Eva. 'He's always reading or talking about books. I've told him he doesn't know what the real world is like.'

In the Mobile Murder Headquarters Wilt was learning. He sat opposite Inspector Flint whose face was registering increasing incredulity.

'Now, we'll just go over that again,' said the Inspector. 'You say that what those men saw down that hole was in actual fact an inflatable plastic doll with a vagina.'

'The vagina is incidental,' said Wilt, calling forth reserves of inconsequence.

'That's as maybe,' said the Inspector. 'Most dolls don't have them but . . all right, we'll let that pass. The point I'm trying to get at is that you're quite positive there isn't a real live human being down there.'

'Positive,' said Wilt, 'and if there were it is doubtful if it would still be alive now.'

The Inspector studied him unpleasantly. 'I don't need you to point that out to me,' he said. 'If there was the faintest possibility of whatever it is down there being alive I wouldn't be sitting here, would I?'

'No,' said Wilt.

'Right. So now we come to the next point. How is it that what those men saw, they say a woman and you say a doll . . . that this thing was wearing clothes, had hair and even more remark-

90

ably had its head bashed in and one hand stretched up in the air?'

'That was the way it fell,' said Wilt. 'I suppose the arm got caught up on the side and lifted up.'

'And its head was bashed in?'

'Well, I did drop a lump of mud on it,' Wilt admitted, 'that would account for that.'

'You dropped a lump of mud on its head?'

'That's what I said,' Wilt agreed.

'I know that's what you said. What I want to know is why you felt obliged to drop a lump of mud on the head of an inflatable doll that had, as far as I can gather, never done you any harm.'

Wilt hesitated. That damned doll had done him a great deal of harm one way and another but this didn't seem an opportune moment to go into that. 'I don't know really,' he said finally, 'I just thought it might help.'

'Help what?'

'Help . . . I don't know. I just did it, that's all. I was drunk at the time.'

'All right, we'll come back to that in a minute. There's still one question you haven't answered. If it was a doll, why was it wearing clothes?'

Wilt looked desperately round the caravan and met the eyes of the police stenographer. There was a look in them that didn't inspire confidence. Talk about lack of suspension of disbelief.

'You're not going to believe this,' Wilt said. The Inspector looked at him and lit a cigarette.

'Well?'

'As a matter of fact I had dressed it up,' Wilt said, squirming with embarrassment.

'You had dressed it up?'

'Yes,' said Wilt.

'And may one enquire what purpose you had in mind when you dressed it up?'

'I don't know exactly.'

The Inspector sighed significantly. 'Right. We go back to the beginning. We have a doll with a vagina which you dress up and bring down here in the dead of night and deposit at the bottom of a thirty-foot hole and drop lumps of mud on its head. Is that what you're saying?'

'Yes,' said Wilt.

'You wouldn't prefer to save everyone concerned a lot of time and bother by admitting here and now that what is at present resting, hopefully at peace, under twenty tons of concrete at the bottom of that pile hole is the body of a murdered woman?'

'No,' said Wilt, 'I most definitely wouldn't.'

Inspector Flint sighed again. 'You know, we're going to get to the bottom of this thing,' he said. 'It may take time and it may take expense and God knows it's taking patience but when we do get down there—'

'You're going to find an inflatable doll,' said Wilt.

'With a vagina?'

'With a vagina.'

In the Staff Room Peter Braintree staunchly defended Wilt's innocence. 'I tell you I've known Henry well for the past seven years and whatever has happened he had nothing to do with it.'

Mr Morris, the Head of Liberal Studies, looked out of the window sceptically. 'They've had him in there since ten past two. That's four hours,' he said. 'They wouldn't do that unless they thought he had some connection with the dead woman.'

'They can think what they like. I know Henry and even if the poor sod wanted to he's incapable of murdering anyone.'

'He did punch that printer on Tuesday. That shows he's capable of irrational violence.'

'Wrong again. The printer punched him,' said Braintree.

'Only after Wilt had called him a snivelling fucking moron,' Mr Morris pointed out. 'Anyone who goes into Printers Three and calls one of them that needs his head examined. They killed poor old Pinkerton, you know. He gassed himself in his car.'

'They had a damned good try at killing old Henry come to that.'

'Of course, that blow might have affected his brain,' said Mr Morris, with morose satisfaction. 'Concussion can do funny things to a man's character. Change him overnight from a nice quiet inoffensive little fellow like Wilt into a homicidal maniac

92

who suddenly goes berserk. Stranger things have happened.'

'I daresay Henry would be the first to agree with you,' said Braintree. 'It can't be very pleasant sitting in that caravan being questioned by detectives. I wonder what they're doing to him.'

'Just asking questions. Things like "How have you been getting on with your wife?" and "Can you account for your movements on Saturday night?" They start off gently and then work up to the heavy stuff later on.'

Peter Braintree sat in silent horror. Eva. He'd forgotten all about her and as for Saturday night he knew exactly what Henry had said he had been doing before he turned up on the doorstep covered with mud and looking like death . . .

'All I'm saying,' said Mr Morris, 'is that it seems very strange to me that they find a dead body at the bottom of a shaft filled with concrete and the next thing you know they've got Wilt in that Murder HQ for questioning. Very strange indeed. I wouldn't like to be in his shoes.' He got up and left the room and Peter Braintree sat on wondering if there was anything he should do like phone a lawyer and ask him to come round and speak to Henry. It seemed a bit premature and presumably Henry could ask to see a lawyer himself if he wanted one.

Inspector Flint lit another cigarette with an air of insouciant menace. 'How well do you get on with your wife?' he asked.

Wilt hesitated. 'Well enough,' he said.

'Just well enough? No more than that?'

'We get along just fine,' said Wilt, conscious that he had made an error.

'I see. And I suppose she can substantiate your story about this inflatable doll.'

'Substantiate it?'

'The fact that you made a habit of dressing it up and carrying on with it.'

'I didn't make a habit of anything of the sort,' said Wilt indignantly.

'I'm only asking. You were the one who first raised the fact that it had a vagina. I didn't. You volunteered the information and naturally I assumed . . .'

'What did you assume?' said Wilt. 'You've got no right . . .'

93

'Mr Wilt,' said the Inspector, 'put yourself in my position. I am investigating a case of suspected murder and a man comes along and tells me that what two eye-witnesses describe as the body of a well-nourished woman in her early thirties . . .'

'In her early thirties? Dolls don't have ages. If that bloody doll was more than six months old. . . .'

'Please, Mr Wilt, if you'll just let me continue. As I was saying we have a prima facie case of murder and you admit yourself to having put a doll with a vagina down that hole. Now if you were in my shoes what sort of inference would you draw from that?'

Wilt tried to think of some totally innocent interpretation and couldn't.

'Wouldn't you be the first to agree that it does look a bit peculiar?'

Wilt nodded. It looked horribly peculiar.

'Right,' continued the Inspector. 'Now if we put the nicest possible interpretation on your actions and particularly on your emphasis that this doll had a vagina—'

'I didn't emphasize it. I only mentioned the damned thing to indicate that it was extremely lifelike. I wasn't suggesting I made a habit of . . .' He stopped and looked miserably at the floor.

'Go on, Mr Wilt, don't stop now. It often helps to talk.'

Wilt stared at him frantically. Talking to Inspector Flint wasn't helping him one iota. 'If you're implying that my sex life was confined to copulating with an inflatable fucking doll dressed in my wife's clothes. . . .'

'Hold it there,' said the Inspector, stubbing out his cigarette significantly. 'Ah, so we've taken another step forward. You admit then that whatever is down that hole is dressed in your wife's clothes? Yes or no.'

'Yes,' said Wilt miserably.

Inspector Flint stood up. 'I think it's about time we all went and had a little chat with Mrs Wilt,' he said, 'I want to hear what she has to say about your funny little habits.'

'I'm afraid that's going to be a little difficult,' said Wilt.

'Difficult?'

'Well you see the thing is she's gone away.'

'Gone away?' said the Inspector. 'Did I hear you say that Mrs Wilt has gone away?'

94

'Yes.'

'And where has Mrs Wilt gone to?'

'That's the trouble. I don't know.'

'You don't know?'

'No, I honestly don't,' said Wilt.

'She didn't tell you where she was going?'

'No. She just wasn't there when I got home.'

'She didn't leave a note or anything like that?'

'Yes,' said Wilt, 'as a matter of fact she did.'

'Right, well let's just go up to your house and have a look at that note.'

'I'm afraid that's not possible,' said Wilt. 'I got rid of it.'

'You got rid of it?' said the Inspector. 'You got rid of it? How?'

Wilt looked pathetically across at the police stenographer. 'To tell the truth I wiped my bottom with it,' he said.

Inspector Flint gazed at him demonically. 'You did what?'

'Well, there was no toilet paper in the lavatory so I . . .' he stopped. The Inspector was lighting yet another cigarette. His hands were shaking and he had a distant look in his eyes that suggested he had just peered over some appalling abyss. 'Mr Wilt,' he said when he had managed to compose himself, 'I trust I am a reasonably tolerant man, a patient man and a humane man, but if you seriously expect me to believe one word of your utterly preposterous story you must be insane. First you tell me you put a doll down that hole. Then you admit that it was dressed in your wife's clothes. Now you say that she went away without telling you where she was going and finally to cap it all you have the temerity to sit there and tell me that you wiped your arse with the one piece of solid evidence that could substantiate your statement.'

'But I did,' said Wilt.

'Balls,' shouted the Inspector. 'You and I both know where Mrs Wilt has gone and there's no use pretending we don't. She's down at the bottom of that fucking hole and you put her there.'

'Are you arresting me?' Wilt asked as they walked in a tight group across the road to the police car.

'No,' said Inspector Flint, 'you're just helping the police with their enquiries. It will be on the news tonight.'

95

'My dear Braintree, of course we'll do all we can,' said the Vice-Principal. 'Wilt has always been a loyal member of staff and there has obviously been some dreadful mistake. I'm sure you needn't worry. The whole thing will right itself before long.'

'I hope you're right,' said Braintree, 'but there are complicating factors. For one thing there's Eva . . .'

'Eva? Mrs Wilt? You're not suggesting . . .'

'I'm not suggesting anything. All I'm saying is . . . well, she's missing from home. She walked out on Henry last Friday.'

'Mrs Wilt walked . . . well I hardly knew her, except by reputation of course. Wasn't she the woman who broke Mr Lockyer's collar-bone during a part-time Evening Class in Judo some years back?'

'That was Eva,' said Braintree.

'She hardly sounds the sort of woman who would allow Wilt to put her down . . .'

'She isn't,' said Braintree hastily. 'If anyone was liable to be murdered in the Wilt household it was Henry. I think the police should be informed of that.'

They were interrupted by the Principal who came in with a copy of the evening paper. 'You've seen this I suppose,' he said, waving it distraughtly. 'It's absolutely appalling.' He put the paper down on the desk and indicated the headlines. MURDERED WOMAN BURIED IN CONCRETE AT TECH. LECTURER HELPING POLICE.

'Oh dear,' said the Vice-Principal. 'Oh dear. How very unfortunate. It couldn't have come at a worse moment.'

'It shouldn't have come at all,' snapped the Principal. 'And that's not all. I've already had half a dozen phone calls from parents wanting to know if we make a habit of employing murderers on the full-time staff. Who is this fellow Wilt anyway?'

'He's in Liberal Studies,' said the Vice-Principal. 'He's been with us ten years.'

'Liberal Studies. I might have guessed it. If they're not poets manqué they're Maoists or . . . I don't know where the hell Morris gets them from. And now we've got a blasted murderer. God knows what I'm going to tell the Education Committee tonight. They've called an emergency meeting for eight.'

'I must say I resent Wilt being called a murderer,' said

96

Braintree loyally. 'There is nothing to suggest that he has murdered anyone.'

The Principal studied him for a moment and then looked back at the headlines. 'Mr Braintree, when someone is helping the police with their enquiries into a murder it may not be proven that he is a murderer but the suggestion is there.'

'This certainly isn't going to help us to get the new CNAA degree off the ground,' intervened the Vice-Principal tactfully. 'We've got a visit from the Inspection Committee scheduled for Friday.'

'From what the police tell me it isn't going to help get the new Administration block off the ground either,' said the Principal. 'They say it's going to take at least three days to bore down to the bottom of that pile and then they'll have to drill through the concrete to get the body out. That means they'll have to put a new pile down and we're already well behind schedule and our building budget has been halved. Why on earth couldn't he have chosen somewhere else to dispose of his damned wife?'

'I don't think . . .' Braintree began.

'I don't care what you think,' said the Principal, 'I'm merely telling you what the police think.'

Braintree left them still wrangling and trying to figure out ways and means of counteracting the adverse publicity the case had already brought the Tech. He went down to the Liberal Studies office and found Mr Morris in a state of despair. He was trying to arrange stand-in lecturers for all Wilt's classes.

'But he'll probably be back in the morning,' Braintree said.

'Like hell he will,' said Mr Morris 'When they take them in like that they keep them. Mark my words. The police may make mistakes, I'm not saying they don't, but when they act this swiftly they're onto a sure thing. Mind you, I always thought Wilt was a bit odd.'

'Odd? I've just come from the VP's office. You want to hear what the Principal's got to say about Liberal Studies staff.'

'Christ,' said Mr Morris, 'don't tell me.'

'Anyway what's so odd about Henry?'

'Too meek and mild for my liking. Look at the way he accepted remaining a Lecturer Grade Two all these years.'

'That was hardly his fault.'

'Of course it was his fault. All he had to do was threaten to resign and go somewhere else and he'd have got promotion like a shot. That's the only way to get on in this place. Make your presence felt.'

'He seems to have done that now,' said Braintree. 'The Principal is already blaming him for throwing the building programme off schedule and if we don't get the Joint Honours degree past the CNAA, Henry's going to be made the scapegoat. It's too bad. Eva should have had more sense than to walk out on him like that.'

Mr Morris took a more sombre view. 'She'd have shown a damned sight more sense if she'd walked out on him before the sod took it into his head to beat her to death and dump her down that bloody shaft. Now who the hell can I get to take Gasfitters One tomorrow?'

Chapter 10

At 34 Parkview Avenue Wilt sat in the kitchen with Clem while the detectives ransacked the house. 'You're not going to find anything incriminating here,' he told Inspector Flint.

'Never you mind what we're going to find. We're just having a look.'

He sent one detective upstairs to examine Mrs Wilt's clothes or what remained of them.

'If she went away she'd have taken half her wardrobe,' he said. 'I know women. On the other hand if she's pushing up twenty tons of premix she wouldn't need more than what she's got on.'

Eva's wardrobe was found to be well stocked. Even Wilt had to admit that she hadn't taken much with her.

'What was she wearing when you last saw her?' the Inspector asked.

'Lemon loungers,' said Wilt.

'Lemon what?'

'Pyjamas,' said Wilt, adding to the list of incriminating evidence against him. The Inspector made a note of the fact in his pocketbook.

'In bed, was she?'

'No,' said Wilt. 'Round at the Pringsheims.'

'The Pringsheims? And who might they be?'

'The Americans I told you about who live in Rossiter Grove.'

'You haven't mentioned any Americans to me,' said the Inspector.

'I'm sorry. I thought I had. I'm getting muddled. She went away with them.'

'Oh did she? And I suppose we'll find they're missing too?'

'Almost certainly,' said Wilt. 'I mean if she was going away with them they must have gone too and if she isn't with them I can't imagine where she has got to.'

'I can,' said the Inspector looking with distasteful interest at a stain on a sheet one of the detectives had found in the dirty

99

linen basket. By the time they left the house the incriminating evidence consisted of the sheet, an old dressing-gown cord that had found its way mysteriously into the attic, a chopper that Wilt had once used to open a tin of red lead, and a hypodermic syringe which Eva had got from the vet for watering cacti very precisely during her Indoor Plant phase. There was also a bottle of tablets with no label on it.

'How the hell would I know what they are?' Wilt asked when confronted with the bottle. 'Probably aspirins. And anyway it's full.'

'Put it with the other exhibits,' said the Inspector. Wilt looked at the box.

'For God's sake, what do you think I did with her? Poisoned her, strangled her, hacked her to bits with a chopper and injected her with Biofood?'

'What's Biofood?' asked Inspector Flint with sudden interest.

'It's stuff you feed plants with,' said Wilt. 'The bottle's on the windowsill.'

The Inspector added the bottle of Biofood to the box. 'We know what you did with her, Mr Wilt,' he said. 'It's how that interests us now.'

They went out to the police car and drove round to the Pringsheims' house in Rossiter Grove. 'You just sit in the car with the constable here while I go and see if they're in,' said Inspector Flint and went to the front door. Wilt sat and watched while he rang the bell. He rang again. He hammered on the doorknocker and finally he walked round through the gate marked Tradesman's Entrance to the kitchen door. A minute later he was back and fumbling with the car radio.

'You've hit the nail on the head all right, Wilt,' he snapped. 'They've gone away. The place is a bloody shambles. Looks like they've had an orgy. Take him out.'

The two detectives bundled Wilt, no longer Mr Wilt but plain Wilt and conscious of the fact, out of the car while the Inspector called Fenland Constabulary and spoke with sinister urgency about warrants and sending something that sounded like the D brigade up. Wilt stood in the driveway of 12 Rossiter Grove and wondered what the hell was happening to him. The order of things on which he had come to depend was disintegrating around him.

100

'We're going in the back way,' said the Inspector. 'This doesn't look good.'

They went down the path to the kitchen door and round to the back garden. Wilt could see what the Inspector had meant by a shambles. The garden didn't look at all good. Paper plates lay about the lawn or, blown by the wind, had wheeled across the garden into honeysuckle or climbing rose while paper cups, some squashed and some still filled with Pringsheim punch and rainwater, littered the ground. But it was the beefburgers that gave the place its air of macabre filth. They were all over the lawn, stained with coleslaw so that Wilt was put in mind of Clem.

'The dog returns to his vomit,' said Inspector Flint evidently reading his mind. They crossed the terrace to the lounge windows and peered through. If the garden was bad the interior was awful.

'Smash a pane in the kitchen window and let us in,' said the Inspector to the taller of the two detectives. A moment later the lounge window slid back and they went inside.

'No need for forcible entry,' said the detective. 'The back door was unlocked and so was this window. They must have cleared out in a hell of a hurry.'

The Inspector looked round the room and wrinkled his nose. The smell of stale pot, sour punch and candle smoke still hung heavily in the house.

'If they went away,' he said ominously and glanced at Wilt.

'They must have gone away,' said Wilt who felt called upon to make some comment on the scene, 'no one would live in all this mess for a whole weekend without . . .'

'Live? You did say "live" didn't you?' said Flint stepping on a piece of burnt beefburger.

'What I meant . . .'

'Never mind what you meant, Wilt. Let's see what's happened here.'

They went into the kitchen where the same chaos reigned and then into another room. Everywhere it was the same. Dead cigarette ends doused in cups of coffee or ground out on the carpet. Pieces of broken record behind the sofa marked the end of Beethoven's Fifth. Cushions lay crumpled against the wall. Burnt-out candles hung limply post-coital from bottles. To add a final touch to the squalor someone had drawn a portrait of Princess Anne on the wall with a red felt pen. She was surrounded by helmeted policemen and underneath was written. THE FUZZ AROUND OUR ANNY THE ROYAL FAMLYS FANNY THE PRICK IS DEAD LONG LIVE THE CUNT. Sentiments that were doubtless perfectly acceptable in Women's Lib circles but were hardly calculated to establish the Pringsheims very highly in Inspector Flint's regard.

'You've got some nice friends, Wilt,' he said.

'No friends of mine,' said Wilt, with feeling. 'The sods can't even spell.'

They went upstairs and looked in the big bedroom. The bed was unmade, clothes, mostly underclothes, were all over the floor or hung out of drawers and an unstoppered bottle of Joy lay on its side on the dressing-table. The room stank of perfume.

'Jesus wept,' said the Inspector, eyeing a pair of jockstraps belligerently. 'All that's missing is some blood.'

They found it in the bathroom. Dr Scheimacher's cut hand had rained bloodstains in the bath and splattered the tiles with dark blotches. The bathroom door with its broken frame was hanging from the bottom hinge and there were spots of blood on the paintwork.

'I knew it,' said the Inspector, studying their message and that written in lipstick on the mirror above the washbasin. Wilt looked at it too. It seemed unduly personal.

WHERE WILT FAGGED AND EVA RAN WHO WAS THEN THE MALE CHAUVINIST PIG?

'Charming,' said Inspector Flint. He turned to look at Wilt whose face was now the colour of the tiles. 'I don't suppose you'd know anything about that. Not your handiwork?'

'Certainly not,' said Wilt.

'Nor this?' said the Inspector, pointing to the bloodstains in the bath. Wilt shook his head. 'And I suppose this has nothing to do with you either?' He indicated a diaphragm that had been nailed to the wall above the lavatory seat. WHERE THE B SUCKS THERE SUCK I UNDERNEATH A DUTCH CAP NICE AND DRY. Wilt stared at the thing in utter disgust.

'I don't know what to say,' he muttered. 'It's all so awful.'

'You can say that again,' the Inspector agreed, and turned to more practical matters. 'Well, she didn't die in here.'

102

'How can you tell?' asked the younger of the two detectives.

'Not enough blood.' The Inspector looked round uncertainly. 'On the other hand one hard bash . . .' They followed the bloodstains down the passage to the room where Wilt had been dollknotted.

'For God's sake don't touch anything,' said the Inspector, easing the door open with his sleeve, 'the fingerprint boys are going to have a field day here.' He looked inside at the toys.

'I suppose you butchered the children too,' he said grimly.

'Children?' said Wilt, 'I didn't know they had any.'

'Well if you didn't,' said the Inspector, who was a family man, 'the poor little buggers have got something to be thankful for. Not much by the look of things but something.'

Wilt poked his head round the door and looked at the Teddy Bear and the rocking horse. 'Those are Gaskell's,' he said, 'he likes to play with them.'

'I thought you said you didn't know they had any children?'

'They haven't. Gaskell is Dr Pringsheim. He's a biochemist and a case of arrested development according to his wife.' The Inspector studied him thoughtfully. The question of arrest had become one that needed careful consideration.

'I don't suppose you're prepared to make a full confession now?' he asked without much hope.

'No I am not,' said Wilt.

'I didn't think you would be, Wilt,' said the Inspector. 'All right, take him down to the Station. I'll be along later.'

The detectives took Wilt by the arms. It was the last straw.

'Leave me alone,' he yelled. 'You've got no right to do this. You've got—'

'Wilt,' shouted Inspector Flint, 'I'm going to give you one last chance. If you don't go quietly I'm going to charge you here and now with the murder of your wife.'

Wilt went quietly. There was nothing else to do.

'The screw?' said Sally. 'But you said it was the con rod.'

'So I was wrong,' said Gaskell. 'She cranks over.'

'It, G, it. It cranks over.'

'OK, It cranks over so it can't be a con rod. It could be something got tangled with the propshaft.'

'Like what?'

'Like weeds.'

'Why don't you go down and have a look yourself?'

'With these glasses?' said Gaskell, 'I wouldn't be able to see anything.'

'You know I can't swim,' said Sally. 'I have this leg.'

'I can swim,' said Eva.

'We'll tie a rope round you. That way you won't drown,' said Gaskell, 'all you've got to do is go under and feel if there's anything down there.'

'We know what's down there,' said Sally. 'Mud is.'

'Round the propshaft,' said Gaskell. 'Then if there is you can take it off.'

Eva went into the cabin and put on the bikini.

'Honestly, Gaskell, sometimes I think you're doing this on purpose. First it's the con rod and now it's the screw.'

'Well, we've got to try everything. We can't just sit here,' said Gaskell, 'I'm supposed to be back in the lab tomorrow.'

'You should have thought of that before,' said Sally. 'Now all we need is a goddam Albatross.'

'If you ask me we've got one,' said Gaskell, as Eva came out of the cabin and put on a bathing cap.

'Now where's the rope?' she asked. Gaskell looked in a locker and found some. He tied it round her waist and Eva clambered over the side into the water.

'It's ever so cold,' she giggled.

'That's because of the Gulf stream,' said Gaskell, 'it doesn't come this far round.'

Eva swam out and put her feet down.

'It's terribly shallow and full of mud.'

She waded round hanging onto the rope and groped under the stern of the cruiser.

'I can't feel anything,' she called.

'It will be further under,' said Gaskell, peering down at her. Eva put her head under water and felt the rudder.

'That's the rudder,' said Gaskell.

'Of course it is,' said Eva, 'I know that, silly. I'm not stupid.'

She disappeared under the boat. This time she found the propeller but there was nothing wrapped round it.

'It's just muddy, that's all,' she said, when she resurfaced. 'There's mud all along the bottom.'

104

'Well there would be wouldn't there,' said Gaskell. Eva waded round to the side. 'We just happen to be stuck on a mudbank.'

Eva went down again but the propshaft was clear too. 'I told you so,' said Sally, as they hauled Eva back on board. 'You just made her do it so you could see her in her plastic kini all covered with mud. Come, Botticelli baby, let Sally wash you off.'

'Oh Jesus,' said Gaskell. 'Penis arising from the waves.' He went back to the engine and looked at it uncertainly. Perhaps there was a blockage in the fuel line. It didn't seem very likely but he had to try something. They couldn't stay stuck on the mudbank forever.

On the foredeck Sally was sponging Eva down.

'Now the bottom half, darling,' she said untying the string.

'Oh, Sally. No, Sally.'

'Labia babia.'

'Oh, Sally, you are awful.'

Gaskell struggled with the adjustable wrench. All this Touch Therapy was getting to him. And the plastic.

At the County Hall the Principal was doing his best to pacify the members of the Education Committee who were demanding a full Enquiry into the recruitment policy of the Liberal Studies Department.

'Let me explain,' he said patiently, looking round at the Committee, which was a nice balance of business interests and social commitment. 'The 1944 Education Act laid down that all apprentices should be released from their places of employment to attend Day Release Classes at Technical Colleges . . .'

'We know all that,' said a building contractor, 'and we all know it's a bloody waste of time and public money. This country would be a sight better off if they were left to get on with their jobs.'

'The courses they attend,' continued the Principal before anyone with a social conscience could intervene, 'are craft-oriented with the exception of one hour, one obligatory hour of Liberal Studies. Now the difficulty with Liberal Studies is that no one knows what it means.'

'Liberal Studies means,' said Mrs Chatterway, who prided

herself on being an advocate of progressive education, in which role she had made a substantial contribution to the illiteracy rate in several previously good primary schools, 'providing socially deprived adolescents with a firm grounding in liberal attitudes and culturally extending topics . . .'

'It means teaching them to read and write,' said a company director. 'It's no good having workers who can't read instructions.'

'It means whatever anyone chooses it to mean,' said the Principal hastily. 'Now if you are faced with the problem of having to find lecturers who are prepared to spend their lives going into classrooms filled with Gasfitters or Plasterers or Printers who see no good reason for being there, and keeping them occupied with a subject that does not, strictly speaking, exist, you cannot afford to pick and choose the sort of staff you employ. That is the crux of the problem.'

The Committee looked at him doubtfully.

'Am I to understand that you are suggesting that Liberal Studies teachers are not devoted and truly creative individuals imbued with a strong sense of vocation?' asked Mrs Chatterway belligerently.

'No,' said the Principal, 'I am not saying that at all. I am merely trying to make the point that Liberal Studies lecturers are not as other men are. They either start out odd or they end up odd. It's in the nature of their occupation.'

'But they are all highly qualified,' said Mrs Chatterway, 'they all have degrees.'

'Quite. As you say they all hold degrees. They are all qualified teachers but the stresses to which they are subject leave their mark. Let me put it this way. If you were to take a heart transplant surgeon and ask him to spend his working life docking dogs' tails you would hardly expect him to emerge unscathed after ten years' work. The analogy is exact, believe me, exact.'

'Well, all I can say,' protested the building contractor, 'is that not all Liberal Studies lecturers end up burying their murdered wives at the bottom of pile shafts.'

'And all I can say,' said the Principal, 'is that I am extremely surprised more don't.'

The meeting broke up undecided.

Chapter 11

As dawn broke glaucously over East Anglia Wilt sat in the Interview Room at the central Police Station isolated from the natural world and in a wholly artificial environment that included a table, four chairs, a detective sergeant and a fluorescent light on the ceiling that buzzed slightly. There were no windows, just pale green walls and a door through which people came and went occasionally and Wilt went twice to relieve himself in the company of a constable. Inspector Flint had gone to bed at midnight and his place had been taken by Detective Sergeant Yates who had started again at the beginning.

'What beginning?' said Wilt.

'At the very beginning.'

'God made heaven and earth and all . . .'

'Forget the wisecracks,' said Sergeant Yates.

'Now that,' said Wilt, appreciatively, 'is a more orthodox use of wise.'

'What is?'

'Wisecrack. It's slang but it's good slang wisewise if you get my meaning.'

Detective Sergeant Yates studied him closely. 'This is a sound-proof room,' he said finally.

'So I've noticed,' said Wilt.

'A man could scream his guts out in here and no one outside would be any the wiser.'

'Wiser?' said Wilt doubtfully. 'Wisdom and knowledge are not the same thing. Someone outside might not be aware that . . .'

'Shut up,' said Sergeant Yates.

Wilt sighed. 'If you would just let me get some sleep . . .'

'You'll get some sleep when you tell us why you murdered your wife, where you murdered her and how you murdered her.'

'I don't suppose it will do any good if I tell you I didn't murder her.'

Sergeant Yates shook his head.

'No,' he said. 'We know you did. You know you did. We know where she is. We're going to get her out. We know you put her there. You've at least admitted that much.'

'I keep telling you I put an inflatable . . .'

'Was Mrs Wilt inflatable?'

'Was she fuck,' said Wilt.

'Right, so we'll forget the inflatable doll crap . . .'

'I wish to God I could,' said Wilt. 'I'll be only too glad when you get down there and dig it out. It will have burst of course with all that concrete on it but it will still be recognizably an inflatable plastic doll.'

Sergeant Yates leant across the table. 'Let me tell you something. When we do get Mrs Wilt out of there, don't imagine she'll be unrecognizable.' He stopped and stared intently at Wilt. 'Not unless you've disfigured her.'

'Disfigured her?' said Wilt with a hollow laugh. 'She didn't need disfiguring the last time I saw her. She was looking bloody awful. She had on these lemon pyjamas and her face was all covered with . . .' He hesitated. There was a curious expression on the Sergeant's face.

'Blood?' he suggested. 'Were you going to say "blood"?'

'No,' said Wilt, 'I most certainly wasn't. I was going to say powder. White powder and scarlet lipstick. I told her she looked fucking awful.'

'You must have had a very happy relationship with her,' said the Sergeant. 'I don't make a habit of telling my wife she looks fucking awful.'

'You probably don't have a fucking awful-looking wife,' said Wilt making an attempt to conciliate the man.

'What I have or don't have by way of a wife is my business. She lies outside the domain of this discussion.'

'Lucky old her,' said Wilt, 'I wish to God mine did.' By two o'clock they had left Mrs Wilt's appearance and got onto teeth and the question of identifying dead bodies by dental chart.

'Look,' said Wilt wearily, 'I daresay teeth fascinate you but at this time of night I can do without them.'

'You wear dentures or something?'

'No. No, I don't,' said Wilt, rejecting the plural.

'Did Mrs Wilt?'

'No,' said Wilt, 'she was always very . . .'

'I thank you,' said Sergeant Yates, 'I knew it would come out in the end.'

'What would?' said Wilt, his mind still on teeth.

'That "was". The past tense. That's the giveaway. Right, so you admit she's dead. Let's go on from there.'

'I didn't say anything of the sort. You said "Did she wear dentures?" and I said she didn't . . .'

'You said "She was." It's that "was" that interests me. If you had said "is" it would have been different.'

'It might have sounded different,' said Wilt, rallying his defences, 'but it wouldn't have made the slightest difference to the facts.'

'Which are?'

'That my wife is probably still around somewhere alive and kicking . . .'

'You don't half give yourself away, Wilt,' said the Sergeant. 'Now it's "probably" and as for "kicking" I just hope for your sake we don't find she was still alive when they poured that concrete down on top of her. The Court wouldn't take kindly to that.'

'I doubt if anyone would,' said Wilt. 'Now when I said "probably" what I meant was that if you had been held in custody for a day and half the night being questioned on the trot by detectives you'd begin to wonder what had happened to your wife. It might even cross your mind that, all evidence to the contrary, she might not be alive. You want to try sitting on this side of the table before you start criticizing me for using terms like "probable". Anything more improbable than being accused of murdering your wife when you know for a fact that you haven't you can't imagine.'

'Listen, Wilt,' said the Sergeant, 'I'm not criticizing you for your language. Believe me I'm not. I'm merely trying as patiently as I can to establish the facts.'

'The facts are these,' said Wilt. 'Like a complete idiot I made the mistake of dumping an inflatable doll down the bottom of a pile shaft and someone poured concrete in and my wife is away from home and . . .'

'I'll tell you one thing,' Sergeant Yates told Inspector Flint when he came on duty at seven in the morning. 'This one is a hard nut to crack. If you hadn't told me he hadn't a record I'd have sworn he was an old hand and a good one at that. Are you sure Central Records have got nothing on him?' Inspector Flint shook his head.

'He hasn't started squealing for a lawyer yet?'

'Not a whimper. I tell you he's either as nutty as a fruit cake or he's been through this lot before.'

And Wilt had. Day after day, year in year out. With Gasfitters One and Printers Three, with Day Release Motor Mechanics and Meat Two. For ten years he had sat in front of classes answering irrelevant questions, discussing why Piggy's rational approach to life was preferable to Jack's brutishness, why Pangloss' optimism was so unsatisfactory, why Orwell hadn't wanted to shoot that blasted elephant or hang that man, and all the time fending off verbal attempts to rattle him and reduce him to the state poor old Pinkerton was in when he gassed himself. By comparison with Bricklayers Four, Sergeant Yates and Inspector Flint were child's play. If only they would let him get some sleep he would go on running inconsequential rings round them.

'I thought I had him once,' the Sergeant told Flint as they conferred in the corridor. 'I had got him onto teeth.'

'Teeth?' said the Inspector.

'I was just explaining we can always identify bodies from their dental charts and he almost admitted she was dead. Then he got away again.'

'Teeth, eh? That's interesting. I'll have to pursue that line of questioning. It may be his weak link.'

'Good luck on you,' said the Sergeant. 'I'm off to bed.'

'Teeth?' said Wilt. 'We're not going through that again are we? I thought we'd exhausted that topic. The last bloke wanted to know if Eva had them in the past tense. I told him she did and . . .'

'Wilt,' said Inspector Flint, 'I am not interested in whether or not Mrs Wilt had teeth. I presume she must have done. What I want to know is if she still has them. Present tense.'

'I imagine she must have,' said Wilt patiently. 'You'd better ask her when you find her.'

'And when we find her will she be in a position to tell us?'

110

'How the hell should I know? All I can say is that if for some quite inexplicable reason she's lost all her teeth there'll be the devil to pay. I'll never hear the end of it. She's got a mania for cleaning the things and sticking bits of dental floss down the loo. You've no idea the number of times I've thought I'd got worms.'

Inspector Flint sighed. Whatever success Sergeant Yates had had with teeth, it was certainly eluding him. He switched to other matters.

'Let's go over what happened at the Pringsheims' party again,' he said.

'Let's not,' said Wilt who had so far managed to avoid mentioning his contretemps with the doll in the bathroom. 'I've told you five times already and it's wearing a bit thin. Besides it was a filthy party. A lot of trendy intellectuals boosting their paltry egos.'

'Would you say you were an introverted sort of man, Wilt? A solitary type of person?'

Wilt considered the question seriously. It was certainly more to the point than teeth.

'I wouldn't go that far,' he said finally. 'I'm fairly quiet but I'm gregarious too. You have to be to cope with the classes I teach.'

'But you don't like parties?'

'I don't like parties like the Pringsheims', no.'

'Their sexual behaviour outrages you? Fills you with disgust?'

'Their sexual behaviour? I don't know why you pick on that. Everything about them disgusts me. All that crap about Women's Lib for one thing when all it means to someone like Mrs Pringsheim is that she can go around behaving like a bitch on heat while her husband spends the day slaving over a hot test tube and comes home to cook supper, wash up and is lucky if he's got enough energy to wank himself off before going to sleep. Now if we're talking about real Women's Lib that's another matter. I've got nothing against . . .'

'Let's just hold it there,' said the Inspector. 'Now two things you said interest me. One, wives behaving like bitches on heat. Two, this business of you wanking yourself off.'

'Me?' said Wilt indignantly. 'I wasn't talking about myself.'

'Weren't you?'

'No, I wasn't.'

'So you don't masturbate?'

'Now look here, Inspector. You're prying into areas of my private life which don't concern you. If you want to know about masturbation read the Kinsey Report. Don't ask me.'

Inspector Flint restrained himself with difficulty. He tried another tack. 'So when Mrs Pringsheim lay on the bed and asked you to have intercourse with her . . .'

'Fuck is what she said,' Wilt corrected him.

'You said no?'

'Precisely,' said Wilt.

'Isn't that a bit odd?'

'What, her lying there or me saying no?'

'You saying no.'

Wilt looked at him incredulously.

'Odd?' he said. 'Odd? A woman comes in here and throws herself flat on her back on this table, pulls up her skirt and says "Fuck me, honey, prick me to the quick." Are you going to leap onto her with a "Whoopee, let's roll baby"? Is that what you mean by not odd?'

'Jesus wept, Wilt,' snarled the Inspector, 'you're walking a fucking tightrope with my patience.'

'You could have fooled me,' said Wilt. 'All I do know is that your notion of what is odd behaviour and what isn't doesn't begin to make sense with me.'

Inspector Flint got up and left the room. 'I'll murder the bastard, so help me God I'll murder him,' he shouted at the Duty Sergeant. Behind him in the Interview Room Wilt put his head on the table and fell asleep.

At the Tech Wilt's absence was making itself felt in more ways than one. Mr Morris had had to take Gasfitters One at nine o'clock and had come out an hour later feeling that he had gained fresh insight into Wilt's sudden excursion into homicide. The Vice-Principal was fighting off waves of crime reporters anxious to find out more about the man who was helping the police with their enquiries into a particularly macabre and newsworthy crime. And the Principal had begun to regret his criticisms of Liberal Studies to the Education Committee. Mrs Chatterway had phoned to say that she had found his remarks in the worst of taste and had hinted that she might well ask for an enquiry into the running of the Liberal Studies Department. But it was at the meeting of the Course Board that there was most alarm.

'The visitation of the Council for National Academic Awards takes place on Friday,' Dr Mayfield, head of Sociology, told the committee. 'They are hardly likely to approve the Joint Honours degree in the present circumstances.'

'If they had any sense they wouldn't approve it in any circumstances,' said Dr Board. 'Urban Studies and Medieval Poetry indeed. I know academic eclecticism is the vogue these days but Helen Waddell and Lewis Mumford aren't even remotely natural bedfellows. Besides the degree lacks academic content.'

Dr Mayfield bristled. Academic content was his strong point. 'I don't see how you can say that,' he said. 'The course has been structured to meet the needs of students looking for a thematic approach.'

'The poor benighted creatures we manage to lure away from universities to take this course wouldn't know a thematic approach if they saw one,' said Dr Board. 'Come to think of it I wouldn't either.'

'We all have our limitations,' said Dr Mayfield suavely.

'Precisely,' said Dr Board, 'and in the circumstances we should recognize them instead of concocting Joint Honours degrees which don't make sense for students who, if their A-level results are anything to go by, haven't any in the first place. Heaven knows I'm all for educational opportunity but—'

'The point is,' interjected Dr Cox, Head of Science, 'that it is not the degree course as such that is the purpose of the visitation. As I understand it they have given their approval to the degree in principle. They are coming to look at the facilities the College provides and they are hardly likely to be impressed by the presence of so many murder squad detectives. That blue caravan is most off-putting.'

'In any case with the late Mrs Wilt structured into the foundations . . .' began Dr Board.

'I am doing my best to get the police to remove her from . . .'

'The syllabus?' asked Dr Board.

'The premises,' said Dr Mayfield. 'Unfortunately they seem to have hit a snag.'

'A snag?'

'They have hit bedrock at eleven feet.'

Dr Board smiled. 'One wonders why there was any need for thirty-foot piles in the first instance if there is bedrock at eleven,' he murmured.

'I can only tell you what the police have told me,' said Dr Mayfield. 'However they have promised to do all they can to be off the site by Friday. Now I would just like to run over the arrangements again with you. The Visitation will start at eleven with an inspection of the library. We will then break up into groups to discuss Faculty libraries and teaching facilities with particular reference to our ability to provide individual tuition . . .'

'I shouldn't have thought that was a point that needed emphasizing,' said Dr Board. 'With the few students we're likely to get we're almost certain to have the highest teacher to student ratio in the country.'

'If we adopt that approach the Committee will gain the impression that we are not committed to the degree. We must provide a united front,' said Dr Mayfield, 'we can't afford at this stage to have divisions among ourselves. This degree could mean our getting Polytechnic status.'

There were divisions too among the men boring down on the building site. The foreman was still at home under sedation suffering nervous exhaustion brought on by his part in the cementation of a murdered woman and it was left to Barney to superintend operations. 'There was this hand, see . . .' he told the Sergeant in charge.

'On which side?'

'On the right,' said Barney.

'Then we'll go down on the left. That way if the hand is sticking out we won't cut it off.'

They went down on the left and cut off the main electricity cable to the canteen.

'Forget that bleeding hand,' said the Sergeant, 'we go down on the right and trust to luck. Just so long as we don't cut the bitch in half.'

114

They went down on the right and hit bedrock at eleven feet.

'This is going to slow us up no end,' said Barney, 'who would have thought there'd be rock down there.'

'Who would have thought some nut would incorporate his missus in the foundation of a college of further education where he worked,' said the Sergeant.

'Gruesome,' said Barney.

In the meantime the staff had as usual divided into factions. Peter Braintree led those who thought Wilt was innocent and was joined by the New Left on the grounds that anyone in conflict with the fuzz must be in the right. Major Millfield reacted accordingly and led the Right against Wilt on the automatic assumption that anyone who incurred the support of the Left must be in the wrong and that anyway the police knew what they were doing. The issue was raised at the meeting of the Union called to discuss the annual pay demand. Major Millfield proposed a motion calling on the union to support the campaign for the reintroduction of capital punishment. Bill Trent countered with a motion expressing solidarity with Brother Wilt. Peter Braintree proposed that a fund be set up to help Wilt with his legal fees. Dr Lomax, Head of Commerce, argued against this and pointed out that Wilt had, by dismembering his wife, brought the profession into disrepute. Braintree said Wilt hadn't dismembered anyone and that even the police hadn't suggested he had, and there was such a thing as a law against slander. Dr Lomax withdrew his remark. Major Millfield insisted that there were good grounds for thinking Wilt had murdered his wife and that anyway Habeas Corpus didn't exist in Russia. Bill Trent said that capital punishment didn't either. Major Millfield said, 'Bosh.' In the end, after prolonged argument, Major Millfield's motion on hanging was passed by a block vote of the Catering Department while Braintree's proposal and the motion of the New Left were defeated, and the meeting went on to discuss a pay increase of forty-five per cent to keep Teachers in Technical Institutes in line with comparably qualified professions. Afterwards Peter Braintree went down to the Police Station to see if there was anything Henry wanted.

'I wonder if I might see him,' he asked the Sergeant at the desk.

'I'm afraid not, sir,' said the Sergeant, 'Mr Wilt is still helping us with our enquiries.'

'But isn't there anything I can get him? Doesn't he need anything?'

'Mr Wilt is well provided for,' said the Sergeant, with the private reservation that what Wilt needed was his head read.

'But shouldn't he have a solicitor?'

'When Mr Wilt asks for a solicitor he will be allowed to see one,' said the Sergeant, 'I can assure you that so far he hasn't asked.'

And Wilt hadn't. Having finally been allowed three hours sleep he had emerged from his cell at twelve o'clock and had eaten a hearty breakfast in the police canteen. He returned to the Interview Room, haggard and unshaven, and with his sense of the improbable markedly increased.

'Now then, Henry,' said Inspector Flint, dropping an official octave nomenclaturewise in the hope that Wilt would respond, 'about this blood.'

'What blood?' said Wilt, looking round the aseptic room.

'The blood on the walls of the bathroom at the Pringsheims' house. The blood on the landing. Have you any idea how it got there? Any idea at all?'

'None,' said Wilt, 'I can only assume that someone was bleeding.'

'Right,' said the Inspector, 'who?'

'Search me,' said Wilt.

'Quite, and you know what we've found?'

Wilt shook his head.

'No idea?'

'None,' said Wilt.

'Bloodspots on a pair of grey trousers in your wardrobe,' said the Inspector. 'Bloodspots, Henry, bloodspots.'

'Hardly surprising,' said Wilt, 'I mean if you looked hard enough you'd be bound to find some bloodspots in anyone's wardrobe. The thing is I wasn't wearing grey trousers at that party. I was wearing blue jeans.'

'You were wearing blue jeans? You're quite sure about that?'

'Yes.'

'So the bloodspots on the bathroom wall and the bloodspots

116

on your grey trousers have nothing to do with one another?'

'Inspector,' said Wilt, 'far be it from me to teach you your own business but you have a technical branch that specializes in matching bloodstains. Now may I suggest that you make use of their skills to establish . . .'

'Wilt,' said the Inspector, 'Wilt, when I need your advice on how to conduct a murder investigation I'll not only ask for it but I'll resign from the force.'

'Well?' said Wilt.

'Well what?'

'Do they match? Do the bloodstains match?'

The Inspector studied him grimly. 'If I told you they did?' he asked.

Wilt shrugged. 'I'm not in any position to argue,' he said. 'If you say they do, I take it they do.'

'They don't,' said Inspector Flint, 'but that proves nothing,' he continued before Wilt could savour his satisfaction. 'Nothing at all. We've got three people missing. There's Mrs Wilt at the bottom of that shaft . . . No, don't say it, Wilt, don't say it. There's Dr Pringsheim and there's Mrs Fucking Pringsheim.'

'I like it,' said Wilt appreciatively, 'I definitely like it.'

'Like what?'

'Mrs Fucking Pringsheim. It's apposite.'

'One of these days, Wilt,' said the Inspector softly, 'you'll go too far.'

'Patiencewise? To use a filthy expression,' asked Wilt.

The Inspector nodded and lit a cigarette.

'You know something, Inspector,' said Wilt, beginning to feel on top of the situation, 'you smoke too much. Those things are bad for you. You should try . . .'

'Wilt,' said the Inspector, 'in twenty-five years in the service I have never once resorted to physical violence while inter-rogating a suspect but there comes a time, a time and a place and a suspect when with the best will in the world . . .' He got up and went out. Wilt sat back in his chair and looked up at the fluorescent light. He wished it would stop buzzing. It was getting on his nerves.

Chapter 12

On Eel Stretch—Gaskell's map-reading had misled him and they were nowhere near Frogwater Reach or Fen Broad—the situation was getting on everyone's nerves. Gaskell's attempts to mend the engine had had the opposite effect. The cockpit was flooded with fuel oil and it was difficult to walk on deck without slipping.

'Jesus, G, anyone would think to look at you that this was a goddam oil rig,' said Sally.

'It was that fucking fuel line,' said Gaskell, 'I couldn't get it back on.'

'So why try starting the motor with it off?'

'To see if it was blocked.'

'So now you know. What you going to do about it? Sit here till the food runs out? You've gotta think of something.'

'Why me? Why don't you come up with something?'

'If you were any sort of a man . . .'

'Shit,' said Gaskell. 'The voice of the liberated woman. Comes the crunch and all of a sudden I've got to be a man. What's up with you, man–woman? You want us off of here, you do it. Don't ask me to be a man, uppercase M, in an emergency. I've forgotten how.'

'There must be some way of getting help,' said Sally.

'Oh sure. You just go up top and take a crowsnest at the scenery. All you'll get is a beanfeast of bullrushes.' Sally climbed on top of the cabin and scanned the horizon. It was thirty feet away and consisted of an expanse of reeds.

'There's something over there looks like a church tower,' she said. Gaskell climbed up beside her.

'It is a church tower. So what?'

'So if we flashed a light or something someone might see it.'

'Brilliant. A highly populated place like the top of a church tower there's bound to be people just waiting for us to flash a light.'

'Couldn't we burn something?' said Sally, 'somebody would see the smoke and . . .'

'You crazy? You start burning anything with all that fuel oil floating around they'll see something all right. Like an exploding cruiser with bodies.'

'We could fill a can with oil and put it over the side and float it away before lighting it.'

'And set the reedbeds on fire? What the hell do you want? A fucking holocaust?'

'G baby, you're just being unhelpful.'

'I'm using my brains is all,' said Gaskell. 'You keep coming up with bright ideas like that you're going to land us in a worse mess than we're in already.'

'I don't see why,' said Sally.

'I'll tell you why,' said Gaskell, 'because you went and stole this fucking *Hesperus*. That's why.'

'I didn't steal it. I . . .'

'You tell the fuzz that. Just tell them. You start setting fire to reedbeds and they'll be all over us asking questions. Like whose boat this is and how come you're sailing someone else's cruiser . . . So we got to get out of here without publicity.'

It started to rain.

'That's all we need. Rain,' said Gaskell. Sally went down into the cabin where Eva was tidying up after lunch. 'God, G's hopeless. First he lands us on a mudbank in the middle of nowhere, then he gefucks the motor but good and now he says he doesn't know what to do.'

'Why doesn't he go and get help?' asked Eva.

'How? Swimming? G couldn't swim that far to save his life.'

'He could take the airbed and paddle down to the open water,' said Eva. 'He wouldn't have to swim.'

'Airbed? Did I hear you say airbed? What airbed?'

'The one in the locker with the lifejackets. All you've got to do is blow it up and . . .'

'Honey you're the practicallest,' said Sally, and rushed outside. 'G, Eva's found a way for you to go and get help. There's an airbed in the locker with the lifejackets.' She rummaged in the locker and took out the airbed.

'You think I'm going anywhere on that damned thing you've got another think coming,' said Gaskell.

'What's wrong with it?'

'In this weather? You ever tried to steer one of those things? It's bad enough on a sunny day with no wind. Right now I'd end up in the reeds and anyhow the rain's getting on my glasses.'

'All right, so we wait till the storm blows over. At least we know how to get off here.'

She went back into the cabin and shut the door. Outside Gaskell squatted by the engine and toyed with the wrench. If only he could get the thing to go again.

'Men,' said Sally contemptuously, 'claim to be the stronger sex but when the chips are down it's us women who have to bail them out.'

'Henry's impractical too,' said Eva. 'It's all he can do to mend a fuse. I do hope he isn't worried about me.'

'He's having himself a ball,' said Sally.

'Not Henry. He wouldn't know how.'

'He's probably having it off with Judy.'

Eva shook her head. 'He was just drunk, that's all. He's never done anything like that before.'

'How would you know?'

'Well he is my husband.'

'Husband hell. He just uses you to wash the dishes and cook and clean up for him. What does he give you? Just tell me that.'

Eva struggled with her thoughts inarticulately. Henry didn't give her anything very much. Not anything she could put into words. 'He needs me,' she said finally.

'So he needs you. Who needs needing? That's the rhetoric of female feudalism. So you save someone's life, you've got to be grateful to them for letting you? Forget Henry. He's a jerk.'

Eva bristled. Henry might not be very much but she didn't like him insulted.

'Gaskell's nothing much to write home about,' she said and went into the kitchen. Behind her Sally lay back on the bunk and opened the centre spread of *Playboy*. 'Gaskell's got bread,' she said.

'Bread?'

'Money, honey. Greenstuff. The stuff that makes the world go round Cabaretwise. You think I married him for his looks? Oh no. I can smell a cool million when it comes by me and I do mean buy me.'

120

'I could never marry a man for his money,' said Eva primly. 'I'd have to be in love with him. I really would.'

'So you've seen too many movies. Do you really think Gaskell was in love with me?'

'I don't know. I suppose he must have been.'

Sally laughed. 'Eva baby you are naïve. Let me tell you about G. G's a plastic freak. He'd fuck a goddam chimpanzee if you dressed it up in plastic.'

'Oh honestly. He wouldn't,' said Eva. 'I don't believe it.'

'You think I put you on the Pill for nothing? You go around in that bikini and Gaskell's drooling over you all the time—if I wasn't here he'd have raped you.'

'He'd have a hard time,' said Eva, 'I took Judo classes.'

'Well he'd try. Anything in plastic drives him crazy. Why do you think he had that doll?'

'I wondered about that.'

'Right. You can stop wondering,' said Sally.

'I still don't see what that has to do with you marrying him,' said Eva.

'Then let me tell you a little secret. Gaskell was referred to me . . .'

'Referred?'

'By Dr Freeborn. Gaskell had this little problem and he consulted Dr Freeborn and Dr Freeborn sent him to me.'

Eva looked puzzled. 'But what were you supposed to do?'

'I was a surrogate,' said Sally.

'A surrogate?'

'Like a sex counsellor,' said Sally. 'Dr Freeborn used to send me clients and I would help them.'

'I wouldn't like that sort of job,' said Eva, 'I couldn't bear to talk to men about sex. Weren't you embarrassed?'

'You get used to it and there are worse ways of earning a living. So G comes along with his little problem and I straightened him out but literally and we got married. A business arrangement. Cash on the tail.'

'You mean you . . .'

'I mean I have Gaskell and Gaskell has plastic. It's an elastic relationship. The marriage with the two-way stretch.'

Eva digested this information with difficulty. It didn't seem right somehow. 'Didn't his parents have anything to say about it?' she asked. 'I mean did he tell them about you helping him and all that?'

'Say? What could they say? G told them he'd met me at summer school and Pringsy's greedy little eyes popped out of his greasy little head. Baby, did that fat little man have penis projection. Sell? He could sell anything. The Rockefeller Centre to Rockefeller. So he accepted me. Old Ma Pringsheim didn't. She huffed and she puffed and she blew but this little piggy stayed right where the bank was. G and me went back to California and G graduated in plastic and we've been bio-degradable ever since.'

'I'm glad Henry isn't like that,' said Eva. 'I couldn't live with a man who was queer.'

'G's not queer, honey. Like I said he's a plastic freak.'

'If that's not queer I don't know what is,' said Eva.

Sally lit a cigarillo.

'All men get turned on by something,' she said. 'They're manipulable. All you've got to do is find the kink. I should know.'

'Henry's not like that. I'd know if he was.'

'So he makes with the doll. That's how much you know about Henry. You telling me he's the great lover?'

'We've been married twelve years. It's only natural we don't do it as often as we used to. We're so busy.'

'Busy lizzie. And while you're housebound what's Henry doing?'

'He's taking classes at the Tech. He's there all day and he comes home tired.'

'Takes classes takes asses. You'll be telling me next he's not a sidewinder.'

'I don't know what you mean,' said Eva.

'He has his piece on the side. His secretary knees up on the desk.'

'He doesn't have a secretary.'

'Then students prudence. Screws their grades up. I know. I've seen it. I've been around colleges too long to be fooled.'

'I'm sure Henry would never . . .'

'That's what they all say and then bingo, it's divorce and bobbysex and all you're left to look forward to is menopause and peeking through the blinds at the man next door and waiting for the Fuller Brush man.'

122

'You make it all sound so awful,' said Eva. 'You really do.'

'It is, Eva teats. It is. You've got to do something about it before it's too late. You've got to liberate yourself from Henry. Make the break and share the cake. Otherwise it's male domination doomside.'

Eva sat on the bunk and thought about the future. It didn't seem to hold much for her. They would never have any children now and they wouldn't ever have much money. They would go on living in Parkview Avenue and paying off the mortgage and maybe Henry would find someone else and then what would she do? And even if he didn't, life was passing her by.

'I wish I knew what to do,' she said presently. Sally sat up and put her arm round her.

'Why don't you come to the States with us in November?' she said. 'We could have such fun.'

'Oh I couldn't do that,' said Eva. 'It wouldn't be fair to Henry.'

No such qualms bothered Inspector Flint. Wilt's intransigence under intense questioning merely indicated that he was harder than he looked.

'We've had him under interrogation for thirty-six hours now,' he told the conference of the Murder Squad in the briefing room at the Police Station, 'and we've got nothing out of him. So this is going to be a long hard job and quite frankly I have my doubts about breaking him.'

'I told you he was going to be a hard nut to crack,' said Sergeant Yates.

'Nut being the operative word,' said Flint. 'So it's got to be concrete evidence.'

There was a snigger which died away quickly. Inspector Flint was not in a humorous mood.

'Evidence, hard evidence is the only thing that is going to break him. Evidence is the only thing that is going to bring him to trial.'

'But we've got that,' said Yates. 'It's at the bott . . .'

'I know exactly where it is, thank you Sergeant. What I am talking about is evidence of multiple murder. Mrs Wilt is accounted for. Dr and Mrs Pringsheim aren't. Now my guess is that he murdered all three and that the other two bodies are . . .' He stopped and opened the file in front of him and hunted through it for Notes on Violence and the Break-Up of Family Life. He studied them for a moment and shook his head. 'No,' he muttered, 'it's not possible.'

'What isn't, sir?' asked Sergeant Yates. 'Anything is possible with this bastard.'

But Inspector Flint was not to be drawn. The notion was too awful.

'As I was saying,' he continued, 'what we need now is hard evidence. What we have got is purely circumstantial. I want more evidence on the Pringsheims. I want to know what happened at that party, who was there and why it happened and at the rate we're going with Wilt we aren't going to get anything out of him. Snell, you go down to the department of Biochemistry at the University and get what you can on Dr Pringsheim. Find out if any of his colleagues were at that party. Interview them. Get a list of his friends, his hobbies, his girl friends if he had any. Find out if there is any link between him and Mrs Wilt that would suggest a motive. Jackson, you go up to Rossiter Grove and see what you can get on Mrs Pringsheim . . .'

By the time the conference broke up detectives had been despatched all over town to build up a dossier on the Pringsheims. Even the American Embassy had been contacted to find out what was known about the couple in the States. The murder investigation had begun in earnest.

Inspector Flint walked back to his office with Sergeant Yates and shut the door. 'Yates,' he said, 'this is confidential. I wasn't going to mention it in there but I've a nasty feeling that I know why that sod is so bloody cocky. Have you ever known a murderer sit through thirty-six hours of questioning as cool as a cucumber when he knows we've got the body of his victim pinpointed to the nearest inch?'

Sergeant Yates shook his head. 'I've known some pretty cool customers in my time and particularly since they stopped hanging but this one takes the biscuit. If you ask me he's a raving psychopath.'

Flint dismissed the idea. 'Psychopaths crack easy,' he said. 'They confess to murders they haven't committed or they confess to murders they have committed, but they confess. This

124

Wilt doesn't. He sits there and tells me how to run the investigation. Now take a look at this.' He opened the file and took out Wilt's notes. 'Notice anything peculiar?'

Sergeant Yates read the notes through twice.

'Well, he doesn't seem to think much of our methods,' he said finally. 'And I don't much like this bit about low level of intelligence of average policeman.'

'What about Point Two D?' said the Inspector, 'Increasing use of sophisticated methods such as diversionary tactics by criminals. Diversionary tactics. Doesn't that suggest anything to you?'

'You mean he's trying to divert our attention away from the real crime to something else?'

Inspector Flint nodded. 'What I mean is this. I wouldn't mind betting that when we do get down to the bottom of that fucking pile we're going to find an inflatable doll dressed up in Mrs Wilt's clothes and with a vagina. That's what I think.'

'But that's insane.'

'Insane? It's fucking diabolical,' said the Inspector. 'He's sitting in there like a goddamn dummy giving as good as he gets because he knows he's got us chasing a red herring.'

Sergeant Yates sat down mystified. 'But why? Why draw attention to the murder in the first place? Why didn't he just lie low and act normally?'

'What, and report Mrs Wilt as missing? You're forgetting the Pringsheims. A wife goes missing, so what? Two of her friends go missing and leave their house in a hell of a mess and covered with bloodstains. That needs explaining, that does. So he puts out a false trail . . .'

'But that still doesn't help him,' objected the Sergeant. 'We dig up a plastic doll. Doesn't mean we're going to halt the investigation.'

'Maybe not but it gives him a week while the other bodies disintegrate.'

'You think he used an acid bath like Haigh?' asked the Sergeant. 'That's horrible.'

'Of course it's horrible. You think murder's nice or something? Anyway the only reason they got Haigh was that stupid bugger told them where to look for the sludge. If he'd kept his trap shut for another week they wouldn't have found anything.

The whole lot would have been washed away. Besides I don't know what Wilt's used. All I do know is he's an intellectual, a clever sod and he thinks he's got it wrapped up. First we take him in for questioning, maybe even get him remanded and when we've done that, we go and dig up a plastic inflatable doll. We're going to look right Charlies going into court with a plastic doll as evidence of murder. We'll be the laughing stock of the world. So the case gets thrown out of court and what happens when we pick him up a second time for questioning on the real murders? We'd have the Civil Liberties brigade sinking their teeth into our throats like bleeding vampire bats.'

'I suppose that explains why he doesn't start shouting for a lawyer,' said Yates.

'Of course it does. What does he want with a lawyer now? But pull him in a second time and he'll have lawyers falling over themselves to help him. They'll be squawking about police brutality and victimization. You won't be able to hear yourself speak. His bloody lawyers will have a field day. First plastic dolls and then no bodies at all. He'll get clean away.'

'Anyone who can think that little lot up must be a madman,' said the Sergeant.

'Or a fucking genius,' said Flint bitterly. 'Christ what a case.' He stubbed out a cigarette resentfully.

'What do you want me to do? Have another go at him.'

'No, I'll do that. You go up to the Tech and chivvy his boss there into saying what he really thinks of Wilt. Get any little bit of dirt on the blighter you can. There's got to be something in his past we can use.'

He went down the corridor and into the Interview Room. Wilt was sitting at the table making notes on the back of a statement form. Now that he was beginning to feel, if not at home in the Police Station, at least more at ease with his surroundings, his mind had turned to the problem of Eva's disappearance. He had to admit that he had been worried by the bloodstains in the Pringsheims' bathroom. To while away the time he had tried to formulate his thoughts on paper and he was still at it when Inspector Flint came into the room and banged the door.

'Right, so you're a clever fellow, Wilt,' he said, sitting down and pulling the paper towards him. 'You can read and write

126

and you've got a nice logical and inventive mind so let's just see what you've written here. Who's Ethel?'

'Eva's sister,' said Wilt. 'She's married to a market gardener in Luton. Eva sometimes goes over there for a week.'

'And "Blood in the bath"?'

'Just wondering how it got there.'

'And "Evidence of hurried departure".'

'I was simply putting down my thoughts about the state of the Pringsheims' house,' said Wilt.

'You're trying to be helpful?'

'I'm here helping you with your enquiries. That's the official term isn't it?'

'It may be the official term, Wilt, but in this case it doesn't correspond with the facts.'

'I don't suppose it does very often,' said Wilt. 'It's one of those expressions that covers a multitude of sins.'

'And crimes.'

'It also happens to ruin a man's reputation,' said Wilt. 'I hope you realize what you're doing to mine by holding me here like this. It's bad enough knowing I'm going to spend the rest of my life being pointed out as the man who dressed a plastic doll with a cunt up in his wife's clothes and dropped it down a pile hole without everyone thinking I'm a bloody murderer as well.'

'Where you're going to spend the rest of your life nobody is going to care what you did with that plastic doll,' said the Inspector.

Wilt seized on the admission.

'Ah, so you've found it at last,' he said eagerly. 'That's fine. So now I'm free to go.'

'Sit down and shut up,' snarled the Inspector. 'You're not going anywhere and when you do it will be in a large black van. I haven't finished with you yet. In fact I'm only just beginning.'

'Here we go again,' said Wilt. 'I just knew you'd want to start at the beginning again. You fellows have primary causes on the brain. Cause and effect, cause and effect. Which came first, the chicken or the egg, protoplasm or demiurge? I suppose this time it's going to be what Eva said when we were dressing to go to the party.'

'This time,' said the Inspector, 'I want you to tell me precisely why you stuck that damned doll down that hole.'

'Now that is an interesting question,' said Wilt, and stopped. It didn't seem a good idea to try to explain to Inspector Flint in the present circumstances just what he had had in mind when he dropped the doll down the shaft. The Inspector didn't look the sort of person who would understand at all readily that a husband could have fantasies of murdering his wife without actually putting them into effect. It would be better to wait for Eva to put in an appearance in the flesh before venturing into that uncharted territory of the wholly irrational. With Eva present Flint might sympathize with him. Without her he most certainly wouldn't.

'Let's just say I wanted to get rid of the beastly thing,' he said.

'Let's not say anything of the sort,' said Flint. 'Let's just say you had an ulterior motive for putting it there.'

Wilt nodded. 'I'll go along with that,' he said.

Inspector Flint nodded encouragingly. 'I thought you might. Well, what was it?'

Wilt considered his words carefully. He was getting into deep waters.

'Let's just say it was by way of being a rehearsal.'

'A rehearsal? What sort of rehearsal?'

Wilt thought for a moment.

'Interesting word "rehearsal",' he said. 'It comes from the old French, *rehercer*, meaning . . .'

'To hell with where it comes from,' said the Inspector, 'I want to know where it ends up.'

'Sounds a bit like a funeral too when you come to think of it,' said Wilt, continuing his campaign of semantic attrition.

Inspector Flint hurled himself into the trap. 'Funeral? Whose funeral?'

'Anyone's,' said Wilt blithely. 'Hearse, rehearse. You could say that's what happens when you exhume a body. You rehearse it though I don't suppose you fellows use hearses.'

'For God's sake,' shouted the Inspector. 'Can't you ever stick to the point? You said you were rehearsing something and I want to know what that something was.'

'An idea, a mere idea,' said Wilt, 'one of those ephemera of mental fancy that flit like butterflies across the summer land-

128

scape of the mind blown by the breezes of association that come like sudden showers . . . I rather like that.'

'I don't,' said the Inspector, looking at him bitterly. 'What I want to know is what you were rehearsing. That's what I'd like to know.'

'I've told you. An idea.'

'What sort of idea?'

'Just an idea,' said Wilt. 'A mere . . .'

'So help me God, Wilt,' shouted the Inspector, 'if you start on these fucking butterflies again I'll break the unbroken habit of a lifetime and wring your bloody neck.'

'I wasn't going to mention butterflies this time,' said Wilt reproachfully, 'I was going to say that I had this idea for a book . . .'

'A book?' snarled Inspector Flint. 'What sort of book? A book of poetry or a crime story?'

'A crime story,' said Wilt, grateful for the suggestion.

'I see,' said the Inspector. 'So you were going to write a thriller. Well now, just let me guess the outline of the plot. There's this lecturer at the Tech and he has this wife he hates and he decides to murder her . . .'

'Go on,' said Wilt, 'you're doing very well so far.'

'I thought I might be,' said Flint delightedly. 'Well, this lecturer thinks he's a clever fellow who can hoodwink the police. He doesn't think much of the police. So he dumps a plastic doll down a hole that's going to be filled with concrete in the hope that the police will waste their time digging it out and in the meantime he's buried his wife somewhere else. By the way, where did you bury Mrs Wilt, Henry? Let's get this over once and for all. Where did you put her? Just tell me that. You'll feel better when it's out.'

'I didn't put her anywhere. If I've told you that once I've told you a thousand times. How many more times have I got to tell you I don't know where she is.'

'I'll say this for you, Wilt,' said the Inspector, when he could bring himself to speak. 'I've known some cool customers in my time but I have to take my hat off to you. You're the coolest bastard it's ever been my unfortunate experience to come across.'

Wilt shook his head. 'You know,' he said, 'I feel sorry for you,

Inspector, I really do. You can't recognize the truth when it's staring you in the face.'

Inspector Flint got up and left the room. 'You there,' he said to the first detective he could find. 'Go into that Interview Room and ask that bastard questions and don't stop till I tell you.'

'What sort of questions?'

'Any sort. Just any. Keep asking him why he stuffed an inflatable plastic doll down a pile hole. That's all. Just ask it over and over and over again. I'm going to break that sod.'

He went down to his office and slumped into his chair and tried to think.

Chapter 13

At the Tech Sergeant Yates sat in Mr Morris' office. 'I'm sorry to disturb you again,' he said, 'but we need some more details on this fellow Wilt.'

The Head of Liberal Studies looked up with a haggard expression from the timetable. He had been having a desperate struggle trying to find someone to take Bricklayers Four. Price wouldn't do because he had Mechanics Two and Williams wouldn't anyway. He had already gone home the day before with a nervous stomach and was threatening to repeat the performance if anyone so much as mentioned Bricklayers Four to him again. That left Mr Morris himself and he was prepared to be disturbed by Sergeant Yates for as long as he liked if it meant he didn't have to take those bloody bricklayers.

'Anything to help,' he said, with an affability that was in curious contrast to the haunted look in his eyes. 'What details would you like to know?'

'Just a general impression of the man, sir,' said the Sergeant. 'Was there anything unusual about him?'

'Unusual?' Mr Morris thought for a moment. Apart from a preparedness to teach the most awful Day Release Classes year in and year out without complaint he could think of nothing unusual about Wilt. 'I suppose you could call what amounted to a phobic reaction to *The Lord of the Flies* a bit unusual but then I've never much cared for . . .'

'If you'd just wait a moment, sir,' said the Sergeant busying himself with his notebook. 'You did say "phobic reaction" didn't you?'

'Well what I meant was . . .'

'To flies, sir?'

'To *The Lord of the Flies*. It's a book,' said Mr Morris, now uncertain that he had been wise to mention the fact. Policemen were not noticeably sensitive to those niceties of literary taste that constituted his own definition of intelligence. 'I do hope I haven't said the wrong thing.'

'Not at all, sir. It's these little details that help us to build up a picture of the criminal's mind.'

Mr Morris sighed. 'I'm sure I never thought when Mr Wilt came to us from the University that he would turn out like this.'

'Quite so, sir. Now did Mr Wilt ever say anything disparaging about his wife?'

'Disparaging? Dear me no. Mind you he didn't have to. Eva spoke for herself.' He looked miserably out of the window at the pile-boring machine.

'Then in your opinion Mrs Wilt was not a very likable woman?'

Mr Morris shook his head. 'She was a ghastly woman,' he said.

Sergeant Yates licked the end of his ballpen.

'You did say "ghastly" sir?'

'I'm afraid so. I once had her in an evening class for Elementary Drama.'

'Elementary?' said the Sergeant, and wrote it down.

'Yes, though elemental would have been more appropriate in Mrs Wilt's case. She threw herself into the parts rather too vigorously to be wholly convincing. Her Desdemona to my Othello is something I am never likely to forget.'

'An impetuous woman, would you say?'

'Let me put it this way,' said Mr Morris, 'had Shakespeare written the play as Mrs Wilt interpreted it, Othello would have been the one to be strangled.'

'I see, sir,' said the Sergeant, 'then I take it she didn't like black men.'

'I have no idea what she thought about the racial issue,' said Mr Morris, 'I am talking of her physical strength.'

'A powerful woman, sir?'

'Very,' said Mr Morris with feeling.

Sergeant Yates looked puzzled. 'It seems strange a woman like that allowing herself to be murdered by Mr Wilt without putting up more of a struggle,' he said thoughtfully.

'It seems incredible to me,' Mr Morris agreed, 'and what is more it indicates a degree of fanatical courage in Henry that his behaviour in this department never led me to suspect. I can only suppose he was insane at the time.'

132

Sergeant Yates seized on the point. 'Then it is your considered opinion that he was not in his right mind when he killed his wife?'

'Right mind? I can think of nothing rightminded about killing your wife and dumping her body . . .'

'I meant sir,' said the Sergeant, 'that you think Mr Wilt is a lunatic.'

Mr Morris hesitated. There were a good many members of his department whom he would have classified as mentally unbalanced but he hardly liked to advertise the fact. On the other hand it might help poor Wilt.

'Yes, I suppose so,' he said finally for at heart he was a kindly man. 'Quite mad. Between ourselves, Sergeant, anyone who is prepared to teach the sort of bloodyminded young thugs we get can't be entirely sane. And only last week Wilt got into an altercation with one of the Printers and was punched in the face. I think that may have had something to do with his subsequent behaviour. I trust you will treat what I say in the strictest confidence. I wouldn't want . . .'

'Quite so, sir,' said Sergeant Yates. 'Well, I needn't detain you any longer.'

He returned to the Police Station and reported his findings to Inspector Flint.

'Nutty as a fruitcake,' he announced. 'That's his opinion. He's quite positive about it.'

'In that case he had no right to employ the sod,' said Flint. 'He should have sacked the brute.'

'Sacked him? From the Tech? You know they can't sack teachers. You've got to do something really drastic before they give you the boot.'

'Like murdering three people, I suppose. Well as far as I'm concerned they can have the little bastard back.'

'You mean he's still holding out?'

'Holding out? He's counterattacking. He's reduced me to a nervous wreck and now Bolton says he wants to be relieved. Can't stand the strain any longer.'

Sergeant Yates scratched his head. 'Beats me how he does it,' he said. 'Anyone would think he was innocent. I wonder when he'll start asking for a lawyer.'

'Never,' said Flint. 'What does he need a lawyer for? If I had

133

a lawyer in there handing out advice I'd have got the truth out of Wilt hours ago.'

As night fell over Eel Stretch the wind increased to Gale Force Eight. Rain hammered on the cabin roof, waves slapped against the hull and the cabin cruiser, listing to starboard, settled more firmly into the mud. Inside the cabin the air was thick with smoke and bad feelings. Gaskell had opened a bottle of vodka and was getting drunk. To pass the time they played Scrabble.

'My idea of hell,' said Gaskell, 'is to be huis closed with a couple of dykes.'

'What's a dyke?' said Eva.

Gaskell stared at her. 'You don't know?'

'I know the sort they have in Holland . . .'

'Yoga bear,' said Gaskell, 'you are the naïvest. A dyke is—'

'Forget it, G,' said Sally. 'Whose turn to play?'

'It's mine,' said Eva. 'I . . . M . . . P spells Imp.'

'O . . . T . . . E . . . N . . . T spells Gaskell,' said Sally.

Gaskell drank some more vodka. 'What the hell sort of game we supposed to be playing? Scrabble or some sort of Truth group?'

'Your turn,' said Sally.

Gaskell put D . . . I . . . L . . . D on the O. 'Try that for size.'

Eva looked at it critically.

'You can't use proper names,' she said. 'You wouldn't let me use Squeezy.'

'Eva teats, dildo is not a proper name. It's an improper thing. A surrogate penis.'

'A what?'

'Never mind what it is,' said Sally. 'Your turn to play.' Eva studied her letters. She didn't like being told what to do so often and besides she still wanted to know what a dyke was. And a surrogate penis. In the end she put L . . . O . . . V on the E.

'Is a many-splendoured thing,' said Gaskell and put D . . . I . . . D on the L and O.

'You can't have two of them,' said Eva. 'You've got one Dildo already.'

'This one's different,' said Gaskell, 'it's got whiskers.'

'What difference does that make?'

134

'Ask Sally. She's the one with penis envy.'

'You asshole,' said Sally and put F . . . A . . . G . . . G . . . O on the T. 'Meaning you.'

'Like I said. Truth Scrabble,' said Gaskell. 'Trubble for short. So why don't we just have an encounter group instead. Let the truth hang out like it is.'

Eva used the F to make Faithful. Gaskell followed with Hooker and Sally went Insane.

'Great,' said Gaskell, 'Alphabetical I Ching.'

'Wunderkind, you slay me,' said Sally.

'Go Zelda yourself,' said Gaskell and slid his hand up Eva's thigh.

'Keep your hands to yourself,' said Eva and pushed him away. She put S and N on the I. Gaskell made Butch with the B.

'And don't tell me it's a proper name.'

'Well it's certainly not a word I've heard,' said Eva.

Gaskell stared at her and then roared with laughter.

'Now I've heard it all,' he said. 'Like cunnilingus is a cough medicine. How dumb can you get?'

'Go look in the mirror,' said Sally.

'Oh sure. So I married a goddam lesbian whore who goes round stealing other people's wives and boats and things. I'm dumb. But boobs here beats me. She's so fucking hypocritical she pretends she's not a dyke . . .'

'I don't know what a dyke is,' said Eva.

'Well let me inform you, fatso. A dyke is a lesbian.'

'Are you calling me a lesbian?' said Eva.

'Yes,' said Gaskell.

Eva slapped him across the face hard. Gaskell's glasses came off and he sat down on the floor.

'Now G . . .' Sally began but Gaskell had scrambled to his feet.

'Right you fat bitch,' he said. 'You want the truth you're going to get it. First off, you think husband Henry got into that doll off his own bat, well let me tell you . . .'

'Gaskell, you just shut up,' shouted Sally.

'Like hell I will. I've had about enough of you and your rotten little ways. I picked you out of a cathouse . . .'

'That's not true. It was a clinic,' screamed Sally, 'a clinic for sick perverts like you.'

Eva wasn't listening. She was staring at Gaskell. He had

135

called her a lesbian and had said Henry hadn't got into that doll of his own accord.

'Tell me about Henry,' she shouted. 'How did he get into that doll?'

Gaskell pointed at Sally. 'She put him there. That poor goof wouldn't know . . .'

'You put him there?' Eva said to Sally. 'You did?'

'He tried to make me, Eva. He tried to—'

'I don't believe it,' Eva shouted. 'Henry isn't like that.'

'I tell you he did. He . . .'

'And you put him in that doll?' Eva screamed and launched herself across the table at Sally. There was a splintering sound and the table collapsed. Gaskell scudded sideways onto the bunk and Sally shot out of the cabin. Eva got to her feet and moved forward towards the door. She had been tricked, cheated and lied to. And Henry had been humiliated. She was going to kill that bitch Sally. She stepped out into the cockpit. On the far side Sally was a dark shadow. Eva went round the engine and lunged at her. The next moment she had slipped on the oily deck and Sally had darted across the cockpit and through the door into the cabin. She slammed the door behind her and locked it. Eva Wilt got to her feet and stood with the rain running down her face and as she stood there the illusions that had sustained her through the week disappeared. She saw herself as a fat, silly woman who had left her husband in pursuit of a glamour that was false and shoddy and founded on brittle talk and money. And Gaskell had said she was a lesbian. The full nausea of knowing what Touch Therapy had meant dawned on Eva. She staggered to the side of the boat and sat down on a locker.

And slowly her self-disgust turned back to anger, and a cold hatred of the Pringsheims. She would get her own back on them. They would be sorry they had ever met her. She got up and opened the locker and took out the lifejackets and threw them over the side. Then she blew up the airbed, dropped it into the water and climbed over herself. She let herself down into the water and lay on the airbed. It rocked alarmingly but Eva was not afraid. She was getting her revenge on the Pringsheims and she no longer cared what happened to her. She paddled off through the little waves pushing the lifejackets in front of her. The wind was behind her and the airbed moved easily. In five

136

minutes she had turned the corner of the reeds and was out of sight of the cruiser. Somewhere in the darkness ahead there was the open water where they had seen the dinghies and beyond it land.

Presently she found herself being blown sideways into the reeds. The rain stopped and Eva lay panting on the airbed. It would be easier if she got rid of the lifejackets. She was far enough from the boat for them to be well hidden. She pushed them into the reeds and then hesitated. Perhaps she should keep one for herself. She disentangled a jacket from the bunch and managed to put it on. Then she lay face down on the airbed again and paddled forward down the widening channel.

Sally leant against the cabin door and looked at Gaskell with loathing.

'You stupid jerk,' she said. 'You had to open your big mouth. So what the hell are you going to do now?'

'Divorce you for a start,' said Gaskell.

'I'll alimony you for all the money you've got.'

'Fat chance. You won't get a red cent,' Gaskell said and drank some more vodka.

'I'll see you dead first,' said Sally.

Gaskell grinned. 'Me dead? Anyone's going to die round here, it's you. Booby baby is out for blood.'

'She'll cool off.'

'You think so? Try opening that door if you're so sure. Go on, unlock it.'

Sally moved away from the door and sat down.

'This time you've really bought yourself some trouble,' said Gaskell. 'You had to pick a goddam prizefighter.'

'You go out and pacify her,' said Sally.

'No way. I'd as soon play blind man's bluff with a fucking rhinoceros.' He lay back on the bunk and smiled happily. 'You know there's something really ironical about all this. You had to go and liberate a Neanderthal. Women's Lib for paleolithics. She Tarzan, you Jane. You've bought yourself a piece of zoo.'

'Very funny,' said Sally. 'And what's your role?'

'Me Noah. Just be thankful she hasn't got a gun.' He pulled a pillow up under his head and went to sleep.

Sally sat on staring at his back venomously. She was frightened.

Eva's reaction had been so violent that it had destroyed her confidence in herself. Gaskell was right. There had been something primeval in Eva Wilt's behaviour. She shuddered at the thought of that dark shape moving towards her in the cockpit. Sally got up and went into the galley and found a long sharp knife. Then she went back into the cabin and checked the lock on the door and lay down on her bunk and tried to sleep. But sleep wouldn't come. There were noises outside. Waves lapped against the side of the boat. The wind blew. God, what a mess it all was! Sally clutched her knife and thought about Gaskell and what he had said about divorce.

Peter Braintree sat in the office of Mr Gosdyke, Solicitor, and discussed the problem. 'He's been in there since Monday and it's Thursday now. Surely they've no right to keep him there so long without his seeing a solicitor.'

'If he doesn't ask for one and if the police want to question him and he is prepared to answer their questions and refuses to demand his legal rights I don't really see that there is anything I can do about it,' said Mr Gosdyke.

'But are you sure that that is the situation?' asked Braintree.

'As far as I can ascertain that is indeed the situation. Mr Wilt has not asked to see me. I spoke to the Inspector in charge, you heard me, and it seems quite clear that Mr Wilt appears, for some extraordinary reason, to be prepared to help the police with their enquiries just as long as they feel his presence at the Police Station is necessary. Now if a man refuses to assert his own legal rights then he has only himself to blame for his predicament.'

'But are you absolutely certain that Henry has refused to see you? I mean the police could be lying to you.'

Mr Gosdyke shook his head. 'I have known Inspector Flint for many years,' he said, 'and he is not the sort of man to deny a suspect his rights. No, I'm sorry, Mr Braintree. I would like to be of more assistance but frankly, in the circumstances, I can do nothing. Mr Wilt's predilection for the company of police officers is quite incomprehensible to me, but it disqualifies me from interfering.'

'You don't think they're giving him third degree or anything of that sort?'

138

'My dear fellow, third degree? You've been watching too many old movies on the TV. The police don't use strong-arm methods in this country.'

'They've been pretty brutal with some of our students who have been on demos,' Braintree pointed out.

'Ah, but students are quite another matter and demonstrating students get what they deserve. Political provocation is one thing but domestic murders of the sort your friend Mr Wilt seems to have indulged in come into a different category altogether. I can honestly say that in all my years in the legal profession I have yet to come across a case in which the police did not treat a domestic murderer with great care and not a little sympathy. After all, they are nearly all married men themselves, and in any case Mr Wilt has a degree and that always helps. If you are a professional man, and in spite of what some people may say lecturers in Technical Colleges are members of a profession if only marginally, then you can rest assured that the police will do nothing in the least untoward. Mr Wilt is perfectly safe.'

And Wilt felt safe. He sat in the Interview Room and contemplated Inspector Flint with interest.

'Motivation? Now there's an interesting question,' he said. 'If you had asked me why I married Eva in the first place I'd have some trouble trying to explain myself. I was young at the time and . . .'

'Wilt,' said the Inspector, 'I didn't ask you why you married your wife. I asked you why you decided to murder her.'

'I didn't decide to murder her,' said Wilt.

'It was a spontaneous action? A momentary impulse you couldn't resist? An act of madness you now regret?'

'It was none of those things. In the first place it was not an act. It was mere fantasy.'

'But you do admit that the thought crossed your mind?'

'Inspector,' said Wilt, 'if I acted upon every impulse that crossed my mind I would have been convicted of child rape, buggery, burglary, assault with intent to commit grievous bodily harm and mass murder long ago.'

'All those impulses crossed your mind?'

'At some time or other, yes,' said Wilt.

'You've got a bloody odd mind.'

'Which is something I share with the vast majority of mankind. I daresay that even you in your odd contemplative moments have . . .'

'Wilt,' said the Inspector, 'I don't have odd contemplative moments. Not until I met you anyhow. Now then, you admit you thought of killing your wife . . .'

'I said the notion had crossed my mind, particularly when I have to take the dog for a walk. It is a game I play with myself. No more than that.'

'A game? You take the dog for a walk and think of ways and means of killing Mrs Wilt? I don't call that a game. I call it premeditation.'

'Not badly put,' said Wilt with a smile, 'the meditation bit. Eva curls up in the lotus position on the living-room rug and thinks beautiful thoughts. I take the bloody dog for a walk and think dreadful ones while Clem defecates on the grass verge in Grenville Gardens. And in each case the end result is just the same. Eva gets up and cooks supper and washes up and I come home and watch the box or read and go to bed. Nothing has altered one way or another.'

'It has now,' said the Inspector. 'Your wife has disappeared off the face of the earth together with a brilliant young scientist and his wife, and you are sitting here waiting to be charged with their murder.'

'Which I don't happen to have committed,' said Wilt. 'Ah well, these things happen. The moving finger writes and having writ . . .'

'Fuck the moving finger. Where are they? Where did you put them? You're going to tell me.'

Wilt sighed. 'I wish I could,' he said, 'I really do. Now you've got that plastic doll . . .'

'No we haven't. Not by a long chalk. We're still going down through solid rock. We won't get whatever is down there until tomorrow at the earliest.'

'Something to look forward to,' said Wilt. 'Then I suppose you'll let me go.'

'Like hell I will. I'll have you up for remand on Monday.'

'Without any evidence of murder? Without a body? You can't do that.'

140

Inspector Flint smiled. 'Wilt,' he said, 'I've got news for you. We don't need a body. We can hold you on suspicion, we can bring you up for trial and we can find you guilty without a body. You may be clever but you don't know your law.'

'Well I must say you fellows have an easy job of it. You mean you can go out in the street and pick up some perfectly innocent passer-by and lug him in here and charge him with murder without any evidence at all?'

'Evidence? We've got evidence all right. We've got a blood-spattered bathroom with a busted-down door. We've got an empty house in a filthy mess and we've got some bloody thing or other down that pile hole and you think we haven't got evidence. You've got it wrong.'

'Makes two of us,' said Wilt.

'And I'll tell you another thing, Wilt. The trouble with bastards like you is that you're too clever by half. You overdo things and you give yourselves away. Now if I'd been in your shoes, I'd have done two things. Know what they are?'

'No,' said Wilt, 'I don't.'

'I'd have washed that bathroom down, number one, and number two I'd have stayed away from that hole. I wouldn't have tried to lay a false trail with notes and making sure the caretaker saw you and turning up at Mr Braintree's house at midnight covered in mud. I'd have sat tight and said nothing.'

'But I didn't know about those bloodstains in the bathroom and if it hadn't been for that filthy doll I wouldn't have dumped the thing down the hole. I'd have gone to bed. Instead of which I got pissed and acted like an idiot.'

'Let me tell you something else, Wilt,' said the Inspector. 'You *are* an idiot, a fucking cunning idiot but an idiot all the same. You need your head read.'

'It would make a change from this lot,' said Wilt.

'What would?'

'Having my head read instead of sitting here and being insulted.'

Inspector Flint studied him thoughtfully. 'You mean that?' he asked.

'Mean what?'

'About having your head read? Would you be prepared to undergo an examination by a qualified psychiatrist?'

'Why not?' said Wilt. 'Anything to help pass the time.'

'Quite voluntarily, you understand. Nobody is forcing you to, but if you want . . .'

'Listen, Inspector, if seeing a psychiatrist will help to convince you that I have not murdered my wife I'll be only too happy to. You can put me on a lie detector. You can pump me full of truth drugs. You can . . .'

'There's no need for any of that other stuff,' said Flint, and stood up. 'A good shrink will do very nicely. And if you think you can get away with guilty but insane, forget it. These blokes know when you're malingering madness.' He went to the door and paused. Then he came back and leant across the table.

'Tell me, Wilt,' he said. 'Tell me just one thing. How come you sit there so coolly? Your wife is missing, we have evidence of murder, we have a replica of her, if you are to be believed, under thirty feet of concrete and you don't turn a hair. How do you do it?'

'Inspector,' said Wilt. 'If you had taught Gasfitters for ten years and been asked as many damnfool questions in that time as I have, you'd know. Besides you haven't met Eva. When you do you'll see why I'm not worried. Eva is perfectly capable of taking care of herself. She may not be bright but she's got a built-in survival kit.'

'Jesus, Wilt, with you around for twelve years she must have had something.'

'Oh she has. You'll like Eva when you meet her. You'll get along like a house on fire. You've both got literal minds and an obsession with trivia. You can take a wormcast and turn it into Mount Everest.'

'Wormcast? Wilt, you sicken me,' said the Inspector, and left the room.

Wilt got up and walked up and down. He was tired of sitting down. On the other hand he was well satisfied with his performance. He had surpassed himself and he took pride in the fact that he was reacting so well to what most people would consider an appalling predicament. But to Wilt it was something else, a challenge, the first real challenge he had had to meet for a long time. Gasfitters and Plasterers had challenged him once but he had learnt to cope with them. You jollied them along. Let them talk, ask questions, divert them, get them going,

142

accept their red herrings and hand out a few of your own, but above all you had to refuse to accept their preconceptions. Whenever they asserted something with absolute conviction as a self-evident truth like all wogs began at Calais, all you had to do was agree and then point out that half the great men in English history had been foreigners like Marconi or Lord Beaverbrook and that even Churchill's mother had been a Yank or talk about the Welsh being the original Englishmen and the Vikings and the Danes and from that lead them off through Indian doctors to the National Health Service and birth control and any other topic under the sun that would keep them quiet and puzzled and desperately trying to think of some ultimate argument that would prove you wrong.

Inspector Flint was no different. He was more obsessive but his tactics were just the same. And besides he had got hold of the wrong end of the stick with a vengeance and it amused Wilt to watch him trying to pin a crime on him he hadn't committed. It made him feel almost important and certainly more of a man than he had done for a long, long time. He was innocent and there was no question about it. In a world where everything else was doubtful and uncertain and open to scepticism the fact of his innocence was sure. For the first time in his adult life Wilt knew himself to be absolutely right, and the knowledge gave him a strength he had never supposed he possessed. And besides there was no question in his mind that Eva would turn up eventually, safe and sound, and more than a little subdued when she realized what her impulsiveness had led to. Serve her right for giving him that disgusting doll. She'd regret that to the end of her days. Yes, if anybody was going to come off badly in this affair it was dear old Eva with her bossyness and her busyness. She'd have a job explaining it to Mavis Mottram and the neighbours. Wilt smiled to himself at the thought. And even the Tech would have to treat him differently in future and with a new respect. Wilt knew the liberal conscience too well not to suppose that he would appear anything less than a martyr when he went back. And a hero. They would bend over backwards to convince themselves that they hadn't thought him as guilty as hell. He'd get promotion too, not for being a good teacher but because they would need to salve their fragile consciences. Talk about killing the fatted calf.

Chapter 14

At the Tech there was no question of killing the fatted calf, at least not for Henry Wilt. The imminence of the CNAA visitation on Friday, coinciding as it apparently would with the resurrection of the late Mrs Wilt, was causing something approaching panic. The Course Board met in almost continuous session and memoranda circulated so furiously that it was impossible to read one before the next arrived.

'Can't we postpone the visit?' Dr Cox asked. 'I can't have them in my office discussing bibliographies with bits of Mrs Wilt being dug out of the ground outside the window.'

'I have asked the police to make themselves as inconspicuous as possible,' said Dr Mayfield.

'With conspicuous lack of success so far,' said Dr Board. 'They couldn't be more in evidence. There are ten of them peering down that hole at this very moment.'

The Vice-Principal struck a brighter note. 'You'll be glad to hear that we've managed to restore power to the canteen,' he told the meeting, 'so we should be able to lay on a good lunch.'

'I just hope I feel up to eating,' said Dr Cox. 'The shocks of the last few days have done nothing to improve my appetite and when I think of poor Mrs Wilt . . .'

'Try not to think of her,' said the Vice-Principal, but Dr Cox shook his head.

'You try not to think of her with a damned great boring machine grinding away outside your office window all day.'

'Talking about shocks,' said Dr Board, 'I still can't understand how the driver of that mechanical corkscrew managed to escape electrocution when they cut through the power cable.'

'Considering the problems we are faced with, I hardly think that's a relevant point just at present,' said Dr Mayfield. 'What we have got to stress to the members of the CNAA committee is that this degree is an integrated course with a fundamental substructure grounded thematically on a concomitance of cultural and sociological factors in no way unsuperficially disparate and with a solid quota of academic content to give students an intellectual and cerebral . . .'

'Haemorrhage?' suggested Dr Board.

Dr Mayfield regarded him balefully. 'I really do think this is no time for flippancy,' he said angrily. 'Either we are committed to the Joint Honours degree or we are not. Furthermore we have only until tomorrow to structure our tactical approach to the visitation committee. Now, which is it to be?'

'Which is what to be?' asked Dr Board. 'What has our commitment or lack of it to do with structuring, for want of several far better words, our so-called tactical approach to a committee which, since it is coming all the way from London to us and not vice versa, is presumably approaching us?'

'Vice-Principal,' said Dr Mayfield, 'I really must protest. Dr Board's attitude at this late stage in the game is quite incomprehensible. If Dr Board . . .'

'Could even begin to understand one tenth of the jargon Dr Mayfield seems to suppose is English he might be in a better position to express his opinion,' interrupted Dr Board. 'As it is, "incomprehensible" applies to Dr Mayfield's syntax, not to my attitude. I have always maintained . . .'

'Gentlemen,' said the Vice-Principal, 'I think it would be best if we avoided inter-departmental wrangles at this point in time and got down to business.'

There was a silence broken finally by Dr Cox. 'Do you think the police could be persuaded to erect a screen round that hole?' he asked.

'I shall certainly suggest that to them,' said Dr Mayfield. They passed on to the matter of entertainment.

'I have arranged for there to be plenty of drinks before lunch,' said the Vice-Principal, 'and in any case lunch will be judiciously delayed to allow them to get into the right mood so the afternoon sessions should be cut short and proceed, hopefully, more smoothly.'

'Just so long as the Catering Department doesn't serve Toad in the Hole,' said Dr Board.

The meeting broke up acrimoniously.

So did Mr Morris' encounter with the Crime Reporter of the *Sunday Post*.

'Of course I didn't tell the police that I employed homicidal maniacs as a matter of policy,' he shouted at the reporter. 'And in any case what I said was, as I understood it, to be treated in the strictest confidence.'

'But you did say you thought Wilt was insane and that quite a number of Liberal Studies lecturers were off their heads?'

Mr Morris looked at the man with loathing. 'To put the record straight, what I said was that some of them were . . .'

'Off their rockers?' suggested the reporter.

'No, not off their rockers,' shouted Mr Morris. 'Merely, well, shall we say, slightly unbalanced.'

'That's not what the police say you said. They say quote . . .'

'I don't care what the police say I said. I know what I said and what I didn't and if you're implying . . .'

'I'm not implying anything. You made a statement that half your staff are nuts and I'm trying to verify it.'

'Verify it?' snarled Mr Morris. 'You put words into my mouth I never said and you call that verifying it?'

'Did you say it or not? That's all I'm asking. I mean if you express an opinion about your staff . . .'

'Mr MacArthur, what I think about my staff is my own affair. It has absolutely nothing to do with you or the rag you represent.'

'Three million people will be interested to read your opinion on Sunday morning,' said Mr MacArthur, 'and I wouldn't be at all surprised if this Wilt character didn't sue you if he ever gets out of the copshop.'

'Sue me? What the hell could he sue me for?'

'Calling him a homicidal maniac for a start. Banner headlines HEAD OF LIBERAL STUDIES CALLS LECTURER HOMICIDAL MANIAC should be good for fifty thousand. I'd be surprised if he got less.'

Mr Morris contemplated destitution. 'Even your paper would never print that,' he muttered, 'I mean Wilt would sue you too.'

'Oh we're used to libel actions. They're run-of-the-mill for us. We pay for them out of petty cash. Now if you'd be a bit more cooperative . . .' He left the suggestion in mid-air for Mr Morris to digest.

'What do you want to know?' he asked miserably.

'Got any juicy drug scene stories for us?' asked Mr Mac-

146

Arthur. 'You know the sort of thing. LOVE ORGIES IN LECTURES. That always gets the public. Teenyboppers having it off and all that. Give us a good one and we'll let you off the hook about Wilt.'

'Get out of my office!' yelled Mr Morris.

Mr MacArthur got up. 'You're going to regret this,' he said and went downstairs to the students' canteen to dig up some dirt on Mr Morris.

'Not tests,' said Wilt adamantly. 'They're deceptive.'

'You think so?' said Dr Pittman, consultant psychiatrist at the Fenland Hospital and professor of Criminal Psychology at the University. Being plagiocephalic didn't help either.

'I should have thought it was obvious,' said Wilt. 'You show me an ink-blot and I think it looks like my grandmother lying in a pool of blood, do you honestly think I'm going to be fool enough to say so? I'd be daft to do that. So I say a butterfly sitting on a geranium. And every time it's the same. I think what it does look like and then say something completely different. Where does that get you?'

'It is still possible to infer something from that,' said Dr Pittman.

'Well, you don't need a bloody ink-blot to infer, do you?' said Wilt. Dr Pittman made a note of Wilt's interest in blood. 'You can infer things from just looking at the shape of people's heads.'

Dr Pittman polished his glasses grimly. Heads were not things he liked inferences to be drawn from. 'Mr Wilt,' he said, 'I am here at your request to ascertain your sanity and in particular to give an opinion as to whether or not I consider you capable of murdering your wife and disposing of her body in a singularly revolting and callous fashion. I shall not allow anything you may say to influence my ultimate and objective findings.'

Wilt looked perplexed. 'I must say you're not giving yourself much room for manoeuvre. Since we've dispensed with mechanical aids like tests I should have thought what I had to say would be the only thing you could go on. Unless of course you're going to read the bumps on my head. Isn't that a bit old fashioned?'

'Mr Wilt,' said Dr Pittman, 'the fact that you clearly have a sadistic streak and take pleasure in drawing attention to other people's physical infirmities in no way disposes me to conclude you are capable of murder . . .'

'Very decent of you,' said Wilt, 'though frankly I'd have thought anyone was capable of murder given the right, or to be precise the wrong, circumstances.'

Dr Pittman stifled the impulse to say how right he was. Instead he smiled prognathously. 'Would you say you were a rational man, Henry?' he asked.

Wilt frowned. 'Just stick to Mr Wilt if you don't mind. This may not be a paid consultation but I prefer a little formality.'

Dr Pittman's smile vanished. 'You haven't answered my question.'

'No, I wouldn't say I was a rational man,' said Wilt.

'An irrational one perhaps?'

'Neither the one wholly nor the other wholly. Just a man.'

'And a man is neither one thing nor the other?'

'Dr Pittman, this is your province not mine but in my opinion man is capable of reasoning but not of acting within wholly rational limits. Man is an animal, a developed animal, though come to think of it all animals are developed if we are to believe Darwin. Let's just say man is a domesticated animal with elements of wildness about him . . .'

'And what sort of animal are you, Mr Wilt?' said Dr Pittman. 'A domesticated animal or a wild one?'

'Here we go again. These splendidly simple dual categories that seem to obsess the modern mind. Either/Or Kierkegaard as that bitch Sally Pringsheim would say. No, I am not wholly domesticated. Ask my wife. She'll express an opinion on the matter.'

'In what respect are you undomesticated?'

'I fart in bed, Dr Pittman. I like to fart in bed. It is the trumpet call of the anthropoid ape in me asserting its territorial imperative in the only way possible.'

'In the only way possible?'

'You haven't met Eva,' said Wilt. 'When you do you'll see that assertion is her forte not mine.'

'You feel dominated by Mrs Wilt?'

'I *am* dominated by Mrs Wilt.'

'She bullies you? She assumes the dominant role?'

'Eva is, Dr Pittman. She doesn't have to assume anything. She just is.'

'Is what?'

'Now there's the rub,' said Wilt. 'What's today? You lose track of time in this place.'

'Thursday.'

'Well, today being Thursday, Eva is Bernard Leach.'

'Bernard Leach?'

'The potter, Dr Pittman, the famous potter,' said Wilt. 'Now tomorrow she'll be Margot Fonteyn and on Saturday we play bridge with the Mottrams so she'll be Omar Sharif. On Sunday she's Elizabeth Taylor or Edna O'Brien depending on what the Colour Supplements have in store for me and in the afternoon we go for a drive and she's Eva Wilt. It's about the only time in the week I meet her and that's because I'm driving and she's got nothing to do but sit still and nag the pants off me.'

'I begin to see the pattern,' said Dr Pittman. 'Mrs Wilt was . . . is given to role-playing. This made for an unstable relationship in which you couldn't establish a distinctive and assertive role as a husband . . .'

'Dr Pittman,' said Wilt, 'a gyroscope may, indeed must, spin but in doing so it achieves a stability that is virtually unequalled. Now if you understand the principle of the gyroscope you may begin to understand that our marriage does not lack stability. It may be damned uncomfortable çoming home to a centrifugal force but it bloody well isn't unstable.'

'But just now you told me that Mrs Wilt did not assume a dominant role. Now you tell me she is a forceful character.'

'Eva is not forceful. She is a force. There's a difference. And as for character, she has so many and so varied it's difficult to keep up with them all. Let's just say she throws herself into whoever she is with an urgency and compulsiveness that is not always appropriate. You remember that series of Garbo pictures they showed on TV some years back? Well, Eva was La Dame Aux Camélias for three days after that and she made dying of TB look like St Vitus' dance. Talk about galloping consumption.'

'I begin to get the picture,' said Dr Pittman making a note that Wilt was a pathological liar with sado-masochistic tendencies.

'I'm glad somebody does,' said Wilt. 'Inspector Flint thinks I murdered her and the Pringsheims in some sort of bloodlust and disposed of their bodies in some extraordinary fashion. He mentioned acid. I mean it's crazy. Where on earth does one get nitric acid in the quantities necessary to dissolve three dead bodies, and one of them overweight at that? I mean it doesn't bear thinking about.'

'It certainly doesn't,' said Dr Pittman.

'In any case do I look like a murderer?' continued Wilt cheerfully. 'Of course I don't. Now if he'd said Eva had slaughtered the brutes, and in my opinion someone should have done years ago, I'd have taken him seriously. God help the poor sods who happen to be around when Eva takes it into her head she's Lizzie Borden.'

Dr Pittman studied him predaciously.

'Are you suggesting that Dr and Mrs Pringsheim were murdered by your wife?' he asked. 'Is that what you're saying?'

'No,' said Wilt, 'I am not. All I'm saying is that when Eva does things she does them wholeheartedly. When she cleans the house she cleans it. Let me tell you about the Harpic. She's got this thing about germs . . .'

'Mr Wilt,' said Dr Pittman hastily, 'I am not interested in what Mrs Wilt does with the Harpic. I have come here to understand you. Now then, do you make a habit of copulating with a plastic doll? Is this a regular occurrence?'

'Regular?' said Wilt. 'Do you mean a normal occurrence or a recurring one? Now your notion of what constitutes a normal occurrence may differ from mine . . .'

'I mean, do you do it often?' interrupted Dr Pittman.

'Do it?' said Wilt. 'I don't do it at all.'

'But I understood you to have placed particular emphasis on the fact that this doll had a vagina?'

'Emphasis? I didn't have to emphasize the fact. The beastly thing was plainly visible.'

'You find vaginas beastly?' said Dr Pittman stalking his prey into the more familiar territory of sexual aberration.

'Taken out of context, yes,' said Wilt sidestepping, 'and with plastic ones you can leave them in context and I still find them nauseating.'

By the time Dr Pittman had finished the interview he was

150

uncertain what to think. He got up wearily and made for the door.

'You've forgotten your hat, doctor,' said Wilt holding it out to him. 'Pardon my asking but do you have them specially made for you?'

'Well?' said Inspector Flint when Dr Pittman came into his office. 'What's the verdict?'

'Verdict? That man should be put away for life.'

'You mean he's a homicidal maniac?'

'I mean that no matter how he killed her Mrs Wilt must have been thankful to go. Twelve years married to that man . . . Good God, it doesn't bear thinking about.'

'Well, that doesn't get us much forrader,' said the Inspector, when the psychiatrist had left having expressed the opinion that while Wilt had the mind of an intellectual jackrabbit he couldn't in all honesty say that he was criminally insane. 'We'll just have to see what turns up tomorrow.'

Chapter 15

What turned up on Friday was seen not only by Inspector Flint, Sergeant Yates, twelve other policemen, Barney and half a dozen construction workers, but several hundred Tech students standing on the steps of the Science block, most of the staff and by all eight members of the CNAA visitation committee who had a particularly good view from the windows of the mock hotel lounge used by the Catering Department to train waiters and to entertain distinguished guests. Dr Mayfield did his best to distract their attention.

'We have structured the foundation course to maximize student interest,' he told Professor Baxendale, who headed the committee, but the professor was not to be diverted. His interest was maximized by what was being unstructured from the foundations of the new Admin block.

'How absolutely appalling,' he muttered as Judy protruded from the hole. Contrary to Wilt's hopes and expectations she had not burst. The liquid concrete had sealed her in too well for that and if in life she had resembled in many particulars a real live woman, in death she had all the attributes of a real dead one. As the corpse of a murdered woman she was entirely convincing. Her wig was matted and secured to her head at an awful angle by the concrete. Her clothes clung to her and cement to them while her legs had evidently been contorted to the point of mutilation and her outstretched arm had, as Barney had fore-told, a desperate appeal about it that was most affecting. It also made it exceedingly difficult to extricate her from the hole. The legs didn't help, added to which the concrete had given her a substance and stature approximate to that of Eva Wilt.

'I suppose that's what they mean by rigor mortice,' said Dr Board, as Dr Mayfield desperately tried to steer the conversation back to the Joint Honours degree.

'Dear Lord,' muttered Professor Baxendale. Judy had eluded the efforts of Barney and his men and had slumped back down the hole. 'To think what she must have suffered. Did you see that damned hand?'

Dr Mayfield had. He shuddered. Behind him Dr Board sniggered. 'There's a divinity that shapes our ends, rough-hew them how we will,' he said gaily. 'At least Wilt has saved himself the cost of a gravestone. All they'll have to do is prop her up with Here Stands Eva Wilt, Born So and So, Murdered last Saturday carved across her chest. In life monumental, in death a monument.'

'I must say, Board,' said Dr Mayfield, 'I find your sense of humour singularly ill-timed.'

'Well they'll never be able to cremate her, that's for certain,' continued Dr Board. 'And the undertaker who can fit that little lot into a coffin will be nothing short of a genius. I suppose they could always take a sledgehammer to her.'

In the corner Dr Cox fainted.

'I think I'll have another whisky if you don't mind,' said Professor Baxendale weakly. Dr Mayfield poured him a double. When he turned back to the window Judy was protruding once more from the hole.

'The thing about embalming,' said Dr Board, 'is that it costs so much. Now I'm not saying that thing out there is a perfect likeness of Eva Wilt as I remember her . . .'

'For heaven's sake, do you have to go on about it?' snarled Dr Mayfield, but Dr Board was not to be stopped. 'Quite apart from the legs there seems to be something odd about the breasts. I know Mrs Wilt's were large but they do seem to have inflated. Probably due to the gases. They putrefy, you know, which would account for it.'

By the time the committee went into lunch they had lost all appetite for food and most of them were drunk.

Inspector Flint was less fortunate. He didn't like being present at exhumations at the best of times and particularly when the corpse on whose behalf he was acting showed such a marked inclination to go back where she came from. Besides he was in two minds whether it was a corpse or not. It looked like a corpse and it certainly behaved like a corpse, albeit a very heavy one, but there was something about the knees that suggested that all was not anatomically as it should have been with whatever it was they had dug up. There was a double-jointedness and a certain lack of substance where the legs stuck forwards at right angles that seemed to indicate that Mrs Wilt had lost not only her life but both kneecaps as well. It was this mangled quality that made Barney's job so difficult and exceedingly distasteful. After the body had dropped down the hole for the fourth time Barney went down himself to assist from below.

'If you sods drop her,' he shouted from the depths, 'you'll have two dead bodies down here so hang onto that rope whatever happens. I'm going to tie it round her neck.'

Inspector Flint peered down the shaft. 'You'll do no such thing,' he shouted, 'we don't want her decapitated. We need her all in one piece.'

'She is all in one bloody piece,' came Barney's muffled reply, 'that's one thing you don't have to worry about.'

'Can't you tie the rope around something else?'

'Well I could,' Barney conceded, 'but I'm not going to. A leg is more likely to come off than her head and I'm not going to be underneath her when it goes.'

'All right,' said the Inspector, 'I just hope you know what you're doing, that's all.'

'I'll tell you one thing. The sod who put her down here knew what he was doing and no mistake.'

But this fifth attempt failed, like the previous four, and Judy was lowered into the depths where she rested heavily on Barney's foot.

'Go and get that bloody crane,' he shouted, 'I can't stand much more of this.'

'Nor can I,' muttered the Inspector, who still couldn't make up his mind what it was he was supposed to be disinterring; a doll dressed up to look like Mrs Wilt or Mrs Wilt dressed up to look like something some demented sculptor forgot to finish. What few doubts he had had about Wilt's sanity had been entirely dispelled by what he was presently witnessing. Any man who could go to the awful lengths Wilt had gone to render, and the word was entirely apposite whichever way you took it, either his wife or a plastic doll with a vagina, both inaccessible and horribly mutilated must be insane.

Sergeant Yates put his thoughts into words. 'You're not

154

going to tell me now that the bastard isn't off his rocker,' he said, as the crane was moved into position and the rope lowered and attached to Judy's neck.

'All right, now take her away,' shouted Barney.

In the dining-room only Dr Board was enjoying his lunch. The eight members of the CNAA committee weren't. Their eyes were glued to the scene below.

'I suppose it could be said she was *in statue pupillari*,' said Dr Board, helping himself to some more Lemon Meringue, 'in which case we stand *in loco parentis*. Not a pleasant thought, gentlemen. Not that she was ever a very bright student. I once had her for an Evening Class in French literature. I don't know what she got out of *Fleurs du Mal* but I do remember thinking that Baudelaire . . .'

'Dr Board,' said Dr Mayfield drunkenly, 'for a so-called cultured man you are entirely without feeling.'

'Something I share with the late Mrs Wilt, by the look of things,' said Dr Board, glancing out of the window, 'and while we are still on the subject, things seem to be coming to a head. They do indeed.'

Even Dr Cox, recently revived and coaxed into having some mutton, looked out of the window. As the crane slowly winched Judy into view the Course Board and the Committee rose and went to watch. It was an unedifying sight. Near the top of the shaft Judy's left leg caught in a crevice while her outstretched arm embedded itself in the clay.

'Hold it,' shouted Barney indistinctly, but it was too late. Unnerved by the nature of his load or in the mistaken belief that he had been told to lift harder, the crane driver hoisted away. There was a ghastly cracking sound as the noose tightened and the next moment Judy's concrete head, capped by Eva Wilt's wig, looked as if it was about to fulfil Inspector Flint's prediction that she would be decapitated. In the event he need not have worried. Judy was made of sterner stuff than might have been expected. As the head continued to rise and the body to remain firmly embedded in the shaft Judy's neck rose to the occasion. It stretched.

'Dear God,' said Professor Baxendale frantically, 'will it never end?'

155

Dr Board studied the phenomenon with increasing interest. 'It doesn't look like it,' he said. 'Mind you we do make a point of stretching our students, eh Mayfield?'

But Dr Mayfield made no response. As Judy took on the configuration of an ostrich that had absentmindedly buried its head in a pail of cement he knew that the Joint Honours degree was doomed.

'I'll say this for Mrs Wilt,' said Dr Board, 'she do hold on. No one could call her stiff-necked. Attenuated possibly. One begins to see what Modigliani was getting at.'

'For God's sake stop,' yelled Dr Cox hysterically, 'I think I'm going off my head.'

'Which is more than can be said for Mrs Wilt,' said Dr Board callously.

He was interrupted by another awful crack as Judy's body finally gave up the struggle with the shaft. With a shower of clay it careered upwards to resume a closer relationship with the head and hung naked, pink and, now that the clothes and the concrete had been removed, remarkably lifelike at the end of the rope some twenty feet above the ground.

'I must say,' said Dr Board, studying the vulva with relish, 'I've never had much sympathy with necrophilia before but I do begin to see its attractions now. Of course it's only of historical interest but in Elizabethan times it was one of the perks of an executioner . . .'

'Board,' screamed Dr Mayfield, 'I've known some fucking swine in my time . . .'

Dr Board helped himself to some more coffee. 'I believe the slang term for it is liking your meat cold.'

Underneath the crane Inspector Flint wiped the mud from his face and peered up at the awful object swinging above him. He could see now that it was only a doll. He could also see why Wilt had wanted to bury the beastly thing.

'Get it down. For God's sake get it down,' he bawled, as the press photographers circled round him. But the crane driver had lost his nerve. He shut his eyes, pulled the wrong lever and Judy began a further ascent.

'Stop it, stop it, that's fucking evidence,' screamed the Inspector, but it was already too late. As the rope wound through the final pulley Judy followed. The concrete cap disintegrated, her head slid between the rollers and her body began to swell. Her legs were the first to be affected.

'I've often wondered what elephantiasis looked like,' said Dr Board, 'Shelley had a phobia about it, I believe.'

Dr Cox certainly had. He was gibbering in a corner and the Vice-Principal was urging him to pull himself together.

'An apt expression,' observed Dr Board, above the gasps of horror as Judy, now clearly twelve months pregnant, continued her transformation. 'Early Minoan, wouldn't you say Mayfield?'

But Dr Mayfield was past speech. He was staring dementedly at a rapidly expanding vagina some fourteen inches long and eight wide. There was a pop and the thing became a penis, an enormous penis that swelled and swelled. He was going mad. He knew he was.

'Now that,' said Dr Board, 'takes some beating. I've heard about sex-change operations for men but . . .'

'Beating?' screamed Dr Mayfield, 'Beating? You can stand there cold-bloodedly and talk about . . .'

There was a loud bang. Judy had come to the end of her tether. So had Dr Mayfield. The penis was the first thing to go. Dr Mayfield the second. As Judy deflated he hurled himself at Dr Board only to sink to the ground gibbering.

Dr Board ignored his colleague. 'Who would have thought the old bag had so much wind in her?' he murmured, and finished his coffee. As Dr Mayfield was led out by the Vice-Principal, Dr Board turned to Professor Baxendale.

'I must apologize for Mayfield,' he said, 'I'm afraid this Joint Honours degree has been too much for him and to tell the truth I have always found him to be fundamentally unsound. A case of dementia post Cox I daresay.'

Inspector Flint drove back to the Police Station in a state bordering on lunacy.

'We've been made to look idiots,' he snarled at Sergeant Yates. 'You saw them laughing. You heard the bastards.' He was particularly incensed by the press photographers who had asked him to pose with the limp remnants of the plastic doll.

'We've been held up to public ridicule. Well, my God, somebody's going to pay.'

He hurled himself out of the car and lunged down the passage to the Interview Room. 'Right, Wilt,' he shouted, 'you've had your little joke and a bloody nasty one it was too. So now we're going to forget the niceties and get to the bottom of this business.'

Wilt studied the torn piece of plastic. 'Looks better like that if you ask me,' he said. 'More natural if you know what I mean.'

'You'll look bloody unnatural if you don't answer my questions,' yelled the Inspector. 'Where is she?'

'Where is who?' said Wilt.

'Mrs Fucking Wilt. Where did you put her?'

'I've told you. I didn't put her anywhere.'

'And I'm telling you you did. Now either you're going to tell me where she is or I'm going to beat it out of you.'

'You can beat me up if you like,' said Wilt, 'but it won't do you any good.'

'Oh yes it will,' said the Inspector and took off his coat.

'I demand to see a solicitor,' said Wilt hastily.

Inspector Flint put his jacket on again. 'I've been waiting to hear you say that. Henry Wilt, I hereby charge you with . . .'

Chapter 16

In the reeds Eva greeted the dawn of another day by blowing up the airbed for the tenth time. It had either sprung a leak or developed a fault in the valve. Whichever it was it had made her progress exceedingly slow and had finally forced her to take refuge in the reeds away from the channel. Here, wedged between the stems, she had spent a muddy night getting off the airbed to blow it up and getting back on to try and wash off the sludge and weeds that had adhered to her when she got off. In the process she had lost the bottom half of her lemon loungers and had torn the top half so that by dawn she resembled less the obsessive housewife of 34 Parkview Avenue than a finalist in the heavyweight division of the Ladies Mudwrestling Championship. In addition she was exceedingly cold and was glad when the sun came up bringing with it the promise of a hot summer day. All she had to do now was to find her way to land or open water and get someone to . . . At this point Eva became aware that her appearance was likely to cause some embarrassment. The lemon loungers had been sufficiently outré to make her avoid walking down the street when she had had them on; with them largely off she certainly didn't want to be seen in public. On the other hand she couldn't stay in the reeds all day. She plunged on, dragging the airbed behind her, half swimming but for the most part trudging through mud and water. At last she came out of the reeds into open water and found herself looking across a stretch to a house, a garden that sloped down to the water's edge, and a church. It seemed a long way across but there was no boat in sight. She would have to swim across and just hope that the woman who lived there was sympathetic and better still large enough to lend her some clothes until she got home. It was at this point that Eva discovered that she had left her handbag somewhere in the reeds. She remembered having it during the night but it must have fallen off the airbed when she was blowing it up. Well she couldn't go back and look for it now. She would just have to go on without it and ring Henry up and tell him to come out in the car and get her. He could bring some clothes too. Yes, that was it. Eva Wilt climbed onto the airbed and began to paddle across. Halfway over the airbed went down for the eleventh time. Eva abandoned it and struggled on in the lifejacket. But that too impeded her progress and she finally decided to take it off. She trod water and tried to undo it and after a struggle managed to get it off. In the process the rest of the lemon loungers disintegrated so that by the time she reached the bank Eva Wilt was exhausted and quite naked. She crawled into the cover of a willow tree and lay panting on the ground. When she had recovered she stood up and looked around. She was at the bottom of the garden and the house was a hundred yards away up the hill. It was a very large house by Eva's standards, and not the sort she would feel at home in at the best of times. For one thing it appeared to have a courtyard with stables at the back and to Eva, whose knowledge of large country houses was confined to what she had seen on TV, there was the suggestion of servants, gentility and a social formality that would make her arrival in the nude rather heavy going. On the other hand the whole place looked decidedly run down. The garden was overgrown and unkempt; ornamental bushes which might once have been trimmed to look like birds and animals had reverted to strange and vaguely monstrous shapes; rusted hoops leant half-hidden in the grass of an untended croquet lawn; a tennis net sagged between posts and an abandoned greenhouse boasted a few panes of lichened glass. Finally there was a dilapidated boathouse and a rowing boat. All in all the domain had a sinister and imposing air to it which wasn't helped by the presence of a small church hidden among trees to the left and a neglected graveyard beyond an old iron fence. Eva peered out from the weeping willow and was about to leave its cover when the French windows opened and a man came out onto the terrace with a pair of binoculars and peered through them in the direction of Eel Stretch. He was wearing a black cassock and a dog collar. Eva went back behind the tree and considered the awkwardness of her situation and lack of attire. It was all extremely embarrassing. Nothing on earth would make her go up to the house, the Vicarage, with nothing on. Parkview Avenue hadn't prepared her for situations of this sort.

160

Rossiter Grove hadn't prepared Gaskell for the situation he found when Sally woke him with 'Noah baby, it's drywise topside. Time to fly the coop.'

He opened the cabin door and stepped outside to discover that Eva had already flown and had taken the airbed and the lifejackets with her.

'You mean you left her outside all night?' he said. 'Now we're really up Shit Creek. No paddle, no airbed, no goddam lifejackets, no nothing.'

'I didn't know she'd do something crazy like take off with everything,' said Sally.

'You leave her outside in the pouring rain all night she's got to do something. She's probably frozen to death by now. Or drowned.'

'She tried to kill me. You think I was going to let her in when she's tried to do that. Anyhow it's all your fault for shooting your mouth off about that doll.'

'You tell that to the law when they find her body floating downstream. You just explain how come she goes off in the middle of a storm.'

'You're just trying to scare me,' said Sally. 'I didn't make her go or anything.'

'It's going to look peculiar if something has happened to her is all I'm saying. And you tell me how we're going to get off of here now. You think I'm going swimming without a lifejacket you're mistaken. I'm no Spitz.'

'My hero,' said Sally.

Gaskell went into the cabin and looked in the cupboard by the stove. 'And another thing. We've got a food problem. And water. There's not much left.'

'You got us into this mess. You think of a way out,' said Sally.

Gaskell sat down on the bunk and tried to think. There had to be some way of letting people know they were there and in trouble. They couldn't be far from land. For all he knew dry land was just the other side of the reeds. He went out and climbed on top of the cabin but apart from the church spire in the distance he could see nothing beyond the reeds. Perhaps if they got a piece of cloth and waved it someone would spot it. He went down and fetched a pillow case and spent twenty minutes waving it above his head and shouting. Then he returned to the cabin and got out the chart and pored over it in a vain attempt to discover where they were. He was just folding the map up when he spotted the pieces of Scrabble still lying on the table. Letters. Individual letters. Now if they had something that would float up in the air with letters on it. Like a kite. Gaskell considered ways of making a kite and gave it up. Perhaps the best thing after all was to make smoke signals. He fetched an empty can from the kitchen and filled it with fuel oil from beside the engine and soaked a handkerchief in it and clambered up on the cabin roof. He lit the handkerchief and tried to get the oil to burn but when it did there was very little smoke and the tin got too hot to hold. Gaskell kicked it into the water where it fizzled out.

'Genius baby,' said Sally, 'you're the greatest.'

'Yea, well if you can think of something practical let me know.'

'Try swimming.'

'Try drowning,' said Gaskell.

'You could make a raft or something.'

'I could hack this boat of Scheimacher's up. That's all we need.'

'I saw a movie once where there were these gauchos or Romans or something and they came to a river and wanted to cross and they used pigs' bladders,' said Sally.

'Right now all we don't have is a pig,' said Gaskell.

'You could use the garbage bags in the kitchen,' said Sally. Gaskell fetched a plastic bag and blew it up and tied the end with string. Then he squeezed it. The bag went down.

Gaskell sat down despondently. There had to be some simple way of attracting attention and he certainly didn't want to swim out across that dark water clutching an inflated garbage bag. He fiddled with the pieces of Scrabble and thought once again about kites. Or balloons. Balloons.

'You got those rubbers you use?' he asked suddenly.

'Jesus, at a time like this you get a hard on,' said Sally. 'Forget sex. Think of some way of getting us off here.'

'I have,' said Gaskell, 'I want those skins.'

'You going to float downriver on a pontoon of condoms?'

'Balloons,' said Gaskell. 'We blow them up and paint letters on them and float them in the wind.'

162

'Genius baby,' said Sally and went into the toilet. She came out with a sponge bag. 'Here they are. For a moment there I thought you wanted me.'

'Days of wine and roses,' said Gaskell, 'are over. Remind me to divorce you.' He tore a packet open and blew a contraceptive up and tied a knot in its end.

'On what grounds?'

'Like you're a lesbian,' said Gaskell and held up the dildo. 'This and kleptomania and the habit you have of putting other men in dolls and knotting them. You name it, I'll use it. Like you're a nymphomaniac.'

'You wouldn't dare. Your family would love it, the scandal.'

'Try me,' said Gaskell and blew up another condom.

'Plastic freak.'

'Bull dyke.'

Sally's eyes narrowed. She was beginning to think he meant what he said about divorce and if Gaskell divorced her in England what sort of alimony would she get? Very little. There were no children and she had the idea that British courts were mean in matters of money. So was Gaskell and there was his family too. Rich and mean. She sat and eyed him.

'Where's your nail varnish?' Gaskell asked when he had finished and twelve contraceptives cluttered the cabin.

'Drop dead,' said Sally and went out on deck to think. She stared down at the dark water and thought about rats and death and being poor again and liberated. The rat paradigm. The world was a rotten place. People were objects to be used and discarded. It was Gaskell's own philosophy and now he was discarding her. And one slip on this oily deck could solve her problems. All that had to happen was for Gaskell to slip and drown and she would be free and rich and no one would ever know. An accident. Natural death. But Gaskell could swim and there had to be no mistakes. Try it once and fail and she wouldn't be able to try again. He would be on his guard. It had to be certain and it had to be natural.

Gaskell came out on deck with the contraceptives. He had tied them together and painted on each one a single letter with nail varnish so that the whole read HELP SOS HELP. He climbed up on the cabin roof and launched them into the air. They floated up for a moment, were caught in the light breeze

163

and sagged sideways down onto the water. Gaskell pulled them in on the string and tried again. Once again they floated down onto the water.

'I'll wait until there's some more wind,' he said, and tied the string to the rail where they bobbed gently. Then he went into the cabin and lay on the bunk.

'What are you going to do now?' Sally asked.

'Sleep. Wake me when there's a wind.'

He took off his glasses and pulled a blanket over him.

Outside Sally sat on a locker and thought about drowning. In bed.

'Mr Gosdyke,' said Inspector Flint, 'you and I have had dealings for a good many years now and I'm prepared to be frank with you. I don't know.'

'But you've charged him with murder,' said Mr Gosdyke.

'He'll come up for remand on Monday. In the meantime I am going on questioning him.'

'But surely the fact that he admits burying a lifesize doll . . .'

'Dressed in his wife's clothes, Gosdyke. In his wife's clothes. Don't forget that.'

'It still seems insufficient to me. Can you be absolutely sure that a murder has been committed?'

'Three people disappear off the face of the earth without a trace. They leave behind them two cars, a house littered with unwashed glasses and the leftovers of a party . . . you should see that house . . . a bathroom and landing covered with blood . . .'

'They could have gone in someone else's car.'

'They could have but they didn't. Dr Pringsheim didn't like being driven by anyone else. We know that from his colleagues at the Department of Biochemistry. He had a rooted objection to British drivers. Don't ask me why but he had.'

'Trains? Buses? Planes?'

'Checked, rechecked and checked again. No one answering to their description used any form of public or private transport out of town. And if you think they went on a bicycle ride, you're wrong again. Dr Pringsheim's bicycle is in the garage. No, you can forget their going anywhere. They died and Mr Smart Alec Wilt knows it.'

'I still don't see how you can be so sure,' said Mr Gosdyke.

164

Inspector Flint lit a cigarette. 'Let's just look at his actions, his admitted actions and see what they add up to,' he said. 'He gets a lifesize doll . . .'

'Where from?'

'He says he was given it by his wife. Where he got it from doesn't matter.'

'He says he first saw the thing at the Pringsheims' house.'

'Perhaps he did. I'm prepared to believe that. Wherever he got it, the fact remains that he dressed it up to look like Mrs Wilt. He puts it down that hole at the Tech, a hole he knows is going to be filled with concrete. He makes certain he is seen by the caretaker when he knows that the Tech is closed. He leaves a bicycle covered with his fingerprints and with a book of his in the basket. He leaves a trail of notes to the hole. He turns up at Mr Braintree's house at midnight covered with mud and says he's had a puncture when he hasn't. Now you're not going to tell me that he hadn't got something in mind.'

'He says he was merely trying to dispose of that doll.'

'And he tells me he was rehearsing his wife's murder. He's admitted that.'

'Yes, but only in fantasy. His story to me is that he wanted to get rid of that doll,' Mr Gosdyke persisted.

'Then why the clothes, why blow the thing up and why leave it in such a position it was bound to be spotted when the concrete was poured down? Why didn't he cover it with earth if he didn't want it to be found? Why didn't he just burn the bloody thing or leave it by the roadside? It just doesn't make sense unless you see it as a deliberate plan to draw our attention away from the real crime.' The Inspector paused. 'Well now, the way I see it is that something happened at that party we don't know anything about. Perhaps Wilt found his wife in bed with Dr Pringsheim. He killed them both. Mrs Pringsheim puts in an appearance and he kills her too.'

'How?' said Mr Gosdyke. 'You didn't find that much blood.'

'He strangled her. He strangled his own wife. He battered Pringsheim to death. Then he hides the bodies somewhere, goes home and lays the doll trail. On Sunday he disposes of the real bodies . . .'

'Where?'

'God alone knows, but I'm going to find out. All I know is

that a man who can think up a scheme like this one is bound to have thought of somewhere diabolical to put the real victims. It wouldn't surprise me to learn that he spent Sunday making illegal use of the crematorium. Whatever he did you can be sure he did it thoroughly.'

But Mr Gosdyke remained unconvinced. 'I wish I knew how you could be so certain,' he said.

'Mr Gosdyke,' said the Inspector wearily, 'you have spent two hours with your client. I have spent the best part of the week and if I've learnt one thing from the experience it is this, that sod in there knows what he is doing. Any normal man in his position would have been worried and alarmed and downright frightened. Any innocent man faced with a missing wife and the evidence we've got of murder would have had a nervous breakdown. Not Wilt. Oh no, he sits in there as bold as you please and tells me how to conduct the investigation. Now if anything convinces me that that bastard is as guilty as hell that does. He did it and I know it. And what is more, I'm going to prove it.'

'He seems a bit worried now,' said Mr Gosdyke.

'He's got reason to be,' said the Inspector, 'because by Monday morning I'm going to get the truth out of him even if it kills him and me both.'

'Inspector,' said Mr Gosdyke getting to his feet, 'I must warn you that I have advised my client not to say another word and if he appears in Court with a mark on him . . .'

'Mr Gosdyke, you should know me better than that. I'm not a complete fool and if your client has any marks on him on Monday morning they will not have been made by me or any of my men. You have my assurance on that.'

Mr Gosdyke left the Police Station a puzzled man. He had to admit that Wilt's story hadn't been a very convincing one. Mr Gosdyke's experience of murderers was not extensive but he had a shrewd suspicion that men who confessed openly that they had entertained fantasies of murdering their wives ended by admitting that they had done so in fact. Besides his attempt to get Wilt to agree that he'd put the doll down the hole as a practical joke on his colleagues at the Tech had failed hopelessly. Wilt had refused to lie and Mr Gosdyke was not used to clients who insisted on telling the truth.

166

Inspector Flint went back into the Interview Room and looked at Wilt. Then he pulled up a chair and sat down.

'Henry,' he said with an affability he didn't feel, 'you and I are going to have a little chat.'

'What, another one?' said Wilt. 'Mr Gosdyke has advised me to say nothing.'

'He always does,' said the Inspector sweetly, 'to clients he knows are guilty. Now are you going to talk?'

'I can't see why not? I'm not guilty and it helps to pass the time.'

Chapter 17

It was Friday and as on every other day in the week the little church at Waterswick was empty. And as on every other day of the week the Vicar, the Reverend St John Froude, was drunk. The two things went together, the lack of a congregation and the Vicar's insobriety. It was an old tradition dating back to the days of smuggling when Brandy for the Parson had been about the only reason the isolated hamlet had a vicar at all. And like so many English traditions it died hard. The Church authorities saw to it that Waterswick got idiosyncratic parsons whose awkward enthusiasms tended to make them unsuitable for more respectable parishes and they, to console themselves for its remoteness and lack of interest in things spiritual, got alcoholic. The Rev St John Froude maintained the tradition. He attended to his duties with the same Anglo-Catholic Fundamentalist fervour that had made him so unpopular in Esher and turned an alcoholic eye on the activities of his few parishioners who, now that brandy was not so much in demand, contented themselves with the occasional boatload of illegal Indian immigrants.

Now as he finished a breakfast of eggnog and Irish coffee and considered the iniquities of his more egregious colleagues as related in the previous Sunday's paper he was startled to see something wobbling above the reeds on Eel Stretch. It looked like balloons, white sausage-shaped balloons that rose briefly and then disappeared. The Rev St John Froude shuddered, shut his eyes, opened them again and thought about the virtues of abstinence. If he was right and he didn't know whether he wanted to be or not, the morning was being profaned by a cluster of contraceptives, inflated contraceptives, wobbling erratically where by the nature of things no contraceptive had ever wobbled before. At least he hoped it was a cluster. He was so used to seeing things in twos when they were in fact ones that he couldn't be sure if what looked like a cluster of inflated contraceptives wasn't just one or better still none at all.

He reeled off to his study to get his binoculars and stepped out onto the terrace to focus them. By that time the manifestation had disappeared. The Rev St John Froude shook his head mournfully. Things and in particular his liver had reached a pretty pickle for him to have hallucinations so early in the morning. He went back into the house and tried to concentrate his attention on a case involving an Archdeacon in Ongar who had undergone a sex-change operation before eloping with his verger. There was matter there for a sermon if only he could think of a suitable text.

At the bottom of the garden Eva Wilt watched his retreat and wondered what to do. She had no intention of going up to the house and introducing herself in her present condition. She needed clothes, or at least some sort of covering. She looked around for something temporary and finally decided on some ivy climbing up the graveyard fence. With one eye on the Vicarage she emerged from the willow tree and scampered across to the fence and through the gate into the churchyard. There she ripped some ivy off the trunk of a tree and, carrying it in front of her rather awkwardly, made her way surreptitiously up the overgrown path towards the church. For the most part her progress was masked from the house by the trees but once or twice she had to crouch low and scamper from tombstone to tombstone in full view of the Vicarage. By the time she reached the church porch she was panting and her sense of impropriety had been increased tenfold. If the prospect of presenting herself at the house in the nude offended her on grounds of social decorum, going into a church in the raw was positively sacrilegious. She stood in the porch and tried frantically to steel herself to go in. There were bound to be surplices for the choir in the vestry and dressed in a surplice she could go up to the house. Or could she? Eva wasn't sure about the significance of surplices and the Vicar might be angry. Oh dear it was all so awkward. In the end she opened the church door and went inside. It was cold and damp and empty. Clutching the ivy to her she crossed to the vestry door and tried it. It was locked. Eva stood shivering and tried to think. Finally she went outside and stood in the sunshine trying to get warm.

In the Staff Room at the Tech, Dr Board was holding court. 'All things considered I think we came out of the whole business

169

rather creditably,' he said. 'The Principal has always said he wanted to put the college on the map and with the help of friend Wilt it must be said he has succeeded. The newspaper coverage has been positively prodigious. I shouldn't be surprised if our student intake jumped astonishingly.'

'The committee didn't approve our facilities,' said Mr Morris, 'so you can hardly claim their visit was an unqualified success.'

'Personally I think they got their money's worth,' said Dr Board. 'It's not every day you get the chance to see an exhumation and an execution at the same time. The one usually precedes the other and certainly the experience of seeing what to all intents and purposes was a woman turn in a matter of seconds into a man, an instantaneous sex change, was, to use a modern idiom, a mind-blowing one.'

'Talking of poor Mayfield,' said the Head of Geography, 'I understand he's still at the Mental Hospital.'

'Committed?' asked Dr Board hopefully.

'Depressed. And suffering from exhaustion.'

'Hardly surprising. Anyone who can use language . . . abuse language like that is asking for trouble. Structure as a verb, for example.'

'He had set great store by the Joint Honours degree and the fact that it has been turned down . . .'

'Quite right too,' said Dr Board. 'The educative value of stuffing second-rate students with fifth-rate ideas on subjects as diverse as Medieval Poetry and Urban Studies escapes me. Far better that they should spend their time watching the police dig up the supposed body of a woman coated in concrete, stretch her neck, rip all her clothes off her, hang her and finally blow her up until she explodes. Now that is what I call a truly educational experience. It combines archaeology with criminology, zoology with physics, anatomy with economic theory, while maintaining the students' undivided attention all the time. If we must have Joint Honours degrees let them be of that vitality. Practical too. I'm thinking of sending away for one of those dolls.'

'It still leaves unresolved the question of Mrs Wilt's disappearance,' said Mr Morris.

'Ah, dear Eva,' said Dr Board wistfully. 'Having seen so

170

much of what I imagined to be her I shall, if I ever have the pleasure of meeting her again, treat her with the utmost courtesy. An amazingly versatile woman and interestingly proportioned. I think I shall christen my doll Eva.'

'But the police still seem to think she is dead.'

'A woman like that can never die,' said Dr Board. 'She may explode but her memory lingers on indelibly.'

In his study the Rev St John Froude shared Dr Board's opinion. The memory of the large and apparently naked lady he had glimpsed emerging from the willow tree at the bottom of his garden like some disgustingly oversized nymph and scuttling through the churchyard was not something he was ever likely to forget. Coming so shortly after the apparition of the inflated contraceptives it leant weight to the suspicion that he had been overdoing things on the alcohol side. Abandoning the sermon he had been preparing on the apostate Archdeacon of Ongar— he had had 'By their fruits ye shall know them' in mind as a text—he got up and peered out of the window in the direction of the church and was wondering if he shouldn't go down and see if there wasn't a large fat naked lady there when his attention was drawn to the reeds across the water. They were there again, those infernal things. This time there could be no doubt about it. He grabbed his binoculars and stared furiously through them. He could see them much more clearly than the first time and much more ominously. The sun was high in the sky and a mist rose over Eel Stretch so that the contraceptives had a luminescent sheen about them, an insubstantiality that was almost spiritual in its implications. Worse still, there appeared to be something written on them. The message was clear if incomprehensible. It read PEESOP. The Rev St John Froude lowered his binoculars and reached for the whisky bottle and considered the significance of PEESOP etched ectoplasmically against the sky. By the time he had finished his third hurried glass and had decided that spiritualism might after all have something to be said for it though why you almost always found yourself in touch with a Red Indian who was acting by proxy for an aunt which might account for the mis-spelling of Peasoup while removing some of the less attractive ingredients from the stuff, the wind had changed the letters

171

round. This time when he looked the message read EELPOPS. The Vicar shuddered. What eel was popping and how?

'The sins of the spirit,' he said reproachfully to his fourth glass of whisky before consulting the oracle once more. POSHELLS was followed by HEPOLP to be succeeded by SHHLPSPO which was even worse. The Rev St John Froude thrust his binoculars and the bottle of whisky aside and went down on his knees to pray for deliverance, or at least for some guidance in interpreting the message. But every time he got up to see if his wish had been granted the combination of letters was as meaningless as ever or downright threatening. What, for instance, did HELLSPO signify? Or SLOSHHEEL? Finally, determined to discover for himself the true nature of the occurrence, he put on his cassock and wove off down the garden path to the boathouse.

'They shall rue the day,' he muttered as he climbed into the rowing boat and took the oars. The Rev St John Froude held firm views on contraception. It was one of the tenets of his Anglo-Catholicism.

In the cabin cruiser Gaskell slept soundly. Around him Sally made her preparations. She undressed and changed into the plastic bikini. She took a silk square from her bag and put it on the table and she fetched a jug from the kitchen and leaning over the side filled it with water. Finally she went into the toilet and made her face up in the mirror. When she emerged she was wearing false eyelashes, her lips were heavily red and pancake make-up obscured her pale complexion. She was carrying a bathing-cap. She crossed to the door of the galley and put an arm up and stuck her hip out.

'Gaskell baby,' she called.

Gaskell opened his eyes and looked at her. 'What the hell gives?'

'Like it, baby?'

Gaskell put on his glasses. In spite of himself he did like it. 'You think you're going to wheedle round me, you're wrong...'

Sally smiled. 'Conserve the verbiage. You turn me on, biodegradable baby.' She moved forward and sat on the bunk beside him.

172

'What are you trying to do?'

'Make it up, babykink. You deserve a curve.' She fondled him gently. 'Like the old days. Remember?'

Gaskell remembered and felt weak. Sally leant forward and pressed him down onto the bunk.

'Surrogate Sally,' she said and unbuttoned his shirt.

Gaskell squirmed. 'If you think . . .'

'Don't think, kink,' said Sally and undid his jeans. 'Only erect.'

'Oh God,' said Gaskell. The perfume, the plastic, the mask of a face and her hands were awakening ancient fantasies. He lay supine on the bunk staring at her while Sally undressed him. Even when she rolled him over on his face and pulled his hands behind his back he made no resistance.

'Bondage baby,' she said softly and reached for the silk square.

'No, Sally, no,' he said weakly. Sally smiled grimly and tied his hands together, winding the silk between his wrists carefully before tightening it. When she had finished Gaskell whimpered. 'You're hurting me.'

Sally rolled him over. 'You love it,' she said and kissed him. She sat back and stroked him gently. 'Harder, baby, real hard. Lift me lover sky high.'

'Oh Sally.'

'That's my baby and now the waterproof.'

'There's no need. I like it better without.'

'But I do, G. I need it to prove you loved me till death did us part.' She bent over and rolled it down.

Gaskell stared up at her. Something was wrong.

'And now the cap.' She reached over and picked up the bathing-cap.

'The cap?' said Gaskell. 'Why the cap? I don't want that thing on.'

'Oh but you do, sweetheart. It makes you look girlwise.' She fitted the cap over his head. 'Now into Sallia inter alia.' She undid the bikini and lowered herself onto him. Gaskell moaned and stared up at her. She was lovely. It was a long time since she had been so good. But he was still frightened. There was a look in her eyes he hadn't seen before. 'Untie me,' he pleaded, 'you're hurting my arm.'

But Sally merely smiled and gyrated. 'When you've come and gone, G baby. When you've been.' She moved her hips. 'Come, bum, come quick.'

Gaskell shuddered.

'Finished?'

He nodded. 'Finished,' he sighed.

'For good, baby, for good,' said Sally. 'That was it. You're past the last.'

'Past the last?'

'You've come and gone, G, come and gone. It's Styxside for you now.'

'Stickside?'

'S for Sally, T for Terminal, Y for You and X for Exit. All that's left is this.' She reached over and picked up the jug of muddy water. Gaskell turned his head and looked at it.

'What's that for?'

'For you, baby. Mudders milk.' She moved up his body and sat on his chest. 'Open your mouth.'

Gaskell Pringsheim stared up at her frantically. He began to writhe. 'You're mad. You're crazy.'

'Now just lie quietly and it won't hurt. It will soon be over, lover. Natural death by drowning. In bed. You're making history.'

'You bitch, you murderous bitch. . . .'

'Cerberuswise,' said Sally, and poured the water into his mouth. She put the jug down and pulled the cap down over his face.

The Rev St John Froude rowed surprisingly steadily for a man with half a bottle of whisky inside him and wrath in his heart, and the nearer he got to the contraceptives the greater his wrath became. It wasn't simply that he had been given a quite unnecessary fright about the state of his liver by the sight of the things (he could see now that he was close to them that they were real), it was rather that he adhered to the doctrine of sexual non-intervention. God, in his view, had created a perfect world if the book of Genesis was to be believed and it had been going downhill ever since. And the book of Genesis *was* to be believed or the rest of the Bible made no sense at all. Starting from this fundamentalist premise the Rev St John Froude had progressed erratically by way of Blake, Hawker, Leavis and a number of obscurantist theologians to the conviction that the miracles of modern science were the works of the devil, that salvation lay in eschewing every material advance since the Renaissance, and one or two before, and that nature was infinitely less red in tooth and claw than modern mechanized man. In short he was convinced that the end of the world was at hand in the shape of a nuclear holocaust and that it was his duty as a Christian to announce the fact. His sermons on the subject had been of such a vividly horrendous fervour as to lead to his exile in Waterswick. Now as he rowed up the channel into Eel Stretch he fulminated silently against contraception, abortion and the evils of sexual promiscuity. They were all symptoms and causes and causative symptoms of the moral chaos which life on earth had become. And finally there were trippers. The Rev St John Froude loathed trippers. They fouled the little Eden of his parish with their boats, their transistors, and their unabashed enjoyment of the present. And trippers who desecrated the prospect from his study window with inflated contraceptives and meaningless messages were an abomination. By the time he came in sight of the cabin cruiser he was in no mood to be trifled with. He rowed furiously across to the boat, tied up to the rail and, lifting his cassock over his knees, stepped aboard.

In the cabin Sally stared down at the bathing-cap. It deflated and inflated, expanded and was sucked in against Gaskell's face and Sally squirmed with pleasure. She was the liberatedest woman in the world, but the liberatedest. Gaskell was dying and she would be free to be with a million dollars in the kitty. And no one would ever know. When he was dead she would take the cap off and untie him and push his body over the side into the water. Gaskell Pringsheim would have died a natural death by drowning. And at that moment the cabin door opened and she looked up at the silhouette of the Rev St John Froude in the cabin doorway.

'What the hell . . .' she muttered and leapt off Gaskell.

The Rev St John Froude hesitated. He had come to say his piece and say it he would but he had clearly intruded on a very naked woman with a horribly made-up face in the act of

175

making love to a man who as far as a quick glance enabled him to tell had no face at all.

'I . . .' he began and stopped. The man on the bunk had rolled onto the floor and was writhing there in the most extraordinary fashion. The Rev St John Froude stared down at him aghast. The man was not only faceless but his hands were tied behind his back.

'My dear fellow,' said the Vicar, appalled at the scene and looked up at the naked woman for some sort of explanation. She was staring at him demonically and holding a large kitchen knife. The Rev St John Froude stumbled back into the cockpit as the woman advanced towards him holding the knife in front of her with both hands. She was clearly quite demented. So was the man on the floor. He rolled about and dragged his head from side to side. The bathing-cap came off but the Rev St John Froude was too busy scrambling over the side into his rowing boat to notice. He cast off as the ghastly woman lunged towards him and began to row away, his original mission entirely forgotten. In the cockpit Sally stood screaming abuse at him and behind her a shape had appeared in the cabin door. The Vicar was grateful to see that the man had a face now, not a nice face, a positively horrible face but a face for all that, and he was coming up behind the woman with some hideous intention. The next moment the intention was carried out. The man hurled himself at her, the knife dropped onto the deck, the woman scrabbled at the side of the boat and then slid forward into the water. The Rev St John Froude waited no longer. He rowed vigorously away. Whatever appalling orgy of sexual perversion he had interrupted he wanted none of it and painted women with knives who called him a mother-fucking son of a cuntsucker among other things didn't elicit his sympathy when the object of their obscene passions pushed them into the water. And in any case they were Americans. The Rev St John Froude had no time for Americans. They epitomized everything he found offensive about the modern world. Imbued with a new disgust for the present and an urge to hit the whisky he rowed home and tied up at the bottom of the garden.

Behind him in the cabin cruiser Gaskell ceased shouting. The priest who had saved his life had ignored his hoarse pleas for

176

further help and Sally was standing waist-deep in water beside the boat. Well she could stay there. He went back into the cabin, turned so that he could lock the door with his tied hands and then looked around for something to cut the silk scarf with. He was still very frightened.

'Right,' said Inspector Flint, 'so what did you do then?'
'Got up and read the Sunday papers.'
'After that?'
'I ate a plate of All-Bran and drank some tea.'
'Tea? You sure it was tea? Last time you said coffee.'
'Which time?'
'The last time you told it.'
'I drank tea.'
'What then?'
'I gave Clem his breakfast.'
'What sort?'
'Chappie.'
'Last time you said Bonzo.'
'This time I say Chappie.'
'Make up your mind. Which sort was it?'
'What the fuck does it matter which sort it was?'
'It matters to me.'
'Chappie.'
'And when you had fed the dog.'
'I shaved.'
'Last time you said you had a bath.'
'I had a bath and then I shaved. I was trying to save time.'
'Forget the time, Wilt, we've got all the time in the world.'
'What time is it?'
'Shut up. What did you do then?'
'Oh for God's sake, what does it matter. What's the point of going over and over the same things?'
'Shut up.'
'Right,' said Wilt, 'I will.'
'When you had shaved what did you do?'
Wilt stared at him and said nothing.
'When you had shaved?'
But Wilt remained silent. Finally Inspector Flint left the room and sent for Sergeant Yates.

'He's clammed up,' he said wearily. 'So what do we do now?'

'Try a little physical persuasion?'

Flint shook his head. 'Gosdyke's seen him. If he turns up in Court on Monday with so much as a hair out of place, he'll be all over us for brutality. There's got to be some other way. He must have a weak spot somewhere but I'm damned if I can find it. How does he do it?'

'Do what?'

'Keep talking and saying nothing. Not one bloody useful thing. That sod's got more opinions on every topic under the flaming sun than I've got hairs on my head.'

'If we keep him awake for another forty-eight hours he's bound to crack up.'

'He'll take me with him,' said Flint. 'We'll both go into court in straitjackets.'

In the Interview Room Wilt put his head on the table. They would be back in a minute with more questions but a moment's sleep was better than none. Sleep. If only they would let him sleep. What had Flint said? 'The moment you sign a confession, you can have all the sleep you want.' Wilt considered the remark and its possibilities. A confession. But it would have to be plausible enough to keep them occupied while he got some rest and at the same time so impossible that it would be rejected by the court. A delaying tactic to give Eva time to come back and prove his innocence. It would be like giving Gasfitters Two *Shane* to read while he sat and thought about putting Eva down the pile shaft. He should be able to think up something complicated that would keep them frantically active. How had he killed them? Beat them to death in the bathroom? Not enough blood. Even Flint had admitted that much. So how? What was a nice gentle way to go? Poor old Pinkerton had chosen a peaceful death when he stuck a tube up the exhaust pipe of his car . . . That was it. But why? There had to be a motive. Eva was having it off with Dr Pringsheim? With that twit? Not in a month of Sundays. Eva wouldn't have looked twice at Gaskell. But Flint wasn't to know that. And what about that bitch Sally? All three having it off together? Well at least it would explain why he killed them all and it would provide the sort of motive Flint would understand. And

178

besides it was right for that kind of party. So he got this pipe . . . What pipe? There was no need for a pipe. They were in the garage to get away from everyone else. No, that wouldn't do. It had to be the bathroom. How about Eva and Gaskell doing it in the bath? That was better. He had bust the door down in a fit of jealousy. Much better. Then he had drowned them. And then Sally had come upstairs and he had had to kill her too. That explained the blood. There had been a struggle. He hadn't meant to kill her but she had fallen in the bath. So far so good. But where had he put them? It had to be something good. Flint wasn't going to believe anything like the river. Somewhere that made sense of the doll down the hole. Flint had it firmly fixed in his head that the doll had been a diversionary tactic. That meant that time entered into their disposal.

Wilt got up and asked to go to the toilet. As usual the constable came with him and stood outside the door.

'Do you have to?' said Wilt. 'I'm not going to hang myself with the chain.'

'To see you don't beat your meat,' said the constable coarsely.

Wilt sat down. Beat your meat. What a hell of an expression. It called to mind Meat One. Meat One? It was a moment of inspiration. Wilt got up and flushed the toilet. Meat One would keep them busy for a long time. He went back to the pale green room where the light buzzed. Flint was waiting for him.

'You going to talk now?' he asked.

Wilt shook his head. They would have to drag it out of him if his confession was to be at all convincing. He would have to hesitate, start to say something, stop, start again, appeal to Flint to stop torturing him, plead and start again. This trout needed tickling. Oh well, it would help to keep him awake.

'Are you going to start again at the beginning?' he asked.

Inspector Flint smiled horribly. 'Right at the beginning.'

'All right,' said Wilt, 'have it your own way. Just don't keep asking me if I gave the dog Chappie or Bonzo. I can't stand all that talk about dog food.'

Inspector Flint rose to the bait. 'Why not?'

'It gets on my nerves,' said Wilt, with a shudder.

The Inspector leant forward. 'Dog food gets on your nerves?' he said.

Wilt hesitated pathetically. 'Don't go on about it,' he said. 'Please don't go on.'

'Now then which was it, Bonzo or Chappie?' said the Inspector, scenting blood.

Wilt put his head in his hands. 'I won't say anything. I won't. Why must you keep asking me about food? Leave me alone.' His voice rose hysterically and with it Inspector Flint's hopes. He knew when he had touched the nerve. He was on to a good thing.

Chapter 18

'Dear God,' said Sergeant Yates, 'but we had pork pies for lunch yesterday. It's too awful.'

Inspector Flint rinsed his mouth out with black coffee and spat into the washbasin. He had vomited twice and felt like vomiting again.

'I knew it would be something like that,' he said with a shudder, 'I just knew it. A man who could pull that doll trick had to have something really filthy up his sleeve.'

'But they may all have been eaten by now,' said the Sergeant. Flint looked at him balefully.

'Why the hell do you think he laid that phoney trail?' he asked. 'To give them plenty of time to be consumed. His expression "consumed", not mine. You know what the shelf life of a pork pie is?'

Yates shook his head.

'Five days. Five days. So they went out on Tuesday which leaves us one day to find them or what remains of them. I want every pork pie in East Anglia picked up. I want every fucking sausage and steak and kidney pie that went out of Sweetbreads Meat Factory this week found and brought in. And every tin of dog food.'

'Dog food?'

'You heard me,' said Inspector Flint staggering out of the washroom. 'And while you're about it you'd better make it cat food too. You never know with Wilt. He's capable of leading us up the garden path in one important detail.'

'But if they went into pork pies what's all this about dog food?'

'Where the hell do you think he put the odds and ends and I do mean ends?' Inspector Flint asked savagely. 'You don't imagine he was going to have people coming in and complaining they'd found a tooth or a toenail in the Sweetbreads pie they had bought that morning. Not Wilt. That swine thinks of everything. He drowns them in their own bath. He puts them in plastic garbage bags and locks the bags in the garage while he goes home and sticks the doll down that fucking hole. Then on Sunday he goes back and picks them up and spends the day at the meat factory all by himself . . . Well if you want to know what he did on Sunday you can read all about it in his statement. It's more than my stomach can stand.'

The Inspector went back hurriedly into the washroom. He'd been living off pork pies since Monday. The statistical chances of his having partaken of Mrs Wilt were extremely high.

When Sweetbreads Meat and Canning Factory opened at eight, Inspector Flint was waiting at the gate. He stormed into the manager's office and demanded to speak to him.

'He's not here yet,' said the secretary. 'Is there anything I can do for you?'

'I want a list of every establishment you supply with pork pies, steak and kidney pies, sausages and dog food,' said the Inspector.

'I couldn't possibly give you that information,' said the secretary. 'It's extremely confidential.'

'Confidential? What the hell do you mean confidential?'

'Well I don't know really. It's just that I couldn't take it on myself to provide you with inside information. . . .' She stopped. Inspector Flint was staring at her with a quite horrible expression on his face.

'Well, miss,' he said finally, 'while we're on the topic of inside information, it may interest you to know that what has been inside your pork pies is by way of being inside information. Vital information.'

'Vital information? I don't know what you mean. Our pies contain perfectly wholesome ingredients.'

'Wholesome?' shouted the Inspector. 'You call three human bodies wholesome? You call the boiled, bleached, minced and cooked remains of three murdered bodies wholesome?'

'But we only use . . .' the secretary began and fell sideways off her chair in a dead faint.

'Oh for God's sake,' shouted the Inspector, 'you'd think a silly bitch who can work in an abattoir wouldn't be squeamish. Find out who the manager is and where he lives and tell him to come down here at the double.'

182

He sat down in a chair while Sergeant Yates rummaged in the desk. 'Wakey, wakey,' he said, prodding the secretary with his foot. 'If anyone has got a right to lie down on the job, it's me. I've been on my feet for three days and nights and I've been an accessory after the fact of murder.'

'An accessory?' said Yates. 'I don't see how you can say that.'

'Can't you? Well what would you call helping to dispose of parts of a murder victim? Concealing evidence of a crime?'

'I never thought of it that way,' said Yates.

'I did,' said the Inspector, 'I can't think of anything else.'

In his cell Wilt stared up at the ceiling peacefully. He was astonished that it had been so easy. All you had to do was tell people what they wanted to hear and they would believe you no matter how implausible your story might be. And three days and nights without sleep had suspended Inspector Flint's disbelief with a vengeance. Then again Wilt's hesitations had been timed perfectly and his final confession a nice mixture of conceit and matter-of-factness. On the details of the murder he had been coldly precise and in describing their disposal he had been a craftsman taking pride in his work. Every now and then when he got to a difficult spot he would veer away into a manic arrogance at once boastful and cowardly with 'You'll never be able to prove it. They'll have disappeared without trace now.' And the Harpic had come in useful once again, adding a macabre touch of realism about evidence being flushed down thousands of U-bends with Harpic being poured after it like salt from a salt cellar. Eva would enjoy that when he told her about it, which was more than could be said for Inspector Flint. He hadn't even seen the irony of Wilt's remark that while he had been looking for the Pringsheims they had been under his nose all the time. He had been particularly upset by the crack about gut reactions and the advice to stick to health foods in future. Yes, in spite of his tiredness Wilt had enjoyed himself watching the Inspector's bloodshot eyes turn from glee and gloating self-satisfaction to open amazement and finally undisguised nausea. And when finally Wilt had boasted that they would never be able to bring him to trial without the evidence, Flint had responded magnificently.

'Oh yes, we will,' he had shouted hoarsely, 'if there is one single pie left from that batch we'll get it and when we do the Lab boys will . . .'

'Find nothing but pork in it,' said Wilt before being dragged off to his cell. At least that was the truth and if Flint didn't believe it that was his own fault. He had asked for a confession and he had got one by courtesy of Meat One, the apprentice butchers who had spent so many hours of Liberal Studies explaining the workings of Sweetbreads Meat Factory to him and had actually taken him down there one afternoon to show him how it all worked. Dear lads. And how he had loathed them at the time. Which only went to show how wrong you could be about people. Wilt was just wondering if he had been wrong about Eva and perhaps she was dead when he fell asleep.

In the churchyard Eva watched the Rev St John Froude walk down to the boathouse and start rowing towards the reeds. As soon as he had disappeared she made her way up the path towards the house. With the Vicar out of the way she was prepared to take the risk of meeting his wife. She stole through the doorway into the courtyard and looked about her. The place had a dilapidated air about it and a pile of empty bottles in one corner, whisky and gin bottles, seemed to indicate that he might well be unmarried. Still clutching her ivy, she went across to the door, evidently the kitchen door, and knocked. There was no answer. She crossed to the window and looked inside. The kitchen was large, distinctly untidy and had all the hallmarks of a bachelor existence about it. She went back to the door and knocked again and she was just wondering what to do now when there was the sound of a vehicle coming down the drive.

Eva hesitated for a second and then tried the door. It was unlocked. She stepped inside and shut the door as a milk van drove into the courtyard. Eva listened while the milkman put down several bottles and then drove away. Then she turned and went down the passage to the front hall. If she could find the phone she could ring Henry and he could come out in the car and fetch her. She would go back to the church and wait for him there. But the hall was empty. She poked her head into several rooms with a good deal of care and found them largely bare of furniture or with dustcovers over chairs and sofas. The place

184

was incredibly untidy too. Definitely the Vicar was a bachelor. Finally she found his study. There was a phone on the desk. Eva went over and lifted the receiver and dialled Ipford 66066. There was no reply. Henry would be at the Tech. She dialled the Tech number and asked for Mr Wilt.

'Wilt?' said the girl on the switchboard. 'Mr Wilt?'

'Yes,' said Eva in a low voice.

'I'm afraid he's not here,' said the girl.

'Not there? But he's got to be there.'

'Well he isn't.'

'But he's got to be. It's desperately important I get in touch with him.'

'I'm sorry but I can't help you,' said the girl.

'But . . .' Eva began and glanced out of the window. The Vicar had returned and was walking up the garden path towards her. 'Oh God,' she muttered and put the phone down hurriedly. She turned and rushed out of the room in a state of panic. Only when she had made her way back along the passage to the kitchen did it occur to her that she had left her ivy behind in the study. There were footsteps in the passage. Eva looked frantically around, decided against the courtyard and went up a flight of stone steps to the first floor. There she stood and listened. Her heart was palpitating. She was naked and alone in a strange house with a clergyman and Henry wasn't at the Tech when he should have been and the girl on the switchboard had sounded most peculiar almost as though there was something wrong with wanting to speak to Henry. She had no idea what to do.

In the kitchen the Rev St John Froude had a very good idea what he wanted to do: expunge for ever the vision of the inferno to which he had been lured by those vile things with their meaningless messages floating across the water. He dug a fresh bottle of Teachers out of the cupboard and took it back to his study. What he had witnessed had been so grotesque, so evidently evil, so awful, so prescient of hell itself that he was in two minds whether it had been real or simply a waking nightmare. A man without a face, whose hands were tied behind his back, a woman with a painted face and a knife, the language . . . The Rev St John Froude opened the bottle and was about to pour a glass when his eye fell on the ivy Eva had left on the chair. He put the bottle down hastily and stared at the leaves. Here was another mystery to perplex him. How had a clump of ivy got onto the chair in his study? It certainly hadn't been there when he had left the house. He picked it up gingerly and put it on his desk. Then he sat down and contemplated it with a growing sense of unease. Something was happening in his world that he could not understand. And what about the strange figure he had seen flitting between the tombstones? He had quite forgotten her. The Rev St John Froude got up and went out onto the terrace and down the path to the church.

'On a Sunday?' shouted the manager of Sweetbreads. 'On a Sunday? But we don't work on a Sunday. There's nobody here. The place is shut.'

'It wasn't last Sunday and there was someone here, Mr Kidney,' said the Inspector.

'Kidley, please,' said the manager, 'Kidley with an L.'

The Inspector nodded. 'OK Mr Kidley, now what I'm telling you is that this man Wilt was here last Sunday and he . . .'

'How did he get in?'

'He used a ladder against the back wall from the car park.'

'In broad daylight? He'd have been seen.'

'At two o'clock in the morning, Mr Kidney.'

'Kidley, Inspector, Kidley.'

'Look Mr Kidley, if you work in a place like this with a name like that you're asking for it.'

Mr Kidley looked at him belligerently. 'And if you're telling me that some bloody maniac came in here with three dead bodies last Sunday and spent the day using our equipment to convert them into cooked meat edible for human consumption under the Food Regulations Act I'm telling you that that comes under the head of . . . Head? What did he do with the heads? Tell me that?'

'What do you do with heads, Mr Kidley?' asked the Inspector.

'That rather depends. Some of them go with the offal into the animal food bins . . .'

'Right. So that's what Wilt said he did with them. And you keep those in the No. 2 cold storage room. Am I right?'

186

Mr Kidley nodded miserably. 'Yes,' he said, 'we do.' He paused and gaped at the Inspector. 'But there's a world of difference between a pig's head and a . . .'

'Quite,' said the Inspector hastily, 'and I daresay you think someone was bound to spot the difference.'

'Of course they would.'

'Now I understand from Mr Wilt that you have an extremely efficient mincing machine . . .'

'No,' shouted Mr Kidley desperately. 'No, I don't believe it. It's not possible. It's . . .'

'Are you saying he couldn't possibly have . . .'

'I'm not saying that. I'm saying he shouldn't have. It's monstrous. It's horrible.'

'Of course it's horrible,' said the Inspector. 'The fact remains that he used that machine.'

'But we keep our equipment meticulously clean.'

'So Wilt says. He was definite on that point. He says he cleaned up carefully afterwards.'

'He must have done,' said Mr Kidley. 'There wasn't a thing out of place on Monday morning. You heard the foreman say so.'

'And I also heard this swine Wilt say that he made a list of where everything came from before he used it so that he could put it back exactly where he'd found it. He thought of everything.'

'And what about our reputation for hygiene? He didn't think of that, did he? For twenty-five years we've been known for the excellence of our products and now this has to happen. We've been at the head of . . .' Mr Kidley stopped suddenly and sat down.

'Now then,' said the Inspector, 'what I have to know is who you supply to. We're going to call in every pork pie and sausage . . .'

'Call them in? You can't call them in,' screamed Mr Kidley, 'they've all gone.'

'Gone? What do you mean they've gone?'

'What I say. They've gone. They've either been eaten or destroyed by now.'

'Destroyed? You're not going to tell me that there aren't any left. It's only five days since they went out.'

187

Mr Kidley drew himself up. 'Inspector, this is an old-fashioned firm and we use traditional methods and a Sweetbreads pork pie is a genuine pork pie. It's not one of your ersatz pies with preservatives that . . .'

It was Inspector Flint's turn to slump into a chair. 'Am I to understand that your fucking pies don't keep?' he asked.

Mr Kidley nodded. 'They are for immediate consumption,' he said proudly. 'Here today, gone tomorrow. That's our motto. You've seen our advertisements of course.'

Inspector Flint hadn't.

'Today's pie with yesterday's flavour, the traditional pie with the family filling.'

'You can say that again,' said Inspector Flint.

Mr Gosdyke regarded Wilt sceptically and shook his head. 'You should have listened to me,' he said, 'I told you not to talk.'

'I had to say something,' said Wilt. 'They wouldn't let me sleep and they kept asking me the same stupid questions over and over again. You've no idea what that does to you. It drives you potty.'

'Frankly, Mr Wilt, in the light of the confession you have made I find it hard to believe there was any need to. A man who can, of his own free will, make a statement like this to the police is clearly insane.'

'But it's not true,' said Wilt, 'it's all pure invention.'

'With a wealth of such revolting detail? I must say I find that hard to believe. I do indeed. The bit about hips and thighs . . . It makes my stomach turn over.'

'But that's from the Bible,' said Wilt, 'and besides I had to put in the gory bits or they wouldn't have believed me. Take the part where I say I sawed their . . .'

'Mr Wilt, for God's sake . . .'

'Well, all I can say is you've never taught Meat One. I got it all from them and once you've taught them life can hold few surprises.'

Mr Gosdyke raised an eyebrow. 'Can't it? Well I think I can disabuse you of that notion,' he said solemnly. 'In the light of this confession you have made against my most earnest advice, and as a result of my firm belief that every word in it is true, I

188

am no longer prepared to act on your behalf.' He collected his papers and stood up. 'You will have to get someone else.'

'But, Mr Gosdyke, you don't really believe all that nonsense about putting Eva in a pork pie, do you?' Wilt asked.

'Believe it? A man who can conceive of such a disgusting thing is capable of anything. Yes I do and what is more so do the police. They are this moment scouring the shops, the pubs and the supermarkets and dustbins of the entire county in search of pork pies.'

'But if they find any it won't do any good.'

'It may also interest you to know that they have impounded five thousand cans of Dogfill, an equal number of Catkin and have begun to dissect a quarter of a ton of Sweetbreads Best Bangers. Somewhere in that little lot they are bound to find some trace of Mrs Wilt, not to mention Dr and Mrs Pringsheim.'

'Well, all I can say is that I wish them luck,' said Wilt.

'And so d, I,' said Mr Gosdyke disgustedly and left the room. Behind him Wilt sighed. If only Eva would turn up. Where the hell could she have got to?

At the Police Laboratories Inspector Flint was getting restive. 'Can't you speed things up a bit?' he asked.

T' Head of the Forensic Department shook his head. 'It's like looking for a needle in a haystack,' he said, glancing significantly at another batch of sausages that had just been brought in. 'So far not a trace. This could take weeks.'

'I haven't got weeks,' said the Inspector, 'he's due in Court on Monday.'

'Only for remand and in any case you've got his statement.' But Inspector Flint had his doubts about that. He had been looking at that statement and had noticed a number of discrepancies about it which fatigue, disgust and an overwhelming desire to get the filthy account over and done with before he was sick had tended to obscure at the time. For one thing Wilt's scrawled signature looked suspiciously like Little Tommy Tucker when examined closely and there was a QNED beside it, which Flint had a shrewd idea meant Quod Non Erat Demonstrandum, and in any case there were rather too many references to pigs for his policeman's fancy and fuzzy pigs at that. Finally the information that Wilt had made a special request for two pork pies for lunch and had specified Sweetbreads in particular suggested an insane cannibalism that might fit in with what he had said he had done but seemed to be carrying things too far. The word 'provocation' sprang to mind and since the episode of the doll Flint had been rather conscious of bad publicity. He read through the statement again and couldn't make up his mind about it. One thing was quite certain. Wilt knew exactly how Sweetbreads factory worked. The wealth of detail he had supplied proved that. On the other hand Mr Kidley's incredulity about the heads and the mincing machine had seemed, on inspection, to be justified. Flint had looked gingerly at the beastly contraption and had found it difficult to believe that even Wilt in a fit of homicidal mania could have . . . Flint put the thought out of his mind. He decided to have another little chat with Henry Wilt. Feeling like death warmed up he went back to the Interview Room and sent for Wilt.

'How's it going?' said Wilt when he arrived. 'Had any luck with the frankfurters yet? Of course you could always try your hand at black puddings . . .'

'Wilt,' interrupted the Inspector, 'why did you sign that statement Little Tommy Tucker?'

Wilt sat down. 'So you've noticed that at last, have you? Very observant of you I must say.'

'I asked you a question.'

'So you did,' said Wilt. 'Let's just say I thought it was appropriate.'

'Appropriate?'

'I was singing, I think that's the slang term for it isn't it, for my sleep, so naturally . . .'

'Are you telling me you made all that up?'

'What the hell do you think I did? You don't seriously think I would inflict the Pringsheims and Eva on an unsuspecting public in the form of pork pies, do you? I mean there must be some limits to your credulity.'

Inspector Flint glared at him. 'My God, Wilt,' he said, 'if I find you've deliberately fabricated a story . . .'

'You can't do very much more,' said Wilt. 'You've already charged me with murder. What more do you want? You drag me in here, you humiliate me, you shout at me, you keep me

190

awake for days and nights bombarding me with questions about dog food, you announce to the world that I am helping you in your enquiries into a multiple murder thus leading every citizen in the country to suppose that I have slaughtered my wife and a beastly biochemist and . . .'

'Shut up,' shouted Flint, 'I don't care what you think. It's what you've done and what you've said you've done that worries me. You've gone out of your way to mislead me. . . .'

'I've done nothing of the sort,' said Wilt. 'Until last night I had told you nothing but the truth and you wouldn't accept it. Last night I handed you, in the absurd shape of a pork pie, a lie you wanted to believe. If you crave crap and use illegal methods like sleep deprivation to get it you can't blame me for serving it up. Don't come in here and bluster. If you're stupid that's your problem. Go and find my wife.'

'Someone stop me from killing the bastard,' yelled Flint, as he hurled himself from the room. He went to his office and sent for Sergeant Yates. 'Cancel the pie hunt. It's a load of bull,' he told him.

'Bull?' said the Sergeant uncertainly.

'Shit,' said Flint. 'He's done it again.'

'You mean . . .'

'I mean that that little turd in there has led us up the garden path again.'

'But how did he know about the factory and all that?'

Flint looked up at him pathetically. 'If you want to know why he's a walking encyclopedia, you go and ask him yourself.'

Sergeant Yates went out and returned five minutes later. 'Meat One,' he announced enigmatically.

'Meet won?'

'A class of butchers he used to teach. They took him round the factory.'

'Jesus,' said Flint, 'is there anybody that little swine hasn't taught?'

'He says they were most instructive.'

'Yates, do me a favour. Just go back and find out all the names of the classes he's taught. That way we'll know what to expect next.'

'Well I have heard him mention Plasterers Two and Gasfitters One . . .'

'All of them, Yates, all of them. I don't want to be caught out with some tale about Mrs Wilt being got rid of in the Sewage Works because he once taught Shit Two.' He picked up the evening paper and glanced at the headlines. POLICE PROBE PIES FOR MISSING WIFE.

'Oh my God,' he groaned. 'This is going to do our public image no end of good.'

At the Tech the Principal was expressing the same opinion at a meeting of the Heads of Departments.

'We've been held up to public ridicule,' he said. 'First it is popularly supposed that we make a habit of employing lecturers who bury their unwanted wives in the foundations of the new block. Secondly we have lost all chance of attaining Polytechnic status by having the Joint Honours degree turned down by the CNAA on the grounds that those facilities we do provide are not such as befit an institution of higher learning. Professor Baxendale expressed himself very forcibly on that point and particularly on a remark he heard from one of the senior staff about necrophilia . . .'

'I merely said . . .' Dr Board began.

'We all know what you said, Dr Board. And it may interest you to know that Dr Cox in his lucid moments is still refusing cold meat. Dr Mayfield has already tendered his resignation. And now to cap it all we have this.'

He held up a newspaper, across the top of whose second page there read SEX LECTURES STUN STUDENTS.

'I hope you have all taken good note of the photograph,' said the Principal bitterly, indicating a large and unfortunately angled picture of Judy hanging from the crane. 'The article goes on . . . well never mind. You can read it for yourselves. I would merely like answers to the following questions. Who authorized the purchase of thirty copies of *Last Exit From Brooklyn* for use with Fitters and Turners?'

Mr Morris tried to think who had taken FTs. 'I think that must have been Watkins,' he said. 'He left us last term. He was only a part-time lecturer.'

'Thank God we were spared him full-time,' said the Principal. 'Secondly which lecturer makes a habit of advocating to Nursery Nurses that they wear . . . er . . . Dutch Caps all the time?'

192

'Well Mr Sedgwick is very keen on them,' said Mr Morris.

'Nursery Nurses or Dutch Caps?' enquired the Principal.

'Possibly both together?' suggested Dr Board sotto voce.

'He's got this thing against the Pill,' said Mr Morris.

'Well please ask Mr Sedgwick to see me in my office on Monday at ten. I want to explain the terms under which he is employed here. And finally, how many lecturers do you know of who make use of Audio Visual Aid equipment to show blue movies to the Senior Secs?'

Mr Morris shook his head emphatically. 'No one in my department,' he said.

'It says here that blue movies have been shown,' said the Principal, 'in periods properly allocated to Current Affairs.'

'Wentworth did show them *Women in Love*,' said the Head of English.

'Well never mind. There's just one more point I want to mention. We are not going to conduct an Evening Class in First Aid with particular reference to the Treatment of Abdominal Hernia for which it was proposed to purchase an inflatable doll. From now on we are going to have to cut our coats to suit our cloth.'

'On the grounds of inflation?' asked Dr Board.

'On the grounds that the Education Committee has been waiting for years for an opportunity to cut back our budget,' said the Principal. 'That opportunity has now been given them. The fact that we have been providing a public service by keeping, to quote Mr Morris, "a large number of mentally unbalanced and potentially dangerous psychopaths off the streets" unquote seems to have escaped their notice.'

'I presume he was referring to the Day Release Apprentices,' said Dr Board charitably.

'He was not,' said the Principal. 'Correct me if I am wrong, Morris, but hadn't you in mind the members of the Liberal Studies Department?'

The meeting broke up. Later that day Mr Morris sat down to compose his letter of resignation.

Chapter 19

From the window of an empty bedroom on the first floor of the Vicarage, Eva Wilt watched the Rev St John Froude walk pensively down the path to the church. As soon as he had passed out of sight she went downstairs and into the study. She would phone Henry again. If he wasn't at the Tech he must be at home. She crossed to the desk and was about to pick up the phone when she saw the ivy. Oh dear, she had forgotten all about the ivy and she had left it where he was bound to have seen it. It was all so terribly embarrassing. She dialled 34 Parkview Avenue and waited. There was no reply. She put the phone down and dialled the Tech. And all the time she watched the gate into the churchyard in case the Vicar should return.

'Fenland College of Arts and Technology,' said the girl on the switchboard.

'It's me again,' said Eva, 'I want to speak to Mr Wilt.'

'I'm very sorry but Mr Wilt isn't here.'

'But where is he? I've dialled home and . . .'

'He's at the Police Station.'

'He's what?' Eva said.

'He's at the Police Station helping the police with their enquiries . . .'

'Enquiries? What enquiries?' Eva shrieked.

'Didn't you know?' said the girl. 'It's been in all the papers. He's been and murdered his wife . . .'

Eva took the phone from her ear and stared at it in horror. The girl was still speaking but she was no longer listening. Henry had murdered his wife. But she was his wife. It wasn't possible. She couldn't have been murdered. For one horrible moment Eva Wilt felt sanity slipping from her. Then she put the receiver to her ear again.

'Are you there?' said the girl.

'But I am his wife,' Eva shouted. There was a long silence at the other end and she heard the girl telling someone that there

194

was a crazy woman on the line who said she was Mrs Wilt and what ought she to do.

'I tell you I am Mrs Wilt. Mrs Eva Wilt,' she shouted but the line had gone dead. Eva put the phone down weakly. Henry at the Police Station . . . Henry had murdered her . . . Oh God. The whole world had gone mad. And here she was naked in a vicarage at . . . Eva had no idea where she was. She dialled 999.

'Emergency Services. Which department do you require?' said the operator.

'Police,' said Eva. There was a click and a man's voice came on.

'Police here.'

'This is Mrs Wilt,' said Eva.

'Mrs Wilt?'

'Mrs Eva Wilt. Is it true that my husband has murdered . . . I mean has my husband . . . oh dear I don't know what to say.'

'You say you're Mrs Wilt, Mrs Eva Wilt?' said the man.

Eva nodded and then said, 'Yes.'

'I see,' said the man dubiously. 'You're quite sure you're Mrs Wilt?'

'Of course I'm sure. That's what I'm ringing about.'

'Might I enquire where you're calling from?'

'I don't know,' said Eva. 'You see I'm in this house and I've got no clothes and . . . oh dear.' The Vicar was coming up the path onto the terrace.

'If you could just give us the address.'

'I can't stop now,' said Eva and put the phone down. For a moment she hesitated and then grabbing the ivy from the desk she rushed out of the room.

'I tell you I don't know where she is,' said Wilt, 'I expect you'll find her under missing persons. She has passed from the realm of substantiality into that of abstraction.'

'What the hell do you mean by that?' asked the Inspector, reaching for his cup of coffee. It was eleven o'clock on Saturday morning but he persisted. He had twenty-eight hours to get to the truth.

'I always warned her that Transcendental Meditation carried potential dangers,' said Wilt, himself in a no-man's-land between sleeping and waking. 'But she would do it.'

'Do what?'

'Meditate transcendentally. In the lotus position. Perhaps she has gone too far this time. Possibly she has transmogrified herself.'

'Trans what?' said Inspector Flint suspiciously.

'Changed herself in some magical fashion into something else.'

'Jesus, Wilt, if you start on those pork pies again . . .'

'I was thinking of something more spiritual, Inspector, something beautiful.'

'I doubt it.'

'Ah, but think. Here am I sitting in this room with you as a direct result of going for walks with the dog and thinking dark thoughts about murdering my wife. From those hours of idle fancy I have gained the reputation of being a murderer without committing a murder. Who is to say but that Eva whose thoughts were monotonously beautiful has not earned herself a commensurately beautiful reward? To put it in your terms, Inspector, we get what we ask for.'

'I fervently hope so, Wilt,' said the Inspector.

'Ah,' said Wilt, 'but then where is she? Tell me that. Mere speculation will not do . . .'

'Me tell you?' shouted the Inspector upsetting his cup of coffee. 'You know which hole in the ground you put her in or which cement mixer or incinerator you used.'

'I was speaking metaphorically . . . I mean rhetorically,' said Wilt. 'I was trying to imagine what Eva would be if her thoughts such as they are took on the substance of reality. My secret dream was to become a ruthless man of action, decisive, unhindered by moral doubts or considerations of conscience, a Hamlet transformed into Henry the Fifth without the patriotic fervour that inclines one to think that he would not have approved of the Common Market, a Caesar . . .'

Inspector Flint had heard enough. 'Wilt,' he snarled, 'I don't give a damn what you wanted to become. What I want to know is what has become of your wife.'

'I was just coming to that,' said Wilt. 'What we've got to establish first is what I am.'

'I know what you are, Wilt. A bloody word merchant, a verbal contortionist, a fucking logic-chopper, a linguistic

196

Houdini, an encyclopedia of unwanted information . . .'
Inspector Flint ran out of metaphors.

'Brilliant, Inspector, brilliant. I couldn't have put it better myself. A logic-chopper, but alas not a wife one. If we follow the same line of reasoning Eva in spite of all her beautiful thoughts and meditations has remained as unchanged as I. The ethereal eludes her. Nirvana slips ever from her grasp. Beauty and truth evade her. She pursues the absolute with a fly-swatter and pours Harpic down the drains of Hell itself . . .'

'That's the tenth time you have mentioned Harpic,' said the Inspector, suddenly alive to a new dreadful possibility. 'You didn't . . .'

Wilt shook his head. 'There you go again. So like poor Eva. The literal mind that seeks to seize the evanescent and clutches fancy by its non-existent throat. That's Eva for you. She will never dance Swan Lake. No management would allow her to fill the stage with water or install a double bed and Eva would insist.'

Inspector Flint got up. 'This is getting us nowhere fast.'

'Precisely,' said Wilt, 'nowhere at all. We are what we are and nothing we can do will alter the fact. The mould that forms our natures remains unbroken. Call it heredity, call it chance . . .'

'Call it a load of codswallop,' said Flint and left the room. He needed his sleep and he intended to get it.

In the passage he met Sergeant Yates.

'There's been an emergency call from a woman claiming to be Mrs Wilt,' the Sergeant said.

'Where from?'

'She wouldn't say where she was,' said Yates. 'She just said she didn't know and that she had no clothes on . . .'

'Oh one of those,' said the Inspector. 'A bloody nutter. What the hell are you wasting my time for? As if we didn't have enough on our hands without that.'

'I just thought you'd want to know. If she calls again we'll try and get a fix on the number.'

'As if I cared,' said Flint and hurried off in search of his lost sleep.

The Rev St John Froude spent an uneasy day. His investigation of the church had revealed nothing untoward and there was

197

no sign that an obscene ritual (a Black Mass had crossed his mind) had been performed there. As he walked back to the Vicarage he was glad to note that the sky over Eel Stretch was empty and that the contraceptives had disappeared. So had the ivy on his desk. He regarded the space where it had been with apprehension and helped himself to whisky. He could have sworn there had been a sprig of ivy there when he had left. By the time he had finished what remained in the bottle his mind was filled with weird fancies. The Vicarage was strangely noisy. There were odd creaks from the staircase and inexplicable sounds from the upper floor as if someone or something was moving stealthily about but when the Vicar went to investigate the noises ceased abruptly. He went upstairs and poked his head into several empty bedrooms. He came down again and stood in the hall listening. Then he returned to his study and tried to concentrate on his sermon, but the feeling that he was not alone persisted. The Rev St John Froude sat at his desk and considered the possibility of ghosts. Something very odd was going on. At one o'clock he went down the hall to the kitchen for lunch and discovered that a pint of milk had disappeared from the pantry and that the remains of an apple pie that Mrs Snape who did his cleaning twice weekly had brought him had also vanished. He made do with baked beans on toast and tottered upstairs for his afternoon nap. It was while he was there that he first heard the voices. Or rather one voice. It seemed to come from his study. The Rev St John Froude sat up in bed. If his ears weren't betraying him and in view of the morning's weird events he was inclined to believe that they were he could have sworn someone had been using his telephone. He got up and put on his shoes. Someone was crying. He went out onto the landing and listened. The sobbing had stopped. He went downstairs and looked in all the rooms on the ground floor but, apart from the fact that a dust cover had been removed from one of the armchairs in the unused sitting-room, there was no sign of anyone. He was just about to go upstairs again when the telephone rang. He went into the study and answered it.

'Waterswick Vicarage,' he mumbled.

'This is Fenland Constabulary,' said a man. 'We've just had a call from your number purporting to come from a Mrs Wilt.'

'Mrs Wilt?' said the Rev St John Froude. 'Mrs Wilt? I'm

afraid there must be some mistake. I don't know any Mrs Wilt.'

'The call definitely came from your phone, sir.'

The Rev St John Froude considered the matter. 'This is all very peculiar,' he said, 'I live alone.'

'You are the Vicar?'

'Of course I'm the Vicar. This is the Vicarage and I am the Vicar.'

'I see, sir. And your name is?'

'The Reverend St John Froude. F . . . R . . . O . . . U . . . D . . . E.'

'Quite sir, and you definitely don't have a woman in the house.'

'Of course I don't have a woman in the house. I find the suggestion distinctly improper. I am a . . .'

'I'm sorry, sir, but we just have to check these things out. We've had a call from Mrs Wilt, at least a woman claiming to be Mrs Wilt, and it came from your phone . . .'

'Who is this Mrs Wilt? I've never heard of a Mrs Wilt.'

'Well sir, Mrs Wilt . . . it's a bit difficult really. She's supposed to have been murdered.'

'Murdered?' said the Rev St John Froude. 'Did you say "murdered"?'

'Let's just say she is missing from home in suspicious circumstances. We're holding her husband for questioning.'

The Rev St John Froude shook his head. 'How very unfortunate,' he murmured.

'Thank you for your help, sir,' said the Sergeant. 'Sorry to have disturbed you.'

The Rev St John Froude put the phone down thoughtfully. The notion that he was sharing the house with a disembodied and recently murdered woman was not one that he had wanted to put to his caller. His reputation for eccentricity was already sufficiently widespread without adding to it. On the other hand what he had seen on the boat in Eel Stretch bore, now that he came to think of it, all the hallmarks of murder. Perhaps in some extraordinary way he had been a witness to a tragedy that had already occurred, a sort of post-mortem déja vu if that was the right way of putting it. Certainly if the husband were being held for questioning the murder must have taken place

199

before . . . In which case . . . The Rev St John Froude stumbled through a series of suppositions in which Time with a capital T, and appeals for help from beyond the grave figured largely. Perhaps it was his duty to inform the police of what he had seen. He was just hesitating and wondering what to do when he heard those sobs again and this time quite distinctly. They came from the next room. He got up, braced himself with another shot of whisky and went next door. Standing in the middle of the room was a large woman whose hair straggled down over her shoulders and whose face was ravaged. She was wearing what appeared to be a shroud. The Rev St John Froude stared at her with a growing sense of horror. Then he sank to his knees.

'Let us pray,' he muttered hoarsely.

The ghastly apparition slumped heavily forward clutching the shroud to its bosom. Together they kneeled in prayer.

'Check it out? What the hell do you mean "check it out"?' said Inspector Flint who objected strongly to being woken in the middle of the afternoon when he had had no sleep for thirty-six hours and was trying to get some. 'You wake me with some damned tomfoolery about a vicar called Sigmund Freud . . .'

'St John Froude,' said Yates.

'I don't care what he's called. It's still improbable. If the bloody man says she isn't there, she isn't there. What am I supposed to do about it?'

'I just thought we ought to get a patrol car to check, that's all.'

'What makes you think . . .'

'There was definitely a call from a woman claiming to be Mrs Wilt and it came from that number. She's called twice now. We've got a tape of the second call. She gave details of herself and they sound authentic. Date of birth, address, Wilt's occupation, even the right name of their dog and the fact that they have yellow curtains in the lounge.'

'Well, any fool can tell that. All they've got to do is walk past the house.'

'And the name of the dog. It's called Clem. I've checked that and she's right.'

'She didn't happen to say what she'd been doing for the past week did she?'

200

'She said she'd been on a boat,' said Yates. 'Then she rang off.'

Inspector Flint sat up in bed. 'A boat? What boat?'

'She rang off. Oh and another thing, she said she takes a size ten shoe. She does.'

'Oh shit,' said Flint. 'All right, I'll come on down.' He got out of bed and began to dress.

In his cell Wilt stared at the ceiling. After so many hours of interrogation his mind still reverberated with questions. 'How did you kill her? Where did you put her? What did you do with the weapon?' Meaningless questions continually reiterated in the hope they would finally break him. But Wilt hadn't broken. He had triumphed. For once in his life he knew himself to be invincibly right and everyone else totally wrong. Always before he had had doubts. Plasterers Two might after all have been right about there being too many wogs in the country. Perhaps hanging was a deterrent. Wilt didn't think so but he couldn't be absolutely certain. Only time would tell. But in the case of Regina *versus* Wilt *re* the murder of Mrs Wilt there could be no question of his guilt. He could be tried, found guilty and sentenced, it would make no difference. He was innocent of the charge and if he was sentenced to life imprisonment the very enormity of the injustice done to him would compound his knowledge of his own innocence. For the very first time in his life Wilt knew himself to be free. It was as though the original sin of being Henry Wilt, of 34 Parkview Avenue, Ipford, lecturer in Liberal Studies at the Fenland College of Arts and Technology, husband of Eva Wilt and father of none, had been lifted from him. All the encumbrances of possessions, habits, salary and status, all the social conformities, the niceties of estimation of himself and other people which he and Eva had acquired, all these had gone. Locked in his cell Wilt was free to be. And whatever happened he would never again succumb to the siren calls of self-effacement. After the flagrant contempt and fury of Inspector Flint, the abuse and the opprobrium heaped on him for a week, who needed approbation? They could stuff their opinions of him. Wilt would pursue his independent course and put to good use his evident gifts of inconsequence. Give him a life sentence and a progressive prison governor and Wilt would drive the man mad within a month by the sweet reasonableness of his refusal to obey the prison rules. Solitary confinement and a regime of bread and water, if such punishments still existed, would not deter him. Give him his freedom and he would apply his new-found talents at the Tech. He would sit happily on committees and reduce them to dissensions by his untiring adoption of whatever argument was most contrary to the consensus opinion. The race was not to the swift after all, it was to the indefatigably inconsequential and life was random, anarchic and chaotic. Rules were made to be broken and the man with the grasshopper mind was one jump ahead of all the others. Having established this new rule, Wilt turned on his side and tried to sleep but sleep wouldn't come. He tried his other side with equal lack of success. Thoughts, questions, irrelevant answers and imaginary dialogues filled his mind. He tried counting sheep but found himself thinking of Eva. Dear Eva, damnable Eva, ebullient Eva and Eva the irrepressibly enthusiastic. Like him she had sought the Absolute, the Eternal Truth which would save her the bother of ever having to think for herself again. She had sought it in Pottery, in Transcendental Meditation, in Judo, on trampolines and most incongruously of all in Oriental Dance. Finally she had tried to find it in sexual emancipation, Women's Lib and the Sacrament of the Orgasm in which she could forever lose herself. Which, come to think of it, was what she appeared to have done. And taken the bloody Pringsheims with her. Well she would certainly have some explaining to do when and if she ever returned. Wilt smiled to himself at the thought of what she would say when she discovered what her latest infatuation with the Infinite had led to. He'd see to it that she had cause to regret it to her dying day.

On the floor of the sitting-room at the Vicarage Eva Wilt struggled with the growing conviction that her dying day was already over and done with. Certainly everyone she came into contact with seemed to think she was dead. The policeman she had spoken to on the phone had seemed disinclined to believe her assertion that she was alive and at least relatively well and had demanded proofs of her identity in the most disconcerting fashion. Eva had retreated stricken from the encounter with her confidence in her own continuing existence seriously undermined and it had only needed the reaction of the Rev St John Froude to her appearance in his house to complete her misery. His frantic appeals to the Almighty to rescue the soul of our dear departed, one Eva Wilt, deceased, from its present shape and unendurable form had affected Eva profoundly. She knelt on the carpet and sobbed while the Vicar stared at her over his glasses, shut his eyes, lifted up a shaky voice in prayer, opened his eyes, shuddered and generally behaved in a manner calculated to cause gloom and despondency in the putative corpse and when in a last desperate attempt to get Eva Wilt, deceased, to take her proper place in the heavenly choir he cut short a prayer about 'Man that is born of Woman hath but a short time to live and is full of misery' and struck up 'Abide with me' with many a semi-quaver, Eva abandoned all attempt at self-control and wailed 'Fast falls the eventide' most affectingly. By the time they had got to 'I need thy presence every passing hour' the Rev St John Froude was of an entirely contrary opinion. He staggered from the room and took sanctuary in his study. Behind him Eva Wilt, espousing her new role as deceased with all the enthusiasm she had formerly bestowed on trampolines, judo and pottery, demanded to know where death's sting was and where, grave, thy victory. 'As if I bloody knew,' muttered the Vicar and reached for the whisky bottle only to find that it too was empty. He sat down and put his hands over his ears to shut out the dreadful noise. On the whole 'Abide with me' was the last hymn he should have chosen. He'd have been better off with 'There is a green hill far away'. It was less open to misinterpretation.

When at last the hymn ended he sat relishing the silence and was about to investigate the possibility that there was another bottle in the larder when there was a knock on the door and Eva entered.

'Oh Father I have sinned,' she shrieked, doing her level best to wail and gnash her teeth at the same time. The Rev St John Froude gripped the arms of his chair and tried to swallow. It was not easy. Then overcoming the reasonable fear that delirium tremens had come all too suddenly he managed to speak. 'Rise, my child,' he gasped as Eva writhed on the rug before him, 'I will hear your confession.'

Chapter 20

Inspector Flint switched the tape recorder off and looked at Wilt.

'Well?'

'Well what?' said Wilt.

'Is that her? Is that Mrs Wilt?'

Wilt nodded. 'I'm afraid so.'

'What do you mean you're afraid so? The damned woman is alive. You should be fucking grateful. Instead of that you sit there saying you're afraid so.'

Wilt sighed. 'I was just thinking what an abyss there is between the person as we remember and imagine them and the reality of what they are. I was beginning to have fond memories of her and now . . .'

'You ever been to Waterswick?'

Wilt shook his head. 'Never.'

'Know the Vicar there?'

'Didn't even know there was a vicar there.'

'And you wouldn't know how she got there?'

'You heard her,' said Wilt. 'She said she'd been on a boat.'

'And you wouldn't know anyone with a boat, would you?'

'People in my circle don't have boats, Inspector. Maybe the Pringsheims have a boat.'

Inspector Flint considered the possibility and rejected it. They had checked the boatyards out and the Pringsheims didn't have a boat and hadn't hired one either.

On the other hand the possibility that he had been the victim of some gigantic hoax, a deliberate and involved scheme to make him look an idiot, was beginning to take shape in his mind. At the instigation of this infernal Wilt he had ordered the exhumation of an inflatable doll and had been photographed staring lividly at it at the very moment it changed sex. He had instituted a round-up of pork pies unprecedented in the history of the country. He wouldn't be at all surprised if Sweetbreads instituted legal proceedings for the damage done to their previously unspotted reputation. And finally he had held an

204

apparently innocent man for questioning for a week and would doubtless be held responsible for the delay and additional cost in building the new Administration block at the Tech. There were, in all probability, other appalling consequences to be considered, but that was enough to be going on with. And he had nobody to blame but himself. Or Wilt. He looked at Wilt venomously.

Wilt smiled. 'I know what you're thinking,' he said.

'You don't,' said the Inspector. 'You've no idea.'

'That we are all the creatures of circumstance, that things are never what they seem, that there's more to this than meets . . .'

'We'll see about that,' said the Inspector.

Wilt got up. 'I don't suppose you'll want me for anything else,' he said. 'I'll be getting along home.'

'You'll be doing no such thing. You're coming with us to pick up Mrs Wilt.'

They went out into the courtyard and got into a police car. As they drove through the suburbs, past the filling stations and factories and out across the fens Wilt shrank into the back seat of the car and felt the sense of freedom he had enjoyed in the Police Station evaporate. And with every mile it dwindled further and the harsh reality of choice, of having to earn a living, of boredom and the endless petty arguments with Eva, of bridge on Saturday nights with the Mottrams and drives on Sundays with Eva, reasserted itself. Beside him, sunk in sullen silence, Inspector Flint lost his symbolic appeal. No longer the mentor of Wilt's self-confidence, the foil to his inconsequentiality, he had become a fellow sufferer in the business of living, almost a mirror-image of Wilt's own nonentity. And ahead, across this flat bleak landscape with its black earth and cumulus skies, lay Eva and a lifetime of attempted explanations and counter-accusations. For a moment Wilt considered shouting 'Stop the car. I want to get out', but the moment passed. Whatever the future held he would learn to live with it. He had not discovered the paradoxical nature of freedom only to succumb once more to the servitude of Parkview Avenue, the Tech and Eva's trivial enthusiasms. He was Wilt, the man with the grasshopper mind.

Eva was drunk. The Rev St John Froude's automatic reaction

to her appalling confession had been to turn from whisky to 150% Polish spirit which he kept for emergencies and Eva, in between agonies of repentance and the outpourings of lurid sins, had wet her whistle with the stuff. Encouraged by its effect, by the petrified benevolence of the Vicar's smile and by the growing conviction that if she was dead eternal life demanded an act of absolute contrition while if she wasn't it allowed her to avoid the embarrassment of explaining what precisely she was doing naked in someone else's house, Eva confessed her sins with an enthusiasm that matched her deepest needs. This was what she had sought in judo and pottery and Oriental dance, an orgiastic expiation of her guilt. She confessed sins she had committed and sins she hadn't, sins that had occurred to her and sins she had forgotten. She had betrayed Henry, she had wished him dead, she had lusted after other men, she was an adulterated woman, she was a lesbian, she was a nymphomaniac. And interspersed with these sins of the flesh there were sins of omission. Eva left nothing out. Henry's cold suppers, his lonely walks with the dog, her lack of appreciation for all he had done for her, her failure to be a good wife, her obsession with Harpic . . . everything poured out. In his chair the Rev St John Froude sat nodding incessantly like a toy dog in the back window of a car, raising his head to stare at her when she confessed to being a nymphomaniac and dropping it abruptly at the mention of Harpic, and all the time desperately trying to understand what had brought a fat naked—the shroud kept falling off her—lady, no definitely not lady, woman to his house with all the symptoms of religious mania upon her.

'My child, is that all?' he muttered when Eva finally exhausted her repertoire.

'Yes, Father,' sobbed Eva.

'Thank God,' said the Rev St John Froude fervently and wondered what to do next. If half the things he had heard were true he was in the presence of a sinner so depraved as to make the ex-Archdeacon of Ongar a positive saint. On the other hand there were incongruities about her sins that made him hesitate before granting absolution. A confession full of falsehoods was no sign of true repentance.

'I take it that you are married,' he said doubtfully, 'and that Henry is your lawful wedded husband?'

'Yes,' said Eva. 'Dear Henry.'

Poor sod, thought the Vicar but he was too tactful to say so. 'And you have left him?'

'Yes.'

'For another man?'

Eva shook her head. 'To teach him a lesson,' she said with sudden belligerence.

'A lesson?' said the Vicar, trying frantically to imagine what sort of lesson the wretched Mr Wilt had learnt from her absence. 'You did say a lesson?'

'Yes,' said Eva, 'I wanted him to learn that he couldn't get along without me.'

The Rev St John Froude sipped his drink thoughtfully. If even a quarter of her confession was to be believed her husband must be finding getting along without her quite delightful. 'And now you want to go back to him?'

'Yes,' said Eva.

'But he won't have you?'

'He can't. The police have got him.'

'The police?' said the Vicar. 'And may one ask what the police have got him for?'

'They say he's murdered me,' said Eva.

The Rev St John Froude eyed her with new alarm. He knew now that Mrs Wilt was out of her mind. He glanced round for something to use as a weapon should the need arise and finding nothing better to choose from than a plaster bust of the poet Dante and the bottle of Polish spirit, picked up the latter by its neck. Eva held her glass out.

'Oh you are awful,' she said. 'You're getting me tiddly.'

'Quite,' said the Vicar and put the bottle down again hastily. It was bad enough being alone in the house with a large, drunk, semi-naked woman who imagined that her husband had murdered her and who confessed to sins he had previously only read about without her jumping to the conclusion that he was deliberately trying to make her drunk. The Rev St John Froude had no desire to figure prominently in next Sunday's *News of the World*.

'You were saying that your husband murdered . . .' He stopped. That seemed an unprofitable subject to pursue.

'How could he have murdered me?' asked Eva. 'I'm here in the flesh, aren't I?'

'Definitely,' said the Vicar. 'Most definitely.'

'Well then,' said Eva. 'And anyway Henry couldn't murder anyone. He wouldn't know how. He can't even change a fuse in a plug. I have to do everything like that in the house.' She stared at the Vicar balefully. 'Are you married?'

'No,' said the Rev St John Froude, wishing to hell that he was.

'What do you know about life if you aren't married?' asked Eva truculently. The Polish spirit was getting to her now and with it there came a terrible sense of grievance. 'Men. What good are men? They can't even keep a house tidy. Look at this room. I ask you.' She waved her arms to emphasize the point and the dustcover dropped. 'Just look at it.' But the Rev St John Froude had no eyes for the room. What he could see of Eva was enough to convince him that his life was in danger. He bounded from the chair, trod heavily on an occasional table, overturned the wastepaper basket and threw himself through the door into the hall. As he stumbled away in search of sanctuary the front door bell rang. The Rev St John Froude opened it and stared into Inspector Flint's face.

'Thank God, you've come,' he gasped, 'she's in there.'

The Inspector and two uniformed constables went across the hall. Wilt followed uneasily. This was the moment he had been dreading. In the event it was better than he had expected. Not so for Inspector Flint. He entered the study and found himself confronted by a large naked woman.

'Mrs Wilt . . .' he began but Eva was staring at the two uniformed constables.

'Where's my Henry?' Eva shouted. 'You've got my Henry.' She hurled herself forward. Unwisely the Inspector attempted to restrain her.

'Mrs Wilt, if you'll just . . .' A blow on the side of his head ended the sentence.

'Keep your hands off me,' yelled Eva, and putting her knowledge of Judo to good use hurled him to the floor. She was about to repeat the performance with the constables when Wilt thrust himself forward.

'Here I am, dear,' he said. Eva stopped in her tracks. For a moment she quivered and, seen from Inspector Flint's viewpoint, appeared to be about to melt. 'Oh Henry,' she said, 'what have they been doing to you?'

208

'Nothing at all, dear,' said Wilt. 'Now get your clothes on. We're going home.' Eva looked down at herself, shuddered and allowed him to lead her out of the room.

Slowly and wearily Inspector Flint got to his feet. He knew now why Wilt had put that bloody doll down the hole and why he had sat so confidently through days and nights of interrogation. After twelve years of marriage to Eva Wilt the urge to commit homicide if only by proxy would be overwhelming. And as for Wilt's ability to stand up to cross-examination . . . it was self-evident. But the Inspector knew too that he would never be able to explain it to anyone else. There were mysteries of human relationships that defied analysis. And Wilt had stood there calmly and told her to get her clothes on. With a grudging sense of admiration Flint went out into the hall. The little sod had guts, whatever else you could say about him.

They drove back to Parkview Avenue in silence. In the back seat Eva, wrapped in a blanket, slept with her head lolling on Wilt's shoulder. Beside her Henry Wilt sat proudly. A woman who could silence Inspector Flint with one swift blow to the head was worth her weight in gold and besides that scene in the study had given him the weapon he needed. Naked and drunk in a vicar's study . . . There would be no questions now about why he had put that doll down the hole. No accusations, no recriminations. The entire episode would be relegated to the best forgotten. And with it would go all doubts about his virility or his ability to get on in the world. It was checkmate. For a moment Wilt almost lapsed into sentimentality and thought of love before recalling just how dangerous a topic that was. He would be better off sticking to indifference and undisclosed affection. 'Let sleeping dogs lie,' he muttered.

It was an opinion shared by the Pringsheims. As they were helped from the cruiser to a police launch, as they climbed ashore, as they explained to a sceptical Inspector Flint how they had come to be marooned for a week in Eel Stretch in a boat that belonged to someone else, they were strangely uncommunicative. No they didn't know how the door of the bathroom had been bust down. Well maybe there had been an accident. They had been too drunk to remember. A doll? What doll? Grass?

209

You mean marijuana? They had no idea. In their house?

Inspector Flint let them go finally. 'I'll be seeing you again when the charges have been properly formulated,' he said grimly. The Pringsheims left for Rossiter Grove to pack. They flew out of Heathrow next morning.

Chapter 21

The Principal sat behind his desk and regarded Wilt incredulously. 'Promotion?' he said. 'Did I hear you mention the word "promotion"?'

'You did,' said Wilt. 'And what is more you also heard "Head of Liberal Studies" too.'

'After all you've done? You mean to say you have the nerve to come in here and demand to be made Head of Liberal Studies?'

'Yes,' said Wilt.

The Principal struggled to find words to match his feelings. It wasn't easy. In front of him sat the man who was responsible for the series of disasters that had put an end to his fondest hopes. The Tech would never be a Poly now. The Joint Honours degree's rejection had seen to that. And then there was the adverse publicity, the cut in the budget, his battles with the Education Committee, the humiliation of being heralded as the Principal of Dollfuckers Hall . . .

'You're fired!' he shouted.

Wilt smiled. 'I think not,' he said. 'Here are my terms . . .'

'Your what?'

'Terms,' said Wilt. 'In return for my appointment as Head of Liberal Studies, I shall not institute proceedings against you for unfair dismissal with all the attendant publicity that would entail. I shall withdraw my case against the police for unlawful arrest. The contract I have here with the *Sunday Post* for a series of articles on the true nature of Liberal Studies—I intend to call them Exposure to Barbarism—will remain unsigned. I will cancel the lectures I had promised to give for the Sex Education Centre. I will not appear on *Panorama* next Monday. In short I will abjure the pleasures and rewards of public exposure . . .'

The Principal raised a shaky hand. 'Enough,' he said, 'I'll see what I can do.'

Wilt got to his feet. 'Let me know your answer by lunchtime,' he said. 'I'll be in my office.'

'Your office?' said the Principal.

'It used to belong to Mr Morris,' said Wilt and closed the door. Behind him the Principal picked up the phone. There had been no mistaking the seriousness of Wilt's threats. He would have to hurry.

Wilt strolled down the corridor to the Liberal Studies Department and stood looking at the books on the shelves. There were changes he had in mind. *The Lord of the Flies* would go and with it *Shane, Women in Love*, Orwell's *Essays* and *Catcher in the Rye*, all those symptoms of intellectual condescension, those dangled worms of sensibility. In future Gasfitters One and Meat Two would learn the how of things not why. How to read and write. How to make beer. How to fiddle their income tax returns. How to cope with the police when arrested. How to make an incompatible marriage work. Wilt would give the last two lessons himself. There would be objections from the staff, even threats of resignation, but it would make no difference. He might well accept several resignations from those who persisted in opposing his ideas. After all you didn't require a degree in English literature to teach Gasfitters the how of anything. Come to think of it, they had taught him more than they had learnt from him. Much more. He went into Mr Morris' empty office and sat down at the desk and composed a memorandum to Liberal Studies Staff. It was headed Notes on a System of Self-Teaching for Day Release Classes. He had just written 'non-hierarchical' for the fifth time when the phone rang. It was the Principal.

'Thank you,' said the new Head of Liberal Studies.

Eva Wilt walked gaily up Parkview Avenue from the doctor's office. She had made breakfast for Henry and Hoovered the front room and polished the hall and cleaned the windows and Harpicked the loo and been round to the Harmony Community Centre and helped with Xeroxing an appeal for a new play group and done the shopping and paid the milkman and been to the doctor to ask if there was any point in taking a course of fertility drugs and there was. 'Of course we'll have to do tests,'

212

the doctor had told her, 'but there's no reason to think they'd prove negative. The only danger is that you might have sex-tuplets.' It wasn't a danger to Eva. It was what she had always wanted, a house full of children. And all at once. Henry would be pleased. And so the sun shone brighter, the sky was bluer, the flowers in the gardens were rosier and even Parkview Avenue itself seemed to have taken on a new and brighter aspect. It was one of Eva Wilt's better days.

The Wilt Alternative

To Bill and Tina Baker

Chapter 1

It was Enrolment Week at the Tech. Henry Wilt sat at a table in Room 467 and stared into the face of the earnest woman opposite him and tried to look interested.

'Well, there is a vacancy in Rapid Reading on Monday evenings,' he said. 'If you'll just fill in the form over there . . .' He waved vaguely in the direction of the window but the woman was not to be fobbed off.

'I would like to know a little more about it. I mean it does help, doesn't it?'

'Help?' said Wilt refusing to be drawn into sharing her enthusiasm for self-improvement. 'It depends what you mean by help.'

'My problem has always been that I'm such a slow reader I can't remember what the beginning of a book was about by the time I've finished it,' said the woman. 'My husband says I'm practically illiterate.'

She smiled forlornly and implied a breaking marriage which Wilt could save by encouraging her to spend her Monday evenings away from home and the rest of the week reading books rapidly. Wilt doubted the therapy and tried to shift the burden of counselling somewhere else.

'Perhaps you would be better off taking Literary Appreciation,' he suggested.

'I did that last year and Mr Fogerty was wonderful. He said I had potential.'

Stifling the impulse to tell her that Mr Fogerty's notion of potential had nothing to do with literature and was more physical in its emphasis—though what the hell he could see in this earnest creature was a mystery—Wilt surrendered.

'The purpose of Rapid Reading,' he said going into the patter, 'is to improve your reading skills both in speed and retention of what you have read. You will find that you concentrate more the faster you go and that . . .'

He went on for five minutes delivering the set speech he had learnt by heart over four years of enrolling potential Rapid Readers. In front of him the woman changed visibly. This was what she had come to hear, the gospel of evening-class improvement. By the time Wilt had finished and she had filled in the form there was a new buoyancy about her.

There was less about Wilt. He sat on for the rest of the two hours listening to other similar conversations at other tables and wondering how the devil Bill Paschendaele managed to maintain his proselytizing fervour for An Introduction To Fenland Sub-Culture after twenty years. The fellow positively glowed with enthusiasm. Wilt shuddered and enrolled six more Rapid Readers with a lack of interest that was calculated to dishearten all but the most fanatical. In the intervals he thanked God he didn't have to teach the subject any longer and was simply there to lead the sheep into the fold. As Head of Liberal Studies Wilt had passed beyond Evening Classes into the realm of timetables, committees, memoranda, wondering which of his staff was going to have a nervous breakdown next, and the occasional lecture to Foreign Students. He had Mayfield to thank for the latter. While the rest of the Tech. had been badly affected by financial cuts the Foreign Students paid for themselves and Dr Mayfield, now Head of Academic Development, had created an empire of Arabs, Swedes, Germans, South Americans and even several Japanese who marched from one lecture room to another pursuing an understanding of the English language and more impossibly English Culture and Customs, a hodge-podge of lectures which came under the heading of Advanced English For Foreigners. Wilt's contribution was a weekly discourse on British Family Life which afforded him the opportunity to discuss his own family life with a freedom and frankness which would have infuriated Eva and embarrassed Wilt himself had he not known that his students lacked the insight to understand what he was telling them. The discrepancy between Wilt's appearance and the facts had baffled even his closest friends. In front of eighty foreigners he was assured of anonymity. He was assured of anonymity, period. Sitting in Room 467 Wilt could while away the time speculating on the ironies of life.

In room after room, on floor above floor, in departments all over the Tech., lecturers sat at tables, people asked questions, received concerned answers and finally filled in the forms that ensured that lecturers would keep their jobs for at least another year. Wilt would keep his for ever. Liberal Studies couldn't fail for lack of students. The Education Act saw to that. Day Release Apprentices had to have their weekly hour of progressive opinions whether they liked it or not. Wilt was safe, and if it hadn't been for the boredom he would have been a happy man. The boredom and Eva.

Not that Eva was boring. Now that she had the quads to look after Eva Wilt's enthusiasms had widened to include every 'Alternative' under the sun. Alternative Medicine alternated with Alternative Gardening and Alternative Nutrition and even various Alternative Religions so that Wilt, coming home from each day's lack of choice at the Tech., could never be sure what was in store for him except that it was not what it had been the night before. About the only constant was the din made by the quads. Wilt's four daughters had taken after their mother. Where Eva was enthusiastic and energetic they were inexhaustible and quadrupled her multiple enthusiasms. To avoid arriving home before they were in bed Wilt had taken to walking to and from the Tech. and was resolutely unselfish about using the car. To add to his problems, Eva had inherited a legacy from an aunt and since Wilt's salary had doubled they had moved from Parkview Avenue to Willington Road and a large house in a large garden. The Wilts had moved up the social scale. It was not an improvement, in Wilt's opinion, and there were days when he hankered for the old times when Eva's enthusiasms had been slightly muted by what the neighbours might think. Now, as the mother of four and the matron of a mansion, she no longer cared. A dreadful self-confidence had been born.

And so at the end of his two hours Wilt took his register of new students to the office and wandered along the corridor of the Administration Block towards the stairs. He was going down when Peter Braintree joined him.

'I've just enrolled fifteen landlubbers for Nautical Navigation. What about that to start the year off with a bang?'

'The bang starts tomorrow with Mayfield's bloody course

219

board meeting,' said Wilt. 'Tonight was as nothing. I tried to dissuade several insistent women and four pimply youths from taking Rapid Reading and failed. I wonder we don't run a course on how to solve *The Times* crossword puzzle in fifteen minutes flat. It would probably boost their confidence more than beating the track record for *Paradise Lost*.'

They went downstairs and crossed the hall where Miss Pansak was still recruiting for Beginners' Badminton.

'Makes me feel like a beer,' said Braintree. Wilt nodded. Anything to delay going home. Outside, stragglers were still coming in and cars were parked densely along Post Road.

'What sort of time did you have in France?' asked Braintree.

'The sort of time you would expect with Eva and the brood in a tent. We were asked to leave the first camp-site after Samantha had let down the guy ropes on two tents. It wouldn't have been so bad if the woman inside one hadn't had asthma. That was on the Loire. In La Vendée we were stuck next to a German who had fought on the Russian front and was suffering from shell-shock. I don't know if you've ever been woken in the night by a man screaming about *Flammenwerfern* but I can tell you it's unnerving. That time we moved on without being asked.'

'I thought you were going down to the Dordogne. Eva told Betty she'd been reading a book about three rivers and it was simply enthralling.'

'The reading may have been but the rivers weren't,' said Wilt, 'not the one we were next to. It rained and of course Eva had to have the tent in what amounted to a tributary. It was bad enough putting the thing up dry. Weighed a ton then, but moving it out of a flashflood up a hundred yards of bramble banks at twelve o'clock at night when the damned thing was sodden . . .' Wilt stopped. The memory was too much for him.

'And I suppose it went on raining,' said Braintree sympathetically. 'That's been our experience, anyway.'

'It did,' said Wilt. 'For five whole days. After that we moved into a hotel.'

'Best thing to do. You can eat decent meals and sleep in comfort.'

'You can perhaps. We couldn't. Not after Samantha shat in

220

the bidet. I wondered what the stench was sometime around 2 a.m. Anyway let's talk about something civilized.'

They went into The Pig In A Poke and ordered pints.

'Of course all men are selfish,' said Mavis Mottram as she and Eva sat in the kitchen at Willington Road. 'Patrick hardly ever gets home until after eight and he always has an excuse about the Open University. It's nothing of the sort, or if it is it's some divorcee student who wants extra coition. Not that I mind any longer. I said to him the other night, "If you want to make a fool of yourself running after other women that's your affair but don't think I'm going to take it lying down. You can go your way and I'll go mine." '

'What did he say to that?' Eva asked, testing the steam iron and starting on the quads' dresses.

'Oh just something stupid about not wanting it standing up anyway. Men are so coarse. I can't think why we bother with them.'

'I sometimes wish Henry was a bit coarser,' said Eva pensively. 'He always was lethargic but now he claims he's too tired because he walks to the Tech. every day. It's six miles so I suppose he could be.'

'I can think of another reason,' said Mavis bitterly. 'Still waters etcetera . . .'

'Not with Henry. I'd know. Besides, ever since the quads were born he's been very thoughtful.'

'Yes, but what's he been thoughtful about? That's what you have to ask yourself, Eva.'

'I meant he's been considerate to me. He gets up at seven and brings me tea in bed and at night he always makes me Horlicks.'

'If Patrick started acting like that I'd be very suspicious,' said Mavis. 'It doesn't sound natural.'

'It doesn't, does it, but that's Henry all over. He's really kind. The only thing is he isn't very masterful. He says it's because he's surrounded by five women and he knows when he's beaten.'

'If you go ahead with this au pair girl plan that will make six,' said Mavis.

'Irmgard isn't a proper au pair girl. She's renting the top-floor flat and says she'll help around the house whenever she can.'

'Which, if the Everards' experience with their Finn is anything to go by, will be never. She stayed in bed till twelve and practically ate them out of house and home.'

'Finns are different,' said Eva. 'Irmgard is German. I met her at the Van Donkens' World Cup Protest Party. You know they raised nearly a hundred and twenty pounds for the Tortured Tupamaros.'

'I didn't think there were any Tupamaros in Argentina any more. I thought they had all been killed off by the army.'

'These are the ones who escaped,' said Eva. 'Anyway I met Miss Mueller and mentioned that we had this top flat and she was ever so eager to have it. She'll do all her own cooking and things.'

'Things? Did you ask her what things she had in mind?'

'Well, not exactly, but she says she wants to study a lot and she's very keen on physical fitness.'

'And what does Henry have to say about her?' asked Mavis moving closer to her real concern.

'I haven't told him yet. You know what he's like about having other people in the house, but I thought if she stays in the flat in the evenings and keeps out of his way . . .'

'Eva dear,' said Mavis with advanced sincerity, 'I know this is none of my business but aren't you tempting fate just a little?'

'I can't see how. I mean it's such a good arrangement. She can baby-sit when we want to go out, and the house is far too big for us and nobody ever goes up to the flat.'

'They will with her up there. You'll have all sorts of people coming through the house and she's bound to have a record player. They all do.'

'Even if she does we won't hear it. I've ordered rush matting from Soales and I went up the other day with the transistor and you can hardly hear a thing.'

'Well, it's your affair, dear, but if I had an au pair girl in the house with Patrick around I'd want to be able to hear some things.'

'I thought you said you'd told Patrick he could do what he liked?'

'I didn't say in my house,' said Mavis. 'He can do what he

likes elsewhere but if I ever caught him playing Casanova at home he'd live to regret it.'

'Well, Henry is different. I don't suppose he will even notice her,' said Eva complacently. 'I've told her he's very quiet and home-loving and she says all she wants is peace and quiet herself.'

With the private thought that Miss Irmgard Mueller was going to find living in the same house as Eva and the quads neither peaceful nor quiet, Mavis finished her coffee and got up to go. 'All the same I would keep an eye on Henry,' she said. 'He may be different but I wouldn't trust a man further than I could throw him. And my experience of foreign students is that they come over here to do a lot more than learn the English language.'

She went out to her car and drove home wondering what there was about Eva's simplicity that was so sinister. The Wilts were an odd couple, but since their move to Willington Road Mavis Mottram's dominance had diminished. The days when Eva had been her protégée in flower-arranging were over and Mavis was frankly jealous. On the other hand Willington Road was definitely in one of the best neighbourhoods in Ipford and there were social advantages to be gained from knowing the Wilts.

At the corner of Regal Gardens her headlights picked Wilt out as he walked slowly home and she called out to him. But he was deep in thought and didn't hear her.

As usual Wilt's thoughts were dark and mysterious and made the more so by the fact that he didn't understand why he had them. They had to do with strange violent fantasies that welled up inside him, with dissatisfactions which could only be partly explained by his job, his marriage to a human dynamo, the dislike he felt for the atmosphere of Willington Road where everyone else was something important in high-energy physics or low-temperature conductivity and made more money than he did. And after all these explicable grounds for grumbling there was the feeling that his life was largely meaningless and that beyond the personal there was a universe which was random, chaotic and yet had some weird coherence about it which he would never fathom. Wilt speculated on the paradox of material progress and spiritual decadence and as usual came to no conclusion except that beer on an empty stomach didn't agree with him. One consolation was that now Eva was into Alternative Gardening he was likely to get a good supper and the quads would be fast asleep. If only the little buggers didn't wake in the night. Wilt had had his fill of broken sleep in the early years of breast-feeding and bottle-warming. Those days were largely over now and, apart from Samantha's occasional bout of sleepwalking and Penelope's bladder problem, his nights were undisturbed. And so he made his way along under the trees that lined Willington Road and was greeted by the smell of casserole from the kitchen. Wilt felt relatively cheerful.

Chapter 2

He left the house next morning in a far more despondent mood. 'I should have been warned by that casserole that she had some bloody ominous message to impart,' he muttered as he set off for the Tech. And Eva's announcement that she had found a lodger for the top flat had been ominous indeed. Wilt had been alert to the possibility ever since they had bought the house but Eva's immediate enthusiasms—gardening, herbalism, progressive playgrouping for the quads, redecorating the house and designing the ultimate kitchen—had postponed any decision about the top flat. Wilt had hoped that the matter would be forgotten. Now she had let the rooms without even bothering to tell him Wilt felt distinctly aggrieved. Worse still, he had been outwitted by the decoy of that splendid stew. When Eva wanted to cook she could, and Wilt had finished his second helping and a bottle of his better Spanish burgundy before she had announced this latest disaster. It had taken Wilt several seconds before he could focus on the problem.

'You've done what?' he said.

'Let it to a very nice young German girl,' said Eva. 'She's paying fifteen pounds a week and promises to be very quiet. You won't even know she's there.'

'I bloody well will. She'll have lovers fumbling their lascivious way up and down stairs all night and the house will reek of sauerkraut.'

'It won't. There's an extractor fan in the kitchenette up there and she's entitled to have boyfriends so long as they behave themselves nicely.'

'Nicely! Show me some loutish lover behaving nicely and I'll show you a camel with four humps. . . .'

'They're called dromedaries,' said Eva using the tactic of muddled information that usually distracted Wilt and lured him into correcting her. But Wilt was too distracted already to bother.

'They're not. They're called fucking foreigners and I'm using fucking properly for once and if you think I want to lie in bed every night listening to some ruddy Latin prove his virility by imitating Popocatepetl in eruption on an inner sprung mattress eight feet above my head—'

'Dunlopillo,' said Eva. 'You never get things right.'

'Oh yes I do,' snarled Wilt. 'I knew this was in the wind ever since your bloody aunt had to die and leave you a legacy and you had to buy this miniature hotel. I knew then that you would turn it into some foul commune.'

'It's not a commune and anyway Mavis says the extended family was one of the good things about the old days.'

'She'd know all about extended families, Mavis would. Patrick has been extending his family for as long as I can remember, and into other people's.'

'Mavis has given him an ultimatum,' said Eva. 'She's not putting up with his carryings on any longer.'

'And I'm giving you an ultimatum,' said Wilt. 'One squeak out of those bedsprings up there, one whiff of pot, one twang of a guitar, one giggle on the stairs and I'll extend this family by finding digs in town until Miss Schickelgruber has moved out.'

'Her name isn't Schickelwhatchamacallit. It's Mueller. Irmgard Mueller.'

'So was one of Hitler's nastier Obergruppenführers and all I'm saying is—'

'You're just jealous,' said Eva. 'If you were a proper man and hadn't got hang-ups about sex from your parents you wouldn't get so hot under the collar about what other people do.'

Wilt regarded her balefully. Whenever Eva wanted to subdue him she launched a sexual offensive. Wilt retired to bed defeated. Discussions of his sexual inadequacies tended to result in his having to prove Eva wrong practically and after that stew he didn't feel up to it.

He didn't feel up to much by the time he reached the Tech. next morning. The quads had fought their usual intersororial war about who was going to wear what dress before being dragged off to playgroup and there had been another letter

226

in *The Times* from Lord Longford demanding the release of Myra Hindley, the Moors murderess, from prison on the grounds that she was now thoroughly reformed, a convinced Christian and a socially valuable citizen. 'In which case she can prove her social value and Christian charity by staying in prison and helping her fellow-convicts,' had been Wilt's infuriated reaction. The other news was just as depressing. Inflation was up again. Sterling down. North Sea gas would run out in five years and the Rhodesians had just massacred fifty more blacks while the blacks had butchered more missionaries. All in all the world was in its usual filthy mess and now he had to listen to Dr Mayfield extol the virtues of the Advanced Course in English For Foreigners for several intolerably boring hours before dealing with complaints from his Liberal Studies lecturers about the way he had done the timetable.

One of the worst things about being Head of Liberal Studies was that he had to spend a large part of his summer vacation fitting classes into rooms and lecturers into classes, and when he had finished and had defeated the Head of Art who wanted Room 607 for Life Studies while Wilt needed it for Meat Three, he was still faced with a hassle at the beginning of the year and had to readjust the timetable because Mrs Fyfe couldn't make Tuesday at 2 with DMT One because her husband . . . It was on such occasions that Wilt wished he was back teaching *The Lord of the Flies* to Gasfitters instead of running the department. But his salary was good, the rates on Willington Road were exorbitant, and for the rest of the year he could spend much of his time sitting in his office dreaming.

He could sit through most committee meetings in a coma too but Dr Mayfield's course board was the one exception. Wilt had to stay awake to prevent Mayfield lumbering him with several more lectures in his relative absence. Besides, Dr Board would start the term off with a row.

He did. Mayfield had only just begun to stress the need for a more student-oriented curriculum with special emphasis on socio-economic awareness when Dr Board intervened.

'Codswallop,' he said. 'The business of my department is to teach English students how to speak German, French, Spanish and Italian, not to explain the origins of their own languages to a whole lot of aliens, and as for socio-economic awareness, I suggest that Dr Mayfield has his priorities wrong. If the Arabs I had last year were anything to go by they were economically aware to the nth degree about the purchasing power of oil and so socially backward that it will take more than a three-year course to persuade the sods that stoning women to death for being unfaithful isn't cricket. Perhaps if we had three hundred years . . .'

'Dr Board, this meeting may well last as long if you keep interrupting,' said the Vice-Principal. 'Now if Dr Mayfield will just continue . . .'

The Head of Academic Development continued for another hour, and was all set for the entire morning when the Head of Engineering objected.

'I see that several of my staff are scheduled to deliver lectures on British Engineering Achievements in the Nineteenth Century. Now I would like to inform Dr Mayfield and this board that my department consists of engineers, not historians, and quite frankly they see no reason why they should be asked to lecture on topics outside their field.'

'Hear, hear,' said Dr Board.

'What is more, I would like to be informed why so much emphasis is being placed on a course for foreigners at the expense of our own British students.'

'I think I can answer that,' said the Vice-Principal. 'Thanks to the cuts that have been imposed on us by the local authority we have been forced to subsidize our existing non-paying courses and staff numbers by expanding the foreign sector where students pay substantial fees. If you want the figures of the profit we made last year . . .'

But no one took up the invitation. Even Dr Board was momentarily silenced.

'Until such time as the economy improves,' continued the Vice-Principal, 'a great many lecturers are only going to keep their jobs because we are running this course. What is more, it may well be possible to expand Advanced English for Foreigners into a degree course approved by the CNAA. I think you will all agree that anything which increases our chances of becoming a Polytechnic is to everyone's advantage.'

228

The Vice-Principal stopped and looked round the room but nobody demurred. 'In which case all that remains is for Dr Mayfield to allocate the new lectures to the various departmental heads.'

Dr Mayfield distributed xeroxed lists. Wilt studied his new burden and found that it included The Development of Liberal and Progressive Social Attitudes in English Society, 1688 to 1978, and was just about to protest when the Head of Zoology got in first.

'I see here that I am down for Animal Husbandry and Agriculture with special reference to Intensive Farming of Pigs, Hens, and Stock-Rearing.'

'The subject has ecological significance—'

'And is student-oriented,' said Dr Board. 'Battery Education or possibly Hog Raising by Continuous Assessment. Perhaps we could even run a course on Composting.'

'Don't,' said Wilt with a shudder. Dr Board looked at him with interest.

'Your magnificent wife?' he enquired.

Wilt nodded dolefully. 'Yes, she has taken up—'

'If I may just get back to my original objection instead of hearing about Mr Wilt's matrimonial problems,' said the Head of Zoology. 'I want to make it absolutely clear now that I am not qualified to lecture on Animal Husbandry. I am a zoologist not a farmer and what I know about Stock-Rearing is zero.'

'We must all extend ourselves,' said Dr Board. 'After all if we are to acquire the doubtful privilege of calling ourselves a Polytechnic we must put the College before personal interest.'

'Perhaps you haven't seen what you're down to teach, Board,' Zoology continued, 'Sementic Influences . . . shouldn't that be Semantic, Mayfield?'

'Must be the typist's error,' said Mayfield. 'Yes it should read Semantic Influences on Current Sociological Theories. The bibliography includes Wittgenstein, Chomsky and Wilkes . . .'

'It doesn't include me,' said Board. 'You can count me out. I don't care if we descend to the level of a primary school but I am not going to mug up Wittgenstein or Chomsky for the benefit of anyone.'

'Well then, don't talk about my having to extend myself,' said the Head of Zoology. 'I am not going into a lecture room filled with Moslems to explain, even with my limited knowledge of the subject, the advantages of raising pigs in the Persian Gulf.'

'Gentlemen, while recognizing that there are one or two minor amendments necessary to the lecture titles I think they can be ironed out—'

'Wiped out more likely,' said Dr Board. The Vice-Principal ignored his interruption. '—and the main thing is to keep the lectures in their present format while presenting them at a level suitable for the individual students.'

'I'm still not mentioning pigs,' said Zoology.

'You don't have to. You can do an elementary series of talks on plants,' said the Vice-Principal wearily.

'Great. And will someone tell me how in God's name I can even begin to talk in an elementary way about Wittgenstein? I had an Iraqi last year who couldn't even spell his own name, so what's the poor bugger going to do with Wittgenstein?' said Dr Board.

'And if I may just bring another subject up,' said a lecturer from the English department rather diffidently, 'I think we are going to have something of a communications problem with the eighteen Japanese and the young man from Tibet.'

'Oh really,' said Dr Mayfield. 'A communications problem. You know, it might be as well to add a lecture or two on Intercommunicational Discourse. It's the sort of subject which is likely to appeal to the Council for National Academic Awards.'

'It may appeal to them but it certainly doesn't to me,' said Board, 'I've always said they were the scourings of the Academic world.'

'Yes, and we've already heard you on the subject,' said the Vice-Principal. 'And now to get back to the Japanese and the young man from Tibet. You did say Tibet, didn't you?'

'Well, I said it, but I can't be too sure,' answered the English lecturer. 'That's what I meant about a communications problem. He doesn't speak a word of English and my Tibetanese isn't exactly fluent. It's the same with the Japanese.'

The Vice-Principal looked round the room. 'I suppose it is too much to expect anyone here to have a smattering of Japanese?'

230

'I've got a bit,' said the Head of Art, 'but I'm damned if I'm going to use it. When you've spent four years in a Nip prisoner-of-war camp the last thing you want is to have to talk to the bastards in later life. My digestive system is still in a hell of a mess.'

'Perhaps you could tutor our Chinese student instead. Tibet is part of China now and if we include him with the four girls from Hong Kong . . .'

'We'll be able to advertise Take-Away Degrees,' said Dr Board and provoked another acrimonious exchange which lasted until lunchtime.

Wilt returned to his office to find that Mrs Fyfe couldn't take Mechanical Technicians at 2 on Tuesday because her husband had . . . It was exactly as he had anticipated. The Tech.'s year had begun as it always did. It continued in the same trying vein for the next four days. Wilt attended meetings on Interdepartmental Course Collaboration, gave a seminar to student teachers from the local training college on The Meaning of Liberal Studies, which was a contradiction in terms as far as he was concerned, was lectured by a Sergeant from the Drug Squad on Pot Plant Recognition and Heroin Addiction and finally managed to fit Mrs Fyfe into Room 29 with Bread Two on Monday at 10 a.m. And all the time he brooded over Eva and her wretched lodger.

While Wilt busied himself lethargically at the Tech., Eva put her own plans implacably into operation. Miss Mueller arrived two mornings later and installed herself inconspicuously in the flat; so inconspicuously that it took Wilt two more days to realize she was there, and then only the delivery of nine milk bottles where there were usually eight gave him the clue. Wilt said nothing but waited for the first hint of gaiety upstairs before launching his counter-offensive of complaints.

But Miss Mueller lived up to Eva's promise. She was exceedingly quiet, came in unobtrusively when Wilt was still at the Tech. and left in the morning after he had begun his daily walk. By the end of a fortnight he was beginning to think his worst fears were unjustified. In any case, he had his lectures to foreign students to prepare and the teaching term had finally started. The question of the lodger receded into the background as he tried to think what the hell to tell Mayfield's Empire, as Dr Board called it, about Progressive Social Attitudes in English Society since 1688. If Gasfitters were any indication there had been a regression, not a progressive development. The bastards had graduated to queer-bashing.

Chapter 3

But if Wilt's fears were premature they were not long being realized. He was sitting one Saturday evening in the Piagetory, the purpose-built summerhouse at the bottom of the garden in which Eva had originally tried to play conceptual games with the 'wee ones', a phrase Wilt particularly detested, when the first blow fell.

It was less a blow than a revelation. The summerhouse was nicely secluded, set back among old apple trees with an arbour of clematis and climbing roses to hide it from the world and Wilt's consumption of homemade beer from Eva. Inside, it was hung with dried herbs. Wilt didn't approve of the herbs but he preferred them in their hung form rather than in the frightful infusions Eva sometimes tried to inflict on him, and they seemed to have the added advantage of keeping the flies from the compost heap at bay. He could sit there with the sun dappling the grass around and feel at relative peace with the world, and the more beer he drank the greater that peace became. Wilt prided himself on the effect of his beer. He brewed it in a plastic dustbin and occasionally fortified it with vodka before bottling it in the garage. After three bottles even the quads' din somehow receded and became almost natural, a chorus of whines, squeals and laughter, usually malicious when someone fell off the swing, but at least distant. And even that distraction was absent this evening. Eva had taken them to the ballet in the hope that early exposure to Stravinsky would turn Samantha into a second Margot Fonteyn. Wilt had his doubts about Samantha and Stravinsky. As far as he was concerned his daughter's talents were more suitable for an all-in wrestler, and Stravinsky's genius was overrated. It had to be if Eva approved it. Wilt's own taste ran to Mozart and Mugsy Spanier, an eclecticism Eva couldn't understand but which allowed him to annoy her by switching from a piano sonata she was enjoying to twenties jazz which she didn't.

Anyway, this evening there was no need to play his tape-recorder. It was sufficient to sit in the summerhouse and know that even if the quads woke him at five next morning he could still stay in bed until ten, and he was just uncorking his fourth bottle of fortified lager when his eye caught sight of a figure on the wooden balcony outside the dormer window of the top-floor flat. Wilt's hand on the bottle loosened and a moment later he was groping for the binoculars Eva had bought for bird-watching. He focused on the figure through a gap in the roses and forgot about beer. All his attentions was riveted on Miss Irmgard Mueller.

She was standing looking out over the trees to the open country beyond, and from where Wilt sat and focused he had a particularly interesting view of her legs. There was no denying that they were shapely legs. In fact they were startlingly shapely legs and her thighs . . . Wilt moved up, found her breasts beneath a cream blouse entrancing, and finally reached her face. He stayed there. It wasn't that Irmgard—Miss Mueller and that bloody lodger were instantaneously words of the past—was an attractive young woman. Wilt had been faced by attractive young women at the Tech. for too many years, young women who ogled him and sat with their legs distractingly apart, not to have built up sufficient sexual antibodies to deflect their juvenile charms. But Irmgard was not a juvenile. She was a woman, a woman of around twenty-eight, a beautiful woman with glorious legs, discreet and tight breasts, 'unsullied by suckling' was the phrase that sprang to Wilt's mind, with firm neat hips, even her hands grasping the balcony rail were some-how delicately strong with tapering fingers, lightly tanned as by some midnight sun. Wilt's mind spun into meaningless metaphors far removed from Eva's washing-up mitts, the canyon wrinkles of her birth-pocked belly, the dugs that haunched her flaccid hips and all the physical erosion of twenty years of married life. He was swept into fancy by this splendid creature, but above all by her face.

Irmgard's face was not simply beautiful. In spite of the beer Wilt might have withstood the magnetism of mere beauty. He was defeated by the intelligence of her face. In fact there were imperfections in that face from a purely physical point of view. It was too strong for one thing, the nose was a shade retroussé to be commercially perfect, and the mouth too generous but it

234

was individual, individual and intelligent and sensitive and mature and thoughtful and . . . Wilt gave up the addition in despair and as he did so it seemed to him that Irmgard was gazing down into his two adoring eyes, or anyway into the binoculars, and that a subtle smile played about her gorgeous lips. Then she turned away and went back into the flat. Wilt dropped the binoculars and reached trancelike for the beer bottle. What he had just seen had changed his view of life.

He was no longer Head of Liberal Studies, married to Eva, the father of four quarrelsome repulsive daughters, and thirty-eight. He was twenty-one again, a bright, lithe young man who wrote poetry and swam on summer mornings in the river and whose future was alight with achieved promise. He was already a great writer. The fact that being a writer involved writing was wholly irrelevant. It was being a writer that mattered and Wilt at twenty-one had long since settled his future in advance by reading Proust and Gide, and then books on Proust and Gide and books about books on Proust and Gide, until he could visualize himself at thirty-eight with a delightful anguish of anticipation. Looking back on those moments he could only compare them to the feeling he now had when he came out of the dentist's surgery without the need for any fillings. On an intellectual plane, of course. Spiritual, with smoke-filled, cork-lined rooms and pages of illegible but beautiful prose littering, almost fluttering from, his desk in some deliciously nondescript street in Paris. Or in a white-walled bedroom on white sheets entwined with a tanned woman with the sun shining through the shutters and shimmering on the ceiling from the azure sea somewhere near Hyères. Wilt had tasted all these pleasures in advance at twenty-one. Fame, fortune, the modesty of greatness, bons mots drifting effortlessly from his tongue over absinthe, allusions tossed and caught, tossed back again like intellectual shuttlecocks, and the intense walk home through dawn-deserted streets in Montparnasse.

About the only thing Wilt had eschewed from his borrowings off Proust and Gide had been small boys. Small boys and plastic dustbins. Not that he could see Gide buggering about brewing beer anyway, let alone in plastic dustbins. The sod was probably a teetotaller. There had to be some deficit to make up for the small boys. So Wilt had lifted Frieda from Lawrence while hoping to hell he didn't get TB, and had endowed her with a milder temperament. Together they had lain on the sand making love while the ripples of the azure sea broke over them on an empty beach. Come to think of it, that must have been about the time he saw *From Here to Eternity* and Frieda had looked like Deborah Kerr. The main thing was she had been strong and firm and in tune, if not with the infinite as such, with the infinite variations of Wilt's particular lusts. Only they hadn't been lusts. Lust was too insensitive a word for the sublime contortions Wilt had had in mind. Anyway, she had been a sort of sexual muse, more sex than muse, but someone to whom he could confide his deepest perceptions without being asked who Rochefou . . . what's-his-name was which was about as near being a blasted muse as Eva ever got. And now look at him, lurking in a bleeding Spockery drinking himself into a beer belly and temporary oblivion on something pretending to be lager that he'd brewed in a plastic dustbin. It was the plastic that got Wilt. At least a dustbin was appropriate for the muck but it could have had the dignity of being a metal one. But no, even that slight consolation had been denied him. He'd tried one and had damned near poisoned himself. Never mind that. Dustbins weren't important and what he had just seen had been his Muse. Wilt endowed the word with a capital M for the first time in seventeen disillusioning years and then promptly blamed the bloody lager for this lapse. Irmgard wasn't a muse. She was probably some dumb, handsome bitch whose Vater was Lager-meister of Cologne and owned five Mercedes. He got up and went into the house.

When Eva and the quads returned from the theatre he was sitting morosely in front of the television ostensibly watching football but inwardly seething with indignation at the dirty tricks life played on him.

'Now then you show Daddy how the lady danced,' said Eva, 'and I'll put the supper on.'

'She was ever so beautiful, Daddy,' Penelope told him. 'She went like this and there was this man and he . . .' Wilt had to sit through a replay of *The Rite of Spring* by four small lumpish girls who hadn't been able to follow the story anyway and who took turns to try to do a pas de deux off the arm of his chair.

'Yes, well, I can see she must have been brilliant from your performance,' said Wilt. 'Now if you don't mind I want to see who wins . . .'

But the quads took no notice and continued to hurl themselves about the room until Wilt was driven to take refuge in the kitchen.

'They'll never get anywhere if you don't take an interest in their dancing,' said Eva.

'They won't get anywhere anyway if you ask me and if you call that dancing I don't. It's like watching hippos trying to fly. They'll bring the bloody ceiling down if you don't look out.'

Instead Emmeline banged her head on the fireguard and Wilt had to put a blob of Savlon on the scratch. To complete the evening's miseries Eva announced that she had asked the Nyes round after supper.

'I want to talk to him about the Organic Toilet. It's not working properly.'

'I don't suppose it's meant to,' said Wilt. 'The bloody thing is a glorified earth closet and all earth closets stink.'

'It doesn't stink. It has a composty smell, that's all, but it doesn't give off enough gas to cook with and John said it would.'

'It gives off enough gas to turn the downstairs loo into a death-chamber if you ask me. One of these days some poor bugger is going to light a cigarette in there and blow us all to Kingdom Come.'

'You're just biased against the Alternative Society in general,' said Eva. 'And who was it who was always complaining about my using chemical toilet cleaner? You were. And don't say you didn't.'

'I have enough trouble with society as it is without being bunged into an alternative one, and, while we are on the subject, there must be an alternative to poisoning the atmosphere with methane and sterilizing it with Harpic. Frankly I'd say Harpic had something to recommend it. At least you could flush the bloody stuff down the drain. I defy anyone to flush Nye's filthy crap-digester with anything short of dynamite. It's a turd-encrusted drainpipe with a barrel at the bottom.'

'It has to be like that if you're going to put natural goodness back into the earth.'

'And get food poisoning,' said Wilt.

'Not if you compost it properly. The heat kills all the germs before you empty it.'

'I don't intend to empty it. You had the beastly thing installed and you can risk your life in the cellar disgorging it when it's good and ready. And don't blame me if the neighbours complain to the Health Department again.'

They argued on until supper and Wilt took the quads up to bed and read them *Mr Gumpy* for the umpteenth time. By the time he came down the Nyes had arrived and were opening a bottle of stinging-nettle wine with an alternative corkscrew John Nye had fashioned from an old bedspring.

'Ah, hullo Henry,' he said with that bright, almost religious goodwill which all Eva's friends in the Self-Sufficiency world seemed to affect. 'Not a bad vintage, 1976, though I say it myself.'

'Wasn't that the year of the drought?' asked Wilt.

'Yes, but it takes more than a drought to kill stinging-nettles. Hardy little fellows.'

'Grow them yourself?'

'No need to. They grow wild everywhere. We just gathered them from the wayside.'

Wilt looked doubtful. 'Mind telling which side of the way you harvested this particular *cru*?'

'As far as I remember it was between Ballingbourne and Umpston. In fact, I'm sure of it.' He poured a glass and handed it to Wilt.

'In that case I wouldn't touch the stuff myself,' said Wilt handing it back. 'I saw them cropspraying there in 1976. These nettles weren't grown organically. They've been contaminated.'

'But we've drunk gallons of the wine,' said Nye. 'It hasn't done us any harm.'

'Probably won't feel the effects until you're sixty,' said Wilt, 'and then it will be too late. It's the same with fluoride, you know.'

And having delivered himself of this dire warning he went through to the lounge, now rechristened by Eva the 'Being Room', and found her deep in conversation with Bertha Nye about the joys and deep responsibilities of motherhood. Since the Nyes were childless and lavished their affection on humus, two pigs, a dozen chickens and a goat, Bertha was receiving

238

Eva's glowing account with a stoical smile. Wilt smiled stoically back and wandered out through the french windows to the summerhouse and stood in the darkness looking hopefully up at the dormer window. But the curtains were drawn. Wilt sighed, thought about what might have been and went back to hear what John Nye had to say about his Organic Toilet.

'To make the methane you have to maintain a steady temperature, and of course it would help if you had a cow.'

'Oh, I don't think we could keep a cow here,' said Eva. 'I mean we haven't the ground and . . .'

'I can't see you getting up at five every morning to milk it,' said Wilt, determined to put a stop to the awful possibility that 9 Willington Road might be turned into a smallholding. But Eva was back on the problem of the methane conversion.

'How do you go about heating it?' she asked.

'You could always install solar panels,' said Nye. 'All you need are several old radiators painted black and surrounded with straw and you pump water through them . . .'

'Wouldn't want to do that,' said Wilt. 'We'd need an electric pump and with the energy crisis what it is I have moral scruples about using electricity.'

'You don't need to use a significant amount,' said Bertha. 'And you could always work a pump off a Savonius rotor. All you require are two large drums . . .'

Wilt drifted off into his private reverie, awakening from it only to ask if there was some way of getting rid of the filthy smell from the downstairs loo, a question calculated to divert Eva's attention away from Savonius rotors, whatever they were.

'You can't have it every way, Henry,' said Nye. 'Waste not want not is an old motto, but it still applies.'

'I don't want that smell,' said Wilt. 'And if we can't produce enough methane to burn the pilot light on the gas stove without turning the garden into a stockyard, I don't see much point in wasting time stinking the house out.'

The problem was still unresolved when the Nyes left.

'Well, I must say you weren't very constructive,' said Eva as Wilt began undressing. 'I think those solar radiators sound very sensible. We could save all our hot water bills in the summer and if all you need are some old radiators and paint . . .'

'And some damned fool on the roof fixing them there. You

239

can forget it. Knowing Nye, if he stuck them up there they'd fall off in the first gale and flatten someone underneath, and anyway with the summers we've had lately we'd be lucky to get away without having to run hot water up to them to stop them freezing and bursting and flooding the top flat.'

'You're just a pessimist,' said Eva, 'you always look on the worst side of things. Why can't you be positive for once in your life.'

'I'm a ruddy realist,' said Wilt, 'I've come to expect the worst from experience. And when the best happens I'm delighted.'

He climbed into bed and turned out the bedside lamp. By the time Eva bounced in beside him he was pretending to be asleep. Saturday nights tended to be what Eva called Nights of Togetherness, but Wilt was in love and his thoughts were all about Irmgard. Eva read another chapter on Composting and then turned her light out with a sigh. Why couldn't Henry be adventurous and enterprising like John Nye? Oh well, they could always make love in the morning.

But when she woke it was to find the bed beside her empty. For the first time since she could remember Henry had got up at seven on a Sunday morning without being driven out of bed by the quads. He was probably downstairs making her a pot of tea. Eva turned over and went back to sleep.

Wilt was not in the kitchen. He was walking along the path by the river. The morning was bright with autumn sunlight and the river sparkled. A light wind ruffled the willows and Wilt was alone with his thoughts and his feelings. As usual his thoughts were dark while his feelings were expressing themselves in verse. Unlike most modern poets Wilt's verse was not free. It scanned and rhymed. Or would have done if he could think of something that rhymed with Irmgard. About the only word that sprang to mind was Lifeguard. After that there was yard, sparred, barred and lard. None of them seemed to match the sensitivity of his feelings. After three fruitless miles he turned back and trudged towards his responsibilities as a married man. Wilt didn't want them.

Chapter 4

He didn't much want what he found on his desk on Monday morning. It was a note from the Vice-Principal asking Wilt to come and see him at, rather sinisterly, 'your earliest, repeat earliest, convenience'.

'Bugger my convenience,' muttered Wilt. 'Why can't he say "immediately" and be done with it?'

With the thought that something was amiss and that he might as well get the bad news over and done with as quickly as possible, he went down two floors and along the corridor to the Vice-Principal's office.

'Ah Henry, I'm sorry to bother you like this,' said the Vice-Principal, 'but I'm afraid we've had some rather disturbing news about your department.'

'Disturbing?' said Wilt suspiciously.

'Distinctly disturbing. In fact all hell has been let loose up at County Hall.'

'What are they poking their noses into this time? If they think they can send any more advisers like the last one we had who wanted to know why we didn't have combined classes of bricklayers and nursery nurses so that there was sexual equality you can tell them from me . . .'

The Vice-Principal held up a protesting hand. 'That has nothing to do with what they want this time. It's what they don't want. And, quite frankly, if you had listened to their advice about multi-sexed classes this wouldn't have happened.'

'I know what would have,' said Wilt. 'We'd have been landed with a lot of pregnant nannies and—'

'If you would just listen a moment. Never mind nursery nurses. What do you know about buggering crocodiles?'

'What do I know about . . . did I hear you right?'

The Vice-Principal nodded. 'I'm afraid so.'

'Well if you want a frank answer I shouldn't have thought it was possible. And if you're suggesting . . .'

'What I am telling you, Henry, is that someone in your

department has been doing it. They've even made a film of it.'

'Film of it?' said Wilt, still grappling with the appalling zoological implications of even approaching a crocodile, let alone buggering the brute.

'With some apprentice class,' continued the Vice-Principal, 'and the Education Committee have heard about it and want to know why.'

'I can't say I blame them,' said Wilt, 'I mean you'd have to be a suicidal candidate for Krafft-Ebing to proposition a fucking crocodile and while I know I've got some demented sods as part-timers I'd have noticed if any of them had been eaten. Where the hell did he get the crocodile from?'

'No use asking me,' said the Vice-Principal. 'All I know is that the Committee insist on seeing the film before passing judgment.'

'Well they can pass what judgments they like,' said Wilt, 'just so long as they leave me out of it. I accept no responsibility for any filming that's done in my department and if some maniac chooses to screw a crocodile, that's his business, not mine. I never wanted all those TV cameras and cines they foisted onto us. They cost a fortune to run and some damned fool is always breaking the things.'

'Whoever made this film should have been broken first if you ask me,' said the Vice-Principal. 'Anyway, the Committee want to see you in Room 80 at six and I'd advise you to find out what the hell has been going on before they start asking you questions.'

Wilt went wearily back to his office desperately trying to think which of the lecturers in his department was a reptile-lover, a follower of *nouvelle vague* brutalism in films and clean off his rocker. Pasco was undoubtedly insane, the result, in Wilt's opinion, of fourteen years continuous effort to get Gasfitters to appreciate the linguistic subtleties of *Finnegans Wake*, but although he had twice spent a year's medical sabbatical in the local mental hospital he was relatively amiable and too hamfisted to use a cine-camera, and as for crocodiles . . . Wilt gave up and went along to the Audio-Visual Aid room to consult the register.

'I'm looking for some blithering idiot who's made a film about crocodiles,' he told Mr Dobble, the A.V.A. caretaker. Mr Dobble snorted.

242

'You're a bit late. The Principal's got that film and he's carrying on something horrible. Mind you, I don't blame him. I said to Mr Macaulay when it came back from processing, "Blooming pornography and they pass that through the labs. Well I'm not letting that film out of here until it's been vetted." That's what I said and I meant it.'

'Vetted being the operative word,' said Wilt caustically. 'And I don't suppose it occurred to you to let me see it first before it went to the Principal?'

'Well, you don't have no control over the buggers in your department, do you Mr Wilt?'

'And which particular bugger made this film?'

'I'm not one for naming names but I will say this, Mr Bilger knows more about it than meets the eye.'

'Bilger? That bastard. I knew he was punch-drunk politically but what the hell's he want to make a film like this for?'

'No names, no packdrill,' said Mr Dobble, 'I don't want any trouble.'

'I do,' said Wilt and went out in pursuit of Bill Bilger. He found him in the staff-room drinking coffee and deep in dialectics with his acolyte, Joe Stoley, from the History Department. Bilger was arguing that a truly proletarian consciousness could only be achieved by destabilizing the fucking linguistic infrastructure of a fucking fascist state fucking hegemony.

'That's fucking Marcuse,' said Stoley rather hesitantly following Bilger into the semantic sewer of destabilization.

'And this is Wilt,' said Wilt. 'If you've got a moment to spare from discussing the millennium I'd like a word with you.'

'I'm buggered if I'm taking anyone else's class,' said Bilger adopting a sound trade-union stance. 'It's not my stand-in period you know.'

'I'm not asking you to do any extra work. I am simply asking you to have a private word with me. I realize this is infringing your inalienable right as a free individual in a fascist state to pursue happiness by stating your opinions but I'm afraid duty calls.'

'Not my bloody duty, mate,' said Bilger.

'No. Mine,' said Wilt. 'I'll be in my office in five minutes.'

'More than I will,' Wilt heard Bilger say as he headed towards the door but Wilt knew better. The man might swagger and pose to impress Stoley but Wilt still had the sanction of altering the timetable so that Bilger started the week at nine on Monday morning with Printers Three and ended it at eight on Friday evening with part-time Cooks Four. It was about the only sanction he possessed, but it was remarkably effective. While he waited he considered tactics and the composition of the Education Committee. Mrs Chatterway was bound to be there defending to the last her progressive opinion that teenage muggers were warm human beings who only needed a few sympathetic words to stop them from beating old ladies over the head. On her right there was Councillor Blighte-Smythe who would, given half a chance, have brought back hanging for poaching and probably the cat o' nine tails for the unemployed. In between these two extremes there were the Principal who hated anything or anyone who upset his leisurely schedule, the Chief Education Officer, who hated the Principal, and finally Mr Squidley, a local builder, for whom Liberal Studies was an anathema and a bloody waste of time when the little blighters ought to have been putting in a good day's work carrying hods of bricks up blooming ladders. All in all the prospect of coping with the Education Committee was a grim one. He would have to handle them tactfully.

But first there was Bilger. He arrived after ten minutes and entered without knocking. 'Well?' he asked sitting down and staring at Wilt angrily.

'I thought we had better have this chat in private,' said Wilt. 'I just wanted to enquire about the film you made with a crocodile. I must say it sounds most enterprising. If only all Liberal Studies lecturers would use the facilities provided by the local authority to such effect . . .' He left the sentence with a tag end of unspoken approval. Bilger's hostility softened.

'The only way the working classes are going to understand how they're being manipulated by the media is to get them to make films themselves. That's all I do.'

'Quite so,' said Wilt, 'and by getting them to film someone buggering a crocodile helps them to develop a proletarian consciousness transcending the false values they've been inculcated with by a capitalist hierarchy?'

'Right, mate,' said Bilger enthusiastically. 'Those fucking things are symbols of exploitation.'

'The bourgeoisie biting its conscience off, so to speak.'

'You've said it,' said Bilger, snapping at the bait.

Wilt looked at him in bewilderment. 'And what classes have you done this . . . er . . . fieldwork with?'

'Fitters and Turners Two. We got this croc thing in Nott Road and . . .'

'In Nott Road?' said Wilt, trying to square his knowledge of the street with docile and presumably homosexual crocodiles.

'Well, it's street theatre as well,' said Bilger, warming to his task. 'Half the people who live there need liberating too.'

'I daresay they do, but I wouldn't have thought encouraging them to screw crocodiles was exactly a liberating experience. I suppose as an example of the class struggle . . .'

'Here,' said Bilger, 'I thought you said you'd seen the film?'

'Not exactly. But news of its controversial content has reached me. Someone said it was almost sub-Buñuel.'

'Really? Well, what we did is we got this toy crocodile, you know, the ones kiddies put pennies in and they get the privilege of a ride on them . . .'

'A *toy* crocodile? You mean you didn't actually use a real live one?'

'Of course we bloody didn't. I mean who'd be loony enough to rivet a real fucking crocodile? He might have been bitten.'

'Might?' said Wilt. 'I'd have said the odds on any self-respecting crocodile . . . Anyway, do go on.'

'So one of the lads gets on this plastic toy thing and we film him doing it.'

'Doing it? Let's get this quite straight. Don't you mean buggering it?'

'Sort of,' said Bilger. 'He didn't have his prick out or anything like that. There was nowhere he could have put it. No, all he did was simulate buggering the thing. That way he was symbolically screwing the whole reformist welfare statism of the capitalist system.'

'In the shape of a rocking crocodile?' said Wilt. He leant back in his chair and wondered yet again how it was that a supposedly intelligent man like Bilger, who had after all been to university and was a graduate, could still believe the world would be a better place once all the middle classes had been put up against a wall and shot. Nobody ever seemed to learn anything from the past. Well, Mr Bloody Bilger was going to learn something from the present. Wilt put his elbows on the desk.

'Let's get the record clear once and for all,' he said. 'You definitely consider it part of your duties as a Liberal Studies lecturer to teach apprentices Marxist-Leninist-Maoist-crocodile-buggerism and any other -Ism you care to mention?'

Bilger's hostility returned. 'It's a free country and I've a right to express my own personal opinions. You can't stop me.'

Wilt smiled at these splendid contradictions. 'Am I trying to?' he asked innocently. 'In fact you may not believe this, but I am willing to provide you with a platform on which to state them fully and clearly.'

'That'll be the day,' said Bilger.

'It is, Comrade Bilger, believe me it is. The Education Committee is meeting at six. The Chief Education Officer, the Principal, Councillor Blighte-Smythe—'

'That militaristic shit. What's he know about education? Just because they gave him the M.C. in the war he thinks he can go about trampling on the faces of the working classes.'

'Which, considering he has a wooden leg, doesn't say much for your opinion of the proletariat, does it?' said Wilt warming to his task. 'First you praise the working class for their intelligence and solidarity, then you reckon they are so dumb they can't tell their own interests from a soap advert on TV and have to be forcibly politicized, and now you tell me that a man who lost his leg can trample all over them. The way you talk they sound like morons.'

'I didn't say that,' said Bilger.

'No, but that seems to be your attitude and if you want to express yourself on the subject more lucidly you may do so to the Committee at six. I am sure they will be most interested.'

'I'm not going before any fucking Committee. I know my rights and—'

'This is a free country, as you keep telling me. Another splendid contradiction, and considering the country allows you to go around getting teenage apprentices to simulate fucking toy crocodiles I'd say a free fucking society just about sums it up. I just wish sometimes we were living in Russia.'

'They'd know what to do with blokes like you, Wilt,' said Bilger. 'You're just a deviationist reformist swine.'

246

'Deviationist, coming from you, is great,' shouted Wilt, 'and with their draconian laws anyone who went about filming Russian fitters buggering crocodiles would end up smartly in the Lubianka and wouldn't come out until they had put a bullet in the back of his mindless head. Either that or they would lock you up in some nuthouse and you'd probably be the only inmate who wasn't sane.'

'Right, Wilt,' Bilger shouted back, leaping from his chair, 'that does it. You may be Head of Department but if you think you can insult lecturers I know what I'm going to do. Lodge a complaint with the union.' He headed for the door.

'That's right,' yelled Wilt, 'run for your collective mummy and while you're about it tell the secretary you called me a deviationist swine. They'll appreciate the term.'

But Bilger was already out of the office and Wilt was left with the problem of finding some plausible excuse to offer the Committee. Not that he would have minded getting rid of Bilger but the idiot had a wife and three children and certainly couldn't expect help from his father, Rear-Admiral Bilger. It was typical of that kind of intellectual radical buffoon that he came from what was known as 'a good family'.

In the meantime he had to finish preparing his lecture to the Advanced Foreigners. Liberal and Progressive attitudes be damned. From 1688 to 1978, almost three hundred years of English history compressed into eight lectures, and all with Dr Mayfield's bland assumption that progress was continuous and that liberal attitudes were somehow independent of time and place. What about Ulster? A fat lot of liberal attitudes applied there in 1978. And the Empire hadn't exactly been a model of liberalism. The most you could say about it was that it hadn't been as bloody awful as the Belgian Congo or Angola. But then Mayfield was a sociologist and what he knew about history was dangerous. Not that Wilt knew much himself. And why English Liberalism? Mayfield seemed to think that the Welsh and Scots and Irish didn't exist, or if they did that they weren't progressive and liberal too.

Wilt got out a ballpoint and jotted down notes. They had nothing at all to do with Mayfield's proposed course. He was still rambling speculatively on when lunchtime came. He went down to the canteen and ate what was called curry and rice at a table by himself and returned to his office with fresh ideas. This time they concerned the influence of the Empire on England. Curry, baksheesh, pukka, posh, polo, thug—words that had infiltrated the English language from farflung outposts where the Wilts of a previous age had lorded it with an arrogance and authority he found it hard to imagine. He was interrupted in these pleasantly nostalgic speculations by Mrs Rosery, the Department secretary, who came to say that Mr Germiston was sick and couldn't take Electronic Technicians Three and that Mr Laxton, his stand-in, had done a swop with Mrs Vaugard without telling anyone and she wasn't available because she had previously made an appointment at the dentist and . . .

Wilt went downstairs and crossed to the hut where Electronic Technicians were sitting in a stupor of pub-lunch beer. 'Right,' he said sitting down behind the table, 'Now what have you been doing with Mr Germiston?'

'Haven't done a bloody thing with him,' said a red-headed youth in the front. 'He isn't worth it. One punch up the snout and . . .'

'What I meant,' said Wilt before redhead could go into the details of what would happen to Germiston in a fight, 'was what has he been talking to you about so far this term?'

'Fucking darkies,' said another technician.

'Not literally, I trust,' said Wilt hoping that his irony would not lead to a discussion of interracial sex. 'You mean race relations?'

'I mean spades. That's what I mean. Nignogs, wogs, foreigners, all them buggers what come in here and take jobs away from decent white blokes. What I say is . . .'

But he was interrupted by another ET 3. 'You don't want to listen to what he says. Joe's a member of the National Front—'

'What's so wrong with that?' demanded Joe. 'Our policy is to keep—'

'Out of politics,' said Wilt. 'That's my policy and I mean to stick with it. What you say outside is your affair but in the classroom we'll discuss something else.'

'Yeah, well you ought to tell old Germ-Piston that. He spends his bloody life telling us we got to be christians and love our

248

neighbours like ourselves. Well if he lived in our street he'd know different. We got a load of Jamrags two doors off and they play bongo drums and dustbins till four in the ruddy morning. If old Germy knows a way of loving that din all fucking night he must be blooming deaf.'

'You could always ask them to quieten down a bit or stop at eleven,' said Wilt.

'What, and get a knife in the guts for the privilege? You must be joking.'

'Then the police . . .'

Joe looked at him incredulously. 'A bloke four doors down went to the fuzz and you know what happened to him?'

'No,' said Wilt.

'Had his car tyres slashed two days later. That's what. And did the cops want to know? Did they fuck.'

'Well I can see you've got a problem,' Wilt had to admit.

'Yeah, and we know how to solve it too,' said Joe.

'You're not going to solve it by sending them back to Jamaica,' said the Technician who was anti the National Front. 'The ones in your street didn't come from there anyway. They was born in Brixton.'

'Brixton Nick if you ask me.'

'You're just prejudiced.'

'So would you be if you didn't get a night's kip in a month.' The battle raged on while Wilt sat contemplating the class. It was just as he had remembered it from his old days. You got the apprentices going and then left them to it, only prodding them into further controversy with a provocative comment when the argument flagged. And these were the selfsame apprentices the Bilgers of this world wanted to instil with political consciousness as if they were proletarian geese to be force-fed to produce a totalitarian pâté de foie gras.

But already Electronic Technicians Three had veered away from race and were arguing about last year's Cup Final. They seemed to have stronger feelings about football than politics. At the end of the hour Wilt left them and made his way across to the auditorium to deliver his lecture to Advanced Foreigners. To his horror he found the place packed. Dr Mayfield had been right in saying that the course was popular and immensely profitable. Looking up the rows, Wilt made a mental note that he was probably about to address several million poundsworth of oil wells, steelworks, shipyards and chemical industries scattered from Stockholm to Tokyo via Saudi Arabia and the Persian Gulf. Well, the blighters had come to learn about England and the English attitudes and he might as well give them their money's worth.

Wilt stepped up to the rostrum, arranged his few notes, tapped the microphone so that several loud booms issued from the loudspeakers at the back of the auditorium and began his lecture.

'It may come as something of a surprise to those of you who come from more authoritarian societies that I intend to ignore the title of the course of lectures I am supposed to be giving, namely The Development of Liberal and Progressive Social Attitudes in English Society from 1688 to the present day, and to concentrate on the more essential problem, not to say the enigma, of what constitutes the nature of being English. It is a problem that has baffled the finest foreign minds for centuries and I have no doubt that it will baffle you. I have to admit that I myself, although English, remain bewildered by the subject and I have no reason to suppose that I will be any clearer in my mind at the end of these lectures than I am now.'

Wilt paused and looked at his audience. Their heads were bent over notebooks and their ballpoints scribbled away. It was what he had come to expect. They would dutifully write down everything he had to tell them as unthinkingly as previous groups he had lectured, but somewhere among them there might be one person who would puzzle over what he had to say. He would give them all something to puzzle over this time.

'I will start with a list of books which are essential reading, but before I do so I will draw your attention to an example of the Englishness I hope to explore. It is that I have chosen to ignore the subject I am supposed to be teaching and have taken a topic of my own choice. I am also confining myself to England and ignoring Wales, Scotland, and what is popularly known as Great Britain. I know less about Glasgow than I do about New Delhi, and the inhabitants of those parts would feel insulted were I to include them among the English. In particular I shall avoid discussing the Irish. They are wholly beyond my comprehension as an Englishman and their methods of settling

250

disputes are not ones that appeal to me. I will only repeat what Metternich, I believe, had to say about Ireland, that it is England's Poland.' Wilt paused again and allowed the class to make another wholly inconsequential note. If the Saudis had ever heard of Metternich he would be very surprised.

'And now the book list. The first is *The Wind in the Willows* by Kenneth Grahame. This gives the finest description of English middle-class aspirations and attitudes to be found in English literature. You will find that it deals entirely with animals, and that these animals are all male. The only women in the book are minor characters, one a bargewoman and the others a jailer's daughter and her aunt, and strictly speaking they are irrelevant. The main characters are a Water Rat, a Mole, a Badger and a Toad, none of whom is married or evinces the slightest interest in the opposite sex. Those of you who come from more torrid climates, or who have sauntered through Soho, may find this lack of sexual motif surprising. I can only say that its absence is entirely in keeping with the values of middle-class family life in England. For those students who are not content with aspirations and attitudes but wish to study the subject in greater, if prurient, depth I can recommend certain of the daily newspapers, and in particular the Sunday ones. The number of choirboys indecently assaulted annually by vicars and church-wardens may lead you to suppose that England is a deeply religious country. I incline to the view held by some that . . .'

But whatever view Wilt was about to incline to, the class never learnt. He stopped in mid-sentence and stared down at a face in the third row. Irmgard Mueller was one of his students. Worse still, she was looking at him with a curious intensity and had not bothered to take any notes. Wilt gazed back and then looked down at his own notes and tried to think what to say next. But all the ideas he had so ironically rehearsed had disintegrated. For the first time in a long career of improvisation, Wilt dried up. He stood at the rostrum with sweating hands and looked at the clock. He had to say something for the next forty minutes, something intense and serious and . . . yes, even significant. That dread word of his sensitive youth burped to the surface. Wilt steeled himself.

'As I was saying,' he stammered just as his audience began to whisper among themselves, 'none of the books I have recommended will do more than scratch the surface of the problem of being English . . . or rather of knowing the nature of the English.' For the next half an hour he strung disjointed sentences together and finally muttering something about pragmaticism gathered his notes together and ended the lecture. He was just climbing down from the stage when Irmgard left her seat and approached him.

'Mr Wilt,' she said, 'I want to say how interesting I found your lecture.'

'Very good of you to say so,' said Wilt dissembling his passion.

'I was particularly interested in what you said about the parliamentary system only seeming to be democratic. You are the first lecturer we have had who has put the problem of England in the context of social reality and popular culture. You were very illuminating.'

It was an illuminated Wilt who floated out of the auditorium and up the steps to his office. There could be no doubt about it now. Irmgard was not simply beautiful. She was also radiantly intelligent. And Wilt had met the perfect woman twenty years too late.

Chapter 5

He was so preoccupied with this new and exhilarating problem that he was twenty minutes late for the meeting of the Education Committee and arrived as Mr Dobble was leaving with the film projector and the air of a man who has done his duty by putting the cat among the pigeons.

'Don't blame me, Mr Wilt,' he said as Wilt scowled, 'I'm only here to . . .'

Wilt ignored him and entered the room to find the Committee arranging themselves around a long table. A solitary chair was placed conspicuously at the far end and, as Wilt had foreseen, they were all there, the Principal, the Vice-Principal, Councillor Blighte-Smythe, Mrs Chatterway, Mr Squidley and the Chief Education Officer.

'Ah, Wilt,' said the Principal by way of unenthusiastic greeting. 'Take a seat.'

Wilt steeled himself to avoid the solitary chair and sat down beside the Education Officer. 'I gather you want to see me about the anti-pornographic film made by a member of the Liberal Studies Department,' he said, trying to take the initiative.

The Committee glared at him.

'You can cut the anti for a start,' said Councillor Blighte-Smythe, 'what we have just seen buggers . . . er . . . beggars belief. The thing is downright pornography.'

'I suppose it might be to someone with a fetish about crocodiles,' said Wilt. 'Personally, since I haven't had the chance to see the film, I can't say how it would affect me.'

'But you did say it was anti-pornographic,' said Mrs Chatterway whose progressive opinions invariably put her at odds with the Councillor and Mr Squidley, 'and as Head of Liberal Studies you must have sanctioned it. I'm sure the Committee would like to hear your reasons.'

Wilt smiled wryly. 'I think the title of Head of Department

253

needs some explaining, Mrs Chatterway,' he began, only to be interrupted by Blighte-Smythe.

'So does this fuc . . . filthy film we've just had to see. Let's stick to the issue,' he snapped.

'It happens to be the issue,' said Wilt. 'The mere fact that I am called Head of Liberal Studies doesn't mean I am in a position to control what the members of my so-called staff do.'

'We know what they ruddy well do,' said Mr Squidley, 'and if any man on my workforce started doing what we've watched I'd soon give him the boot.'

'Well, it's rather different in education,' said Wilt. 'I can lay down guidelines in regard to teaching policy, but I think the Principal will agree that no Head of Department can sack a lecturer for failing to follow them.' Wilt looked at the Principal for confirmation. It came regretfully. The Principal would happily have sacked Wilt years ago. 'True,' he muttered.

'You mean to tell us you can't get rid of the pervert who made this film?' demanded Blighte-Smythe.

'Not unless he continually fails to turn up for his teaching periods, is habitually drunk, or openly cohabits with students, no,' said Wilt.

'Is that true?' Mr Squidley asked the Education Officer.

'I'm afraid so. Unless we can prove blatant incompetence or sexual immorality involving a student, there's no way of removing a full-time lecturer.'

'If getting a student to bugger a crocodile isn't sexual immorality I'd like to know what is,' said Councillor Blighte-Smythe.

'As I understand it the object in question was not a proper crocodile and there was no actual intercourse,' said Wilt, 'and in any case the lecturer merely recorded the event on film. He didn't participate himself.'

'He'd have been arrested if he had,' said Mr Squidley. 'It's a wonder the sod wasn't lynched.'

'Aren't we in danger of losing the central theme of this meeting?' asked the Principal. 'I believe Mr Ranlon has some other questions to raise.'

The Education Officer shuffled his notes. 'I would like to ask Mr Wilt what his policy guidelines are in regard to Liberal Studies. They may have some bearing on a number of complaints

254

we have received from members of the public.' He glared at Wilt and waited.

'It might help if I knew what those complaints were,' said Wilt stalling for time but Mrs Chatterway intervened.

'Surely the purpose of Liberal Studies has always been to inculcate a sense of social responsibility and concern for others in the young people in our care, many of whom have themselves been deprived of a progressive education.'

'Depraved would be a better word if you ask me,' said Councillor Blighte-Smythe.

'Nobody did,' barked Mrs Chatterway. 'We all know very well what your views are.'

'Perhaps if we heard what Mr Wilt's views are . . .' suggested the Education Officer.

'Well, in the past Liberal Studies consisted largely of keeping day-release apprentices quiet for an hour by getting them to read books,' said Wilt. 'In my opinion they didn't learn anything and the system was a waste of time.' He halted in the hope that the Councillor would say something to infuriate Mrs Chatterway. Mr Squidley squashed the hope by agreeing with him.

'Always was and always will be. I've said it before and I'll say it again. They'd be better employed doing a proper day's work instead of wasting ratepayers' money loafing in classrooms.'

'Well at least we have some measure of agreement,' said the Principal pacifically. 'As I understand it Mr Wilt's guideline has been a more practical one. Am I right, Wilt?'

'The policy of the department has been to teach apprentices how to do things. I believe in interesting them in . . .'

'Crocodiles?' enquired Councillor Blighte-Smythe.

'No,' said Wilt.

The Education Officer looked down the list in front of him. 'I see here that your notion of practical education includes home brewing.'

Wilt nodded.

'May one ask why? I shouldn't have thought encouraging adolescents to become alcoholics served any educational purpose.'

'It serves to keep them out of pubs for a start,' said Wilt. 'And in any case Gas Engineers Four are not adolescents. Half of them are married men with children.'

255

'And does the course in home brewing extend to the manu- facture of illicit stills?'

'Stills?' said Wilt.

'For making spirit.'

'I don't think anyone in my department would have the expertise. As it is the stuff they brew is . . .'

'According to Customs and Excise almost pure alcohol,' said the Education Officer. 'Certainly the forty-gallon drum they unearthed from the basement of the Engineering block had to be burnt. In the words of one Excise officer, you could run a car on the muck.'

'Perhaps that's what they intended it for,' said Wilt.

'In which case,' continued the Education Officer, 'it hardly seemed appropriate to have labelled several bottles Chateau Tech. V.S.O.P.'

The Principal looked at the ceiling and prayed but the Education Officer hadn't finished.

'Would you mind telling us about the class you have organ- ized for Caterers on Self Sufficiency?'

'Well, actually it's called Living Off The Land,' said Wilt.

'Quite so. The land in question being Lord Podnorton's.'

'Never heard of him.'

'He has heard of this institution. His head gamekeeper caught two apprentice cooks in the act of decapitating a pheasant with the aid of a ten-foot length of plastic tubing through which had been looped a strand of piano wire stolen from the Music Department, which probably accounts for the fact that fourteen pianos have had to be restrung in the past two terms.'

'Good Lord, I thought they had been vandalized,' muttered the Principal.

'Lord Podnorton was under the same misapprehension about his greenhouses, four cold frames, a currant cage . . .'

'Well, all I can say,' interrupted Wilt, 'is that breaking into greenhouses wasn't part of the syllabus for Living Off The Land. I can assure you of that. I got the idea from my wife who is very keen on composting . . .'

'No doubt you got the next course from her too. I have here a letter from Mrs Tothingford complaining that we conduct classes in karate for nannies. Perhaps you would like to explain that.'

256

'We do have a course called Rape Retaliation for Nursery Nurses. We thought it wise in the light of the rising tide of violence.'

'Very sensible too,' said Mrs Chatterway, 'I heartily approve.'

'Perhaps you do,' said the Education Officer looking at her critically over his glasses, 'Mrs Tothingford doesn't. Her letter is addressed from the hospital where she is being treated for a broken collar-bone, a dislocated Adam's apple, and internal injuries inflicted on her by her nanny last Saturday night. You're not going to tell me that Mrs Tothingford is a rapist?'

'She might be,' said Wilt. 'Have you asked her if she is a lesbian? It's been known for—'

'Mrs Tothingford happens to be the mother of five and wife of . . .' He consulted the letter.

'Three?' asked Wilt.

'Judge Tothingford, Wilt,' snarled the Education Officer. 'And if you're suggesting that a judge's wife is a lesbian I would remind you that there is such a thing as slander.'

'There's such a thing as a married lesbian too,' said Wilt. 'I knew one once. She lived down our . . .'

'We are not here to discuss your deplorable acquaintances.'

'I thought you were. After all you asked me here to talk about a film made by a lecturer in my department and while I would not call him a friend I am vaguely acquainted . . .'

He was silenced by a kick under the table from the V.-P.

'Is that the end of the casualty list?' asked the Principal hopefully.

'I could go on almost indefinitely, but I won't,' said the Education Officer. 'What it all adds up to is that the Liberal Studies Department is not only failing in its supposed function of instilling a sense of social responsibility in day-release apprentices but is actively fostering anti-social behaviour . . .'

'That's not my fault,' said Wilt angrily.

'You are responsible for the way your department is run, and as such answerable to the Local Authority.'

Wilt snorted. 'Local Authority, my foot. If I had any authority at all this film would never have been made. Instead of that I am lumbered with lecturers I didn't appoint and can't fire, half of whom are raving revolutionaries or anarchists, and the other half couldn't keep order if the students were in straitjackets and you expect me to be answerable for everything that happens.'

Wilt looked at the members of the Committee and shook his head. Even the Education Officer was looking somewhat abashed.

'The problem is clearly a very complex one,' said Mrs Chatterway, who had swung round to Wilt's defence since hearing about the Rape Retaliation Course for Nursery Nurses. 'I think I can speak for the entire Committee when I say we appreciate the difficulties Mr Wilt faces.'

'Never mind what Mr Wilt faces,' intervened Blighte-Smythe. 'We are going to face a few difficulties ourselves if this thing ever gets out. If the press got wind of the story . . .'

Mrs Chatterway blanched at the prospect while the Principal covered his eyes. Wilt noted their reactions with interest.

'I don't know,' he said cheerfully. 'I'm all in favour of public debates on issues of educational importance. Parents ought to know the way their children are being taught. I've got four daughters and . . .'

'Wilt,' said the Principal violently, 'the Committee has generously agreed that you cannot be held wholly responsible for these deplorable incidents. I don't think we need detain you further.'

But Wilt remained seated and pursued his advantage. 'I take it then that you're not willing to bring this regrettable affair to the attention of the media. Well, if that is your decision . . .'

'Listen, Wilt,' snarled the Education Officer, 'if one word of this is leaked to the press or is discussed in any public form I'll see . . . Well, I wouldn't like to be in your shoes.'

Wilt stood up. 'I don't like being in them at the moment,' he said. 'You call me in here and cross-examine me about something I can't prevent because you refuse to give me any real authority and then when I propose making this disgraceful state of affairs a public issue you start threatening me. I've half a mind to complain to the union.' And having delivered this terrible threat he headed for the door.

'Wilt,' shouted the Principal, 'we haven't finished yet.'

'Nor have I,' said Wilt and opened the door. 'I find this whole attempt to cover up a matter of serious public concern most reprehensible. I do indeed.'

'Christ,' said Mrs Chatterway uncharacteristically calling for Divine guidance. 'You don't think he means it, do you?'

'I have long since given up trying to think what Wilt means,' said the Principal miserably. 'All I can be certain about is that I wish to God we'd never employed him.'

Chapter 6

'You'd be committing promotional suicide,' Peter Braintree told Wilt as they sat over pints in The Glassblower's Arms later that evening.

'I feel like committing real suicide,' said Wilt, ignoring the pork pie Braintree had just bought him. 'And it's no use trying to tempt me with pork pies.'

'You've got to have some supper. In your condition it's vital.'

'In my condition, nothing is vital. On the one hand I am forced to fight battles with the Principal, the Chief Education Officer and his foul Committee on behalf of lunatics like Bilger who want a bloody revolution, and on the other, after I have spent years thrusting down predatory lusts for Senior Secretaries, Miss Trott and the occasional Nursery Nurse, Eva has to introduce into the house the most splendid, the most ravishing woman she can find. You may not believe me . . . remember that summer and the Swedes?'

'The ones you had to teach *Sons and Lovers* to?'

'Yes,' said Wilt, 'four weeks of D. H. Lawrence and thirty delectable Swedish girls. Well, if that wasn't a baptism of lust I don't know what is. And I came through unscathed. I went home to Eva every evening unblemished. If the sex war was openly declared I'd have won the Marital Medal for chastity beyond the call of duty.'

'Well we've all had to go through that phase,' said Braintree.

'And what exactly do you mean by "that phase"?' asked Wilt stiffly.

'The body beautiful, boobs, bottoms, the occasional glimpse of thigh. I remember once . . .'

'I prefer not to hear your loathsome fantasies,' said Wilt. 'Some other time perhaps. With Irmgard it's different. I am not talking about the merely physical. We relate.'

'Good God, Henry . . .' said Braintree, flabbergasted.

'Exactly. When did you hear me use that dreaded word before?'

'Never.'

'You're hearing it now. And if that doesn't indicate the fearful predicament I'm in, nothing will.'

'It does,' said Braintree. 'You're . . .'

'In love,' said Wilt.

'I was going to say out of your mind.'

'It amounts to the same thing. I am caught in the horns of a dilemma. I use that cliché advisedly, though to be perfectly frank horns don't come into it. I am married to a formidable, frenetic and basically insensitive wife . . .'

'Who doesn't understand you. We've heard all this before.'

'Who does understand me. And you haven't,' said Wilt and drank some more beer bitterly.

'Henry, someone has been putting stuff in your tea,' said Braintree.

'Yes, and we all know who that is. Mrs Crippen.'

'Mrs Crippen? What the hell are you talking about?'

'Has it ever occurred to you,' said Wilt pointedly shoving the pork pie down the counter, 'what would have happened if Mrs Crippen, instead of being childless and bullying her husband and generally being in the way, had had quads? I can see it hasn't. Well, it has to me. Ever since I taught that course on Orwell and the Art of the English Murder, I have gone into the subject deeply on my way home to an Alternative Supper consisting of uncooked soya sausage and homegrown sorrel washed down with dandelion coffee and I've come to certain conclusions.'

'Henry, this is verging on paranoia,' said Braintree sternly.

'Is it? Then answer my question. If Mrs Crippen had had quads who would have ended up under the cellar floor? Dr Crippen. No, don't interrupt. You are not aware of the change that maternity has brought to Eva. I am. I live in an oversize house with an oversize mother and four daughters and I can tell you that I have had an insight into the female of the species which is denied more fortunate men and I know when I'm not wanted.'

'What the hell are you on about now?'

'Two more pints please,' Wilt told the barman, 'and kindly return that pie to its cage.'

'Now look here, Henry, you're letting your imagination run

away with you,' said Braintree. 'You're not seriously suggesting that Eva is setting out to poison you?'

'I won't go quite that far,' said Wilt, 'though the thought did cross my mind when Eva moved into Alternative Fungi. I soon put a stop to that by getting Samantha to taste them first. I may be redundant but the quads aren't. Not in Eva's opinion anyway. She sees her litter as being potential geniuses. Samantha is Einstein, Penelope's handiwork with a felt-pen on the sitting-room wall suggested she was a feminine Michelangelo, Josephine hardly needs an introduction with a name like that. Need I go on?'

Braintree shook his head.

'Right,' continued Wilt, despondently helping himself to the fresh beer. 'As a male I have performed my biological function and just when I was settling down relatively happily to pre-mature senility Eva, with an infallible intuition, which I might add I never suspected, brings to live under the same roof a woman who possesses all those remarkable qualities, intelligence, beauty, a spiritual sensitivity and a radiance . . . all I can say is that Irmgard is the epitome of the woman I should have married.'

'And didn't,' said Braintree emerging from the beer-mug where he had taken refuge from Wilt's ghastly catalogue. 'You are lumbered with Eva and . . .'

'Lumbered is exact,' said Wilt. 'When Eva gets into bed . . . I'll spare you the sordid details. Suffice it to say that she's twice the man I am. He relapsed into silence and finished his pint.

'Anyway, I still say you'd be making a hell of a mistake if you brought the Tech. any more bad publicity,' said Braintree, to change a distressing subject. 'Let sleeping dogs lie is my motto.'

'Mine too if people didn't sleep with crocs on film,' said Wilt. 'As it is that bastard Bilger has the gall to tell me I'm a deviationist swine and a lackey of capitalistic fascism . . . thank you, I will have another pint . . . and all the time I'm protecting the sod. I've half a mind to make a public issue of the whole damned thing. Only half a mind, because Toxted and his gang of National Front thugs are just waiting for a chance to have a punch-up and I'm not going to be their hero thank you very much.'

262

'I saw our little Hitler pinning up a poster in the canteen this morning,' said Braintree.

'Oh really, what's he advocating this time? Castration for coolies or bring back the rack?'

'Something to do with Zionism,' said Braintree. 'I'd have ripped the thing down if he hadn't had a bodyguard of Bedouins. He's moved in with the Arabs now, you know.'

'Brilliant,' said Wilt, 'absolutely brilliant. That's what I like about these maniacs of the right and left, they're so bloody inconsistent. There's Bilger who sends his children to a private school and lives in a ruddy great house his father bought him and he goes round advocating world revolution from the driving seat of a Porsche that must have cost six thousand if it cost a penny and he calls me a fascist pig. I'm just recovering from that one when I bang into Toxted who is a genuine fascist and lives in a council house and wants to send anyone with a pigmentation problem back to Islamabad even though they were actually born in Clapham and haven't been out of England since, and who does he team up with? A bunch of ruddy sheikhs with more oil dollars under their burnouses than he's had hot dinners, can't speak more than three words of English, and own half Mayfair. Add the fact that they're semites and he's so anti-semitic he makes Eichmann look like a Friend of Israel, and then tell me how his bloody mind ticks. I'm damned if I know. It's enough to drive a rational man to drink.'

As if to give point to this remark Wilt ordered two more pints.

'You've had six already,' said Braintree doubtfully. 'Eva will give you hell when you get home.'

'Eva gives me hell, period,' said Wilt. 'When I consider how my life is spent . . .'

'Yes, well I'd just as soon you didn't,' said Braintree, 'there's nothing worse than an introspective drunk.'

'I was quoting from the first line of "Testament of Beauty" by Robert Bridges,' said Wilt. 'Not that it's relevant. And I may be introspective but I am not introspectively drunk. I am merely pissed. If you'd had the sort of day I've had and were faced with the prospect of climbing into bed with Eva in a foul temper you would seek oblivion in beer too. Added to which is the knowledge that ten feet above my head, separated only by a ceiling, a floor and some wall-to-wall rush matting, will be lying the most beautiful, intelligent, radiant, sensitive creature . . .'

'If you mention the word Muse again, Henry . . .' said Braintree threateningly.

'I don't intend to,' said Wilt. 'Such ears as yours are far too coarse. Come to think of it, that almost rhymes. Has it ever occurred to you that English is a language most naturally fitted for poetry which rhymes?'

Wilt launched into this more agreeable topic and finished two more beers. By the time they left The Glassblower's Arms Braintree was too drunk to drive home.

'I'll leave the car here and fetch it in the morning,' he told Wilt, who was propping up a telegraph pole, 'and if I were you I'd ring for a taxi. You're not even fit to walk.'

'I shall commune with nature,' said Wilt, 'I have no intention of hastening the time between now and reality. With any luck it'll be asleep by the time I get back.'

And he wobbled off in the direction of Willington Road, stopping occasionally to steady himself against a gatepost and twice to pee into someone else's garden. On the second occasion he mistook a rosebush for a hydrangea and scratched himself rather badly and was sitting on the grass verge attempting to use a handkerchief as a tourniquet when a police car pulled up beside him. Wilt blinked into the flashlight which shone in his face before travelling down to the bloodstained handkerchief.

'Are you all right?' asked the voice behind the flashlight, rather too obsequiously for Wilt's taste.

'Does it look like it?' he asked truculently. 'You find a bloke sitting on the kerb tying a handkerchief round the remains of his once-proud manhood and you ask a bloody fool question like that?'

'If you don't mind, sir, I'd lay off the abusive language,' said the policeman. 'There's a law against using it on the public highway.'

'There ought to be a law about planting ruddy rosebushes next to the fucking pavement,' said Wilt.

'And may one ask what you were doing to the rose, sir?'

'One may,' said Wilt, 'if one can't bloody well surmise for one's ruddy self, one may indeed.'

264

'Mind telling me, then?' said the policeman taking out a notebook. Wilt told him with a wealth of description and a volubility that brought the lights on in several houses down the road. Ten minutes later he was helped out of the police car into the station. 'Drunk and disorderly, using abusive language, disturbing the peace . . .'

Wilt intervened. 'Peace my bloody foot,' he shouted. 'That was no Peace. We've got a Peace in our front garden and it hasn't got thorns a foot long. And anyway I wasn't disturbing it. You want to try partial circumcision on flaming floribunda to find out what disturbs what. All I was doing was quietly relieving myself or in plain language having a slash when that infernal thicket of climbing cat's claws took it into its vegetable head to have a slash at me and if you don't believe me, go back and try for yourselves . . .'

'Take him down to the cells,' said the desk sergeant to prevent Wilt upsetting an elderly woman who had come in to report the loss of her Pekinese. But before the two constables could drag Wilt away to a cell they were interrupted by a shout from Inspector Flint's office. The Inspector had been called back to the station by the arrest of a long-suspected burglar and was happily interrogating him when the sound of a familiar voice reached him. He erupted from his office and stared lividly at Wilt.

'What the hell is he doing here?' he demanded.

'Well, sir . . .' one constable began but Wilt broke loose.

'According to your goons I was attempting to rape a rosebush. According to me I was having a quiet pee . . .'

'Wilt,' yelled the Inspector, 'if you've come down here to make my life a misery again, forget it. And as for you two, take a good look at this bastard, a very good, long look and unless you catch him in the act of actually murdering someone, or better still wait until you've seen him do it, don't lay a finger on the brute. Now get him out of here.'

'But, sir—'

'I said out,' shouted Flint. 'I meant out. That thing you've just brought in is a human virus of infective insanity. Get him out of here before he turns this station into a madhouse.'

'Well, I like that,' Wilt protested. 'I get dragged down here on a trumped-up charge . . .'

He was dragged out again while Flint went back to his office and sat abstractedly thinking about Wilt. Visions of that damned doll still haunted his mind and he would never forget the hours he had spent interrogating the little sod. And then there was Mrs Eva Wilt whose corpse he had supposed to be buried under thirty tons of concrete while all the time the wretched woman was drifting down the river on a motor cruiser. Together the Wilts had made him look an idiot and there were jokes in the canteen about inflatable dolls. One of these days he would get his revenge. Yes, one of these days . . . He turned back to the burglar with a new sense of purpose.

On the doorstep of his house in Willington Road Wilt sat staring up at the clouds and meditating on love and life and the differing impressions he made on people. What had Flint called him? An infective virus . . . a human virus of infective . . . The word recalled Wilt to his own injury.

'Might get tetanus or something,' he muttered and fumbled in his pocket for the doorkey. Ten minutes later, still wearing his jacket but without trousers and pants, Wilt was in the bathroom soaking his manhood in a toothmug filled with warm water and Dettol when Eva came in.

'Have you any idea what time it is? It's—' She stopped and stared in horror at the toothmug.

'Three o'clock,' said Wilt, trying to steer the conversation back to less controversial matters, but Eva's interest in the time had vanished.

'What on earth are you doing with that thing?' she gasped. Wilt looked down at the toothmug.

'Well, now that you come to mention it, and despite all circum . . . circumstantial evidence to the contrary, I am not . . . well, actually I am trying to disinfect myself. You see—'

'Disinfect yourself?'

'Yes . . . well,' said Wilt conscious that there was an element of ambiguity about the explanation, 'the thing is . . .'

'In my toothmug,' shouted Eva. 'You stand there with your thingamajig in my toothmug and admit you're disinfecting yourself? And who was the woman, or didn't you bother to ask her name?'

'It wasn't a woman. It was . . .'

266

'Don't tell me. I don't want to know. Mavis was right about you. She said you didn't just walk home. She said you spent your evenings with some other woman.'

'It wasn't another woman. It was . . .'

'Don't lie to me. To think that after all these years of married life you have to resort to whores and prostitutes . . .'

'It wasn't a whore in that sense,' said Wilt. 'I suppose you could say hips and haws but it's spelt differently and . . .'

'That's right, try to wriggle out of it . . .'

'I'm not wriggling out of anything. I got caught in a rose-bush . . .'

'Is that what they call themselves nowadays? Rosebushes?' Eva stopped and stared at Wilt with fresh horror.

'As far as I know they've always called themselves rose-bushes,' said Wilt, unaware that Eva's suspicions had hit a new low. 'I don't see what else you can call them.'

'Gays? Faggots? How about them for a start?'

'What?' shouted Wilt, but Eva was not to be stopped.

'I always knew there was something wrong with you, Henry Wilt,' she bawled, 'and now I know what. And to think that you come back and use my toothmug to disinfect yourself. How low can you get?'

'Listen,' said Wilt, suddenly conscious that his Muse was privy to Eva's appalling innuendos, 'I can prove it was a rose-bush. Take a look if you don't believe me.'

But Eva didn't wait. 'Don't think you're spending another night in my house,' she shouted from the passage. 'Never again! You can take yourself back to your boyfriend and . . .'

'I have had about as much as I can take from you,' yelled Wilt emerging in hot pursuit. He was brought up short by the sight of Penelope standing wide-eyed in the passage.

'Oh, shit,' said Wilt and retreated to the bathroom again. Outside he could hear Penelope sobbing and Eva hysterically pretending to calm her. A bedroom door opened and closed. Wilt sat on the edge of the bath and cursed. Then he emptied the toothmug down the toilet, dried himself distractedly on a towel and used the Elastoplast. Finally he squeezed toothpaste onto the electric toothbrush and was busily brushing his teeth when the bedroom door opened again and Eva rushed out.

'Henry Wilt, if you're using that toothbrush to . . .'

'Once and for all,' yelled Wilt with a mouthful of foam, 'I am sick and tired of your vile insinuations. I have had a long and tiring day and—'

'I can believe that,' bawled Eva.

'For your information I am simply brushing my teeth prior to climbing into bed and if you think I am doing anything else . . .' He was interrupted by the toothbrush. The end jumped off and fell into the washbasin.

'Now what are you doing?' Eva demanded.

'Trying to get the brush out of the plughole,' said Wilt, an explanation that led to further recriminations, a brief and un-even encounter at the top of the stairs and finally a disgruntled Wilt being shoved out through the kitchen door with a sleeping-bag and told to spend the rest of the night in the summerhouse.

'I won't have you perverting the minds of the wee ones,' Eva shouted through the door, 'and tomorrow I'm seeing a lawyer.'

'As if I bloody care,' Wilt shouted back and wove down the garden to the summerhouse. For a while he stumbled about in the darkness trying to find the zip in the sleeping-bag. It didn't appear to have one. Wilt sat down on the floor and got his feet into the thing and was just wriggling his way down it when a sound from behind the summerhouse startled him into silence. Someone was making his way through the orchard from the field beyond. Wilt sat still in the darkness and listened. There could be no doubt about it. There was a rustle of grass, and a twig broke. Silence again. Wilt peered over the edge of the window and as he did so the lights in the house went out. Eva had gone to bed again. The sound of someone walking cautiously through the orchard began once more. In the summerhouse Wilt's imagination was toying with burglars and what he would do if someone tried to break into the house, when he saw close outside the window a dark figure. It was joined by a second. Wilt crouched lower in the summerhouse and cursed Eva for leaving him without his trousers and . . .

But a moment later his fears had gone. The two figures were moving confidently across the lawn and one of them had spoken in German. It was Irmgard's voice that reached Wilt and re-assured him. And as the figures disappeared round the side of the house Wilt wriggled down into the sleeping-bag with the relatively comfortable thought that at least his Muse had been

268

spared that insight into English family life which Eva's denunciations would have revealed. On the other hand, what was Irmgard doing out at this time of night and who was the other person? A wave of self-pitying jealousy swept over Wilt before being dislodged by more practical considerations. The summerhouse floor was hard, he had no pillow and the night had suddenly become extremely chilly. He was damned if he was going to spend the rest of it outside. And anyway the keys to the front door were still in his jacket pocket. Wilt climbed out of the sleeping-bag and fumbled for his shoes. Then dragging the sleeping-bag behind him he made his way across the lawn and round to the front door. Once inside he took off his shoes and crossed the hall to the sitting-room and ten minutes later was fast asleep on the sofa.

When he awoke Eva was banging things about in the kitchen while the quads, evidently gathered round the breakfast table, were discussing the events of the night. Wilt stared at the curtains and listened to the muffled questions of his daughters and Eva's evasive answers. As usual she was garnishing downright lies with mawkish sentimentality.

'Your father wasn't very well last night, darling,' he heard her say. 'He had the collywobbles in his tummy that's all and when he gets like that he says things . . . Yes, I know mumsy said things too, Hennypenny. I was . . . What did you say, Samantha? . . . I said that? . . . Well he can't have had it in the toothmug because tummies won't go in little things like that . . . Tummies, darling . . . You can't get collywobbles anywhere else . . . Where did you learn that word, Samantha? . . . No he didn't and if you go to playgroup and tell Miss Oates that daddy had his . . .'

Wilt buried his head under the cushions to shut out the conversation. The bloody woman was doing it again, lying through her teeth to four damned girls who spent so much of their time trying to deceive one another they could spot a lie a mile off. And harping on about Miss Oates was calculated to make them compete to see who could be the first to tell the old bag and twenty-five other toddlers that daddy spent the night with his penis in a toothmug. By the time that story had been disseminated through the neighbourhood it would be common

269

knowledge that the notorious Mr Wilt was some sort of tooth-mug fetishist.

He was just cursing Eva for her stupidity and himself for having drunk too much beer when the further consequences of too much beer made themselves felt. He needed a pee and badly. Wilt clambered out of the sleeping-bag. In the hall Eva could be heard hustling the quads into their coats. Wilt waited until the front door had closed behind them and then hobbled across the hall to the downstairs toilet. It was only then that full magnitude of his predicament became apparent. Wilt stared down at a large and extremely tenacious piece of sticking-plaster.

'Damn,' said Wilt, 'I must have been drunker than I thought. When the hell did I put that on?' There was a gap in his memory. He sat down on the toilet and wondered how on earth to get the bloody thing off without doing himself any more injury. From past experience of sticking-plaster he knew the best method was to wrench the stuff off with one swift jerk. It didn't seem advisable now.

'Might pull the whole bloody lot off,' he muttered. The safest thing would be to find a pair of scissors. Wilt emerged cautiously from the toilet and peered over the banisters. Just so long as he didn't meet Irmgard coming down from the flat in the attic. Considering the hour she had got back it was extremely unlikely. She was probably still in bed with some beastly boyfriend. Wilt went upstairs and into the bedroom. Eva kept some nail-scissors in the dressing table. He found them and was sitting on the edge of the bed when Eva returned. She headed upstairs, hesitated a moment on the landing and then entered the bedroom.

'I thought I'd find you here,' she said crossing the room to the curtains. 'I knew the moment my back was turned you'd sneak into the house. Well don't think you can worm your way out of this one because you can't. I've made up my mind.'

'What mind?' said Wilt.

'That's right. Insult me,' said Eva, pulling the curtains back and flooding the room with sunshine.

'I am not insulting you,' snarled Wilt, 'I am merely asking a question. Since I can't get it into your empty head that I am not a raving arse-bandit—'

'Language, language,' said Eva.

270

'Yes, language. It's a means of communication, not just a series of moos, coos and bleats the way you use it.'

But Eva was no longer listening. Her attention was riveted on the scissors. 'That's right. Cut the horrid thing off,' she squawked and promptly burst into tears. 'To think that you had to go and . . .'

'Shut up,' yelled Wilt. 'Here I am in imminent danger of bursting and you have to start howling like a banshee. If you had used your bloody head instead of a perverted imagination last night I wouldn't have been in this predicament.'

'What predicament?' asked Eva between sobs.

'This,' shouted Wilt waving his agonized organ.

Eva glanced at it curiously. 'What did you do that for?' she asked.

'To stop the damned thing from bleeding. I have told you repeatedly that I caught it on a rosebush but you had to jump to idiotic conclusions. Now I can't get this bloody sticking-plaster off and I've got a gallon of beer backed up behind it.'

'You really meant it about the rosebush then?'

'Of course I did. I spend my life telling the truth and nothing but the truth and nobody ever believes me. For the last time I was having a pee next to a rosebush and I got snagged in the fucking thing. That is the simple truth, unembroidered, ungarnished and unexaggerated.'

'And you want the sticking-plaster off?'

'What the hell have I been saying for the last five minutes? I not only want it off. I need it off before I burst.'

'That's easy,' said Eva. 'All you've got to do . . .'

Chapter 7

Twenty-five minutes later Wilt hobbled through the door of the Accident Centre at the Ipford Hospital, pale, pained and horribly embarrassed. He made his way to the desk and looked into the unsympathetic and obviously unimaginative eyes of the admissions clerk.

'I'd like to see a doctor,' he said with some difficulty.

'Have you broken something?' asked the woman.

'Sort of,' said Wilt, conscious that his conversation was being monitored by a dozen other patients with more obvious but less distressing injuries.

'What do you mean, sort of?'

Wilt eyed the woman and tried to convey wordlessly that his was a condition that required discretion. The woman was clearly extraordinarily obtuse.

'If it's not a break, cut or wound requiring immediate attention, or a case of poisoning you should consult your own doctor.' Wilt considered these options and decided that 'wound requiring immediate attention' fitted the bill.

'Wound,' he said.

'Where?' asked the woman picking up a ballpen and a pad of forms.

'Well . . .' said Wilt even more hoarsely than before. Half the other patients seemed to have brought their wives or mothers.

'I said where?' said the woman impatiently.

'I know you did,' whispered Wilt. 'The thing is . . .'

'I haven't got all day, you know.'

'I realize that,' said Wilt, 'it's just that . . . well I . . . Look, would you mind if I explained the situation to a doctor? You see . . .' But the woman didn't. In Wilt's opinion she was either a sadist or mentally deficient.

'I have to fill in this form and if you won't tell me where the wound is . . .' She hesitated and looked at Wilt suspiciously, 'I

272

thought you said it was a break. Now you say it's a wound. You'd better make up your mind. I haven't got all day, you know.'

'Nor, at this rate, have I,' said Wilt irritated by the repetition. 'In fact if something isn't done almost immediately I may well pass out in front of you.'

The woman shrugged. People passing out in front of her were evidently part of her daily routine. 'I still have to state whether it is a wound or a break and its location and if you won't tell me what it is and where it is I can't admit you.'

Wilt glanced over his shoulder and was about to say that he had had his penis practically scalped by his bloody wife when he caught the eyes of several middle-aged women who were paying close attention to the exchange. He changed his tactic hastily.

'Poison,' he muttered.

'Are you quite sure?'

'Of course I'm sure,' said Wilt. 'I took the stuff, didn't I?'

'You also claimed you had a break and then a wound. Now you say you've taken all three . . . I mean you've taken poison. And it's no good looking at me like that. I'm only doing my job, you know.'

'At the speed you're doing it I wonder anyone gets in here at all before they're actually dead,' snapped Wilt, and instantly regretted it. The woman was staring at him with open hostility. The look on her face suggested that as far as Wilt was concerned he had just expressed her most ardent hope.

'Look,' said Wilt trying to pacify the bitch, 'I'm sorry if I seem agitated . . .'

'Rude, more like.'

'Have it your own way. Rude then. I apologize but if you had just swallowed poison, fallen on your arm and broken it and suffered a wound in your posterior you'd be a bit agitated.'

To lend some sort of credibility to this list of catastrophes he raised his left arm limply and supported it with his right hand. The woman regarded it doubtfully and took up the ballpen again.

'Did you bring the bottle with you?' she asked.

'Bottle?'

'The bottle containing the poison you claim to have taken.'

273

'What would I do that for?'

'We can't help you unless we know what sort of poison you took.'

'It didn't say what sort of poison it was on the bottle,' said Wilt. 'It was in a lemonade bottle in the garage. All I know is that it was poison.'

'How?'

'How what?'

'How do you know it was poison?'

'Because it didn't taste like lemonade,' said Wilt frantically, aware that he was getting deeper and deeper into a morass of diagnostic confusion.

'Because something doesn't taste like lemonade it doesn't necessarily mean it's poisonous,' said the woman, exercising an indefatigable logic. 'Only lemonade tastes like lemonade. Nothing else does.'

'Of course it doesn't. But this stuff didn't simply not taste like lemonade. It tasted like deadly poison. Probably cyanide.'

'Nobody knows what cyanide tastes like,' said the woman continuing to batter Wilt's defences. 'Death is instantaneous.'

Wilt glared at her bleakly. 'All right,' he said finally, 'forget the poison. I've still got a broken arm and a wound that requires immediate attention. I demand to see a doctor.'

'Then you'll have to wait your turn. Now where did you say this wound was?'

'On my backside,' said Wilt, and spent the next hour regretting it. To substantiate his claim he had to stand while the other patients were treated and the admissions clerk continued to eye him with a mixture of outright suspicion and dislike. In an effort to avoid her eye Wilt tried to read the paper over the shoulder of a man whose only apparent claim to be in need of urgent attention was a bandaged toe. Wilt envied him and, not for the first time, considered the perversity of circumstances which rendered him incapable of being believed.

It wasn't as simple as Byron had suggested with his 'Truth is stranger than fiction'. If his own experience was anything to go by, truth and fiction were equally unacceptable. Some element of ambiguity in his own character, perhaps the ability to see every side of every problem, created an aura of insincerity around him and made it impossible for anyone to believe what

274

he was saying. The truth, to be believed, had first to be plausible and probable, to fall into some easy category of predigested opinion. If it didn't conform to the expected, people refused to believe it. But Wilt's mind did not conform. It followed possibilities wherever they led in labyrinths of speculation beyond most people's ken. Certainly beyond Eva's. Not that Eva ever speculated. She leapt from one opinion to another without that intermediate stage of bewilderment which was Wilt's perpetual condition. In her world, every problem had an answer; in Wilt's, every problem had about ten, each of them in direct contradiction to all the others. Even now in this bleak waiting-room where his own immediate misery might have been expected to spare him concern for the rest of the world, Wilt's febrile intelligence found material to speculate upon.

The headlines in the paper OIL DISASTER: SEA BIRDS THREATENED dominated a page filled with apparently minor horrors. Apparently because they occupied such little space. There had been another terrorist raid on a security truck. The driver had been threatened with a rocket launcher and a guard had been callously shot through the head. The murderers had got away with £250,000 but this was of less importance than the plight of seagulls threatened by an oil slick off the coast. Wilt noted this distinction and wondered how the widow of the shot guard felt about her late husband's relegation to second place in public concern compared to the sea birds. What was it about the modern world that wildlife took precedence over personal misery? Perhaps the human species was so fearful of extinction that it no longer cared what happened to individuals, but closed collective ranks and saw the collision of two supertankers as a foretaste of its own eventual fate. Or perhaps . . .

Wilt was interrupted from this reverie by the sound of his name and looking up from the paper his eyes met those of a hatchet-faced nurse who was talking to the admissions clerk. The nurse disappeared and a moment later the admissions clerk was joined by an elderly and evidently important specialist, if his retinue of young doctors, a Sister and two nurses was anything to go by. Wilt watched unhappily while the man studied his record of injuries, looked over his spectacles at Wilt as at some specimen beneath his dignity to treat, nodded to one of the housemen and, smiling sardonically, departed.

'Mr Wilt,' called the young doctor. Wilt stepped cautiously forward.

'If you'll just go through to a cubicle and wait,' said the doctor.

'Excuse me, doctor,' said Wilt, 'I would like a word with you in private.'

'In due course, Mr Wilt, we will have words in private and now if you have nothing better to do kindly go through to a cubicle.' He turned on his heel and walked down the corridor. Wilt was about to hobble after him when the admissions clerk stopped him.

'Accident cubicles are that way,' she said pointing to curtains down another corridor. Wilt grimaced at her and went down to a cubicle.

At Willington Road Eva was on the telephone. She had called the Tech. to say that Wilt was unavoidably detained at home by sickness and was now in conference with Mavis Mottram.

'I don't know what to think,' said Eva miserably. 'I mean it seemed so unlikely and when I found out he was really hurt I felt so awful.'

'My dear Eva,' said Mavis, who knew exactly what to think, 'you are far too ready to blame yourself and of course Henry exploits that. I mean that doll business must have given you some indication that he was peculiar.'

'I don't like to think about that,' said Eva. 'It was so long ago and Henry has changed since then.'

'Men don't change fundamentally and Henry is at a dangerous age. I warned you when you insisted on taking that German au pair girl.'

'That's another thing. She's not an au pair. She's paying much more rent than I asked for the flat but she won't help in the house. She has enrolled in the Foreigners' Course at the Tech. and she speaks perfect English already.'

'What did I tell you, Eva? She never mentioned anything about the Tech. when she came to you for a room, did she?'

'No,' said Eva.

'It wouldn't surprise me to find that Henry knew her already and told her you were letting the attic.'

276

'But how could he? He seemed very surprised and angry when I told him.'

'My dear, I hate to say this but you always look on the good side of Henry. Of course he would pretend to be surprised and angry. He knows exactly how to manipulate you and if he had seemed pleased you'd have known there was something wrong.'

'I suppose so,' said Eva doubtfully.

'And as for knowing her before,' continued Mavis, waging war vicariously against her Patrick by way of Wilt, 'I seem to remember he spent a lot of time at the Tech. at the beginning of the summer vac and that's when the foreign students enrol.'

'But Henry doesn't have anything to do with that department. He was busy on the timetable.'

'He doesn't have to belong to the department to meet the slut, and for all you know when he was supposed to be doing the timetable the two of them were doing something quite different in his office.'

Eva considered this possibility only to dismiss it. 'Henry isn't like that, and anyway I would have noticed the change in him,' she said.

'My dear, what you have got to realize is that all men are like that. And I didn't notice any change in Patrick until it was too late. He'd been having an affair with his secretary for over a year before I knew anything about it,' said Mavis. 'And then it was only when he blew his nose on her panties that I got an inkling what was going on.'

'Blew his nose on her *what*?' said Eva, intrigued by the extraordinary perversion the statement conjured up.

'He had a streaming cold and at breakfast one morning he took out a pair of red panties and blew his nose on them,' said Mavis. 'Of course I knew then what he had been up to.'

'Yes, well you would, wouldn't you?' said Eva. 'What did he say when you asked him?'

'I didn't ask him. I knew. I told him that if he thought he could provoke me into divorcing him he was quite mistaken because . . .'

Mavis chattered on about her Patrick while Eva's mind turned slowly as she listened. There was something in her memory of the night that was coming to the surface. Something to do with

Irmgard Mueller. After that awful row with Henry she hadn't been able to sleep. She had lain awake in the darkness wondering why Henry had to . . . well of course now she knew he hadn't but at the time . . . Yes, that was it, the time. At four o'clock she had heard someone come upstairs very quietly and she had been sure it was Henry and then there had been sounds of creaking from the steps up to the attic and she had known it was Irmgard coming home. She remembered looking at the luminous dial of the alarm clock and seeing the hands at four and twelve and for a moment she had thought they pointed to twenty past twelve only Henry had come in at three and . . . She had drifted off to sleep with a question half-formed in her mind. Now, against Mavis' chatter, the question completed itself. Had Henry been out with Irmgard? It wasn't like Henry to come in so late. She couldn't remember when he had done it before. And Irmgard certainly didn't behave like an au pair girl. She was too old for one thing, and she had so much money. But Mavis Mottram interrupted this slow train of thought by stating the conclusion Eva was moving towards.

'I know I'd keep an eye on that German girl,' she said. 'And if you take my advice you'll get rid of her at the end of the month.'

'Yes,' said Eva. 'Yes, I'll think about that, Mavis. Thank you for being so sympathetic.'

Eva put the phone down and stared out of the bedroom window at the beech tree that stood on the front lawn. It had been one of the first things to attract her to the house, the copper beech in the front garden, a large comfortable solid tree with roots that stretched as far underground as the branches did above. She had read that somewhere, and the balance between branches seeking the light and roots searching for water had seemed so right and so, somehow, organic, as to explain what she wanted from the house and could give it in return.

And the house had seemed right too. A big house with high ceilings and thick walls and a garden and orchard in which the quads could grow up happily and at a further remove from unsettling reality than Parkview Road would have allowed. But Henry hadn't liked the move. She had had to force it on him and he had never succumbed to the call of the domesticated wildness of the orchard or the sense of social invulnerability she

278

had found in the house and Willington Road. Not that Eva was a snob but she didn't like anyone to look down on her and now they couldn't. Even Mavis didn't patronize her any longer and that story about Patrick and the panties was something Mavis would never have told her if she had still been living two streets away. Anyway, Mavis was a bitch. She was always running Patrick down and if he was unfaithful physically Mavis was morally disloyal. Henry had said she committed adultery by gossip, and there was something in what he said. But there was also something in what Mavis said about Irmgard Mueller. She would keep an eye on her. There was a strange coldness about her—and what did she mean by saying she would help around the house and then suddenly enrolling at the Tech?

With an unusual sense of depression Eva made herself some coffee and then polished the hall floor and Hoovered the stair-carpet and tidied the living-room and put the dirty clothes in the washing-machine and brushed the rim of the Organic Toilet and did all those jobs which had to be done before she collected the quads from play school. She had just finished and was brushing her hair in the bedroom when she heard the front door open and close and footsteps on the stairs. That couldn't be Henry. He never came up two at a time and anyway with his dooda in bandages he probably wouldn't come up at all. Eva crossed to the bedroom door and looked out at a startled young man on the landing.

'What do you think you're doing?' she asked in some alarm.

The young man raised his hands. 'Please, I am here for Miss Mueller,' he said with a thick foreign accent. 'She has borrowed me the key.' He held it up in front of him as evidence.

'She had no right to,' said Eva annoyed at herself for being so alarmed, 'I don't want people walking in and out without knocking.'

'Yes,' said the young man, 'I understand you. But Miss Mueller have told me I can work on my studies in her rooms. Where I am living too much noise.'

'All right, I don't mind you working here but I don't want any noise either,' said Eva and went back into the bedroom. The young man went on up the narrow steps to the attic while Eva finished brushing her hair with a suddenly lighter mind. If

Irmgard invited rather good-looking young men to her room, she was unlikely to be interested in Henry. And the young man had been decidedly handsome. With a sigh which combined regret that she was not younger and more attractive herself, and relief that her marriage wasn't threatened, she went downstairs.

Chapter 8

At the Tech. Wilt's absence from the weekly meeting of Heads of Departments met with mixed reactions. The Principal was particularly alarmed.

'What with?' he asked the secretary who brought Eva's message that Wilt was sick.

'She didn't make that clear. She just said he would be incapacitated for a few days.'

'Would it were years,' murmured the Principal, and called the meeting to order. 'I have no doubt you have all heard the distressing news about the . . . er . . . film made by a Liberal Studies lecturer,' he said. 'I can't see there's much to be gained from discussing its implications for the College.'

He looked cheerlessly round the room. Only Dr Board seemed inclined to disagree. 'What I haven't been able to make out is whether it was a male or a female crocodile,' he said.

The Principal regarded him with disgust. 'In actual fact it was a toy one. As far as I know, they are not noticeably differentiated by sex.'

'No, I suppose not,' said Dr Board. 'Still it raises an interesting point—'

'Which, I feel sure, the rest of us would prefer not to discuss,' said the Principal.

'On the grounds of least said, soonest mended?' said Board. 'Though for the life of me I can't understand how the star of this film could be induced to—'

'Board,' said the Principal with dangerous patience, 'we are here to discuss academic matters, not the obscene aberrations of lecturers in the Liberal Studies Department.'

'Hear, hear,' said the Head of Catering. 'When I think that some of my girls are exposed to the influence of such disgusting perverts I can only say that I think we should consider very seriously the possibility of doing away with Liberal Studies altogether.'

There was a general murmur of approval. Dr Board was the exception.

'I can't see why you should blame Liberal Studies as a whole,' he said, 'and having had a look at some of your girls I should say—'

'Don't, Board, don't,' said the Principal.

Dr Mayfield took up the issue. 'This deplorable incident only reinforces my opinion that we should extend the parameters of our academic content to include courses of wider intellectual significance.'

For once Dr Board agreed with him. 'I suppose we could run an evening class in Reptile Sodomy,' he said. 'It might have the side-effect, if that is the right expression, of attracting a number of crocophiliacs, and on a more theoretical level doubt-less a course on Bestiality Down The Ages might have a certain eclectic appeal. Have I said something wrong, Principal?'

But the Principal was beyond speech. The V.-P. stepped into the breach.

'The first essential is to see that this regrettable affair doesn't become public knowledge.'

'Well, considering that it took place in Nott Road—'

'Shut up, Board,' shouted the Principal, 'I have stood just about all I can stand of your infernal digressions. One more word out of you and I shall demand either your resignation or my own from the Education Committee. And if need be both. You can make your choice. Shut up or get out.'

Dr Board shut up.

At the Accident Centre Wilt was finding he had no choice at all. The doctor who finally arrived at his cubicle to attend to him was accompanied by a formidable Sister and two male nurses. Wilt regarded him balefully from the couch on which he had been told to lie.

'You've taken your time,' he grumbled. 'I've been lying here in agony for the last hour and . . .'

'Then we must get a move on,' said the doctor. 'We'll start with the poison first. A stomach wash-out will . . .'

'What?' said Wilt, sitting up on the couch in horror.

'It won't take more than a minute,' said the doctor. 'Just lie back while Sister inserts the tube.'

282

'Oh no! Nothing doing,' said Wilt, bolting from the couch into a corner of the cubicle as the nurse closed in with a length of rubber pipe. 'I haven't taken poison.'

'It says on your admittance sheet that you have,' said the doctor. 'You are Mr Henry Wilt, I take it?'

'Yes,' said Wilt, 'but you needn't take it that I have taken poison. I can assure you . . .' He dodged round the couch to avoid the Sister, only to find himself grabbed from behind by the two male nurses.

'I swear that—' Wilt's denial died on his lips as he was pushed back onto the couch. The pipe hovered over his mouth. Wilt stared villainously at the doctor. The man seemed to be smiling in a singularly sadistic manner.

'Now then, Mr Wilt, you will kindly cooperate.'

'Won't,' grunted Wilt through clenched teeth. Behind him the Sister held his head and waited.

'Mr Wilt,' said the doctor, 'you arrived here this morning and stated quite adamantly and of your own free will that you had swallowed poison, broken your arm and had suffered a wound that required immediate attention. Is that not so?'

Wilt debated how to answer. It seemed safest not to open his mouth. He nodded and then tried to shake his head.

'Thank you. Not only that but you were impolite, to put it mildly, to the lady at the desk.'

'Wasn't,' said Wilt only to regret both his rudeness and this attempt to state his case. Two hands attempted to insert the tube. Wilt bit the thing.

'Have to use the left nostril,' said the doctor.

'No you fucking don't,' yelled Wilt, but it was too late. As the pipe slid up his nose and, by the feel of it, expanded in his throat, Wilt's protests came to an unintelligible end. He writhed and gurgled.

'You may find the next part slightly uncomfortable,' said the doctor with evident pleasure. Wilt stared at the man murderously and would, had the infernal pipe not prevented him, have stated forcibly that he found the present part bloody terrible. He was just burbling his protest when the curtains parted and the admissions clerk came in.

'I thought you might want to see this, Mrs Clemence,' said the doctor. 'Go ahead, Sister.' The Sister went ahead while

Wilt silently promised himself that if he didn't suffocate first or burst he would wipe the smile off that sadistic doctor's face just as soon as this ghastly experience was over. By the time it was Wilt's condition prevented him from doing anything except moan feebly. Only the Sister's suggestion that perhaps to be on the safe side they ought to give him an oil enema into the bargain provided him with the strength to state his case.

'I came here to have my penis attended to,' he whispered hoarsely.

The doctor consulted his record sheet. 'It doesn't make any mention of your penis here,' he said. 'It states quite clearly that . . .'

'I know what it states,' squeaked Wilt. 'I also know that if you were forced to go into a waiting-room filled with middle-class mothers and their skateboard-suicidal sons and had to announce at the top of your voice to that harridan there that you needed stitches in the top of your prick you'd have been less than reluctant to do it.'

'I'm not standing here listening to a lunatic call me a harridan,' said the clerk.

'And I wasn't standing out there shouting the odds about what had happened to my penis for all the bloody world to hear. I asked to see a doctor but you wouldn't let me. Deny that if you can.'

'I asked you if you had broken a limb, suffered a wound that required—'

'I know what you asked me,' yelled Wilt, 'don't I just. I can quote it word for word. Well, for your information a penis is not a limb, not in my case anyway. I suppose it comes into the category of an appendage and if I'd said I had damaged my appendage you'd have asked me which one and where and how and on what occasion and with whom and then sent me round to the VD clinic and . . .'

'Mr Wilt,' interrupted the doctor, 'we are extremely busy here and if you come and refuse to state exactly what is wrong with you . . .'

'I get a fucking stomach-pump stuffed down my gullet for my pains,' shouted Wilt. 'And what happens if some poor bugger who is deaf and dumb comes in? I suppose you let him die on the waiting-room floor or whip his tonsils out to teach

284

him to speak up for himself in future. And they call this the National Health Service. It's a fucking bureaucratic dictatorship. That's what I call it.'

'Never mind what it's called, Mr Wilt. If there is something really the matter with your penis we're quite prepared to look at it.'

'I'm not,' said the admissions clerk firmly, and disappeared through the curtains. Wilt lay back on the couch and removed his pants.

The doctor observed him cautiously.

'Mind telling me what you've got wound round it?' he asked.

'Bloody handkerchief,' said Wilt and slowly untied the makeshift bandage.

'Good God,' said the doctor, 'I see what you mean about an appendage. Would it be asking too much to enquire how you got your penis into this condition?'

'Yes,' said Wilt, 'it would. Everyone I've told so far hasn't believed me and I'd rather not go through that drill again.'

'Drill?' asked the doctor pensively. 'You're surely not implying that this injury was inflicted by a drill? I don't know what you think, Sister, but from where I stand it looks as though our friend here had a rather too intimate relationship with a mincing machine.'

'And from where I lie it feels like it,' said Wilt. 'And if it will help to cut the badinage let me tell you that my wife was largely responsible.'

'Your wife?'

'Listen, doctor,' said Wilt, 'if it's all the same to you I'd just as soon not go into details.'

'Can't say I blame you,' said the doctor scrubbing his hands. 'If my wife did that to me I'd divorce the bitch. Were you having intercourse at the time?'

'No comment,' said Wilt deciding that silence was the best policy. The doctor donned surgical gloves and drew his own ghastly conclusions. He loaded a hypodermic.

'After what you've already been through,' he said approaching the couch, 'this isn't going to hurt at all.'

Wilt bounded off the couch again. 'Hold it,' he shouted. 'If you imagine for one moment that you're going to stick that

285

surgical hornet into my private fucking parts you can think again. And what's that for?'

The Sister had picked up an aerosol can.

'Just a mild disinfectant and freezer. I'll spray it on first and you won't feel the little prick.'

'Won't I? Well let me tell you that I want to feel it. If I'd wanted anything else I'd have let nature take its course and I wouldn't be here now. And what's she doing with that razor?'

'Sterilizing it. We've got to shave you.'

'Have you just? I've heard that one before, and while we're on the subject of sterilizing I'd like to hear your views on vasectomy.'

'I'm pretty neutral on the subject,' said the doctor.

'Well I'm not,' snarled Wilt from the corner. 'In fact I am distinctly biased not to say prejudiced. What are you laughing about?' The muscular Sister was smiling. 'You're not some damned women's libber, are you?'

'I'm a working woman,' said the Sister, 'and my politics are my own affair. They don't enter into the matter.'

'And I'm a working man and I want to remain that way and politics do enter into the matter. I've heard what they get up to in India and if I walk out of here with a transistor, no balls and jabbering like an incipient mezzo-soprano I warn you I shall return with a meat cleaver and you'll both learn what social genetics are all about.'

'Well, if that is your attitude,' said the doctor, 'I suggest you try private medicine, Mr Wilt. You get what you pay for that way. I can only assure you . . .'

It took ten minutes to lure Wilt back onto the couch and five seconds to get him off it again clutching his scrotum.

'Freezer,' he squealed. 'My God, you meant it too. What the hell do you think I've got down there, a packet of freezable peas?'

'We'll just wait until the anaesthetic takes effect,' said the doctor. 'It shouldn't be long now.'

'It isn't,' squawked Wilt peering down. 'It's bloody disappearing. I came in here to have minor medication, not a sex-change operation, and if you think my wife is going to be happy having a husband with a clitoris you sorely misjudge the woman.'

'I'd say you had already misjudged her,' said the doctor

286

cheerfully. 'Any woman who can inflict that sort of damage on her husband deserves what she gets.'

'She may but I don't,' said Wilt frantically. 'I happen . . . What's she doing with that tube?'

The Sister was unwrapping a catheter.

'Mr Wilt,' said the doctor, 'we are going to insert this . . .'

'No, you're not,' shouted Wilt. 'I may be shrinking rapidly in parts but I'm not Alice in Wonderland or a fucking dwarf with chronic constipation. I heard what she said about an oil enema and I'm not having one.'

'No one intends giving you an enema. This will simply enable you to pass water through the bandages. Now kindly get back on the couch before I have to call for assistance.'

'What do you mean pass water simply?' asked Wilt cautiously, climbing onto the couch. The doctor explained, and this time it took four male nurses to hold Wilt down. Throughout the operation he kept up a barrage of obscene observations and it was only the threat of a general anaesthetic that caused him to lower his voice. Even then his remark that the doctor and the Sister were less fitted for medicine than for off-shore oil drilling could be heard in the waiting-room.

'That's right, send me out into the world like a bleeding petrol pump,' he said when he was finally allowed to go. 'There's such a thing as the dignity of man, you know.'

The doctor looked at him sceptically. 'In the light of your behaviour I'll reserve my opinion on the matter. Call in again next week and we'll see how you're coming along.'

'The only reason I'll be back is if I don't come again,' said Wilt bitterly. 'From now on I'll see the family doctor.' He hobbled out to a telephone and called for a taxi.

By the time he got home the anaesthetic was beginning to wear off. He went wearily upstairs and climbed into bed. He was lying there staring at the ceiling and wondering why he was not as other men presumably were when it came to bearing pain manfully, and wishing he was, when Eva returned with the quads.

'You do look awful,' she said encouragingly as she stood by the bed.

'I am awful,' said Wilt. 'Why I should be married to a female circumcisionist, God alone knows.'

'Perhaps it will teach you not to drink so much in future.'

'It's already taught me not to let you get your mitts near my waterworks,' said Wilt. 'And I mean waterworks.'

Even Samantha had to contribute to his misery. 'When I grow up I'm going to be a nurse, daddy.'

'Bounce on the bed like that again and you won't grow up to be anything,' snarled Wilt on the recoil.

Downstairs the telephone rang.

'If it's the Tech. again, what shall I tell them?' asked Eva.

'Again? I thought I told you to say I was sick.'

'I did but they've phoned back several times.'

'Tell them I'm still sick,' said Wilt. 'Just don't mention what with.'

'They probably know anyway by now. I saw Rowena Blackthorn at play school and she said she was sorry to hear about your accident,' said Eva, going downstairs.

'And which of you quadraphonic loudspeakers blurted the good news about daddy's whatsit to Mrs Blackthorn's little prodigy?' asked Wilt, turning a terrible eye on the quads.

'I didn't,' said Samantha smugly.

'You just egged Penelope on to, I suppose. I know that look on your mug.'

'It wasn't Penny. It was Josephine. She played with Robin and they were playing mummies and daddies . . .'

'Well when you get a little older you'll learn that there's no such thing as playing mummies and daddies. You will find instead that there is a war between the sexes and that you, my sweethearts, being females of the species, invariably win.'

The quads retreated from the bedroom and could be heard conferring on the landing. Wilt edged his way out of bed in search of a book and was just getting back with *Nightmare Abbey*, which was sufficiently unromantic to suit his mood, when Emmeline was pushed into the room.

'What do you want now? Can't you see I'm ill?'

'Please daddy,' said Emmeline, 'Samantha wants to know why you've got that bag tied to your leg.'

'Oh she does, does she?' said Wilt with dangerous calmness. 'Well you can tell Samantha and through her Miss Oates and her animal minders that your daddy wears a bag on his leg and a pipe up his prick because your mummsyfuckingwumsy took it

288

into her empty head to try to rip off daddywaddy's genitalia on the end of a strip of fucking sticking-plaster. And if Miss Oates doesn't know what genitalia are tell her from me that they're the adult equivalent of a male stork only its spelt with a fucking L. Now get out of my sight before I add hernia, hypertension and multiple infanticide to my other infernal problems.'

The children fled. Downstairs Eva slammed the phone down and shouted.

'Henry Wilt. . . .'

'Shut up,' yelled Wilt. 'One more comment out of anybody in this house and I won't be responsible for my actions.'

And for once he was obeyed. Eva went through to the kitchen and put the kettle on for tea. If only Henry would be more masterful when he was up and about and well.

Chapter 9

For the next three days Wilt was off work. He mooched about the house, sat in the Spockery and speculated on the nature of a world in which Progress with a capital P conflicted with Chaos and man with a small M was continually at loggerheads with Nature. In Wilt's view it was one of life's great paradoxes that Eva, who was forever accusing him of being cynical and non-progressive, should succumb so readily to the recessive call of nature in the shape of compost heaps, Organic Toilets, home weaving and anything that smacked of the primitive while at the same time maintaining an unshakable optimism in the future. For Wilt there was only the eternal present, a succession of present moments, not so much moving forward as aggregating behind him like a reputation. And if in the past his reputation had suffered some nasty blows, his latest misfortune had already added to his legend. From Mavis Mottram the ripples of gossip had spread out across Ipford's educational suburbia, gaining fresh credence and additional attributes with each re-telling. By the time the story reached the Braintrees it had already incorporated the crocodile film by way of the Tech., Blighte-Smythe, and Mrs Chatterway, and rumour had it that Wilt was about to be arrested for grossly indecent behaviour with a circus alligator which had only managed to preserve its virginity by biting Wilt's member.

'That's typical of this bloody town,' Peter Braintree told his wife, Betty, when she brought this version home. 'Henry has merely to take a few days off from the Tech. and the grapevine is buzzing with absolute lies.'

'Grapevines don't buzz,' said Betty. 'There's no smoke—'

'Without some evil-minded moron adding two and two together and coming up with fifty-nine. There's a bloke called Bilger in Liberal Studies who did make a film in which a plastic crocodile figures largely as a rape victim. Point one. Henry has to give some explanation to the Education Committee that will prevent Comrade Bilger's numerous offspring having to leave their private school because daddy is on the dole. Point two. Point three is that Wilt is taken ill next day . . .'

'Not according to Rowena Braintree. It's common knowledge Henry's penis has been mauled.'

'Where?'

'Where what?'

'Where is it common knowledge?'

'At the play group. The quads have been reporting progress on papa's dingaling daily.'

'Great,' said Braintree. 'For once common knowledge about sums it up. Henry's dutiful daughters wouldn't know a penis from a marrow-bone. Eva sees to that. She may be into self-sufficiency but it doesn't extend to sex. Not after the Prings-heims, and I can't see Henry in the role of Flash Harry. If anything, he's a bit of a prude.'

'Not where his language is concerned,' said Betty.

'His use of "fucking" as an adjective is the simple consequence of years of teaching apprentices. In the average bloke's sentence it serves as a sort of hyphen. If you listened to me more carefully you'd hear it at least twenty times in an average day. As I was saying, whatever's the matter with Henry he is *not* into croco-diles. Anyway, I'll pop round this evening and see what is up.'

But when he arrived at Willington Road that evening there was no sign of Wilt. Several cars were parked in the driveway, among them an Aston-Martin which looked out of place in the company of the Nyes' methane-converted Ford and Mavis Mottram's battered Minor. Braintree made his way across the obstacle course of cast-off clothing and the quad's toys that cluttered the hall and found Eva in the conservatory, chairing what appeared to be a committee on the problems of the Third World.

'The issue that seems to be overlooked is that Marangan medicine has an important part to play in providing an alter-native to chemically derived drug treatment in the West,' Roberta Smott was saying as Braintree hesitated behind the bean flyscreen, 'I don't think we should forget that in helping the Marangans we are also helping ourselves in the long term.'

Braintree tiptoed away as John Nye launched into an im-passioned plea for the preservation of Marangan agricultural

291

methods and particularly the use of human excreta as fertilizer. 'It has all the natural goodness of . . .'

Braintree slipped through the kitchen door, skirted the Fertility Retainer or compost bin outside, and went down the Bio/Dynamic kitchen garden to the summerhouse where he found Wilt lurking behind a cascade of dried herbs. He was reclining on a deckchair and wearing what looked suspiciously like a muslin bell-tent.

'As a matter of fact it's one of Eva's maternity gowns,' he said when Braintree enquired. 'In its time it has doubled as a wigwam, the interior sheet of a kingsize sleeping-bag, and the canopy of the camping loo. I rescued it from the mountain of clothing Eva's inflicting on her equatorial village.'

'I wondered what they were on about in there. Is this some sort of Oxfam exercise?'

'You're out of date. Eva's into Alternative Oxfam. Personal Assistance for Primitive People. Appropriately P.A.P.P. for short. You adopt some tribe in Africa or New Guinea and then load them with overcoats that would be unsuitably hot on a windy day in February here, write letters to the local witch-doctor asking his advice about herbal cures for chilblains, or better still frostbite, and generally twin Willington Road and the Ipford Brigade of the Anti-Male Chauvinist League with a cannibal community who go in for female circumcision with a rusty flint.'

'I didn't know you could circumcise females and anyway a rusty flint is out,' said Braintree.

'So are clitorises in Maranga,' said Wilt. 'I've tried to tell Eva but you know what she is. The noble savage is the latest vogue and it's nature worship run riot. If the Nyes had their way they'd import cobras to keep down rats in central London.'

'He was on about human faeces as a substitute for Growmore when I passed through. The man's an anal fanatic.'

'Religious,' said Wilt, 'I swear they sing Nearer My Turd to Thee before taking herbal communion at the compost heap every Sunday morning.'

'On a more personal note,' said Braintree, 'just exactly what is the matter with you?'

'I'd prefer not to discuss it,' said Wilt.

292

'All right, but why the . . . er . . . maternity drag?'

'Because it has none of the inconvenience of trousers,' said Wilt. 'There are depths of suffering you have yet to plumb. I use that word advisedly.'

'What, suffering?'

'Plumb,' said Wilt. 'If it hadn't been for all that beer we drank the other night I wouldn't be in this awful condition.'

'I notice you're not drinking your usual foul home-brewed lager.'

'I am not drinking anything in large quantities. In fact I am rationing myself to a thimble every four hours in the hope that I can sweat it out instead of peeing razor blades.'

Braintree smiled. 'Then there is some truth in the rumour,' he said.

'I don't know about the rumour,' said Wilt, 'but there's certainly truth in the description. Razor blades is exact.'

'Well, you'll be interested to hear that the gossip-mongers are thinking of awarding a medal to the croc that took the bit between its teeth. That's the version that's going the rounds.'

'Let it,' said Wilt. 'Nothing could be further from the truth.'

'Christ, you haven't got syphilis or something ghastly like that, have you?'

'Unfortunately not. I understand the modern treatment for syphilis is relatively painless. My condition isn't. And I've had all the fucking treatment I can stand. There are a number of people in this town I could cheerfully murder.'

'Oh dear,' said Braintree, 'things do sound grim.'

'They are,' said Wilt. 'They reached their nadir of grimness at four o'clock this morning when that little bitch Emmeline climbed into bed and stepped on my septic tank. It's bad enough being a human hose pipe but to be awakened in the dead hours of the night to find yourself peeing backwards is an experience that throws a new and terrible light on the human condition. Have you ever had a non-euphemistically wet dream in reverse?'

'Certainly not,' said Braintree with a shudder.

'Well I have,' said Wilt. 'And I can tell you that it destroys what few paternal feelings a father has. If I hadn't been in convulsions I'd have been charged with quadricide by now. Instead I have added volumes to Emmeline's vile vocabulary and Miss Mueller must be under the impression that English

293

sex life is sado-masochistic in the extreme. God alone knows what she thought of the din we made last night.'

'And how is our Inspiration these days? Still musing?' asked Braintree.

'Evasive. Distinctly evasive. Mind you in my present condition I try not to be too conspicuous myself.'

'If you will go around in Eva's maternity gowns I can't say I'm surprised. It's enough to make anyone wonder.'

'Well, I'm puzzled too,' said Wilt. 'I can't make the woman out. Do you know she has a succession of disgustingly rich young men traipsing through the house?'

'That accounts for the Aston-Martin,' said Braintree. 'I wondered who had inherited a fortune.'

'Yes, but it doesn't account for the wig.'

'What wig?'

'The car belongs to some Casanova from Mexico. He wears a walrus moustache, Chanel Number something or other, and worst of all a wig. I have observed it closely through the binoculars. He takes it off when he gets up there.'

Wilt handed Braintree the binoculars and indicated the attic flat.

'I can't see anything. The venetian blinds are down,' said Braintree after a minute's observation.

'Well I can tell you he does wear a wig and I'd like to know why.'

'Probably because he's bald. That's the usual reason.'

'Which is precisely why I ask the question. Lothario Zapata isn't. He has a perfectly good head of hair, and yet when he gets up to the flat he takes his wig off.'

'What sort of wig?'

'Oh, a black shaggy thing,' said Wilt. 'Underneath he's blond. You've got to admit it's peculiar.'

'Why don't you ask your Irmgard? Could be she has a penchant for blond young men with wigs.'

But Wilt shook his head. 'In the first place because she leaves the house before I'm up and relatively about, and secondly because my sense of self-preservation tells me that anything in the way of sexual stimulation could have the most dire and possibly irreversible consequences. No, I prefer to speculate from afar.'

294

'Very wise,' said Braintree. 'I hate to think what Eva would do if she found you knew you were passionately in love with the au pair.'

'If what she has done for lesser reasons is anything to go by so do I,' said Wilt and left it at that.

'Any message for the Tech?' asked Braintree.

'Yes,' said Wilt, 'just tell them that I'll be back in circulation . . . Christ, what a word . . . when it's safe for me to sit down without back-firing.'

'I doubt if they'll understand what you mean.'

'I don't expect them to. I have emerged from this ordeal with the firm conviction that the last thing anyone will believe is the truth. It is far safer to lie in this vile world. Just say I am suffering from a virus. Nobody knows what a virus is but it covers a multitude of ailments.'

Braintree went back to the house leaving Wilt thinking dark thoughts about the truth. In a godless, credulous, violent and random world it was the only touchstone he had ever possessed and the only weapon. But like all his weapons it was double-edged and, from recent experience, served as much to harm him as to enlighten others. It was something best kept to oneself, a personal truth, probably meaningless in the long run but at least providing a moral self-sufficiency more effective than Eva's practical attempts to the same end in the garden. Having reached that conclusion and condemned Eva's world concern and P.A.P.P., Wilt turned these findings on their head and accused himself of a quietism and passivity in the face of an underfed and deprived world. Eva's actions might not be more than sops to a liberal conscience but for all that they helped to sustain conscience and set an example to the quads which his own apathy denied. Somewhere there had to be a golden mean between charity beginning at home and improving the lot of starving millions. Wilt was damned if he knew where that mean was. It certainly wasn't to be found in doctrinaire shits like Bilger. Even John and Bertha Nye were trying to make a better world, not destroy a bad one. And what was he, Henry Wilt, doing? Nothing. Or rather, turning into a beer-swilling, self-pitying Peeping Tom without a worthwhile achievement to his credit. As if to prove that he had at least the courage of his garb, Wilt left the summerhouse and walked back to the house in full view of the conservatory, only to discover that the meeting had ended and Eva was putting the quads to bed.

When she came downstairs she found Wilt sitting at the kitchen table stringing runner beans.

'Wonders never cease,' she said. 'After all these years you're actually helping in the kitchen. You're not feeling ill or something?'

'I wasn't,' said Wilt, 'but now you mention it . . .'

'Don't go. There's something I want to discuss with you.'

'What?' said Wilt, stopping in the doorway.

'Upstairs,' said Eva, raising her eyes to the ceiling meaningfully.

'Upstairs?'

'You know what,' said Eva, increasing the circumspection.

'I don't,' said Wilt. 'At least I don't think I do, and if your tone of voice means anything, I don't want to. If you suppose for one moment I'm mechanically capable of . . .'

'I don't mean us. I mean them.'

'Them?'

'Miss Mueller and her friends.'

'Oh, them,' said Wilt and sat down again. 'What about them?'

'You must have heard,' said Eva.

'Heard what?' said Wilt.

'Oh, you know. You're just being difficult.'

'Lord,' said Wilt, 'we're back in Winnie-The-Pooh language. If you mean has it dawned on my semi-consciousness that they occasionally copulate, why don't you say so?'

'It's the children I'm thinking of,' said Eva. 'I'm not sure it's good for them to live in an environment where there's so much of what you just said going on.'

'If it didn't they wouldn't be here at all. And anyway your primitive penfriends are great ones for a bit of icketyboo, to use an expression that will suitably baffle Josephine. She usually comes straight out with—'

'Henry,' said Eva warningly.

'Well she does. Frequently. I heard her only yesterday tell Penelope to go—'

'I don't want to hear,' said Eva.

'I didn't either, come to that,' said Wilt, 'but the fact remains

296

that the younger generation mature rather more rapidly in words and deeds than we did. When I was ten I still thought fuck was something father did with a hammer when he hit his thumb instead of the nail. Now it's common parlance at four . . .'

'Never mind that,' said Eva. 'Your father's language left much to be desired.'

'At least in my father's case it was his language. In your old man it was the whole person. I've often wondered how your mother could bring herself . . .'

'Henry Wilt, you'll leave my family out of this. I want to know what you think we should do about Miss Mueller.'

'Why ask me? You invited her to come and live here. You didn't consult me. And I certainly didn't want the damned woman. Now that she's turned out to be some sort of international sex fiend, according to you, who's likely to infect the children with premature nymphomania, I get dragged in . . .'

'All I want is your advice,' said Eva.

'Then here it is,' said Wilt. 'Tell her to get the hell out.'

'But that's the difficulty. She's given a month's rent in advance. I haven't put it in the bank yet, but still . . .'

'Well, give it back to her for Christ's sake. If you don't want the bag give her the boot.'

'It seems so inhospitable really,' said Eva. 'I mean she's foreign and far from home.'

'Not far enough from my home,' said Wilt, 'and all her boyfriends seem to be Croesus Juniors. She can shack up with them or stay at Claridges. My advice is to give her money back and bung her out.' And Wilt went through to the living-room and sat in front of the television until supper was ready.

In the kitchen Eva made up her mind. Mavis Mottram had been wrong again. Henry wasn't in the least interested in Miss Mueller and she could give the money to P.A.P.P. So there was no need to ask the lodger to leave. Perhaps if she just suggested that things could be heard through the ceiling or . . . Anyway it was nice to know Henry hadn't been up to anything nasty. Which only went to show that she shouldn't listen to what Mavis had to say. Henry was a good husband in spite of his funny ways. It was a happy Eva who called Wilt to his supper that evening.

Chapter 10

It was a surprisingly happy Wilt who left Dr Scally's surgery the following Wednesday. After an initial bout of jocularity about Wilt's injuries the removal of the bandages and the pipeline had proceeded comparatively painlessly.

'Absolutely no need for all this in my opinion,' said the doctor, 'but those young fellows up at the hospital like to make a thorough job of things while they're about it.'

A remark that almost persuaded Wilt to lodge an official complaint with the Health Ombudsman. Dr Scally was against it.

'Think of the scandal, my dear fellow, and strictly speaking they were within their rights. If you will go round saying you've been poisoned . . .'

It was a persuasive argument and with the doctor's promise that he'd soon be as right as rain provided he didn't overdo things with his missus, Wilt emerged into the street feeling, if not on top of the world, at least half-way up it. The sun was shining on autumnal leaves, small boys were collecting conkers underneath the chestnuts in the park, and Dr Scally had given him a doctor's certificate keeping him away from the Tech. for another week. Wilt strolled into town, spent an hour browsing in the second-hand bookshop, and was about to go home when he remembered he had to deposit Miss Mueller's advance in the bank. Wilt turned bankwards and felt even better. His brief infatuation for her had evaporated. Irmgard was just another silly foreign student with more money than sense, a taste for expensive cars and young men of every nationality.

And so he walked up the bank steps airily and went to the counter where he wrote out a deposit slip and handed it to the cashier. 'My wife has a special account,' he explained. 'It's a deposit account in the name of Wilt. Mrs H. Wilt. I've forgotten the number but it's for an African tribe and I think it's called . . .' But the cashier was clearly not listening. He was busy counting the notes and while Wilt watched he stopped several times.

298

Finally with a brief 'Excuse me, sir,' he opened the hatch at the back of his cubicle and disappeared through it. Several customers behind Wilt moved to the next cashier, leaving him with that vague sense of unease he always felt when he cashed a cheque and the clerk before stamping the back glanced at a list of customers who were presumably grossly overdrawn. But this time he was paying money in, not taking it out, and it wasn't possible for notes to bounce.

It was. Wilt was just beginning to work up some resentment at being kept waiting when a bank messenger approached him.

'If you wouldn't mind stepping into the manager's office, sir,' he said with a slightly threatening politeness. Wilt followed him across the foyer and into the manager's office.

'Mr Wilt?' said the manager. Wilt nodded. 'Do take a seat.' Wilt sat and glared at the cashier who was standing beside the manager's desk. The notes and the deposit slip lay on the blotting pad in front of him.

'I'd be glad if you would tell me what this is all about,' said Wilt with growing alarm. Behind him the bank messenger had taken up a position by the door.

'I think we'll reserve any comment until the police arrive,' said the manager.

'What do you mean "the police arrive"?'

The manager said nothing. He stared at Wilt with a look that managed to combine sorrow and suspicion.

'Now look here,' said Wilt, 'I don't know what's going on but I demand . . .'

Wilt's protest died away as the manager eyed the pile of notes on the desk.

'Good Lord, you're not suggesting they're forged?'

'Not forged, Mr Wilt, but as I said before when the police arrive you'll have a chance to explain matters. I'm sure there's some perfectly reasonable explanation. Nobody for one moment suspects you . . .'

'Of what?' said Wilt.

But again the bank manager said nothing. Apart from the noise of traffic outside there was silence and the day which only a few minutes before had seemed full of good cheer and hope suddenly became grey and horrid. Wilt searched his mind frantically for an explanation but could think of nothing, and he was about to protest that they had no right to keep him there when there was a knock on the door and the bank messenger opened it cautiously. Inspector Flint, Sergeant Yates and two sinister plainclothes men entered.

'At last,' said the manager. 'This is really very awkward. Mr Wilt here is an old and respected customer . . .'

His defence died out. Flint was staring at Wilt.

'I didn't think there could be two Wilts in the same town,' he said triumphantly. 'Now then—'

But he was interrupted by the older of the two plainclothes men. 'If you don't mind, Inspector, we'll handle this,' he said with a brisk authority and almost a charm of manner that was even more alarming than the bank manager's previous coolness. He moved to the desk, picked up some of the notes and studied them. Wilt watched him with increasing concern.

'Would you mind telling us how you came by these five-pound notes, sir?' said the man. 'By the way, my name is Misterson.'

'They're a month's rent in advance from our lodger,' said Wilt. 'I came here to deposit them in my wife's P.A.P.P. account. . . .'

'Pap, sir? Pap account?' said the smooth Mr Misterson.

'It stands for Personal Assistance for Primitive People,' said Wilt. 'My wife is the treasurer of the local branch. She's adopted a tribe in Africa and . . .'

'I understand, Mr Wilt,' said Misterson, casting a cold eye on Inspector Flint who had just muttered 'Typical'. He sat down and hitched his chair closer to Wilt. 'You were saying that this money came from the lodger and was destined for your wife's deposit account. What sort of lodger is this?'

'Female,' said Wilt slipping into cross-examination brevity.

'And her name, sir?'

'Irmgard Mueller.'

The two plainclothes men exchanged a look. Wilt followed it and said hastily, 'She's German.'

'Yes sir. And would you be able to identify her?'

'Identify her?' said Wilt. 'I'd be hard put not to. She's been living in the attic for the last month.'

'In which case if you'll kindly come to the station we'd be glad if you would look at some photographs,' said Misterson pushing back his chair.

300

'Now wait a moment. I want to know what this is all about,' said Wilt. 'I've been to that police station and frankly I don't want to go there again.' He stayed resolutely in his chair.

Mr Misterson reached in his pocket and took out a plastic licence which he opened.

'If you'll take a good look at this.'

Wilt did and felt sick. It stated that Superintendent Misterson of the Anti-Terrorist Branch was empowered . . . Wilt got up unsteadily and moved towards the door. Behind him the Superintendent was giving Inspector Flint, Sergeant Yates and the bank manager their orders. No one was to leave the office, there were to be no outgoing phone calls, maximum security and business as usual. Even the bank messenger was to remain where he was.

'And now Mr Wilt if you'll just walk out quite normally and follow me. We don't want to attract attention.'

Wilt followed him out and across the bank to the door and was hesitating there wondering what to do when a car drew up. The Superintendent opened the door and Wilt got in. Five minutes later he was sitting at a table being handed photographs of young women. It was twenty past twelve when he finally picked Miss Irmgard Mueller out.

'Are you absolutely certain?' asked the Superintendent.

'Of course I am,' said Wilt irritably. 'Now I don't know who she is or what the wretched woman has done but I'd be glad if you would go and arrest her or something. I want to get home to my lunch.'

'Quite so, sir. And is your wife in the house?'

Wilt looked at his watch. 'I don't see what that's got to do with it. As a matter of fact she will now be on her way back from play school with the children and . . .'

The Superintendent sighed. It was a long ominous sigh. 'In that case I'm afraid there won't be any question of an arrest just yet,' he said. 'I take it that Miss . . . er . . . Mueller is in the house.'

'I don't know,' said Wilt, 'she was when I left this morning, and today being Wednesday she doesn't have any lectures, so she probably is. Why don't you go round and find out?'

'Because, sir, your lodger just happens to be one of the most

301

dangerous woman terrorists in the world. I think that is self-explanatory.'

'Oh my God,' said Wilt, suddenly feeling very weak.

Superintendent Misterson leant across the desk. 'She has at least eight killings to her credit and she's suspected of being the mastermind . . . I'm sorry to use such melodramatic terms but in the event they happen to fit. As I was saying she has organized several bombings and we now know she's been involved in the hijacking of a security van in Gantrey last Tuesday. A man died in the attack. You may have read about the case.'

Wilt had. In the waiting-room at the Accident Centre. It had seemed then one of those remote and disgusting acts of gratuitous violence which made the morning paper such depressing reading. And yet because he read about it the murder of a security guard had been invested with a reality which it lacked in the present circumstances. Mastermind, terrorist, killings—words spoken casually in an office by a bland man with a paisley tie and a brown tweed suit. Like some country solicitor, Superintendent Misterson, was the last person he would have expected to use such words and it was this incongruity which was so alarming. Wilt stared at the man and shook his head.

'I'm afraid it's true,' said the Superintendent.

'But the money . . .'

'Marked, sir. Marked and numbered. Bait in a trap.'

Wilt shook his head again. The truth was unbearable. 'What are you going to do? My wife and children are at home by now and if she's there . . . and there are all those other foreigners in the house too.'

'Would you mind telling us how many other . . . er . . . foreigners are there, sir?'

'I don't know,' said Wilt, 'it varies from day to day. There's a stream of them coming and going. Jesus wept.'

'Now, sir,' said the Superintendent briskly, 'what's your usual routine? Do you normally go home for lunch?'

'No. I usually have it at the Tech. but just at the moment I'm off work and yes, I suppose I do.'

'So your wife will be surprised if you don't come home?'

'I doubt it,' said Wilt. 'Sometimes I drop into a pub for sandwiches.'

302

'And you don't telephone first?'

'Not always.'

'What I am trying to ascertain, sir, is whether your wife will evince any alarm were you not to come home now or contact her.'

'She won't,' said Wilt. 'The only time she'll be alarmed is when she knows we've been providing accommodation for . . . What is the name of this bloody woman anyway?'

'Gudrun Schautz. And now, sir, I'll have some lunch sent up from the canteen and we'll make preparations.'

'What preparations?' asked Wilt but the Superintendent had left the room and the other plainclothes man seemed disinclined to talk. Wilt regarded the slight bulge under the man's right armpit and tried to stifle his growing feeling of insanity.

In the kitchen at Willington Road Eva was busy giving the quads their lunch.

'We won't wait for daddy,' she said, 'he'll probably be back a little later.'

'Will he bring his bagpipe home?' asked Josephine.

'Bagpipe, dear? Daddy doesn't have a bagpipe.'

'He's been wearing one,' said Penelope.

'Yes, but not the sort you play.'

'I saw some men in dresses playing bagpipes at the show,' said Emmeline.

'Kilts, dear.'

'I saw daddy playing with his pipe in the summerhouse,' said Penelope, 'and he was wearing mummy's dress too.'

'Well he wasn't playing with it in the same way, Penny,' argued Eva, wondering privately what way Wilt had been playing with it.

'Bagpipes make a horrid noise anyway,' maintained Emmeline.

'And daddy made a horrid noise when you got into bed . . .'

'Yes, dear, he was having a bad dream.'

'He called it a wet dream, mummy. I heard him.'

'Well that's a bad dream too,' said Eva. 'Now then, what did you do at school today?'

But the quads were not to be diverted from the absorbing topic of their father's recent misfortune. 'Roger's mummy told him daddy must have something wrong with his bladder to have a pipe,' said Penelope. 'What's a bladder, mummy?'

'I know,' shouted Emmeline, 'it's a pig's tummy and that's what they make bagpipes out of because Sally told me.'

'Daddy's not a pig . . .'

'That's enough of that,' said Eva firmly, 'we won't talk about daddy any more. Now eat your cod's roe.'

'Roger says cod's roe is baby fishes,' said Penelope. 'I don't like it.'

'Well it's not. Fishes don't have babies. They lay eggs.'

'Do sausages lay eggs, mummy?' asked Josephine.

'Of course they don't, darling. Sausages aren't alive.'

'Roger says his daddy's sausage lays eggs and his mummy wears something . . .'

'I don't care to hear what Roger says any more,' said Eva torn between curiosity about the Rawstons and revulsion at her offsprings' encyclopedic knowledge. 'It's not nice to talk about such things.'

'Why not, mummy?'

'Because it isn't,' said Eva unable to think of a suitably progressive argument to silence them. Caught between her own indoctrinated sense of niceness and her opinion that children's innate curiosity should never be thwarted, Eva struggled through lunch wishing that Henry were there to put a stop to their questions with a taciturn growl. But Henry still wasn't there at two o'clock when Mavis phoned to remind her that she had promised to pick her up on the way to the Symposium on Alternative Painting in Thailand.

'I'm sorry but Henry isn't back,' said Eva. 'He went to the doctor's this morning and I expected him home for lunch. I can't leave the children.'

'Patrick's got the car today,' said Mavis, 'his own is in for a service and I was relying on you.'

'Oh well, I'll go and ask Mrs de Frackas to baby-sit for half an hour,' said Eva, 'she's always volunteering to sit and Henry's bound to be back shortly.'

She went next door and presently old Mrs de Frackas was sitting in the summerhouse surrounded by the quads reading them the story of Rikki Tikki Tavi. The widow of Major-General de Frackas, at eighty-two her memories of girlhood

304

days in India were rather better than on topics of more recent occurrence. Eva drove off happily to pick up Mavis.

By the time Wilt had finished his lunch he had picked out two more terrorists from the mug shots as being frequent visitors to the house, and the police station had seen the arrival of several large vans containing a large number of surprisingly agile men in a motley of plain clothes. The canteen had been turned into a briefing centre and Superintendent Misterson's authority had been superseded by a Major (name undisclosed) of Special Ground Services.

'The Superintendent here will explain the initial stages of the operation,' said the Major condescending, 'but before he does I want to stress that we are dealing with some of the most ruthless killers in Europe. They must on no account escape. At the same time we naturally want to avoid bloodshed if at all possible. However, it has to be said that in the circumstances we are entitled to shoot first and ask questions afterwards if the target is able to answer. I have that authority from the Minister.' He smiled bleakly and sat down.

'After the house has been surrounded,' said the Superintendent, 'Mr Wilt will enter and hopefully effect the exit of his family. I want nothing done to prevent that first essential requirement. The second factor to take into account is that we have a unique opportunity to arrest at least three leading terrorists and possibly more, and again, hopefully, Mr Wilt will enable us to know how many members of the group are in the house at the moment of time of his exit. I'll go ahead with my side and leave the rest to the Major.'

He left the canteen and went up to the office where Wilt was finishing his Queen's pudding with the help of mouthfuls of coffee. Outside the door he met the SGS surgeon and para-psychologist who had been studying Wilt covertly.

'Nervous type,' he said gloomily. 'Couldn't be worse material. Sort of blighter who'd funk a jump from a tethered balloon.'

'Fortunately he doesn't have to jump from a tethered balloon,' said the Superintendent. 'All he has to do is enter the house and find an excuse for taking his family out.'

'All the same I think he ought to have a shot of something

to stiffen his backbone. We don't want him dithering on the doorstep. Give the game away.'

He marched off to fetch his bag while the Superintendent went in to Wilt. 'Now then,' he said with alarming cheerfulness, 'all you've got to do . . .'

'Is enter a house filled with killers and ask my wife to come out. I know,' said Wilt.

'Nothing very difficult about that.'

Wilt looked at him incredulously. 'Nothing difficult?' said Wilt in a vaguely soprano voice. 'You don't know my bloody wife.'

'I haven't had the privilege yet,' admitted the Superintendent.

'Precisely,' said Wilt. 'Well, when and if you do you'll discover that if I go home and ask her to come out she'll think of a thousand reasons for staying in.'

'Difficult woman, sir?'

'Oh no, nothing difficult about Eva. Not at all. She's just bloody awkward, that's all.'

'I see, sir, and if you suggested she didn't go out you think she might in fact do so?'

'If you want my opinion,' said Wilt, 'if I do that she'll think I'm off my rocker. I mean what would you do if you were sitting peacefully at home and your wife came in and suggested out of the blue that you didn't go out when it had never occurred to you to go out in the first place? You'd think there was something fucking odd going on, wouldn't you?'

'I suppose I would,' said the Superintendent. 'Never thought of it like that before.'

'Well you'd better start now,' said Wilt, 'I'm not going . . .' He was interrupted by the entrance of the Major and two other officers wearing jeans, T-shirts with UP THE I.R.A. printed on them, and carrying rather large handbags.

'If we might just interrupt a moment,' said the Major, 'we would like Mr Wilt to draw a detailed plan of the house, vertical section and then horizontal.'

'What for?' said Wilt unable to take his eyes off the T-shirts.

'In the event that we have to storm the house, sir,' said the Major, 'we need to get the killing angles right. Don't want to go in and find the loo's in the wrong place and what not.'

306

'Listen, mate,' said Wilt, 'you go down Willington Road with those T-shirts and handbags you won't reach my house. You'll be bloody lynched by the neighbours. Mrs Fogin's nephew was blown up in Belfast and Professor Ball's got a thing about gays. His wife married one.'

'Better change into the KEEP CLAPHAM WHITE shirts, chaps,' said the Major.

'Better not,' said Wilt. 'Mr and Mrs Bokani at Number 11 would be onto Race Relations like the clappers. Can't you think of something neutral?'

'Mickey Mouse, sir?' suggested one of the officers.

'Oh, all right,' said the Major grumpily, 'one Mickey Mouse and the rest Donald Ducks.'

'Christ,' said Wilt, 'I don't know how many men you've got but if you're going to flood the neighbourhood with Donald Ducks armed to the teeth with whatever you have in those gigantic handbags you'll have a whole lot of schizophrenic infants on your conscience.'

'Never mind that,' said the Major, 'you leave the tactical angle to us. We've had experience before of this sort of operation and all we want from you is a detailed plan of the domestic terrain.'

'Talk about calling a spade an earth-inverting horticultural implement,' said Wilt. 'I never thought I'd live to hear my home called a domestic terrain.'

He picked up a pencil but the Superintendent intervened. 'Look, if we don't get Mr Wilt back to the house soon, someone may begin wondering where he is,' he protested.

As if to reinforce this argument the phone rang.

'It's for you,' said the Major. 'Some bugger called Flint who says he's holed up in the bank.'

'I thought I told you not to make any outgoing calls,' the Superintendent said angrily into the phone. 'Relieve themselves? Of course they can . . . An appointment at three with Mr Daniles? Who's he? . . . Oh shit . . . Where? . . . Well, empty the wastepaper basket for Chrissake . . . I don't have to tell you where. I should have thought that was patently obvious . . . What do you mean it's going to look peculiar? . . . Do they have to cross the entire bank? . . . I know all about the smell. Get hold of an aerosol or something . . . Well if he objects detain the sod. And Flint, see if someone has a bucket and use that in future.'

He slammed down the phone and turned back to the Major. 'Things are steaming up at the bank and if we don't move swiftly—'

'Someone's going to smell a rat?' suggested Wilt. 'Now, do you want me to draw my house or not?'

'Yes,' said the Major, 'and fast.'

'There's no need to adopt that tone,' said Wilt. 'You may be eager to have a battle on my property but I want to know who's going to pay for the damage. My wife's a very particular woman and if you start killing people all over the carpet in the living-room . . .'

'Mr Wilt,' said the Major with determined patience, 'we shall do everything we can to avoid any violence on your property. It is for precisely that reason we need a detailed plan of the domestic . . . er . . . the house.'

'I think if we leave Mr Wilt to draw the plan . . .' said the Superintendent and nodded towards the door. The Major followed him out and they conferred in the corridor.

'Listen,' said the Superintendent, 'I've already had a report from your trick-cyclist that the little bastard's a mass of nerves and if you're going to start bullying him . . .'

'Superintendent,' said the Major, 'it may interest you to know that I have a casualty allowance of ten on this op and if he's one of them I shan't be sorry. War Office approval.'

'And if we don't get him in there, and his wife and children out, you'll have used up six of your quota,' snapped the Superintendent.

'All I can say is that a man who puts his living-room carpet before his country and the Western World . . .' He would have said a lot more had it not been for the arrival of the para-psychologist with a cup of coffee.

'Fixed him a spot of nervebracer,' he said cheerfully. 'Should see him through.'

'I certainly hope so,' said the Superintendent. 'I could do with something myself.'

'No need to worry about it working,' said the Major. 'Used it myself once in County Armagh when I had to defuse a bloody

308

great bomb. Bugger went off before I could get to it but by God I felt good all the same.'

The medic went into the office and presently reappeared with the empty cup. 'In like a lamb, out like a lion,' he said. 'No trouble at all.'

Chapter 11

Ten minutes later Wilt lived up to the prediction. He left the police station of his own free will and entered the Superintendent's car quite cheerfully.

'Just drop me off at the bottom of the road and I'll find my own way home,' he said. 'No need for you to bother to drive right up to the house.'

The Superintendent looked at him doubtfully. 'I hadn't intended to. The object of the exercise is for you to go into the house without arousing suspicion and persuade your wife to come out by telling her you've met this herbalist in a pub and he's invited you all round to look at his collection of plants. You've got that straight?'

'Wilco,' said Wilt.

'Wilco?'

'And what's more,' continued Wilt, 'if that doesn't flush the bitch out I'll take the children and leave her to stew in her own juice.'

'Stop the car, driver,' said the Superintendent hastily.

'What for?' said Wilt. 'You don't expect me to walk two miles? When I said you could drop me off I didn't mean here.'

'Mr Wilt,' said the Superintendent, 'I must impress on you the seriousness of the situation. Gudrun Schautz is undoubtedly armed and she won't hesitate to shoot. The woman is a professional killer.'

'So what? Bloody woman comes into my house having killed people all over the place and expects me to give her bed and board. Like hell I will. Driver, drive on.'

'Oh God,' said the Superintendent, 'trust the army to cock this one up.'

'Want me to turn back, sir?' asked the driver.

'Certainly not,' said Wilt. 'The sooner I can get my family out and the army in the better. No need to look like that. Everything's going to be roger over and out.'

'I wouldn't be at all surprised,' said the Superintendent

310

despondently. 'All right, drive on. Now then, Mr Wilt, for God's sake stick to your story about the herbalist. The fellow's name is . . .'

'Falkirk,' said Wilt automatically. 'He lives at Number 45 Barrabas Road. He has recently returned from South America with a collection of plants including tropical herbs previously uncultivated in this country . . .'

'At least he knows his lines,' muttered the Superintendent as they turned into Farringdon Avenue and pulled into the kerb. Wilt got out, slammed the car door with unnecessary violence and marched off down Willington Road. Behind him the Superintendent watched miserably and cursed the para-psychologist.

'Must have given him some sort of chemical kamikaze mixture,' he told the driver.

'There's still time to stop him, sir,' said the driver. But there wasn't. Wilt had dived into the gate of his house and disappeared. As soon as he had gone a head popped out of the hedge beside the car.

'Don't want to give the game away, old boy,' said an officer wearing the uniform of a Gas Inspector. 'If you'll just toddle along I'll call HQ and tell them the subject has entered the danger zone . . .'

'Oh no you won't,' snarled the Superintendent as the officer twiddled with the knobs of his walkie-talkie, 'there's to be strict radio silence until the family are safely out.'

'My orders are . . .'

'Countermanded as of now,' said the Superintendent. 'Innocent lives are at stake and I'm not having them jeopardized.'

'Oh all right,' said the officer. 'Anyway we've got the area sealed off. Not even a rabbit could get out of there now.'

'It's not simply a question of anyone getting out. We want as many to get in before we move.'

'Rightho, want to bag the lot of them eh? Nothing like going the whole hog, what!'

The officer disappeared into the hedge and the Superintendent drove on.

'Lions, lambs, and now fucking rabbits and hogs,' he told the driver, 'I wish to heaven the Special Ground Services hadn't

311

been called in. They seem to have animals on the brain.'

'Comes of recruiting them from the huntin' an' shootin' set, I expect, sir,' said the driver. 'Wouldn't like to be in that bloke Wilt's shoes.'

In the garden of Number 9 Willington Road Wilt did not share his apprehensions. Stiffened by the parapsychologist's nervebracer he was in no mood to be trifled with. Bloody terrorists coming into his house without so much as a by-your-leave. Well, he'd soon show them the door. He marched resolutely up to the house and opened the front door before realizing that the car wasn't outside. Eva must be out with the quads. In which case there was no need for him to go in. 'To hell with that,' said Wilt to himself, 'this is my house and I'm entitled to do what I damned well please in it.' He went into the hall and shut the door. The house was silent and the living-room empty. Wilt went through the kitchen and wondered what to do next. In normal circumstances he would have left, but circumstances were not normal. To Wilt's intoxicated way of thinking they called for stern measures. The bloody army wanted a battle on his domestic terrain, did they? Well, he'd soon put a stop to that. Domestic terrain indeed! If people wanted to kill one another they could jolly well do it somewhere else. Which was all very fine, but how to persuade them? Well, the simplest way was to go up to the attic and heave Miss Bloody Schautz/Mueller's suitcases and clobber out into the front garden. That way when she came home she'd get the message and take herself off to someone else's domestic terrain.

With this simple solution in mind Wilt went upstairs and climbed the steps to the attic door only to find it locked. He went down to the kitchen, found the spare key and went back. For a moment he hesitated outside the door before knocking. There was no reply. Wilt unlocked the door and went inside.

The attic flat consisted of three rooms, a large bedsitter with the balcony looking down onto the garden, a kitchenette and beyond it a bathroom. Wilt shut the door behind him and looked around. The bedsitter which had occupied his former Muse was unexpectedly tidy. Gudrun Schautz might be a ruthless terrorist but she was also house-proud. Clothes hung neatly in a wall closet and the cups and saucers in the kitchen were all washed

312

and set on shelves. Now, where would she have put her suit-cases? Wilt looked round and tried another cupboard before remembering that Eva had moved the cold-water cistern to a higher position under the roof when the bathroom had been put in. There was a door to it somewhere.

He found it beside the stove in the kitchenette and crawled through only to discover that he had to stoop along under the eaves on a narrow plank to reach the storage space. He groped about in the darkness and found the lightswitch. The suitcases were in a row beside the cistern. Wilt made his way along and grabbed the handle of the first bag. It felt incredibly heavy. Also distinctly lumpy. Wilt dragged it down from the shelf and it dropped with a metallic thud onto the plank at his feet. He wasn't going to lug that back across the rafters. Wilt fumbled with the catches and finally opened the bag.

All his doubts about Miss Schautz/Mueller's profession vanished. He was looking down on some sort of sub-machine gun, a mound of revolvers, boxes of ammunition, a typewriter and what appeared to be grenades. And as he looked he heard the sound of a car outside. It had pulled into the drive and even to his untrained ear it sounded like the Aston-Martin. Cursing himself for not listening to his innate cowardice, Wilt struggled to get back along the plank to the door but the bag was in the way. He banged his head on the rafters above and was about to crawl over the bag when it occurred to him that the sub-machine gun might be loaded and could well go off if he prodded it in the wrong place. Best get the damned thing out. Again, that was easier said than done. The barrel got caught in the end of the bag and by the time he had disentangled it he could hear foot-steps on the wooden stairs below. Too late to do anything now except switch the light off. Leaning forward across the bag and holding the machine gun at arm's length Wilt joggled the switch up with the muzzle before crouching down in the darkness.

Outside in the garden the quads had had a marvellous after-noon with old Mrs de Frackas. She had read them the story about Rikki Tikki Tavi, the mongoose, and the two cobras, and had then taken them into her house to show them what a stuffed cobra looked like (she had one in a glass case and it bared its fangs most realistically) and had told them about her own childhood in India before sitting them down to tea in her conservatory. For once the quads had behaved themselves. They had picked up from Eva a proper sense of Mrs de Frackas' social standing and in any case the old lady's voice had a distinctly firm ring to it—or as Wilt had once put it, if at eighty-two she could no longer break a sherry glass at fifty paces she could still make a guard dog whimper at forty. It was certainly true that the milkman had long since given up trying to collect his payment on a weekly basis. Mrs de Frackas belonged to a generation that had paid when it felt so inclined; the old lady sent her cheque only twice a year, and then it was wrong. The milk company did not dispute it. The widow of the late Major-General de Frackas, D.S.O. etcetera was a personage to whom people deferred and it was one of Eva's proudest boasts that she and the old lady got on like a house on fire. Nobody else in Willington Road did and it was almost entirely because Mrs de Frackas loved children and considered Eva, in spite of her obvious lack of breeding, to be an excellent mother that she smiled on the Wilts. To be precise, she seldom smiled on Wilt, evidently regarding him as an accident in the family process and one that, if her observation of his activities in the summerhouse of an evening was correct, drank. Since the Major-General had died of cirrhosis or as she bluntly said, hob-nailed liver, Wilt's solitary communion with the bottle only increased her regard for Eva and concern for the children. Being also rather deaf she thought them delightful girls, an opinion that was shared by no one else in the district.

And so this bright sunny afternoon Mrs de Frackas sat the quads in her conservatory and served tea, happily unaware of the gathering drama next door. Then she allowed them to play with the tiger rug in her drawing-room and even to knock over a potted palm before deciding it was time to go home. The little procession went out of the front gate and into Number 9 just as Wilt began his search in the attic. In the bushes on the opposite side of the road the officer whom the Superintendent had warned not to use his radio watched them enter the house and was desperately praying that they would come out again straightaway when the Aston-Martin drove up. Gudrun Schautz and two young men got out, opened the boot and took out several suitcases while the officer dithered but before he could make up his mind to tackle them in the open they had hurried in the front door. Only then did he break radio silence.

'Female target and two males have entered the zone,' he told the Major who was making a round of the S.G.S. men posted at the bottom of the Wilts' garden. 'No present withdrawal of civilian occupants. Request instructions.'

In response the Major threaded his way through the gardens of Numbers 4 and 2 and accompanied by two privates carrying a theodolite and a striped pole promptly set this up on the pavement and began to take sightings down Willington Road while carrying on a conversation with the officer in the hedge.

'What do you mean you couldn't stop them?' demanded the Major when he learnt that the quads and an old lady had left the house next door and gone into the Wilts'. But before the officer could think of an answer they were interrupted by Professor Ball.

'What's the meaning of all this?' he demanded, regarding the two long-haired privates and the theodolite with equal distaste.

'Just making a survey for the new road extension,' said the Major improvising hastily.

'Road extension? What road extension?' said the Professor transferring his disgust to the handbag the Major had over his shoulder.

'The proposed road extension to the by-pass,' said the Major.

Professor Ball's voice rose. 'By-pass? Did I hear you say there's a proposal to put a road through here to the by-pass?'

'Only doing my job, sir,' said the Major, wishing to hell the old fool would get lost.

'And what job is that?' demanded the Professor, taking a notebook from his pocket.

'Surveyor's Department, Borough Engineering.'

'Really? And your name?' asked the Professor with a nasty glint in his eye. He wetted the end of his ballpen with his tongue while the Major hesitated.

'Palliser, sir,' said the Major. 'And now, sir, if you don't mind, we've got to get on.'

'Don't let me disturb you, Mr Palliser.' The Professor turned and stalked into his house. He returned a moment later with a heavy stick.

'It may interest you to know, Mr Palliser,' he said brandishing the stick, 'that I happen to sit on the Highways and Planning Committee of the City Council. Note the word "city", Mr Palliser. And we don't have a Borough Engineering Department. We have a City one.'

'Slip of the tongue, sir,' said the Major trying to keep one eye on the Wilts' house while conscious of the threat of the stick.

'And I suppose it was another slip of the tongue that you said that the City of Ipford was proposing to build an extension of this road to the by-pass . . .'

'It's just a vague idea, sir,' said the Major.

Professor Ball laughed dryly. 'It must indeed be vague considering we don't yet have a by-pass and that as Chairman of the Highways and Planning Committee I would be the first to hear of any proposed alterations to the existing roads. What's more, I happen to know a great deal about the use of theodolites and you don't look through the wrong end. Now then, you will kindly remain where you are until the police arrive. My housekeeper has already phoned . . .'

'If I could have a word with you in private,' said the Major fumbling frantically in his handbag for his credentials. But Professor Ball knew an impostor when he saw one and, as Wilt had predicted, his reaction to men who carried handbags was violent. With the descent of his stick the Major's credentials tipped from his handbag and clattered on the ground. They included one walkie-talkie, two revolvers and a teargas grenade.

'Fuck,' said the Major, stooping to retrieve his armoury, but Professor Ball's stick was in action again. This time it caught the Major on the back of the neck and sent him sprawling in the gutter. Behind him the private in charge of the theodolite moved swiftly. Throwing himself on the Professor he pinned his left arm behind his back and with a karate chop knocked the stick from his right hand.

'If you'll just come quietly, sir,' he said, but that was the last thing Professor Ball intended to do. Safety, from men pretending to be surveyors who carried revolvers and grenades, lay in

316

making as much noise as he could and Willington Road was aroused from its suburban torpor by yells of 'Help! Murder! Call the police!'

'For God's sake gag the old bastard,' shouted the Major still scrabbling for his revolvers but it was too late. Across the road a face appeared at the attic skylight, was followed by a second, and before the Professor could be removed in silence they had disappeared.

Squatting in the darkness beside the water tank Wilt was only dimly aware that something odd was happening in the street. Gudrun Schautz had decided to take a bath and the tank was rumbling and hissing but he could hear the reactions of her companions clearly enough.

'Police!' one of them yelled. 'Gudrun, the police are here.'

Another voice shouted from the balcony room. 'There are more in the garden with rifles.'

'Downstairs quickly. We take them on the ground.'

Footsteps clattered down the wooden staircase while Gudrun Schautz from the bathroom shouted instructions in German and then remembered to bawl them in English.

'The children,' she shouted, 'hold the children.'

It was too much for Wilt. Disregarding the bag and the machine gun he was holding he hurled himself at the door, fell through it into the kitchen and promptly sprayed the ceiling with bullets by accidentally pulling the trigger. The effect was quite remarkable. In the bathroom Gudrun Schautz screamed, downstairs the terrorists began firing into the back garden and at the little group including Professor Ball across the street, and from both the street and the back garden the S.G.S. returned their fire fourfold, smashing windows, adding new holes in the leaves of Eva's Swiss Cheese plant and generally pock-marking the walls of the living-room where Mrs de Frackas and the quads were enjoying a Western on TV until the Mexican rug on the wall behind them was dislodged and covered their heads.

'Now then, children,' she said calmly, 'there's no need to be alarmed. We'll just lie on the floor until whatever's happening stops.' But the quads were not in the least alarmed. Inured by continual gunfights on television they were perfectly at home in the middle of a real one.

317

The same could hardly be said for Wilt. As the plaster from the perforated ceiling drifted down onto him he scrambled to his feet and was making for the stairs when a burst of small-arms fire heading through the back windows of the landing and out the front deterred him. Still clutching the sub-machine gun, he stumbled back into the kitchen and then realized that the infernal Fräulein Schautz was behind him in the bathroom. She had stopped screaming and might at any moment emerge with a gun. 'Lock the bitch in,' was his first thought but since the key was on the inside . . . Wilt looked round for an alternative and found it in a kitchen chair which he jammed under the door handle. To make this doubly secure he tore the flex from a table-lamp in the main room and dragged it through before tying a loop to the handle and attaching the other end to the leg of the electric stove. Then having secured his rear he made another sortie to the stairs, but the battle below still raged. He was just about to risk going down when a head appeared on the landing, a head and shoulders carrying the same sort of weapon he had just used. Wilt didn't hesitate. He slammed the door of the flat, pushed up the safety lock and then dragged a bed from the wall and lodged it against the door. Finally he picked up his own gun and waited. If anyone tried to come through the door he would pull the trigger. But then just as suddenly as the battle had begun it ceased.

Silence reigned in Willington Road, a short, blissful, healthy silence. Wilt stood in the attic and listened breathlessly, wondering what to do next. It was decided for him by Gudrun Schautz trying the door of the bathroom. He edged into the kitchen and pointed the gun at the door.

'One more move in there and I fire,' he said, and even to Wilt his voice had a strange and unnaturally menacing, almost unrecognizable sound to it. To Gudrun Schautz it held the authentic tone of a man behind a gun. The doorhandle stopped wriggling. On the other hand there was someone at the top of the stairs trying to get into the flat. With a facility that astonished him Wilt turned and pulled the trigger and once more the flat resounded to a burst of gunfire. None of the bullets hit the door. They spattered the wall of the bedsitter while the sub-machine gun juddered in Wilt's hands. The bloody thing seemed to have a will of its own and it was a horrified Wilt who finally took his

318

finger off the trigger and put the gun gingerly down on the kitchen table. Outside someone descended the stairs with remarkable rapidity but there was no other sound.

Wilt sat down and wondered what the hell was going to happen next.

Chapter 12

Much the same question was occupying Superintendent Misterson's mind.

'What the hell's going on?' he demanded of the dishevelled Major who arrived with Professor Ball and the two pseudo-surveyors at the corner of Willington Road and Farringdon Avenue. 'I thought I told you nothing must be done until the children were safely out of the house.'

'Don't look at me,' said the Major. 'This old fool had to poke his fucking nose in.'

He fingered the back of his neck and eyed the Professor with loathing.

'And who might you be?' Professor Ball asked the Superintendent.

'A police officer.'

'Then kindly do your duty and arrest these bandits. Come down the road with a damned theodolite and handbags filled with guns and tell me they're from the Roads Department and indulge in gun battles . . .'

'Anti-Terrorist Squad, sir,' said the Superintendent and showed him his pass. Professor Ball regarded it bleakly.

'A likely story. First I'm assaulted by . . .'

'Oh, get the old bugger out of here,' snarled the Major. 'If he hadn't interfered we'd have—'

'Interfered? Interfered indeed! I was exercising my right to make a citizen's arrest of these impostors when they start shooting into a perfectly ordinary house across the street and . . .' Two uniformed constables arrived to escort the Professor, still protesting angrily, to a waiting police car.

'You heard the damned man,' said the Major in response to the Superintendent's reiterated request for someone to please tell him what the hell had gone wrong. 'We were waiting for the children to come out when he arrives on the scene and blows the gaff. That's what happened. The next thing you know the sods

320

were firing from the house, and by the sound of it using some damnably powerful weapons.'

'Right, so what you are saying is that the children are still in the house, Mr Wilt is still there, and so are a number of terrorists. Is that correct?'

'Yes,' said the Major.

'And all this in spite of your guarantee that you wouldn't do anything to jeopardize the lives of innocent civilians?'

'I didn't do a damned thing. I happened to be lying in the gutter when the balloon went up. And if you expect my men to sit quietly and let themselves be shot at by thugs using automatic weapons you're asking too much of human nature.'

'I suppose so,' the Superintendent conceded. 'Oh well, we'll just have to go into the usual siege routine. Any idea how many terrorists were in there?'

'Too bloody many for my liking,' said the Major looking to his men for confirmation.

'One of them was firing through the roof, sir,' said one of the privates. 'A burst of fire came through the tiles right at the beginning.'

'And I wouldn't say they were short of ammo. Not the way they were loosing off.'

'All right. First thing is to evacuate the street,' said the Superintendent. 'Don't want any more people involved than we can help.'

'Sounds as if someone else is already involved,' said the Major as the muffled burst of Wilt's second experiment with the machine gun echoed from Number 9. 'What the hell are they doing firing inside the house?'

'Probably started on the hostages,' said the Superintendent gloomily.

'Hardly likely, old chap. Not unless one of them tried to escape. Oh by the way I don't know if I mentioned it but there's a little old lady in there too. Went in with the four girls.'

'Went in with the four—' the Superintendent began lividly before being interrupted by his driver with the message that Inspector Flint had called from the bank to know if it was all right for him to leave now as it was closing time and the bank staff . . .

The Superintendent unleashed his fury on Flint via the driver, and the Major made good his escape. Presently little groups of refugees from Willington Road were making their way circuitously out of the area while more armed men moved in to take their place. An armoured car with the Major perched safely on its turret rumbled past.

'HQ and Communications Centre are at Number 7,' he shouted. 'My signal chappies have rigged you up with a direct line in.'

He drove on before the Superintendent could think of a suitable retort. 'Damned military getting in the way all the time,' he grumbled and gave orders for parabolic listening devices to be brought up and for tape recorders and voiceprint analysers to be installed at the Communications Centre. In the meantime Farringdon Avenue was cordoned off by uniformed police at road blocks and a Press Briefing Room established at the Police Station.

'Got to give the public their pound of vicarious flesh,' he told his men, 'but I don't want any TV cameramen inside the area. The sods inside the house will be watching and frankly if I had my way there would be press and TV silence. These swine thrive on publicity.'

Only then did he make his way down Willington Road to Number 7 to begin the dialogue with the terrorists.

Eva drove home from Mavis Mottram's in a bad temper. The Symposium on Alternative Painting in Thailand had been cancelled because the artist-cum-lecturer had been arrested and was awaiting extradition proceedings for drug smuggling and instead Eva had had to sit through two hours of discussion on Alternative Childbirth about which, since she had given birth to four overweight infants in the course of forty minutes, she considered she knew more than the lecturer. To add to her irritation, several ardent advocates of abortion had used the occasion to promote their views and Eva had violent feelings about abortion.

'It's unnatural,' she told Mavis afterwards in the Coffee House with that simplicity her friends found so infuriating. 'If people don't want children they shouldn't have them.'

'Yes, dear,' said Mavis, 'but it's not as easy as all that.'

'It is. They can have their babies adopted by parents who

322

can't have any. There are thousands of couples like that.'

'Yes but in the case of teenage girls . . .'

'Teenage girls shouldn't have sex. I didn't.'

Mavis looked at her thoughtfully. 'No, but you're the exception, Eva. The modern generation is much more demanding than we were. They're physically more mature.'

'Perhaps they are, but Henry says they're mentally retarded.'

'Of course, he would know,' said Mavis but Eva was impervious to such slights.

'If they weren't they would take precautions.'

'But you're the one who is always going on about the pill being unnatural.'

'And so it is. I just meant they wouldn't allow boys to go so far. After all once they're married they can have as much as they like.'

'That's the first time I've heard you say that, dear. You're always complaining that Henry is too tired to bother.'

In the end Eva had had to riposte with a reference to Patrick Mottram and Mavis had seized the opportunity to catalogue his latest infidelities.

'Anyone would think the whole world revolved round Patrick,' Eva grumbled to herself as she drove away from Ms Mottram's house. 'And I don't care what anyone thinks, I still say abortion is wrong.' She turned into Farringdon Avenue and was immediately stopped by a policeman. A barrier had been erected across the road and several police cars were parked against the kerb.

'Sorry, ma'am, but you'll have to go back. No one is allowed through,' a uniformed constable told her.

'But I live here,' said Eva. 'I'm only going as far as Willington Road.'

'That's where the trouble is.'

'What trouble?' asked Eva, her instincts suddenly alert. 'Why have they got that barbed wire across the road?'

A sergeant walked across as Eva opened the door of the car and got out.

'Now then, if you'll kindly turn round and drive back the way you came,' he said.

'Says she lives in Willington Road,' the constable told him. At that moment two S.G.S. men armed with automatic weapons came round the corner and entered Mrs Granberry's garden by way of her flowerbed of prize begonias. If anything was needed to confirm Eva's worst fears this was it.

'Those men have got guns,' she said. 'Oh my God, my children! Where are my children?'

'You'll find everyone from Willington Road in the Memorial Hall. Now what number do you live at?'

'Number 9. I left the quads with Mrs de Frackas and—'

'If you'll just come this way, Mrs Wilt,' said the sergeant gently and started to take her arm.

'How did you know my name?' Eva asked, staring at the sergeant with growing horror. 'You called me Mrs Wilt.'

'Now please keep calm. Everything is going to be all right.'

'No, it isn't.' And Eva threw his hand aside and began running down the road before being stopped by four policemen and dragged back to a car.

'Get the medic and a policewoman,' said the sergeant. 'Now you just sit in the back, Mrs Wilt.' Eva was forced into a police car.

'What's happened to the children? Somebody tell me what's happened.'

'The Superintendent will explain. They're quite safe so don't worry.'

'If they're safe why can't I go to them? Where's Henry? I want my Henry.'

But instead of Wilt she got the Superintendent who arrived with two policewomen and a doctor.

'Now then, Mrs Wilt,' said the Superintendent, 'I'm afraid I've got some bad news for you. Not that it couldn't be worse. Your children are alive and quite safe, but they're in the hands of several armed men and we're trying to get them out of the house safely.'

Eva stared at him wildly. 'Armed men? What armed men?'

'Some foreigners.'

'You mean they're being held *hostage*?'

'We can't be too sure just yet. Your husband is with them.'

The doctor intervened. 'I'm just going to give you a sedative, Mrs Wilt,' he began but Eva recoiled in the back seat.

'No you aren't. I'm not taking anything. You can't make me.'

324

'If you'll just calm down . . .'

But Eva was adamant, and too strong to be easily given an injection in the confined space. After the doctor had had the hypodermic syringe knocked from his hand for the second time he gave up.

'All right, Mrs Wilt, you needn't take anything,' said the Superintendent. 'If you'll just sit still we'll drive you back to the police station and keep you fully informed of any developments.'

And in spite of Eva's protests that she wanted to stay where she was or even go down to the house she was driven away with an escort of two policewomen.

'Next time you want me to sedate that damned woman I'll get a tranquillizer gun from the Zoo,' said the doctor, nursing his wrist. 'And if you're sensible you'll keep her in a cell. If she gets loose she could foul things up properly.'

'As if they weren't already,' said the Superintendent and made his way back to the Communications Centre. It was situated in Mrs de Frackas' drawing-room and there incongruously, set among mementos of life in Imperial India, antimacassars, potted plants and beneath the ferocious portrait of the late Major-General, the S.G.S. and the Anti-Terrorist Squad had collaborated to install a switchboard, a telephone amplifier, tape recorders and the voiceprint analyser.

'All ready to go, sir,' said the detective in charge of the apparatus. 'We've hooked into the line next door.'

'Have you got the listening devices in position?'

'Can't do that yet,' said the Major. 'No windows on this side and we can't move in across the lawn. Have a shot after dark, provided those buggers haven't got night sights.'

'Oh well, put me through,' said the Superintendent. 'The sooner we begin the dialogue the sooner everyone will be able to go home. If I know my job they'll start with a stream of abuse. So everyone stand by to be called a fascist shit.'

In the event he was mistaken. It was Mrs de Frackas who answered.

'This is Ipford 23 . . . I'm afraid I haven't got my glasses with me but I think it's . . . Now, young man . . .'

There was a brief pause during which Mrs de Frackas was evidently relieved of the phone.

'My name is Misterson, Superintendent Misterson,' said the Superintendent finally.

'Lying pig of a fascist shit,' shouted a voice, at last fulfilling his prediction. 'You think we are going to surrender, shitface, but you are wrong. We die first, you understand. Do you hear me, pig?'

The Superintendent sighed and said he did.

'Right. Get that straight in your pigshit fascist head. No way we surrender. If you want us you come in and kill us and you know what that means.'

'I don't think anyone wants . . .'

'What you want, pig, you don't get. You do what we want or people get hurt.'

'That's what I'm waiting to hear, what you want,' said the Superintendent, but the terrorists were evidently in consultation and after a minute the phone in the house was slammed down.

'Well, at least we know the little old lady hasn't been hurt and by the sound of things the children are all right.'

The Superintendent crossed to a coffee-dispenser and poured himself a cup.

'Bit of a bore being called a pig all the time,' said the Major sympathetically. 'You'd think they could come up with something slightly more original.'

'Don't you believe it. They're on a marxist millennium ego-trip, kamikaze style, and what few brains they have they laundered years ago. That sounded like Chinanda, the Mexican.'

'Intonation and accent was right,' said the sergeant on the tape recorder.

'What's his record?' asked the Major.

'The usual. Rich parents, good education, flunked University and decided to save the world by knocking people off. To date, five. Specializes in car bombs, and crude ones at that. Not a very sophisticated laddie, our Miguel. Better get that tape through to the analysts. I want to hear their verdict on his stress pattern. And now we settle down to the long slog.'

'You expect him to call back with demands?'

'No. Next time we'll have the charming Fräulein Schautz. She's the one with the brains up top.'

It was an unintentionally apt description. Trapped in the

326

bathroom, Gudrun Schautz had spent much of the afternoon wondering what had happened and why no one had either killed her or come to arrest her. She had also considered methods of escape but was hampered by the lack of her clothes, which she had left in the bedsitter, and by Wilt's threat that if she made one more move he would fire. Not that she knew it was Wilt who had made it. What she had heard of his domestic life through the floor above his bedroom had done nothing to suggest he was capable of any sort of heroism. He was simply an effete, degenerate and cowardly little Englishman who was bullied by his stupid wife.

Fräulein Schautz might speak English fluently but her understanding of the English was hopelessly deficient. Given the chance Wilt would have agreed in large measure with this assessment of his character but he was too preoccupied to waste time on introspection. He was trying to guess what had happened downstairs during the shooting. He had no way of knowing if the quads were still in the house, and only the presence of armed men at the bottom of the garden and across the road in front of the house told him that the terrorists were still on the ground floor. From the balcony window he could look down at the summerhouse where he had spent so many idle evenings regretting his wasted gifts and longing for a woman who turned out in reality to be less a Muse than a private executioner. Now the summerhouse was occupied by men with guns while the field beyond was ringed with coils of barbed wire. The view from the skylight over the kitchen was even less encouraging. An armoured car had stationed itself outside the front gate with its gun turret turned towards the house, and there were more armed men in Professor Ball's garden.

Wilt climbed down and was wondering rather hysterically what the hell to do next when the telephone rang. He went into the main room and picked the extension up in time to hear Mrs de Frackas end her brief statement. Wilt listened to the tide of abuse wash over the uncomplaining Superintendent and felt briefly for the man. It sounded just like Bilger in one of his tirades, only this time the men downstairs had guns. They probably had the quads too. Wilt couldn't be certain but Mrs de Frackas' presence suggested as much. Wilt listened to see if his own name was mentioned and was relieved that it wasn't. When the one-sided conversation ended Wilt replaced his receiver very cautiously and with a slight feeling of optimism. It was very slight, a mere reaction from the tension and from a sudden sense of power. It wasn't the power of the gun but rather that of knowledge, what he knew and what nobody else apparently knew; that the attic was occupied by a man whose killing capacity was limited to flies and whose skill with firearms was less murderous than suicidal. About the only thing Wilt knew about machine guns and revolvers was that bullets came out the barrel when you pulled the trigger. But if he knew nothing about the workings of firearms the terrorists clearly had no idea what had happened in the attic. For all they knew the place was filled with armed policemen and the shots he had fired so accidentally could have killed Fräulein Bloody Schautz. If that were the case they would make no attempt to rescue her. Anyway, the illusion that the flat was held by desperate men who could kill without a moment's hesitation seemed definitely worth maintaining. He was just congratulating himself when the opposite thought occurred to him. What the hell would happen if they *did* discover he was up there?

Wilt slumped into a chair and considered this frightful possibility. If the quads were downstairs . . . Oh God . . . and all it needed was that blasted Superintendent to get on the phone and ask if Mr Wilt was all right. The mere mention of his name would be enough. The moment the swine downstairs realized he was up there they would kill the children. And even if they didn't they would threaten to unless he came down, which was much the same thing. Wilt's only answer to such an ultimatum would be to threaten to kill the Schautz bitch if they touched the children. That would be no sort of threat. He was incapable of killing anyone and even if he were it wouldn't save the children. Lunatics who supposed that they were adding to the sum total of human happiness by kidnapping, torturing and killing politicians and businessmen and who, when cornered, sheltered behind women and children, wouldn't listen to reason. All they wanted was maximum publicity for their cause and the murder of the quads would guarantee they got it. And then there was the theory of terrorism. Wilt had heard Bilger expound it in the staff-room and had been sickened by it then. Now he was panic-stricken. There had to be something he could do.

328

Well, first he could get the rest of the guns out of the bag in the storeroom and try to find out how to use them. He got up and went through the kitchen to the cupboard door and dragged the bag down. Inside were two revolvers, an automatic, four spare magazines for the sub-machine gun, several boxes of ammunition and three hand grenades. Wilt put the collection on the table, decided he didn't like the look of the hand grenades and put them back in the bag. It was then that he spotted a scrap of paper in the side pocket of the bag. He pulled it out and saw that he was holding what purported to be a COMMUNIQUE OF THE PEOPLE'S ARMY GROUP 4. That at least was the title but the space underneath was blank. Evidently no one had bothered to fill in the details. Probably nothing to communicate.

All the same it was interesting, very interesting. If this bunch were Group 4 it suggested that Groups 1, 2 and 3 were somewhere else and that there were possibly Groups 5, 6 and 7. Even more perhaps. On the other hand there might not be. The tactics of self-aggrandizement were not lost on Wilt. It was typical of tiny minorities to claim they were part of a much larger organization. It boosted their morale and helped to confuse the authorities. Then again it was just possible that a great many other groups did exist. How many? Ten, twenty? And with this sort of cell structure, one group would not know the members of another group. That was the whole point about cells. If one was captured and questioned there was no way of betraying anyone else. And with this realization Wilt lost interest in the arsenal on the table. There were more effective weapons than guns.

Wilt took out a pen and began to write. Presently he closed the kitchen door and picked up the phone.

Chapter 13

Superintendent Misterson was enjoying a moment of quiet and comfortable relaxation on the mahogany seat of Mrs de Frackas' toilet when the telephone rang in the drawing-room and the sergeant came through to say that the terrorists were back on the line.

'Well, that's a good sign,' said the Superintendent, emerging hurriedly. 'They don't usually start the dialogue quite so quickly. With any luck we'll get them to listen to reason.'

But his illusions on that score were quickly dispersed. The squawk that issued from the amplifier was strange in the extreme. Even the Major's face, usually a blank mask of calculated inanity, registered bewilderment. Made weirdly falsetto by fear and guttural by the need to sound foreign, and preferably German, Wilt's voice alternately whimpered and snarled a series of extraordinary demands.

'Zis is communiqué Number Vun of ze People's Alternative Army. Ve demand ze immediate release of all comrades held illegally in British prisons vizout trial. You understand?'

'No,' said the Superintendent, 'I certainly don't.'

'Fascistic schweinfleisch,' shouted Wilt. 'Zecond, ve demand . . .'

'Now hold on,' said the Superintendent, 'we don't have any of your . . . er . . . comrades in prison. We can't possibly meet your . . .'

'Lying pigdog,' yelled Wilt, 'Günther Jong, Erica Grass, Friederich Böll, Heinrich Musil to namen eine few. All in British prisons. You release wizin funf hours. Zecond, ve demand ze immediate haltings of all false reportings on television, transistor radios und der newspapers financed by capitalistic-militarische-liberalistic-pseudo-democratische-multi-nazionalistische und finanzialistische conspirationialistische about our fightings here for freedom, ja. Dritte, ve demand ze immediate withdrawal of alles militaristic truppen aus der garden unter den linden und die strasse Villington Road.

Vierte, ve demand ze safe conduct for ze People's Alternative Army cadres and ze exposing of ze deviationist and reformist class treachery of ze C.I.A.-Zionist-nihilistische murderers naming zemselves falsely People's Army Group Four who are threatening ze lives of women and children in ze propaganda attempt to deceive ze proletarian consciousness for ze true liberationist struggle for world freedom. End of communiqué.'

The line went dead.

'What the fuck was all that about?' asked the Major.

'I'm buggered if I know,' said the Superintendent with a glazed look in his eyes. 'Something's definitely screwy. If my ears and that sod's ghastly accent didn't deceive me he seemed to think Chinanda and the Schautz crowd are CIA agents working for Israel. Isn't that what he seemed to be saying?'

'It's what he said, sir,' said the sergeant. 'People's Army Group Four are the Schautz brigade and this bloke was blasting off at them. Could be we've got a splinter group in the People's Alternative Army.'

'Could be we've got a raving nut,' said the Superintendent. 'Are you positive that little lot came from the house?'

'Can't have come from anywhere else, sir. There's only one line in and we're hooked to it.'

'Somebody's got their wires crossed if you ask me,' said the Major, 'unless the Schautz crowd have come up with something new.'

'It's certainly new for a terrorist group to demand no TV or press coverage. That's one thing I do know,' muttered the Superintendent. 'What I don't know is where the hell he got that list of prisoners we're supposed to release. To the best of my knowledge we're not holding anyone called Günther Jong.'

'Might be worth checking that out, old boy. Some of these things are kept hush-hush.'

'If it's that top secret I can't see the Home Office blurting the fact out now. Anyway, let's hear that gobbledygook again.'

But for once the sophisticated electronic equipment failed them.

'I can't think what's wrong with the recorder, sir,' said the sergeant, 'I could have sworn I had it on.'

'Probably blew a fuse when that maniac came on the line,' said the Major, 'I know I damned near did.'

'Well, see the bloody thing works next time,' snapped the Superintendent, 'I want to get a voiceprint of this other bunch.' He poured himself another cup of coffee and sat waiting.

If there was confusion among the Anti-Terrorist Squad and the S.G.S. following Wilt's extraordinary intervention, there was chaos in the house. On the ground floor Chinanda and Baggish had barricaded themselves into the kitchen and the front hall while the children and Mrs de Frackas had been bundled down into the cellar. The telephone in the kitchen was on the floor out of the line of fire and it had been Baggish who had picked it up and listened to the first part. Alarmed by the look on Baggish's face, Chinanda had grabbed the receiver and had heard himself described as an Israeli nihilistic murderer working for the C.I.A. in a propaganda attempt to deceive proletarian consciousness.

'It's a lie,' he shouted at Baggish who was still trying to square a demand by the People's Alternative Army for the release of comrades held in British prisons with his previous belief that the attic flat was occupied by men from the Anti-Terrorist Squad.

'How do you mean a lie?'

'What they say. That we are C.I.A.-Zionists.'

'A lie?' yelled Baggish, desperately searching for a more extreme word to describe such a gross distortion of the truth. 'It's . . . Who said that?'

'Someone saying he was the People's Alternative Army.'

'But the People's Alternative Army demanded the release of prisoners held illegally by the British imperialists.'

'They did?'

'I heard them. First they say that and then they attack the false reporting on TV and then they demand all troops to be withdrawn.'

'Then why call us C.I.A.-Zionist murderers?' demanded Chinanda. 'And where are these people?'

They looked suspiciously at the ceiling.

'They're up there, you think?' asked Baggish.

But, like the Superintendent, Chinanda didn't know what to think.

'Gudrun is up there. When we came down there was shooting.'

332

'So maybe Gudrun is dead,' said Baggish. 'Is a trick to fool us.'

'Could be,' said Chinanda, 'British intelligence is clever. They know how to use psycho-warfare.'

'So what we do now?'

'We make our own demands. We show them we are not fooled.'

'If I might just interrupt for a moment,' said Mrs de Frackas, emerging from the cellar, 'it's time I gave the quadruplets their supper.'

The two terrorists looked at her lividly. It was bad enough having the house ringed with troops and police, but when to add to their troubles they had to cope with incomprehensible demands from someone representing the People's Alternative Army and at the same time were confronted by Mrs de Frackas' imperturbable self-assurance, they felt the need to assert their superior authority.

'Listen, old woman,' said Chinanda waving an automatic under her nose for emphasis, 'we give the orders here and you do what we say. You don't we kill you.'

But Mrs de Frackas was not to be so easily deterred. Over a long lifetime in which she had been bullied by governesses, shot at by Afghans, bombed out of two houses in two World Wars and had had to face an exceedingly liverish husband across the breakfast table for several decades, she had developed a truly remarkable resilience and, more usefully, a diplomatic deafness.

'I'm sure you will,' she said cheerfully, 'and now I'll see where Mrs Wilt keeps the eggs. I always think that children can't have enough eggs, don't you? So good for the digestive system.' And ignoring the automatic she bustled about the kitchen peering into cupboards. Chinanda and Baggish conferred in undertones.

'I kill the old bitch now,' said Baggish. 'That way she learns we're not bluffing.'

'That way we don't get out of here. We keep her and the children we got a chance and we keep up the propaganda war.'

'Without TV we got no propaganda war to keep up,' said Baggish. 'That was one of the demands of People's Alternative Army. No TV, no radio, no newspapers.'

'So we demand the opposite, full publicity,' said Chinanda, and picked up the phone. Upstairs Wilt who had been lying on the floor with the telephone to his ear answered it.

'Zis is People's Alternative Army. Communiqué Two. Ve demand . . .'

'No you don't. We do the demanding,' shouted Chinanda, 'we know British psycho-warfare.'

'Zionist pigs. Ve know CIA murderers,' countered Wilt. 'Ve are fighting for ze liberation of all peoples.'

'We are fighting for the liberation of Palestine . . .'

'So are ve. All peoples ve fight for.'

'If you would kindly make up your minds who is fighting for what,' intervened the Superintendent, 'we might be able to talk more reasonably.'

'Fascist police pig,' bellowed Wilt. 'Ve no discuss viz you. Ve know who ve are dealing viz.'

'I wish to God I did,' said the Superintendent, only to be told by Chinanda that the People's Army Group was—

'Revisionistic-deviationist lumpen schwein,' interjected Wilt. 'Ze revolutionary army of ze people rejects ze fascistic holding of hostages und . . .' He was interrupted by bangs from the bathroom which tended to contradict his argument and gave Chinanda the opportunity to state his demands. They included five million pounds, a jumbo jet and the use of an armoured car to take them to the airport. Wilt, having shut the kitchen door to drown out Gudrun Schautz's activities, came back in time to up the ante.

'Six million pounds and two armoured cars . . .'

'You can make it a round ten million for all I care,' said the Superintendent, 'it won't make any difference. I'm not bargaining.'

'Seven million or we kill the hostages. You have till eight in the morning to agree or we die with the hostages,' shouted Chinanda, and slammed down the phone before Wilt could make a further bid. Wilt replaced his own receiver with a sigh and tried to think what on earth to do now. There was no doubt in his mind that the terrorists downstairs would carry out their threat unless the police gave way. And it was just as certain that the police had no intention of providing an armoured car or a jet. They would simply play for time in the hope of breaking the terrorists' morale. If they didn't succeed and the children died along with their captors it would hardly matter to the authorities. Public policy dictated that terrorists' demands must never be met. In the past Wilt had agreed. But now private policy dictated anything that would save his family. To reinforce the need for some new plan, Fräulein Schautz sounded as though she was ripping up the linoleum in the bathroom. For a moment Wilt considered threatening to fire through the doorway if she didn't stop, but decided against it. It was no damned use. He was incapable of killing anyone except by accident. There had to be some other way.

In the Communications Centre ideas were in short supply too. As the echo of the last conflicting demands died away the Superintendent shook his head wearily.

'I said this was a bag of maggots and by God it is. Will someone kindly tell me what the hell is going on in there?'

'No use looking at me, old boy,' said the Major, 'I'm simply here to hold the ring while you Anti-Terrorist chappies establish rapport with the blighters. That's the drill.'

'It may be the drill but considering we seem to be dealing with two competing sets of world-changers it's fucking near impossible. Isn't there some way we can get a separate line to each group?'

'Don't see how, sir,' said the sergeant. 'The People's Alternative Army seem to be using the extension phone from upstairs and the only way would be to get into the house.'

The Major studied Wilt's clumsy map. 'I could call a chopper up and land some of my lads on the roof to take the bastards out.'

Superintendent Misterson looked at him suspiciously. 'By "take out" I don't suppose you mean literally?'

'Literally? Oh, see what you mean. No. Doubt it. Bound to be a bit of schemozzle, what!'

'Which is precisely what we've got to avoid. Now, if someone can come up with a scheme whereby I can talk to one group without being drowned out by the other I'd be grateful.'

But instead there was a buzz on the intercom. The sergeant listened and then spoke. 'The psychos and the idiot brigade on the line, sir. Want to know if it's OK to move in.'

335

'I suppose so,' said the Superintendent.

'Idiot brigade?' said the Major.

'Ideological Warfare Analysis and the Psychological Advisers. Home Office insists we use them and sometimes they come up with a sensible suggestion.'

'Christ,' said the Major. 'Damned if I know what the world is coming to. First they call the army a peace-keeping force and now Scotland Yard has to have psychoanalysts to do their sleuthing for them. Rum.'

'The People's Alternative Army are back on the line,' said the sergeant. Once more a barrage of abuse issued from the telephone amplifier but this time Wilt had changed his tactics. His guttural German had been doing things to his vocal cords and his new accent was a less demanding but equally less convincing Irish brogue.

'Bejasus it will be nobody's fault but your own if we have to shoot the poor innocent creature Irmgard Mueller herself before eight in the morning if the wee babies are not returned to their mam, look you.'

'What?' said the Superintendent baffled by this new threat.

'I wouldn't want to be repeating meself for the likes of reactionary pigs like yourself but if you're deaf I'll say it again.'

'Don't,' said the Superintendent firmly, 'We got the message first time.'

'Well I'll be hoping those Zionist spalpeens will have got the message too begorrah.'

A muffled flow of Spanish seemed to indicate that Chinanda had heard.

'Well then that'll be all. I wouldn't want to be running up too big a telephone bill now would I?' And Wilt slammed the phone down. It was left to the Superintendent to interpret this ultimatum to Chinanda as best he could, a difficult process made almost impossible by the terrorist's insistence that the People's Alternative Army was a gang of fascist police pigs under the Superintendent's command.

'We know you British use psychological warfare. You are experts,' he shouted, 'we are not to be so easily deceived.'

'But I assure you, Miguel . . .'

'Don't try bluffing me by calling me Miguel so I think you

336

are my friend. We understand your tactics. First you threaten and then you keep us talking . . .'

'Well as a matter of fact I'm not keeping . . .'

'Shut your mouth, pig. I'm doing the talking now.'

'That's all I was going to say,' protested the Superintendent. 'But I want you to know there are no police . . .'

'Bullshit. You tried to trap us and now you threaten to kill Gudrun. Right, we do not respond to your threats. You kill Gudrun, we kill the hostages.'

'I'm not in a position to stop whoever is holding Fräulein Schautz . . .'

'You keep trying the bluff but it doesn't work. We know how clever you British imperialists are.' And Chinanda too slammed the phone down.

'I must say he seems to have a rather higher opinion of the British Empire than I have,' said the Major. 'I mean I can't actually see where we've got one, unless you count Gibraltar.'

But the Superintendent was in no mood to discuss the extent of the Empire. 'There's something demented about this bloody siege,' he muttered. 'First we need to get a separate telephone link through to the lunatics in that top flat. That's number one priority. If they shoot . . . What on earth did he call the Schautz woman, sergeant?'

'I think the expression was "the poor innocent creature Irmgard Mueller", sir? Do you want me to play the tape back?'

'No,' said the Superintendent, 'we'll wait for the analysts. In the meantime request use of helicopter to drop a field telephone onto the balcony of the flat. That way we'll at least get some idea who's up there.'

'Field telephone incorporating TV camera, sir?' asked the sergeant.

The Superintendent nodded. 'Second priority is to move the listening devices into position.'

'Can't do that until it gets dark,' said the Major. 'Not having my chaps shot down unless they're allowed to shoot back.'

'Well, we'll just have to wait,' said the Superintendent. 'That's always the way with these beastly sieges. Just a question of sitting and waiting. Though I must say this is the first time I've had to deal with two lots of terrorists at once.'

'Makes you feel sorry for those poor children,' said the Major. 'What they must be going through doesn't bear thinking about.'

Chapter 14

But for once his sympathy was wasted. The quads were having a wonderful time. After the initial excitement of windows being shattered by bullets and the terrorists firing from the kitchen and the front hall, they had been bundled down into the cellar with Mrs de Frackas. Since the old lady refused to be flustered and seemed to regard the events upstairs as perfectly normal, the quads had taken the same attitude. Besides the cellar was usually forbidden territory, Wilt objecting to their visiting it on the ostensible grounds that the Organic Toilet was insanitary and dangerously explosive, while Eva barred the quads because she kept her stock of preserved fruit down there and the chest freezer was filled with homemade ice cream. The quads had made a bee-line for the ice cream and had finished a large carton before Mrs de Frackas' eyes had got accustomed to the dim light. By then the quads had found other interesting things to occupy their attention. A large coal bunker and a pile of logs gave them the opportunity to get thoroughly filthy. Eva's store of organically grown apples provided them with a second course after the ice cream, and they would undoubtedly have drunk themselves into a stupor on Wilt's homebrew if Mrs de Frackas hadn't put her foot down on a broken bottle first.

'You're not to go into that part of the cellar,' she said looking severely at the evidence of Wilt's inexpert brewing in the shape of several exploded bottles. 'It isn't safe.'

'Then why does daddy drink it?' asked Penelope.

'When you get a little older you'll learn that men do a great many things that aren't very sensible or safe,' said Mrs de Frackas.

'Like wearing a bag on the end of their wigwags?' asked Josephine.

'Well I wouldn't quite know about that, dear,' said Mrs de Frackas evidently torn between curiosity and a desire not to enquire too closely into the Wilts' private life.

'Mummy said the doctor made him wear it,' continued

Josephine adding an unmentionable disease to the old lady's dossier of Wilt's faults.

'And I stepped on it and daddy screamed,' said Emmeline proudly. 'He screamed ever so loudly.'

'I'm sure he did, dear,' said Mrs de Frackas, trying to imagine the reaction of her late and liverish husband had any child been so unwise as to step on his penis. 'Now let's talk about something nice.'

The distinction was wasted on the quads. 'When daddy comes home from the doctor mummy says his wigwag will be better and he won't say "Fuck" when he goes weewee.'

'Say what, dear?' asked Mrs de Frackas, adjusting her hearing aid in the hope that it rather than Samantha had been at fault. The quads in unison disillusioned her.

'Fuck, fuck, fuck,' they squealed. Mrs de Frackas turned her hearing aid down.

'Well, really,' she said, 'I don't think you should use that word.'

'Mummy says we mustn't too but Michael's daddy told him . . .'

'I don't want to hear,' said Mrs de Frackas hastily. 'In my young days children didn't talk about such things.'

'How did babies get born then?' asked Penelope.

'In the usual way, dear, only we were brought up not to mention such things.'

'What things?' demanded Penelope.

Mrs de Frackas regarded her dubiously. It was beginning to dawn on her that the Wilt quads were not quite such nice children as she had supposed. In fact they were distinctly unnerving. 'Just things,' she said finally.

'Like cocks and cunts?' asked Emmeline.

Mrs de Frackas eyed her with disgust. 'You could put it like that, I suppose,' she said stiffly. 'Though frankly I'd prefer it if you didn't.'

'If you don't put it like that how do you put it?' asked the indefatigable Penelope.

Mrs de Frackas searched her mind in vain for an alternative. 'I don't quite know,' she said, surprised at her own ignorance. 'I suppose the matter never arose.'

'Daddy's does,' said Josephine, 'I saw it once.'

340

Mrs de Frackas turned her disgusted attention on the child and tried to stifle her own curiosity. 'You did?' she said involuntarily.

'He was in the bathroom with mummy and I looked through the keyhole and daddy's . . .'

'It's time you had baths too,' said Mrs de Frackas, getting to her feet before Josephine could divulge any further details of the Wilts' sexual life.

'We haven't had supper yet,' said Samantha.

'Then I'll get you some,' said Mrs de Frackas and went up the cellar steps to hunt for eggs. By the time she returned with a tray the quads were no longer hungry. They had finished a jar of pickled onions and were halfway through their second packet of dried figs.

'You've still got to have scrambled eggs,' said the old lady resolutely. 'I didn't go to the trouble of making them to have them wasted, you know.'

'You didn't make them,' said Penelope. 'Mummy hens made them.'

'And daddy hens are called cocks,' squealed Josephine but Mrs de Frackas, having just outfaced two armed bandits, was in no mood to be defied by four foul-minded girls.

'We won't discuss that any further, thank you,' she said, 'I've had quite enough.'

It was shortly apparent that the quads had too. As she shooed them up the cellar steps Emmeline was complaining that her tummy hurt.

'It will soon stop, dear,' said Mrs de Frackas, 'and it doesn't help to hiccup like that.'

'Not hiccuping,' retorted Emmeline, and promptly vomited on the kitchen floor. Mrs de Frackas looked around in the semi-darkness for the light switch and had just found it and turned it on when Chinanda cannoned into her and switched it off.

'What are you trying to do? Get us all killed?' he yelled.

'Not all of us,' said Mrs de Frackas, 'and if you don't look where you're going . . .'

A crash as the terrorist slid across the kitchen floor on a mixture of half-digested pickled onions and dried figs indicated that Chinanda hadn't.

'It's no use blaming me,' said Mrs de Frackas, 'and you shouldn't use language like that in front of children. It sets a very bad example.'

'I set an example all right,' shouted Chinanda, 'I spill your guts.'

'I rather think somebody is doing that already,' retorted the old lady as the other three quads, evidently sharing Emmeline's inability to cope with quite so eclectic a diet, followed her example. Presently the kitchen was filled with four howling and vomit-stained small girls, a very unappetizing smell, two demented terrorists and Mrs de Frackas at her most imperious. To add to the confusion Baggish had deserted his post in the front hall and had dashed in threatening to kill the first person who moved.

'I have no intention of moving,' said Mrs de Frackas, 'and since the only person who is happens to be that creature grovelling in the corner I suggest you put him out of his misery.'

From the direction of the sink Chinanda could be heard disentangling himself from Eva's Kenwood mixer which had joined him on the floor.

Mrs de Frackas turned the light on again. This time no one objected, Chinanda because he had been momentarily stunned and Baggish because he was too dismayed by the state of the kitchen.

'And now,' said the old lady, 'if you've quite finished I'll take the children up for their bath before putting them to bed.'

'Bed?' yelled Chinanda getting unsteadily to his feet. 'Nobody goes upstairs. You all sleep down in the cellar. Go down there now.'

'If you really suppose for one moment that I am going to allow these poor children to go down that cellar again in their present condition and without being thoroughly washed you're very much mistaken.'

Chinanda jerked the cord on the venetian blind and cut out the view from the garden.

'Then you wash them in here,' he said pointing to the sink.

'And where do you propose to be?'

'Where we can see what you are doing.'

Mrs de Frackas snorted derisively. 'I know your sort, and if you think I am going to expose their pure little bodies to your lascivious gaze . . .'

'What the hell is she saying?' demanded Baggish.

Mrs de Frackas turned her contempt on him. 'And yours too, don't I just. I haven't been through the Suez Canal and Port Said for nothing you know.'

Baggish stared at her. 'Port Said? The Suez Canal? I never been to Egypt in my life.'

'Well I have. And I know what I know.'

'So what are we talking about? You know what you know. I don't know what you know.'

'Postcards,' said Mrs de Frackas. 'I don't think I need say any more.'

'You haven't said anything yet. First the Suez Canal, then Port Said and now postcards. Will someone tell me what the hell these things have to do with washing children?'

'Well if you must know, I mean dirty postcards. I might also mention donkeys but I won't. And now if you'll both leave the room . . .'

But the implications of Mrs de Frackas' imperial prejudices had slowly dawned on Baggish.

'You mean pornography? What century you think you're living in? You want pornography you go to London. Soho is full—'

'I don't want pornography and I don't intend to discuss the matter further.'

'Then you go down the cellar before I kill you,' yelled the enraged Baggish. But Mrs de Frackas was too old to be persuaded by mere threats and it took bodily pressure to shove her through the cellar door with the quads. As they went down the steps Emmeline could be heard asking why the nasty man didn't like donkeys.

'I tell you the English are mad,' said Baggish. 'Why did we have to choose this crazy house?'

'It chose us,' said Chinanda miserably, and switched out the light.

But if Mrs de Frackas had decided to ignore the fact that her life was in danger, upstairs in the flat Wilt was now acutely aware that his previous tactics had backfired on him. To have

343

invented the People's Alternative Army had served to confuse things for a while, but his threat to execute, or more accurately to murder Gudrun Schautz had been a terrific mistake. It put a time limit on his bluff. Looking back over forty years Wilt's record of violence was limited to the occasional and usually unsuccessful bout with flies and mosquitoes. No, to have issued that ultimatum had been almost as stupid as not getting out of the house when the going was good. Now it was distinctly bad, and the sounds coming from the bathroom suggested that Gudrun Schautz had torn up the lino and was busy on the floorboards. If she escaped and joined the men below she would add an intellectual fervour to their evidently stupid fanaticism. On the other hand he could think of no way of stopping her short of threatening to fire through the bathroom door, and if that didn't work . . . There had to be an alternative method. What if he opened the door himself and somehow persuaded her that it wasn't safe to go downstairs? In that way he could keep the two groups separate and provided they couldn't communicate with one another Fräulein Schautz would be hard put to it to influence her blood-brothers down below. Well, that was easy enough to do.

Wilt crossed to the telephone and jerked the cord from the wall. So far so good but there was still the little matter of the guns. The notion of sharing the flat with a woman who had cold-bloodedly murdered eight people was not an attractive one in any circumstances, but when that flat contained enough firearms to eliminate several hundred it became positively suicidal. The guns would have to go too. But where? He could hardly drop the damned things out of the window. The effect of a shower of revolvers, grenades and a sub-machine gun on the terrorists was likely to encourage them to come up and find out what the hell was going on. Anyway, the grenades might go off and there were enough misunderstandings floating around already without adding exploding grenades. The best thing would be to hide them. Very gingerly Wilt put his armoury back into the flight bag and went through the kitchen to the attic space. Gudrun Schautz was now definitely busy on the floorboards and under cover of the noise Wilt climbed up and edged his way along to the water cistern. There he lowered the bag into the water before replacing the cover. Then, having checked

344

to make quite sure that he hadn't missed a gun, he steeled himself for the next move. It was, he considered, about as safe as opening the cage of a tiger at the zoo and inviting the thing to come out, but it had to be done and in an insane situation only an act of total lunacy could save the children. Wilt went through the kitchen to the bathroom door.

'Irmgard,' he whispered. Miss Schautz went on with her work of demolishing the bathroom floor. Wilt took another deep breath and whispered more loudly. Inside work ceased and there was silence.

'Irmgard,' said Wilt, 'is that you?'

There was a movement and then a quiet voice spoke. 'Who is there?'

'It's me,' said Wilt, sticking to the obvious and wishing to hell it wasn't, 'Henry Wilt.'

'Henry Wilt?'

'Yes. They've gone.'

'Who have gone?'

'I don't know. Whoever they were. You can come out now.'

'Come out?' asked Gudrun Schautz in a tone of voice that suggested the total bewilderment Wilt wanted.

'I'll undo the door.'

Wilt began to remove the flex from the doorhandle. It was difficult in the growing darkness but after several minutes he had undone the wire and removed the chair.

'It's OK now,' he said. 'You can come out.'

But Gudrun Schautz made no move. 'How do I know it's you?' she asked.

'I don't know,' said Wilt, glad of this opportunity to delay matters, 'it just is.'

'Who is with you?'

'No one. They've gone downstairs.'

'You keep saying "They". Who are these "They"?'

'I've no idea. Men with guns. The whole house is filled with men with guns.'

'So why are you here?' asked Miss Schautz.

'Because I can't be somewhere else,' said Wilt truthfully. 'You don't think I want to be here? They've been shooting at one another. I could have been killed. I don't know what the hell's going on.'

There was a silence from the bathroom. Gudrun Schautz was having difficulty working out what was going on too. In the darkness of the kitchen Wilt smiled to himself. Keep this up and he'd have the bitch bombed out of her mind.

'And no one is with you?' she asked.

'Of course not.'

'Then how did you know I was in the bathroom?'

'I heard you having a bath,' said Wilt, 'and then all these people started shouting and shooting and . . .'

'Where were you?'

'Look,' said Wilt deciding to change his tactics, 'I don't see why you keep asking me these questions. I mean I've taken the trouble to come up here and undo the door and you won't come out and you keep on about who they are and where I was and all that as if I knew. As a matter of fact I was having a nap in the bedroom and . . .'

'A nap? What is a nap?'

'A nap? Oh, a nap. Well it's a sort of after-lunch snooze. Sleep, you know. Anyway when all the hullabaloo started, the shooting and so on, and I heard you shout "Get the children," and I thought how jolly kind of you that was . . .'

'Kind of me? You thought that kind of me?' asked Miss Schautz with a distinctly strangulated disbelief.

'I mean putting the children first instead of your own safety. Most people wouldn't have thought of saving the children, would they?'

A gurgling noise from the bathroom indicated that Gudrun Schautz hadn't thought of this interpretation of her orders and was having to make readjustments in her attitude to Wilt's intelligence.

'No, that is so,' she said finally.

'Well naturally after that I couldn't leave you locked up here, could I?' continued Wilt, realizing that talking like some idiotic chinless wonder had its advantages. 'Noblesse oblige and all that, what!'

'Noblesse oblige?'

'You know, one good turn deserves another and whatnot,' said Wilt. 'So as soon as the coast was clear I sort of came out from under the bed and hopped up here.'

'What coast?' demanded Miss Schautz suspiciously.

346

'When the blighters up here decided to go downstairs,' said Wilt. 'Seemed the safest place to be. Anyway, why don't you come out and have a chair. It must be jolly uncomfortable in there.'

Miss Schautz considered this proposition and the fact that Wilt sounded like a congenital idiot and took the risk.

'I haven't any clothes on,' she said opening the door an inch.

'Gosh,' said Wilt, 'I'm awfully sorry. Hadn't thought of that. I'll go and get you something.'

He went into the bedroom and rummaged in a cupboard and having found what felt like a raincoat in the darkness took it back.

'Here's a coat,' he said handing it through the doorway. 'Don't like to turn the bedroom light on in case those blokes downstairs see it and start pooping off again with their guns. Mind you I've locked the door and barricaded it so they'd have a job getting in.'

In the bathroom Miss Schautz put on the raincoat and cautiously came out to find Wilt pouring boiling water from the electric kettle into a teapot.

'Thought you'd like a nice cup of tea,' he said. 'Know I would.'

Behind him Gudrun Schautz tried to comprehend what had happened. From the moment she had been locked in the bathroom she had been convinced that the flat was occupied by policemen. Now it seemed whoever had been there had gone and this weak and stupid Englishman was making tea as if nothing was wrong. Wilt's admission that he had spent the afternoon cowering under the bed in the room below had been convincingly ignominious and had helped to confirm the impression she had gathered from his previous nocturnal exchanges with Frau Wilt that he was no sort of threat. On the other hand she had to find out how much he knew.

'These men with guns,' she said, 'what sort of men are they?'

'Well I wasn't really in a very good position to see them,' said Wilt, 'being under the bed and so on. Some of them were wearing boots and some weren't, if you see what I mean.'

Gudrun Schautz didn't. 'Boots?'

'Not shoes. Do you take sugar, by the way?'

'No.'

'Very wise,' said Wilt, 'awfully bad for the teeth. Anyway here's your cup. Oh I am sorry. Here, let me get a cloth and wipe you down.'

And in the close confines of the little kitchen Wilt groped for a cloth and presently was mopping Gudrun Schautz's coat down where he had deliberately spilt the tea.

'You can stop now,' she said as Wilt transferred the attentions of the towel from her breasts to lower areas.

'Righto, and I'll pour another cup.'

She squeezed past him into the bedroom while Wilt considered what other domestic accidents he could provoke to distract her attention. There was always sex, of course, but in the circumstances it hardly seemed likely that the bitch would be particularly interested in it and, even if she were, the notion of making love with a professional murderess would make arousal extremely difficult. Whisky droop was bad enough, terror droop was infinitely worse. Still, flattery might help, and she certainly had nice boobs. Wilt took another cup of tea through to the bedroom and found her looking out of the balcony window into the garden.

'I shouldn't go over there,' he said, 'there are more maniacs outside with Donald Duck shirts on.'

'Donald Duck shirts?'

'And guns,' said Wilt. 'If you ask me the whole bloody place has gone loony.'

'And have you no idea what is happening?'

'Well I heard somebody shouting about Israelis, but it doesn't seem likely somehow, does it? I mean what on earth would Israelis want to come swarming all over Willington Road for?'

'Oh my God,' said Gudrun Schautz. 'So what do we do?'

'Do?' said Wilt. 'I don't see there is much we can do really. Except drink our tea and make ourselves inconspicuous. It's all probably some ghastly mistake or other. I can't think what else it can be, can you?'

Gudrun Schautz could, and did, but to admit it to this idiot before she had the power to terrify him into doing what she wanted didn't seem a good idea. She headed for the kitchen and began to climb into the attic space. Wilt followed, sipping his tea. 'Of course I did try phoning the police,' he said, dropping his chin even more gormlessly.

Miss Schautz stopped in her tracks. 'The police? You phoned the police?'

'Couldn't actually,' said Wilt, 'some blighter had pulled the phone out of the wall. Can't think why. I mean with all that shooting going on . . .'

But Gudrun Schautz was no longer listening. She was clambering along the plank towards the luggage and Wilt could hear her rummaging among the suitcases. So long as the bitch didn't look in the water tank. To distract her attention Wilt poked his head through the door and switched off the light.

'Better not show a light,' he explained as she stumbled about in the pitch darkness cursing, 'don't want anyone to know we're up here. Best just to lie low until they go away.'

A stream of incomprehensible but evidently malevolent German greeted this suggestion, and after fruitlessly groping about for the bag for several more minutes Gudrun Schautz climbed down into the kitchen, breathing heavily.

Wilt decided to strike again. 'No need to be so upset, my dear. After all, this is England and nothing nasty can happen to you here.'

He placed a comforting arm round her shoulders. 'And anyway you've got me to look after you. Nothing to worry about.'

'Oh my God,' she said and suddenly began to shake with silent laughter. The thought that she had only this weak and stupid little coward to look after her was too much for the murderess. Nothing to worry about! The phrase suddenly took on a new and horribly inverted meaning and like a revelation she saw its truth, a truth she had been fighting against all her life. The only thing she had to worry about was nothing. Gudrun Schautz looked into oblivion, an infinity of nothingness and was filled with terror. With a desperate need to escape the vision she clung to Wilt and her raincoat hung open.

'I say . . .' Wilt began, realizing this new threat but Gudrun Schautz's mouth closed over his, her tongue flickering, while her hand dragged his fingers up to a breast. The creature who had brought only death into the world was now turning in her panic to the most ancient instinct of all.

Chapter 15

Gudrun Schautz was not the only person in Ipford to look oblivion in the face. The manager of Wilt's bank had spent an exceedingly disturbing afternoon with Inspector Flint who kept assuring him that it was of national importance that he shouldn't phone his wife to cancel their dinner engagement and refusing to allow him to communicate with his staff and several clients who had made appointments to see him. The manager had found these aspersions on his discretion insulting and Flint's presence positively lethal to his reputation for financial probity.

'What the hell do you imagine the staff are thinking with three damned policemen closeted in my office all day?' he demanded, dropping the diplomatic language of banking for more earthy forms of address. He had been particularly put out by having to choose between urinating in a bucket procured from the care-taker or suffer the indignity of being accompanied by a police-man every time he went to the toilet.

'If a man can't pee in his own bank without having some bloody gendarme breathing down his neck all I can say is that things have come to a pretty pass.'

'Very aptly put, sir,' said Flint, 'but I'm only acting under orders and if the Anti-Terrorist Squad say a thing's in the national interest then it is.'

'I can't see how it's in the national interest to stop me relieving myself in private,' said the manager. 'I shall see that a complaint goes to the Home Office.'

'You do that small thing,' said Flint, who had his own reasons for feeling disgruntled. The intrusion of the Anti-Terrorist Squad into his patch had undermined his authority. The fact that Wilt was responsible only maddened him still further and he was just speculating on Wilt's capacity for disrupting his life when the phone rang.

'I'll take it if you don't mind,' he said and lifted the receiver.

'Mr Fildroyd of Central Investment on the line, sir,' said the telephonist.

350

Flint looked at the bank manager. 'Some bloke called Fildroyd. Know anyone of that name?'

'Fildroyd? Of course I do.'

'Is he to be trusted?'

'Good Lord, man, Fildroyd to be trusted? He's in charge of the entire bank's investment policy.'

'Stocks and shares, eh?' asked Flint who had once had a little flutter in Australian bauxite and wasn't likely to forget the experience. 'In that case I wouldn't trust him further than I could throw him.'

He relayed this opinion in only slightly less offensive terms to the girl on the switchboard. A distant rumble suggested that Mr Fildroyd was on the line.

'Mr Fildroyd wants to know who's speaking,' said the girl.

'Well you just tell Mr Fildroyd that it's Inspector Flint of the Fenland Constabulary and if he knows what's good for him he'll keep his trap shut.'

He put the phone down and turned to the manager who was looking distinctly seedy. 'What's the matter with you?' Flint asked.

'Matter? Nothing, nothing at all. Only that you've just led the entire Central Investment Division to suppose I'm suspected of some serious crime.'

'Landing me with Mr Henry Wilt is a serious crime,' said Flint bitterly, 'and if you want my opinion this whole thing's a put-up job on Wilt's part to get himself another slice of publicity.'

'As I understood it Mr Wilt was the innocent victim of—'

'Innocent victim my foot. The day that sod's innocent I'll stop being a copper and take holy fucking orders.'

'Charming way of expressing yourself, I must say,' said the bank manager.

But Flint was too engrossed in a private line of speculation to note the sarcasm. He was recalling those hideous days and nights during which he and Wilt had been engaged in a dialogue on the subject of Mrs Wilt's disappearance. There were still dark hours before dawn when Flint would wake sweating at the memory of Wilt's extraordinary behaviour and swearing that one day he would catch the little sod out in a serious crime. And today had seemed the ideal opportunity, or would have done if the Anti-Terrorist Squad hadn't intervened. Well, at least they were having to cope with the situation but if Flint had had his way he would have discounted all that talk about German au pairs as so much hogwash and remanded Wilt in custody on a charge of being in possession of stolen money, never mind where he said he had got it from.

But when at five he left the bank and returned to the police station it was to discover that Wilt's account seemed yet again to correspond, however implausibly, with the facts.

'A siege?' he said to the desk sergeant. 'A siege at Willington Road? At Wilt's house?'

'Proof of the pudding's in there, sir,' said the sergeant indicating an office. Flint crossed to the window and glanced in.

Like some monolith to maternity Eva Wilt sat motionless on a chair staring into space, her mind evidently absent and with her children in the house in Willington Road. Flint turned away and for the umpteenth time wondered what it was about this woman and her apparently insignificant husband that had brought them together and by some strange fusion of incompatibility had turned them into a catalyst for disaster. It was a recurring enigma, this marriage between a woman whom Wilt had once described as a centrifugal force and a man whose imagination fostered bestial fantasies involving murder, rape, and those bizarre dreams that had come to light during the hours of his interrogation. Since Flint's own marriage was as conventionally happy as he could wish, the Wilts' was less a marriage in his eyes than some rather sinister symbiotic arrangement of almost vegetable origin, like mistletoe growing on an oak tree. There was certainly a vegetable-looking quality about Mrs Wilt sitting there in silence in the office and Inspector Flint shook his head sadly.

'Poor woman's in shock,' he said, and hurried away to discover for himself what was actually happening at Willington Road.

But as usual his diagnosis was wrong. Eva was not in a state of shock. She had long since realized that it was pointless telling the policewomen who were sitting with her that she wanted to go home, and now her mind was calmly and rather menacingly working on practical things. Out there in the gathering darkness

352

her children were at the mercy of murderers and Henry was probably dead. Nothing was going to stop her from joining the quads and saving them. Beyond that goal she had not looked, but a brooding violence seeped through her.

'Perhaps you would like some friend to come and sit with you,' one of the policewomen suggested. 'Or we could come with you to a friend's house.'

But Eva shook her head. She didn't want sympathy. She had her own reserves of strength to cope with her misery. In the end a social worker arrived from the welfare hostel.

'We've got a nice warm room for you,' she said with an extruded cheerfulness that had served in the past to irritate a number of battered wives, 'and you needn't worry about nighties and toothbrushes and things like that. Everything you want will be provided for you.'

'It won't,' thought Eva but she thanked the policewomen and followed the social worker out to her car and sat docilely beside her as they drove away. And all the time the woman chattered on, asking questions about the quads and how old they were and saying how difficult it must be bringing up four girls at the same time as if the continually repeated assumption that nothing extraordinary had happened would somehow re-create the happy, humdrum world Eva had seen disintegrate round her that afternoon. Eva hardly heard her. The trite words were so grotesquely at odds with the instincts moving within her that they merely added anger to her terrible resolve. No silly woman who didn't have children could know what it meant to have them threatened and she wasn't going to be lulled into a passive acceptance of the situation.

At the corner of Dill Road and Persimmon Street she caught sight of a billboard outside a newsagent's shop. TERRORIST SIEGE LATEST.

'I want a newspaper,' said Eva abruptly and the woman pulled to the kerb.

'It won't tell you anything you don't know already,' she said.

'I know that. I just want to see what they're saying,' said Eva and opened the door of the car. But the woman stopped her.

'You just sit here and I'll get one for you. Would you like a magazine too?'

'Just the paper.'

And with the sad thought that even in terrible tragedies some people found solace by seeing their names in print the social worker crossed the pavement to the shop and went in. Three minutes later she came out and had opened the car door before she realized that the seat beside her was empty. Eva Wilt had disappeared into the night.

By the time Inspector Flint had made his way past the road blocks in Farringdon Avenue and with the help of an S.G.S. man had clambered across several gardens to the Communications Centre he had begun to have doubts about his theory that the whole business was yet another hoax on Wilt's part. If it was it had gone too far this time. The armoured car in the road and the spotlights that had been set up round Number 9 indicated how seriously the Anti-Terrorist Squad and Special Ground Services were taking the siege. In the conservatory at the back of Mrs de Frackas' house men were assembling strange looking equipment.

'Parabolic listening devices. P.L.D.s for short,' explained a technician. 'Once we've installed them we'll be able to hear a cockroach fart in any room in the house.'

'Really? I had no idea cockroaches farted,' said Flint. 'One lives and learns.'

'We'll learn what those bastards are saying and just where they are.'

Flint went through the conservatory into the drawing-room and found the Superintendent and the Major listening to the adviser on International Terrorist Ideology who was discussing the tapes.

'If you want my opinion,' said Professor Maerlis gratuitously, 'I would have to say that the People's Alternative Army represents a sub-faction or splinter group of the original cadre known as the People's Army Group. I think I would go so far.'

Flint took a seat in a corner and was pleased to note that the Superintendent and Major seemed to share his bewilderment.

'Are you saying that they're actually part of the same group?' asked the Superintendent.

'Specifically, no,' said the Professor. 'I can only surmise from the inherent contradictions expressed in their communiqués that there is a strong difference of opinion as to the tactical approach

354

while at the same time the two groups share the same underlying ideological assumptions. Owing, however, to the molecular structure of terrorist organizations the actual identification of a member of one group by another member of another group or sub-faction of the same group remains extremely problematical.'

'The whole fucking situation is extremely problematical, come to that,' said the Superintendent. 'So far we've had two communiqués from what sounds like a partially castrated German, one from an asthmatic Irishman, demands from a Mexican for a jumbo jet and six million quid, a counter-demand from the Kraut for seven million, not to mention a stream of abuse from an Arab and everyone accusing everyone else of being a CIA agent working for Israel and who's fighting for whose freedom.'

'Beats me how they can begin to talk about freedom when they're holding innocent children and an old lady hostage and threatening to kill them,' said the Major.

'There I must disagree with you,' said the Professor. 'In terms of Neo-Hegelian post-Marxist political philosophy the freedom of the individual can only reside within the parameters of a collectively free society. The People's Army Groups regard themselves as in the forefront of total freedom and equality and as such are not bound to observe the moral norms which restrict the actions of lackeys of imperialist, fascist and neo-colonialist oppression.'

'Listen, old boy,' said the Major angrily removing his Afro wig, 'just whose side are you on anyway?'

'I am merely stating the theory. If you want a more precise analysis . . .' began the Professor nervously, only to be interrupted by the Head of the Psychological Warfare team who had been working on the voiceprints.

'From our analysis of the stress factors revealed in these tape recordings we are of the opinion that the group holding Fräulein Schautz are emotionally more disturbed than the two other terrorists,' he announced, 'and frankly I think we should concentrate on reducing their anxiety level.'

'Are you saying the Schautz woman is likely to be shot?' asked the Superintendent.

The Psychologist nodded. 'It's rather baffling actually. We've hit something rather odd with that lot, a variation from the normal pattern of speech reactions and I must admit I think she's the one who's most likely to get it in the neck.'

'No skin off my nose if she does,' said the Major, 'she's had it coming to her.'

'There'll be skin off everyone's nose if that happens,' said the Superintendent. 'My instructions are to keep this thing cool and if they start killing their hostages all hell will be let loose.'

'Yes,' said the Professor, 'a very interesting dialectical situation. You must understand that the theory of terrorism as a progressive force in world history demands the exacerbation of class warfare and the polarizing of political opinion. Now in terms of simple effectiveness we must say that the advantage lies with People's Army Group Four and not with the People's Alternative Army.'

'Say that again,' said the Major.

The Professor obliged. 'Put quite simply it is politically better to kill these children than eliminate Fräulein Schautz.'

'That may be your opinion,' said the Major, his fingers twitching on the butt of his revolver, 'but if you know what's good for you you won't express it round here again.'

'I was talking only in terms of political polarization,' said the Professor nervously. 'Only a very small minority will be perturbed if Fräulein Schautz dies but the effect of liquidating four small children, and coterminously conceived female siblings at that, would be considerable.'

'Thank you, Professor,' said the Superintendent hastily. And before the Major could decipher this sinister pronouncement he had ushered the adviser on Terrorist Ideologies out of the room.

'It's blasted eggheads like him who've ruined this country,' said the Major. 'To hear him talk you'd think there were two sides to every damned question.'

'Which is exactly the opposite of what we're getting on the voiceprints,' said the psychologist. 'Our analysis seems to indicate that there's only one spokesman for the People's Alternative Army.'

'One man?' said the Superintendent incredulously. 'Didn't sound like one man to me. More like half-a-dozen insane ventriloquists.'

'Precisely. Which is why we think you should try to lower

356

the anxiety level of that group. We may well be dealing with a split personality. I'll play the tapes again and perhaps you'll see what I mean.'

'Must you? Oh well . . .'

But the sergeant had switched the recorder on and once again the cluttered drawing-room echoed to guttural snarls and whimpers of Wilt's communiqués. In a dark corner Inspector Flint who had been on the point of dozing off suddenly sprang to his feet.

'I knew it,' he shouted triumphantly, 'I knew it. I just knew it had to be and by God it is!'

'Had to be what?' asked the Superintendent.

'Henry Fucking Wilt who was behind this foul-up. And there's the proof on those tapes.'

'Are you sure, Inspector?'

'I'm more than that. I'm positive. I'd know that little sod's voice if he imitated an Eskimo in labour.'

'I don't think we have to go that far,' said the psychological adviser. 'Are you telling us you know the man we've just heard?'

'Know him?' said Flint. 'Of course I know the bastard. I ought to after what he did for me. And now he's having you lot on.'

'I must say I find it hard to believe,' said the Superintendent. 'A more inoffensive little man you couldn't wish to meet.'

'I could,' said Flint with feeling.

'But he had to be drugged up to the eyeballs before we could get him to go back in,' said the Major.

'Drugged? What with?' said the psychologist.

'No idea. Some little concoction our medic brews up for blighters with a streak of yellow. Works wonders with the bomb-disposal chappies.'

'Well it wouldn't appear to have worked quite so well in this case,' said the psychologist nervously, 'but it certainly accounts for the remarkable readings we've been getting. We could well have a case of chemically induced schizophrenia on our hands.'

'I wouldn't bother too much about the "chemically induced" if I were you,' said Flint. 'Wilt's a nutter anyway. I'll give a hundred to one he set this thing up from the start.'

'You can't seriously be suggesting that Mr Wilt deliberately went out of his way to put his own children in the hands of

357

a bunch of international terrorists,' said the Superintendent. 'When I discussed the matter with him he seemed genuinely astonished and disturbed.'

'What Wilt seems and what Wilt is are two entirely separate things. I can tell you this much though. Any man who can dress an inflatable doll up in his wife's clothes and ditch the thing at the bottom of a pile hole under thirty tons of quick-set concrete isn't—'

'Excuse me, sir,' interrupted the sergeant, 'message just come through from the station that Mrs Wilt has flown the coop.'

The four men looked at him in despair.

'She's what?' said the Superintendent.

'Escaped from custody, sir. Nobody seems to know where she is.'

'It fits,' said Flint, 'it fits and no mistake.'

'Fits? What fits for Chrissake?' asked the Superintendent, who was beginning to feel distinctly peculiar himself.

'The pattern, sir. Next thing we'll hear is that she was last seen on a motor cruiser going down the river, only she won't be.'

The Superintendent stared at him dementedly. 'And you call that a pattern? Oh my God.'

'Well, it's the sort of the thing Wilt would come up with, believe me. That little bugger can think up more ways of taking a perfectly sane and sensible situation and turning it into a raving nightmare than any villain I've ever met.'

'But there's got to be some motive for his actions.'

Flint laughed abruptly. 'Motive? With Henry Wilt? Not on your life. You can think of a thousand good motives, ten thousand if you like, for what he does but at the end of the day he'll come up with the one explanation you never even dreamt of. Wilt's the nearest thing to Ernie you could wish to meet.'

'Ernie?' said the Superintendent. 'Who the hell is Ernie?'

'That ruddy computer they use for the premium bonds, sir. You know, the one that picks numbers out at random. Well, Wilt's a random man, if you know what I mean.'

'I don't think I want to,' said the Superintendent. 'I thought all I had to cope with was a nice simple ordinary siege, instead of which this thing is developing into a madhouse.'

'While we're on that subject,' said the psychologist, 'I really

358

do think it's very important to resume communications with the people in the top flat. Whoever is up there and holding the Schautz woman is in a highly disturbed state. She could be in grave danger.'

'No "could" about it,' said Flint. 'Is.'

'All right. I suppose we'll have to risk it,' said the Superintendent. 'Give the go-ahead for the helicopter to move in with a field telephone, sergeant.'

'Any orders regarding Mrs Wilt, sir?'

'You'd better ask the Inspector here. He seems to be the expert on the Wilt family. What sort of woman is Mrs Wilt? And don't say she's a random one.'

'I wouldn't really like to say,' said Flint, 'except that she's a very powerful woman.'

'What do you think she plans to do then? She obviously didn't leave the police station without some aim in mind.'

'Well, knowing Wilt as well as I do, sir, I have to admit I've grave doubts about her having a mind at all. Any normal woman would have been in a nut-house years ago living with a man like that.'

'You're not suggesting she's some sort of psychopath as well?'

'No, sir,' said Flint, 'all I'm saying is that she can't have any nerves worth speaking about.'

'That's a big help. So we've got a bunch of terrorists armed to the teeth, some sort of nutter in the shape of Wilt and a woman on the loose with a hide like a rhino. Put that little lot together and we've got ourselves one hell of a combination. All right, sergeant, put out an alert for Mrs Wilt and see that they take her into custody before anyone else gets hurt.'

The Superintendent crossed to the window and looked at the Wilts' house. Under the glare of the floodlights it stood out against the night sky like a monument erected to commemorate the stolidity and unswerving devotion to boredom of English middle-class life. Even the Major was moved to comment.

'Sort of suburban son-et-lumière, what?' he murmured.

'Lumière perhaps,' said the Superintendent, 'but at least we're spared the son.'

But not for long. From somewhere seemingly close at hand there came a series of terrible wails. The Wilt quads were giving tongue.

Chapter 16

A mile away Eva Wilt moved towards her home with a fixed resolve that was wholly at variance with her appearance. The few people who noticed her as she bustled down narrow streets saw only an ordinary housewife in a hurry to fix her husband's supper and put the children to bed. But beneath her homely look Eva Wilt had changed. She had shed her cheerful silliness and her borrowed opinions and had only one thought in mind. She was going home and no one was going to stop her. What she would do when she got there she had no idea, and in a vague way she was aware that home was not simply a place. It was also what she was, the wife of Henry Wilt and mother of the quads, a working woman descended from a line of working women who had scrubbed floors, cooked meals and held families together in spite of illnesses and deaths and the vagaries of men. It wasn't a clearly defined thought but it was there driving her forward almost by instinct. But with instinct there came thought.

They would be waiting for her in Farringdon Avenue so she would avoid it. Instead she would cross the river by the iron footbridge and go round by Barnaby Road and then across the fields where she had taken the children blackberrying only two months ago and enter the garden at the back. And then? She would have to wait and see. If there was any way of entering the house and joining the children she would take it. And if the terrorists killed her it was better than losing the quads. The main thing was that she would be there to protect them. Beneath this uncertain logic there was rage. Like her thoughts it was vague and diffuse and focused as much on the police as on the terrorists. If anything she blamed the police more. To her the terrorists were criminals and murderers and the police were there to save the public from such people. That was their job, and they hadn't done it properly. Instead they had allowed her children to be taken hostage and were now playing a sort of game in which the quads were merely pieces. It was

360

a simple view but Eva's mind saw things simply and straight-forwardly. Well, if the police wouldn't act she would.

It was only when she reached the footbridge over the river that she saw the full magnitude of the problem facing her. Half a mile away the house in Willington Road stood in an aura of white light. Around it the street lamps glimmered dimly and the other houses were black shadows. For a moment she paused, gripping the handrail and wondering what to do, but there was no point in hesitating. She had to go on. She went down the iron steps and along Barnaby Road until she came to the footpath across the field. She went through and followed it until she reached the muddy patch by the next gate. A group of bullocks stirred in the darkness near her but Eva had no fear of cattle. They were part of the natural world to which she felt she properly belonged.

But on the far side of the gate everything was unnatural. Against the sinister white glare of the floodlights she could see men with guns and when she had climbed the gate she stooped down and spotted the coils of barbed wire. They ran right across the field from Farringdon Avenue. Willington Road had been sealed off. Again instinct provoked cunning. There was a ditch to her left and if she made her way along it . . . But there would be a man there to stop her. She needed something to divert his attention. The bullocks would do. Eva opened the gate and then trudging through the mud shooed the beasts into the next field before closing the gate again. She shooed them still further and the bullocks scattered and were presently moving slowly forward in their usual inquisitive way. Eva scrambled down into the ditch and began to wade along it. It was a muddy ditch, half filled with water and as she went weeds gathered round her knees and the occasional bramble scratched her face. Twice she put her hand into clumps of stinging-nettles but Eva hardly felt them. Her mind was too occupied with other problems. Mainly the lights. They glared at the house with a brilliance that made it seem unreal and almost like looking at a photographic negative where all the tones were reversed and windows which should have shone with light were black squares against a lighter background. And all the time from somewhere across the field there came the incessant beat of an engine. Eva peered over the edge of the ditch and made

361

out the dark shape of a generator. She knew what it was because John Nye had once explained how electricity was made when he had been trying to persuade her to install a Savonius rotor which ran off windpower. So that was how they were lighting the house. Not that it helped her. The generator was out in the middle of the field and she couldn't possibly reach it. Anyway, the bullocks were proving a useful distraction. They had gathered in a group round one of the armed men and he was trying to get rid of them. Eva went back into the ditch and stumbling along came to the barbed wire.

As she had expected it coiled down into the water and it was only by reaching down the full length of her arm that she could find the bottom strand. She pulled it up and then stooping down so that she was almost submerged managed to wriggle her way underneath. By the time she reached the hedge that ran along the backs of all the gardens she was soaked to the skin and her hands and legs were covered with mud, but the cold didn't affect her. Nothing mattered except the fear that she would be stopped before she reached the house. And there were bound to be more armed men in the garden.

Eva stood knee-deep in the mud and waited and watched. Noises came to her out of the night. There was certainly some-one in Mrs Haslop's garden. The smell of cigarette smoke told her so but her main attention was fixed on her own back garden and the lights that blazed her home into a fearful isolation. A man moved from the back of the summerhouse and crossed to the gate into the field. Eva watched him stroll away towards the generator. And still she waited with the cunning that sprang from some deep instinct. Another man moved behind the summerhouse, a match flared in the darkness as he lit a cigarette, and Eva, like some primeval amphibian, climbed slowly from the ditch and on her hands and knees crawled forward along the hedge. All the time her eyes were fixed on the glowing tip of the cigarette. By the time she reached the gate she could see the man's face each time he took a deep puff, and the gate was open. It swung slightly in the breeze, never quite shutting. Eva began to crawl through it when her knee touched something cylindrical and slippery. She felt down with a hand and found a thick plastic-coated cable. It ran through the gateway to the three floodlights stationed on the lawn. All she had to do was cut it and the lights would go off. And there were secateurs in the greenhouse. But if she used them she might electrocute herself. Better to take the axe with the long handle and that was by the woodpile on the far side of the summerhouse. If only the man with the cigarette would go she could reach it in no time. But what would make him move? If she threw a stone at the greenhouse he would certainly investigate.

Eva felt around on the path and had just found a piece of flint when the need for throwing it ended. A loud chattering noise was coming from behind her and turning her head she could make out the shape of a helicopter coming low over the field. And the man had moved. He was on his feet and had walked round the summerhouse so that his back was towards her. Eva crawled through the gate, got to her feet and ran for the woodpile. On the other side of the summerhouse the man didn't hear her. The helicopter was nearer now and its rotors drowned her movements. Already Eva had the axe and had returned to the cable and as the helicopter passed overhead she swung the axe down. A moment later the house had disappeared and the night had become intensely dark. She stumbled forward, trampled across the herb garden and reached the lawn before she realized that she seemed to be in the middle of a tornado. Above her the helicopter blades thrashed the air, the machine veered sideways, something swung past her head and a moment later there came the sound of breaking glass. Mrs de Frackas' conservatory was being demolished. Eva stopped in her tracks and threw herself flat on the lawn. From inside the house there came the rattle of automatic fire, and bullets riddled the summer-house. She was in the middle of some awful battle and every-thing had suddenly gone horribly wrong.

In Mrs de Frackas' conservatory Superintendent Misterson had been watching the helicopter moving in towards the balcony window with the field telephone dangling beneath it, when the world had suddenly vanished. After the brilliance of the flood-lights he could see nothing but he could still feel and hear and before he could grope his way back into the drawing-room he both felt and heard. He certainly felt the field telephone on the side of his head and he vaguely heard the sound of breaking glass. A second later he was on the tiled floor and the whole damned place seemed to be cascading glass, potted geraniums, *begonia semperflorens* and soilless compost. It was the latter that prevented him from expressing his true feelings.

'You bleeding maniac . . .' he began before choking in the dust storm. The Superintendent rolled onto his side and tried to avoid the debris but things were still falling from the shelves and Mrs de Frackas' treasured Cathedral Bell plant had detached itself from the wall and had draped him with tendrils. Finally as he tried to fight his way out of this home-grown jungle a large Camellia 'Donation' in a heavy clay pot toppled from its pedestal and put an end to his misery. The Head of the Anti-Terrorist Squad lay comfortably unconscious on the tiles and made no comment.

But in the Communications Centre comments flew thick and fast. The Major yelled orders to the helicopter pilot while two operators wearing headphones were clutching their ears and screaming that some fucking lunatic was bouncing on the parabolic listening devices. Only Flint remained cool and comparatively detached. Ever since he had first learnt that Wilt was involved in the case he had known that something appalling was bound to happen. In Flint's mind the name Wilt spelt chaos, a sort of cosmic doom against which there was no protection, except possibly prayer, and now that catastrophe had struck he was secretly pleased. It proved his premonition right and the Superintendent's optimism entirely wrong. And so while the Major ordered the helicopter pilot to get the hell out, Flint picked his way through the rubble in the conservatory and disentangled his unconscious superior from the foliage.

'Better call an ambulance,' he told the Major as he dragged the injured man into the Communications Centre, 'the Super looks as if he's bought it.'

The Major was too busy to be concerned. 'That's your business, Inspector,' he said. 'I've got to see those swine don't get away.'

'Sounds as though they're still in the house,' said Flint as the sporadic firing continued from Number 9, but the Major shook his head.

364

'Doubt it. Could have left a suicide squad to cover their retreat, or rigged up a machine gun with a timing device to fire at intervals. Can't trust the buggers an inch.'

Flint radioed for medical help and ordered two constables to carry the Superintendent through the neighbouring gardens to Farringdon Avenue, a process that was impeded by the S.G.S. men searching for escaping terrorists. It was half an hour before silence descended on Willington Road and the listening devices had confirmed that there was still human presence in the house.

There was also apparently something vertebrate lying on the Wilts' lawn. Flint, returning from the ambulance, found the Major grasping a revolver and preparing to make a sortie.

'Got one of the bastards by the sound of things,' he said as a massive heartbeat issued from an amplifier linked to a listening device. 'Going out to bring him in. Probably wounded in the cross-fire.'

He dashed out into the darkness and a few minutes later there was a yell, the sound of a violent struggle involving an extremely vigorous object and sections of the fence between the two gardens. Flint switched the amplifier off. Now that the massive heartbeat had gone there were other even more disturbing sounds coming from the machine. But what was finally dragged through the shattered conservatory was worst of all. Never the most attractive of women in Flint's eyes, Eva Wilt daubed in mud, weeds and soaked to the skin which showed through her torn dress in several places, now presented a positively prehistoric appearance. She was still struggling as the six S.G.S. men bundled her into the room. The Major followed with a black eye.

'Well at least we've got one of the swine,' he said.

'I'm not one of the swine,' shouted Eva, 'I'm Mrs Wilt. You've no right to treat me like this.'

Inspector Flint retreated behind a chair. 'It's certainly Mrs Wilt,' he said. 'Mind telling us what you were trying to do?'

From the carpet Eva regarded him with loathing.

'I was trying to join my children. I've got a right to.'

'I've heard that one before,' said Flint. 'You and your rights. I suppose Henry put you up to this?'

'He did nothing of the sort. I don't even know what's

365

happened to him. For all I know he's dead.' And she promptly burst into tears.

'All right, you can let her go now, chaps,' said the Major at last convinced that his captive was not one of the terrorists. 'You could have got yourself killed, you know.'

Eva ignored him and got to her feet. 'Inspector Flint, you're a father yourself. You must know what it means to be separated from your loved ones in their hour of need.'

'Yes, well . . .' said the Inspector awkwardly. Weeping Neanderthal women aroused mixed emotions in him and in any case his particular loved ones were two teenage louts with an embarrassing taste for vandalism. He was grateful for an interruption from one of the technicians in charge of the listening devices.

'Getting something peculiar, Inspector,' he said. 'Want to hear it?'

Flint nodded. Anything was better than appeals for sympathy from Eva Wilt. It wasn't. The technician switched the amplifier on.

'That's coming from Boom Number 4,' he explained as a series of grunts, groans, ecstatic cries and the insistent creaking of bedsprings issued from the loudspeaker.

'Boom Number 4? That's not a boom, that's a . . .'

'Sounds like a fucking sex maniac, begging the lady's pardon,' said the Major. But Eva was listening too intently to care.

'Where's it coming from?'

'Attic flat, sir. The one where you-know-who is.'

But the subterfuge was wasted on Eva. 'Yes, I do,' she shrieked, 'that's my Henry. I'd know that moan anywhere.'

A dozen disgusted eyes turned on her but Eva was unabashed. After all she had been through in so short a time this new revelation destroyed the last vestiges of her social discretion.

'He's making love to some other woman. Just wait till I lay my hands on him,' she screamed in fury and would have dashed out into the night again if she hadn't been seized.

'Handcuff the bitch,' shouted the Inspector, 'and take her back to the station and see she doesn't get out again. I want maximum security this time and I don't mean maybe.'

'Doesn't sound as if her husband does either, come to that,' said the Major as Eva was dragged off and the unequivocal evidence of Wilt's first affair continued to pulsate through the Communications Centre. Flint emerged from behind the chair and sat down.

'Well at least she's proved me right. I said the little bastard was in this thing up to his eyeballs.'

The Major shuddered. 'I can think of pleasanter ways of putting it, but it rather sounds as if you're right.'

'Of course I am,' said Flint smugly. 'I know friend Wilt's little tricks.'

'I'm glad I don't,' said the Major. 'If you ask me we ought to get the psycho to analyse this little lot.'

'It's all going down on the tape, sir,' said the radio man.

'In that case turn that filthy din off,' said Flint. 'I've got enough on my hands without having to listen to Wilt having it off.'

'Couldn't agree more,' said the Major, struck by the accuracy of the term, 'the fellow must have nerves of steel. Dashed if I could get it up in the circumstances.'

'You'd be surprised what that little bugger can get up to in any circumstances,' said Flint, 'and married to that maternal mastodon of his, is it any wonder? I'd just as soon go to bed with a giant clam as climb in with Eva Wilt.'

'I suppose there's something in that,' said the Major fingering his black eye cautiously. 'She certainly packs one hell of a punch. Can't stay around. Got to go and get those floodlights going again.'

He wandered out and Flint sat on wondering what to do. Now that the Superintendent was out of action he supposed he must be in charge of the case. It was not a promotion he wanted. About the only consolation he could find was the thought that Henry Wilt was about to get his final come-uppance.

In fact Wilt was concentrating his mind on just the opposite. The state of his manhood, so recently repaired, demanded it. Besides, adultery was not his forte and he had never found the process of making love when he didn't feel up to it at all appealing. And since when he felt like it Eva usually didn't, reserving her moments of passion until the quads were safely asleep and Wilt would have been given half a chance, he had become accustomed to a sort of split sexuality in which he did one thing while thinking about another. Not that Eva was satisfied with one thing. Her interest, while more single-minded than his, was infinitely eclectic in matters of procedure and Wilt had learnt to accept being bent, crushed, twisted and generally contorted along lines suggested by the manuals Eva consulted. They had titles like *How to Keep your Marriage Young* or *Making Love the Natural Way*. Wilt had objected that their marriage wasn't young and that there was nothing natural about risking strangulated hernia by using the coitus position advocated by Dr Eugene van Yonk. Not that his arguments ever did any good. Eva replied by making unpleasant references to his adolescence and unwarranted accusations about what he did in the bathroom when she wasn't there and in the end he had been driven to prove his normality by doing what he considered thoroughly abnormal. But if Eva had been vigorously experimental in bed Gudrun Schautz was a demented carnivore.

From the moment in the kitchen when she had first latched onto him in a frenzy of blatant lust, Wilt had been bitten, scratched, licked, chewed and sucked with a violence and lack of discrimination that was frankly insulting, not to say dangerous, and which had led him to wonder why the bitch bothered to shoot people when she could just as easily have done them to death in more lawful and decidedly nastier ways. Anyway, nobody in his right mind could sensibly accuse him of being an unfaithful husband. If anything, quite the opposite; only the most dutiful and conscientious family man would have put himself so much at risk as to get voluntarily into bed with a wanted murderess. Wilt found the adjective singularly inappropriate and it was only by concentrating his imagination on Eva when he had first met her that he could evoke a modicum of desire. It was this flaccid response that provoked Gudrun Schautz. The bitch was not only a murderess; she managed to combine political terror with the expectation that Wilt was a male chauvinist pig who would launch himself into her without a second thought.

Wilt's views on the matter were different. It was one of the tenets of his confused philosophy that you didn't mess about with other women once you were married. And bouncing up and down on an extremely nubile young woman undoubtedly came into the category of messing about. On the other hand

368

there was the interesting paradox that he was spiritually closer to Eva now than when he was actually making love to her and thinking about something else. More practically there wasn't a hope in hell of having an orgasm. The catheter had put paid to that for the time being. He could bounce away until the cows came home, but he was no more going to put his penis to the test of a genuine erection than fly. To prevent this dreadful possibility he alternated his vision of a youthful Eva with images of himself and the execrable Schautz lying on the autopsy table in a terminal coitus interruptus. Considering the din they were making it seemed all too likely and it was certainly a most effective anti-aphrodisiac. Besides, it had the additional advantage of confusing the Schautz woman. She was evidently accustomed to more committed lovers and Wilt's erratic fervour threw her.

'You like it some other way, Liebling?' she asked as Wilt receded for the umpteenth time.

'In the bath,' said Wilt who had suddenly become conscious that the terrorists below might decide to take a hand and that baths were more bulletproof than beds. Gudrun Schautz laughed. 'So funny, ja. In the bath!'

At that moment the floodlights went out and the roar of the helicopter could be heard. The noise seemed to spur her to a new frenzy of lust.

'Quick, quick,' she moaned, 'they're coming.'

'Buggered if I am,' muttered Wilt but the murderess was too busy trying to exorcise oblivion to hear him and as Mrs de Frackas' conservatory disintegrated and rapid gunfire sounded below he was hurtled once more into a maelstrom of lust that had nothing to do with real sex at all. Death was going through the motions of life and Wilt, unaware that his part in this grisly performance was being monitored for posterity, did his best to play his role. He tried thinking about Eva again.

Chapter 17

Downstairs in the kitchen Chinanda and Baggish were having a hard time thinking at all. All the complexities of life from which they had tried to escape into the idiotic and murderous fanaticism of terror seemed suddenly to have combined against them. They fired frantically into the darkness, and for one proud moment imagined they had hit the helicopter. Instead, the thing had apparently bombed the house next door. When they finally stopped shooting they were assailed by the yells of quads in the cellar. To make matters worse, the kitchen had become a health hazard. Eva's highly polished tiles were a slick of vomit and after Baggish had twice landed on his backside they had retreated to the hall to consider their next move. It was then that they heard the extraordinary noises emanating from the attic.

'They're raping Gudrun,' said Baggish and would have gone to her rescue if Chinanda hadn't stopped him.

'It's a trap the police pigs are setting. They want to get us upstairs and then they rush the house and rescue the hostages. We stay down here.'

'With that noise? How long do you think we can go on with all that yelling? We each need to sleep by turns and with them crying is impossible.'

'So we stop them,' said Chinanda and led the way down to the cellar where Mrs de Frackas was sitting on a wooden chair while the quads demanded mummy.

'Shut up, you hear me! You want to see your mummy you stop that noise,' Baggish shouted. But the quads only yelled the louder.

'I should have thought coping with small children would have been an essential part of your training,' said Mrs de Frackas unsympathetically. Baggish rounded on her. He still hadn't got over her suggestion that his proper métier was selling dirty postcards in Port Said.

'You make them quiet yourself,' he told her, waving his automatic in her face, 'or else we—'

'My dear boy, there are some things you have yet to learn,' said the old lady. 'By the time you reach my age dying is so imminent that I can't be bothered to worry about it. In any case I have always been an advocate of euthanasia. So much more sensible, don't you think, than putting one on a drip or one of those life-support machines or whatever they call them. I mean, who wants to keep a senile old person alive when she's no use to anyone?'

'I don't,' said Baggish fervently. Mrs de Frackas looked at him with interest.

'Besides, being a Moslem, you'd be doing me a favour. I've always understood that death in battle was a guarantee of salvation according to the Prophet, and while I can't say I'm actually battling I should have thought being shot by a murderer amounts to the same thing.'

'We are not murderers,' shouted Baggish, 'we are freedom fighters against international imperialism!'

'Which serves to prove my point,' continued Mrs de Frackas imperturbably. 'You're fighting and I am self-evidently a product of the Empire. If you kill me I should, according to your philosophy, go straight to heaven.'

'We are not here to discuss philosophy,' said Chinanda. 'You stupid old woman, what do you know about the suffering of the workers?'

Mrs de Frackas turned her attention to his clothes. 'Rather more than you do by the cut of your coat, young man. It may not be obvious but I spent several years working in a children's hospital in the slums of Calcutta and I think I know what misery means. Have you ever done a hard day's work in your life?'

Chinanda evaded the question. 'But what did you do about this misery?' he yelled, poking his face close to hers. 'You washed your conscience in the hospital and then went back and lived in luxury.'

'I had three square meals a day if that's what you mean by luxury. I certainly couldn't have afforded the sort of expensive car you drive around in,' riposted the old lady. 'And while we're on the subject of washing, I think it might help to quieten the children if you allowed me to bath them.'

371

The terrorists looked at the quads and tended to agree. The quads were not a pleasant sight.

'OK, we bring you water down and you can wash them here,' said Chinanda, who went up to the darkened kitchen and finally found a plastic bucket under the sink. He filled it with water and brought it down with a bar of soap. Mrs de Frackas looked into the bucket doubtfully.

'I said "Wash them." Not dye them.'

'Die them? What do you mean die them?'

'Take a look for yourself,' said Mrs de Frackas. The two terrorists did, and were appalled. The bucket was filled with dark blue water.

'Now they're trying to poison us,' yelled Baggish and headed up the stairs to register this fresh complaint against the Anti-Terrorist Squad.

Inspector Flint took the call. 'Poison you? By putting something in the water supply? I can assure you I know nothing about it.'

'Then how come it's blue?'

'I've no idea. Are you sure the water's blue?'

'I know fucking well it's blue,' shouted Baggish. 'We turn the tap and the water comes out blue. You think we're idiots or something.'

Flint hesitated but suppressed his true opinion in the interest of the hostages. 'Never mind what I think,' he said, 'all I'm saying is that we have done absolutely nothing to the water supply and—'

'Lying pig,' shouted Baggish. 'First you try trapping us by raping Gudrun and now you poison the water. We don't wait any longer. The water is clean in one hour and you let Gudrun go or we execute the old woman.'

He slammed the phone down, leaving Flint more mystified than ever. 'Raping Gudrun? The man's off his head. I wouldn't touch the bitch with a bargepole and how I can be in two places at the same time defeats me. And now he's saying the water's gone blue.'

'Could be they're on drugs,' said the sergeant. 'Gets them hallucinating sometimes, especially when they're under stress.'

'Stress? Don't talk to me about stress,' said Flint and turned

372

his anger on a P.L.D. operator. 'And what the hell are you smirking about?'

'They're trying it out in the bath now, sir. Wilt's idea. Randy little sod.'

'If you're seriously suggesting that a couple copulating in a bath can turn the rest of the water in the house blue, think again,' snapped Flint.

He leant his head back against an antimacassar and shut his eyes. His mind was churning with opinions. Wilt was mad. Wilt was a terrorist. Wilt was a mad terrorist. Wilt was possessed. Wilt was a bloody enigma. Only the last was certain, that and the Inspector's fervent wish that Wilt was a thousand miles away and that he had never heard of the bastard. Finally he roused himself.

'All right, I want that helicopter back and this time no balls-ups. The house is floodlit and it's going to stay that way. All they have to do is land that telephone through the balcony window and considering what they've done here that should be child's play. Tell the pilot he can rip the roof off if he wants to but I want a line through to that flat and fast. That's the only way we're going to find out exactly what Wilt's playing at.'

'Will do,' said the Major, and began issuing fresh instructions.

'He's playing politics now, sir,' said the operator. 'Makes Marx sound like a right-winger. Want to hear?'

'I suppose I'd better,' said Flint miserably, and the loud-speaker was switched on. Through the crackle Wilt could be heard expounding violently.

'We must annihilate the capitalist system lock stock and barrel. There must be no hesitation in exterminating the last vestiges of the ruling class and instilling a proletarian conscious-ness into the minds of the workers. This can best be achieved by exposing the fascistic nature of pseudo-democracy through the praxis of terror against the police and the lumpen executives of international finance. Only by demonstrating the fundamental antithesis between . . .'

'Christ, he sounds like a bloody textbook,' said Flint with unintentional accuracy. 'We've got a pocket Mao in the attic. Right, get these tapes through to the Idiot Brigade. Perhaps they can tell us what a lumpen executive is.'

'Helicopter's on its way,' said the Major. 'The telephone's

373

fitted with a micro-television camera. If all goes well we'll soon see what's going on up there.'

'As if I wanted to,' said Flint and retreated to the safety of the downstairs toilet.

Five minutes later the helicopter swirled across the orchard at the bottom of the garden, poised for a moment over Number 9, and a field telephone swung through the balcony window into the flat. As the pilot lifted the machine away a trail of wire spun out behind it like the thread of a mechanical spider.

Flint emerged from the toilet to find that Chinanda was back on the phone.

'Wants to know why we haven't cleared the water, sir,' said the operator.

Inspector Flint sat down with a sigh and took the call. 'Now listen, Miguel,' he began, imitating the friendly approach of the Superintendent, 'you may not believe this—'

A stream of abuse indicated all too clearly that the terrorist didn't.

'All right, I accept all that,' said Flint when the epithets dried up. 'But what I'm saying is that we aren't in the attic. We haven't put anything in the water.'

'Then why are you supplying them with weapons by helicopter?'

'That wasn't a weapon. It happened to be a telephone so we can talk to them . . . Yes, I daresay it doesn't sound likely. I'm the first to agree . . . No, we haven't. If anyone has it's the . . .'

'People's Alternative Army,' prompted the sergeant.

'The People's Alternative Army,' repeated Flint. 'They must have put something in the water, Miguel . . . What? . . . You don't like being called Miguel . . . Well as a matter of fact I don't particularly like being called fuzzpig . . . Yes, I heard you. I heard you the first time. And if you'll get off the line I'll talk to the bastards up there.'

And Flint slammed down the phone. 'All right, now get me through to the attic. And make it snappy. Time's running out.'

It was to run out for a further quarter of an hour. The sudden reappearance of the helicopter just when the Wilt alternative had switched from sex to politics had thrown Wilt's tactics out

374

of joint. Having softened his victim up on the physical level he had begun confusing her still more by quoting the egregious Bilger at his most Marcusian. It hadn't been too difficult, and in any case Wilt had speculated on the injustice of human existence over many years. His dealings with Plasterers Four had taught him that he belonged to a relatively privileged society. Plasterers earned more than he did, and Printers were positively rich, but allowing for these discrepancies it was still true that he had been born into an affluent country with a favoured climate and sophisticated political institutions developed over the centuries. Above all an industrial society. The vast majority of mankind lived in abject poverty, were riddled with curable disease which went uncured, were subject to despotic govern-ments and lived in terror and in danger of dying by starvation. To the extent that anyone tried to change this inequity, Wilt sympathized. Eva's Personal Assistance for Primitive People might be ineffectual but it had at least the merit of being personal and moving in the right direction. Terrorizing the innocent and murdering men, women and children was both ineffectual and barbaric. What difference was there between the terrorists and their victims? Only one of opinion. Chinanda and Gudrun Schautz came from wealthy families and Baggish, whose father had been a shopkeeper in Beirut, could hardly be called poor. None of these self-appointed executioners had been driven to murder by the desperation of poverty, and as far as Wilt could tell their fanaticism had its roots in no specific cause. They weren't trying to drive the British from Ulster, the Israelis from the Golan Heights or even the Turks from Cyprus. They were political poseurs whose enemy was life. In short they were murderers by personal choice, psychopaths who camouflaged their motives behind a screen of utopian theory. Power was their kick, the power to inflict pain and to terrify. Even their own readiness to die was a sort of power, some sick and infantile form of masochism and expiation of guilt, not for their filthy crimes, but for being alive at all. Beyond that there were doubt-less other motives concerned with parents or toilet training. Wilt didn't care. It was enough that they were carriers of the same political rabies that had driven Hitler to construct Auschwitz and kill himself in the bunker, or the Cambodians to murder one another by the million. As such they were beyond the pale of sympathy. Wilt had his children to protect and only his wits to help him.

And so, in a desperate attempt to keep Gudrun Schautz isolated and uncertain, he mouthed Marcusian dogma until the helicopter interrupted his recital. As the telephone encased in a wooden box swung through the window Wilt hurled himself to the floor in the kitchen.

'Back into the bathroom,' he yelled convinced that the thing was some sort of tear-gas bomb. But Gudrun Schautz was already there. Wilt crawled through to her.

'They know we're here,' she whispered.

'They know I'm here,' said Wilt, grateful to the police for seeming to provide proof that he was a wanted man. 'What would they want with you?'

'They locked me in the bathroom. Why would they do that if they didn't want me?'

'Why would they do it if they did?' asked Wilt. 'They'd have dragged you out straightaway.' He paused and looked hard at her in the light reflected from the ceiling. 'But how did they get on to me? I ask myself that question. Who told them?'

Gudrun Schautz looked back and asked herself a great many questions. 'Why do you look at me? I don't know what you are talking about.'

'No?' said Wilt, deciding the time was ripe to switch to full-scale mania. 'That's what you say now. You come to my house when everything is going so good with the plan and now suddenly the Israelis arrive and everything is kaput. No assassination of the Queen, no use for the nerve-gas, no annihilation of the entire pseudo-democratic parliamentary cadres in the House of Commons at one fell swoop, no . . .'

In the living-room the telephone interrupted this insane catalogue. Wilt listened to it with relief. So did Gudrun Schautz. The paranoia which was part of her make-up was beginning to assume new proportions in her mind with every shift in Wilt's position.

'I'll answer it,' she said but Wilt glared at her ferociously.

'Informer,' he snarled, 'you've done enough harm already. You will stay where you are. That's your only hope.'

And leaving her to work out this strange logic, Wilt crawled through the kitchen and opened the box.

376

'Listen you fascist pig swine,' he yelled before Flint could get a word in edgeways, 'don't think you're going to sweet-talk the People's Alternative Army into one of your lying dialogues. We demand—'

'Shut up, Wilt,' snapped the Inspector. Wilt shut up. So the sods knew. In particular, Flint knew. Which would have been good news if he hadn't had a bloody murderess breathing down his neck. 'So there's no use trying to bluff us. For your information, if you want to see your daughters alive again you had better stop trying to poison your little comrades on the ground floor.'

'Trying to what?' asked Wilt, stunned by this new accusation into using his normal voice.

'You heard me. You've been doctoring the water supply and they want it undoctored as of now.'

'Doctoring the . . .' Wilt began before remembering he couldn't talk openly in present company.

'The water supply,' said Flint. 'They've set a deadline for it to be cleared and it runs out in half an hour. And I do mean deadline.'

There was a moment's silence while Wilt tried to think. There must have been something in that bloody hold-all that was poisonous. Perhaps the terrorists carried their own supply of cyanide. He'd have to get the bag out but in the meantime he had to maintain his lunatic stand. He fell back on his earlier approach.

'We make no deals,' he shouted. 'If our demands aren't met by eight in the morning the hostage dies.'

There was the sound of laughter at the other end of the line. 'Pull the other one, Wilt,' said Flint. 'How are you going to kill her? Screw her to death perhaps?'

He paused to let this information sink in before continuing, 'We've got every little antic you've been up to on tape. It's going to sound great when we play it back in court.'

'Shit,' said Wilt, this time impersonally.

'Mrs Wilt particularly enjoyed it. Yes, you heard me right. Now then, are you going to clear that water or do you want your daughters to have to drink it?'

'All right, I agree. You have the aircraft waiting on the runway and I don't move from here until the car arrives. One

driver and no tricks or the woman dies with me. You understand?'

'No,' said Flint beginning to feel confused himself but Wilt
had ended the conversation. He was sitting on the floor trying
to think himself out of this new dilemma. He couldn't do anything about the water tank with the Schautz woman watching.
He would have to continue his bluff. He went back into the
kitchen and found her standing uncertainly by the bathroom
door.

'So now you know,' he said.

Gudrun Schautz didn't. 'Why did you say you would kill me?'
she asked.

'Why do you think?' said Wilt, plucking up sufficient courage
to move towards her with something approximating to menace.
'Because you are an informer? Without you the plan . . .'

But Gudrun Schautz had heard enough. She retreated into
the bathroom, slammed the door and bolted it. This little man
was insane. The whole situation was insane. Nothing made any
sort of sense, and contradiction piled on contradiction so that
the outcome was an incomprehensible flux of impressions. She
sat on the toilet and tried to think her way through the chaos.
If this weird man with his talk of assassinating the Queen was
wanted by the police, and everything seemed to point in that
direction, however illogically, there was something to be said
for seeming to be his hostage. The British police weren't
supposed to be fools but they might free her without asking
too many awkward questions. It was the only chance she had.
And through the door she could hear Wilt muttering to himself
alarmingly. He had started to wire the doorhandle again.

When he had finished Wilt climbed back into the attic space
and was presently elbow-deep in the water tank. It was certainly
a very murky colour and when he finally managed to drag the
hold-all out his arm was blue. Wilt laid the bag on the floor
and began to rummage through its contents. At the bottom he
found a portable typewriter and a large ink pad with a rubber
stamp. There was nothing to suggest poison, but the typewriter
ribbon and the ink pad had certainly polluted the water. Wilt
went back to the kitchen and turned on the tap. 'No wonder
the buggers thought they were being doctored,' he muttered and,
leaving the tap running, climbed back into the roof space. By

378

the time he had crawled round the back of the tank with the hold-all and hidden it under the fibreglass insulation the dawn was beginning to compete with the floodlights. He emerged, went through to the living-room, lay down on the sofa and wondered what to do next.

Chapter 18

And so Day Two of the siege of Willington Road began. The sun rose, the floodlights faded, Wilt nodded fitfully in a corner of the attic, Gudrun Schautz lay in the bathroom, Mrs de Frackas sat in the cellar, and the quads huddled together under a pile of sacks in which Eva had once stored 'organic' potatoes. Even the two terrorists snatched some sleep, while in the Communications Centre the Major, installed on a camp bed, snored and twitched in his sleep like a hound dreaming of the hunt. Elsewhere in Mrs de Frackas' house several Anti-Terrorist men had made themselves comfortable. The sergeant in charge of the listening devices was curled on a sofa and Inspector Flint had commandeered the main bedroom. But for all this human inactivity the electronic sensors relayed information to the tapes and via them to the computer and the Psycho-Warfare team, while the field telephone, like some audio-visual Trojan horse, monitored Wilt's breathing and scanned his movements through its TV camera eye.

Only Eva didn't sleep. She lay in a cell in the police station staring at the dim lightbulb in the ceiling and kept the duty sergeant in a state of uncertainty by demanding to see her solicitor. It was a request he didn't know how to refuse. Mrs Wilt was not a criminal and to the best of his knowledge there were no legal grounds for keeping her locked in a cell. Even genuine villains were allowed to see their solicitors, and after fruitlessly trying to contact Inspector Flint the sergeant gave in.

'You can use the telephone in here,' he told her, and discreetly left her in the office to make as many calls as she chose. If Flint didn't like it he could lump it. The duty sergeant wasn't laying his own head on the chopping-block for anyone.

Eva made a great many phone calls. Mavis Mottram was woken at four and was mollified to learn that the only reason Eva hadn't contacted her before was because she was being held illegally by the police.

'I never heard anything so scandalous in my life. You poor thing. Now don't worry we'll have you out of there in no time,' she said, and promptly woke Patrick to tell him to get in touch with the Chief Constable, the local M.P. and his friends at the B.B.C.

'I won't have any friends at the Beeb if I call them at half-past four.'

'Nonsense,' said Mavis, 'it will give them plenty of time to get it on the early-morning news.'

The Braintrees were woken too. This time Eva horrified them by describing how she had been assaulted by the police and asked them if they knew anyone who could help. Peter Braintree phoned the secretary of the League of Personal Liberties and, as an afterthought, every national newspaper with the story.

And Eva continued her calls. Mr Gosdyke, the Wilts' solicitor, was dragged from his bed to answer the phone and promised to come to the police station at once.

'Don't say anything to anyone,' he advised her, in the firm belief that Mrs Wilt must have committed some crime. Eva ignored his advice. She spoke to the Nyes, the Principal of the Tech. and as many people as she could think of, including Dr Scully. She had just finished when the B.B.C. called back and Eva gave a taped interview as the mother of the quadruplets held by the terrorists who was herself being held by the police for no good reason.

From that moment on a crescendo of protest gathered. The Home Secretary was woken by his Permanent Under-Secretary with the news that the B.B.C. was refusing his request not to broadcast the interview in the national interest on the grounds that the illegal detention of the hostages' mother was diametrically opposed to the national interest. From there the information reached the Police Commissioner, who was held responsible for the activities of the Anti-Terrorist Squad, and even the Ministry of Defence, whose Special Ground Services had assaulted Mrs Wilt in the first place.

Eva hit the radio news at seven and the headlines of every paper in time for the morning rush hour, and by half-past seven the Ipford police station was more obviously besieged by press men, TV cameras, photographers, Eva's friends and onlookers, than the house in Willington Road. Even Mr Gosdyke's

381

scepticism had evaporated in the face of the sergeant's confession that he did not know why Mrs Wilt was in custody.

'Don't ask me what she's supposed to have done,' said the sergeant. 'I was ordered to keep her in the cells by Inspector Flint. If you want any further information, ask him.'

'I intend to,' said Mr Gosdyke. 'Where is he?'

'At the siege. I can try and get him on the phone for you.'

And so it was that Flint, who had finally snatched some sleep with the happy thought that he had at long last got that little bastard Wilt where he wanted him, up to his eyes in a genuine crime, suddenly found that the tables had been turned on him.

'I didn't say arrest her. I said she was to be held in custody under the Terrorism Act.'

'Are you suggesting for one moment that my client is a terrorist suspect?' demanded Mr Gosdyke. 'Because if you are . . .'

Inspector Flint considered the law on slander and decided he wasn't. 'She was being kept in custody for her own safety,' he equivocated. Mr Gosdyke doubted it.

'Well, having seen the state she's in all I can say is that it's my considered opinion that she would have been safer outside the police station than in it. She has obviously been badly beaten, dragged through the mud, and, if I'm any judge of the matter, several hedges into the bargain, has suffered multiple abrasions to the hands and legs and is in a state of nervous exhaustion. Now are you going to allow her to leave or do I have to apply for . . .'

'No,' said Flint hastily, 'of course she can go, but I'm not taking any responsibility for her safety if she comes here.'

'I hardly need any assurances from you on that score,' said Mr Gosdyke, and escorted Eva out of the police station. She was greeted by a barrage of questions and cameras.

'Mrs Wilt, is it correct that the police beat you up?'

'Yes,' said Eva before Mr Gosdyke could interject that she was making no comments.

'Mrs Wilt, what do you intend to do now?'

'I'm going home,' said Eva, but Mr Gosdyke hustled her into the car.

'That's out of the question, my dear. You must have some friends you can stay with for the time being.'

382

From the crowd Mavis Mottram was trying to make herself heard. Eva ignored her. She had begun thinking about Henry and that awful German girl in bed together, and the last person she wanted to talk to now was Mavis. Besides, at the back of her mind she still blamed Mavis for insisting on going to that stupid seminar. If she had stayed at home none of this would have happened.

'I'm sure the Braintrees won't mind my going there,' she said, and presently she was sitting in their kitchen sipping coffee and telling Betty all about it.

'Are you sure, Eva?' said Betty. 'I mean, it doesn't sound at all like Henry?'

Eva nodded tearfully. 'It did. They have these loudspeaker things all round the house and they can hear everything that's going on inside.'

'I must say I can't understand.'

Nor could Eva. It wasn't simply that it was unlike Henry to be unfaithful; it wasn't Henry at all. Henry never even looked at other women. She had always known he didn't and there had been times when she had been almost irritated by his lack of interest. It somehow deprived her of the little jealousy she was entitled to as his wife, and there was also the suspicion that his lack of interest extended to her too. Now she felt doubly betrayed.

'You'd think he'd be far too worried about the children,' she went on. 'They're downstairs and there he is up in the flat with that creature . . .' Eva broke down and wept openly.

'What you need is a bath and then a good sleep,' said Betty, and Eva allowed herself to be led upstairs to the bathroom. But as she lay in the hot water, instinct and thought combined again. She was going home. She had to, and this time she would go in broad daylight. She got out of the bath, dried herself, and put on the maternity dress which was the only thing Betty Braintree had been able to find that would fit her, and went downstairs. She had made up her mind what to do.

In the temporary conference room which had once been Major-General de Frackas' private den, Inspector Flint, the Major and the members of the Psycho-Warfare team sat looking at a television set which had been placed incongruously in the middle of the Battle of Waterloo. The late Major-General's obsession with toy soldiers and their precise deployment on a large ping-pong table where they had been gathering dust since his death added a surrealist element to the extraordinary sights and sounds being relayed by the TV camera in the field telephone next door. The Wilt alternative had entered a new phase, one in which he had apparently gone clean off his rocker.

'Mad as a March hare,' said the Major as Wilt, horribly distorted by the fish-eye lens, loomed and dwarfed as he strode about the attic mouthing words that made no sense at all. Even Flint found it hard not to accept the verdict.

'What the hell does "Life is prejudicial to Infinity" mean?' he asked Dr Felden, the psychiatrist.

'I need to hear more before I express a definite opinion,' said the doctor.

'I'm damned if I do,' muttered the Major, 'it's like peering into a padded cell.'

On the screen Wilt could be seen shouting something about fighting for the religion of Allah and death to all unbelievers. He then made some extremely disturbing noises which suggested a village idiot having trouble with a fishbone, and disappeared into the kitchen. There was a moment's silence before he began chanting, 'The bells of hell go tingalingaling for you but not for me,' in a frightening falsetto. When he reappeared he was armed with a bread knife and yelling, 'There's a crocodile in the cupboard, mother and its eating up your coat. Bats and lizards braving blizzards keep the world afloat.' Finally he lay on the bed and giggled.

Flint leant across the sunken road and switched the set off. 'Much more of that and I'll go off my head too,' he muttered. 'All right, you've seen and heard the sod, and I want to know your opinion as to the best way of handling him.'

'Looked at from the standpoint of a coherent political ideology,' said Professor Maerlis, 'I must confess that I find it hard to express an opinion.'

'Good,' said the Major, who still harboured the suspicion that the professor shared the views of the terrorists.

'On the other hand the transcripts of the tapes made last night indicate definite evidence that Mr Wilt has a profound knowledge of terrorist theory and was apparently engaged in a conspiracy to assassinate the Queen. What I don't understand is where the Israelis come in.'

'That could easily be a symptom of paranoia,' said Dr Felden. 'A very typical example of persecution mania.'

'Never mind about the "could be",' said Flint, 'is the bugger mad or not?'

'Difficult to say. In the first place the subject may well be suffering the after-effects of the drugs he was given yesterday before entering the house. I have ascertained from the so-called medical officer who administered it that the concoction consisted of three parts Valium, two Sodium Amytal, a jigger of Bromide and what he chose to call a bouquet of Laudanum. He couldn't specify the actual quantities involved, but in my opinion it says something for Mr Wilt's constitution that he is still alive.'

'Says something for the canteen coffee that the bugger drank it without noticing,' said Flint. 'Anyway, do we get him on the blower and ask him what he has done with the Schautz woman or not?'

Dr Felden toyed with a lead Napoleon pensively. 'On the whole I am against the idea. If Fräulein Schautz is still alive I wouldn't want to be responsible for introducing the notion of murdering her to a man in Mr Wilt's condition.'

'That's a big help. So when those swine demand her release again I suppose I'll have to tell them she's being held by a lunatic.' And wishing to God the replacement for the Head of the Anti-Terrorist Squad would arrive before mass murder began next door, Flint went through to the Communications Centre.

'No go,' he told the sergeant. 'The Idiot Brigade reckon we're dealing with a homicidal maniac.'

It was more or less the reaction that Wilt wanted. He had spent a miserable night pondering his next move. So far he had played a number of roles—a revolutionary terrorist group, a grateful father, a chinless wonder, an erratic lover and a man who had intended to assassinate the Queen—and with each fresh fabrication he had seen Gudrun Schautz's sense of certainty waver. Stoned out of her mind by the drug of revolutionary dogma, she was incapable of adjusting to a world of absurd fantasy. And Wilt's world was absurd; it always had been and

385

as far as he could tell it always would be. It was fantastic and absurd that Bilger had made the bloody film about the crocodile but it was true, and Wilt had spent his adult life surrounded by pimply youths who thought they were God's gift to women, and by lecturers who imagined that they could convert Plasterers and Motor Mechanics into sensitive human beings by forcing them to read *Finnegan's Wake* or instil them with a truly proletarian consciousness by handing out dollops of *Das Kapital*. And Wilt himself had been through the gamut of fantasy, those internal dreams of being a great writer which had been re-awakened by his first glimpse of Irmgard Mueller and, on a previous occasion, the cold-blooded murderer of Eva. And for eighteen years he had lived with a woman who had changed roles almost as frequently as she changed her clothes. With such a wealth of experience behind him Wilt could produce new fantasies at a moment's notice just so long as he wasn't called upon to give them greater credibility by doing anything more practical than gloss them with words. Words were his medium and had been through all the years at the Tech. With Gudrun Schautz locked in the bathroom he was free to use them to his heart's content and her discomfort. Provided those creatures down below didn't start doing anything violent.

But Baggish and Chinanda had their hands full with another form of bizarre behaviour. The quads had woken early to renew their assault on Eva's freezer and stock of bottled fruit, and Mrs de Frackas had given up the unequal battle to keep them moderately clean. She had spent an exceedingly uncomfortable night on the wooden chair and her rheumatism had given her hell. In the end she had been driven to drink, and since the only drink available was Wilt's patented homebrew the results had been remarkable.

From the first appalling mouthful the old lady wondered what the hell had hit her. It wasn't simply that the stuff tasted foul, so foul that she had immediately taken another shot to try to wash her mouth out, it was also extremely potent. Having choked down a second mouthful Mrs de Frackas looked at the bottle with downright disbelief. It was impossible to suppose that anyone had seriously distilled the stuff for human consumption, and for a moment or two she considered the awful possibility

386

that Wilt had, for some diabolical reason of his own, laid up a binful of undiluted paint stripper. It didn't seem likely somehow, but then again what she had just swallowed hadn't seemed likely either. It had seared its way down her gullet with all the virulence of a powerful toilet-cleaner going to work on a neglected U-bend. Mrs de Frackas examined the label and felt reassured. The muck proclaimed itself 'Lager' and while the title was in blatant disregard of the facts, whatever the bottle contained was meant to be drunk. The old lady took another mouthful and instantly forgot her rheumatism. It was impossible to concentrate on two ailments simultaneously.

By the time she had finished the bottle she had difficulty concentrating on anything. The world had suddenly become a delightful place and all it needed to make it even better was more of the same. She swayed back to the wine store and selected a second bottle and was in the process of unscrewing the top when the thing exploded. Doused with beer and holding the neck of the bottle Mrs de Frackas was about to try a third when she caught sight of several larger bottles in the bottom rack. She pulled one out and saw that it had once contained champagne. What it contained now she couldn't imagine but at least it seemed safer to open and less likely to fragment than the beer bottles. She took two bottles out into the cellar and tried to uncork them. It was easier said than done. Wilt had fastened the corks down with Sellotape and what looked like the remnants of a wire coathanger.

'Need some pliers,' she muttered as the quads gathered round with interest.

'That's daddy's best,' said Josephine. 'He wouldn't like it if you drank it.'

'No dear, I daresay he wouldn't,' said the old lady with a belch that suggested her stomach was of the same opinion.

'He calls it his four-star BB,' said Penelope. 'But mummy says it ought to be called peepee.'

'Does she?' said Mrs de Frackas with mounting disgust.

'That's because he has to get up in the night when he's drunk it.'

Mrs de Frackas relaxed. 'We wouldn't want to do anything that would upset your father,' she said, 'and anyway, champagne needs to be chilled.'

She went back to the bins, returned with two opened bottles that had proved less explosive than the others, and sat down again. The quads were gathered round the freezer but the old lady was too busy to care what they were doing. By the time she had finished the third bottle the Wilt quads were octuplets in her eyes and she was having difficulty focusing. In any case she had begun to understand what Eva had meant about peepee. Wilt's homebrew was making its presence felt. Mrs de Frackas got up, fell over and finally crawled up the steps to the door. The damned thing was locked.

'Let me out,' she shouted, and banged on the door. 'Let me out this inshtant.'

'What you want?' demanded Baggish.

'Never you mind what I want. Itsh what I need that matters and thatsh no concern of yours.'

'Then you stay where you are.'

'I shan't be reshponsible for what happens if I do,' said Mrs de Frackas.

'What you mean?'

'Young man, there are shome things better left unshaid and I don't intend dishcushing them with you.'

Through the door the two terrorists could be heard struggling with slurred English sentences. 'Things better left unshed' had them baffled, while 'not be reshponshible for what happens' sounded faintly ominous, and they had already been alarmed by several popping noises and the crunch of glass from the cellar.

'We want to know what happens if we don't let you out,' said Chinanda finally.

Mrs de Frackas was in no doubt. 'I shall almosht shertainly burst,' she yelled.

'You what?'

'Burst, burst, burst. Like a bomb,' screamed the old lady, now convinced she was in the terminal stage of diuresis. A muttered conversation took place in the kitchen.

'You come out with your hands up,' Chinanda ordered, and unlocked the door before backing away into the hall and aiming his automatic. But Mrs de Frackas was no longer in a condition to obey. She was trying to reach one of several doorknobs and missing. From the bottom of the steps the quads watched in

388

fascination. They were used to Wilt's occasional bouts of booziness but they had never seen anyone paralytically drunk before.

'For Heaven's shake shomeone open the door,' Mrs de Frackas burbled.

'I will,' squealed Samantha and a rush of competing girls fought their way over the old lady for the privilege. By the time Penelope had won and the quads had cascaded over her into the kitchen the old lady had lost all interest in toilets. She lay across the threshold and, raising her head with difficulty, delivered her verdict on the quads.

'Do me a favour, shomeone, and shoot the little shits,' she gurgled before passing out. The terrorists didn't hear her. They knew now what she had meant about a bomb. Two devastating explosions came from the cellar and the air was filled with frozen peas and broad beans. In the freezer Wilt's BB had finally burst.

Chapter 19

Eva had been busy too. She had spent part of the morning on the phone to Mr Gosdyke and the rest arguing with Mr Symper, the local representative of the League of Personal Liberties. He was a very earnest and concerned young man, and in the normal course of events, would have been dismayed at the outrageous behaviour of the police in putting at risk the lives of a senior citizen and four impressionable children by refusing to meet the legitimate demands of the freedom fighters besieged in Number 9 Willington Road. Instead, Eva's treatment at the hands of the police had put Symper in the extremely uncomfortable position of having to look at the problem from her point of view.

'I do understand the case you're making, Mrs Wilt,' he said forced by her bruised appearance to subdue his bias in favour of radical foreigners, 'but you must admit you are free.'

'Not to enter my own house. I am not at liberty to do that. The police won't let me.'

'Now if you want us to take up your case against the police for infringing your liberty by holding you in custody, we'll . . .'

Eva didn't. 'I want to enter my own home.'

'I do sympathize with you, but you see our organization aims to protect the individual from the infringement of her personal liberty by the police and in your case . . .'

'They won't let me go home,' said Eva. 'If that isn't infringing my personal liberty I don't know what is.'

'Yes, well I do see that.'

'Then do something about it.'

'I don't really know what I can do about it,' said Mr Symper.

'You knew what to do when the police stopped a container truck of deep-frozen Bangladeshis outside Dover,' said Betty. You organized a protest rally and . . .'

'That was quite different,' said Mr Symper, bridling. 'The Customs officials had no right to insist that the refrigeration

390

unit be turned on. They were suffering from acute frostbite. And besides, they were in transit.'

'They shouldn't have labelled themselves cod fillets, and anyhow you argued that they were simply coming to join their families in Britain.'

'They were in transit to their families.'

'And so is Eva, or should be,' said Betty. 'If anyone has a right to join her family it's Eva.'

'I suppose we could apply for a court order,' said Mr Symper sighing for less domestic issues, 'that would be the best way.'

'It wouldn't,' said Eva, 'it would be slowest. I am going home now and you are coming with me.'

'I beg your pardon?' said Mr Symper, whose concern didn't extend to becoming a hostage himself.

'You heard me,' said Eva, and loomed over him with a ferocity that put in question his ardent feminism, but before he could make a plea for his own personal liberty he was being hustled out of the house. A crowd of reporters had gathered there.

'Mrs Wilt,' said a man from the *Snap*, 'our readers would like to hear how it feels as the mother of quads to know that your loved ones are being held hostage.'

Eva's eyes bulged in her head. 'Feel?' she asked. 'You want to know how I feel?'

'That's right,' said the man, licking his ballpen, 'human interest—'

He got no further. Eva's feelings had passed beyond the stage of words or human interest. Only actions could express them. Her hand came up, descended in a karate chop and as he fell her knee caught him in the stomach.

'That's how it feels,' said Eva as he rolled into a foetal position on the flowerbed. 'Tell your readers that.' And she marched the now thoroughly cowed Mr Symper to his car and pushed him in.

'I am going home to my children,' she told the other reporters. 'Mr Symper of the League of Personal Liberties is accompanying me and my solicitor is waiting for us.'

And without another word she got into the driver's seat. Ten minutes later, followed by a small convoy of press cars, they reached the road block in Farringdon Road to find Mr Gosdyke arguing ineffectually with the police sergeant.

'I'm afraid it's no use, Mrs Wilt. The police have orders to let no one through.'

Eva snorted. 'This is a free country,' she said, dragging Mr Symper out of the car with a grip that contradicted her statement. 'If anyone tries to stop me from going home we will take the matter to the courts, to the Ombudsman and to Parliament. Come along, Mr Gosdyke.'

'Now hold it, lady,' said the sergeant, 'my orders . . .'

'I've taken your number,' said Eva, 'and I shall sue you personally for denying me free access to my children.'

And pushing the unwilling Mr Symper before her she marched through the gap in the barbed wire, followed cautiously by Mr Gosdyke. Behind them a cheer went up from the crowd of reporters. For a moment the sergeant was too stunned to react and by the time he reached for his walkie-talkie the trio had turned the corner into Willington Road. They were stopped halfway down by two armed S.G.S. men.

'You've no right to be here,' one of them shouted. 'Don't you know there's a siege on?'

'Yes,' said Eva, 'which is why we're here. I'm Mrs Wilt, this is Mr Symper of the League of Personal Liberties and Mr Gosdyke is here to handle negotiations. Now kindly take us to . . .'

'I don't know anything about this,' said the soldier. 'All I know is that we've got orders to shoot . . .'

'Then shoot me,' said Eva defiantly, 'and see where that gets you.'

The S.G.S. man hesitated. Shooting mothers wasn't included in Queen's Rules and Regulations, and Mr Gosdyke looked too respectable to be a terrorist.

'All right, come this way,' he said, and escorted them into Mrs de Frackas' house to be greeted abusively by Inspector Flint.

'What the fuck's going on?' he yelled. 'I thought I gave orders for you to stay away.'

Eva pushed Mr Gosdyke forward. 'Tell him,' she said.

Mr Gosdyke cleared his throat and looked uncomfortably round the room. 'As Mrs Wilt's legal representative,' he said, 'I have come to inform you that she demands to join her family. Now to the best of my knowledge there is nothing in law to prevent her from entering her own home.'

392

Inspector Flint goggled at him. 'Nothing?' he spluttered.

'Nothing in law,' said Mr Gosdyke.

'Bugger the law,' shouted Flint. 'You think those sods in there give a tuppenny fuck for the law?'

Mr Gosdyke conceded the point.

'Right,' continued Flint, 'so there's a houseful of armed terrorists who'll blow the heads off her four blasted daughters if anyone so much as goes near the place. That's all. Can't you get that into her thick skull?'

'No,' said Mr Gosdyke bluntly.

The Inspector sagged into a chair and looked balefully at Eva. 'Mrs Wilt,' he said, 'tell me something. You don't by any chance happen to belong to some suicidal religious cult, do you? No? I just wondered. In that case let me explain the situation to you in simple four-letter words that even you will understand. Inside your house there are—'

'I know all that,' said Eva, 'I've heard it over and over again and I don't care. I demand the right to enter my own home.'

'I see. And I suppose you intend walking up to the front door and ringing the bell?'

'I don't,' said Eva, 'I intend to be dropped in.'

'Dropped in?' said Flint with a gleam of incredulous hope in his eyes, 'did you really say "dropped in"?'

'By helicopter,' explained Eva, 'the same way you dropped that telephone in to Henry last night.'

The Inspector held his head in his hands and tried to find words.

'And it's no use your saying you can't,' continued Eva, 'because I've seen it done on telly. I wear a harness and the helicopter . . .'

'Oh my God,' said Flint, closing his eyes to shut out this appalling vision. 'You can't be serious.'

'I can,' said Eva.

'Mrs Wilt, if, and I repeat if, you were to enter the house by the means you have described, will you be good enough to tell me how you think it would help your four daughters?'

'Never you mind.'

'But I do mind, I mind very much. In fact I'll go so far as to say that I mind what happens to your children rather more than you appear to and . . .'

'Then why aren't you doing something about it? And don't say you are, because you aren't. You're sitting in here with all this transistor stuff listening to them being tortured and you like it.'

'Like it? Like it?' yelled the Inspector.

'Yes, like it,' Eva yelled back. 'It gives you a feeling of importance and what's more you've got a dirty mind. You enjoyed listening to Henry in bed with that woman and don't say you didn't.'

Inspector Flint couldn't. Words failed him. The only ones that sprang to mind were obscene and almost certain to lead to an action for slander. Trust this bloody woman to bring her solicitor and the sod from the Personal Liberties mob with her. He rose from his chair and stumbled through to the toy-room, slamming the door behind him. Professor Maerlis, Dr Felden and the Major were sitting watching Wilt pass the time by idly examining his glans penis for signs of incipient gangrene on the television screen. Flint switched the unnerving image off.

'You're not going to believe this,' he mouthed, 'but that bloody Mrs Wilt is demanding that we use the helicopter to swing her through the attic window on the end of a rope so she can join her fucking family.'

'I hope you're not going to allow it,' said Dr Felden. 'After what she threatened to do to her husband last night I hardly think it's advisable.'

'Don't tempt me,' said Flint. 'If I thought I could sit here and watch her tear the little shit limb from limb . . .' He broke off to savour the thought.

'Damned plucky little woman,' said the Major. 'Blowed if I'd choose to swing into that house on the end of a rope. Well, not without a lot of covering fire anyhow. Still, there's something to be said for it.'

'What?' said Flint wondering how the hell anyone could call Mrs Wilt a little woman.

'Diversionary tactics, old man. Can't think of anything more likely to unnerve the buggers than the sight of that woman dangling from a helicopter. Know it would scare the pants off me.'

'I daresay. But since that doesn't happen to be the purpose of the exercise I'd like some more constructive suggestion.'

394

From the other room Eva could be heard shouting that she'd send a telegram to the Queen if she wasn't allowed to join her family.

'That's all we need,' said Flint. 'We've got the press baying for blood and there hasn't been a decent mass suicide for months. She'll hit the headlines.'

'Certainly hit that window with a hell of a bang,' said the Major practically. 'Then we could rush the sods and—'

'No! Definitely no,' shouted Flint and dashed into the Communications Centre. 'All right, Mrs Wilt, I am going to try to persuade the two terrorists holding your daughters to allow you to join them. If they refuse that's their business. I can't do more.'

He turned to the sergeant on the switchboard. 'Get the two wogs on the phone and let me know when they've finished their Fascist Pig Overture.'

Mr Symper felt called upon to protest. 'I really do think these racialist remarks are quite unnecessary,' he said. 'In fact they are illegal. To call foreigners wogs—'

'I'm not calling foreigners wogs. I'm calling two fucking murderers wogs and don't tell me I shouldn't call them murderers either,' said Flint as Mr Symper tried to interject. 'A murderer is a murderer is a murderer and I've had about as much as I can take.'

So, it seemed, had the two terrorists. There was no preliminary tirade of abuse. 'What do you want?' Chinanda asked.

Flint took the phone. 'I have a proposal to make,' he said. 'Mrs Wilt, the mother of the four children you are holding, has volunteered to come in to look after them. She is unarmed and is prepared to meet any conditions you may choose to make.'

'Say that again,' said Chinanda. The Inspector repeated the message.

'Any conditions?' said Chinanda incredulously.

'Any. You name them, she'll meet them,' said Flint looking at Eva, who nodded.

A muttered conference took place in the kitchen next door made practically inaudible by the squeals of the quads and the occasional moan from Mrs de Frackas. Presently the terrorist came back on the line.

395

'Here are our conditions. The woman must be naked first of all. You hear me, naked.'

'I hear what you say but I can't say I understand . . .'

'No clothes on. So we see she has no weapons. Right?'

'I'm not sure Mrs Wilt will agree . . .'

'I do,' said Eva adamantly.

'Mrs Wilt agrees,' said Flint with a sigh of disgust.

'Second. Her hands are tied above her head.'

Again Eva nodded.

'Third. Her legs are tied.'

'Her legs are tied?' said Flint. 'How the hell is she going to walk if her legs are tied?'

'Long rope. Half metre between ankles. No running.'

'I see. Yes, Mrs Wilt agrees. Anything else?'

'Yes,' said Chinanda. 'As soon as she comes in, out go the children.'

'I beg your pardon?' said Flint. 'Did I hear you say "Out go the children"? You mean you don't want them?'

'Want them!' yelled Chinanda. 'You think we want to live with four dirty, filthy, disgusting little animals who shit all over the floor and piss . . .'

'No,' said Flint, 'I take your point.'

'So you can take the fucking little fascist shit-machines too,' said Chinanda, and slammed the phone down.

Inspector Flint turned to Eva with a happy smile. 'Mrs Wilt, I didn't say it, but you heard what the man said.'

'And he'll live to regret it,' said Eva with blazing eyes. 'Now, where do I undress?'

'Not in here,' said Flint firmly. 'You can use the bedrooms upstairs. The sergeant here will tie your hands and legs.'

While Eva went up to undress the Inspector consulted the Psycho-Warfare Team. He found them at odds with one another. Professor Maerlis argued that by exchanging four co-terminously conceived siblings for one woman whom the world would scarcely miss, there was propaganda advantage to be gained from the swop. Dr Felden disagreed.

'It's evident that the terrorists are under considerable pressure from the girls,' he said. 'Now, by relieving them of that psycho-logical burden we may well be giving them a morale boost.'

396

'Never mind about their morale,' said Flint. 'If the bitch goes in she'll be doing me a favour and after that the Major here can mount Operation Slaughterhouse for all I care.'

'Whacko,' said the Major.

Flint went back to the Communications Centre, averted his eyes from the monstrous revelations of Eva in the raw, and turned to Mr Gosdyke.

'Let's get one thing straight, Gosdyke,' he said. 'I want you to understand that I am totally opposed to your client's actions and am not prepared to take responsibility for what happens.'

Mr Gosdyke nodded. 'I quite understand, Inspector, and I would just as soon not be involved myself. Mrs Wilt, I appeal to you . . .'

Eva ignored him. With her hands tied above her head and with her ankles linked by a short length of rope, she was an awesome sight and not a woman with whom anyone would willingly argue.

'I am ready,' she said. 'Tell them I'm coming.'

She hobbled out of the door and down Mrs de Frackas' drive. In the bushes S.G.S. men blanched and thought wistfully of booby traps in South Armagh. Only the Major, surveying the scene from a bedroom window, gave Eva his blessing. 'Makes a chap proud to be British,' he told Dr Felden. 'By God that woman's got some guts.'

'I must say I find that remark in singularly bad taste,' said the doctor, who was studying Eva from a purely physiological point of view.

There was something of a misunderstanding next door. Chinanda, viewing Eva through the letter-box in the Wilt's front door, had just begun to have second thoughts when a waft of vomit hit him from the kitchen. He opened the door and aimed his automatic.

'Get the children,' he shouted to Baggish, 'I'm covering the woman.'

'You're what?' said Baggish, who had just glimpsed the expanse of flesh that was moving towards the house. But there was no need to fetch the children. As Eva reached the doormat they rushed towards her squealing with delight.

'Back,' yelled Baggish, 'back or I fire!'

It was too late. Eva swayed on the doorstep as the quads clutched at her.

'Oh mummy, you do look funny,' shrieked Samantha, and grabbed her mother's knees. Penelope clambered over the others and flung her arms round Eva's neck. For a moment they swayed uncertainly and then Eva took a step forward, tripped and with a crash fell heavily into the hall. The quads slithered before her across the polished parquet and the hatstand, seismically jolted from the wall, crashed forward against the door and slammed it. The two terrorists stood staring down at their new hostage while Mrs de Frackas raised a drunken head from the kitchen, took one look at the amazing sight and passed out again. Eva heaved herself to her knees. Her hands were still tied above her head but her concern was all for the quads.

'Now don't worry, darlings. Mummy's here,' she said. 'Everything is going to be all right.'

From the safety of the kitchen the two terrorists surveyed the extraordinary scene with dismay. They didn't share her optimism.

'Now what do we do?' asked Baggish. 'Throw the children out the door?'

Chinanda shook his head. He wasn't going within striking distance of this powerful woman. Even with her hands tied above her head there was something dangerous and frightening about Eva, and now she seemed to be edging towards him on bulging knees.

'Stay where you are,' he ordered, and raised his gun. Next to him the telephone rang. He reached for it angrily.

'What do you want now?' he asked Flint.

'I might ask you the same question,' said the Inspector. 'You've got the woman and you said you'd let the children go.'

'If you think I want this fucking woman you're crazy,' Chinanda yelled, 'and the fucking children won't leave her. So now we've got them all.'

What sounded like a chuckle came from Flint. 'Not my fault. We didn't ask for the children. You volunteered to . . .'

'And we didn't ask for this woman,' screamed Chinanda his voice rising hysterically. 'So now we do a deal. You . . .'

'Forget it, Miguel,' said Flint, beginning to enjoy himself.

398

'Deals are out and for your information you'd be doing me a favour shooting Mrs Wilt. In fact you go right ahead and shoot whoever you want, mate, because the moment you do I'm sending my men in and where they shoot you and Comrade Baggish you won't die in a hurry. You'll be . . .'

'Fascist murderer,' screamed Chinanda, and pulled the trigger of his automatic. Bullets spat holes across a chart on the kitchen wall which had until that moment announced the health-giving properties of any number of alternative herbs, most of them weeds. Eva regarded the damage balefully and the quads sent up a terrible wail.

Even Flint was horrified. 'Did you kill her?' he asked, suddenly conscious that his pension came before personal satisfaction.

Chinanda ignored the question. 'So now we deal. You send Gudrun down and have the jet ready in one hour only. From now on we don't play games.'

He slammed the phone down.

'Shit,' said Flint. 'All right, get me Wilt. I've got news for him.'

Chapter 20

But Wilt's tactics had changed again. Having run the gamut of roles from chinless wonder to village idiot by way of revolutionary fanatic, which to his mind was merely a more virulent form of the same species, it had slowly dawned on him he was approaching the destabilization of Gudrun Schautz from the wrong angle. The woman was an ideologue, and a German one at that. Behind her a terrible tradition stretched back into the mists of history, a cultural heritage of solemn, monstrously serious and ponderous *Dichter und Denker*, philosophers, artists, poets and thinkers obsessed with the meaning, significance and process of social and historical development. The word Weltanschauung sprang, or at least lumbered, to mind. Wilt had no idea what it meant and doubted if anyone else knew. Something to do with having a world view and about as charming as Lebensraum which should have meant Living-Room but actually signified the occupation of Europe and as much of Russia as Hitler had been able to lay his hands on. And after Weltanschauung and Lebensraum there came, even less comprehensibly, Weltschmerz or world pity which, considering Fräulein Schautz's propensity for putting bullets into unarmed opponents without a qualm, topped the bill for codswallop. And beyond these dread concepts there were the carriers of the virus, Hegel, Kant, Fichte, Schopenhauer, and Nietzsche who had gone clean off his nut from a combination of syphilis, superman and large ladies in helmets trumpeting into theatrical forests at Bayreuth. Wilt had once waded lugubriously through *Thus Spake Zarathustra* and had come out convinced that either Nietzsche hadn't known what the hell he was on about or, if he had, he had kept it very verbosely to himself. And Nietzsche was sprightly by comparison with Hegel and Schopenhauer, tossing off meaningless maxims with an abandon that was positively joyful. If you wanted the real hard stuff Hegel was your man, while Schopenhauer hit a nadir of gloom that made

King Lear sound like an hysterical optimist under the influence of laughing gas. In short, Gudrun Schautz's weak spot was happiness. He could blather on about the horrors of the world until he was blue in the face but she wouldn't bat an eyelid. What was needed to send her reeling was a dose of undiluted good cheer, and Wilt beneath his armour of domestic grumbling was at heart a cheerful man.

And so while Gudrun Schautz cowered in the bathroom and Eva stumbled across the threshold downstairs he bombarded his captive audience with good tidings. The world was a splendid place.

Gudrun Schautz disagreed. 'How can you say that when millions are starving?' she demanded.

'The fact that I can say it means that I'm not starving,' said Wilt, applying the logic he had learnt with Plasterers Two, 'and anyway now that we know they're starving means we can do something about it. Things would be much worse if we didn't know. We couldn't send them food for one thing.'

'And who is sending food?' she asked unwisely.

'To the best of my knowledge the wicked Americans,' said Wilt. 'I'm sure the Russians would if they could grow enough but they don't so they do the next best thing and send them Cubans and tanks to take their minds off their empty stomachs. In any case, not everyone is starving and you've only got to look around you to see what fun it is to be alive.'

Gudrun Schautz's view of the bathroom didn't include fun. It looked uncommonly like a prison cell. But she didn't say so.

'I mean, take me for example,' continued Wilt. 'I have a wonderful wife and four adorable daughters . . .'

A snort from the bathroom indicated that there were limits to the Schautz woman's credulity.

'Well, you may not think so,' said Wilt, 'but I do. And even if I didn't you've got to admit that the quads love life. They may be a trifle exuberant for some people's taste, but no one can say they're unhappy.'

'And Mrs Wilt is a wonderful wife?' said Gudrun Schautz with advanced scepticism.

'As a matter of fact I couldn't ask for a better,' said Wilt. 'You may not believe me but—'

'Believe you? I have heard what she calls you and you are always fighting.'

'Fighting?' said Wilt. 'Of course we have our little differences of opinion, but that is essential for a happy marriage. It's what we British call give and take. In Marxist terms I suppose you'd call it thesis, antithesis and synthesis. And the synthesis in our case is happiness.'

'Happiness,' snorted Gudrun Schautz. 'What is happiness?'

Wilt considered the question and the various ways he could answer it. On the whole it seemed wisest to steer clear of the metaphysical and stick to everyday things. 'In my case it happens to be walking to the Tech. on a frosty morning with the sun shining and the ducks waddling and knowing I don't have any committee meetings and teaching and going home by moonlight to a really good supper of beef stew and dumplings and then getting into bed with an interesting book.'

'Bourgeois pig. All you think about is your own comfort.'

'It's not all I think about,' said Wilt, 'but you asked for a definition of happiness and that happens to be mine. If you want me to go on I will.'

Gudrun Schautz didn't but Wilt went on all the same. He spoke of picnics by the river on hot summer days and finding a book he wanted in a secondhand shop and Eva's delight when the garlic she had planted actually managed to show signs of growing and his delight at her delight and decorating the Christmas tree with the quads and waking in the morning with them all over the bed tearing open presents and dancing round the room with toys they had wanted and would probably have forgotten about in a week and . . . Simple family pleasures and surprises which this woman would never know but which were the bedrock of Wilt's existence. And as he re-told them they took on a new significance for him and soothed present horrors with a balm of decency and Wilt felt himself to be what he truly was, a good man in a quiet and unobtrusive way married to a good woman in a noisy and ebullient way. If nobody else saw him like this he didn't care. It was what he was that mattered and what he was grew out of what he did, and for the life of him Wilt couldn't see that he had ever done anyone wrong. If anything he had done a modicum of good.

That wasn't the way Gudrun Schautz viewed things. Hungry,

402

cold and fearful, she heard Wilt tell of simple things with a growing sense of unreality. She had lived too long in a world of bestial actions taken to achieve the ideal society to be able to stand this catechism of domestic pleasures. And the only answers she could give him were to call him a fascist swine and secretly she knew she would be wasting her breath. In the end she stayed silent and Wilt was about to take pity on her and cut short a modified version of the family's holiday in France when the telephone rang.

'All right, Wilt,' said Flint, 'you can forget the travelogue. This is the crunch. Your missus is downstairs with the children and if the Schautz doesn't come down right now you're going to be responsible for a minor massacre.'

'I've heard that one before,' said Wilt. 'And for your information . . .'

'Oh no, you haven't. This time it's for real. And if you don't bring her down, by God, we will. Take a look out the window.' Wilt did. Men were climbing into the helicopter in the field.

'Right,' continued Flint, 'so they'll land on the roof and the first person they'll take out is you. Dead. The Schautz bitch we want alive. Now move.'

'I can't say I like your priorities,' said Wilt, but the Inspector had rung off. Wilt went through the kitchen and untied the bathroom door.

'You can come out now,' he said. 'Your friends downstairs seem to be winning. They want you to join them.'

There was no reply from the bathroom. Wilt tried the door and found it was locked.

'Now listen. You've got to come out. I'm serious. Messrs Baggish and Chinanda are downstairs with my wife and children and the police are prepared to meet their demands.'

Silence suggested that Gudrun Schautz wasn't. Wilt put his ear to the door and listened. Perhaps the wretched creature had escaped somehow or, worse still, committed suicide.

'Are you there?' he asked inanely. A faint whimper reassured him.

'Right. Now then, nobody is going to hurt you. There is absolutely no point in staying in there and . . .' A chair was jammed under the doorhandle on the other side.

'Shit,' said Wilt, and tried to calm himself. 'Please listen to

403

reason. If you don't come out and join them all hell is going to be let loose and someone is going to get hurt. You've got to believe me.'

But Gudrun Schautz had listened to too much unreason already to believe anything. She gibbered faintly in German.

'Yes, well that's a great help,' said Wilt, suddenly conscious that his alternative had gone into overkill. He went back to the living-room and called Flint.

'We've got a problem,' he said before the Inspector stopped him.

'You've got problems, Wilt. Don't include us.'

'Yes, well we've all got problems now,' said Wilt. 'She's in the bathroom and she's locked the door and the way things sound she isn't going to come out.'

'Still your problem,' said Flint. 'You got her in there and you get her out.'

'Now hold on. Can't you persuade those two goons . . .'

'No,' said Flint and ended the discussion. With a weary sigh Wilt went back to the bathroom but the sounds inside didn't suggest that Gudrun Schautz was any more amenable to rational persuasion than before, and after putting his case as forcibly as he could and swearing to God that there were no Israelis downstairs he was driven back to the telephone.

'All I want to know,' said Flint when he answered, 'is whether she's down with Bonnie and Clyde or not. I'm not interested in . . .'

'I'll open the attic door. I'll stand where the buggers can see I'm not armed and they can come up and get her. Now will you kindly put that suggestion to the sods?'

Flint considered the offer in silence for a moment and said he would call back.

'Thank you,' said Wilt and having pulled the bed away from the door lay on it listening to his heart beat. It seemed to be making up for lost time.

Two floors below Chinanda and Baggish were edgy too. Eva's arrival, far from quietening the quads, had aroused their curiosity to new levels of disgusting frankness.

'You've got ever so many wrinkles on your tummy, mummy,' said Samantha, putting into words what Baggish had already noticed with revulsion. 'How did you get them?'

404

'Well, before you were born, dear,' said Eva, who had crossed the Rubicon of modesty by hobbling naked into the house, 'mummy's tummy was much bigger. You see, you were inside it.'

The two terrorists shuddered at the thought. It was bad enough being stuck in a kitchen and hall with these revolting children without being regaled with the physiological intimacies of their pre-natal existence in this extraordinary woman.

'What were we doing inside you?' asked Penelope.

'Growing, dear.'

'What did we eat?'

'You didn't exactly eat.'

'You can't grow unless you eat. You're always telling Josephine she won't grow up big and strong unless she eats her muesli.'

'Don't like muesli,' said Josephine. 'It's got sultanas in it.'

'I know what we ate,' said Samantha with relish, 'blood.'

In the corner by the cellar stairs Mrs de Frackas, in the throes of a stupendous hangover, opened a veined eye.

'I shouldn't be at all surprised,' she mumbled. 'Nearest thing to human vampires I've ever met. Whoever called it baby-sitting? Some damned fool.'

'But we didn't have teeth,' continued Samantha.

'No, dear, you were tied to mummy by your umbilical cords. And what mummy ate went through the cord . . .'

'Things can't go through cords, mummy,' said Josephine. 'Cords are string.'

'Knives can go through string,' said Samantha.

Eva looked at her appreciatively. 'Yes, dear, so they can . . .'

The discussion was cut short by Baggish. 'Shut up and cover yourself,' he shouted throwing the Mexican rug from the living-room at Eva.

'I don't see how I can with my hands tied,' Eva began, but the telephone was ringing. Chinanda answered.

'No more talking. Either . . .' he said before stopping and listening. Behind him Baggish clutched his sub-machine gun and kept a wary eye on Eva.

'What are they saying?'

'That Gudrun won't come down,' said Chinanda. 'They want for us to go up.'

'No way. It's a trap. The police are up there. We know that.'

Chinanda took his hand from the phone. 'No one goes up and Gudrun comes down. Five minutes we give you or . . .'

'I'll go up,' Eva called out. 'The police aren't up there. My husband is. I'll bring them both down.'

The terrorists stared at her. 'Your husband?' they asked in unison. The quads joined in. 'You mean daddy's in the attic? Oh, mummy do bring him down. He's going to be ever so cross with Mrs de Frackas. She drank ever such a lot of daddy's peepee.'

'You can say that again,' moaned the old lady, but Eva ignored the extraordinary statement. She was looking fixedly at the terrorists and willing them to let her go up to the flat.

'I promise you I'll . . .'

'You're lying. You want to go up there to report to the police.'

'I want to go up there to save my children,' said Eva, 'and if you don't believe me tell Inspector Flint that Henry has got to come down now.'

The terrorists moved away down the kitchen and conferred.

'If we can free Gudrun and get rid of this woman and her filthy children it's good,' said Baggish. 'We have the man and the old woman.'

Chinanda disagreed. 'We keep the children. That way the woman does nothing wrong.'

He went back to the phone and repeated Eva's message. 'Five minutes we give you only. The man Wilt comes down . . .'

'Naked,' said Eva, determined to see that Henry shared her discomfort.

'He comes down naked,' Chinanda repeated, 'and with his hands tied . . .'

'He can't tie his own hands,' said Flint practically.

'Gudrun can tie them for him,' answered Chinanda. 'Those are our conditions.'

He put the phone down and sat looking wearily at Eva. The English were strange people. With women like this, why had they ever given up their Empire? He was roused from his reverie. Mrs de Frackas was getting woozily to her feet.

'Sit down,' he shouted at her but the old lady ignored him. She wobbled across to the sink.

406

'Why don't I shoot her?' said Baggish. 'That way they'll know we mean what we say.'

Mrs de Frackas squinted at him with bloodshot eyes. 'Young man,' she said, 'with a head like mine you'd be doing me a favour. Just don't miss.' And to emphasize the point she turned her back on him and stuck her bun under the cold tap.

Chapter 21

In the Communications Centre there was confusion too. Flint was happily relaying the message to Wilt and enjoying his protest that it was bad enough risking death by gunshot but he didn't see why he had to go naked and risk double pneumonia into the bargain and anyway how the hell he was going to tie his own hands together he hadn't the faintest idea, when he was stopped by the new Head of the Anti-Terrorist Squad.

'Hold everything,' the Superintendent told Flint. 'The Idiot Brigade have just come up with a psycho-political profile of Wilt and it looks bad.'

'It's going to look a damned sight worse if the bastard doesn't get down out of that flat in the next three minutes,' said Flint, 'and anyway what the hell is a psycho-political profile?'

'Never mind that now. Just go into a holding pattern with the terrorists on the ground floor.'

Leaving Flint feeling like a flight controller trying to deal with two demented pilots on a collision course, he hurried through to the conference room.

'Right,' he said, 'I've ordered all armed personnel to fall back to lessen the tension. Now do we allow the swop to go ahead or not?'

Dr Felden was in no doubt. 'No,' he said. 'From the data we have accumulated there is no doubt in my mind that Wilt is a latent psychopath with extremely dangerous homicidal tendencies and to let him loose . . .'

'I cannot agree,' said Professor Maerlis. 'The transcripts of the conversations he has been having with the Schautz woman indicate a degree of ideological commitment to post-Marcusian anarchism of the highest possible order. I would go further . . .'

'We haven't time, Professor. In fact we've got precisely two minutes and all I want to know is whether to make the swop.'

'My advice is definitely negative,' said the psychiatrist. 'If we add the subject Wilt together with Gudrun Schautz to the two terrorists holding the children the effect will be explosive.'

'That's a great help,' said the Superintendent. 'We're sitting on a keg of dynamite and . . . yes, Major?'

'I suppose if we got all four of them together on the ground floor we could kill two birds with one stone,' said the Major.

The Superintendent looked at him keenly. He had never understood why the S.G.S. had been called in from the beginning and the Major's lack of obvious logic had him baffled.

'If by that you mean we could slaughter everyone in the house I can't see any reason for going ahead with the exchange. We can do that already. The purpose of the exercise is not to kill anyone at all. I want to know how to avoid a bloodbath, not achieve one.'

But events in the house next door had already moved ahead of him. Far from getting the terrorists into a holding pattern, Flint's message that there was a slight technical hitch had met with an immediate reply that if Wilt didn't come down in exactly one minute he would be the father of triplets. But it had been Eva who had forced Wilt to act.

'Henry Wilt,' she yelled up the stairs, 'if you don't come down this minute I'll . . .'

Flint, with his ear glued to the phone heard Wilt's tremulous 'Yes, dear, I'm coming.' He switched on the monitoring device in the field telephone and could hear Wilt stumbling about undressing and presently his faint steps on the staircase. They were followed a moment later by the heavier tread of Eva coming up. Flint went through to the conference room and announced this latest development.

'I thought I told you . . .' began the Superintendent before sitting down heavily. 'So now we're really into a different ballgame.'

The quads had reached much the same conclusion, though they didn't put it like that. As Wilt moved cautiously across the hall into the kitchen they squealed with delight.

'Daddy's got a wigwag, Mummy's got a cunt. Mummy wee-wees down her legs and Daddy out in front,' they chanted to the amazement of the terrorists and the disgust of Mrs de Frackas.

'How utterly revolting,' she said, combining criticism of their language with her verdict on Wilt. She had never liked him with

409

his clothes on: without them she detested him. Not only was this wretch responsible for the lethal concoction that had made her head behave like a sensient ping-pong ball in a mixing bowl, and was now, by the flaming feel of things, busily at work cauterizing her waterworks but he was presenting a full frontal view of that diabolical organ which had once helped to thrust four of the most loathsome little girls she had ever met onto an already suffering world. And all this with a blatant disregard for those social niceties to which she was accustomed. Mrs de Frackas threw caution to the winds.

'If you think for one moment I intend to remain in a house with a naked man you're much mistaken,' she said and headed for the kitchen door.

'Stay where you are,' shouted Baggish, but Mrs de Frackas had lost what little fear she had ever possessed. She kept on going.

'One more move and I fire,' yelled Baggish. Mrs de Frackas snorted derisively and moved. So did Wilt. As the gun came up he hurled himself and the quads who were clutching him out of the line of fire. It was also out of the kitchen. The cellar door stood open. Wilt and his brood shot through it, cascaded down the steps, slid across the pea-strewn floor and ended up in the coal-heap. Above them a shot rang out, a thud, and the cellar door slammed to as Mrs de Frackas crashed against it and slumped to the ground.

Wilt waited no longer. He had no wish to hear any more shots. He scrambled up the pile of coal and heaved with his shoulders against the iron lid of the chute. Beneath his feet the coal slithered but the cover was moving and his head and shoulders were in the open air. The cover slid forward and Wilt crawled out before dragging each quad up and dropping the lid back in place. For a moment he hesitated. To his right were the kitchen windows, to his left the door, but beyond that were the dustbins and more usefully Eva's Organic Compost Collector. For the first time Wilt regarded the bin with gratitude. No matter what it contained it had space for them all and was, thanks to the insistence of the Health Authorities, constructed of alternative wood or concrete. Wilt hesitated long enough to scoop the quads up under his arms and then dashed for the thing and dropped them in before hurling himself on top of them.

410

'Oh, daddy, this is fun,' squawked Josephine, raising a face that was largely covered with rotten tomato.

'Shut up,' snarled Wilt and shoved her down into the mess. Then, conscious that anyone opening the kitchen door might see them, he burrowed down into the stinking remains of cabbages, fish ends and the household garbage until it was almost impossible to tell where Wilt and the children began and the compost ended.

'It's ever so warm,' squeaked the indefatigable Josephine from beneath a seasoning of decomposing courgettes.

'It will be a sight warmer if you don't keep your trap shut,' said Wilt wishing to hell he had. His mouth was half-filled with eggshell and something that suggested it had once seen the inside of a vacuum cleaner and should have stayed there. Wilt spat the mixture out and as he did so there came the sound of rapid fire from somewhere within the house. The terrorists were shooting at random into the darkness of the cellar. Wilt stopped spitting and wondered what the hell was going to happen to Eva now.

He had no need to worry. In the attic Eva was busy. She had already used the broken glass of the balcony window to cut the ropes on her hands and had untied her legs. Then she had gone through to the kitchen. As Wilt had passed her on the stairs he had whispered something about the bitch being in the bathroom. Eva had said nothing. She was reserving her comments on his behaviour with the bitch until the children were safe and the way to ensure that was to take Gudrun Schautz downstairs and do what the terrorists wanted. But now as she tried the bathroom door she heard the shot that had felled Mrs de Frackas. It was the signal for all the pent-up fury inside her to let itself loose. If any of the children had been murdered, the vile creature she had invited into her house would die too. And if Eva had to die she would take as many of the terrorists as she could with her. Standing in front of the bathroom door she raised a muscular leg. The next moment a further volley of shots came from below and the sole of Eva's foot slammed forward. The door tore from its hinges and the lock splintered. Eva kicked again; the door fell back into the bath and Eva Wilt stepped over it. In the corner by the washbasin crouched a

411

woman as naked as Eva herself. They had nothing else in common. Gudrun Schautz's body bore no marks of birth upon it. It was as smooth and synthetically attractive as the centre-page of a girlie magazine and her face mocked its appeal. From a mask of terror and madness her eyes stared blankly, her cheeks were the colour of putty, and her mouth uttered the meaningless sounds of a terrified animal.

But Eva was beyond pity. She moved forward, ponderously implacable, and then with surprising swiftness her hands struck out and clenched in the woman's hair. For a moment Gudrun Schautz struggled before Eva's knee came up. Gasping for breath and doubled over, Gudrun was dragged from the bathroom and thrown to the kitchen floor. Eva pinned her down with a knee between her shoulder blades and twisting her arms behind her tied her wrists with the electric cord before gagging her with a cloth from the sink. Finally she bound her legs together with a strip of towel.

All this Eva did with as little compunction as she would have trussed a chicken for Sunday lunch. A plan had matured in her mind, a plan that seemed almost to have been waiting for this moment, a plan born of desperation and murder. She turned and foraged in the cupboard under the sink and found what she was looking for, the rope fire escape she had had installed when the flat was first built. It was designed to hang from a hook over the balcony window to save lives in an emergency, but she had a different purpose for it now. And as more shots echoed from below she went swiftly to work. She cut the rope in two and fetched an upright chair which she placed in the middle of the bedroom facing the door. Then she dragged the bed over and wedged it on top of the chair before going back to the kitchen and pulling her captive by the ankles across the room onto the balcony. A minute later she was back with the two lengths of rope and had tied them to the legs of the chair, slid them over the hook and, leaving one slack, threaded the other under the woman's arms, wound it round her body and knotted it. The second she coiled neatly on the floor by the chair and, with unconscious expertise, looped the other end into a noose and slipped it over the terrorist's head and around her throat.

Then Gudrun Schautz, who had put the fear of death into so many other innocent people, came to know its terror herself.

412

For a moment she squirmed on the balcony, but Eva was already back in the room and dragging on the rope round her chest. Gudrun Schautz rose sagging to her feet as Eva hauled. Then she was off the ground and level with the railing. Eva tied the rope to the bed and went back to the balcony and hoisted her over the railing. Below lay the patio and oblivion. Finally Eva removed the gag and returned to the chair. But before sitting down she opened the door to the stairs and loosened the rope from the bed. Grasping it in both hands, she played it out until it had run over the balcony rail and seemed taut. Still grasping it, she pushed the bed off the chair and sat down. Then she let go. For a second it felt as if the chair would lift under the strain but her weight held it down. The moment she was shot or rose from the chair it would hurtle away across the room and the murderess now dangling on the makeshift scaffold would drop to her death by hanging. In her own frighteningly domestic way Eva Wilt had re-established the terrible scales of Justice.

That was hardly the way it looked to the viewers in the Conference Room next door. On the TV screen Eva took on the dimensions of some archetypal Earth Mother and her actions had a symbolic quality surpassing mere reality. Even Dr Felden, whose experience of homicidal maniacs was extensive, was appalled, while Professor Maerlis, witnessing for the first time the awful preparations of a naked hangwoman, was heard to mutter something about a great beast slouching towards Bedlam. But it was the representative of the League of Personal Liberties who reacted most violently. Mr Symper could not believe his eyes.

'Dear God,' he squawked, 'she's going to hang the poor girl. She's out of her mind. Someone must stop her.'

'Can't see why, old boy,' said the Major. 'Always been in favour of capital punishment myself.'

'But it's illegal,' shrieked Mr Symper, and appealed to Mr Gosdyke, but the solicitor had shut his eyes and was considering a plea of diminished responsibility. On the whole he thought it less likely to convince a jury than justified homicide. Self-defence was clearly out. In the view of the wide-angle lens in the field telephone Eva bulked gigantic while Gudrun Schautz had the tiny proportions of one of Major-General de Frackas' toy

413

soldiers. Professor Maerlis as usual took refuge in logic.

'An interesting ideological situation,' he said. 'I cannot think of a clearer example of social polarization. On the one hand we have Mrs Wilt and on the other . . .'

'A headless Kraut by the look of things,' said the Major enthusiastically as Eva, having hauled Gudrun Schautz into the air, shoved her over the balcony railing. 'I don't know what the proper drop for a hanging is but I should have thought forty feet was a bit excessive.'

'Excessive?' squeaked Mr Symper. 'It's positively monstrous. And what's more I take exception to your use of the word "kraut". I shall protest most vehemently to the authorities.'

'Odd bod,' said the Major as the secretary of the League of Personal Liberties rushed from the room. 'Anyone would think Mrs Wilt was the terrorist instead of a devoted mother.'

It was more or less the attitude adopted by Inspector Flint. 'Listen, mate,' he told the distraught Symper, 'you can lead as many protest marches as you fucking well like but don't come yelling at me that Mrs Bloody Wilt is a murderess. You brought her here . . .'

'I didn't know she was going to hang people. I refuse to be party to a private execution.'

'No, well you won't be that. You're an accessory. The bastards on the ground floor have bumped off Wilt and the children by the sound of things. How's that for loss of personal liberties?'

'But they wouldn't have if you had let them go. They . . .'

Flint had heard enough. Much as he had disliked Wilt the thought that this hysterical do-gooder was blaming the police for refusing to give way to the demands of a group of blood-thirsty foreigners was too much for him. He rose from his chair and grabbed Mr Symper by the lapels. 'All right, if that's the way you feel about it I'm sending you next door to persuade the Widow Wilt to come downstairs and let herself be shot by . . .'

'I won't go,' gibbered Mr Symper. 'You've no right . . .'

Flint tightened his grip and was frogmarching him backwards down the hall when Mr Gosdyke interrupted.

'Inspector, something has got to be done immediately. Mrs Wilt is taking the law into her own hands!'

'Good for her,' said Flint. 'This little shit has just volunteered

414

to act as an emissary to our friendly neighbourhood freedom fighters . . .'

'I have done nothing of the sort,' squeaked Mr Symper. 'Mr Gosdyke, I appeal to you to . . .'

The solicitor ignored him. 'Inspector Flint, if you are prepared to give an undertaking that my client will not be held responsible, questioned, taken into custody, charged or placed on remand or in any way proceeded against for what she is evidently about to do . . .'

Flint released the egregious Mr Symper. Years of courtroom procedure told him when he was beaten. He followed Mr Gosdyke into the Conference Room and studied Eva Wilt's astonishing posterior with amazement. Gosdyke's remark about taking the law into her own hands seemed totally inappropriate. She was flattening the damned thing. Flint looked to Dr Felden.

'Mrs Wilt is obviously in an extremely disturbed mental state, Inspector. We must try to reassure her. I suggest you use the telephone. . . .'

'No,' said Professor Maerlis. 'Mrs Wilt may appear from this angle to have the proportions of an attenuated gorilla, but even so I doubt if she could reach the telephone without getting off the chair.'

'And what's so wrong with that?' demanded the Major aggressively. 'The Schautz bitch has it coming to her.'

'Perhaps, but we don't want to make a martyr of her. She already has a very considerable political charisma . . .'

'Bugger her charisma,' said Flint, 'she's had the rest of the Wilt family martyred and we can always claim that her death was accidental.'

The Professor looked at him sceptically. 'You could try, I suppose, but I think you'd have some difficulty persuading the media that a woman who has been suspended from a balcony on the end of two ropes, one of which had been expertly knotted round her neck, and who was subsequently hanged and/or decapitated, died in any meaningfully accidental manner. Of course its up to you but . . .'

'All right, then what the hell do you suggest?'

'Turn a blind eye, old boy,' said the Major. 'After all Mrs Wilt is only human . . .'

415

'Only?' muttered Dr Felden. 'A clearer example of anthromorphism . . .'

'And she's got to answer the call of nature sometime.'

'Call of nature?' shouted Flint. 'She's done that already. She's squatting there like a ruddy performing elephant . . .'

'Pee, old boy, pee,' continued the Major. 'She's got to get up to have a pee sooner or later.'

'Pray later than sooner,' said the psychiatrist. 'The thought of that ghastly shape getting off that chair would be too much to bear.'

'Anyway she's probably got a bladder like a barrage balloon,' said Flint. 'Mind you, she can't be any too warm and there's nothing like cold for making one hit the piss-pot.'

'In which case it's curtains for La Schautz,' said the Major. 'Lets us off the hook, what?'

'I can think of happier ways of putting it,' said the Professor, 'and it would still leave us with the problem of Fräulein Schautz's evident martyrdom.'

Flint left them arguing and went out to look for the Superintendent. As he passed through the Communication Centre he was stopped by the sergeant. A series of squeaks and squelches was coming from one of the listening devices.

'It's the boom aimed at the kitchen window,' the sergeant explained.

'Kitchen window?' said Flint incredulously. 'Sounds more like a squad of mice tap-dancing in a septic tank. What the hell are those squeaks?'

'Children,' said the sergeant. 'Hardly likely, I know, but I've yet to hear one mouse tell another to shut its fucking trap. And it's not coming from inside the house. The two wogs have been complaining that they haven't anyone left to shoot. If you want my opinion . . .'

But Flint was already clambering across the rubble of the conservatory in search of the Superintendent. He found him lying in the grass beside the summerhouse at the bottom of the Wilts' garden, studying Gudrun Schautz's anatomy through a pair of binoculars.

'Extraordinary lengths these lunatics will go to gain some publicity,' he said by way of explanation. 'It's a good thing we've kept the TV cameras out of range.'

416

'She's not up there out of choice,' said Flint. 'It's Mrs Wilt's doing and we've got a chance to take the two swine on the ground floor. They're out of hostages for the time being.'

'Are they really?' said the Superintendent, and transferred his observation to the kitchen windows with some reluctance. A moment later he was refocusing his binoculars on the compost bin.

'Good God,' he muttered, 'I've heard of rapid fermentation but . . . Here, you take a look at that bin by the back door.'

Flint took the binoculars and looked. In close-up he could see what the Superintendent meant by rapid fermentation. The compost was alive. It moved, it heaved, several bean haulms rose and fell, while a beetroot suddenly emerged from the sludge and promptly disappeared again. Finally, and most disconcertingly of all, something that resembled a Hallowe'en pumpkin with matted hair peered over the side of the bin.

Flint closed his eyes, opened them again and found himself looking through a mask of decaying vegetable matter at a very familiar face.

Chapter 22

Five minutes later Wilt was hauled unceremoniously from the compost heap while a dozen armed policemen aimed guns at the kitchen door and windows.

'Bang, bang, you're dead,' squealed Josephine as she was lifted from the mess. A constable bundled her through the hedge and went back for Penelope. Inside the house the terrorists made no move. They were being kept occupied on the phone by Flint.

'You can forget any deals,' he was saying as the Wilt family were led through the conservatory. 'Either you come out with your hands up and no guns or we're coming in firing, and after the first ten bullets you won't know what hit you . . . Christ, what's that revolting smell?'

'It says it's called Samantha,' said the constable who was carrying the foetid child.

'Well take it away and disinfect the beastly thing,' said Flint, groping for a handkerchief.

'I don't want to be disinfected,' bawled Samantha. Flint turned a weary eye on the group and for a moment had the nightmarish feeling that he was looking at something in an advanced state of decomposition. But the vision faded. He could see now that it was simply Wilt clotted with compost.

'Well, look what the cat dragged in. If it isn't Compost Casanova himself, our beanstalk hero of the hour. I've seen some sickening sights in my time but . . .'

'Charming,' said Wilt. 'Considering what I've just been through I can do without cracks about nostalgie de la boue. And what about Eva? She's still in there and if you start shooting . . .'

'Shut up, Wilt,' said Flint, lumbering to his feet. 'For your information, if it weren't for Mrs Wilt's latest enthusiasm for hanging people we'd have been into that house an hour ago.'

'Her enthusiasm for *what*?'

'Someone give him a blanket,' said Flint, 'I've seen enough of this human vegetable to last me a lifetime.' He went into the Conference Room followed by Wilt wrapped rather meagrely in one of Mrs de Frackas' shawls.

'Gentlemen, I'd like you all to meet Mr Henry Wilt,' he told the dumbfounded Psycho-Warfare Team, 'or should I say Comrade Wilt?'

Wilt didn't hear the crack. He was staring at the television screen. 'That's Eva,' he said numbly.

'Yes, well, it takes one to know one, I suppose,' said Flint, 'and on the end of all those ropes is your playmate, Gudrun Schautz. The moment your missus gets up from that chair you're going to find yourself married to the first British female executioner. Now that's fine with me. I'm all in favour of capital punishment and women's lib. Unfortunately these gentlemen don't share my lack of prejudice and home hanging is against the law, so if you don't want to see Mrs Wilt on a charge of justifiable homicide you'd better come up with something quick.' But Wilt sat staring in dismay at the screen. His own alternative terrorism had been tame by comparison with Eva's. She was sitting there calmly waiting to be murdered and had devised a hideous deterrent.

'Can't you call her on the telephone?' he asked finally.

'Use your loaf. The moment she gets off . . .'

'Quite,' said Wilt hastily. 'And I don't suppose there's any way of putting a net or something under Miss Schautz. I mean . . .'

Flint laughed nastily. 'Oh, it's Miss Schautz now, is it? Such modesty. Considering that only a few hours ago you were pork-swording the bitch I must say I find . . .'

'Under duress,' said Wilt. 'You don't think I make a habit of leaping into bed with killers, do you?'

'Wilt,' said Flint, 'what you do in your spare time is no concern of mine. Or wouldn't be if you kept within the limits of the law. Instead of which you fill your house with terrorists and give them lectures in the theory of mass murder.'

'But that was—'

'Don't argue. We've got every word you said on tape. We've built up a psycho . . .'

'Profile,' prompted Dr Felden, studying Wilt in preference to watching Eva on the screen.

'Thank you, doctor. A psycho-profile of you . . .'

'Psycho-political profile,' said Professor Maerlis. 'I would like to hear Mr Wilt explain where he gained such an extensive knowledge of the theory of terrorism.'

Wilt scraped a carrot-peeling from his ear and sighed. It was always the same. No one ever understood him: no one ever would. He was a creature of infinite incomprehensibility and the world was filled with idiots, himself included. And all the time Eva was in danger of being killed and killing. He got wearily to his feet.

'All right, if that's the way you want it I'll go back into the house and put it to those maniacs that . . .'

'Like hell you will,' said Flint. 'You'll stay exactly where you are and come up with a solution to the mess you've got us all into.'

Wilt sat down again. There was no way he could think of to end the stalemate. Happenstance reigned supreme and only chaos could be counted on to determine man's fate.

As if to confirm this opinion there came the sound of a dull rumble from the house nextdoor. It was followed by a violent explosion and the crash of breaking glass.

'My God, the swine have blown themselves up kamikaze-style,' shouted Flint as several toy soldiers toppled on the ping-pong table. He turned and hurried into the Communications Centre with the rest of the Psycho-Warfare Team. Only Wilt remained behind staring fixedly at the television screen. For a moment Eva had seemed to lift from the chair, but she had settled back again and was sitting there as stolidly as ever. From the other room the sergeant could be heard shouting his version of the disaster to Flint.

'I don't know what happened. One moment they were arguing about giving themselves up and claiming we were using poison gas and the next minute the balloon had gone up. I shouldn't think they knew what hit them.'

But Wilt did. With a cheerful smile he stood up and went into the conservatory.

'If you'll just follow me,' he told Flint and the others, 'I can explain everything.'

420

'Hold it there, Wilt,' said Flint. 'Let's get something straight. Are you by any chance suggesting that you're responsible for that explosion?'

'Only in passing,' said Wilt with the sublime confidence of a man who knew he was telling nothing but the truth, 'only in passing. I don't know if you're at all acquainted with the workings of the bio-loo but—'

'Oh shit,' said Flint.

'Precisely, Inspector. Now shit is converted anerobically in the bio-loo or, more properly speaking, the alternative toilet, into methane, and methane is a gas which ignites with the greatest of ease in the presence of air. And Eva has been into self-sufficiency in what you may well call a big way. She had dreams of cooking by perpetual motion, or rather by perpetual motions. So the cooker is hooked to the bio-loo and what goes in one end has got to come out the other and vice versa. Take a boiled egg for instance . . .'

Flint looked incredulously at him. 'Boiled eggs?' he shouted. 'Are you seriously telling me that boiled eggs . . . oh no. No, definitely no. We've been through the pork-pie routine before. You're not fooling me this time. I'm going to get to the bottom of this.'

'Anatomically speaking . . .' began Wilt, but Flint was already floundering through the conservatory into the garden. One glance over the fence was enough to convince him that Wilt was right. The few remaining windows on the ground floor of the house were spattered with blobs of stained yellow paper and something else. But it was the stench that hit him which was so convincing. The Inspector groped for his handkerchief. Two extraordinary figures had lurched through the shattered patio windows. As terrorists they were unrecognizable. Chinanda and Baggish had taken the full force of the bio-loo and were perfect examples of the worth of their own ideology.

'Shits in shits' clothing,' murmured Professor Maerlis, gazing in awe at the human excreta that stumbled about the lawn.

'Hold it there,' shouted the Head of the Anti-Terrorist Squad as his men aimed revolvers at them, 'we've got you covered.'

'Rather an unnecessary injunction if you ask me,' said Dr Felden. 'I've heard of bullshit baffling brains but I've never realized the destabilizing potential of untreated sewage before.'

421

But the two terrorists were past caring about the destruction of pseudo-democratic fascism. Their concern was purely personal. They rolled on the ground in a frantic attempt to rid themselves of the filth while above them Gudrun Schautz looked down with an idiot smile.

As Baggish and Chinanda were dragged to their feet by reluctant policemen Wilt entered the house. He passed through the devastated kitchen and stepped over old Mrs de Frackas and climbed the stairs. On the landing he hesitated.

'Eva,' he called, 'it's me, Henry. It's all right. The children are safe. The terrorists are under arrest. Now don't get up from that chair. I'm coming up.'

'I warn you if this is some sort of trick I won't be responsible for what happens,' shouted Eva.

Wilt smiled to himself happily. That was the old Eva talking in defiance of all logic. He went up to the attic and stood in the doorway looking at her with open admiration. There was nothing silly about Eva now. Sitting naked and unashamed she possessed a strength he would never have.

'Darling,' he began incautiously before stopping. Eva was studying him with frank disgust.

'Don't you "darling" me, Henry Wilt,' she said. 'And how did you get in that filthy state?'

Wilt looked down at his torso. Now that he came to examine it he was in a filthy state. A piece of celery poked rather ambiguously from Mrs de Frackas' shawl.

'Well, as a matter of fact, I was in the compost heap with the children . . .'

'With the children?' shouted Eva furiously. 'In the compost heap?'

And before Wilt could explain she had risen from the chair. As it shot across the room Wilt hurled himself at the rope, clung to it, was slammed against the opposite wall and finally managed to wedge himself behind a wardrobe.

'For Christ's sake, help me pull her up,' he yelled, 'you can't let the bitch hang.'

Eva put her hands on her hips. 'That's your problem. I'm not doing anything to her. You're holding the rope.'

'Only just. And I suppose you're going to tell me that if I really love you I'll let go. Well, let me tell you . . .'

'Don't bother,' shouted Eva. 'I heard you in bed with her. I know what you got up to.'

'Up to?' yelled Wilt. 'The only way I got anything up was by pretending she was you. I know it seems unlikely . . .'

'Henry Wilt, if you think I'm going to stand here and let you insult me . . .'

'I'm not insulting you. I'm paying you the biggest bloody compliment you've ever received. Without you I don't know what I would have done. And now for goodness sake—'

'I know what you did without me,' shouted Eva, 'you made love to that horrible woman . . .'

'Love?' yelled Wilt. 'That wasn't love. That was war. The bitch battened onto me like a sex-starved barnacle and . . .' But it was too late to explain. The wardrobe was shifting and the next moment Wilt, still gripping the rope, rose slowly into the air and moved towards the hook. Behind him came the chair and presently he was crouched up against the ceiling with his head twisted at a curious angle. Eva looked up at him uncertainly. For a second she hesitated, but she couldn't let him stay there and it was wrong to hang the German girl now that the quads were safe.

Eva grabbed Wilt's legs and began to pull. Outside the police had reached Gudrun Schautz and were cutting her down. As the rope broke Wilt fell from his perch and mingled with portions of the chair.

'Oh my poor darling,' said Eva, her voice suddenly taking on a new and, to Wilt, thoroughly alarming solicitude. It was typical of the bloody woman to practically turn him into a cripple and then be conscience-stricken. As she took him in her arms Wilt groaned and decided the time had come to put the boot in diplomatically. He passed out.

On the patio below Gudrun Schautz was unconscious too. Before she could be more than partially strangled she had been lifted down and now the Head of the Anti-Terrorist Squad was giving her the kiss of life rather more passionately than was called for. Flint dragged himself away from this unnatural relationship and cautiously entered the house. A hole in the kitchen floor testified to the destructive force of a ruptured bio-loo. 'Out of their tiny minds,' he muttered behind his handker-

423

chief and slithered through into the hall before climbing the stairs to the attic. The scene that greeted him there confirmed his opinion. The Wilts were clasped in one another's arms. Flint shuddered. He would never understand what these two diabolical people saw in one another. Come to think of it, he didn't want to know. There were some mysteries better left unprobed. He turned back towards his more orderly world where there were no such awful ambiguities and was greeted on the landing by the quads. They were dressed in some clothes they had found in Mrs de Frackas' chest of drawers and wearing hats that had been fashionable before the First World War. As they tried to rush past him Flint stopped them.

'I don't think your mummy and daddy want to be disturbed,' he said, firmly holding to the view that nice children should be spared the sight of their naked parents presumably making love. But the Wilt quads had never been nice.

'What are they doing?' asked Samantha.

Flint swallowed. 'They're . . . er . . . engaged.'

'You mean they're not married?' asked Samantha gleefully adjusting her boa.

'I didn't say that . . .' began Flint.

'Then we're bastards,' squealed Josephine. 'Michael's daddy says if mummies and daddies aren't married their babies are called bastards.'

Flint stared down at the hideously precocious child. 'You can say that again,' he muttered, and went on downstairs. Above him the quads could be heard chanting something about daddies having wigwags and mummies having . . . Flint hurried out of earshot and found the stench in the kitchen a positive relief. Two ambulance men were carrying Mrs de Frackas out on a stretcher. Amazingly she was still alive.

'Bullet lodged in her stays,' said one of the ambulance men. 'Tough old bird. Don't make them like this any more.'

Mrs de Frackas opened a beady eye. 'Are the children still alive?' she asked faintly.

Flint nodded. 'It's all right. They're quite safe. You needn't worry about them.'

'Them?' moaned Mrs de Frackas. 'You can't seriously suppose I'm worried about them. It's the thought that I'll have to live next door to the little savages that . . .'

But the effort to express her horror was too much for her and she sank back on the pillow. Flint followed her out to the ambulance.

'Take me off the drip,' she pleaded as they loaded her inside.

'Can't do that, mum,' said the ambulance man, 'it's against union rules.'

He shut the doors and turned to Flint. 'Suffering from shock, poor old dear. They get like that sometimes. Don't know what they're saying.'

But Flint knew better, and as the ambulance drove away his heart went out to the courageous old lady. He was thinking of asking for a transfer himself.

Chapter 23

It was the end of term at the Tech. Wilt walked across the common with the frost on the grass, ducks waddling by the river and the sun shining out of a cloudless sky. He had no committee meetings to attend and no teaching to do. About the only cloud on the horizon was the possibility that the Principal might congratulate the Wilt family on their remarkable escape from danger. To avert it Wilt had already intimated to the Vice-Principal that such rank hypocrisy would be in the worst of taste. If the Principal were to express his true feelings he would have to admit that he wished to hell the terrorists had carried out their promises.

Dr Mayfield was certainly of this opinion. The Special Branch had been going through the students in Advanced English For Foreigners with a fine-tooth comb and the Anti-Terrorist Squad had detained two Iraquis for questioning. Even the curriculum had been under scrutiny and Professor Maerlis, ably assisted by Dr Board, had submitted a report condemning the seminars on Contemporary Theories of Revolution and Social Change as positively subversive and inciting to violence. And Dr Board had helped to exonerate Wilt.

'Considering the political lunatics he has to cope with in his department it's a wonder Wilt isn't a raving fascist. Take Bilger for example . . .' he had told the Special Branch officer in charge of enquiries. The officer had taken Bilger. He had also screened the film and had viewed it with incredulity.

'If this is the sort of filth you encourage your lecturers to produce it's no bloody wonder the country is in the mess it is,' he told the Principal, who had promptly tried to shift the blame to Wilt.

'I always considered the thing a disgrace,' said Wilt, 'and if you'll check the minutes of the Education Committee meeting you'll see I wanted to make the issue public. I think parents have a right to know when their children are being politically indoctrinated.'

And the minutes had proved him right. From that moment Wilt was given a clean ticket. Officially.

But on the domestic front suspicion still lurked. Eva had taken to waking him in the small hours to demand proof that he loved her.

'Of course I do, damn it,' grunted Wilt. 'How many times do I have to tell you?'

'Actions speak louder than words,' retorted Eva snuggling up to him.

'Oh all right,' said Wilt. And the exercise had done him good. It was a leaner, healthier Wilt who walked briskly to the Tech., and the knowledge that he would never have to take this path again buoyed his spirits. They were moving from Willington Road. The removal van had already arrived when he left and this afternoon the home he returned to would be 45 Oakhurst Avenue. The choice of the new house had been Eva's. It was several steps down the social ladder from Willington Road, but the big house there had bad vibes for her. Wilt deplored the word but agreed. He had always disliked the pretensions of the neighbourhood and Oakhurst Avenue was nicely anonymous.

'At least we'll be away from haute academe and the relicts of Imperial arrogance,' he told Peter Braintree as they sat in The Pig In The Poke after the Principal's pep talk. There had been no mention of Wilt's ordeal and they were celebrating. 'And there's a quiet little pub round the corner so I won't have to brew my own gutrot.'

'Thank heavens for that. But won't Eva pine for the compost heap and all that?'

Wilt drank his beer cheerfully. 'The educative effects of exploding septic tanks have to be seen to be believed,' he said. 'To say that ours revealed the fundamental flaws in the Alternative Society might be going too far but it certainly blew Eva's mind. I've noticed she's taken to medicated toilet paper and it wouldn't surprise me to learn she's making tea with distilled water.'

'But she'll have to find something to occupy her energy.'

Wilt nodded. 'She has. The quads. She's determined to see they don't grow up in the image of Gudrun Schautz. A losing battle, to my way of thinking, but at least I've managed to prise

427

her away from sending them to the Convent. It's remarkable how much better their language has become of late. All in all I have an idea that life is going to be more peaceful from now on.'

But as with so many of Wilt's predictions this one was premature. When, having spent an hour tidying his office, he sauntered contentedly up Oakhurst Avenue it was to find the new house unlit and empty. There was no sign of Eva, the quads or the furniture van. He waited about for an hour and then phoned from a call-box. Eva exploded at the other end.

'Don't blame me,' she shouted, 'the removal men have had to unload the van.'

'Unload the van? What on earth for?'

'Because Josephine hid in the wardrobe and they put that in first, that's why.'

'But they don't have to unload because of that,' said Wilt. 'She wouldn't suffocate and it would teach her a lesson.'

'And what about Mrs de Frackas' cat and the Balls' poodle and Jennifer Willis' four pet rabbits . . .'

'The what?' said Wilt.

'She was playing hostages,' shouted Eva, 'and . . .'

But the coin in the phone box ran out. Wilt didn't bother to put another in. He strolled out along the street wondering what it was about his marriage with Eva that turned everyday events into minor catastrophes. He couldn't bring himself to think what sort of time Josephine was having in the wardrobe. Talk about trauma . . . Oh well, there was nothing like experience. As he passed along Oakhurst Avenue towards the pub Wilt suddenly felt pity for his new neighbours. They still had no idea what was going to hit them.

Wilt on High

Chapter 1

'Days of wine and roses,' said Wilt to himself. It was an inconsequential remark but sitting on the Finance and General Purposes Committee at the Tech needed some relief and for the fifth year running Dr Mayfield had risen to his feet and announced, 'We must put the Fenland College of Arts and Technology on the map.'

'I should have thought it was there already,' said Dr Board, resorting as usual to the literal to preserve his sanity. 'In fact to the best of my knowledge it's been there since 1895 when –'

'You know perfectly well what I mean,' interrupted Dr Mayfield. 'The fact of the matter is that the College has reached the point of no return.'

'From what?' asked Dr Board.

Dr Mayfield turned to the Principal. 'The point I am trying to make –' he began, but Dr Board hadn't finished. 'Is apparently that we are either an aircraft halfway to its destination or a cartographical feature. Or possibly both.'

The Principal sighed and thought about early retirement. 'Dr Board,' he said, 'we are here to discuss ways and means of maintaining our present course structure and staffing levels in the face of the Local Education Authority and Central Government pressure to reduce the College to an adjunct of the Department of Unemployment.'

Dr Board raised an eyebrow. 'Really? I thought we were here to teach. Of course, I may be mistaken but when I first entered the profession, that's what I was led to believe. Now I learn that we're here to maintain course structures, whatever they may be, and staffing levels. In plain English, jobs for the boys.'

'And girls,' said the Head of Catering, who hadn't been listening too carefully. Dr Board eyed her critically.

'And doubtless one or two creatures of indeterminate gender,' he murmured. 'Now, if Dr Mayfield –'

431

'Is allowed to continue,' interrupted the Principal, 'we may arrive at a decision by lunchtime.'

Dr Mayfield continued. Wilt stared out of the window at the new Electronics Building and wondered for the umpteenth time what it was about committees that turned educated and relatively intelligent men and women, all of them graduates of universities, into bitter and boring and argumentative people whose sole purpose seemed to be to hear themselves speak and prove everyone else wrong. And committees had come to dominate the Tech. In the old days, he had been able to come to work and spend his mornings and afternoons trying to teach or at least to awaken some intellectual curiosity in classes of Turners and Fitters or even Plasterers and Printers, and if they hadn't learnt much from him, he had been able to go home in the evening with the knowledge that he had gained something from them.

Now everything was different. Even his title, Head of Liberal Studies, had been changed to that of Communication Skills and Expressive Attainment, and he spent his time on committees or drawing up memoranda and so-called consultative documents or reading similarly meaningless documents from other departments. It was the same throughout the Tech. The Head of Building, whose literacy had always been in some doubt, had been forced to justify classes in Bricklaying and Plastering in a 45-page discussion paper on 'Modular Construction and Internal Surface Application', a work of such monumental boredom and bad grammar, that Dr Board had suggested forwarding it to the RIBA with the recommendation that he be given a Fellowship in Architectural Semanticism – or alternatively Cementicism. There had been a similar row over the monograph submitted by the Head of Catering on 'Dietetic Advances In Multi-Phased Institutional Provisioning', to which Dr Mayfield had taken exception on the grounds that the emphasis on faggots and Queen's Pudding might lead to a misunderstanding in certain quarters. Dr Cox, Head of Science, had demanded to know what a Multi-Phased Institution was, and what the hell was wrong with faggots, he'd been brought up on them. Dr Mayfield had explained he was referring to gays and the Head of Catering had confused the issue still further by denying she was a feminist. Wilt had sat through the controversy in silent wondering, as he did now, at the curious modern assumption that you could alter acts by using words in a different way. A cook was a cook no matter that you call him a Culinary Scientist. And calling a gasfitter a Gaseous and Liquefaction Engineer didn't alter the fact that he had taken a course in Gasfitting.

He was just considering how long it would be before they called him an Educational Scientist or even a Mental Processing Officer, when he was drawn from this reverie by a question of 'contact hours'.

'If I could have a breakdown of departmental timetabling on a real-time contact hour basis,' said Dr Mayfield, 'we could computerize those ·areas of overlap which under present circumstances render our staffing levels unviable on a cost-effective analysis.'

There was a silence while the Heads of Departments tried to figure this out. Dr Board snorted and the Principal rose to the bait. 'Well, Board?' he asked.

'Not particularly,' said the Head of Modern Languages, 'but thank you for enquiring all the same.'

'You know very well what Dr Mayfield wants.'

'Only on the basis of past experience and linguistic guesswork,' said Dr Board. 'What puzzles me in the present instance is his use of the phrase "real-time contact hours". Now according to my vocabulary ...'

'Dr Board,' said the Principal, wishing to God he could sack the man, 'what we want to know is quite simply the number of contact hours the members of your department do per week.'

Dr Board made a show of consulting a small notebook. 'None,' he said finally.

'None?'

'That's what I said.'

'Are you trying to say your staff do no teaching at all? That's a downright lie. If it isn't ...'

'I didn't say anything about teaching and no one asked me to. Dr Mayfield quite specifically asked for "real time" –'

'I don't give a damn about real-time. He means actual.'

'So do I,' said Dr Board, 'and if any of my lecturers have

been touching their students even for a minute, let alone an hour, I'd –'

'Board,' snarled the Principal, 'you're trying my patience too far. Answer the question.'

'I have. Contact means touching, and a contact hour must therefore mean a touching hour. Nothing more and nothing less. Consult any dictionary you choose, and you'll find it derives directly from the Latin, *contactus*. The infinitive is *contigere* and the past participle *contactum*, and whichever way you look at it, it still means touch. It cannot mean to teach.'

'Dear God,' said the Principal, through clenched teeth, but Dr Board hadn't finished.

'Now I don't know what Dr Mayfield encourages in Sociology and for all I know he may go in for touch teaching, or, what I believe is called in the vernacular "group groping", but in my department . . .'

'Shut up,' shouted the Principal, now well beyond the end of his tether. 'You will all submit in writing the number of teaching hours, the actual teaching hours, each member of your department does . . .'

As the meeting broke up, Dr Board walked down the corridor with Wilt. 'It's not often one can strike a blow for linguistic accuracy,' he said, 'but at least I've thrown a spanner in Mayfield's clockwork mind. The man's mad.'

It was a theme Wilt took up with Peter Braintree in the public bar of The Pig In A Poke half an hour later.

'The whole system is loony,' he said over a second pint, 'Mayfield's given up empire-building with degree courses and he's on a cost-effectiveness kick now.'

'Don't tell me,' said Braintree. 'We've already lost half our textbook allocation this year, and Foster and Carston have been bullied into early retirement. At this rate I'll end up teaching *King Lear* to a class of sixty with eight copies of the play to go round.'

'At least you're teaching something. You want to try Expressive Attainment with Motor Mechanics Three. Expressive Attainment! The sods know all there is to be known about cars in the first place, and I haven't a clue what Expressive

Attainment means. Talk about wasting the taxpayers' money. And anyway, I spend more of my time on committees than I do supposedly teaching. That's what galls me.'

'How's Eva?' asked Braintree, recognizing Wilt's mood and trying to change the subject.

'*Plus ça change, plus c'est la même chose.* Mind you, that's not entirely true. At least she's off Suffrage for Little Children and Votes at Eleven Plus. After those two blokes from PIE came round soliciting and went away with thick ears.'

'Pie?'

'Pedophile Information Exchange. Used to be called child molesters. These two sods made the mistake of trying to get Eva's support for lowering the age of consent to four. I could have told them four was an unlucky number round our way, considering what the quads get up to. By the time Eva had finished with them, they must have thought 45 Oakhurst Avenue was part of some bloody zoo, and they'd broached the topic with a tigress in cub.'

'Serve the swine right.'

'Didn't serve Mr Birkenshaw right though. Samantha promptly organized the other three into CAR, otherwise known as Children Against Rape, and set up a target in the garden. Luckily the neighbours put their communal feet down before one of the little boys in the street got himself castrated. The quads were just warming up with penknives. Well, actually, they were Sabatier knives from the kitchen, and they'd got quite good with them. Emmeline could hit the damned thing's scrotum at eighteen feet, and Penelope punctured it at ten.'

'It?' said Braintree faintly.

'Mind you, it was a bit oversize. They made it out of an old football bladder and two tennis balls. But it was the penis that got the neighbours up in arms. And Mr Birkenshaw. I didn't know he had a foreskin like that. Come to think of it, I doubt if anyone else in the street did either. Not until Emmeline wrote his name on the damned French letter and fixed wrapping paper from the Christmas cake round the end and the wind carried it ten gardens at peak viewing time on Saturday afternoon. It ended up hanging from the cherry tree

435

in Mrs Lorrimer's on the corner. That way you could see BIRKENSHAW down all four streets quite clearly.'

'Good Lord,' said Braintree. 'What on earth did Mr Birkenshaw have to say about it?'

'Not much yet,' said Wilt, 'he's still in shock. Spent most of Saturday night at the cop shop trying to convince them he isn't the Phantom Flasher. They've been trying to catch that lunatic for years and this time they thought they'd got him.'

'What? Birkenshaw? They're out of their tinies, the man's a Town Councillor.

'Was,' said Wilt. 'I doubt if he'll stand again. Not after what Emmeline told the policewoman. Said she knew his prick looked like that because he'd lured her into his back garden and waggled the thing at her.'

'Lured her?' said Braintree dubiously. 'With all due respect to your daughters, Henry, I wouldn't have said they were exactly lurable. Ingenious, perhaps, and ...'

'Diabolical,' said Wilt. 'Don't think I mind what you say about them. I have to live with the hell-cats. Of course she wasn't lured. She's had a vendetta with his little pussy for months because it comes and knocks the stuffing out of ours. She was probably trying to poison the brute. Anyway, she was in his garden and according to her he waggled it. Not his version of course. Claimed he always pees on the compost heap and if little girls choose to lurk ... Anyway, that didn't go down with the policewoman very well either. Said it was unhygienic.'

'Where was Eva while this was going on.'

'Oh, here and there,' said Wilt airily. 'Apart from practically accusing Mr Birkenshaw of being related to the Yorkshire Ripper ... I managed to stop that one going down in the police report by saying she was hysterical. Talk about drawing fire. At least I had the policewoman there to protect me and as far as I know the law of slander doesn't apply to ten-year-olds. If it does, we'll have to emigrate. As it is, I'm having to work nights to keep them at that blasted school for so-called gifted children. The cost is astronomic.'

'I thought Eva was getting something off by helping out there.'

'Helped out is more accurate. In fact, ordered off the

436

premises,' said Wilt and asked for two more pints.

'What on earth for? I'd have thought they'd have been only too glad to have someone as energetic as Eva as an unpaid ancillary cleaning up and doing the cooking.'

'Not when the said ancillary takes it into her head to brighten up their micro-computers with metal polish. Anyway, she screwed the lot and it was a miracle we didn't have to replace them. Mind you, I wouldn't have minded handing over the ones we've got in the house. The place is a deathtrap of I triple E cables and floppy discs, and I can never get near the TV. And when I do, something called a dot matrix printer goes off somewhere and sounds like a hornets' nest in a hurry. And all for what? So that four girls of average if fiendish intelligence can steal a march on snotty-nosed small boys in the scholastic rat-race.'

'We're just old-fashioned,' said Braintree with a sigh. 'The fact is the computer's here to stay and children know how to use them and we don't. Even the language.'

'Don't talk to me about that gobbledygook. I used to think a poke was a crude form of sex. Instead it's something numerical in a programme and a programme's not what it was. Nothing is. Even bugs and bytes. And to pay for this electronic extravaganza, I spend Tuesday night at the prison teaching a bloody gangster what I don't know about E. M. Forster and Fridays at Baconheath Airbase giving lectures on British Culture and Institutions to a load of Yanks with time on their hands till Armageddon.'

'I shouldn't let the news of that leak out to Mavis Mottram,' said Braintree as they finished their beer and left the pub. 'She's taken up Banning the Bomb with a vengeance. She's been on to Betty about it and I'm surprised she hasn't roped Eva in.'

'She tried but it didn't work, for a change. Eva's too busy worrying about the quads to get involved in demonstrations.'

'All the same, I'd keep quiet about the airbase job. You don't want Mavis picketing your house.'

But Wilt wasn't sure. 'Oh, I don't know. It might make us slightly more popular with the neighbours. At the moment they've got it into their thick heads that I'm either a potential mass-murderer or a left-wing revolutionary because I teach at the Tech. Being picketed by Mavis on the wholly false grounds that I'm in favour of the Bomb might improve my image.' They walked back to the Tech by way of the cemetery.

At 45 Oakhurst Avenue, it was one of Eva Wilt's better days. There were days, better days and one of those days. Days were just days when nothing went wrong and she drove the quads to school without too much quarrelling, and came home to do the housework and went shopping and had a tuna-fish salad for lunch and did some mending afterwards and planted something in the garden and picked the children up from school and nothing particularly nasty happened. On one of those days everything went wrong. The quads quarrelled before, during and after breakfast, Henry lost his temper with them and she found herself having to defend them when she knew all the time he was right, the toast got stuck in the toaster and she was late getting the girls to school and something went wrong with the Hoover or the loo wouldn't flush and nothing seemed to be right with the world, so that she was tempted to have a glass of sherry before lunch and that was no good because then she'd want a nap afterwards and the rest of the day would be spent trying to catch up with what she had to do. But on one of her better days she did all the things she did on days and was somehow uplifted by the thought that the quads were doing wonderfully well at The School for The Mentally Gifted and would definitely get scholarships and go on to become doctors or scientists or something really creative, and that it was lovely to be alive in an age when all this was possible and not like it had been when she was a girl and had to do what she was told. It was on such days that she even considered having her mother to live with them instead of being in the old people's home in Luton and wasting all that money. Only considered it, of course, because Henry couldn't stand the old lady and had threatened to walk out and find himself digs if she ever stayed more than three days in the house.

'I'm not having that old bag polluting the atmosphere with her fags and her filthy habits,' he had shouted so loudly that even Mrs Hoggart, who had been in the bathroom at the time, didn't need her hearing aid to get the gist of the message.

'And another thing. The next time I come down to breakfast and find she's been lacing the teapot with brandy, and my brandy at that, I'll strangle the old bitch.'

'You've got no right to talk like that. After all, she is family –'

'Family?' yelled Wilt, 'I'll say she's family. Your fucking family, not mine. I don't foist my father on you –'

'Your father smells like an old badger,' Eva had retaliated, 'he's unhygienic. At least Mother washes.'

'And doesn't she need to, considering all the muck she smears on her beastly mug. Webster wasn't the only one to see the skull beneath the skin. I was trying to shave the other morning . . .'

'Who's Webster?' demanded Eva before Wilt could repeat the disgusting account of Mrs Hoggart's emergence from behind the shower curtain in the altogether.

'Nobody. It's from a poem, and talking about uncorseted breasts the old hag . . .'

'Don't you dare call her that. She's my mother and one day you'll be old and helpless and need –'

'Yes, well maybe, but I'm not helpless now and the last thing I need is that old Dracula in drag haunting the house and smoking in bed. It's a wonder she didn't burn the place down with that flaming duvet.'

It was the memory of that terrible outburst and the smouldering duvet that had prevented Eva from giving in to her better-day intentions. Besides, there had been truth in what Henry had said, even if he had put it quite horribly. Eva's feelings for her mother had always been ambiguous and part of her wish to have her in the house sprang from the desire for revenge. She'd show her what a really good mother was. And so on one of her better days, she telephoned her and told the old lady how wonderfully the quads were getting on and what a happy atmosphere there was in the home and how even Henry related to the children – Mrs Hoggart invariably broke into a hacking cough at this point – and on the best of days, invited her over for the weekend only to regret it almost as soon as she'd put the phone down. By then it had become one of those days.

But today she resisted the temptation and went round to

Mavis Mottram's to have a heart-to-heart with her before lunch. She just hoped Mavis wouldn't try recruiting her for the Ban the Bomb demo.

Mavis did. 'It's no use your saying you have your hands full with the quads, Eva,' she said, when Eva had pointed out that she couldn't possibly leave the children with Henry, and what would happen if she were sent to prison. 'If there's a nuclear war you won't have any children. They'll all be dead in the first second. I mean Baconheath puts us in a first-strike situation. The Russians would be forced to take it out to protect themselves and we'd all go with it.'

Eva tried to puzzle this out. 'I don't see why we'd be a first-strike target if the Russians were being attacked,' she said finally, 'wouldn't it be a second strike?'

Mavis sighed. It was always so difficult to get things across to Eva. It always had been, and with the barrier of the quads behind which to retreat, it was practically impossible nowadays. 'Wars don't start like that. They start over trivial little things like the Archduke Ferdinand being assassinated at Sarajevo in 1914,' she said, putting it as simply as her work with the Open University allowed. But Eva was not impressed.

'I don't call assassinating people trivial,' she said. 'It's wicked and stupid.'

Mavis cursed herself. She ought to have remembered that Eva's experience with terrorists had prejudiced her against political murders. 'Of course it is. I'm not saying it isn't. What I'm –'

'It must have been terrible for his wife,' said Eva, pursuing her line of domestic consequences.

'Since she happened to be killed with him, I don't suppose she cared all that much,' said Mavis bitterly. There was something quite horribly anti-social about the whole Wilt family but she ploughed on. 'The whole point I'm trying to make is that the most terrible war in the history of mankind, up till then, happened because of an accident. A man and his wife were shot by a fanatic, and the result was that millions of ordinary people died. That sort of accident could happen again, and this time there'd be no one left. The human race would be extinct. You don't want that to happen, do you?'

Eva looked unhappily at a china figurine on the mantelshelf.

440

She knew it had been a mistake to come anywhere near Mavis on one of her better days. 'It's just that I don't see what I can do to stop it,' she said and threw Wilt into the fray. 'And anyway, Henry says the Russians won't stop making the bomb and they've got nerve gas too, and Hitler had as well, and he'd have used it if he'd known we hadn't during the war.' Mavis took the bait.

'That's because he's got a vested interest in things staying the way they are,' she said. 'All men have. That's why they're against the women's peace movement. They feel threatened because we're taking the initiative and in a sense the bomb is symbolic of the male orgasm. It's potency on a mass destruction level.'

'I hadn't thought of it like that,' said Eva, who wasn't quite sure how a thing that killed everyone could be a symbol of an orgasm. 'And after all, he used to be a member of CND.'

'"Used to",' sniffed Mavis, 'but not any longer. Men just want us to be passive and stay in a subordinate sex role.'

'I'm sure Henry doesn't. I mean he's not very active sexually,' said Eva, still preoccupied with exploding bombs and orgasms.

'That's because you're a normal person,' said Mavis. 'If you hated sex he'd be pawing you all the time. Instead, he maintains his power by refusing you your rights.'

'I wouldn't say that.'

'Well, I would, and it's no use your claiming anything different.'

It was Eva's turn to look sceptical. Mavis had complained too often in the past about her husband's numerous affairs. 'But you're always saying Patrick's too sex-oriented.'

'Was,' said Mavis with rather sinister emphasis. 'His days of gadding about are over. He's learning what the male menopause is like. Prematurely.'

'Prematurely? I should think it must be. He's only forty-one, isn't he?'

'Forty,' said Mavis, 'but he's aged lately, thanks to Dr Kores.'

'Dr Kores? You don't mean to say Patrick went to her after that dreadful article she wrote in the *News*? Henry burnt the paper before the girls could read it.'

'Henry would. That's typical. He's anti freedom of information.'

'Well, it wasn't a very nice article, was it? I mean it's all very well to say that men are ... well ... only biological sperm banks but I don't think it's right to want them all neutered after they've had two children. Our cat sleeps all day and he's –'

'Honestly, Eva, you're so naïve. She didn't say anything about neutering them. She was simply pointing out that women have to suffer all the agonies of childbirth, not to mention the curse, and with the population explosion the world will face mass starvation unless something's done.'

'I can't see Henry being done. Not that way,' said Eva. 'He won't even let anyone talk about vasectomy. Says it has unwanted side-effects.'

Mavis snorted. 'As if the Pill didn't too, and far more dangerous ones. But the multi-national pharmaceutical corporations couldn't care less. All they are interested in is profits and they're controlled by men too.'

'I suppose so,' said Eva, who'd got used to hearing about multi-national companies though she still didn't know exactly what they were, and was completely at a loss with 'pharmaceutical'. 'All the same, I'm surprised Patrick agreed.'

'Agreed?'

'To have a vasectomy.'

'Who said anything about him having a vasectomy?'

'But you said he went to Dr Kores.'

'*I* went,' said Mavis grimly. 'I thought to myself, "I've had just about enough of you gallivanting about with other women, my boy, and Dr Kores may be able to help." And I was right. She gave me something to reduce his sex drive.'

'And he took it?' said Eva, genuinely astounded now.

'Oh, he takes it all right. He's always been keen on vitamins, especially Vitamin E. So I just swapped the capsules in the bottle. They're some sort of hormone or steroid and he takes one in the morning and two at night. Of course, they're still in the experimental stage but she told me they'd worked very well with pigs and they can't do any harm. I mean he's put on some weight and he's complained about his teats being a bit swollen, but he's certainly quietened down a lot. He never

442

goes out in the evening. Just sits in front of the telly and dozes off. It's made quite a change.'

'I should think it has,' said Eva, remembering how randy Patrick Mottram had always been. 'But are you really sure it's safe?'

'Absolutely. Dr Kores assured me they're going to use it on gays and transvestites who are frightened of a sex-change operation. It shrinks the testicles or something.'

'That doesn't sound very nice. I wouldn't want Henry's shrinking.'

'I daresay not,' said Mavis, who had once made a pass at Wilt at a party, and still resented the fact that he hadn't responded. 'In his case she could probably give you something to stimulate him.'

'Do you really think so?'

'You can always try,' said Mavis. 'Dr Kores does understand women's problems and that's more than you can say for most doctors.'

'But I didn't think she was a proper doctor like Dr Buchman. Isn't she something in the University?'

Mavis Mottram stifled an impulse to say that, yes, she was a consultant in animal husbandry at that, which should suit Henry Wilt's needs even better than Patrick's.

'The two aren't mutually incompatible, Eva. I mean there is a medical school at the University, you know. Anyway, the point is, she's set up a clinic for women with problems, and I do think you'd find her very sympathetic and helpful.'

By the time Eva left and returned to 45 Oakhurst Avenue and a lunch of celery soup with bran magi-mixed into it, she was convinced. She would phone Dr Kores and go and see her about Henry. She was also rather pleased with herself. She had managed to divert Mavis from the depressing topic of the Bomb and on to alternative medicine and the need for women to determine the future because men had made such a mess of the past. Eva was all for that, and when she drove down to fetch the quads it was definitely one of her better days. New possibilities were burgeoning all over the place.

Chapter 2

They were burgeoning all over the place for Wilt as well, but he wouldn't have put the day into the category of one of his better ones. He had returned to his office smelling of The Pig In A Poke's best bitter and hoping he could do some work on his lecture at the airbase without being disturbed, only to find the County Advisor on Communication Skills waiting for him with another man in a dark suit. 'This is Mr Scudd from the Ministry of Education,' said the Advisor. 'He's making a series of random visits to Colleges of Further Education on behalf of the Minister, to ascertain the degree of relevance of certain curricula.'

'How do you do,' said Wilt, and retreated behind his desk. He didn't like the County Advisor very much, but it was as nothing to his terror of men in dark grey suits, and three-piece ones at that, who acted on behalf of the Minister of Education. 'Do take a seat.'

Mr Scudd stood his ground. 'I don't think there's anything to be gained from sitting in your office discussing theoretical assumptions,' he said. 'My particular mandate is to report my observations, my personal observations, of what is actually taking place on the classroom floor.'

'Quite,' said Wilt, hoping to hell nothing was actually taking place on any of his classroom floors. There had been a singularly nasty incident some years before when he'd had to stop what had the makings of a multiple rape of a rather too attractive student teacher by Tyres Two, who'd been inflamed by a passage in *By Love Possessed* which had been recommended by the Head of English.

'Then if you'll lead the way,' said Mr Scudd and opened the door. Behind him, even the County Advisor had assumed a hangdog look. Wilt led the way into the corridor.

'I wonder if you'd mind commenting on the ideological bias of your staff,' said Mr Scudd, promptly disrupting Wilt's desperate attempt to decide which class it would be safest to take the man into. 'I noticed you had a number of books on Marxism–Leninism in your office.'

'As a matter of fact, I do,' said Wilt and bided his time. If the sod had come on some sort of political witch-hunt, the emollient response seemed best. That way the bastard would land with his bum in the butter, but fast.

'And you consider them suitable reading matter for the working-class apprentices?'

'I can think of worse,' said Wilt.

'Really? So you admit to a left-wing tendency in your teaching.'

'Admit? I didn't admit to anything. You said I had books on Marxism–Leninism in my office. I don't see what that's got to do with what I teach.'

'But you also said you could think of worse reading material for your students,' said Mr Scudd.

'Yes,' said Wilt, 'that's exactly what I said.' The bloke was really getting on his wick now.

'Would you mind amplifying that statement?'

'Glad to. How about *Naked Lunch* for starters?'

'*Naked Lunch?*'

'Or *Last Exit From Brooklyn*. Nice healthy reading stuff for young minds, don't you think?'

'Dear God,' muttered the County Advisor, who had gone quite ashen.

Mr Scudd didn't look any too good either, though he inclined to puce rather than grey. 'Are you seriously telling me that you regard those two revolting books ... that you encourage the reading of books like that?'

Wilt stopped outside a lecture room in which Mr Ridgeway was fighting a losing battle with a class of first-year A-level students who didn't want to hear what he thought about Bismark. 'Who said anything about encouraging students to read any particular books?' he asked above the din.

Mr Scudd's eyes narrowed. 'I don't think you quite understand the tenor of my questions,' he said, 'I am here ...' He stopped. The noise coming from Ridgeway's class made conversation inaudible.

'So I've noticed,' shouted Wilt.

The County Advisor staggered to intervene. 'I really think, Mr Wilt,' he began, but Mr Scudd was staring maniacally through the glass pane at the class. At the back, a youth had just passed what looked suspiciously like a joint to a girl with yellow hair in Mohawk style who could have done with a bra.

'Would you say this was a typical class?' he demanded and turned back to Wilt to make himself heard.

'Typical of what?' said Wilt, who was beginning to enjoy the situation. Ridgeway's inability to interest or control supposedly high motivated A-level students would prepare Scudd nicely for the docility of Cake Two and Major Millfield.

'Typical of the way your students are allowed to behave.'

'My students? Nothing to do with me. That's History, not Communication Skills.' And before Mr Scudd could ask what the hell they were doing standing outside a classroom with bedlam going on inside, Wilt had walked on down the corridor. 'You still haven't answered my question,' said Mr Scudd when he had caught up.

'Which one?'

Mr Scudd tried to remember. The sight of that bloody girl had thrown his concentration. 'The one about the pornographic and revoltingly violent reading matter,' he said finally.

'Interesting,' said Wilt. 'Very interesting.'

'What's interesting?'

'That you read that sort of stuff. I certainly don't.'

They went up a staircase and Mr Scudd made use of the handkerchief he kept folded for decoration in his breast pocket. 'I don't read that filth,' he said breathlessly when they reached the top landing.

'Glad to hear it,' said Wilt.

'And I'd be glad to hear why you raised the issue.' Mr Scudd's patience was on a short leash.

'I didn't,' said Wilt, who, having reached the classroom in which Major Millfield was taking Cake Two, had reassured himself that the class was as orderly as he'd hoped. 'You raised it in connection with some historical literature you found in my office.'

'You call Lenin's *State and Revolution* historical literature? I most certainly don't. It's communist propaganda of a particularly virulent kind, and I find the notion that it's being fed to young minds in your department extremely sinister.'

Wilt permitted himself a smile. 'Do go on,' he said. 'There's nothing I enjoy more than listening to a highly trained intelligence leapfrogging common sense and coming to the wrong conclusions. It gives me renewed faith in parliamentary democracy.'

Mr Scudd took a deep breath. In a career spanning some thirty years of uninterrupted authority and bolstered by an inflation-linked pension in the near future, he had come to have a high regard for his own intelligence and he had no intention of having it disparaged now. 'Mr Wilt,' he said, 'I would be grateful to know what conclusions I am supposed to draw from the observation that the Head of Communication Skills at this College has a shelf full of works of Lenin in his office.'

'Personally, I'd be inclined not to draw any,' said Wilt, 'but if you press me ...'

'I most certainly do,' said Mr Scudd.

'Well, one thing's for certain. I wouldn't suppose that the bloke was a raving Marxist.'

'Not a very positive answer.'

'Not a very positive question, come to that,' said Wilt. 'You asked me what conclusions I'd arrive at and when I tell you I wouldn't arrive at any, you're still not satisfied. I don't see what more I can do.'

But before Mr Scudd could reply, the County Advisor forced himself to intervene. 'I think Mr Scudd simply wants to know if there's any political bias in the teaching in your department.'

'Masses,' said Wilt.

'Masses?' said Mr Scudd.

'Masses?' echoed the County Advisor.

'Absolutely stuffed with it. In fact, if you were to ask me ...'

'I am,' said Mr Scudd. 'That's precisely what I'm doing.'

'What?' said Wilt.

'Asking you how much political bias there is,' said Mr Scudd, having recourse to his handkerchief again.

'In the first place, I've told you, and in the second, I thought you said you didn't think there was anything to be gained from discussing theoretical assumptions and you'd come to see for yourself what went on on the classroom floor. Right?' Mr Scudd swallowed and looked desperately at the County Advisor, but Wilt went on. 'Right. Well you just take a shuftie in there where Major Millfield is having a class with Fulltime Caterers brackets Confectionery and Bakery close brackets Year Two, affectionately known as Cake Two, and then come and tell me how much political bias you've managed to squeeze out of the visit.' And without waiting for any further questions, Wilt went back down the stairs to his office.

'Squeeze out?' said the Principal two hours later. 'You have to ask the Minister of Education's Personal Private Secretary how much political bias he can squeeze out of Cake Two?'

'Oh, is that who he was, the Minister of Education's own Personal Private Secretary?' said Wilt. 'Well, what do you know about that? Now if he'd been an HMI ...'

'Wilt,' said the Principal with some difficulty, 'if you think that bastard isn't going to lumber us with one of Her Majesty's Inspectors – in fact I shouldn't be surprised if the entire Inspectorate doesn't descend upon us – and all thanks to you, you'd better think again.'

Wilt looked round at the ad hoc committee that had been set up to deal with the crisis. It consisted of the Principal, the V-P, the County Advisor and, for no apparent reason, the Bursar. 'It's no skin off my nose how many Inspectors he rustles up. Only too glad to have them.'

'You may be but I rather doubt ...' The Principal hesitated. The County Advisor's presence didn't make for a free flow of opinion on the deficiencies of other departments. 'I take it that any remarks I make will be treated as off the record and entirely confidential,' he said finally.

'Absolutely,' said the County Advisor, 'I'm only interested in Liberal Studies and ...'

'How nice to hear that term used again. That's the second time this afternoon,' said Wilt.

'And you might have added the bloody studies,' snarled the Advisor, 'instead of leaving the wretched man with the impression that that other idiot lecturer was a fee-paying member of the Young Liberals and a personal friend of Peter Tatchell.'

'Mr Tatchell isn't a Young Liberal,' said Wilt. 'To the best of my knowledge he's a member of the Labour Party, left of centre of course, but ...'

'And a fucking homosexual.'

'I've no idea. Anyway, I thought the compassionate word was "gay".'

'Shit,' muttered the Principal.

'Or that if you prefer,' said Wilt, 'though I'd hardly describe the term as compassionate. Anyway, as I was saying ...'

'I am not interested in what you are saying. It's what you said in front of Mr Scudd that matters. You deliberately led him to believe that this College, instead of being devoted to Further Education ...'

'I like that "devoted". I really do,' interrupted Wilt.

'Yes, devoted to Further Education, Wilt, and you led him to think we employ nobody but paid-up members of the Communist Party and at the other extreme a bunch of lunatics from the National Front.'

'Major Millfield isn't a member of any party to the best of my knowledge,' said Wilt. 'The fact that he was discussing the social implications of immigration policies –'

'Immigration policies!' exploded the County Advisor. 'He was doing no such thing. He was talking about cannibalism among wogs in Africa and some swine who keeps heads in his fridge.'

'Idi Amin,' said Wilt.

'Never mind who. The fact remains that he was demonstrating a degree of racial bias that could get him prosecuted by the Race Relations Board and you had to tell Mr Scudd to go in and listen.'

'How the hell was I to know what the Major was on about? The class was quiet and I had to warn the other lecturers that the sod was on his way. I mean if you choose to pitch up out of the blue with a bloke who's got no official status ...'

'Official status?' said the Principal. 'I've already told you Mr Scudd just happens to be –'

'Oh, I know all that and it still doesn't add up. The point is he walks into my office with Mr Reading here, noses his way through the books on the shelf, and promptly accuses me of being an agent of the bleeding Comintern.'

'And that's another thing,' said the Principal. 'You deliberately left him with the impression that you use Lenin's whatever it was called ...'

'*The State and Revolution*,' said Wilt.

'As teaching material with day-release apprentices. Am I right, Mr Reading?'

The County Advisor nodded weakly. He still hadn't recovered from those heads in the fridge or the subsequent visit to Nursery Nurses who had been deep in a discussion on the impossible and utterly horrifying topic of post-natal abortion for the physically handicapped. The bloody woman had been in favour of it.

'And that's just the beginning,' continued the Principal, but Wilt had had enough.

'The end,' he said. 'If he'd bothered to be polite, it might have been different but he wasn't. And he wasn't even observant enough to see that those Lenin books belong to the History Department, were stamped to that effect, and were covered with dust. To the best of my knowledge, they've been on that shelf ever since my office was changed and they used to use them for the A-level special subject on the Russian Revolution.'

'Then why didn't you tell him that?'

'Because he didn't ask. I don't see why I should volunteer information to total strangers.'

'What about *Naked Lunch*? You volunteered that all right,' said the County Advisor.

'Only because he asked for worse reading material and I couldn't think of anything more foul.'

'Thank the Lord for small mercies,' murmured the Principal.

'But you definitely stated that the teaching in your department is stuffed – yes, you definitely used the word "stuffed" – with political bias. I heard you myself,' continued the County Advisor.

'Quite right too,' said Wilt. 'Considering I'm lumbered with forty-nine members of staff, including part-timers, and all the teaching they ever do is to natter away to classes and keep them quiet for an hour, I should think their political opinions must cover the entire spectrum, wouldn't you?'

'That isn't the impression you gave him.'

'I'm not here to give impressions,' said Wilt, 'I'm a teacher as a matter of unquestionable fact, not a damned public-relations expert. All right, now I've got to take a class of Electronics Engineers for Mr Stott who's away ill.'

'What's the matter with him?' asked the Principal inadvertently.

'Having another nervous breakdown. Understandably,' said Wilt and left the room.

Behind him the members of the Committee looked wanly at the door. 'Do you really imagine this man Scudd will get the Minister to call for an enquiry?' asked the Vice-Principal.

'That's what he told me,' said the Advisor. 'There are certain to be questions in the House after what he saw and heard. It wasn't simply the sex that got his goat, though that was bad enough in all conscience. The man's a Catholic and the emphasis on contraception –'

'Don't,' whispered the Principal.

'No, the thing that really upset him was being told to go and fuck himself by a drunken lout in Motor Mechanics Three. And Wilt, of course.'

'Isn't there something we can do about Wilt?' the Principal asked despairingly as he and the Vice-Principal returned to their offices.

'I don't see what,' said the V–P. 'He inherited half his staff and since he can't get rid of them, he has to do what he can.'

'What Wilt can do is land us with questions in Parliament, the total mobilization of Her Majesty's Inspectorate and a public enquiry into the way this place is run.'

'I shouldn't have thought they'd go to the lengths of a public enquiry. This man Scudd may have influence but I very much doubt ...'

'I wouldn't. I saw the swine before he left and he was practically demented. What in God's name is post-natal abortion anyway?'

'Sounds rather like murder ...' the Vice-Principal began, but the Principal was way ahead of him on a thought process that would lead to his forced retirement. 'Infanticide. That's it. Wanted to know if I was aware that we were running a course on Infanticide for future Nannies and asked if we had an evening class for Senior Citizens on Euthanasia or Do-It-Yourself Suicide. We haven't, have we?'

'Not to my knowledge.'

'If we had I'd ask Wilt to run it. That bloody man will be the end of me.'

At the Ipford Police Station, Inspector Flint shared his feelings. Wilt had already screwed his chances of becoming a Superintendent and Flint's misery had been compounded by the career of one of his sons, Ian, who had left school and home before taking his A-levels, and after graduating on marijuana and a suspended prison sentence had gone on to be seized by Customs and Excise loaded with cocaine at Dover. 'Bang goes any hope of promotion,' Flint had said morosely when his son was sent down for five years, and had brought down on his own head the wrath of Mrs Flint who blamed him for her son's delinquency. 'If you hadn't been so interested in your own blooming work and getting on and all, and had taken a proper father's interest in him, he wouldn't be where he is now,' she had shouted at him, 'but no, it had to be Yes Sir, No Sir, Oh certainly Sir, and any rotten night work you could get. And week-ends. And what did Ian ever see of his own father? Nothing. And when he did it was always this crime or that villain and how blooming clever you'd been to nick him. That's what your career's done for your family. B. all.'

And for once in his life, Flint wasn't sure she wasn't right. He couldn't bring himself to put it more positively than that. He'd always been right. Or in the right. You had to be to be a good copper, and he certainly hadn't been a bent one. And his career had had to come first.

'You can talk,' he'd said somewhat gratuitously, since it was about the only thing he'd ever allowed her to do apart from the shopping and washing up and cleaning the house and whining on about Ian, feeding the cat and the dog and generally skivvying for him. 'If I hadn't worked my backside off, we wouldn't have the house or the car and you wouldn't have been able to take the little bastard to the Costa ...'

'Don't you dare call him that!' Mrs Flint had shouted, putting the hot iron on his shirt and scorching it in her anger.

'I'll call him what I bloody well like. He's a rotten villain like all the rest of them.'

'And you're a rotten father. About the only thing you ever did as a father was screw me, and I mean screw, because it wasn't anything else as far as I was concerned.' Flint had taken himself out of the house and back to the police station thinking dark thoughts about women and how their place was in the home, or ought to be, and he was going to be the laughing-stock of the Fenland Constabulary with cracks about him visiting the nick over in Bedford to see his own home-grown convict and a drug pusher at that, and what he'd do to the first sod who called him Snowy and harrying ... And all the time there was, on the very edge of his mind, a sense of grievance against Henry fucking Wilt. It had always been there, but now it came back stronger than ever: Wilt had buggered his career with that doll of his and then the siege. Oh, yes, he'd almost admired Wilt at one stage but that was a long time ago, a very long time indeed. The little sod was sitting pretty in his house at Oakhurst Avenue and a good salary at the ruddy Tech, and one day he'd probably be the Principal of the stinking place. Whereas any hope Flint had ever had of rising to Super, and being posted to some place Wilt wasn't, had gone up in smoke. He was stuck with being Inspector Flint for the rest of his natural, and stuck with Ipford. As if to emphasize his lack of any hope, they'd brought Inspector Hodge in as Head of the Drug Squad and a right smart-arse he was too. Oh, they'd tried to butter over the crack, but the Super had called Flint in to tell him personally, and that had to mean something. That he was a dead-beat and they couldn't trust him in the drugs game, because his son was inside. Which had brought on another of his headaches which he'd always thought were migraines, only this time the police doctor had diagnosed hypertension and put him on pills.

'Of course I'm hypertense,' Flint had told the quack. 'With the number of brainy bastards round here who ought to be behind bars, any decent police officer's got to be tense. He wouldn't be any good at nailing the shits if he weren't. It's an occupational hazard.'

'It's whatever you like to call it, but I'm telling you you've got high blood pressure and ...'

'That's not what you said a moment ago,' Flint had flashed

453

back. 'You stated I had tension. Now then, which is it, hyper-tension or high blood pressure?'

'Inspector,' the doctor had said, 'you're not interrogating a suspect now.' (Flint had his reservations about that.) 'And I'm telling you as simply as I can that hypertension and high blood pressure are one and the same thing. I'm putting you on one diuretic a day –'

'One what?'

'It helps you pass water.'

'As if I needed anything to make me do that. I'm up twice in the blasted night as it is.'

'Then you'd better cut down on your drinking. That'll help your blood pressure, too.'

'How? You tell me not to be tense and the one thing that helps is a beer or two in the local.'

'Or eight,' said the doctor, who'd seen Flint in the pub. 'Anyway, it'll bring your weight down.'

'And make me piss less. So you give me a pill to make me piss more and tell me to drink less. Doesn't make sense.'

By the time Inspector Flint left the surgery, he still didn't know what the pills he had to take did for him. Even the doctor hadn't been able to explain how beta-blockers worked. Just said they did and Flint would have to stay on them until he died.

A month later the Inspector could tell the doctor how they worked. 'Can't even type any more,' he said, displaying a pair of large hands with white fingers. 'Look at them. Like bloody celery sticks that have been blanched.'

'Bound to have some side-effects. I'll give you something to relieve those symptoms.'

'I don't want any more of the piss pills,' said Flint. 'Those bleeding things are dehydrating me. I'm on the bloody trot all the time and it's obvious there's not enough blood left in me to get to my fingers. And that's not all. You want to try working some villain over and being taken short just when he's coming up with a confession. I tell you, it's affecting my work.'

The doctor looked at him suspiciously and thought wistfully of the days when his patients didn't answer back and police officers were of a different calibre to Flint. Besides, he didn't

454

like the expression 'working some villain over'. 'We'll just have to try you out on some other medications,' he said, and was startled by the Inspector's reaction.

'Try me out on some other medicines?' he said belligerently. 'Who are you supposed to be treating, me or the bloody medicines? I'm the one with blood pressure, not them. And I don't like being experimented with. I'm not some bleeding dog, you know.'

'I suppose not,' said the doctor, and had doubled the Inspector's dose of beta-blockers but under a different trade name, added some pills to counter the effect on his fingers, and changed the name of the diuretics. Flint had gone back to his office from the chemist feeling like a walking medicine cabinet.

A week later, he was hard put to it to say what he felt like. 'Fucking awful is all I know,' he told Sergeant Yates who'd been unwise enough to enquire. 'I must have passed more bleeding water in the last six weeks than the Aswan Dam. And I've learnt one thing, this bloody town doesn't have enough public lavatories.'

'I should have thought there were enough to be going on with,' said Yates, who'd once had the unhappy experience of being arrested by a uniformed constable while loitering in the public toilets near the cinema in plain clothes trying to apprehend a genuine loo-lounger.

'Well, you can think again,' snapped Flint. 'I was caught short in Canton Street yesterday, and do you think I could find one? Not on your nelly. Had to use a lane between two houses and nearly got nabbed by a woman hanging her washing on the line. One of these days I'll be done for flashing.'

'Talking about flashing, we've had another report of a case down by the river. Tried it out on a woman of fifty this time.'

'Makes a change from those Wilt bitches and Councillor Birkenshaw. Get a good look at the brute?'

'She said she couldn't see it very well because he was on the other side but she had the impression it wasn't very big.'

'It? It?' shouted Flint. 'I'm not interested in it. I'm talking about the bugger's mug. How the hell do you think we're going to identify the maniac. Have a prick parade and ask the victims to go along studying cocks? The next thing you'll be doing is issuing identikits of penises.'

'She couldn't see his face. He was looking down.'

'And peeing, I daresay. Probably on the same fucking tablets I'm doomed to. Anyway, I wouldn't take the evidence of a fifty-year-old blasted woman. They're all sex-mad at that age. I should know. My old woman's practically off her rocker about it and I keep telling her that the ruddy quack's lowered my blood pressure so much I couldn't get the fucking thing up even if I wanted to. Know what she said?'

'No,' said Sergeant Yates, who found the subject rather distasteful, and anyway it was obvious he didn't know what Mrs Flint had said and he didn't want to hear. The whole notion of anyone wanting the Inspector was beyond him. 'She had the gall to tell me to do it the other way.'

'The other way?' said Yates in spite of himself.

'The old soixante-neuf. Disgusting. And probably illegal. And if anyone thinks I'm going to go down at my age, and on my ruddy missus at that, they're clean off their fucking rockers.'

'I should think they'd have to be,' said the Sergeant almost pitifully. He'd always been relatively fond of old Flint, but there were limits. In a frantic attempt to change the topic to something less revolting, he mentioned the Head of the Drug Squad. He was just in time. The Inspector had just begun a repulsive description of Mrs Flint's attempts to stimulate him. 'Hodge? What's that bloody cock-sucker want now?' Flint bawled, still managing to combine the two subjects.

'Phone-tapping facilities,' said Yates. 'Reckons he's on to a heroin syndicate. And a big one.'

'Where?'

'Won't say, not to me any road.'

'What's he want my permission for? Got to ask the Super or the Chief Constable and I don't come into it. Or do I?' It had dawned on Flint that this might be a subtle dig at him about his son. 'If that bastard thinks he's going to take the piss out of me ...' he muttered and stopped.

'I shouldn't think he could,' said Yates, getting his own back, 'not with those tablets you're on.'

But Flint hadn't heard. His mind had veered off along lines

determined more than he knew by beta-blockers, vaso-
dilators and all the other drugs he was on, but which combined
with his natural hatred for Hodge and the accumulated worries
of his job and his family to turn him into an exceedingly nasty
man. If the Head of the Drug Squad thought he was going to
put one over on him he'd got another think coming. 'There
are more ways of stuffing a cat than filling it with cream,' he
said with a gruesome smile.

Sergeant Yates looked at him doubtfully. 'Shouldn't it be
the other way round?' he asked, and immediately regretted
any reference to other way round. He'd had enough of Mrs
Flint's thwarted sex life, and stuffing cats was definitely out.
The old man must be off his rocker.

'Quite right,' said the Inspector. 'We'll fill the bugger with
cream all right. Got any idea who he wants to tap?'

'He's not telling me that sort of thing. He reckons the
uniform branch aren't to be trusted and he doesn't want any
leaks.' The word was too much for Inspector Flint. He shot
out of his chair and was presently finding temporary relief in
the toilet.

By the time he returned to his office, his mood had changed
to the almost dementedly cheerful. 'Tell him we'll give him
all the co-operation he needs,' he told the Sergeant, 'only too
pleased to help.'

'Are you sure?'

'Of course I'm sure. He's only got to come and see me. Tell
him that.'

'If you say so,' said Yates and left the room a puzzled man.
Flint sat on in a state of drug-induced bemusement. There
was only one bright spot on his limited horizon. If that bastard
Hodge wanted to foul up his career by making unauthorized
phone taps, Flint would do all he could to encourage him.
Fortified by this sudden surge of optimism, he absentmindedly helped himself to another beta-blocker.

Chapter 3

But already things were moving in a direction the Inspector would have found even more encouraging. Wilt had emerged from the meeting of the crisis committee rather too pleased with his performance. If Mr Scudd really had the influence with the Minister of Education he had claimed to, there might well be a full-scale inspection by the HMIs. Wilt welcomed the prospect. He had frequently thought about the advantages of such a confrontation. For one thing, he'd be able to demand an explicit statement on what the Ministry really thought Liberal Studies were about. Communication Skills and Expressive Attainment they weren't. Since the day some twenty years before when he'd joined the Tech staff, he'd never had a clear knowledge and nobody had been able to tell him. He'd started off with the peculiar dictum enunciated by Mr Morris, the then Head of Department, that what he was supposed to be doing was 'Exposing Day Release Apprentices to Culture', which had meant getting the poor devils to read *Lord Of The Flies* and *Candide*, and then discuss what they thought the books were about, and countering their opinions with his own. As far as Wilt could see, the whole thing had been counter-productive and as he had expressed it, if anyone was being exposed to anything, the lecturers were being exposed to the collective barbarism of the apprentices which accounted for the number who had nervous breakdowns or became milkmen with degrees. And his own attempt to change the curriculum to more practical matters, like how to fill in Income Tax forms, claim Unemployment Benefit, and generally move with some confidence through the maze of bureaucratic complications that had turned the Welfare State into a piggy-bank for the middle classes and literate skivers, and an incomprehensible and humiliating nightmare of forms and jargon for the provident poor, had been thwarted by the lunatic theories of so-called educa-

458

tionalists of the sixties like Dr Mayfield, and the equally irrational spending policies of the seventies. Wilt had persisted in his protestations that Liberal Studies didn't need video cameras and audio-visual aids galore, but could do with a clear statement from somebody about the purpose of Liberal Studies.

It had been an unwise request. Dr Mayfield and the County Advisor had both produced memoranda nobody could understand, there had been a dozen committee meetings at which nothing had been decided, except that since all the video cameras were available they might as well be used, and that Communication Skills and Expressive Attainment were more suited to the spirit of the times than Liberal Studies. In the event the education cuts had stymied the audio-visual aids and the fact that useless lecturers in more academic departments couldn't be sacked had meant that Wilt had been lumbered with even more deadbeats. If Her Majesty's Inspectors did descend, they might be able to clear the log jam and make some sense, Wilt would be only too pleased. Besides, he rather prided himself on his ability to hold his own in confrontations.

His optimism was premature. Having spent fifty minutes listening to Electronic Engineers explaining the meaning of cable television to him, he returned to his office to find his secretary, Mrs Bristol, in a flap. 'Oh, Mr Wilt,' she said as he came down the corridor. 'You've got to come quickly. She's there again and it's not the first time.'

'What isn't?' asked Wilt from behind a pile of *Shane* he had never used.

'That I've seen her there.'

'Seen whom where?'

'Her. In the loo.'

'Her in the loo?' said Wilt, hoping to hell Mrs Bristol wasn't having another of her 'turns'. She'd once gone all funny-peculiar when one of the girls in Cake Three had announced in all innocence, that she had five buns in the oven. 'I don't know what you're talking about.'

Nor, it appeared, did Mrs Bristol. 'She's got this needle thing and ...' she petered out.

'Needle thing?'

'Syringe,' said Mrs Bristol, 'and it's in her arm and full of blood and ...'

'Oh my God,' said Wilt, and headed past her to the door. 'Which loo?'

'The Ladies' staff one.'

Wilt halted in his tracks. 'Are you telling me one of the members of staff is shooting herself full of heroin in the Ladies' staff lavatory?'

Mrs Bristol *had* gone all funny now. 'I'd have recognized her if she'd been staff. It was a girl. Oh, do something Mr Wilt. She may do herself an injury.'

'You can say that again,' said Wilt, and bolted down the corridor and the flight of stairs to the toilet on the landing and went in. He was confronted by six cubicles, a row of washbasins, a long mirror and a paper-towel dispenser. There was no sign of any girl. On the other hand, the door of the third cubicle was shut and someone was making unpleasant sounds inside. Wilt hesitated. In less desperate circumstances, he might have supposed Mr Rusker, whose wife was a fibre freak, was having one of his problem days again. But Mr Rusker didn't use the Ladies' lavatory. Perhaps if he knelt down he might get a glimpse. Wilt decided against it. (*A*) He didn't want glimpses and (*B*) it had begun to dawn on him that he was, to put it mildly, in a delicate situation and bending down and peeping under doors in ladies' lavatories was open to misinterpretation. Better to wait outside. The girl, if there was a girl and not some peculiar figment of Mrs Bristol's imagination, would have to come out some time.

With one last glance in the trash can for a hypodermic, Wilt tiptoed towards the door. He didn't reach it. Behind him a cubicle door opened. 'I thought so,' a voice shouted, 'a filthy Peeping Tom!' Wilt knew that voice. It belonged to Miss Hare, a senior lecturer in Physical Education, whom he had once likened rather too audibly in the staff-room to Myra Hindley in drag. A moment later, his arm had been wrenched up to the back of his neck and his face was in contact with the tiled wall.

'You little pervert,' Miss Hare continued, jumping to the nastiest, and, from Wilt's point of view, the least desirable conclusion. The last person he'd want to peep at was Miss

460

Hare. Only a pervert would. It didn't seem the time to say so.

'I was just looking –' he began, but Miss Hare quite evidently had not forgotten the crack about Myra Hindley.

'You can keep your explanation for the police,' she screamed, and reinforced the remark by banging his face against the tiles. She was still enjoying the process, and Wilt wasn't, when the door opened and Mrs Stoley from Geography came in.

'Caught the voyeur in the act,' said Miss Hare. 'Call the police.' Against the wall, Wilt tried to offer his point of view and failed. Having Miss Hare's ample knee in the small of his back didn't help and his false tooth had come out.

'But that's Mr Wilt,' said Mrs Stoley uncertainly.

'Of course it's Wilt. It's just the sort of thing you'd expect from him.'

'Well ...' began Mrs Stoley, who evidently hadn't.

'Oh for goodness sake get a move on. I don't want the little runt to escape.'

'Am I trying to?' Wilt mumbled and had his nose rammed against the wall for his pains.

'If you say so,' said Mrs Stoley and left the room only to return five minutes later with the Principal and the V-P. By then, Miss Hare had transferred Wilt to the floor and was kneeling on him.

'What on earth's going on?' demanded the Principal. Miss Hare got up.

'Caught in the act of peeping at my private parts,' she said. 'He was trying to escape when I grabbed him.'

'Wasn't,' said Wilt groping for his false tooth and inadvisedly putting it back in his mouth. It tasted of some extremely strong disinfectant which hadn't been formulated as a mouthwash, and was doing things to his tongue. As he scrambled to his feet, and made a dash for the washbasins, Miss Hare applied a half-nelson.

'For God's sake let go,' yelled Wilt, by now convinced he was about to die of carbolic poisoning. 'This is all a terrible mistake.'

'Yours,' said Miss Hare and cut off his air supply.

The Principal looked dubiously at them. While he might have enjoyed Wilt's discomfiture in other circumstances, the sight of him being strangled by an athletically built woman like Miss Hare whose skirt had come down was more than he could stomach.

'I think it would be best if you let him go,' he said as Wilt's face darkened and his tongue stuck out. 'He seems to be bleeding rather badly.'

'Serves him right,' said Miss Hare, reluctantly letting Wilt breathe again. He stumbled to a basin and turned the tap on.

'Wilt,' said the Principal, 'what is the meaning of this?' But Wilt had his false tooth out again and was trying desperately to wash his mouth out under the tap.

'Hadn't we better wait for the police before he makes a statement?' asked Miss Hare.

'The police?' squawked the Principal and the V-P simultaneously. 'You're not seriously suggesting the police should be called in to deal with this ... er ... affair.'

'I am,' Wilt mumbled from the basin. Even Miss Hare looked startled.

'You are?' she said. 'You have the nerve to come in here and peer at ...'

'Balls,' said Wilt, whose tongue seemed to be resuming its normal size, though it still tasted like a recently sterilized toilet bend.

'How dare you,' shouted Miss Hare, and was on the point of getting to grips with him again when the V-P intervened. 'I think we should hear Wilt's version before we do anything hasty, don't you?' Miss Hare obviously didn't, but she stopped in her tracks. 'I've already told you precisely what he was doing,' she said.

'Yes, well let me tell you what ...'

'He was bending over and looking under the door,' continued Miss Hare remorselessly.

'Wasn't,' said Wilt.

'Don't you dare lie. I always knew you were a pervert. Remember that revolting incident with the doll?' she said, appealing to the Principal. The Principal didn't need reminding but it was Wilt who answered.

'Mrs Bristol,' he mumbled, dabbing his nose with a paper towel, 'Mrs Bristol's the one who started this.'

462

'Mrs Bristol?'

'Wilt's secretary,' explained the V-P.

'Are you suggesting you were looking for your secretary in here?' asked the Principal. 'Is that what you're saying?'

'No, I'm not. I'm saying Mrs Bristol will tell you why I was here and I want you to hear it from her before that damned bulldozer on anabolic steroids starts knocking hell out of me again.'

'I'm not standing here being insulted by a ...'

'Then you'd better pull your skirt up,' said the V-P, whose sympathies were entirely with Wilt.

The little group made their way up the stairs, past a class of English A-level students who'd just ended an hour with Mr Gallen on The Pastoral Element in Wordsworth's *Prelude*, and were consequently unprepared for the urban element of Wilt's bleeding nose. Nor was Mrs Bristol. 'Oh dear, Mr Wilt, what have you done to yourself?' she asked. 'She didn't attack you?'

'Tell them,' said Wilt. 'You tell them.'

'Tell them what?'

'What you told me,' snapped Wilt, but Mrs Bristol was too concerned about his condition and the Principal and the V-P's presence had unnerved her. 'You mean about –'

'I mean ... Never mind what I mean,' said Wilt lividly, 'just tell them what I was doing in the Ladies' lavatory, that's all.'

Mrs Bristol's face registered even more confusion. 'But I don't know,' she said, 'I wasn't there.'

'I know you weren't there, dammit. What they want to know is why I was.'

'Well ...' Mrs Bristol began, and lost her nerve again, 'Haven't you told them?'

'Caesar's ghost,' said Wilt, 'can't you just spit it out. Here I am accused of being a peeping Tom by Miss Burke and Hare over there ...'

'You call me that again and your own mother wouldn't recognize you,' said Miss Hare.

'Since she's been dead for ten years, I don't suppose she would now,' said Wilt, retreating behind his desk. By the time the PE teacher had been restrained, the Principal was trying to make some sense out of an increasingly confused situation. 'Can someone please shed some light on this sordid business?' he asked.

'If anyone can, she can,' said Wilt, indicating his secretary. 'After all, she set me up.'

'Set you up, Mr Wilt? I never did anything of the sort. All I said was there was a girl in the staff toilet with a hypodermic and I didn't know who she was and ...' Intimidated by the look of horror on the Principal's face, she ground to a halt. 'Have I said something wrong?'

'You saw a girl with a hypodermic in the staff toilet? And told Mr Wilt about it?'

Mrs Bristol nodded dumbly.

'When you say "girl" I presume you don't mean a member of the staff?'

'I'm sure it wasn't. I didn't see her face but I'd have known surely. And she had this awful syringe filled with blood and ...' She looked at Wilt for assistance.

'You said she was taking drugs.'

'There was no one in that toilet while I was there,' said Miss Hare, 'I'd have heard them.'

'I suppose it could have been someone with diabetes,' said the V-P, 'some adult student who wouldn't want to use the students' toilet for obvious reasons.'

'Oh quite,' said Wilt, 'I mean we all know diabetics go round with hypodermics full of blood. She was obviously flushing back to get the maximum dose.'

'Flushing back?' said the Principal weakly.

'That's what the junkies do,' said the V-P. 'They inject themselves and then –'

'I don't want to know,' said the Principal.

'Well, if she was taking heroin –'

'Heroin! That's all we need,' said the Principal, and sat down miserably.

'If you ask me,' said Miss Hare, 'the whole thing's a fabrication. I was in there ten minutes ...'

'Doing what?' asked Wilt. 'Apart from attacking me.'

'Something feminine, if you must know.'

'Like taking steroids. Well, let me tell you that when I went down there and I wasn't there more than ...'

464

It was Mrs Bristol's turn to intervene. 'Down, did you say down?'

'Of course I said down. What did you expect me to say? Up?'

'But the toilet's on the fourth floor, not the second. That's where she was.'

'Now you tell us. And where the hell do you think I went?'

'But I always go upstairs,' said Mrs Bristol. 'It keeps me in trim. You know that. I mean one's got to get some exercise and . . .'

'Oh, belt up,' said Wilt, and dabbed his nose with a blood-stained handkerchief.

'Right, let's get this straight,' said the Principal, deciding it was time to exercise some authority. 'Mrs Bristol tells Wilt here there is a girl upstairs injecting herself with something or other and instead of going upstairs, Wilt goes down to the toilet on the second floor and . . .'

'Gets beaten to a pulp by Ms Blackbelt Burke here,' said Wilt who was beginning to regain the initiative. 'And I don't suppose it's occurred to anyone to go up and see if that junkie's still there.'

But the Vice-Principal had already left.

'If that little turd calls me Burke again . . .' said Miss Hare menacingly. 'Anyway, I still think we should call the police. I mean, why did Wilt go downstairs instead of up? I find that peculiar.'

'Because I don't use the Ladies' or, in your case, the Bisexual Toilets, that's why.'

'Oh for God's sake,' said the Principal, 'there's obviously been some mistake and if we all keep calm . . .'

The Vice-Principal returned. 'No sign of her,' he said.

The Principal got to his feet. 'Well, that's that. Evidently there's been some mistake. Mrs Bristol may have imagined . . .' But any aspersions on Mrs Bristol's imagination he was about to make were stopped by the V-P's next words.

'But I did find this in the trash can,' he said, and produced a blood-stained lump of paper towel, which looked like Wilt's handkerchief.

The Principal regarded it with disgust. 'That hardly proves anything. Women do bleed occasionally.'

'Call it a jamrag and be done with it,' said Wilt viciously.

465

He was getting fed up with bleeding himself. Miss Hare turned on him.

'That's typical, you foulmouthed sexist,' she snapped.

'I was merely interpreting what the Principal was ...'

'And more conclusively, this,' interrupted the V-P, this time producing a hypodermic needle.

It was Mrs Bristol's turn to bridle. 'There, what did I tell you. I wasn't imagining anything. There was a girl up there injecting herself and I did see her. Now what are you going to do?'

'Now we mustn't jump to conclusions just because ...' the Principal began.

'Call the police. I demand that you call the police,' said Miss Hare, determined to take this opportunity for airing her opinions about Wilt and Peeping Toms as widely as possible.

'Miss Burke,' said the Principal, flustered into sharing Wilt's feelings about the PE lecturer, 'this is a matter that needs cool heads.'

'Miss Hare's my name and if you haven't the decency ... And where do you think you're going?'

Wilt had taken the opportunity to sidle to the door. 'To the men's toilet to assess the damage you did, then the Blood Transfusion Unit for a refill and after that, if I can make it, to my doctor and the most litigious lawyer I can find to sue you for assault and battery.' And before Miss Hare could reach him, Wilt was off down the corridor and had closeted himself in the Men's toilet.

Behind him Miss Hare vented her fury on the Principal. 'Right, that does it,' she shouted. 'If you don't call the police, I will. I want the facts of this case spelt out loud and clear so that if that little sex-maniac goes anywhere near a lawyer, the public are going to learn the sort of people who teach here. I want this whole disgusting matter dealt with openly.'

It was the last thing the Principal wanted. 'I really don't think that's wise,' he said. 'After all, Wilt could have made a natural mistake.'

Miss Hare wasn't to be mollified. 'The mistake Wilt made wasn't natural. And besides, Mrs Bristol did see a girl taking heroin.'

466

'We don't know that. There could be some quite ordinary explanation.'

'The police will find out soon enough once they've got that syringe,' said Miss Hare adamantly. 'Now then, are you going to phone them or am I?'

'If you put it like that, I suppose we'll have to,' said the Principal, eyeing her with loathing. He picked up the phone.

Chapter 4

In the Men's toilet, Wilt surveyed his face in the mirror. It looked as unpleasant as it felt. His nose was swollen, there were streaks of blood on his chin and Miss Hare had managed to open an old cut above his right eye. Wilt washed his face in a basin and thought dismally about tetanus. Then he took his false tooth out and studied his tongue. It was not, as he had expected, twice its normal size, but it still tasted of disinfectant. He rinsed his mouth out under the tap with the slightly cheering thought that if his taste buds were anything to go by a tetanus germ wouldn't stand an earthly of surviving. After that, he put his tooth back and wondered yet again what it was about him that invited misunderstanding and catastrophe.

The face in the mirror told him nothing. It was a very ordinary face and Wilt had no illusions about it being handsome. And yet for all its ordinariness, it had to be the façade behind which lurked an extraordinary mind. In the past he had liked to think it was an original mind or, at the very least, an individual one. Not that that helped much. Every mind had to be individual and that didn't make everyone accident-prone, to put it mildly. No, the fact of the matter was that he lacked a sense of his own authority.

'You just let things happen to you,' he told the face in the mirror. 'It's about time you made them happen for you.' But as he said it, he knew it would never be like that. He would never be a dominating person, a man of power whose orders were obeyed without question. It wasn't his nature. To be more accurate, he lacked the stamina and drive to deal in details, to quibble over procedure and win allies and out-manoeuvre opponents, in short, to concentrate his attention on the means of gaining power. Worse still, he despised the people who had that drive. Invariably, they limited themselves to a view of the world in which they alone were important

468

and to hell with what other people wanted. And they were everywhere, these committee Hitlers, especially at the Tech. It was about time they were challenged. Perhaps one day he would ...

He was interrupted in this daydream by the entrance of the Vice-Principal. 'Ah, there you are, Henry,' he said, 'I thought I'd better let you know that we've had to call in the police.'

'About what?' asked Wilt, suddenly alarmed at the thought of Eva's reaction if Miss Hare accused him of being a voyeur.

'Drugs in the college.'

'Oh, that. A bit late in the day, isn't it? Been going on ever since I can remember.'

'You mean you knew about it?'

'I thought everyone did. It's common knowledge. Anyway, it's obvious we're bound to have a few junkies with all the students we've got,' said Wilt, and made good his escape while the Vice-Principal was still busy at the urinal. Five minutes later, he had left the Tech and was immersed once more in those speculative thoughts that seemed to occupy so much of his time when he was alone. Why was it, for instance, that he was so concerned with power when he wasn't really prepared to do anything about it? After all, he was earning a comfortable salary – it would have been a really good one if Eva hadn't spent so much of it on the quads' education – and objectively he had nothing to complain about. Objectively. And a fat lot that meant. What mattered was how one felt. On that score, Wilt came bottom even on days when he hadn't had his face mashed by Ms Hare.

Take Peter Braintree for example. He didn't have any sense of futility or lack of power. He had even refused promotion because it would have meant giving up teaching and taking on administrative duties. Instead, he was content to give his lectures on English literature and go home to Betty and the children and spend his evenings playing trains or making model aeroplanes when he'd finished marking essays. And at the weekends, he'd go off to watch a football match or play cricket. It was the same during the holidays. The Braintrees always went off camping and walking and came back cheerful, with none of the rows and catastrophes that seemed an inevitable part of the Wilt family excursions. In his own way, Wilt envied him, while having to admit that his envy was muted by a contempt he knew to be wholly unjustified. In the modern world, in any world, it wasn't enough just to be content and hope that everything would turn out for the best in the end. In Wilt's experience, they turned out for the worst, e.g. Miss Hare. On the other hand, when he did try to do something the result was catastrophic. There didn't seem to be any middle way.

He was still puzzling over the problem when he crossed Bilton Street and walked up Hillbrow Avenue. Here too, the signs told him that almost everyone was content with his lot. The cherry trees were in bloom, and pink and white petals littered the pavement like confetti. Wilt noted each front garden, most of them neat and bright with wallflowers, but some, where academics from the University lived, unkempt and overgrown with weeds. On the corner of Pritchard Street, Mr Sands was busy among his heathers and azaleas, proving to an uninterested world that it was possible for a retired bank manager to find satisfaction by growing acid-loving plants on an alkaline soil. Mr Sands had explained the difficulties to Wilt one day, and the need to replace all the topsoil with peat to lower the pH. Since Wilt had no idea what pH stood for, he hadn't a clue what Mr Sands had been talking out, and in any case, he had been more interested in Mr Sands' character and the enigma of his contentment. The man had spent forty years presumably fascinated by the movement of money from one account to the other, fluctuations in the interest rate and the granting of loans and overdrafts, and now all he seemed prepared to talk about were the needs of his camellias and miniature conifers. It didn't make sense and was just as unfathomable as the character of Mrs Cranley who had once figured so spectacularly in a trial to do with a brothel in Mayfair, but who now sang in the choir at St Stephens and wrote children's stories filled with remorseless whimsy and an appalling innocence. It was all beyond him. He could only deduce one fact from his observations. People could and did change their lives from one moment to the next, and quite fundamentally at that. And if they could, there was no reason why he shouldn't. Fortified with the knowledge, he strode on more confidently and with the determination not to put up with any nonsense from the quads tonight.

As usual he was proved wrong. He had no sooner opened the front door, than he was under siege. 'Ooh, Daddy, what have you done to your face?' demanded Josephine.

'Nothing,' said Wilt, and tried to escape upstairs before the real inquisition could begin. He needed a bath and his clothes stank of disinfectant. He was stopped by Emmeline who was playing with her hamster halfway up.

'Don't step on Percival,' she said, 'she's pregnant.'

'Pregnant?' said Wilt, momentarily nonplussed. 'He can't be. It's impossible.'

'Percival's a she, so it is.'

'A she? But the man at the petshop guaranteed the thing was a male. I asked him specifically.'

'And she's not a thing,' said Emmeline. 'She's an expectant mummy.'

'Better not be,' said Wilt. 'I'm not having the house overrun by an exploding population of hamsters. Anyway, how do you know?'

'Because we put her in with Julian's to see if they'd fight to the death like the book said, and Percival went into a trance and didn't do anything.'

'Sensible fellow,' said Wilt, immediately identifying with Percival in such horrid circumstances.

'She's not a fellow. Mummy hamsters always go into a trance when they want to be done.'

'Done?' said Wilt inadvisedly.

'What you do to Mummy on Sunday mornings and Mummy goes all funny afterwards.'

'Christ,' said Wilt, cursing Eva for not shutting the bedroom door. Besides, the mixture of accuracy and baby-talk was getting to him. 'Anyway, never mind what we do. I want to ...'

'Does Mummy go into a trance, too?' asked Penelope, who was coming down the stairs with a doll in a pram.

'It's not something I'm prepared to discuss,' said Wilt. 'I need a bath and I'm going to have one. And now.'

'Can't,' said Josephine. 'Sammy's having her hair washed. She's got nits. You smell funny too. What's that on your collar?'

'And all down the front of your shirt.' This from Penelope.

'Blood,' said Wilt, endowing the word with as much threat as he could. He pushed past the pram and went into the bedroom, wondering what it was about the quads that gave them some awful sort of collective authority. Four separate daughters wouldn't have had the same degree of assertiveness and the quads had definitely inherited Eva's capacity for making the worst of things. As he undressed, he could hear Penelope bearing the glad tidings of his misfortune to Eva through the bathroom door.

'Daddy's come home smelling of disinfectant and he's cut his face.'

'He's taking off his trousers and there's blood all down his shirt,' Josephine chimed in.

'Oh, great,' said Wilt. 'That ought to bring her out like a scalded cat.'

But it was Emmeline's announcement that Daddy had said Mummy went into a trance when she wanted a fuck that caused the trouble.

'Don't use that word,' yelled Wilt. 'If I've told you once I've told you a thousand times and I never said anything about your bleeding mother going into a trance. I said –'

'What did you call me?' Eva shouted, storming out of the bathroom. Wilt pulled up his Y-fronts again and sighed. On the landing, Emmeline was describing with clinical accuracy the mating habits of female hamsters, and attributing the description to Wilt.

'I didn't call you a bloody hamster. That's a downright lie. I don't know the first thing about the fucking things and I certainly never wanted them in –'

'There you go,' shouted Eva. 'One moment you're telling the children not to use filthy language and the next you're using it yourself. You can't expect them to –'

'I don't expect them to lie. That's far worse than the sort of language they use and anyway Penelope used it first. I –'

'And you've absolutely no right to discuss our sex life with them.'

'I don't and I wasn't,' said Wilt. 'All I said was I didn't want the house overrun by blasted hamsters. The man in the shop sold me that mentally deficient rat as a male, not a bloody breeding machine.'

'Now you're being disgustingly sexist as well,' yelled Eva.

Wilt stared wildly round the bedroom. 'I am not being sexist,' he said finally. 'It just happens to be a well-known fact that hamsters –'

But Eva had seized on his inconsistency. 'Oh yes you are. The way you talk anyone would think women were the only ones who wanted you-know-what.'

'You-know-what my foot. Those four little bints out there know what without you-know-whating –'

'How dare you call your own daughters bints? That's a disgusting word.'

'Fits,' said Wilt, 'and as for their being my own daughters, I can tell you it's –'

'I shouldn't,' said Eva.

Wilt didn't. Push Eva too far and there was no knowing what would happen. Besides, he'd had enough of women's power in action for one day. 'All right, I apologize,' he said. 'It was a stupid thing to say.'

'I should think it was,' said Eva, coming off the boil and picking his shirt off the floor. 'How on earth did you get all this blood on your new shirt?'

'Slipped and fell in the gents,' said Wilt, deciding the time was hardly appropriate for a more accurate account. 'That's why it smells like that.'

'In the gents?' said Eva suspiciously. 'You fell over in the gents?'

Wilt gritted his teeth. He could see any number of awful consequences developing if the truth leaked out but he'd already committed himself.

'On a bar of soap,' he said. 'Some idiot had left it on the floor.'

'And another idiot stepped on it,' said Eva, scooping up Wilt's jacket and trousers and depositing them in a plastic basket. 'You can take these to the dry-cleaners on the way to work tomorrow.'

'Right,' said Wilt, and headed for the bathroom.

'You can't go in there yet. I'm still washing Samantha's

hair and I'm not having you prancing around in the altogether ...'

'Then I'll wear my pants in the shower,' said Wilt and was presently hidden behind the shower curtain listening to Penelope telling the world that female hamsters frequently bit the male's testicles after copulating.

'I wonder they bother to wait. Talk about having your cake and eating it,' muttered Wilt, and absentmindedly soaped his Y-fronts.

'I heard that,' said Eva and promptly turned the hot tap on in the bath. Behind the shower curtain Wilt juddered under a stream of cold water. With a grunt of despair, he wrenched at the cold tap and stepped from the shower.

'Daddy's foaming at his panties,' squealed the quads delightedly.

Wilt lurched at them rabidly. 'Not the only fucking place he'll be foaming if you don't get the hell out of here,' he shouted.

Eva turned the hot tap in the bath off. 'That's no way to set an example,' she said, 'talking like that. You should be ashamed of yourself.'

'Like hell I should. I've had a bloody awful day at the Tech and I've got to go out to the prison to teach that ghastly creature McCullum, and I no sooner step into the bosom of my menagerie than I –'

The front doorbell rang loudly downstairs. 'That's bound to be Mr Leach nextdoor come to complain again,' said Eva.

'Sod Mr Leach,' said Wilt and stepped back under the shower.

This time he learnt what it felt like to be scalded.

Chapter 5

Things were hotting up for other people in Ipford as well. The Principal for one. He had just arrived home and was opening the drinks cabinet in the hope of dulling his memory of a disastrous day, when the phone rang. It was the Vice-Principal. 'I'm afraid I've got some rather disturbing news,' he said with a lugubrious satisfaction the Principal recognized. He connected it with funerals. 'It's about that girl we were looking for ...' The Principal reached for the gin bottle and missed the rest of the sentence. He got back in time to hear something about the boiler-room. 'Say that again,' he said, holding the bottle between his knees and trying to open it with one hand.

'I said the caretaker found her in the boiler-room.'

'In the boiler-room? What on earth was she doing there?'

'Dying,' said the Vice-Principal, affecting an even more sombre tone.

'Dying?' The Principal had the bottle open now and poured himself a large gin. This was even more awful than he expected.

'I'm afraid so.'

'Where is she now?' asked the Principal, trying to stave off the worst.

'Still in the boiler-room.'

'Still in the ... But good God man, if she's in that condition, why the devil haven't you got her to hospital?'

'She isn't in that condition,' said the Vice-Principal and paused. He too had had a hard day. 'What I said was that she was dying. The fact of the matter is that she's dead.'

'Oh, my God,' said the Principal and swigged neat gin. It was better than nothing. 'You mean she died of an overdose?'

'Presumably. I suppose the police will find out.'

The Principal finished the rest of the gin. 'When did this happen?'

'About an hour ago.'

'An hour ago? I was still in my office an hour ago. Why the hell wasn't I told?'

'The caretaker thought she was drunk first of all and fetched Mrs Ruckner. She was taking an ethnic needlework class with Home Economics in the Morris block and –'

'Never mind about that now,' snapped the Principal. 'A girl's dead on the premises and you have to go on about Mrs Ruckner and ethnic needlework.'

'I'm not going on about Mrs Ruckner,' said the Vice-Principal, driven to some defiance, 'I'm merely trying to explain.'

'Oh, all right, I've heard you. So what have you done with her?'

'Who? Mrs Ruckner?'

'No, the damned girl, for God's sake. There's no need to be flippant.'

'If you're going to adopt that tone of voice, you'd better come here and see for yourself,' said the Vice-Principal and put the phone down.

'You bloody shit,' said the Principal, unintentionally addressing his wife who had just entered the room.

At Ipford Police Station the atmosphere was fairly acrimonious too. 'Don't give me that,' said Flint who had returned from a fruitless visit to the Mental Hospital to interview a patient who had confessed (quite falsely) to being the Phantom Flasher. 'Give it to Hodge. He's drugs and I've had my fill of the bloody Tech.'

'Inspector Hodge is out,' said the Sergeant, 'and they specially asked for you. Personally.'

'Pull the other one,' said Flint. 'Someone's hoaxing you. The last person they want to see is me. And it's mutual.'

'No hoax, sir. It was the Vice-Principal himself. Name of Avon. My lad goes there so I know.'

Flint stared at him incredulously. 'Your son goes to that hell-hole? And you let him? You must be out of your mind. I wouldn't let a son of mine within a mile of the place.'

'Possibly not,' said the Sergeant, tactfully avoiding the observation that since Flint's son was doing a five-year stretch, he wasn't likely to be going any place. 'All the same, he's an

476

apprentice plumber. Got day-release classes and he can't opt out of them. There's a law about it.'

'You want my opinion, there ought to be a law stopping youngsters having anything to do with the sods who teach there. When I think of Wilt ...' He shook his head in despair.

'Mr Avon said something about your discreet approach being needed,' the Sergeant went on, 'and anyway, they don't know how she died. I mean, it doesn't have to be an overdose.'

Flint perked up. 'Discreet approach my arse,' he muttered. 'Still, a genuine murder there makes a change.' He lumbered to his feet and went down to the car pool and drove down to Nott Road and the Tech. A patrol car was parked outside the gates. Flint swept past it and parked deliberately in the space reserved for the Bursar. Then with the diminished confidence he always felt when returning to the Tech, he entered the building. The Vice-Principal was waiting for him by the Enquiries Desk. 'Ah, Inspector, I'm so glad you could come.'

Flint regarded him suspiciously. His previous visits hadn't been welcomed. 'All right, where's the body?' he said abruptly and was pleased to see the Vice-Principal wince.

'Er ... in the boiler-room,' he said. 'But first there's the question of discretion. If we can avoid a great deal of publicity it would really be most helpful.'

Inspector Flint cheered up. When the sods started squealing about publicity and the need for discretion, things had got to be bad. On the other hand, he'd had enough lousy publicity from the Tech himself. 'If it's anything to do with Wilt ...' he began, but the Vice-Principal shook his head.

'Nothing like that, I assure you,' he said. 'At least, not directly.'

'What's that mean, not directly?' said Flint warily. With Wilt, nothing was ever direct.

'Well, he was the first to be told that Miss Lynchknowle had taken an overdose but he went to the wrong loo.'

'Went to the wrong loo?' said Flint and bared his teeth in a mock smile. A second later the smile had gone. He'd smelt trouble. 'Miss who?'

'Lynchknowle. That's what I meant about ... well, the need for discretion. I mean ...'

'You don't have to tell me. I know, don't I just,' said Flint rather more coarsely than the Vice-Principal liked. 'The Lord Lieutenant's daughter gets knocked off here and you don't want him to ...' He stopped and looked hard at the V-P. 'How come she was here in the first place? Don't tell me she was shacked up with one of your so-called students.'

'She was one of our students,' said the Vice-Principal, trying to maintain some dignity in the face of Flint's patent scepticism. 'She was Senior Secs Three and ...'

'Senior Sex Three? What sort of course is that, for hell's sake? Meat One was sick enough considering they were a load of butcher's boys, but if your telling me you've been running a class for prostitutes and one of them's Lord Lynchknowle's ruddy daughter ...'

'Senior Secretaries,' spluttered the Vice-Principal, 'a very respectable course. We've always had excellent results.'

'Like deaths,' said Flint. 'All right, let's have a look at your latest victim.'

With the certainty now that he'd done the wrong thing in asking for Flint, the Vice-Principal led the way across the quad.

But the Inspector hadn't finished. 'I hear you've been putting it out as a self-administered OD. Right?'

'OD?'

'Overdose.'

'Of course. You're not seriously suggesting it could have been anything else?'

Inspector Flint fingered his moustache. 'I'm not in a position to suggest anything. Yet. I'm asking why you say she died of drugs.'

'Well, Mrs Bristol saw a girl injecting herself in the staff toilet and went to fetch Wilt ...'

'Why Wilt of all people? Last person I'd fetch.'

'Mrs Bristol is Wilt's secretary,' said the V-P and went on to explain the confused course of events. Flint listened grimly. The only part he enjoyed was hearing how Wilt had been dealt with by Miss Hare. She sounded like a woman after his own heart. The rest fitted in with his preconceptions of the Tech.

'One thing's certain,' he said when the Vice-Principal had

finished, 'I'm not drawing any conclusions until I've made a thorough examination. And I do mean thorough. The way you've told it doesn't make sense. One unidentified girl takes a fix in a toilet and the next thing you know Miss Lynchknowle is found dead in the boiler-room. How come you assume it's the same girl?'

The Vice-Principal said it just seemed logical. 'Not to me it doesn't,' said Flint. 'And what was she doing in the boiler-room?'

The Vice-Principal looked miserably down the steps at the door and resisted the temptation to say she'd been dying. That might work with the Principal but Inspector Flint's manner didn't suggest he'd respond kindly to statements of the obvious. 'I've no idea. Perhaps she just felt like going somewhere dark and warm.'

'And perhaps she didn't,' said Flint. 'Anyway, I'll soon find out.'

'I just hope you will be discreet,' said the V-P, 'I mean it's a very sensitive ...'

'Bugger discretion,' said Flint, 'all I'm interested in is the truth.'

Twenty minutes later, when the Principal arrived, it was all too obvious that the Inspector's search for the truth had assumed quite alarming dimensions. The fact was that Mrs Ruckner, more accustomed to the niceties of ethnic needle-work than resuscitation, had allowed the body to slip behind the boiler: that the boiler hadn't been turned off added a macabre element to the scene. Flint had refused to allow it to be moved until it had been photographed from every possible angle, and he had summoned fingerprint and forensic experts from the Murder Squad along with the police surgeon. The Tech car park was lined with squad cars and an ambulance and the buildings themselves seemed to be infested with policemen. And all this in full view of students arriving for evening classes. To the Principal, it appeared as if the Inspector was intent on attracting the maximum adverse publicity.

'Is the man mad?' he demanded of the Vice-Principal, stepping over a white tape that had been laid on the ground outside the steps to the boiler-room.

479

'He says he's treating it as a murder case until he's proved it isn't,' said the Vice-Principal weakly, 'and I wouldn't go down there if I were you.'

'Why the hell not?'

'Well, for one thing there's a dead body and ...'

'Of course there's a dead body,' said the Principal, who had been in the War and frequently mentioned the fact. 'Nothing to be squeamish about.'

'If you say so. All the same ...'

But the Principal had already gone down the steps into the boiler-room. He was escorted out a moment later looking decidedly unwell. 'Jesus wept! You could have told me they were holding an autopsy on the spot,' he muttered. 'How the hell did she get in that state?'

'I rather think Mrs Ruckner ...'

'Mrs Ruckner? Mrs Ruckner?' gurgled the Principal, trying to equate what he had just seen in some way with the tenuous figure of the part-time lecturer in ethnic needlework and finding it impossible. 'What the hell has Mrs Ruckner got to do with that ... that ...'

But before he could express himself at all clearly, they were joined by Inspector Flint. 'Well, at least we've got a real dead corpse this time,' he said, timing his cheerfulness nicely. 'Makes a change for the Tech, doesn't it?'

The Principal eyed him with loathing. Whatever Flint might feel about the desirability of real dead corpses littering the Tech he didn't share Flint's opinions. 'Now look here, Inspector ...' he began in an attempt to assert some authority.

But Flint had opened a cardboard box. 'I think you had better look in here first,' he said. 'Is this the sort of printed matter you encourage your students to read?'

The Principal stared down into the box with a horrid fascination. If the cover of the top magazine was anything to go by – it depicted two women, a rack and a revoltingly androgynous man clad in chains and a ... the Principal preferred not to think what it looked like – the entire box was filled with printed matter he wouldn't have wanted his students to know about, let alone read.

'Certainly not,' he said, 'that's downright pornography.'

'Hard core,' said Flint, 'and there's more where this little

480

lot came from. Puts a new complexion on things, doesn't it?'

'Dear God,' muttered the Principal, as Flint trotted off across the quad, 'are we to be spared nothing? That bloody man seems to find the whole horrible business positively enjoyable.'

'It's probably because of that terrible incident with Wilt some years back,' said the V-P. 'I don't think he's ever forgotten it.'

'Nor have I,' said the Principal, looking gloomily round at the buildings in which he had once hoped to make a name for himself. And in a sense it seemed he had. Thanks to so many things that were connected, in his mind, with Wilt. It was the one topic on which he would have agreed with the Inspector. The little bastard ought to be locked up.

And in a sense Wilt was. To prevent Eva from learning that he spent Friday evenings at Baconheath Airbase he devoted himself on Mondays to tutoring a Mr McCullum at Ipford Prison and then led her to suppose he had another tutorial with him four evenings later. He felt rather guilty about this subterfuge but excused himself with the thought that if Eva wanted to buy an expensive education plus computers for four daughters, she couldn't seriously expect his salary, however augmented by HM Prison Service, to pay for it. The airbase lectures did that and anyway Mr McCullum's company constituted a form of penance. It also had the effect of assuaging Wilt's sense of guilt. Not that his pupil didn't do his damnedest to instil one. A sociology lecturer from the Open University had given him a solid grounding in that subject and Wilt's attempts to further Mr McCullum's interest in E. M. Forster and *Howards End* were constantly interrupted by the convict's comments on the socio-economically disadvantaged environment which had led him to end up where and what he was. He was also fairly fluent on the class war, the need for a preferably bloody revolution and the total redistribution of wealth. Since he had spent his entire life pursuing riches by highly illegal and unpleasant means, ones which involved the deaths of four people and the use of a blowtorch as a persuader on several gentlemen in his debt, thus earning himself the soubriquet 'Fireworks Harry' and 25 years from a socially

481

prejudiced judge, Wilt found the argument somewhat suspect.

He didn't much like Mr McCullum's changes of mood either. They varied from whining self-pity, and the claim that he was deliberately being turned into a cabbage, through bouts of religious fervour during which the name Longford came up rather too often, and finally to a bloody-minded belligerence when he threatened to roast the fucking narks who'd shopped him. On the whole, Wilt preferred McCullum the cabbage and was glad that the tutorials were conducted through a grill of substantial wire mesh and in the presence of an even more substantial warder. After Miss Hare and the verbal battering he'd had from Eva, he could do with some protection and this evening Mr McCullum's mood had nothing to do with vegetables. 'Listen,' he told Wilt thickly, 'you don't have a clue, do you? Think you know everything but you haven't done time. Same with this E. M. Forster. He was a middle-class scrubber too.'

'Possibly,' said Wilt, recognizing that this was not one of the nights on which to press Mr McCullum too frankly on the need to stick to the subject. 'He was certainly middle-class. On the other hand, this may have endowed him with the sensitivity needed to –'

'Fuck sensitivity. Lived with a pig, that's how sensitive he was, dirty sod.'

Wilt considered this estimation of the private life of the great author dubious. So, evidently, did the warder. 'Pig?' said Wilt, 'I don't think he did you know. Are you sure?'

'Course I'm sure. Fucking pig by the name of Buckingham.'

'Oh, him,' said Wilt, cursing himself for having encouraged the beastly man to read Forster's biography as background material to the novels. He should have realized that any mention of policemen was calculated to put 'Fireworks Harry' in a foul mood. 'Anyway, if we look at his work as a writer, as an observer of the social scene and ...'

McCullum wasn't having any of that. 'The social scene my eye and Betty Martin. Spent more time looking up his own arsehole.'

'Well, metaphorically I suppose you could ...'

'Literally,' snarled McCullum, and turned the pages of the book. 'How about this? January second "... have the illusion

I am charming and beautiful ... blah, blah ... but would powder my nose if I wasn't found out ... blah, blah ... The anus is clotted with hairs ..." And that's in your blooming Forster's diary. A self-confessed narcissistic fairy.'

'Must have used a mirror, I suppose,' said Wilt, temporarily thrown by this revelation. 'All the same his novels reflect ...'

'I know what you're going to say,' interrupted McCullum. 'They have social relevance for their time. Balls. He could have got nicked for what he did, slumming it with one of the State's sodding hatchet men. His books have got about as much social relevance as Barbara bloody Cartland's. And we all know what they are, don't we? Literary asparagus.'

'Literary asparagus?'

'Chambermaid's delight,' said Mr McCullum with peculiar relish.

'It's an interesting theory,' said Wilt, who had no idea what the beastly man was talking about, 'though personally I'd have thought Barbara Cartland's work was pure escapism whereas ...'

'That's enough of that,' interrupted the warder, 'I don't want to hear that word again. You're supposed to be talking about books.'

'Listen to Wilberforce,' said McCullum, still looking fixedly at Wilt, 'bloody marvellous vocabulary he's got, hasn't he?'

Behind him the warder bridled. 'My name's not Wilberforce and you know it,' he snapped.

'Well then, I wasn't talking about you, was I?' said McCullum. 'I mean everyone knows you're Mr Gerard, not some fucking idiot who has to get someone literate to read the racing results for him. Now as Mr Wilt here was saying ...'

Wilt tried to remember. 'About Barbara Cartland being moron fodder,' prompted McCullum.

'Oh yes, well according to your theories, reading romantic novels is even more detrimental to working-class consciousness than ... What's the matter?'

Mr McCullum was smiling horribly at him through the mesh. 'Screw's pissed off,' he hissed. 'Knew he would. Got him on my payroll and his wife reads Barbara Cartland so he couldn't stand to listen. Here, take this.'

Wilt looked at the rolled-up piece of paper McCullum was thrusting through the wire. 'What is it?'

'My weekly essay.'

'But you write that in your notebook.'

'Think of it like that,' said McCullum, 'and stash it fast.'

'I'll do no ...'

Mr McCullum's ferocious expression had returned. 'You will,' he said.

Wilt put the roll in his pocket and 'Fireworks' relaxed. 'Don't make much of a living, do you?' he asked. 'Live in a semi and drive an Escort. No big house with a Jag on the forecourt, eh?'

'Not exactly,' said Wilt, whose taste had never been drawn to Jaguars. Eva was dangerous enough in a small car.

'Right. Well now's your chance to earn 50K.'

'50K?'

'Grand. Cash,' said McCullum and glanced at the door behind him. So did Wilt, hopefully, but there was no sign of the warder. 'Cash?'

'Old notes. Small denominations and no traceability. Right?'

'Wrong,' said Wilt firmly. 'If you think you can bribe me into ...'

'Gob it,' said McCullum with a nasty grunt. 'You've got a wife and four daughters and you live in a brick and mortar, address 45 Oakhurst Avenue. You drive an Escort, pale dog-turd, number-plate HPR 791 N. Bank at Lloyds, account number 0737 ... want me to go on?' Wilt didn't. He got to his feet but Mr McCullum hadn't finished. 'Sit down while you've still got knees,' he hissed. 'And daughters.'

Wilt sat down. He was suddenly feeling rather weak. 'What do you want?' he asked.

Mr McCullum smiled. 'Nothing. Nothing at all. You just go off home and check that piece of paper and everything's going to be just jake.'

'And if I don't?' asked Wilt feeling weaker still.

'Sudden bereavement is a sad affair,' said McCullum, 'very sad. Specially for cripples.'

Wilt gazed through the wire mesh and wondered, not for the first time in his life, though by the sound of things it might be the last, what it was about him that attracted the horrible.

And McCullum was horrible, horrible and evilly efficient. And why should the evil be so efficient? 'I still want to know what's on that paper,' he said.

'Nothing,' said McCullum, 'it's just a sign. Now as I see it Forster was the typical product of a middle-class background. Lots of lolly and lived with his old Ma ...'

'Bugger E. M. Forster's mother,' said Wilt. 'What I want to know is why you think I'm going to ...'

But any hope he had of discussing his future was ended by the return of the warder. 'You can cut the lecture, we're shutting up shop.'

'See you next week, Mr Wilt,' said McCullum with a leer as he was led back to his cell. Wilt doubted it. If there was one thing on which he was determined, it was that he would never see the swine again. Twenty-five years was far too short a sentence for a murdering gangster. Life should mean life and nothing less. He wandered miserably down the passage towards the main gates, conscious of the paper in his pocket and the awful alternatives before him. The obvious thing to do was to report McCullum's threats to the warder on the gate. But the bastard had said he had one warder on his payroll and if one, why not more? In fact, looking back over the months, Wilt could remember several occasions when McCullum had indicated that he had a great deal of influence in the prison. And outside too, because he'd even known the number of Wilt's bank account. No, he'd have to report to someone in authority, not an ordinary screw.

'Had a nice little session with "Fireworks"?' enquired the warder at the end of the corridor with what Wilt considered to be sinister emphasis. Yes, definitely he'd have to speak to someone in authority.

At the main gate it was even worse. 'Anything to declare, Mr Wilt?' said the warder there with a grin, 'I mean we can't tempt you to stay inside, can we?'

'Certainly not,' said Wilt hurriedly.

'You could do worse than join us, you know. All mod cons and telly and the grub's not at all bad nowadays. A nice little cell with a couple of friendly mates. And they do say it's a healthy life. None of the stress you get outside ...'

But Wilt didn't wait to hear any more. He stepped out into

what he had previously regarded as freedom. It didn't seem so free now. Even the houses across the road, bathed in the evening sunshine, had lost their moderate attraction; instead, their windows were empty and menacing. He got into his car and drove a mile along Gill Road before pulling into a side street and stopping. Then making sure no one was watching him, he took the piece of paper out of his pocket and unrolled it. The paper was blank. Blank? That didn't make sense. He held it up to the light and stared at it but the paper was unlined and as far as he could see, had absolutely nothing written on it. Even when he held it horizontally and squinted along it he could make out no indentations on the surface to suggest that a message had been written on it with a matchstick or the blunt end of a pencil. A man was coming towards him along the pavement. With a sense of guilt, Wilt put the paper on the floor and took a road map from the dashboard and pretended to be looking at it until the man had passed. Even then he checked in the rear-view mirror before picking up the paper again. It remained what it had been before, a blank piece of notepaper with a ragged edge as though it had been torn very roughly from a pad. Perhaps the swine had used invisible ink. Invisible ink? How the hell would he get invisible ink in prison? He couldn't unless ... Something in Wilt's literary memories stirred. Hadn't Graham Greene or Muggeridge mentioned using bird-shit as ink when he was a spy in the Second World War? Or was it lemon juice? Not that it mattered much. Invisible ink was meant to be invisible and if that bastard had intended him to read it, he'd have told him how. Unless, of course, the swine was clear round the bend and in Wilt's opinion, anyone who'd murdered four people and tortured others with a blowtorch as part of the process of earning a living had to be bloody well demented. Not that that let McCullum off the hook in the least. The bugger was a murderer whether he was sane or not, and the sooner he fulfilled his own predictions and became a cabbage the better. Pity he hadn't been born one.

With a fresh sense of desperation, Wilt drove on to The Glassblowers' Arms to think things out over a drink.

Chapter 6

'All right, call it off,' said Inspector Flint, helping himself to a plastic cup of coffee from the dispenser and stumping into his office.

'Call it off?' said Sergeant Yates, following him in.

'That's what I said. I knew it was an OD from the start. Obvious. Gave those old windbags a nasty turn all the same, and they could do with a bit of reality. Live in a bloody dream world where everything's nice and hygienic because it's been put into words. That way they don't happen, do they?'

'I hadn't thought of it like that,' said Yates.

The Inspector took a magazine out of the cardboard box and studied a photograph of a threesome grotesquely intertwined. 'Bloody disgusting,' he said.

Sergeant Yates peered over his shoulder. 'You wouldn't think anyone would have the nerve to be shot doing that, would you?'

'Anyone who does that ought to be shot, if you ask me,' said Flint. 'Though mind you they're not really doing it. Can't be. You'd get ruptured or something. Found this little lot in that boiler-room and it didn't do that murky Principal a bit of good. Turned a very queer colour, he did.'

'Not his, are they?' asked Yates.

Flint shut the magazine and dumped it back in the box. 'You never know, my son, you never know. Not with so-called educated people you don't. It's all hidden behind words with them. They look all right from the outside, but it's what goes on in here that's really weird.' Flint tapped his forehead significantly. 'And that's something else again.'

'I suppose it must be,' said Yates. 'Specially when it's hygienic into the bargain.'

Flint looked at him suspiciously. He never knew if Sergeant

Yates was as stupid as he made out. 'You trying to be funny or something?'

'Of course not. Only first you said they lived in a hygienic dream world of words; and then you say they're kinky in the head. I was just putting the two together.'

'Well, don't,' said Flint. 'Don't even try. Just get me Hodge. The Drug Squad can take this mess over, and good luck to them.' The Sergeant went out, leaving Flint studying his pale fingers and thinking weird thoughts of his own about Hodge, the Tech and the possibilities that might result from bringing the Head of the Drug Squad and that infernal institution together. And Wilt. It was an interesting prospect, particularly when he remembered Hodge's request for phone-tapping facilities and his generally conspiratorial air. Kept his cards close to his chest, did Inspector Hodge, and a fat lot of good it had done him so far. Well, two could play at that game, and if ever there was a quicksand of misinformation and inconsequentiality, it had to be the Tech and Wilt. Flint reversed the order. Wilt and the Tech. And Wilt had been vaguely connected with the dead girl, if only by going to the wrong toilet. The word alerted Flint to his own immediate needs. Those bloody pills had struck again.

He hurried down the passage for a pee and as he stood there, standing and staring at the tiled wall and a notice which said, 'Don't drop your cigarette ends in the urinal. It makes them soggy and difficult to light,' his disgust changed to inspiration. There was a lesson to be learned from that notice if he could only see it. It had to do with the connection between a reasonable request and an utterly revolting supposition. The word 'inconsequential' came to mind again. Sticking Inspector Bloody Hodge onto Wilt would be like tying two cats together by their tails and seeing which one came out on top. And if Wilt didn't, Flint had sorely misjudged the little shit. And behind Wilt there was Eva and those foul quads and if that frightful combination didn't foul Hodge's career up as effectively as it had wrecked Flint's, the Inspector deserved promotion. With the delightful thought that he'd be getting his own back on Wilt too, he returned to his office and was presently doodling figures of infinite confusion which was exactly what he hoped to initiate.

488

He was still happily immersed in this daydream of revenge when Yates returned. 'Hodge is out,' he reported. 'Left a message he'd be back shortly.'

'Typical,' said Flint. 'The sod's probably lurking in some coffee bar trying to make up his mind which dolly bird he's going to nail.'

Yates sighed. Ever since Flint had been on those ruddy penis-blockers or whatever they were called, he'd had girls on his mind. 'Why shouldn't he be doing that?' he asked.

'Because that's the way the sod works. A right shoddy copper. Pulls some babe in arms in for smoking pot and then tries to turn her into a supergrass. Been watching too much TV.'

He was interrupted by the preliminary report from the Lab. 'Massive heroin dose,' the technician told him, 'that's for starters. She'd used something else we haven't identified yet. Could be a new product. It's certainly not the usual. Might be "Embalming Fluid" though.'

'Embalming Fluid? What the hell would she be doing with that?' said Flint with a genuine and justified revulsion.

'It's a name for another of these hallucinogens like LSD only worse. Anyway, we'll let you know.'

'Don't,' said Flint. 'Deal direct with Hodge. It's his pigeon now.'

He put the phone down and shook his head sorrowfully. 'Says she fixed herself with heroin and some filth called Embalming Fluid,' he told Yates. 'You wouldn't credit it, would you? Embalming Fluid! I don't know what the world's coming to.'

Fifty miles away, Lord Lynchknowle's dinner had been interrupted by the arrival of a police car and the news of his daughter's death. The fact that it had come between the mackerel pâté and the game pie, and on the wine side, an excellent Montrachet and a Chateau Lafite 1962, several bottles of which he'd opened to impress the Home Secretary and two old friends from the Foreign Office, particularly annoyed him. Not that he intended to let the news spoil his meal by announcing it before he'd finished, but he could foresee an ugly episode with his wife afterwards for no better reason than that he had come back to the table with the rather unfortunate remark that it was nothing important. Of course, he could always excuse himself on the grounds that hospitality came first, and old Freddie was the Home Secretary after all, and he wasn't going to let that Lafite '62 go to waste, but somehow he knew Hilary was going to kick up the devil of a fuss about it afterwards. He sat on over the Stilton in a pensive mood wishing to God he'd never married her. Looking back over the years, he could see that his mother had been right when she'd warned him that there was bad blood in 'that family', the Puckertons.

'You can't breed bad blood out, you know,' she'd said, and as a breeder of bull terriers, she'd known what she was talking about. 'It'll come out in the end, mark my words.'

And it had, in that damned girl Penny. Silly bitch should have stuck to showjumping instead of getting it into her head she was going to be some sort of intellectual and skiving off to that rotten Tech in Ipford and mixing with the scum there. All Hilary's fault, too, for encouraging the girl. Not that she'd see it that way. All the blame would be on his side. Oh well, he'd have to do something to pacify her. Phone the Chief Constable perhaps and get Charles to put the boot in. His eyes wandered round the table and rested moodily on the Home Secretary. That was it, have a word with Freddie before he left and see that the police got their marching orders from the top.

By the time he was able to get the Home Secretary alone, a process that required him to lurk in the darkness outside the cloakroom and listen to some frank observations about himself by the hired waitresses in the kitchen, Lord Lynch-knowle had worked himself up into a state of indignation that was positively public-spirited. 'It's not simply a personal matter, Freddie,' he told the Home Secretary, when the latter was finally convinced Lynchknowle's daughter was dead and that he wasn't indulging that curious taste for which he'd been renowned at school. 'There she was at this bloody awful Tech at the mercy of all these drug pedlars. You've got to put a stop to it.'

'Of course, of course,' said the Home Secretary, backing

into a hatstand and a collection of shooting sticks and umbrellas. 'I'm deeply sorry –'

'It's no use you damned politicians being sorry,' continued Lynchknowle, forcing him back against a clutter of raincoats, 'I begin to understand the man-in-the-street's disenchantment with the parliamentary process.' (The Home Secretary doubted it) 'What's more, words'll mend no fences' (the Home Secretary didn't doubt that) 'and I want action.'

'And you'll have it, Percy,' the Home Secretary assured him, 'I guarantee that. I'll get the top men at Scotland Yard onto it tomorrow first thing and no mistake.' He reached for the little notebook he used to appease influential supporters. 'What did you say the name of the place was?'

'Ipford,' said Lord Lynchknowle, still glowering at him.

'And she was at the University there?'

'At the Tech.'

'Really?' said the Home Secretary, with just enough inflexion in his voice to lower Lord Lynchknowle's resolve.

'All her mother's fault,' he said defensively.

'Quite. All the same, if you will allow your daughters to go to Technical Colleges, not that I'm against them you understand, but a man in your position can't be too careful ...'

In the hall, Lady Lynchknowle caught the phrase.

'What are you two men doing down there?' she asked shrilly.

'Nothing, dear, nothing,' said Lord Lynchknowle. It was a remark he was to regret an hour later when the guests had gone.

'Nothing?' shrieked Lady Lynchknowle, who had by then recovered from the condolences the Home Secretary had offered so unexpectedly. 'You dare to stand there and call Penny's death nothing?'

'I am not actually standing, my dear,' said Lynchknowle from the depths of an armchair. But his wife was not to be deflected so easily.

'And you sat through dinner knowing she was lying there on a marble slab? I knew you were a callous swine but ...'

'What the hell else was I supposed to do?' yelled Lynchknowle, before she could get into her stride. 'Come back to the table and announce that your daughter was a damned junkie? You'd have loved that, wouldn't you? I can just hear you now ...'

491

'You can't,' shrieked his wife, making her fury heard in the servants' quarters. Lynchknowle lumbered to his feet and slammed the door. 'And don't think you're going to –'

'Shut up,' he bawled, 'I've spoken to Freddie and he's putting Scotland Yard onto the case and now I'm going to call Charles. As Chief Constable he can –'

'And what good is that going to do? He can't bring her back to me!'

'Nobody can, dammit. And if you hadn't put the idea into her empty head that she was capable of earning her own living when it was as clear as daylight she was as thick as two short planks, none of this would have happened.' Lord Lychknowle picked up the phone and dialled the Chief Constable.

At The Glassblowers' Arms, Wilt was on the phone too. He had spent the time trying to think of some way to circumvent whatever ghastly plans McCullum had in mind for him without revealing his own identity to the prison authorities. It wasn't easy.

After two large whiskies, Wilt had plucked up enough courage to phone the prison, had refused to give his name and had asked for the Governor's home number. It wasn't in the phone book. 'It's ex-directory,' said the warder in the office.

'Quite,' said Wilt. 'That's why I'm asking.'

'And that's why I can't give it to you. If the Governor wanted every criminal in the district to know where he could be subjected to threats, he'd put it there wouldn't he?'

'Yes,' said Wilt. 'On the other hand, when a member of the public is being threatened by some of your inmates, how on earth is he supposed to inform the Governor that there's going to be a mass breakout?'

'Mass breakout? What do you know about plans for a mass breakout?'

'Enough to want to speak to the Governor.' There was a pause while the warder considered this and Wilt fed the phone with another coin.

'Why can't you tell me?' the warder asked finally.

Wilt ignored the question. 'Listen,' he said with a desperate earnestness that sprang from the knowledge that having come so far he couldn't back down, and that if he didn't convince the man that this was a genuine crisis, McCullum's accomplices would shortly be doing something ghastly to his knees, 'I assure you that this is a deeply serious matter. I wish to speak to the Governor privately. I will call back in ten minutes. All right?'

'It may not be possible to reach him in that time, sir,' said the warder, recognizing the voice of genuine desperation. 'If you can give me your number, I'll get him to call you.'

'It's Ipford 23194,' he said, 'and I'm not joking.'

'No, sir,' said the warder. 'I'll be back to you as soon as I can.'

Wilt put the phone down and wandered back to his whisky at the bar uncomfortably aware that he was now committed to a course of action that could have horrendous consequences. He finished his whisky and ordered another to dull the thought that he'd given the warder the phone number of the pub where he was well-known. 'At least it proved to him that I was being serious,' he thought and wondered what it was about the bureaucratic mentality that made communication so difficult. The main thing was to get in touch with the Governor as soon as possible and explain the situation to him. Once McCullum had been transferred to another prison, he'd be off the hook.

At HM Prison Ipford, the information that a mass escape was imminent was already causing repercussions. The Chief Warder, summoned from his bed, had tried to telephone the Governor. 'The blasted man must be out to dinner somewhere,' he said when the phone had rung for several minutes without being answered. 'Are you certain it wasn't a hoax call?'

The warder on duty shook his head. 'Sounded genuine to me,' he said. 'Educated voice and obviously frightened. In fact, I have an idea I recognized it.'

'Recognized it?'

'Couldn't put a name to it but he sounded familiar somehow. Anyway, if it wasn't genuine, why did he give me his phone number so quick?' The Chief Warder looked at the number and dialled it. The line was engaged. A girl at The Glass-blowers' Arms was talking to her boyfriend. 'Why didn't he give his name?'

'Sounded frightened to death like I told you. Said something about being threatened. And with some of the swine we've got in here ...'

The Chief Warder didn't need telling. 'Right. We're not taking any chances. Put the emergency plan into action pronto. And keep trying to contact the bloody Governor.'

Half an hour later, the Governor returned home to find the phone in his study ringing. 'Yes, what is it?'

'Mass breakout threatened,' the warder told him, 'a man ...' But the Governor wasn't waiting. He'd been living in terror for years that something of this sort was going to happen. 'I'll be right over,' he shouted and dashed for his car. By the time he reached the prison his fears had been turned to panic by the wail of police sirens and the presence on the road of several fire engines travelling at high speed in front of him. As he ran towards the gate, he was stopped by three policemen.

'Where do you think you're going?' a sergeant demanded. The Governor looked at him lividly.

'Since I happen to be the Governor,' he said, 'the Governor of this prison, you understand, I'm going inside. Now if you'll kindly stand aside.'

'Any means of identification, sir?' asked the Sergeant. 'My orders require me to prevent anyone leaving or entering.'

The Governor rummaged through the pockets of his suit and produced a five-pound note and a comb. 'Now look here, officer ...' he began, but the Sergeant was already looking. At the five-pound note. He ignored the comb.

'I shouldn't try that one if I were you,' he said.

'Try what one? I don't seem to have anything else on me.' 'You heard that one, Constable,' said the sergeant, 'Attempting to offer a bribe to –'

'A bribe ... offer a bribe? Who said anything about offering a bribe?' exploded the Governor. 'You ask me for means of identification and when I try to produce some, you start talking about bribes. Ask the warder on the gate to identify me, dammit.' It took another five minutes of protest to get inside the prison and by then his nerves were in no state to deal at all adequately with the situation. 'You've done what?' he screamed at the Chief Warder.

'Moved all the men from the top floors to the cells below, sir. Thought it better in case they got onto the roof. Of course, they're a bit cramped but ...'

'Cramped? They were four to a one-man cell already. You mean to say they're eight now? It's a wonder they haven't started rioting already.' He was interrupted by the sound of screams from C Block. As Prison Officer Blaggs hurried away, the Governor tried to find out what was happening. It was almost as difficult as getting into the prison had been. A battle was apparently raging on the third floor of A Wing. 'That'll be due to putting Fidley and Gosling in with Stanforth and Haydow,' the warder in the office said.

'Fidley and ... Put two child murderers in with a couple of decent honest-to-God armed bank robbers? Blaggs must be mad. How long did it take them to die?'

'I don't think they're dead yet,' said the warder with rather more disappointment in his voice than the Governor approved. 'Last I heard, they'd managed to stop Haydow from castrating Fidley. That was when Mr Blaggs decided to intervene.'

'You mean the lunatic waited?' asked the Governor.

'Not exactly, sir. You see, there was this fire in D Block –'

'Fire in D Block? What fire in D Block?'

'Moore set fire to his mattress, sir, and by the time –' But the Governor was no longer listening. He knew now that his career was at stake. All it needed to finish him was for that lunatic Blaggs to have acted as an accessory to murder by packing all the swine in the Top Security Block into one cell. He was just on his way to make quite certain when Chief Warder Blaggs returned. 'Everything's under control, sir,' he said cheerfully.

'Under control?' spluttered the Governor. 'Under control? If you think the Home Secretary's going to think "under control" means having child killers castrated by other prisoners, I can assure you you're not up-to-date with contemporary regulations. Now then, about Top Security.'

'Nothing to worry about there, sir. They're all sleeping like babes.'

'Odd,' said the Governor. 'If there was going to be an

495

attempted breakout you'd think they were bound to be involved. You're sure they're not shamming?'

'Positive, sir,' said Blaggs proudly. 'The first thing I did, sir, by way of a precaution, was to lace their cocoa with that double-strength sleeping stuff.'

'Sweet Jesus,' moaned the Governor, trying to imagine the consequences of the Chief Warder's experiment in preventive sedation if news leaked out to the Howard League for Penal Reform. 'Did you say "double strength"?'

The Chief Warder nodded. 'Same stuff we had to use on Fidley that time he saw the Shirley Temple film and went bananas. Mind you, he's not going to get a hard-on after tonight, not if he's wise.'

'But that was double-strength phenobarb,' squawked the Governor.

'That's right, sir. So I gave them double strength like it said. Went out like lights they did.'

The Governor could well believe it. 'You've gone and given four times the proper dose to those men,' he moaned, 'probably killed the brutes. That stuff's lethal. I never told you to do that.'

Chief Warder Blaggs looked crestfallen. 'I was only doing what I thought best, sir. I mean those swine are a menace to society. Half of them are psychopathic killers.'

'Not the only psychopaths round here,' muttered the Governor. He was about to order a medical team into the prison to stomach-pump the villains Blaggs had sedated, when the warder by the phone intervened. 'We could always say Wilson poisoned them,' he said, 'I mean, that's what they're terrified of. Remember that time they went on dirty strike and Mr Blaggs here let Wilson do some washing up in the kitchen?'

The Governor did, and would have preferred to forget it. Putting a mass poisoner anywhere near a kitchen had always struck him as insane.

'Did the trick, sir. They come off dirtying their cells double quick.'

'And went on hunger strike instead,' said the Governor.

'And Wilson didn't like it much either, come to that,' said the warder, for whom the incident evidently had pleasant memories. 'Said we'd no right making him wash up in boxing gloves. Proper peeved he was –'

'Shut up,' yelled the Governor, trying to get back to a world of comparative sanity, but he was interrupted by the phone.

'It's for you, sir,' said the Chief Warder significantly.

The Governor grabbed it. 'I understand you have some information to give me about an escape plan,' he said, and realized he was talking to the buzz of a pay phone. But before he could ask the Chief Warder how he knew it was for him, the coin dropped. The Governor repeated his statement.

'That's what I'm phoning about,' said the caller. 'Is there any truth in the rumour?'

'Any truth in the ...' said the Governor. 'How the devil would I know? You were the one to bring the matter up.'

'News to me,' said the man. 'That is Ipford Prison, isn't it?'

'Of course it's Ipford Prison and what's more, I'm the Governor. Who the hell did you think I was?'

'Nobody,' said the man, now sounding decidedly perplexed, 'nobody at all. Well, not nobody exactly but ... well ... you don't sound like a Prison Governor. Anyway, all I'm trying to find out is if there's been an escape or not.'

'Listen,' said the Governor, beginning to share the caller's doubts about his own identity, 'you phoned earlier in the evening with information about an escape plot and –'

'I did? You off your rocker or something? I've been out covering a burst bloody bulkloader on Bliston Road for the last three bloody hours and if you think I've had time to call you, you're bleeding barmy.'

The Governor struggled with the alliteration before realizing something else was wrong. 'And who am I speaking to?' he asked, mustering what little patience he still retained.

'The name's Nailtes,' said the man, 'and I'm from the *Ipford Evening News* and –'

The Governor slammed the phone down and turned on Blaggs. 'A bloody fine mess you've landed us in,' he shouted. 'That was the *Evening News* wanting to know if there's been an escape.'

Chief Warder Blaggs looked dutifully abashed. 'I'm sorry if there's been some mistake ...' he began and brought a fresh torrent of abuse on his head.

'Mistake? Mistake?' yelled the Governor. 'Some maniac rings up with some fucking cock-and-bull story about an escape and you have to poison ...' But further discussion was interrupted by news of a fresh crisis. Three safebreakers, who had been transferred from a cell designed to hold one Victorian convict to another occupied by four Grievous Bodily Harm merchants from Glasgow, known as the Gay Gorbals, had begun to fulfil Wilt's prophesy by escaping and demanding to be closeted with some heterosexual murderers for protection.

The Governor found them arguing their case with warders in B Block. 'We're not going in with a load of arse-bandits and that's a fact,' said the spokesman.

'It's only a temporary move,' said the Governor, himself temporizing. 'In the morning –'

'We'll be suffering from AIDS,' said the safebreaker.

'Aids?'

'Auto-Immune Deficiency Syndrome. We want some good, clean murderer, not those filthy swine with anal herpes. A stretch is one thing and so's a bang to rights but not the sort of stretch those Scotch sods would give us and we're fucked if we're going to be banged to wrong. This is supposed to be a prison, not Dotheboys Hall.'

By the time the Governor had pacified them and sent them back to their own cell, he was beginning to have his doubts about the place himself. In his opinion, the prison felt more like a mad-house. His next visit, this time to Top Security, made an even worse impression. A sepulchral silence hung over the floodlit building and, as the Governor passed from cell to cell, he had the illusion of being in a charnel-house. Wherever he looked, men who in other circumstances he would happily have seen dead, looked as though they were. Only the occasional ghastly snore suggested otherwise. For the rest, the inmates hung over the sides of their beds or lay grotesquely supine on the floor in attitudes that seemed to indicate that rigor mortis had already set in.

'Just let me find the swine who started this little lot,' he muttered. 'I'll ... I'll ... I'll ...' He gave up. There was nothing in the book of legal punishments that would fit the crime.

Chapter 7

By the time Wilt left The Glassblowers' Arms, his desperation had been alleviated by beer and his inability to get anywhere near the phone. He'd moved onto beer after three whiskies, and the change had made it difficult for him to be in two places at the same time, a prerequisite, it seemed, for finding the phone unoccupied. For the first half hour, a girl had been engaged in an intense conversation on reversed charges, and when Wilt had returned from the toilet, her place had been taken by an aggressive youth who had told him to bugger off. After that, there seemed to be some conspiracy to keep him away from the phone. A succession of people had used it and Wilt had ended up sitting at the bar and drinking, and generally arriving at the conclusion that things weren't so bad after all, even if he did have to walk home instead of driving.

'The bastard's in prison,' he told himself as he left the pub. 'And what's more, he's not coming out for twenty years, so what have I got to worry about? Can't hurt me, can he?'

All the same, as he made his way along the narrow streets towards the river, he kept glancing over his shoulder and wondering if he was being followed. But apart from a man with a small dog and a couple who passed him on bicycles, he was alone and could find no evidence of menace. Doubtless that would come later. Wilt tried to figure out a scenario. Presumably, McCullum had given him the piece of paper as a token message, an indication that he was to be some sort of link-man. Well, there was an easy way out of that one; he wouldn't go near the bloody prison again. Might make things awkward as far as Eva was concerned though. He'd just have to make himself scarce on Monday nights and pretend he was still teaching the loathsome McCullum. Shouldn't be too difficult and anyway, Eva was so engrossed in the quads and their so-called development, she hardly noticed what he was doing. The main thing was that he still had the airbase job and that brought the real money in.

But in the meantime, he had more immediate problems to deal with. Like what to tell Eva when he got home. He looked at his watch and saw that it was midnight. After midnight and without the car. Eva would certainly demand an explanation. What a bloody world it was, where he spent his days dealing with idiotic bureaucrats who interfered at the Tech, and was threatened by maniacs in prison, and after all that, came home to be bullied into lying by a wife who didn't believe he'd done a stroke of work all day. And in a bloody world, only the bloody-minded made any mark. The bloody-minded and the cunning. People with drive and determination. Wilt stopped under a street light and looked at the heathers and azaleas in Mr Sands' garden for the second time that day, but this time with a resurgence of those dangerous drives and determinations which beer and the world's irrationality induced in him. He would assert himself. He would do something to distinguish himself from the mass of dull, stupid people who accepted what life handed out to them and then passed on probably into oblivion (Wilt was never sure about that) without leaving more than the fallacious memories of their children and the fading snapshots in the family album. Wilt would be . . . well, anyway, Wilt would be Wilt, whatever that was. He'd have to give the matter some thought in the morning.

In the meantime, he'd deal with Eva. He wasn't going to stand any nonsense about where have you been? or what have you been up to this time? He'd tell her to mind her own . . . No, that wouldn't do. It was the sort of challenge the damned woman was waiting for and would only provoke her into keeping him awake half the night discussing what was wrong with their marriage. Wilt knew what was wrong with their marriage; it had been going on for twenty years and Eva had had quads instead of having one at a time. Which was typical of her. Talk about never doing things by halves. But that was beside the point. Or was it? Perhaps she'd had quads to compensate in some ghastly deterministic and genetical way for marrying only half a man. Wilt's mind shot off on a tangent once again as he considered the fact, if it was one, that after wars the birthrate of males shot up as if nature with a capital N was automatically compensating for their shortage. If Nature was that intelligent, it ought to have known better than to make him attractive to Eva, and vice versa. He was driven from this line of thought by another attribute of Nature. This time its call. Well, he wasn't peeing in a rose bush again. Once was enough.

He hurried up the street and was presently letting himself surreptitiously into 45 Oakhurst Avenue with the resolve that if Eva was awake he would say the car had broken down and he'd taken it to a garage. It was better to be cunning than bloody-minded after all. In the event, there was no need to be anything more than quiet. Eva, who had spent the evening mending the quads' clothes and who had discovered that they had cut imitation flies in their knickers as a blow for sexual equality, was fast asleep. Wilt climbed carefully into bed beside her and lay in the darkness thinking about drive and determination.

Drive and determination were very much in the air at the police station. Lord Lynchknowle's phone call to the Chief Constable, and the news that the Home Secretary had promised Scotland Yard's assistance, had put the skids under the Superintendent and had jerked him from his chair in front of the telly and back to the station for an urgent conference.

'I want results and I don't care how you get them,' he told the meeting of senior officers inadvisedly. 'I'm not having us known as the Fenland equivalent of Soho or Piccadilly Circus or wherever they push this muck. Is that clear? I want action.'

Flint smirked. For once he was glad of Inspector Hodge's presence. Besides, he could honestly claim that he had gone straight to the Tech and had made a very thorough investigation of the cause of death. 'I think you'll find all the preliminary details in my report, sir,' he said. 'Death was due to a massive overdose of heroin and something called Embalming Fluid. Hodge might know.'

'It's Phencyclidine or PCP,' he said. 'Comes under a whole series of names like Super Grass, Hog, Angel Dust and Killer Weed.'

The Superintendent didn't want a catalogue of names. 'What's the filth do, apart from kill kids, of course?'

'It's like LSD only a hell of a sight worse,' said Hodge. 'Puts them into psychosis if they smoke the stuff too much and generally blows their minds. It's bloody murder.'

'So we've gathered,' said the Superintendent. 'Where'd she get it is what I want to know. Me and the Chief Constable *and* the Home Secretary.'

'Hard to say,' said Hodge. 'It's a Yankee habit. Haven't seen it over here before.'

'So she went to the States and bought it there on holiday? Is that what you're saying?'

'She wouldn't have fixed herself with the stuff if she had,' said Hodge, 'she'd have known better. Could have got it from someone in the University, I suppose.'

'Well, wherever she got it,' said the Superintendent grimly, 'I want that source traced, and fast. In fact, I want this town clean of heroin and every other drug before we have Scotland Yard descending on us like a ton of bricks and proving we're nothing but a bunch of country hicks. Those aren't my words, they're the Chief Constable's. Now then, we're quite certain she took this stuff herself? She couldn't have been ... well, given it against her will?'

'Not according to my information,' said Flint, recognizing the attempt to shift the investigation in his direction and clear Lord Lynchknowle's name from any connection with the drug scene. 'She was seen shooting herself with it in one of the Staff toilets at the Tech. If shooting's the right word,' said Flint, and looked across at Hodge, hoping to shift onto him the burden of keeping Scotland Yard at bay while screening the Lynchknowles.

The Superintendent wasn't interested. 'Whatever,' he said. 'So there's no question of foul play?'

Flint shook his head. The whole beastly business of drugs was foul play but now didn't seem the time to discuss the question. What was important from Flint's point of view was to land Hodge with the problem up to his eyebrows. Let him foul this case up and his head really would be on the chopping-block. 'Mind you,' he said, 'I did find it suspicious she was using the Staff toilet. Could be that's the connection.'

'What is?' demanded the Superintendent.

'Well, I'm not saying they are and I'm not saying they're

502

not,' said Flint, with what he liked to think was subtle equivocation. 'All I'm saying is some of the staff could be.'

'Could be what, for Christ's sake?'

'Involved in pushing,' said Flint. 'I mean, that's why it's been so difficult to get a lead on where the stuff's coming from. Nobody'd suspect lecturers to be pushing the muck, would they?' He paused before putting the boot in. 'Take Wilt for example, Mr Henry Wilt. Now there's a bloke I wouldn't trust further than I could throw him and even then I wouldn't turn my back. This isn't the first time we've had trouble over there, you know. I've got a file on that sod as thick as a telephone directory and then some. And he's Head of the Liberal Studies Department at that. You should see some of the drop-outs he's got working for him. Beats me why Lord Lynchknowle let his daughter go to the Tech in the first place.' He paused again. Out of the corner of his eye he could see Inspector Hodge making notes. The bastard was taking the bait. So was the Superintendent.

'You may have something there, Inspector,' he said. 'A lot of teachers are hangovers from the sixties and seventies and that rotten scene. And the fact that she was spotted in the Staff toilet ...' It was this that did it. By the time the meeting broke up, Hodge was committed to a thorough investigation of the Tech and had been given permission to send in undercover agents.

'Let me have a list of the names and I'll forward it to the Chief Constable,' said the Superintendent. 'With the Home Secretary involved, there shouldn't be any difficulty, but for God's sake, get some results.'

'Yes, sir,' said Inspector Hodge, and went off to his office a happy man.

So did Flint. Before leaving the station, he called in on the Head of the Drug Squad with Wilt's file. 'If this is any use ...' he said and dropped it on the desk with apparent reluctance. 'And any other help I can give you, you've only to ask.'

'I will,' said Inspector Hodge, with the opposite intention. If one thing was certain, it was that Flint would get no credit for breaking the case. And so, while Flint drove home and unwisely helped himself to a brown ale before going to bed,

503

Hodge sat on in his office planning the campaign that would lead to his promotion.

He was still there two hours later. Outside, the street lamps had gone off and Ipford slept, but Hodge sat on, his mind already infected with the virus of ambition and hope. He had gone carefully through Flint's report on the discovery of the body and for once he could find no fault with the Inspector's conclusions. They were confirmed by the preliminary report from Forensic. The victim had died from an overdose of heroin mixed with Emblaming Fluid. It was this last which interested Hodge.

'American,' he muttered yet again, and checked with the Police National Computer on the incidence of its use. Negligible, as he had thought. All the same, the drug was extremely dangerous and its spread in the States had been so rapid that it had been described as the syphilis of drug abuse. Crack this case and Hodge's name would be known, not simply in Ipford, but through the Lord Lieutenant to the Home Secretary and ... Hodge's dreams pursued his name before returning to the present. He picked up Wilt's file doubtfully. He hadn't been in Ipford at the time of the Great Doll Case and its ghastly effects on Flint's career, but he'd heard about it in the canteen, where it was generally acknowledged that Mr Henry Wilt had outfoxed Inspector Flint. Made him look a damned fool was the usual verdict, but it had never been clear what Wilt had really been up to. No one in his right mind went round burying inflatable dolls dressed in his wife's clothes at the bottom of piling-holes with twenty tons of concrete on top of them. And Wilt had. It followed that either Wilt hadn't been in his right mind, or that he'd been covering some other crime. Diverting suspicion. Anyway, the sod had got away with whatever he'd been up to and had screwed Flint into the bargain. So Flint had a grudge against the bastard. That was generally acknowledged too.

It was therefore with justified suspicion that Hodge turned to Wilt's file and began to read in detail the transcript of his interrogation. And as he read, a certain grim respect for Wilt grew in his mind. The sod hadn't budged from his story, in spite of being kept awake and deluged with questions. And he had made Flint look the idiot he was. Hodge could see

504

that, just as he could see why Flint had a grudge against him. But above all his own intuition told him that Wilt had to have been guilty of something. Just had to be. And he'd been too clever for the old bugger. Which explained why Flint had been prepared to hand the file over to him. He wanted this Wilt nailed. Only natural. All the same, knowing Flint's attitude to him, Hodge was amazed he had given him the file. Not with all that stuff showing what a moron he was. Must be something else there. Like the old man knew when he was beaten? And certainly he looked it lately. Sounded it too, so maybe giving him the file was tacitly acknowledging the fact. Hodge smiled to himself. He'd always known he was the better man and that his chance to prove it would come. Well, now it bloody well had.

He turned back to Flint's report on Miss Lynchknowle again and read it through carefully. There was nothing wrong with Flint's methods and it was only when he came to the bit about Wilt having gone to the wrong toilet that Inspector Hodge saw where the old man had made a mistake. He read through it again.

'Principal reported Wilt went to toilet on the second floor when he should have gone to the one on fourth floor.' And later 'Wilt's secretary, Mrs Bristol, said she told Wilt to go to Ladies' staff toilet on the fourth floor. Claimed she'd seen girl there before.' It fitted. Another of clever Mr Wilt's little moves, to go to the wrong toilet. But Flint hadn't spotted that or he'd have interviewed the sod. Hodge made a mental note to check Mr Wilt's movements. But surreptitiously. There was no point in putting him on his guard. Hodge made more notes. 'Tech laboratory facilities provide means of making Embalming Fluid. Check,' was one. 'Source heroin,' another. And all the time while he concentrated, part of his mind ran on different lines, involving romantic-sounding places like the 'Golden Triangle' and the 'Golden Crescent', those jungle areas of Thailand and Burma and Laos, or in the case of the 'Golden Crescent', the laboratories of Pakistan from which heroin came into Europe. In Hodge's mind, small dark men, Pakis, Turks, Iranians and Arabs, converged on Britain by donkey or container truck or the occasional ship: always at night, a black and sinister movement of the deadly opiates

505

financed by men who lived in large houses and belonged to country clubs and had yachts. And then there was the Sicilian Connexion with Mafia murders almost daily on the streets of Palermo. And finally the 'pushers' in England, little runts like Flint's son doing his time in Bedford. That again could be an explanation for Flint's change of attitude, his ruddy son. But the romantic picture of distant lands and evil men was the dominant one, and Hodge himself the dominant figure in it, a lone ranger in the war against the most insidious of all crimes.

Reality was different of course, and converged with Hodge's mental geography only in the fact that heroin did come from Asia and Sicily and that an epidemic of terrible addiction had come to Europe, and only the most determined and intelligent police action and international co-operation would bring it to a halt. Which, since the Inspector in spite of his rank was neither intelligent nor possessed of more than a vivid imagination, was where he came unstuck. In place of intelligence, there was only determination, the determination of a man without a family and with few friends, but with a mission. And so Inspector Hodge worked on through the night planning the action he intended to take. It was four in the morning when he finally left the station and walked round the corner to his flat for a few hours' sleep. Even then, he lay in the darkness gloating over Flint's discomfiture. 'The sod's getting his comeuppance,' he thought before falling asleep.

On the other side of Ipford, in a small house with a neat garden distinguished by a nicely symmetrical goldfish pond with a stone cherub in the middle, Inspector Flint would have agreed, though the cause of his problem had rather more to do with brown ale and those bloody piss pills than with Hodge's future. On the latter score, he was quietly confident. He went back to bed wondering if it wouldn't be a wise move to take some leave. He had a fortnight due to him, and anyway he could justifiably claim his doctor had told him to take it easy. A trip to the Costa Brava, or maybe Malta? The only trouble there was that Mrs Flint tended to get randy in the heat. It was about the only time she did these days, thank God. Perhaps Cornwall would be a better bet. On the other hand, it would be a pity to miss watching Hodge come unstuck and if Wilt didn't run rings round the shit, Flint wasn't the man he thought he was. Talk about tying two cats together by their tails!

And so the night wore on. At the Prison, the activities Wilt had initiated went on. At two, another prisoner in D Block set fire to his mattress, only to have it extinguished by an enterprising burglar using the slop bucket. But it was in Top Security that matters were more serious. The Governor had been disconcerted to find two prisoners wide awake in McCullum's cell, and because it was McCullum's cell, he had been wary of entering without at least six warders to ensure his safety, and six warders were hard to find, partly because they shared the Governor's apprehension and partly because they were busy elsewhere. Lacking their support, the Governor was forced to conduct a dialogue with McCullum's companions through the cell door. Known as the Bull and the Bear, they acted as McCullum's bodyguards.

'Why aren't you men asleep?' demanded the Governor.

'Might be if you hadn't turned the ruddy light on,' said the Bull, who had once made the mistake of falling madly in love with a bank manager's wife, only to be betrayed when he had fulfilled her hopes by murdering her husband and robbing the bank of fifty thousand pounds. She had gone on to marry a stockbroker.

'That's no way to speak to me,' said the Governor, peering suspiciously through the peep-hole. Unlike the other two prisoners, McCullum appeared to be fast asleep. One hand hung limply over the side of his bunk, and his face was unnaturally pallid. Considering that the swine was usually a nasty ruddy colour, the Governor was perturbed. If anyone was likely to be involved in an escape plot, he'd have sworn McCullum was. In which case, he'd have been ... The Governor wasn't sure what he'd have been, but he certainly wouldn't have been fast asleep, with his face that ghastly grey colour, while the Bull and the Bear were wide awake. There was something distinctly fishy about his being asleep.

'McCullum,' shouted the Governor, 'McCullum, wake up.'

507

McCullum didn't move. 'Blimey,' said the Bear, sitting up. 'What the fuck's going on?'

'McCullum,' yelled the Governor, 'I am ordering you to wake up.'

'What the fuck's up with you?' yelled the Bull. 'Middle of the bleeding night and some screw has to go off his nut and go round fucking waking people up. We got fucking rights, you know, even if we are in nick and Mac isn't going to like this.'

The Governor clenched his teeth and counted to ten. Being called a screw wasn't what he liked either. 'I am simply trying to ascertain that Mr McCullum is all right,' he said. 'Now will you kindly wake him up.'

'All right? All right? Why shouldn't he be all right?' asked the Bear.

The Governor didn't say. 'It's merely a precautionary measure,' he answered. McCullum's refusal to show any sign of life – and in fact from his attitude and complexion to show just the opposite – was getting to him. If it had been anyone else, he'd have opened the cell door and gone in. But the swine could well be shamming, and with the Bull and the Bear to help him, might be planning to overpower a warder going in to see what was wrong. With a silent curse on the Chief Warder for making his life so difficult, the Governor hurried off to get assistance. Behind him, the Bull and the Bear expressed their feelings about fucking screws who left the fucking light on all fucking night, when it occurred to them that there might be something to be said for checking McCullum after all. The next moment, Top Security was made hellish by their shouts.

'He's fucking dead,' screamed the Bear, while the Bull made a rudimentary attempt to resuscitate McCullum by applying what he thought was artificial respiration, and which in fact meant hurling himself on the body and expelling what remained of breath from his victim's lungs.

'Give him the fucking kiss of life,' ordered the Bear, but the Bull had reservations. If McCullum wasn't dead, he had no intention of bringing him back to consciousness to find he was being kissed, and if he had coughed it, he didn't fancy kissing a corpse.

'Squeamish sod,' yelled the Bear, when the Bull stated his

views on the question. 'Here, let me get at him.' But even then he was put off by McCullum's coldness. 'You bloody murderers,' he shouted through the cell door.

'You've done it this time,' said the Governor. He had found the Chief Warder in the office enjoying a cup of coffee. 'You and your infernal sedatives.'

'Me?' said the Chief Warder.

The Governor took a deep breath. 'Either McCullum's dead or he's shamming very convincingly. Get me ten warders and the doctor. If we hurry, we may be in time to save him.'

They rushed down the passage, but the Chief Warder had yet to be convinced. 'I gave him the same dose as everyone else. He's having you on.'

Even when they had secured the ten warders and were outside the cell door, he delayed matters. 'I suggest you leave this to us, sir,' he said. 'If they take hostages, you ought to be on the outside to conduct negotiations. We're dealing with three extremely dangerous men, you know.' The Governor doubted it. Two seemed more probable.

Chief Warder Blaggs peered into the cell. 'Could have painted his face with chalk or something,' he said. 'He's a right crafty devil.'

'And pissed himself into the bargain?'

'Never does things by halves, does our Mac,' said the Chief Warder. 'All right, stand clear of the door in there. We're coming in.' A moment later the cell was filled with prison officers and in the mêlée that followed, the late McCullum received some post mortem injuries which did nothing to improve his appearance. But there was no doubt he was dead. It hardly needed the prison doctor to diagnose death as due to acute barbiturate poisoning.

'Well, how was I to know that the Bull and the Bear were going to give him their cups of cocoa?' said the Chief Warder plaintively, at a meeting held in the Governor's office to discuss the crisis.

'That's something you're going to have to explain to the Home Office enquiry,' said the Governor.

They were interrupted by a prison officer who announced that a cache of drugs had been found in McCullum's sodden mattress. The Governor looked out at the dawn sky and groaned.

'Oh, and one other thing, sir,' said the warder. 'Mr Coven in the office has remembered where he heard that voice on the telephone. He thought he recognized it at the time. Says it was Mr Wilt.'

'Mr Wilt?' said the Governor. 'Who the hell's Mr Wilt?'

'A lecturer from the Tech or somewhere who's been teaching McCullum English. Comes every Monday.'

'McCullum? Teaching McCullum English? And Coven's certain he was the one who phoned?' In spite of his fatigue, the Governor was wide awake now.

'Definitely, sir. Says he thought it was familiar and naturally when he heard "Fireworks" Harry'd snuffed it, he made the connection.'

So had the Governor. With his career in jeopardy he was prepared to act decisively. 'Right,' he said, casting discretion to the draught that blew under the door. 'McCullum died of food poisoning. That's the official line. Next...'

'What do you mean, "food poisoning"?' asked the prison doctor. 'Death was due to an overdose of phenobarbitone and I'm not going on record as saying –'

'And where was the poison? In his cocoa, of course,' snapped the Governor. 'And if cocoa isn't food, I don't know what is. So we put it out as food poisoning.' He paused and looked at the doctor. 'Unless you want to go down as the doctor who nearly poisoned thirty-six prisoners.'

'Me? I didn't have anything to do with it. That goon went and dosed the sods.' He pointed at Chief Warder Blaggs, but the Chief Warder had spotted the out.

'On your instructions,' he said with a meaningful glance at the Governor. 'I mean I couldn't have laid my hands on that stuff if you hadn't authorized it, could I now? You always keep the drugs cupboard in the dispensary locked, don't you? Be irresponsible not to, I'd have thought.'

'But I never did...' the doctor began, but the Governor stopped him.

'I'm afraid Mr Blaggs has a point there,' he said. 'Of course if you want to dispute the facts with the Board of Enquiry, that is your privilege. And doubtless the Press would make some-

510

thing of it. PRISON DOCTOR INVOLVED IN POISONING CONVICT would look well in the *Sun*, don't you think?'

'If he had drugs in his cell, I suppose we could say he died of an overdose,' said the doctor.

Chapter 8

'There's no use in saying you didn't come home late last night because you did,' said Eva. It was breakfast, and, as usual, Wilt was being cross-examined by his nearest and dearest. On her other days, Eva left it to the quads to make the meal a misery for him by asking questions about computers or bio-chemistry about which he knew absolutely nothing. But this morning the absence of the car had given her the opportunity to get her own questions in.

'I didn't say I didn't come in late,' said Wilt through a mouthful of muesli. Eva was still into organic foods and her home-made muesli, designed to guarantee an adequate supply of roughage, did just that and more.

'That's a double negative,' said Emmeline.

Wilt looked at her balefully. 'I know it is,' he said, and spat out the husk of a sunflower seed.

'Then you weren't telling the truth,' Emmeline continued. 'Two negatives make a positive and you didn't say you had come in late.'

'And I didn't say I hadn't,' said Wilt, struggling with his daughter's logic and trying to use his tongue to get the bran off the top of his dentures. The damned stuff seemed to get everywhere.

'There's no need to mumble,' said Eva. 'What I want to know is where the car is.'

'I've already told you. I left it in a car park. I'll get a mechanic to go round and see what's wrong with the thing.'

'You could have done that last night. How do you expect me to take the girls to school?'

'I suppose they could always walk,' said Wilt, extracting a raisin from his mouth with his fingers and examining it offensively. 'It's an organic form of transportation, you know. Unlike this junior prune which would appear to have led a sedentary life and a sedimentary death. I wonder why it is

512

that health foods so frequently contain objects calculated to kill. Now take this –'

'I am not interested in your comments,' said Eva. 'You're just trying to wriggle out of it and if you expect me to . . .'

'Walk?' interrupted Wilt. 'God forbid. The adipose tissue with which you –'

'Don't you adipose me, Henry Wilt,' Eva began, only to be interrupted by Penelope.

'What's adipose?'

'Mummy is,' said Wilt. 'As to the meaning, it means fat, fatty deposits and appertaining to fat.'

'I am not fat,' said Eva firmly, 'and if you think I'm spending my precious time walking three miles there and three miles back twice a day you're wrong.'

'As usual,' said Wilt. 'Of course. I was forgetting that the gender arrangements of this household leave me in a minority of one.'

'What are gender arrangements?' demanded Samantha.

'Sex,' said Wilt bitterly and got up from the table.

Behind him Eva snorted. She was never prepared to discuss sex in front of the quads. 'It's all very well for you,' she said, reverting to the question of the car which provided a genuine grievance. 'All you have to do is –'

'Catch a bus,' said Wilt, and hurried out of the house before Eva could think of a suitable reply. In fact there was no need. He caught a lift with Chesterton from the Electronics Department and listened to his gripes about financial cuts and why they didn't make them in Communication Skills and get rid of some of those Liberal Studies deadbeats.

'Oh well, you know how it is,' said Wilt as he got out of the car at the Tech. 'We have to make good the inexactitudes of science.'

'I didn't know there were any,' said Chesterton.

'The human element,' said Wilt enigmatically, and went through the library to the lift and his office. The human element was waiting for him.

'You're late, Henry,' said the Vice-Principal.

Wilt looked at him closely. He usually got on rather well with the V-P. 'You're looking pretty late yourself,' he said. 'In fact, if I hadn't heard you speak, I'd say you were a standing corpse. Been whooping it up with the wife?'

The Vice-Principal shuddered. He still hadn't got over the horror of seeing his first dead body in the flesh, rather than on the box, and trying to drown the memory in brandy hadn't helped. 'Where the hell did you get to last night?'

'Oh, here and there, don't you know,' said Wilt. He had no intention of telling the V-P he did extra-mural teaching.

'No, I don't,' said the V-P. 'I tried calling your house and all I got was some infernal answering service.'

'That'd be one of the computers,' said Wilt. 'The quads have this programme. It runs on tape, I think. Quite useful really. Did it tell you to fuck off?'

'Several times,' said the Vice-Principal.

'The wonders of science. I've just been listening to Chesterton praising –'

'And I've just been listening to the Police Inspector,' cut in the V-P, 'on the subject of Miss Lynchknowle. He wants to see you.'

Wilt swallowed. Miss Lynchknowle hadn't anything to do with the prison. It didn't make sense. In any case, they couldn't have got on to him so quickly. Or could they? 'Miss Lynchknowle? What about her?'

'You mean you haven't heard?'

'Heard what?' said Wilt.

'She's the girl who was in the toilet,' said the V-P. 'She was found dead in the boiler-room last night.'

'Oh God,' said Wilt. 'How awful.'

'Quite. Anyway, we had the police swarming all over the place last night and this morning there's a new man here. He wants a word with you.'

They walked down the corridor to the Principal's office. Inspector Hodge was waiting there with another policeman. 'Just a matter of routine, Mr Wilt,' he said when the Vice-Principal had shut the door. 'We've already interviewed Mrs Bristol and several other members of the staff. Now I understand you taught the late Miss Lynchknowle?'

Wilt nodded. His previous experience with the police didn't dispose him to say more than he had to. The sods always chose the most damning interpretation.

'You taught her English?' continued the Inspector.

514

'I teach Senior Secretaries Three English, yes,' said Wilt.

'On Thursday afternoons at 2.15 p.m?'

Wilt nodded again.

'And did you notice anything odd about her?'

'Odd?'

'Anything to suggest that she might be an addict, sir.'

Wilt tried to think. Senior Secretaries were all odd as far as he was concerned. Certainly in the context of the Tech. For one thing, they came from 'better families' than most of his other students and seemed to have stepped out of the fifties with their perms and their talk about Mummies and Daddies who were all wealthy farmers or something in the Army. 'I suppose she was a bit different from the other girls in the class,' he said finally. 'There was this duck, for instance.'

'Duck?' said Hodge.

'Yes, she used to bring a duck she called Humphrey with her to class. Bloody nuisance having a duck in a lesson but I suppose it was a comfort to her having a furry thing like that.'

'Furry?' said Hodge. 'Ducks aren't furry. They have feathers.'

'Not this one,' said Wilt. 'Like a teddy bear. You know, stuffed. You don't think I'd have a live duck shitting all over the place in my class, do you?'

Inspector Hodge said nothing. He was beginning to dislike Wilt.

'Apart from that particular addiction, I can't think of anything else remarkable about her. I mean, she didn't twitch or seem unduly pale or even go in for those sudden changes of mood you tend to find with junkies.'

'I see,' said Hodge, holding back the comment that Mr Wilt seemed exceedingly well-informed on the matter of symptoms. 'And would you say there was much drug-taking at the College?'

'Not to my knowledge,' said Wilt. 'Though, come to think of it, I suppose there must be some with the numbers we've got. I wouldn't know. Not my scene.'

'Quite, sir,' said the Inspector, simulating respect.

'And now, if you don't mind,' said Wilt, 'I have work to do.' The Inspector didn't mind.

'Not much there,' said the Sergeant when he'd left.

'Never is with the really clever sods,' said Hodge.

'I still don't understand why you didn't ask him about going to the wrong toilet and what the secretary said.'

Hodge smiled. 'If you really want to know, it's because I don't intend to raise his suspicions one little iota. That's why. I've been checking on Mr Wilt and he's a canny fellow, he is. Scuppered old Flint, didn't he? And why? I'll tell you. Because Flint was fool enough to do what Wilt wanted. He pulled him in and put him through the wringer and Mr Wilt got away with bloody murder. I'm not getting caught the same way.'

'But he never did commit any murder. It was only a fucking inflatable doll he'd buried,' said the Sergeant.

'Oh, come off it. You don't think the bugger did that without he had a reason? That's a load of bull. No, he was pulling some other job and he wanted a cover, him and his missus, so they fly a kite and Flint falls for it. That old fart wouldn't know a decoy if it was shoved under his bloody snout. He was so busy grilling Wilt about that doll he couldn't see the wood for the trees.'

Sergeant Runk fought his way through the mixed metaphors and came out none the wiser. 'All the same,' he said finally, 'I can't see a lecturer here being into drugs, not pushing anyway. Where's the lifestyle? No big house and car. No country-club set. He doesn't fit the bill.'

'And no big salary here either,' said Hodge. 'So maybe he's saving up for his old age. Anyway, we'll check him out and he won't ever know.'

'I should have thought there were more likely prospects round about,' said the Sergeant. 'What about that Greek restaurant bloke Macropolis or something you've been bugging? We know he's been into heroin. And there's that fly boy down the Siltown Road with the garage we had for GBH. He was on the needle himself.'

'Yea, well he's inside, isn't he? And Mr Macropolis is out of the country right now. Anyway, I'm not saying it is Wilt. She could have been down in London getting it for all we know. In which case, it's off our patch. All I'm saying is, I'm keeping an open mind and Mr Wilt interests me, that's all.'

And Wilt was to interest him still further when they returned to the police station an hour later. 'Super wants to see you,' said the Duty Sergeant. 'He's got the Prison Governor with him.'

'Prison Governor?' said Hodge. 'What's he want?'

'You,' said the Sergeant, 'hopefully.'

Inspector Hodge ignored the crack and went down the passage to the Superintendent's office. When he came out half an hour later, his mind was alive with circumstantial evidence, all of which pointed most peculiarly to Wilt. Wilt had been teaching one of the most notorious gangsters in Britain, now thankfully dead of an overdose of one of his own drugs. (The prison authorities had decided to use the presence of so much heroin in McCullum's mattress as the cause of death, rather than the phenobarb one, much to Chief Warder Blaggs' relief.) Wilt had been closeted with McCullum at the very time Miss Lynchknowle's body had been discovered. And, most significantly of all, Wilt, within an hour of leaving the prison and presumably on learning that the police were busy at the Tech, had rung the prison anonymously with a phoney message about a mass break-out and McCullum had promptly taken an overdose.

If that little lot didn't add up to something approaching a certainty that Wilt was involved, Hodge didn't know one. Anyway, add it to what he already knew of Wilt's past and it was certain. On the other hand, there was still the awkward little matter of proof. It was one of the disadvantages of the English legal system, and one Hodge would happily have dispensed with in his crusade against the underworld, that you had first to persuade the Director of Public Prosecutions that there was a case to be answered, and then go on to present evidence that would convince a senile judge and a jury of do-gooders, half of whom had already been nobbled, that an obvious villain was guilty. And Wilt wasn't an obvious villain. The bastard was as subtle as hell and to send the sod down would require evidence that was as hard as ferro-concrete.

'Listen,' Hodge said to Sergeant Runk and the small team of plain-clothes policemen who constituted his private crime squad, 'I don't want any balls-ups so this has got to be strictly covert and I mean covert. No one, not even the Super, is to know it's going on, so we'll code-name it Flint. That way, no one will suspect. Anyone can say Flint round this station and

517

it doesn't register. That's one. Two is, I want Mr Wilt tailed twenty-four hours continuous. And another tail on his missus. No messing. I want to know what those people do every moment of the day and night from now on in.'

'Isn't that going to be a bit difficult?' asked Sergeant Runk. 'Day *and* night. There's no way we can put a tail in the house and ...'

'Bug it is what we'll do,' said Hodge. 'Later. First off we're going to patternize their lives on a time-schedule basis. Right?'

'Right,' echoed the team. In their time, they had patternized the lives of a fish-and-chip merchant and his family who Hodge had suspected were into hard-core porn; a retired choirmaster – this time for boys; and a Mr and Mrs Pateli for nothing better than their name. In each case the patternizing had failed to confirm the Inspector's suspicions, which were in fact wholly groundless, but had established as incontrovertible facts that the fish-and-chip merchant opened his shop at 6 p.m. except Sundays, that the choirmaster was having a happy and vigorous love affair with a wrestler's wife, and in any case had an aversion amounting almost to an allergy for small boys, and that the Patelis went to the Public Library every Tuesday, that Mr Pateli did full-time unpaid work with the Mentally Handicapped, while Mrs Pateli did Meals on Wheels. Hodge had justified the time and expense by arguing that these were training sessions in preparation for the real thing.

'And this is it,' continued Hodge. 'If we can nail this one down before Scotland Yard takes over we'll be quids in. We're also going into a surveillance mode at the Tech. I'm going over to see the Principal about it now. In the meantime, Pete and Reg can move into the canteen and the Student's Common Room and make out they're mature students chucked out for dope at Essex or some other University.'

Within an hour, Operation Flint was underway. Pete and Reg, suitably dressed in leather garments that would have alarmed the most hardened Hell's Angels, had already emptied the Students' Common Room at the Tech by their language and their ready assumption that everyone there was on heroin. In the Principal's office, Inspector Hodge was having more or less the same effect on the Principal and the V-P, who found the notion that the Tech was the centre for drug distribu-

tion in Fenland particularly horrifying. They didn't much like
the idea of being lumbered with fifteen educationally subnormal coppers as mature students.

'At this time of year?' said the Principal. 'Dammit, it's April.
We don't enrol mature students this term. We don't enrol
any, come to that. They come in September. And anyway,
where the hell would we put them?'

'I suppose we could always call them "Student Teachers",'
said the V-P. 'That way they could sit in on any classes they
wanted to without having to say very much.'

'Still going to look bloody peculiar,' said the Principal. 'And
frankly, I don't like it at all.'

But it was the Inspector's assertion that the Lord Lieutenant,
the Chief Constable and, worst of all, the Home Secretary
didn't like what had been going on at the Tech that turned
the scales.

'God, what a ghastly man,' said the Principal, when Hodge
had left. 'I thought Flint was foul enough, but this one's even
bloodier. What is it about policemen that is so unpleasant?
When I was a boy, they were quite different.'

'I suppose the criminals were, too,' said the V-P. 'I mean,
it can't be much fun with sawn-off shotguns and hooligans
hurling Molotov cocktails at you. Enough to turn any man
bloody.'

'Odd,' said the Principal, and left it at that.

Meanwhile Hodge had put the Wilts under surveillance.
'What's been happening?' he asked Sergeant Runk.

'Wilt's still at the Tech so we haven't been able to pick him
up yet, and his missus hasn't done anything much except the
shopping.'

But even as he spoke, Eva was already acting in a manner
calculated to heighten suspicion. She had been inspired to
phone Dr Kores for an appointment. Where the inspiration
came from she couldn't have said, but it had partly to do with
an article she had read in her supermarket magazine on sex
and the menopause entitled 'No Pause In The Pause, The
Importance of Foreplay In The Forties', and partly with the
glimpse she'd had of Patrick Mottram at the check-out counter
where he usually chatted up the prettiest girl. On this occasion,

he had ogled the chocolate bars instead and had ambled off with the glazed eyes of a man for whom the secret consumption of half a pound of Cadbury's Fruit and Nut was the height of sensual experience. If Dr Kores could reduce the randiest man in Ipford to such an awful condition, there was every possibility she could produce the opposite effect in Henry.

Over lunch, Eva had read the article again and, as always on the subject of sex, she was puzzled. All her friends seemed to have so much of it, either with their husbands or with someone, and obviously it was important, otherwise people wouldn't write and talk so much about it. All the same, Eva still had difficulty reconciling it with the way she'd been brought up. Mind you, her mother had been quite wrong going on about remaining a virgin until she was married. Eva could see that now. She certainly wasn't going to do the same with the quads. Not that she'd have them turn into little tarts like the Hatten girls, wearing make-up at fourteen and going around with rough boys on motorbikes. But later on, when they were eighteen and at university, then it would be all right. They'd need experience before they got married instead of getting married to get ... Eva stopped herself. That wasn't true, she hadn't married Henry just for sex. They'd been genuinely in love. Of course, Henry had groped and fiddled but never nastily like some of the boys she'd gone out with. If anything, he'd been rather shy and embarrassed and she'd had to encourage him. Mavis was right to call her a full-blooded woman. She did like sex but only with Henry. She wasn't going to have affairs, especially not with the quads in the house. You had to set an example and broken homes were bad. On the other hand, so were homes where both parents were always quarrelling and hated one another. So divorce was a good thing too. Not that anything like that threatened her marriage. It was just that she had a right to a more fulfilling love life and if Henry was too shy to ask for help, and he certainly was, she'd have to do it for him. So she had phoned Dr Kores and had been surprised to learn that she could come at half past two.

Eva had set off with an unnoticed escort of two cars and four policemen and had caught the bus at the bottom of Perry Road to Silton and Dr Kores' shambolic herb farm. 'I don't

520

suppose she has time to keep it tidy,' Eva thought as she made her way past a number of old frames and a rusty cultivator to the house. All the same, she was slightly dismayed by the lack of organization. If it had been her garden, it wouldn't have looked like that. But then anything organic tended to go its own way, and Dr Kores did have a reputation as an eccentric. In fact, she had prepared herself to be confronted by some wizened old creature with a plaid shawl when the door opened and a severe woman in a white coat stood looking at her through strangely tinted dark glasses.

'Ms Wilt?' she said. Was there just the hint of a V for the W? But before Eva could consider this question, she was being ushered down the hallway and into a consulting-room. Eva looked round apprehensively as the doctor took a seat behind the desk. 'You are having problems?' she asked.

Eva sat down. 'Yes,' she said, fiddling with the clasp of her handbag and wishing she hadn't made the appointment.

'With your husband I think you said, yes?'

'Well, not with him exactly,' said Eva, coming to Henry's defence. After all, it wasn't his fault he wasn't as energetic as some other men. 'It's just that he's ... well ... not as active as he might be.'

'Sexually active?' Eva nodded.

'How old?' continued Dr Kores.

'You mean Henry? Forty-three. He'll be forty-four next March. He's a –'

But Dr Kores was clearly uninterested in Wilt's astrological sign. 'And the sexual gradient has been steep?'

'I suppose so,' said Eva, wondering what a sexual gradient was.

'Maximum weekly activity please.'

Eva looked anxiously at an Anglepoise lamp and tried to think. 'Well, when we were first married ...' she paused.

'Go on,' Dr Kores ordered.

'Well, Henry did it three times one night I remember,' said Eva, blurting the statement out. 'He only did it once of course.'

The doctor's ballpen stopped. 'Please explain,' she said. 'First you said he was sexually active three times in one night. And second you said he was only once. Are you saying there was seminal ejaculation only on the first occasion?'

521

'I don't really know,' said Eva. 'It's not easy to tell, is it?'

Dr Kores eyed her doubtfully. 'Let me put it another way. Was there a penile spasm at the climax of each episode?'

'I suppose so,' said Eva. 'It's so long ago now and all I remember is that he was ever so tired next day.'

'In which year did this take place?' asked the doctor, having written down 'Penile spasm uncertain.'

'1963. In July,' said Eva. 'I remember that because we were on a walking holiday in the Peak District and Henry said he'd peaked out.'

'Very amusing,' said Dr Kores dryly. 'And that is his maximum sexual attainment?'

'He did it twice in 1970 on his birthday...'

'And the plateau was how many times a week?' asked Dr Kores, evidently determined to prevent Eva from intruding anything remotely human into the discussion.

'The plateau? Oh, well it used to be once or twice but now I'm lucky if it's once a month and sometimes we go even longer.'

Dr Kores licked her thin lips and put the pen down. 'Mrs Wilt,' she said, leaning on the desk and forming a triangle with her fingertips and thumbs. 'I deal exclusively with the problems of the female in a male-dominated social context, and to speak frankly, I find your attitude to your relationship with your husband unduly submissive.'

'Do you really?' said Eva, beginning to perk up. 'Henry always says I'm too bossy.'

'Please,' said the doctor with something approaching a shudder, 'I'm not in the least interested in your husband's opinions or in his person. If you choose to be, that is your business. Mine is to help you as an entirely independent being and, to be truthful, I find your self-objectivization highly distasteful.'

'I'm sorry,' said Eva, wondering what on earth self-objectivization was.

'For instance, you have repeatedly stated that and I quote "He did it three times" and again "He did it twice..."'

'But he did,' Eva protested.

'And who was the "It"? You?' said the doctor vehemently.

'I didn't mean it that way...' Eva began but Dr Kores was

not to be stopped. 'And the very word "did" or "done" is a tacit acceptance of marital rape. What would your husband say if you were to do him?'

'Oh, I don't think Henry'd like that,' said Eva, 'I mean, he's not very big and...'

'If you don't mind,' said the doctor, 'size does not come into it. The question of attitude is predominant. I am only prepared to help you if you make a determined effort to see yourself as the leader in the relationship.' Behind the blue tinted spectacles her eyes narrowed.

'I'll certainly try,' said Eva.

'You will succeed,' said the doctor sibilantly. 'It is of the essence. Repeat after me "I will succeed."'

'I will succeed,' said Eva.

'I am superior,' said Dr Kores.

'Yes,' said Eva.

'Not "Yes",' hissed the doctor, gazing even more peculiarly into Eva's eyes, 'but "I am superior".'

'I am superior,' said Eva obediently.

'Now both.'

'Both,' said Eva.

'Not that. I want you to repeat both remarks. First ...'

'I will succeed,' said Eva, finally getting the message, 'I am superior.'

'Again.'

'I will succeed. I am superior.'

'Good,' said the doctor. 'It is vital that you establish the correct psychic attitude if I am to help you. You will repeat those auto-instructs three hundred times a day. Do you understand?'

'Yes,' said Eva. 'I am superior. I will succeed.'

'Again,' said the doctor.

For the next five minutes Eva sat fixed in her chair and repeated the assertions while Dr Kores stared unblinking into her eyes. 'Enough,' she said finally. 'You understand what this means, of course?'

'Sort of,' said Eva. 'It's to do with what Mavis Mottram says about women taking the leading rôle in the world, isn't it?'

Dr Kores sat back in her chair with a thin smile. 'Ms Wilt,' she said, 'for thirty-five years I have made a continuous study of the sexual superiority of the feminine in the mammalian world. Even as a child, I was inspired by the mating habits of arachnida – my mother was something of an expert in the field before so unfortunately marrying my father, you understand.'

Eva nodded. Fortunately for her she had missed the reference to spiders but she was too fascinated not to understand that whatever Dr Kores was saying was somehow important. She had the future of the quads in mind.

'But,' continued the doctor, 'my own work has been concentrated upon the higher forms of life and, in particular, the infinitely superior talents of the feminine in the sphere of survival. At every level of development, the rôle of the male is subordinate and the female demonstrates an adaptability which preserves the species. Only in the human world, and then solely in the social context rather than the purely biological, has this process been reversed. This reversal has been achieved by the competitive and militaristic nature of society in which the brute force of the masculine has found justification for the suppression of the feminine. Would you agree?'

'Yes, I suppose so,' said Eva, who had found the argument difficult to follow but could see that it made some sort of sense.

'Good,' said Dr Kores. 'And now we have arrived at a world crisis in which the extermination of life on earth has been made probable by the masculine distortion of scientific development for military purposes. Only we women can save the future.' She paused and let Eva savour the prospect. 'Fortunately, science has also put into our hands the means of so doing. The purely physical strength of the male has lost its advantage in the automated society of the present. Man is redundant and with the age of the computer, it is women who will have power. You have, of course, read of the work done at St Andrew's. It is proven that women have the larger corpus collossum than men.'

'Corpus collossum?' said Eva.

'One hundred million brain cells, neural fibre connecting the hemispheres of the brain and essential in the transfer of information. In working with the computer, this interchange has the highest significance. It could well be to the electronic age what the muscle was to the age of the physical . . .'

524

For another twenty minutes, Dr Kores talked on, swinging between an almost demented fervour for the feminine, rational argument and the statement of fact. To Eva, ever prone to accept enthusiasm uncritically, the doctor seemed to embody all that was most admirable about the intellectual world to which she had never belonged. It was only when the doctor seemed to sag in her chair that Eva remembered the reason she had come. 'About Henry...' she said hesitantly.

For a moment, Dr Kores continued to focus on a future in which there were probably no men, before dragging herself back to the present. 'Oh yes, your husband,' she said almost absently. 'You wish for something to stimulate him sexually, yes?'

'If it's possible,' said Eva. 'He's never been...'

But Dr Kores interrupted her with a harsh laugh.

'Ms Wilt,' she said, 'have you considered the possibility that your husband's lack of sexual activity may be only apparent?'

'I don't quite understand.'

'Another woman perhaps?'

'Oh, no,' said Eva. 'Henry isn't like that. He really isn't.'

'Or latent homosexuality?'

'He wouldn't have married me if he'd been like that, would he?' said Eva, now genuinely shocked.

Dr Kores looked at her critically. It was at moments like this that her faith in the innate superiority of the feminine was put to the test. 'It has been known,' she said through clenched teeth and was about to enter into a discussion of the family life of Oscar Wilde when the bell rang in the hall.

'Excuse me a moment,' she said and hurried out. When she returned it was through another door. 'My dispensary,' she explained. 'I have there a tincture which may prove beneficial. The dose is, however, critical. Like many medications, it contains elements that taken in excess will produce definite contra-indication. I must warn you not to exceed the stated dose by as much as five millilitres. I have supplied a syringe for the utmost accuracy in measurement. Within those limits, the tincture will produce the desired result. Beyond them, I cannot be held responsible. You will naturally treat the matter with the utmost confidentiality. As a scientist, I cannot be held responsible for the misapplication of proven formulae.'

Eva put the plastic bottle in her bag and went down the hall. As she passed the rusty cultivator and the broken frames, her mind was in a maelstrom of contradictory impressions. There had been something weird about Dr Kores. It wasn't what she said that was wrong, Eva could see her words made good sense. It was rather in the way she said them and how she behaved. She'd have to discuss it with Mavis. All the same, as she stood at the bus stop she found herself repeating 'I am superior. I will succeed' almost involuntarily.

A hundred yards away, two of Inspector Hodge's plain-clothes men watched her and made notes of the time and place. The patternizing of the Wilts' lives had begun in earnest.

Chapter 9

And it continued. For two days, teams of detectives kept watch on the Wilts and reported back to Inspector Hodge who found the signals unambiguous. Eva's visit to Dr Kores was particularly damning.

'Herb farm? She went to a herb farm in Silton?' said the Inspector incredulously. After forty-eight almost sleepless hours and as many cups of black coffee, he could have done with some alternative medicine himself. 'And she came out with a large plastic bottle?'

'Apparently,' said the detective. Trying to keep up with Eva had taken its toll. So had the quads. 'For all I know, she went in with one. All we saw was her taking the bottle out of her bag when she was waiting for the bus.'

Hodge ignored the logic. As far as he was concerned, suspects who visited herb farms, and had bottles in their bags afterwards, were definitely guilty.

But it was Mavis Mottram's arrival at 45 Oakhurst Avenue later that afternoon that interested him most. 'Subject collects children from school at 3.30,' he read from the written report 'gets home and a woman drives up in a mini.'

'Correct.'

'What's she look like?'

'Forty, if she's a day. Dark hair. Five foot four. Blue anorak and khaki trousers with leg-warmers. Goes in at 3.55, leaving at 4.20.'

'So she could have collected the bottle?'

'Could have, I suppose, but she hadn't got a bag and there was no sign of it.'

'Then what?'

'Nothing till the nextdoor neighbour comes home at 5.30. Look, it's all there in my report.'

'I know it is,' said Hodge, 'I'm just trying to get the picture. How did you know his name was Gamer?'

'Blimey, I'd have to be stone deaf not to, the way she gave it to him, not to mention his wife carrying on something chronic.'

'So what happened?'

'This bloke Gamer goes in the door of 43,' said the detective, 'and five minutes later he's out again like a scalded cat with his wife trying to stop him. Dashes round to the Wilts' and tries to go in the side gate round the back of the house. Grabs the latch on the gate and the next moment he's flat on his back in the flower bed, twitching like he's got St Vitus' dance and his missus is yelling like they've killed him.'

'So what you're saying is the back gate was electrified?' said Hodge.

'I'm not saying it. He did. As soon as he could speak, that is, and had stopped twitching. Mrs Wilt comes out and wants to know what he's doing in her wallflowers. By the time he's got to his feet, just, and is yelling that her fucking hellcats – his words, not mine – have tried to murder him by stealing some statuette he's got in his back garden, and they've put in theirs, and wiring up the back gate to the fucking mains. And Mrs Wilt tells him not to be so silly and kindly not to use filthy language in front of her daughters. After that, things got a bit confusing with him wanting his statue and her saying she hadn't got it, and wouldn't have it if he gave it to her because it's dirty.'

'Dirty?' muttered Hodge. 'What's dirty about it?'

'It's one of those ones of a small boy peeing. Got it on his pond. She practically called him a pervert. And all the time his wife is pleading with him to come on home and never mind the ruddy statue, they can always get another one when they've sold the house. That got to him. "Sell the house?" he yells, "Who to? Even a raving lunatic wouldn't buy a house next to the bloody Wilts." Probably right at that.'

'And what happened in the end?' asked Hodge, making a mental note that he'd have an ally in Mr Gamer.

'She insists he come through the house and see if his statue's there, because she's not going to have her girls called thieves.'

'And he went?' said Hodge incredulously.

'Hesitantly,' said the detective. 'Came out shaken and swearing he'd definitely seen it there and if she didn't believe those kids had tried to kill him, why were all the lights in the house on the blink. That had her, and he pointed out there was a piece of wire still tied to the bootscraper outside the back gate.'

'Interesting,' said Hodge. 'And was there?'

'Must have been, because she got all flustered then, especially when he said it was evidence to show the police.'

'Naturally, with that bottle of dope still in the house,' said Hodge. 'No wonder they'd fixed the back door.' A new theory had been formulated in his mind. 'I tell you we're on to something, this time.'

Even the Superintendent, who shared Flint's view that Inspector Hodge was a greater menace to the public than half the petty crooks he arrested and would gladly have put the sod on traffic duty, had to admit that for once the Inspector seemed to be on the right track. 'This fellow Wilt's got to be guilty of something,' he muttered as he studied the report of Wilt's extraordinary movements during his lunch break.

In fact, Wilt had been on the look-out for McCullum's associates and had almost immediately spotted the two detectives in an unmarked car when he'd walked out of the Tech to pick up the Escort at the back of The Glassblowers' Arms, and had promptly taken evasive action with an expertise he'd learnt from watching old thrillers on TV. As a result, he'd doubled back down side roads, had disappeared up alleyways, had bought a number of wholly unnecessary items in crowded shops and had even bolted in the front doors of Boots and out the back before heading for the pub.

'Returned to the Tech car park at 2.15,' said the Superintendent. 'Where'd he been?'

'I'm afraid we lost him,' said Hodge. 'The man's an expert. All we know is he came back driving fast and practically ran for the building.'

Nor had Wilt's behaviour on leaving the Tech that evening been calculated to inspire confidence in his innocence. Anyone who walked out of the front gate wearing dark glasses, a coat with the collar turned up and a wig (Wilt had borrowed one from the Drama Department) and spent half an hour sitting on a bench by the bowling green on Midway Park, scrutinizing the passing traffic before sneaking back to the Tech car park, had definitely put himself into the category of a prime suspect.

'Think he was waiting for someone?' the Superintendent asked.

'More likely trying to warn them off,' said Hodge. 'They've probably got a system of signalling. His accomplices drive past and see him sitting there and get the message.'

'I suppose so,' said the Superintendent, who couldn't think of anything else that made sense. 'So we can expect an early arrest. I'll tell the Chief Constable.'

'I wouldn't say that, sir,' said Hodge, 'just that we've got a definite lead. If I'm right, this is obviously a highly organized syndicate. I don't want to rush into an early arrest when this man could lead us to the main source.'

'There is that,' said the Superintendent gloomily. He had been hoping that Hodge's handling of the case would prove so inept that he could call in the Regional Crime Squad. Instead the confounded man seemed to be making a success of it. And after that he'd doubtless apply for promotion and get it. Hopefully somewhere else. If not, the Superintendent would apply for a transfer himself. And there was still a chance Hodge would foul things up.

At the Tech, Hodge had. His insistence on putting plain-clothes detectives in, masquerading as apprentices or even more unsatisfactorily as Trainee Teachers, was playing havoc with staff morale.

'I can't stand it,' Dr Cox, Head of Science, told the Principal. 'It's bad enough trying to teach some of the students we get, without having a man poking about who doesn't know the difference between a Bunsen burner and a flamethrower. He practically burnt down the lab. on the third floor. And as for being any sort of teacher...'

'He doesn't have to say anything. After all, they're only here to observe.'

'In theory,' said Dr Cox. 'In practice, he keeps taking my students into corners and asking them if they can get him some Embalming Fluid. Anyone would think I was running a funeral home.'

The Principal explained the term. 'God Almighty, no won-

530

der the wretched fellow asked to stay behind last night to check the chemical inventory.'

It was the same in botany. 'How was I to know she was a policewoman?' Miss Ryfield complained. 'And anyway I had no idea students were growing marijuana as pot plants in the greenhouses. She seems to hold me responsible.' Only Dr Board viewed the situation at all philosophically. Thanks to the fact that none of the policemen spoke French, his department had been spared intrusion.

'After all, it is 1984,' he announced to an ad hoc committee in the staff room, 'and as far as I can tell, discipline has improved enormously.'

'Not in my department,' said Mr Spirey of Building. 'I've had five punch-ups in Plasterers and Bricklayers and Mr Gilders is in hospital with bicycle-chain wounds.'

'Bicycle-chain wounds?'

'Someone called the young thug from the police station a fucking pig and Mr Gilders tried to intervene.'

'And I suppose the apprentices were arrested for carrying offensive weapons?' said Dr Mayfield.

The Head of Building shook his head. 'No, it was the policeman who had the bicycle chain. Mind you, they made a right mess of him afterwards,' he added with some satisfaction.

But it was among Senior Secretaries that Hodge's investigations had been carried out most vigorously. 'If this goes on much longer, our exam results will be appalling,' said Miss Dill. 'You have no idea the effect of having girls taken out of class and interrogated is having on their typing performance. The impression seems to be that the College is a hotbed of vice.'

'Would that it were,' said Dr Board. 'But, as usual, the papers have got it all wrong. Still, page 3 is something.' And he produced a copy of the *Sun* and a photograph of Miss Lynchknowle in the nude, taken in Barbados the previous summer. The caption read DRUG HEIRESS DEAD AT TECH.

'Of course I've seen the papers and the publicity is disgraceful,' said the Principal to the members of the Education Committee. Originally called to discuss the impending visitation of HMIs, it was now more concerned with the new crisis. 'The point I am trying to make is that this is an isolated incident and...'

'It isn't,' said Councillor Blighte-Smythe. 'I have here a list of catastrophes which have bedevilled the College since your appointment. First there was that awful business with the Liberal Studies lecturer who...'

Mrs Chatterway, whose views were indefatigably progressive, intervened. 'I hardly think there's anything to be gained by dwelling on the past,' she said.

'Why not?' demanded Mr Squidley. 'It's time someone was held accountable for what goes on there. As tax- and rate-payers, we have a right to a decent practical education for our children and...'

'How many children do you have at the Tech?' snapped Mrs Chatterway.

Mr Squidley looked at her in disgust. 'None, thank God,' he said. 'I wouldn't let one of my kids anywhere near the place.'

'If we could just keep to the point,' said the Chief Education Officer.

'I am,' said Mr Squidley, 'very much to the point, and the point is that as an employer, I'm not paying good money to have apprentices turned into junkies by a lot of fifth-rate academic drop-outs.'

'I resent that,' said the Principal. 'In the first place, Miss Lynchknowle wasn't an apprentice, and in the second we have some extremely dedicated –'

'Dangerous nutters,' said Councillor Blighte-Smythe.

'I was going to say "dedicated teachers".'

'Which doubtless accounts for the fact that the Minister of Education's secretary is pushing for the appointment of a board of enquiry to investigate the teaching of Marxism-Leninism in the Liberal Studies Department. If that isn't a clear indication something's wrong, I don't know what is.'

'I object. I object most strongly,' said Mrs Chatterway. 'The real cause of the problem lies in spending cuts. If we are to give our young people a proper sense of social responsibility and care and concern –'

'Oh God, not that again,' muttered Mr Squidley. 'If half the louts I have to employ could even read and bloody write...'

The Principal glanced significantly at the Chief Education

532

Officer and felt more comfortable. The Education Committee would come to no sensible conclusions. It never did.

At 45 Oakhurst Avenue, Wilt glanced nervously out of the window. Ever since his lunch break and the discovery that he was being followed, he'd been on edge. In fact, he had driven home with his eyes so firmly fixed on the rear-view mirror that he had failed to notice the traffic lights on Nott Road and had banged into the back of the police car which had taken the precaution of tailing him from the front. The resulting exchange with the two plain-clothes men who were fortunately unarmed had done a lot to confirm his view that his life was in danger.

And Eva had hardly been sympathetic. 'You never do look where you're going,' she said, when he explained why the car had a crumpled bumper and radiator. 'You're just hopeless.'

'You'd feel fairly hopeless if you'd had the sort of day I've had,' said Wilt and helped himself to a bottle of home-brew. He took a swig of the stuff and looked at his glass dubiously.

'Must have left the bloody sugar out, or something,' he muttered, but Eva quickly switched the conversation to the incident with Mr Gamer. Wilt listened half-heartedly. His beer didn't usually taste like that and anyway it wasn't always quite so flat.

'As if girls their age could lift a horrid statue like that over the fence,' said Eva, concluding a singularly biased account of the incident.

Wilt dragged his attention away from his beer. 'Oh, I don't know. That probably explains what they were doing with Mr Boykins' block and tackle the other day. I wondered why they'd become so interested in physics.'

'But to say they'd tried to electrocute him,' said Eva indignantly.

'You tell me why the whole damned house was out,' said Wilt. 'The main fuse was blown, that's why. Don't tell me a mouse got into the toaster again either, because I checked. Anyway, that mouse didn't blow all the fuses and if I hadn't objected to having putrefying mouse savoury for breakfast instead of toast and marmalade, you'd never have noticed.'

'That was quite different,' said Eva. 'The poor thing got in there looking for crumbs. That's why it died.'

'And Mr Gamer damn near died because he was looking for his ruddy garden ornament,' said Wilt. 'And I can tell you who gave your brood that idea, the blooming mouse, that's who. One of these days they'll get the hang of the electric chair and I'll come home and find the Radleys' boy with a saucepan on his head and a damned great cable running to the cooker plug, as dead as a dodo.'

'They'd never do anything like that,' said Eva. 'They know better. You always look on the worst side of things.'

'Reality,' said Wilt, 'that's what I look at and what I see is four lethal girls who make Myra Hindley seem like a suitable candidate for a kindergarten teacher.'

'You're just being horrid,' said Eva.

'So's this bloody beer,' said Wilt as he opened another bottle. He took a mouthful and swore, but his words were drowned by the Magimix which Eva had switched on, in part to make an apple and carrot slaw because it was so good for the quads, but also to express her irritation. Henry could never admit the girls were bright and intelligent and good. They were always bad to him.

So was the beer. Eva's addition of five millilitres of Dr Kores' sexual stimulant to each bottle of Wilt's Best Bitter had given the stuff a new edge to it and, besides, it was flat. 'Must have left the screw top loose on this batch,' Wilt muttered as the Magimix came to a halt.

'What did you say?' Eva asked unpleasantly. She always suspected Wilt of using the cover of the Magimix, or the coffee-grinder to express his true thoughts.

'Nothing at all,' said Wilt, preferring to keep off the topic of beer. Eva was always going on about what it did to his liver and for once he believed her. On the other hand, if McCullum's thugs were going to duff him up, he intended to be drunk when they started, even if the muck did taste peculiar. It was better than nothing.

On the other side of Ipford, Inspector Flint sat in front of the telly and gazed abstractedly at a film on the life-cycle of the giant turtle. He didn't give a damn about turtles or their

534

sex life. About the only thing he found in their favour was that they had the sense not to worry about their offspring and left the little buggers to hatch out on a distant beach or, better still, to get eaten by predators. Anyway, the sods lived two hundred years and presumably didn't have high blood pressure.

Instead, his thoughts reverted to Hodge and the Lynchknowle girl. Having pointed the Head of the Drug Squad towards the morass of inconsequentiality that was Wilt's particular forte, it had begun to dawn on him that he might gain some kudos by solving the case himself. For one thing, Wilt wasn't into drugs. Flint was certain of that. He knew Wilt was up to something – stood to reason – but his copper's instinct told him that drugs didn't fit.

So someone else had supplied the girl with the muck that had killed her. With all the slow persistence of a giant turtle swimming in the depths of the Pacific, Flint went over the facts. The girl dead on heroin and PCP: a definite fact. Wilt teaching that bastard McCullum (also dead from drugs): another fact. Wilt making a phone call to the prison: not a fact, merely a probability. An interesting probability for all that, and if you subtracted Wilt from the case there was absolutely nothing to go on. Flint picked up the paper and looked at the dead girl's photo. Taken in Barbados. Smart set and half of them on drugs. If she'd got the stuff in that circle Hodge hadn't got a hope in hell. They kept their secrets. Anyway, it might be worth checking up on his findings so far. Flint switched off the TV and went into the hall. 'I'm just going out to stretch my legs,' he called out to his wife and was answered by a grim silence. Mrs Flint didn't give a damn what he did with his legs.

Twenty minutes later, he was in his office with the report on the interview with Lord and Lady Lynchknowle in front of him. Naturally, it had never dawned on them that Linda was on drugs. Flint recognized the symptoms and the desire to clear themselves of all blame. 'About as much parental care as those bloody turtles,' he muttered and turned to the interview with the girl who'd shared a flat with Miss Lynchknowle.

This time there was something more positive. No, Penny hadn't been to London for ages. Never went anywhere, in fact, not even home at weekends. Discos occasionally, but generally a loner and had given up her boyfriend at the university before Christmas etcetera. No recent visitors either. Occasionally, she'd go out of an evening to a coffee bar or just wander along by the river. She'd seen her down there twice on her way back from the cinema. Whereabouts exactly? Near the marina. Flint made a note of that, and also of the fact that the Sergeant who'd visited her had asked the right questions. Flint noted the names of some of the coffee bars. There was no point in visiting them, they'd be covered by Hodge and, besides, Flint had no intention of being seen to be interested in the case. Above all, though, he knew he was acting on intuition, the 'smell' of the case which came from his long experience and his knowledge that whatever else Wilt was – and the Inspector had his own views on the matter – he wasn't pushing drugs. All the same, it would be interesting to know if he had made that phone call to the prison on the night McCullum took an overdose. There was something strangely coincidental about that incident, too. It was easy enough to hear the story from Mr Blaggs. Flint had known the Chief Warder for years and had frequently had the pleasure of consigning prisoners to his dubious care.

And so presently he was standing in the pub near the prison discussing Wilt with the Chief Warder with a frankness Wilt would have found only partly reassuring. 'If you want my opinion,' said Mr Blaggs, 'educating villains is anti-social. Only gives them more brains than they need. Makes your job more difficult when they come out, doesn't it?'

Flint had to agree that it didn't make it any easier. 'But you don't reckon Wilt had anything to do with Mac's having a cache of junk in his cell?' he asked.

'Wilt? Never. A bloody do-gooder, that's what he is. Mind you, I'm not saying they're not daft enough, because I know for a fact they are. What I'm saying is, a nick ought to be a prison, not a fucking finishing-school for turning half-witted petty thieves into first-rate bank robbers with degrees in law.'

'That's not what Mac was studying for, is it?' asked Flint.

Mr Blaggs laughed. 'Didn't need to,' he said. 'He had enough cash on the outside, he had a fistful of legal beavers on his payroll.'

536

'So how come Wilt's supposed to have made this phone call?' asked Flint.

'Just what Bill Coven thought, he took the call,' said Blaggs, and looked significantly at his glass. Flint ordered two more pints. 'He just thought he recognized Wilt's voice,' Blaggs continued, satisfied that he was getting his money's worth for information. 'Could have been anyone.'

Flint paid for the beer and tried to think what to ask next. 'And you've got no idea how Mac got his dope then?' he asked finally.

'Know exactly,' said Blaggs proudly. 'Another bloody do-gooder only this time a fucking prison visitor. If you ask me, they should ban all vi –'

'A prison visitor?' interrupted Flint, before the Chief Warder could express his views on a proper prison regime, which involved perpetual solitary confinement for all convicts and mandatory hanging for murderers, rapists and anyone insulting a prison officer. 'You mean a visitor to the prison?'

'I don't. I mean an authorized prison visitor, a bloody licensed busybody. They come in and treat us officers like we've committed the ruddy crimes and the villains are all bloody orphans who didn't get enough teat when they were toddlers. Right, well, this bitch of a PV, name of Jardin, was the one McCullum got to bring his stuff in.'

'Christ,' said Flint. 'What did she do that for?'

'Scared,' said Blaggs. 'Some of Mac's nastier mates on the outside paid her a visit with razors and a bottle of nitric acid and threatened to leave her looking like a cross between a dog's dinner and a leper with acne unless ... You get the message?'

'Yes,' said Flint, who'd begun to sympathize with the prison visitor, though for the life of him he couldn't visualize what a leper with acne looked like. 'And you mean she walked in and announced the fact?'

'Oh dear me, no,' said Blaggs. 'Starts off we've done for Mr – I ask you, *Mister*? – fucking McCullum ourselves. Practically said I'd hanged the sod myself, not that I'd have minded. So we took her down the morgue – of course it just happened the prison quack was doing an autopsy at the time and didn't much like the look of things by the sound of it, using a saw he was, too – and he wasn't having any crap about anyone doing anything to the bugger. Right, well when she'd come to, like, and he's saying the swine died of drug overdose and anyone who said different'd end up in court for slander, she cracked. Tears all over the place and practically down on her knees in front of the Governor. And it all comes out how she's been running heroin into the prison for months. Ever so bleeding sorry and all.'

'I should bloody well think so,' said Flint. 'When's she going to be charged?'

Mr Blaggs drank his beer mournfully. 'Never,' he grunted.

'Never? But smuggling anything, let alone drugs, into a prison is an indictable offence.'

'Don't tell me,' said Blaggs. 'On the other hand, the Governor don't want no scandal, can't afford one with his job up for grabs and anyway, she'd done a social service in a way by shoving the bugger where he belongs.'

'There is that,' said Flint. 'Does Hodge know this?'

The Chief Warder shook his head. 'Like I said, the Governor don't want no publicity. Anyway, she claimed she thought the stuff was talcum powder. Like hell, but you know what a Rumpole would do with a defence like that. Prison authorities entirely to blame, and so on. Negligence, the lot.'

'Did she say where she got the heroin?' asked Flint.

'Picked it up back of a telephone box on the London Road at night. Never saw the blokes who delivered it.'

'And it won't have been any of the lot who'd threatened her either.'

By the time the Inspector left the pub, he was a happy man. Hodge was way off line, and Flint had a conscience-stricken prison visitor to question. He wasn't even worried about the effect of four pints of the best bitter being flushed through his system by those bloody piss-pills. He'd already charted his route home by way of three relatively clean public lavatories.

Chapter 10

But if Flint's mood had changed for the better, Inspector Hodge's hadn't. His interpretation of Wilt's behaviour had been coloured by the accident at the end of Nott Road. 'The bastard's got to know we're onto him, ramming a police car like that,' he told Sergeant Runk, 'so what's he do?'

'Buggered if I know,' said the Sergeant, who preferred early nights and couldn't think at all clearly at one in the morning.

'He goes for an early arrest, knowing we've got no hard evidence and will have to let him go.'

'What's he want us to do that for?'

'Because if we pull him in again he can start squealing about harassment and civil bloody liberties,' said Hodge.

'Seems an odd way of going about things,' said Runk.

'And what about sending your wife out to a herb farm to pick up a load of drugs on the very day after a girl dies of the filth? Isn't that a bit odd too?' Hodge demanded.

'Definitely,' said Runk. 'In fact, I can't think of anything odder. Any normal criminal would lie bloody low.'

Inspector Hodge smiled unpleasantly. 'Exactly. But we're not dealing with any ordinary criminal. That's the point I'm trying to make. We've got one of the cleverest monkeys I've ever had to catch on our hands.'

Sergeant Runk couldn't see it. 'Not if he sends his missus out to get a bottle of the stuff when we're watching her, he's not clever. Downright stupid.'

Hodge shook his head sadly. It was always difficult to get the Sergeant to understand the complexities of the criminal mind. 'Suppose there was nothing remotely like drugs in that bottle she was seen carrying?' he asked.

Sergeant Runk dragged his thoughts back from beds and tried to concentrate. 'Seems a bit of a wasted journey,' was all he could find to say.

'It's also intended to lead us up the garden path,' said Hodge.

'And that's his tactics. You've only to look at Wilt's record to see that. Take that doll caper for instance. He had old Flint by the short and curlies there, and why? Because the stupid fool pulled him in for questioning when all the evidence he had to go on was a blown-up doll of Mrs Wilt down a piling-hole with twenty tons of concrete on top of her. And where was the real Mrs Wilt all that week? Out on a boat with a couple of hippie Yanks who were into drugs up to their eyeballs and Flint lets them flee the country without grilling them about what they'd really been doing down the coast. Sticks out a mile they were smuggling and Wilt had set himself up for a decoy and kept Flint busy digging up a plastic doll. That's how cunning Wilt is.'

'I suppose when you put it like that it makes sense,' said Runk. 'And you reckon he's using the same tactics now.'

'Leopards,' said Hodge.

'Leopards?'

'Don't change their bleeding spots.'

'Oh, them,' said the Sergeant, who could have done without ellipses at that time of night.

'Only this time he's not dealing with some old-fashioned dead-beat copper like Flint,' said Hodge, now thoroughly convinced by the persuasiveness of his argument. 'He's dealing with me.'

'Makes a change. And talking about changes, I'd like to go...'

'To 45 Oakhurst Avenue,' said Hodge decisively, 'that's where you're going. I want Mr Smart-Arse Wilt's car wired for sound and we're calling off the physical observation. This time it's going to be electronic all the way.'

'Not if I have anything to do with it,' said Runk defiantly, 'I've enough sense to know better than start tinkering with a sod like Wilt's car. Besides, I've got a wife and three kids to –'

'What the hell's your family got to do with it?' said Hodge. 'All I'm saying is, we'll go round there while they're asleep –'

'Asleep? A bloke who electrifies his back gate, you think he takes chances with his bloody car? You can do what you like, but I'm buggered if I'm going to meet my Maker charred to a fucking cinder by a maniac who's linked his car to the national grid. Not for you or anyone else.'

540

But Hodge was not to be stopped. 'We can check it's safe,' he insisted.

'How?' asked Runk, who was wide awake now. 'Let a police dog pee against the thing and see if he gets 32,000 volts up his prick? You've got to be joking.'

'I'm not,' said Hodge. 'I'm telling. Go and get the equipment.'

Half an hour later, a desperately nervous Sergeant wearing gum boots and electrically safe rubber gloves eased the door of Wilt's car open. He'd already been round it four times to check there were no wires running from the house and had earthed it with a copper rod. Even so, he was taking no chances and was a trifle surprised that the thing didn't explode.

'All right, now where do you want the tape recorder?' he asked when the Inspector finally joined him.

'Somewhere where we can get at the tape easily,' Hodge whispered.

Runk groped under the dash and tried to find a space. 'Too bloody obvious,' said Hodge. 'Stick it under his seat.'

'Anything you say,' said Runk and stuffed the recorder into the springs. The sooner he was out of the damned car, the better. 'And what about the transmitter?'

'One in the boot and the other...'

'Other?' said Runk. 'You're going to get him picked up by the TV licence-detector vans at this rate. One of these sets has a radius of five miles.'

'I'm not taking chances,' said Hodge. 'If he finds one, he won't look for the other.'

'Not unless he has his car serviced.'

'Put it where no one looks.'

In the end, and then only after a lot of disagreement, the Sergeant attached one radio magnetically in a corner of the boot and was lying under the car searching for a hiding-place for the second when the lights came on in the Wilts' bedroom. 'I told you the swine wouldn't take any chances,' he whispered frantically as the Inspector fought his way in beside him. 'Now we're for it.'

Hodge said nothing. With his face pressed against an oily patch of tarmac and something that smelt disgustingly of cats, he was incapable of speech.

*

So was Wilt. The effect of Dr Kores' sexual stimulant added to his homebrew – Wilt had surreptitiously finished six bottles in an effort to find one that didn't taste peculiar – had been to leave him mentally befuddled and with the distinct impression that something like a battalion of army ants had taken possession of his penis and were busily digging in. Either that, or one of the quads had dementedly shoved the electric toothbrush up it while he was asleep. It didn't seem likely. But then again the sensation he was experiencing didn't seem in the least likely either. As he switched on the bedside lamp and hurled the sheet back to see what on earth was wrong, he glimpsed an expanse of red panties beside him. Eva in red panties? Or was she on fire too?

Wilt stumbled out of bed and fought a losing battle with his pyjama cord before dragging the damned things down without bothering to undo them and pointed the Anglepoise at the offending organ in an effort to identify the cause of his agony. The beastly creature (Wilt had always granted his penis a certain degree of autonomy or, more accurately, had never wholly associated himself with its activities) looked normal enough but it certainly didn't feel normal, not by a long chalk. Perhaps if he put some cold cream on it . . .

He hobbled across to Eva's dressing-table and searched among the jars. Where the hell did she keep the cold cream? In the end, he chose one that called itself a moisturizer. That'd do. It didn't. By the time he'd smeared half the jar on himself and a good deal on the pillow, the burning sensation seemed to have got worse. And whatever was going on was taking place *inside*. The army ants weren't digging in, the sods were digging out. For one insane moment he considered using an aerosol of Flykil to flush them out, but decided against it. God alone knew what a load of pressurized insecticide would do to his bladder and anyway the bloody thing was full enough already. Perhaps if he had a pee . . . Still clutching the moisturizer, he hobbled through to the bathroom. 'Must have been a fucking lunatic who first called it relieving oneself,' he thought when he'd finished. About the only relief he'd found was that he hadn't peed blood and there didn't appear to be any ants in the pan afterwards. And peeing hadn't helped. If anything, it had made things even worse. 'The bloody thing'll

542

ignite in a minute,' Wilt muttered, and was considering using the shower hose as a fire extinguisher when a better idea occurred to him. There was no point in smearing moisturizer on the outside. The stuff was needed internally. But how the hell to get it there? A tube of toothpaste caught his eye. That was what he needed. Oh no, it wasn't. Not with toothpaste. With moisturizer. Why didn't they pack the muck in tubes?

Wilt opened the medicine cupboard and groped among the old razors, the bottles of aspirin and cough mixture for a tube of something vaguely suitable for squeezing up his penis but apart from Eva's hair remover ... 'Sod that for a lark,' said Wilt, who had once accidentally brushed his teeth with the stuff, 'I'm not shoving that defoliant up any place.' It would have to be the moisturizing cream or nothing. And it wasn't going to be nothing. With a fresh and frenzied sense of desperation, he lurched from the bathroom clutching the jar and stumbled downstairs to the kitchen and was presently scrabbling in the drawer by the sink. A moment later he had found what he was looking for.

Upstairs, Eva turned over. For some time she had been vaguely aware that her back was cold but too vaguely to do anything about it. Now she was also aware that the light was on and that the bed beside her was empty and the bedclothes had been flung back. Which explained why she'd been freezing. Henry had evidently gone to the lavatory. Eva pulled the blankets back and lay awake waiting for him to return. Perhaps he'd be in the mood to make love. After all, he'd had two bottles of his beer and Dr Kores' aphrodisiac and she'd put on her red panties and it was much nicer to make love in the middle of the night when the quads were fast asleep than on Sunday mornings when they weren't, and she had to get up and shut the door in case they came in. Even that wasn't guaranteed to work. Eva would always remember one awful occasion when Henry had almost made it and she had suddenly smelt smoke and there'd been a series of screams from the quads. 'Fire! Fire!' they'd yelled, and she and Henry had hurled themselves from the bed and onto the landing in the altogether only to find the quads there with her jam-making pan filled with burning newspaper. It had been one of those rare occasions when she'd had to agree with Henry about the need for a thorough thrashing. Not that the quads had had one. They'd been down the stairs and out of the front door before Wilt could catch them and he'd been unable to pursue them down the street without a stitch of clothing on. No, it was much nicer at night and she was just wondering if she ought to take her panties off now and not wait, when a crash from downstairs put the thought out of her mind.

Eva climbed out of bed and putting a dressing-gown on, went down to investigate. The next moment all thoughts of making love had gone. Wilt was standing in the middle of the kitchen with her cake-icing syringe in one hand and his penis in the other. In fact, the two seemed to be joined together.

Eva groped for words. 'And what do you think you're doing?' she demanded when she could speak.

Wilt turned a crimson face towards her. 'Doing?' he asked, conscious that the situation was one that was open to any number of interpretations and none of them nice.

'That's what I said, doing,' said Eva.

Wilt looked down at the syringe. 'As a matter of fact...' he began, but Eva was ahead of him.

'That's my icing syringe.'

'I know it is. And this is my John Thomas,' said Wilt. Eva regarded the two objects with equal disgust. She would never be able to ice a cake with the syringe again and how she could ever have found anything faintly attractive about Wilt's John Thomas was beyond her. 'And for your information,' he continued, 'that is your moisturizing cream on the floor.'

Eva stared down at the jar. Even by the peculiar standards of 45 Oakhurst Avenue there was something disorientating about the conjunction – and conjunction was the right word – of Wilt's thingamajig and the icing syringe and the presence on the kitchen floor of a jar of her moisturizing cream. She sat down on a stool.

'And for your further information,' Wilt went on, but Eva stopped him. 'I don't want to hear,' she said.

Wilt glared at her lividly. 'And I don't want to feel,' he snarled. 'If you think I find any satisfaction in squirting whatever's in that emulsifier you use for your face up my whatsit at three o'clock in the morning, I can assure you I don't.'

544

'I don't see why you're doing it then,' said Eva, beginning to have an awful feeling herself.

'Because, if I didn't know better, I'd think some bloody sadist had larded my waterworks with pepper, that's why.'

'With pepper?'

'Or ground glass and curry powder,' said Wilt. 'Add a soupçon of mustard gas and you'll have the general picture. Or sensation. Something ghastly anyway. And now if you don't mind...'

But before he could get to work with the icing syringe again Eva had stopped him. 'There must be an antidote,' she said. 'I'll phone Dr Kores.'

Wilt's eyes bulged in his head. 'You'll do what?' he demanded.

'I said I'll —'

'I heard you,' shouted Wilt. 'You said you'd ring that bloody herbal homothrope Dr Kores and I want to know why.'

Eva looked desperately round the kitchen but there was no comfort now to be found in the Magimix or the le Creuset saucepans hanging by the stove and certainly none in the herb chart on the wall. That beastly woman had poisoned Henry and it was all her own fault for having listened to Mavis. But Wilt was staring at her dangerously and she had to do something immediately. 'I just think you ought to see a doctor,' she said. 'I mean, it could be serious.'

'Could be?' yelled Wilt, now thoroughly alarmed. 'It fucking well is and you still haven't told me —'

'Well, if you must know,' interrupted Eva, fighting back, 'you shouldn't have had so much beer.'

'Beer? My God, you bitch, I knew there was something wrong with the muck,' shouted Wilt and hurled himself at her across the kitchen.

'I only meant —' Eva began, and then dodged round the pine table to avoid the syringe. She was saved by the quads.

'What's Daddy doing with cream all over his genitals?' asked Emmeline. Wilt stopped in his tracks and stared at the four faces in the doorway. As usual, the quads were employing tactics that always nonplussed him. To combine the whimsy of 'Daddy', particularly with the inflection Emmeline gave the word, with the anatomically exact was calculated to disconcert him. And why not ask him instead of referring to him so objectively? For a moment he hesitated and Eva seized her opportunity.

'That's nothing to do with you,' she said and ostentatiously shielded them from the sight. 'It's just that your father isn't very well and –'

'That's right,' shouted Wilt, who could see what was coming, 'slap all the blame on me.'

'I'm not blaming you,' said Eva over her shoulder. 'It's –'

'That you lace my beer with some infernal irritant and bloody well poison me, and then you have the gall to tell them I'm not very well. I'll say I'm not well. I'm –'

A hammering sound from the Gamers' wall diverted his attention. As Wilt hurled the syringe at the Laughing Cavalier his mother-in-law had given them when she'd sold her house and which Eva claimed reminded her of her happy childhood there, Eva hustled the quads upstairs. When she came down again, Wilt had resorted to ice-cubes.

'I do think you ought to see a doctor,' she said.

'I should have seen one before I married you,' said Wilt. 'I suppose you realize I might be dead by now. What the hell did you put in my beer?'

Eva looked miserable. 'I only wanted to help our marriage,' she said, 'and Mavis Mottram said –'

'I'll strangle the bitch!'

'She said Dr Kores had helped Patrick and –'

'Helped Patrick?' said Wilt, momentarily distracted from his ice-packed penis. 'The last time I saw him he looked as if he could do with a bra. Said something about not having to shave so much either.'

'That's what I mean. Dr Kores gave Mavis something to cool his sexual ardour and I thought...' She paused. Wilt was looking at her dangerously again.

'Go on, though I'd question the use of "thought".'

'Well, that she might have something that would pep...'

'Pep?' said Wilt. 'Why not say ginger and have done with it? And why the hell should I need pepping up anyway? I'm a working man ... or was, with four damned daughters, not some demented sex pistol of seventeen.'

'I just thought ... I mean it occurred to me if she could do

546

so much for Patrick...' (here Wilt snorted) '... she might be able to help us to have a ... well, a more fulfilling sex life.'

'By poisoning me with Spanish Fly? Some fulfilment that is,' said Wilt. 'Well, let me tell you something now. For your information, I am not some fucking sex processor like that Magimix, and if you want the sort of sex life those idiotic women's magazines you read seem to suggest is your due, like fifteen times a week, you'd better find another husband because I'm buggered if I'm up to it. And the way I feel now, you'll be lucky if I'm ever up to it again.'

'Oh Henry!'

'Sod off,' said Wilt, and hobbled through to the downstairs loo with his mixing bowl of ice cubes. At least they seemed to help and the pain was easing off now.

As the sound of discord inside the house died down, Inspector Hodge and the Sergeant made their way back down Oakhurst Avenue to their car. They hadn't been able to hear what was being said, but the fact that there had been some sort of terrible row had heightened Hodge's opinion that the Wilts were no ordinary criminals. 'The pressure's beginning to tell,' he told Sergeant Runk. 'If we don't find him calling on his friends within a day or two, I'm not the man I think I am.'

'If I don't get some sleep, I won't be either,' said Runk, 'and I'm not surprised that bloke next door wants to sell his house. Must be hell living next to people like that.'

'Won't have to much longer,' said Hodge, but the mention of Mr Gamer had put a new idea in his mind. With a bit of collaboration from the Gamers, he'd be in a position to hear everything that went on in the Wilts' house. On the other hand, with their car transformed into a mobile radio station, he was expecting an early arrest.

Chapter 11

All the following day, while Wilt lay in bed with a hot-water bottle he'd converted into an ice-pack by putting it into the freezer compartment of the fridge and Inspector Hodge monitored Eva's movements about Ipford, Flint followed his own line of investigation. He checked with Forensic and learnt that the high-grade heroin found in McCullum's cell corresponded in every way to that discovered in Miss Lynchknowle's flat and almost certainly came from the same source. He spent an hour with Mrs Jardin, the prison visitor, wondering at the remarkable capacity for self-deception that had already allowed her to put the blame on everyone else for McCullum's death. Society was to blame for creating the villain, the education authorities for his wholly inadequate schooling, commerce and industry for failing to provide him with a responsible job, the judge for sentencing him...

'He was a victim of circumstances,' said Mrs Jardin.

'You might say that about everybody,' said Flint, looking at a corner cupboard containing pieces of silver that suggested Mrs Jardin's circumstances allowed her the wherewithal to be the victim of her own sentimentality. 'For instance, the three men who threatened to carve you up with –'

'Don't,' said Mrs Jardin, shuddering at the memory.

'Well, they were victims too, weren't they? So's a rabid dog, but that's no great comfort when you're bitten by one, and I put drug pushers in that category.' Mrs Jardin had to agree. 'So you wouldn't recognize them again?' asked Flint, 'not if they were wearing stockings over their heads like you said.'

'They were. And gloves.'

'And they took you down the London Road and showed you where the drop was going to be made.'

'Behind the telephone box opposite the turn-off to Brindlay. I was to stop and go into the phone box and pretend to make

548

a call, and then, if no one was about, I had to come out and pick up the package and go straight home. They said they'd be watching me.'

'And I don't suppose it ever occurred to you to go straight to the police and report the matter?' asked Flint.

'Naturally it did. That was my first thought, but they said they had more than one officer on their payroll.'

Flint sighed. It was an old tactic, and for all he knew the sods had been telling the truth. There were bent coppers, a lot more than when he'd joined the force, but then there hadn't been the big gangs and the money to bribe, and if bribery failed, to pay for a contract killing. The good old days when someone was always hanged if a policeman was murdered, even if it was the wrong man. Now, thanks to the do-gooders like Mrs Jardin, and Christie lying in the witness box and getting that mentally subnormal Evans topped for murders Christie himself had committed, the deterrent was no longer there. The world Flint had known had gone by the board, so he couldn't really blame her for giving in to threats. All the same, he was going to remain what he had always been, an honest and hardworking policeman.

'Even so we could have given you protection,' he said, 'and they wouldn't have been bothered with you once you'd stopped visiting McCullum.'

'I know that now,' said Mrs Jardin, 'but at the time I was too frightened to think clearly.'

Or at all, thought Flint, but he didn't say it. Instead, he concentrated on the method of delivery. No one dropped a consignment of heroin behind a telephone kiosk without ensuring it was going to be picked up. Then again, they didn't hang around after the drop. So there had to be some way of communicating. 'What would have happened if you'd been ill?' he asked. 'Just supposing you couldn't have collected the package, what then?'

Mrs Jardin looked at him with a mixture of contempt and bewilderment she evidently felt when faced with someone who concentrated so insistently on practical matters and neglected moral issues. Besides, he was a policeman and ill-educated. Policemen didn't find absolution as victims. 'I don't know,' she said.

But Flint was getting angry. 'Come off the high horse,' he said, 'you can squeal you were forced into being a runner, but we can still charge you with pushing drugs and into a prison at that. Who did you have to phone?'

Mrs Jardin crumbled. 'I don't know his name. I had to call a number and...'

'What number?'

'Just a number. I can't –'

'Get it,' said Flint. Mrs Jardin went out of the room and Flint sat looking at the titles in the bookshelves. They meant very little to him and told him only that she'd read or at least bought a great many books on sociology, economics, the Third World and penal reform. It didn't impress Flint. If the woman had really wanted to do something about the conditions of prisoners, she'd have got a job as a wardress and lived on low wages, instead of dabbling in prison visits and talking about the poor calibre of the staff who had to do society's dirty work. Stick up her taxes to build better prisons and she'd soon start squealing. Talk about hypocrisy.

Mrs Jardin came back with a piece of paper. 'That's the number,' she said, handing it to him. Flint looked at it. A London phone box.

'When did you have to call?'

'They said between 9.30 and 9.40 at night the day before I had to collect the packet.'

Flint changed direction. 'How many times did you collect?'

'Only three.'

He got to his feet. It was no use. They'd know Mac was dead, even if it hadn't been announced in the papers, so there was no point in supposing they'd make another drop, but at least they were operating out of London. Hodge was on the wrong track. On the other hand, Flint himself couldn't be said to be on the right one. The trail stopped at Mrs Jardin and a public telephone in London. If McCullum had still been alive...

Flint left the house and drove over to the prison. 'I'd like to take a look at Mac's list of visitors,' he told Chief Warder Blaggs, and spent half an hour writing names in his notebook, together with addresses.

'Someone in that little lot had to be running messages,' he

550

said when he finished. 'Not that I expect to get anywhere, but it's worth trying.'

Afterwards, back at the Station, he had checked them on the Central Records Computer and cross-referenced for drug dealing, but the one link he was looking for, some petty criminal living in Ipford or nearby, was missing. And he wasn't going to waste his time trying to tackle London. In fact, if he were truthful, he had to admit he was wasting his time even in Ipford except ... except that something told him he wasn't. It nagged at his mind. Sitting in his office, he followed that instinct. The girl had been seen by her flat-mate down by the marina. Several times. But the marina was just another place like the telephone kiosk on the London Road. It had to be something more definite, something he could check out.

Flint picked up the phone and called the Drug Addiction Study Unit at the Ipford Hospital.

By lunchtime, Wilt was up and about. To be exact, he'd been up and about several times during the morning, in part to get another hot-water bottle from the freezer, but more often in a determined effort not to masturbate himself to death. It was all very well Eva supposing she'd benefit from the effects of whatever diabolical irritant she'd added to his homebrew, but to Wilt's way of thinking, a wife who'd damned near poisoned her husband didn't deserve what few sexual benefits he had to offer. Give her an inkling of satisfaction from this experiment and next time he'd land up in hospital with internal bleeding and a permanent erection. As it was, he had a hard time with his penis.

'I'll freeze the damn thing down,' had been Wilt's first thought and for a while it had worked, though painfully. But after a time he had drifted off to sleep and had woken an hour later with the awful impression that he'd taken it into his head to have an affair with a freshly caught Dover Sole. Wilt hurled himself off the thing and had then taken the bottle downstairs to put it back in the fridge before realizing that this wouldn't be particularly hygienic. He was in the process of washing it when the front doorbell rang. Wilt dropped the bottle on the draining-board, retrieved it from the sink when it slithered off and finally tried wedging it between the upturned teapot and a casserole dish in the drying rack, before going to answer the call.

It was not the postman as he expected, but Mavis Mottram. 'What are you doing at home?' she asked.

Wilt sheltered behind the door and pulled his dressing-gown tightly round him. 'Well, as a matter of fact ...' he began.

Mavis pushed past him and went through to the kitchen. 'I just came round to see if Eva could organize the food side of things.'

'What things?' asked Wilt, looking at her with loathing. It was thanks to this woman that Eva had consulted Dr Kores. Mavis ignored the question. In her dual rôle as militant feminist and secretary of Mothers Against The Bomb, she evidently considered Wilt to be part of the male sub-species. 'Is she going to be back soon?' she went on.

Wilt smiled unpleasantly and shut the kitchen door behind him. If Mavis Mottram was going to treat him like a moron, he felt inclined to behave like one. 'How do you know she's not here?' he asked, testing the blade of a rather blunt bread-knife against his thumb.

'The car's not outside and I thought ... well, you usually take it ...' She stopped.

Wilt put the breadknife on the magnetic holder next to the Sabatier ones. It looked out of place. 'Phallic,' he said. 'Interesting.'

'What is?'

'Lawrentian,' said Wilt, and retrieved the icing syringe from a plastic bucket where Eva had been soaking it in Dettol in an attempt to persuade herself she would be able to use the thing again.

'Lawrentian?' said Mavis, beginning to sound genuinely alarmed.

Wilt put the syringe on the counter and wiped his hands. Eva's washing-up gloves caught his eye. 'I agree,' he said and began putting the gloves on.

'What on earth are you talking about?' asked Mavis, suddenly remembering Wilt and the inflated doll. She moved round the kitchen table towards the door and then thought better of it. Wilt in a dressing-gown and no pyjama trousers, and

552

now wearing a pair of rubber gloves and holding a cake-icing syringe, was an extremely disturbing sight. 'Anyway, if you'll ask her to call me, I'll explain about the food side of ...' Her voice trailed off.

Wilt was smiling again. He was also squirting a yellowish liquid into the air from the syringe. Images of some demented doctor in an early horror movie flickered in her mind. 'You were saying something about her not being here,' said Wilt and stepped back in front of the door. 'Do go on.'

'Go on about what?' said Mavis with a distinct quaver.

'About her not being here. I find your interest curious, don't you?'

'Curious?' mumbled Mavis, desperately trying to find some thread of sanity in his inconsequential remarks. 'What's curious about it? She's obviously out shopping and –'

'Obviously?' asked Wilt, and gazed vacantly past her out of the window and down the garden. 'I wouldn't have said anything was obvious.'

Mavis involuntarily followed his gaze and found the back garden almost as sinister as Wilt with washing-up gloves and that bloody syringe. With a fresh effort, she forced herself to turn back and speak normally. 'I'll be off now,' she said and moved forward.

Wilt's fixed smile crumbled. 'Oh, not so soon,' he said. 'Why not put the kettle on and have some coffee? After all, that's what you'd do if Eva was here. You'd sit down and have a nice talk. And you and Eva had so much in common.'

'Had?' said Mavis and wished to God she'd kept her mouth shut. Wilt's awful smile was back again. 'Well, if you'd like a cup yourself, I suppose I've got time.' She crossed to the electric kettle and took it to the sink. The hot-water bottle was lying on the bottom. Mavis lifted it out and experienced another ghastly frisson. The hot-water bottle wasn't simply not hot, it was icy cold. And behind her Wilt had begun to grunt alarmingly. For a moment Mavis hesitated before swinging round. This time there was no mistaking the threat she was facing. It was staring at her from between the folds of Wilt's dressing-gown. With a squeal, she hurled herself at the back door, dragged it open, shot out and with a clatter of dustbin lids, was through the gate and heading for the car.

Behind her Wilt dropped the syringe back into the bucket and tried to get his hands out of the washing-up gloves by pulling on the fingers. It wasn't the best method and it was some time before he'd rid himself of the wretched things and had grabbed the second bottle from the freezer. 'Bugger the woman,' he muttered as he clutched the bottle to his penis and tried to think of what to do next. If she went to the police ... No, she wasn't likely to do that but all the same, it would be as well to take precautions. Regardless of hygiene, he flung the bottle from the sink into the freezer and hobbled upstairs. 'At least we've seen the last of Mavis M,' he thought as he got back into bed. That was some consolation for the reputation he was already doubtless acquiring. As usual, he was entirely wrong.

Twenty minutes later, Eva, who had been intercepted by Mavis on her way home, drove up to the house.

'Henry,' she shouted as soon as she was inside the front door. 'You come straight down here and explain what you were doing with Mavis.'

'Sod off,' said Wilt.

'What did you say?'

'Nothing. I was just groaning.'

'No, you weren't. I distinctly heard you say something,' said Eva on her way upstairs.

Wilt got out of bed and girded his loins with the water bottle. 'Now you just listen to me,' he said before Eva could get a word in, 'I've had all I can stand from everybody, you, Mavis-moron-Mottram, that poisoner Kores, the quads and the bloody thugs who've been following me. In fact the whole fucking modern world with its emphasis on me being nice and docile and passive and everyone else doing their own thing and to hell with the consequences. (A) I am not a thing, and (B) I'm not going to be done any more. Not by you, or Mavis, or, for that matter, the damned quads. And I don't give a tuppenny stuff what received opinions you suck up like some dehydrated sponge from the hacks who write articles on progressive education and sex for geriatrics and health through fucking hemlock –'

'Hemlock's a poison. No one . . .' Eva began, trying to divert his fury.

'And so's the ideological codswallop you fill your head with,' shouted Wilt. 'Permissive cyanide, page three nudes for the so-called intelligentsia or video nasties for the unemployed, all fucking placebos for them that can't think or feel. And if you don't know what a placebo is, try looking it up in a dictionary.'

He paused for breath and Eva grabbed her opportunity. 'You know very well what I think about video nasties,' she said, 'I wouldn't dream of letting the girls see anything like that.'

'Right,' yelled Wilt, 'so how about letting me and Mr bleeding Gamer off the hook. Has it ever occurred to you that you've got genuine non-video actual nasties, pre-pubescent horrors, in those four daughters? Oh no, not them. They're special, they're unique, they're flipping geniuses. We mustn't do anything to retard their intellectual development, like teaching them some manners or how to behave in a civilized fashion. Oh no, we're your modern model parents holding the ring while those four ignoble little savages turn themselves into computer-addicted technocrats with about as much moral sense as Ilse Koch on a bad day.'

'Who's Ilse Koch?' asked Eva.

'Just a mass murderess in a concentration camp,' said Wilt, 'and don't get the idea I'm on a right-wing, flog 'em and hang 'em reactionary high because I'm not, and those idiots don't think either. I'm just mister stick-in-the-middle who doesn't know which way to jump. But my God I do think! Or try to. Now leave me in peace and discomfort and go and tell your mate Mavis that the next time she doesn't want to see an involuntary erection, not to advise you to go anywhere near Castrator Kores.'

Eva went downstairs feeling strangely invigorated. It was a long time since she'd heard Henry state his feelings so strongly and, while she didn't understand everything he'd said, and she certainly didn't think he'd been fair about the quads, it was somehow reassuring to have him assert his authority in the house. It made her feel better about having been to that awful Dr Kores with all her silly talk about . . . what was it? ... 'the sexual superiority of the female in the mammalian world'. Eva didn't want to be superior in everything and anyway, she wasn't just a mammal. She was a human being. That wasn't the same thing at all.

Chapter 12

By the following evening, it would have been difficult to say what Inspector Hodge was. Since Wilt hadn't emerged from the house, the Inspector had spent the best part of two days tracing Eva's progress to and from the school and round Ipford in the bugged Escort.

'It's good practice,' he told Sergeant Runk, as they followed her in a van Hodge had converted to a listening-post.

'For what?' asked the Sergeant, pinning a mark on the town map to indicate that Eva had now parked behind Sainsbury's. She'd already been to Tesco's and Fine Fare. 'So we learn where to get the best discount on washing powder?'

'For when he decides to move.'

'When,' said Runk. 'So far he hasn't been out of the house all day.'

'He's sent her out to check she hasn't got a tail on her,' said Hodge. 'In the meantime, he's lying low.'

'Which you said was just the thing he wasn't doing,' said Runk. 'I said he was and you said...'

'I know what I said. But that was when he knew he was being followed. It's different now.'

'I'll say,' said Runk. 'So the sod sends us on a tour of shopping centres and we haven't got a clue what's going on.'

They had that night. Runk, who had insisted on having the afternoon off for some shut-eye if he was to work at night, retrieved the tape from under the seat and replaced it with a new one. It was one o'clock in the morning. Half an hour later, Hodge, whose childhood had been spent in a house where sex was never mentioned, was listening to the quads discussing Wilt's condition with a frankness that appalled him. If anything was needed to convince him that Mr and Mrs Wilt were died-in-the-wool criminals, it was Emmeline's repeated demand to know why Daddy had been up in the night putting cake icing on his penis. Eva's explanation didn't help either. 'He wasn't feeling very well, dear. He'd had too much beer and he couldn't sleep, so he went down to the kitchen to see if he could ice cake and . . .'

'I wouldn't like the sort of cake he was icing,' interrupted Samantha. 'And anyway, it was face-cream.'

'I know, dear, but he was practising and he spilt it.'

'Up his cock?' demanded Penelope, which gave Eva the opportunity to tell her never to use that word. 'It's not nice,' she said, 'it's not nice to say things like that and you're not going to tell anyone at school.'

'It wasn't very nice of Daddy to use the icing syringe to pump face-cream up his penis,' said Emmeline.

By the time the discussion was over, and Eva had dropped the quads off at the school, Hodge was ashen. Sergeant Runk wasn't feeling very well either.

'I don't believe it, I don't believe a bloody word of it,' muttered the Inspector.

'I wish to God I didn't,' said Runk. 'I've heard some revolting things in my time but that lot takes the cake.'

'Don't mention that word,' Hodge said. 'I still don't believe it. No man in his right mind would do a thing like that. They're having us on.'

'Oh, I don't know. I knew a bloke once who used to butter his wick with strawberry jam and have his missus –'

'Shut up,' shouted Hodge, 'if there's one thing I can't stand it's filth and I've had my fill of that for one night.'

'So's Wilt, by the sound of it,' said Runk, 'walking about with his prick in a jug of ice cubes like that. Can't have been just face-cream or icing-sugar he had in that syringe.'

'Dear God,' said Hodge. 'You're not suggesting he was fixing himself with a cake-icing syringe, are you? He'd be bloody dead by now, and anyhow the fucking thing would leak.'

'Not if he mixed the junk with cold cream. That'd explain it, wouldn't it?'

'It might do,' Hodge admitted. 'I suppose if people can sniff the filthy muck, there's no knowing what they can do with it. Not that it helps us much what he does.'

'Of course it does,' said the Sergeant, who had suddenly seen a way of ending the tedium of sitting through the night in the van. 'It means he's got the stuff in the house.'

'Or up his pipe,' said Hodge.

'Wherever. Anyway, there's bound to be enough around to haul him in and give him a good going over.'

But the Inspector had his sights set on more ambitious targets. 'A fat lot of good that's going to do us,' he said, 'even if he did crack, and if you'd read what he did to old Flint you'd know better –'

'But this'd be different,' Runk interrupted. 'First off, he'd be cold turkey. Don't have to question him. Leave him in a cell for three days without a fix and he'd be bleating like a fucking baa-lamb.'

'Yes, and I know who for,' said the Inspector. 'His ruddy mouthpiece.'

'Yes, but we'd have his missus too, remember. And anyway this time we'd have hard evidence and it would just be a matter of charging him. He wouldn't get bail on a heroin charge.'

'True,' said Hodge grudgingly, 'if we had hard evidence. "If."'

'Well, there's bound to be with him getting the stuff all over his pyjamas like those kids said. Forensic would have an easy time. Take that cake-icing syringe for a starter. And then there are towels and drying-up cloths. Blimey, the place must be alive with the stuff. Even the fleas on the cat must be addicts the way he's been splashing it round.'

'That's what worries me,' said Hodge. 'Whoever heard of a pusher splashing it round? No way. They're too bloody careful. Especially when the heat's on like it is now. You know what I think?' Sergeant Runk shook his head. In his opinion the Inspector was incapable of thought. 'I think the bastard's trying the old come-on. Wants us to arrest him. He's trying to trap us into it. That explains the whole thing.'

'Doesn't explain anything to me,' said Runk despairingly.

'Listen,' said Hodge, 'what we've heard on that tape just now is too bizarre to be credible, right? Right. You've never heard of a junkie fixing his cock and I haven't either. But apparently, this Wilt does. Not only that, but he makes a fucking mess, does it in the middle of the night and with a cake-icing syringe and makes sure his kids find him in the kitchen doing it. For why? Because he wants the little bitches

559

to shoot their mouths off about it in public and for us to hear about it. That's why. Well, I'm not falling for it. I'm going to take my time and wait for Mr Clever Wilt to lead me to his source. I'm not interested in single pushers, this time I'm going to pull in the whole ruddy network.'

And having satisfied himself with this interpretation of Wilt's extraordinary behaviour, the Inspector sat on, savouring his eventual triumph. In his mind's eye, he could see Wilt in the dock with a dozen big-time criminals, none of whom the likes of Flint had ever suspected. They'd be moneyed men with large houses who played golf and belonged to the best clubs, and after sentencing them, the Judge would compliment Inspector Hodge on his brilliant handling of the case. No one would ever call him inefficient again. He'd be famous and his photograph would be in all the papers.

Wilt's thoughts followed rather similar lines, though with a different emphasis. The effects of Eva's enthusiasm for aphrodisiacs were still making themselves felt and, more disastrously, had given him what appeared to be a permanent erection. 'Of course I'm confined to the bloody house,' he said when Eva complained that she didn't want him wandering about in his dressing-gown on her weekly coffee morning. 'You don't expect me to go back to the Tech with the thing sticking out like a ramrod.'

'Well, I don't want you making an exhibition of yourself in front of Betty and the others like you did with Mavis.'

'Mavis got what she deserved,' said Wilt. 'I didn't ask the woman into the house, she just marched in, and anyway if she hadn't put you on to poisoner Kores I wouldn't be wandering around with a coat-hanger strapped to my waist, would I?'

'What's the coat-hanger for?'

'To keep the flipping dressing-gown off the inflamed thing,' said Wilt. 'If you knew what it felt like to have stuff like a heavy blanket rubbing against the end of a pressurized and highly sensitive –'

'I don't want to hear,' said Eva.

'And I don't want to feel,' Wilt retorted. 'Hence the coat-hanger. And what's more, you want to try bending your knees and leaning forward at the same time every time you have to pee. It's bloody agony. As it is I've banged my head on the wall twice and I haven't had a crap in two days. I can't even sit down to read. It's either flat on my back in bed with the wastepaper basket for protection or up and about with the coat-hanger. And up and about it is. At this rate, they'll have to build a special coffin with a periscope when I cough it.'

Eva looked at him doubtfully. 'Perhaps you ought to go and see a doctor if it's that serious.'

'How?' snapped Wilt. 'If you think I'm going to walk down the road looking like a pregnant sex-change artist, forget it. I'd be arrested before I was half-way there and the local rag would have a field day. TECH TEACHER ON PERMANENT HIGH. And you'd really love it if I got called Pumpkin Penis Percy. So you have your Tupperware Party and I'll stick around upstairs.'

Wilt went carefully up to the bedroom and took refuge under the wastepaper basket. Presently, he heard voices from below. Eva's Community Care Committee had begun to arrive. Wilt wondered how many of them had already heard Mavis' version of the episode in the kitchen and were secretly delighted that Eva was married to a homicidal flasher. Not that they would ever admit as much. No, it would be 'Did you hear about poor Eva's awful husband?' or 'I can't think how she can bring herself to stay in the same house with that frightful Henry,' but in fact the target for their malice would be Eva herself. Which was just as it should be, considering that she'd doctored his beer with whatever poison Dr Kores had given her. Wilt lay back and wondered about the doctor and presently fell into a daydream in which he sued her for some enormous sum on the grounds of . . . What sort of grounds were there? Invasion of Penisy? Or Deprivation of Scrotal Rights? Or just plain Poisoning. That wouldn't work because Eva had administered the stuff and presumably if you took it in the correct doses it wouldn't have such awful effects. And, of course, the Kores bitch wasn't to know that Eva never did things by halves. In her book, if a little of something was good for you, twice as much was better. Even Charlie, the cat, knew that, and had developed an uncanny knack of disappearing for several days the moment Eva put down a saucer of cream laced with worm powder. But then Charlie was no fool and evidently still remembered the experience of having his innards scoured out by twice the recommended dosage. The poor brute had come limping back into the house after a week in the bushes at the bottom of the garden looking like a tapeworm with fur and had promptly been put on a high-pilchard diet to build him up.

Well, if a cat could learn from experience, there was no excuse for Wilt. On the other hand, Charlie didn't exactly have to live with Eva, but could shove off at the first sign of trouble. 'Lucky blighter,' Wilt muttered and wondered what would happen if he rang up one night and said he wasn't coming home for a week. He could just imagine the explosion on the other end of the line, and if he put the phone down without coming up with a really plausible explanation, he'd never hear the end of it when he did come home. And why? Because the truth was always too insane or incredible. Just about as incredible as the events of the week which had started with that idiot from the Ministry of Education and had gone on through Miss Hare's use of karate in the Ladies' lavatory to McCullum's threats and the men in the car who'd followed him. Add that little lot together with an overdose of Spanish Fly, and you had a truth no one would believe. Anyway, there was no point in lying there speculating about things he couldn't alter.

'Emulate the cat,' said Wilt to himself and went through to the bathroom to check in the mirror how his penis was getting on. It certainly felt better, and when he removed the wastepaper basket, he was delighted to find it had begun to droop. He had a shower and shaved and by the time Eva's little group had broken up, he was able to go downstairs wearing his trousers. 'How did the hen party go?' he asked.

Eva rose to the provocation. 'I see you're back to your normal sexist self. Anyway, it wasn't any sort of party. We're having that next Friday. Here.'

'Here?'

'That's right. It's going to be a fancy-dress party with prizes for the best costume and a raffle to raise money for the Harmony Community Play-Group.'

'Yes, and I'm sending a bill to all the people you're inviting to pay for the insurance in advance. Remember what happened to the Vurkells when Polly Merton sued them for falling downstairs blind drunk.'

'That was quite different,' said Eva. 'It was all Mary's fault for having a loose stair carpet. She never did look after the house properly. It was always a mess.'

'So was Polly Merton when she hit the hall floor. It was a wonder she wasn't killed,' said Wilt. 'Anyway, that's not the point. The Vurkells' house was wrecked and the insurance company wouldn't pay up because he'd been breaking the by-laws by running an illegal casino with that roulette wheel of his.'

'There you are,' said Eva. 'We're not breaking the law by holding a raffle for charity.'

'I'd check it out if I were you, and you can check me out too,' said Wilt. 'I've had enough trouble with my private parts these last two days without wearing that Francis Drake outfit you rigged me out in last Christmas.'

'You looked very nice in it. Even Mr Persner said you deserved a prize.'

'For wearing your grandmother's camiknickers stuffed with straw, I daresay I did, but I certainly didn't feel nice. In any case, I've got my prisoner to teach that night.'

'You could cancel that for once,' said Eva.

'What, just before the exams? Certainly not,' said Wilt. 'You invite a mob of costumed fools to invade the house for the good of charity without consulting me, you mustn't expect me to stop my charitable work.'

'In that case, you'll be going out tonight then?' said Eva. 'Today's Friday and you've got to keep up the good work, haven't you?'

'Good Lord,' said Wilt, who'd lost track of the days. It *was* Friday and he had forgotten to prepare anything for the lecture to his class at Baconheath. Spurred on by Eva's sarcasm and the knowledge that he'd end up the following Friday in straw-filled camiknickers or even as Puss in Boots in a black leotard which fitted far too tightly, Wilt spent the afternoon working over some old notes on British Culture and Institutions. They were entitled 'The Need For Deference, Paternalism and The Class Structure' and were designed to be provocative.

By six o'clock he had finished his supper, and half an hour later was driving out along the fen roads towards the airbase rather faster then usual. His penis was playing up again and it had only been by strapping it to his lower stomach with a long bandage and a cricket box that he'd been able to make himself comfortable and not provocatively indecent.

Behind him, the two monitoring vans followed his progress and Inspector Hodge was jubilant. 'I knew it. I knew he'd have to move,' he told Sergeant Runk as they listened to the signals coming from the Escort. 'Now we're getting some-where.'

'If he's as smart as you say he is, it could be up the garden path,' said Runk.

But Hodge was consulting the map. The coast lay ahead. Apart from that, there were only a few villages, the bleak flatness of the fens and ... 'Any moment he'll switch west,' he predicted. His hopes had turned to certainty. Wilt was heading for the US Airbase at Baconheath and the American connection was complete.

In Ipford prison, Inspector Flint stared into the Bull's face. 'How many years have you still to do?' he asked. 'Twelve?'

'Not with remission,' said the Bull. 'Only eight. I've got good behaviour.'

'Had,' said Flint. 'You lost that when you knocked Mac off.'

'Knocked Mac off? I never did. That's a bloody lie. I never touched him. He –'

'That's not what the Bear says,' interrupted Flint, and opened a file. 'He says you'd been saving up those sleeping pills so you could murder Mac and take over from him. Want to read his statement? It's all down in black and white and nicely signed. Here, take a dekko.'

He pushed the paper across the table but the Bull was on his feet. 'You can't pull that fucking one on me,' he shouted and was promptly pushed back into his chair by the Chief Warder.

'Can,' said Flint, leaning forward and staring into the Bull's frightened eyes. 'You wanted to take over from McCullum, didn't you? Jealous of him, weren't you? Got greedy. Thought you'd grab a nice little operation run from inside and you'd

564

come out in eight years with a pension as long as your arm all safely stashed away by your widow.'

'Widow?' The Bull's face was ashen now. 'What you mean, widow?'

Flint smiled. 'Just as I say. Widow. Because you aren't ever going to get out now. Eight years back to twelve and a life stretch for murdering Mac adds up to twenty-seven by my reckoning, and for all those twenty-seven years, you're going to be doing solitary for your own protection. I can't see you making it, can you?'

The Bull stared at him pathetically. 'You're setting me up.'

'I don't want to hear your defence,' said Flint, and got to his feet. 'Save the blarney for the court. Maybe you'll get some nice judge to believe you. Especially with your record. Oh, and I shouldn't count on the missus to help. She's been shacked up with Joe Slavey for six months, or didn't you know?'

He moved towards the door, but the Bull had broken. 'I didn't do it, I swear to God I didn't, Mr Flint. Mac was like a brother to me. I'd never . . .'

Flint put the boot in again. 'Plead insanity is my advice,' he said. 'You'll be better off in Broadmoor. Buggered if I'd want Brady or the Ripper as a neighbour for the rest of my natural.' For a moment he paused by the door. 'Let me know if he wants to make a statement,' he said to the Chief Warder. 'I mean, I suppose he could help . . .'

There was no need to go on. Even the Bull had got the message. 'What do you want to know?'

It was Flint's turn to think. Take the pressure off too quickly and all he'd get would be garbage. On the other hand, strike while the iron was hot. 'The lot,' he said. 'How the operations work. Who does what. What the links are. You name it, I want it. Every fucking thing!'

The Bull swallowed. 'I don't know everything,' he said, looking unhappily at the Chief Warder.

'Don't mind me,' said Mr Blaggs. 'I'm not here. Just part of the furniture.'

'Start with how Mac got himself junk,' said Flint. It was best to begin with something he already knew. The Bull told him and Flint wrote it all down with a growing sense of satisfaction. He hadn't known about Prison Officer Lane being bent.

'You'll get me slit for this,' said the Bull when he'd finished with Mrs Jardin, the Prison Visitor.

'I don't know why,' said Flint. 'Mr Blaggs here isn't going to say who told him and it doesn't necessarily have to come out at your trial.'

'Christ,' said the Bull. 'You're not still going on with that, are you?'

'You tell me,' said Flint, maintaining the pressure. By the time he left the prison three hours later, Inspector Flint was almost a happy man. True, the Bull hadn't told him everything, but then he hadn't expected him too. In all likelihood, the fool didn't know much more, but he'd given Flint enough names to be going on with. Best of all, he'd grassed too far to back out, even if the threat of a murder charge lost its effect. The Bull would indeed get himself sliced by some other prisoner if the news ever got out. And the Bear was going to be Flint's next target.

'Being a copper's a dirty business sometimes,' he thought as he drove back to the police station. But drugs and violence were dirtier still. Flint went up to his office and began to check out some names.

Ted Lingon's name rang a bell – two bells, when he put his lists together. And Lingon ran a garage. Promising. But who was Annie Mosgrave?

Chapter 13

'Who?' said Major Glaushof.

'Some guy who teaches English or something evenings. Name of Wilt,' said the Duty Lieutenant. 'H. Wilt.'

'I'll be right over,' said Glaushof. He put the phone down and went through to his wife.

'Don't wait up, honey,' he said, 'I've got a problem.'

'Me too,' said Mrs Glaushof, and settled back to watch Dallas on BBC. It was kind of reassuring to know Texas was still there and it wasn't damp and raining all the time and goddam cold like Baconheath, and people still thought big and did big things. So she shouldn't have married an Airbase Security Officer with a thing going for German Shepherds. And to think he'd seemed so romantic when she'd met him back from Iran. Some security there. She should have known.

Outside, Glaushof climbed into his jeep with the three dogs and drove off between the houses towards the gates to Civilian Quarters. A group of men were standing well back from Wilt's Escort in the parking lot. Glaushof deliberately skidded the jeep to a stop and got out.

'What is it?' he asked. 'A bomb?'

'Jesus, I don't know,' said the Lieutenant, who was listening to a receiver. 'Could be anything.'

'Like he's left his CB on,' a Corporal explained, 'only there's two of them and they're bleeping.'

'Know any Brit who has two CBs running continuously the same time?' asked the Lieutenant. 'No way, and the frequency's wrong. Way too high.'

'So it could be a bomb,' said Glaushof. 'Why the fuck did you let it in?'

In the darkness and under threat of being blown to bits by whatever diabolical device the car concealed, Glaushof edged away. The little group followed him.

567

'Guy comes every Friday, gives his lecture, has coffee and goes on home no problem,' said the Lieutenant.

'So you let him drive right through with that lot buzzing and you don't stop him,' said Glaushof. 'We could have a Beirut bomb blast on our hands.'

'We didn't pick up the bleep till later.'

'Too later,' said Glaushof, 'I'm not taking any chances. I want the sand trucks brought up but fast. We're going to seal that car. Move.'

'It ain't no bomb,' said the Corporal, 'not sending like that. With a bomb the signals would be coming in.'

'Whatever,' said Glaushof, 'it's a breach of security and it's going to be sealed.'

'If you say so, Major,' said the Corporal and disappeared across the parking lot. For a moment, Glaushof hesitated and considered what other action he should take. At least he'd acted promptly to protect the base and his own career. As Base Security Officer, he'd always been against these foreign lecturers coming in with their subversive talks. He'd already discovered a geographer who'd sneaked a whole lot of shit about the dangers to bird-life from noise pollution and kerosene into his lectures on the development of the English landscape. Glaushof had had him busted as a member of Greenpeace. A car with radios transmitting continuously suggested something much more serious. And something much more serious could be just what he needed.

Glaushof ran through a mental checklist of enemies of the Free World: terrorists, Russian spies, subversives, women from Greenham Common ... whatever. It didn't matter. The key thing was that Base Intelligence had fouled things up and it was up to him to rub their faces in the shit. Glaushof smiled to himself at the prospect. If there was one man he detested, it was the Intelligence Officer. Nobody heard of Glaushof, but Colonel Urwin with his line to the Pentagon and his wife in with the Base Commander's so they were invited to play Bridge Saturday nights, oh sure, he was a big noise. And a Yale man. Screw him. Glaushof intended to. 'This guy ... what did you say his name is?' he asked the Lieutenant.

'Wilt,' said the Lieutenant.

'Where are you holding him?'

'Not holding him anyplace,' said the Lieutenant. 'Called you first thing we picked up the signals.'

'So where is he?'

'I guess he's over lecturing someplace,' said the Lieutenant. 'His details are in the guardhouse. Schedule and all.'

They hurried across the parking lot to the gates to the civilian quarters and Glaushof studied the entry in Wilt's file. It was brief and uninformative. 'Lecture Hall 9,' said the Lieutenant. 'You want me to have him picked up?'

'No,' said Glaushof, 'not yet. Just see no one gets out, is all.'

'No way he can except over the new fence,' said the Lieutenant, 'and I don't see him getting far. I've switched the current on.'

'Fine,' said Glaushof. 'So he comes out you stop him.'

'Yes, sir,' said the Lieutenant, and went out to check the guards, while Glaushof picked up the phone and called the Security Patrol. 'I want Lecture Hall 9 surrounded,' he said, 'but nobody to move till I come.'

He sat on staring distractedly at the centrepage of *Playgirl* featuring a male nude which had been pinned to the wall. If this bastard Wilt could be persuaded to talk, Glaushof's career would be made. So how to get him in the right frame of mind? First of all, he had to know what was in that car. He was still puzzling over tactics when the Lieutenant coughed discreetly behind him. Glaushof reacted violently. He didn't like the implications of that cough. 'Did you pin this up?' he shouted at the Lieutenant.

'Negative,' said the Lieutenant, who disliked the question almost as much as Glaushof had hated the cough. 'No, sir, I did not. That's Captain Clodiak.'

'That's Captain Clodiak?' said Glaushof, turning back to examine the picture again. 'I knew she ... he ... You've got to be kidding, Lieutenant. That's not the Captain Clodiak I know.'

'She put it there, sir. She likes that sort of thing.'

'Yes, well I guess she's a pretty feisty woman,' said Glaushof to avoid the accusation that he was discriminatory. In career prospect terms, it was almost as dangerous as being called a faggot. Not almost; it was worse.

'I happen to be Church of God,' said the Lieutenant, 'and that is irreligious according to my denomination.'

But Glaushof wasn't to be drawn into a discussion. 'Could be,' he said. 'Some other time, huh?' He went out and back to the parking lot where the Corporal, now accompanied by a Major and several men from the Demolition and Excavation section, had surrounded Wilt's car with four gigantic dumpers filled with sand, sweeping aside a dozen other vehicles in the process. As he approached, Glaushof was blinded by two searchlights which had suddenly been switched on. 'Douse those mothers,' he shouted, stumbling about in the glare. 'You want them to know in Moscow what we're doing?' In the darkness that followed this pronouncement, Glaushof banged into the wheelhub of one of the dumptrucks.

'Okay, so I go in without lights,' said the Corporal. 'No problem. You think it's a bomb, I don't. Bombs don't transmit CB.' And before Glaushof could remind him to call him 'Sir' in future, the Corporal had walked across to the car.

'Mr Wilt,' said Mrs Ofrey, 'would you like to elucidate on the question of the rôle of women in British society with particular regard to the part played in professional life by the Right Honorable Prime Minister Mrs Thatcher and...'

Wilt stared at her and wondered why Mrs Ofrey always read her questions from a card and why they seldom had anything to do with what he had been talking about. She must spend the rest of the week thinking them up. And the questions always had to do with the Queen and Mrs Thatcher, presumably because Mrs Ofrey had once dined at Woburn Abbey with the Duke and Duchess of Bedford and their hospitality had affected her deeply. But at least this evening he was giving her his undivided attention.

From the moment he'd entered the lecture room, he'd been having problems. The bandage he had wound round his loins had come undone on the drive over, and before he could do anything about it one end had begun to worm its way down his right trouser leg. To make matters worse, Captain Clodiak had come late and had seated herself in front of him with her legs crossed, and had promptly forced Wilt to press himself

570

against the lectern to quell yet another erection or, at least, hide the event from his audience. And by concentrating on Mrs Ofrey, he had so far managed to avoid a second glance at Captain Clodiak.

But there were disadvantages in concentrating so intently on Mrs Ofrey too. Even though she wore enough curiously patterned knitwear to have subsidized several crofters in Western Scotland, and her few charms were sufficiently muted by wool to make some sort of antidote to the terrifying chic of Captain Clodiak – Wilt had already noted the Captain's blouse and what he took to be a combat skirt in shantung silk – Mrs Ofrey was still a woman. In any case, she evidently liked to be socially exclusive and sat by herself to the left of the rest of the class, and by the time he'd got halfway through his lecture, he'd become positively wry-necked in his regard for her. Wilt had switched his attention to an acned clerk from the PX stores whose other courses were karate and aerobics and whose interest in British Culture was limited to unravelling the mysteries of cricket. That hadn't worked too well either, and after ten minutes of almost constant eye-contact and Wilt's deprecating observations on the effect of women's suffrage on the voting patterns in elections since 1928, the man had begun to shift awkwardly in his chair and Wilt had suddenly realized the fellow thought he was being propositioned. Not wanting to be beaten to pulp by a karate expert, he had tried alternating between Mrs Ofrey and the wall behind the rest of the class, but each time it seemed that Captain Clodiak was smiling more significantly. Wilt had clung to the lectern in the hope that he'd manage to get through the hour without ejaculating into his trousers. He was so worried about this that he hardly noticed that Mrs Ofrey had finished her question. 'Would you say that view was correct?' she said by way of a prompt.

'Well ... er ... yes,' said Wilt, who couldn't recall what the question was anyway. Something to do with the Monarchy being a matriarchy. 'Yes, I suppose in a general way I'd go along with you,' he said, wedging himself more firmly against the lectern. 'On the other hand, just because a country has a female ruler, I don't think we can assume it's not male-dominated. After all, we had Queen Boadicea in Pre-Roman

571

Britain and I wouldn't have thought there was an awful lot of Women's Lib about then, would you?'

'I wasn't asking about the feminist movement,' said Mrs Ofrey, with a nasty inflection that suggested she was a pre-Eisenhower American, 'my question was directed to the matriarchal nature of the Monarchy.'

'Quite,' said Wilt, fighting for time. Something desperate seemed to have happened to the cricket box. He'd lost touch with the thing. 'Though just because we've have a number of Queens ... well, I suppose we've had almost as many as we've had kings ... must have had more, come to think of it? Is that right? I mean, each king had to have a queen...'

'Henry VIII had a whole heap of them,' said an astro-navigational expert, whose reading tastes seemed to suggest she would have preferred life in some sort of airconditioned and deodorized Middle Ages. 'He must have been some man.'

'Definitely,' said Wilt, grateful for her intervention. At this rate, the discussion might spread and leave him free to find that damned box again. 'In fact he had five. There was Katherine of...'

'Excuse me asking, Mr Wilt,' interrupted an engineer, 'but do old Queens count as Queens? Like they're widows. Is a King's widow still a Queen?'

'She's a Queen Mother,' said Wilt, who by this time had his hand in his pocket and was searching for the box. 'It's purely titular of course. She –'

'Did you say "titular"?' asked Captain Clodiak, endowing the word with qualities Wilt had never intended and certainly didn't need now. And her voice suited her face. Captain Clodiak came from the South. 'Would you care to amplify what titular means?'

'Amplify?' said Wilt weakly. But before he could answer, the engineer had interrupted again.

'Pardon me breaking in, Mr Wilt,' he said, 'but you've got kind of something hanging out of your leg.'

'I have?' said Wilt, clutching the lectern even more closely. The attention of the entire class was now focused on his right leg. Wilt tried to hide it behind his left.

'And by the look of it I'd say it was something important to you.'

Wilt knew damned well what it was. With a lurch, he let go of the lectern and grabbed his trouser leg in a vain attempt to stop the box but the beastly thing had already evaded him. It hung for a moment almost coyly half out of the trouser cuff and then slid onto his shoe. Wilt's hand shot out and smothered the brute and the next moment he was trying to get it into his pocket. The box didn't budge. Still attached to the bandage by the plaster he had used, it refused to come without the bandage. As Wilt tried to drag it away it became obvious he was in danger of splitting the seam of his trousers. It was also fairly obvious that the other end of the bandage was still round his waist and had no intention of coming off. At this rate, he'd end up half-naked in front of the class and suffering from a strangulated hernia into the bargain. On the other hand, he could hardly stay half-crouching there and any attempt to drag the bloody thing up the inside of his trousers from the top was bound to be misinterpreted. In fact, by the sound of things, his predicament already had been. Even from his peculiar position, Wilt was aware that Captain Clodiak had got to her feet, a bleeper was sounding and the astro-navigator was saying something about codpieces.

Only the engineer was being at all constructive. 'Is that a medical problem you got there?' he asked and missed Wilt's contorted reply that it wasn't. 'I mean, we've got the best facilities for the treatment of infections of the urino-genital tract this side of Frankfurt and I can call up a medic ...'

Wilt relinquished his hold on the box and stood up. It might be embarrassing to have a cricket box hanging out of his trousers but it was infinitely preferable to being examined in his present state by an airbase doctor. God knows what the man would make of a runaway erection. 'I don't need any doctor,' he squawked. 'It's just ... well, I was playing cricket before I came here and in a hurry not to be late I forgot ... Well, I'm sure you understand.'

Mrs Ofrey clearly didn't. With some remark about the niceties of life being wanting, she marched out of the hall in the wake of Captain Clodiak. Before Wilt could say that all he needed was to get to the toilet, the acned clerk had intervened. 'Say, Mr Wilt,' he said, 'I didn't know you were a cricket player. Why, only three weeks ago you were saying you couldn't tell me what you English call a curve ball.'

'Some other time,' said Wilt, 'right now I need to get to ... er ... a washroom.'

'You sure you don't want –'

'Definitely,' said Wilt, 'I am perfectly all right. It's just a ... never mind.'

He hobbled out of the hall and was presently ensconced in a cubicle fighting a battle with the box, the bandage and his trousers. Behind him, the class were discussing this latest manifestation of British Culture with a greater degree of interest than they had shown for Wilt's views on voting patterns. 'I still say he don't know anything about cricket,' said the PX clerk, only to be countered by the navigator and the engineer who were more interested in Wilt's medical condition. 'I had an uncle in Idaho had to wear a support. It's nothing unusual. Fell off a ladder when he was painting the house one spring,' said the engineer. 'Those things can be real serious.'

'I told you, Major,' said the Corporal, 'two radio transmitters, one tape recorder, no bomb.'

'Definitely?' asked Glaushof, trying to keep the disappointment out of his voice.

'Definite,' said the Corporal and was supported in this by the Major from the Demolition and Excavation Section who wanted to know whether he could order his men to move the dumpers back. As they rolled away leaving Wilt's Escort isolated in the middle of the parking lot, Glaushof tried to salvage some opportunity from the situation. After all, Colonel Urwin, the Intelligence Officer, was away for the weekend and in his absence Glaushof could have done with a crisis.

'He had to come in here with that equipment for some reason,' he said, 'transmitting like that. Any ideas on the matter, Major?'

'Could be it's a dummy run to check if they can bring a bomb in and explode it by remote control,' said the Major, whose expertise tended to make him one-track-minded.

'Except he was transmitting, not receiving,' said the Corporal. 'They'd need signals in, not out, for a bomb. And what's with the recorder?'

574

'Not my department,' said the Major. 'Explosively, it's clean. I'll go file my report.'

Glaushof took the plunge. 'With me,' he said. 'You file it with me and no one else. We've got to shroud this.'

'We've done that once already with the safety trucks and quite unnecessarily.'

'Sure,' said Glaushof, 'but we still gotta find out what this is all about. I'm in charge of security and I don't like it, some Limey bastard coming in with all this equipment. Either it's a dummy run like you said, or it's something else.'

'It's got to be something else,' said the Corporal, 'obviously. With the equipment he's using, you could tape lice fucking twenty miles away it's that sensitive.'

'So his wife's getting evidence for a divorce,' said the Major.

'Must be goddam desperate for it,' said the Corporal, 'using two transmitters and a recorder. And that stuff's not general issue. I never seen a civilian using homers that sophisticated.'

'Homers?' said Glaushof, who had been preoccupied by the concept of lice fucking. 'How do you mean, homers?'

'Like they're direction indicators. Signals go out and two guys pick it up on their sets and they've got where he is precise.'

'Jesus!' said Glaushof. 'You mean the Russkies could have sent this guy Wilt in as an agent so they can pin-point right where we are?'

'They're doing that already infra-red by satellite. They don't need some guy coming in waving a radio flag,' said the Corporal. 'Not unless they want to lose him.'

'Lose him? What would they want to do that for?'

'I don't know,' continued the Corporal. 'You're Security, I'm just Technical and why anybody wants to do things isn't my province. All I do know is I wouldn't send any agent of mine any place I didn't want him caught with those signals spelling out he was coming. Like putting a fucking mouse in a room with a cat and it can't stop fucking squeaking.'

But Glaushof was not to be deterred. 'The fact of the matter is this Wilt came in with unauthorized spy equipment and he isn't going out.'

'So they're going to know he's here from those signals,' said the Corporal.

Glaushof glared at him. The man's common sense had become intensely irritating. Here was his opportunity to hit back. 'You don't mean to tell me those radios are still operational?' he shouted.

'Sure,' said the Colonel. 'You tell me and the Major here to check the car for bombs. You didn't say nothing about screwing his transmission equipment. Bombs, you said.'

'Correct,' said the Major. 'That's what you did say. Bombs.'

'I know I said bombs,' yelled Glaushof, 'you think I need telling?' He stopped and turned his attention lividly on the car. If the radios were still working, presumably the enemy already knew they'd been discovered, in which case ... His mind raced on, following lines which led to catastrophe. He had to make a momentous decision, and now. Glaushof did. 'Right, we're going in,' he said, 'and you're going out.'

Five minutes later, in spite of his protests that he wasn't driving any fucking car thirty miles with fucking spooks following his fucking progress, not unless he had a fucking escort, the Corporal drove out of the base. The tape in the recorder had been removed and replaced with a new one, but in all other respects there was nothing to indicate that the car had been tampered with. Glaushof's instructions had been quite explicit. 'You drive right back and dump it outside his house,' he had told the Corporal. 'You've got the Major here with you to bring you back and if there's any problems, he'll take care of them. Those bastards want to know where their boy is they can start looking at home. They're going to have trouble finding him here.'

'Ain't going to have no trouble finding me,' said the Corporal, who knew never to argue with a senior officer. He should have stuck to dumb insolence.

For a moment, Glaushof watched as the two vehicles disappeared across the bleak night landscape. He had never liked it but now it had taken on an even more sinister aspect. It was across those flatlands that the wind blew from Russia non-stop from the Urals. In Glaushof's mind, it was an infected wind which, having blown around the domes and turrets of the Kremlin, threatened the very future of the world. And now somewhere out there someone was listening. Glaushof turned away. He was going to find out who those sinister listeners were.

Chapter 14

'I got the whole place wrapped up, sir, and he's still inside,' said Lieutenant Harah when Glaushof finally reached Lecture Hall 9. Glaushof didn't need telling. He had had enough trouble himself getting through the cordon the Lieutenant had thrown up around the hall and in other circumstances would have expressed himself irritably on the Lieutenant's thoroughness. But the situation was too serious for recrimination, and besides he respected his second-in-command's expertise. As head of the APPS, the Anti Perimeter Penetration Squad, Lieutenant Harah had been through training at Fort Knox, in Panama and had seen action at Greenham Common disguised as a British bobby where he had qualified for a Purple Heart after being bitten in the leg by a mother of four, an experience which had left him with a useful bias against women. Glaushof appreciated his misogyny. At least one man in Baconheath could be relied on not to lay Mona Glaushof and Harah wasn't going to play footsy with any CND women if and when they tried breaking into Baconheath.

On the other hand, he seemed to have gone too far this time. Quite apart from the six hit-squad men in gas masks by the glass fronted door to the lecture hall and a number of others crouching under the windows round the side a small group of women were standing with their heads up against the wall of the next building.

'What are those?' Glaushof asked. He had a nasty suspicion he recognized Mrs Ofrey's Scottish knitwear.

'Suspected women,' said Lieutenant Harah.

'What do you mean "suspected women"?' demanded Glaushof. 'Either they're women or they aren't.'

'They came out dressed as women, sir,' said the Lieutenant, 'doesn't mean to say they are. Could be the terrorist dressed as one. You want me to check them out?'

'No,' said Glaushof, wishing to hell he had given the order

to storm the building before he had put in an appearance himself. It wasn't going to look too good spread-eagling the wife of the Chief Administrative Officer against a wall with a gun at her head, and to have her checked out sexually by Lieutenant Harah would really foul things up. On the other hand even Mrs Ofrey could hardly complain about being rescued from a possible hostage situation.

'You sure there's no way he could have got out?'

'Absolute,' said the Lieutenant. 'I got marksmen on the next block in case he makes the roof and the utilities tunnels are sealed. All we got to do is toss a canister of Agent Incapacitating in there and there's going to be no trouble.'

Glaushof glanced nervously at the row of women and doubted it. There was going to be trouble and maybe it would be better if that trouble could be seen to be serious. 'I'll get those women under cover and then you go in,' he said. 'And no shooting unless he fires first. I want this guy taken for interrogation. You got that?'

'Absolute, sir,' said the Lieutenant. 'He gets a whiff of AI he wouldn't find a trigger to pull if he wanted to.'

'Okay. Give me five minutes and then go,' said Glaushof and crossed to Mrs Ofrey.

'If you ladies will just step this way,' he said, and dismissing the men who were holding them hurried the little group round the corner and into the lobby of another lecture hall. Mrs Ofrey was clearly annoyed.

'What do you mean –' she began but Glaushof raised a hand. 'If you'll just let me explain,' he said, 'I realize you have been inconvenienced but we have an infiltration situation on our hands and we couldn't afford the possibility of you being held hostage.' He paused and was glad to see that even Mrs Ofrey had taken the message. 'How absolutely dreadful,' she murmured.

It was Captain Clodiak's reaction that surprised him. 'Infiltration situation? We just had the usual class no problem,' she said, 'I didn't see anybody new. Are you saying there's somebody in there we don't know about?'

Glaushof hesitated. He had hoped to keep the question of Wilt's identity as a secret agent to himself and not have news of it spreading round the base like wildfire. He certainly didn't

578

want it getting out until he had completed his interrogation and had all the information he needed to prove that the Intelligence Section, and in particular that bland bastard Colonel Urwin, hadn't screened a foreign employee properly. That way the Colonel would take a fall and they could hardly avoid promoting Glaushof. Let Intelligence get wind of what was going on and the plan might backfire. Glaushof fell back on the 'Eyes off' routine.

'I don't think it advisable at this moment in time to elucidate the matter further. This is a top-security matter. Any leak could severely prejudice the defensive capabilities of Strategic Air Command in Europe. I must insist on a total information blackout.'

For a moment the pronouncement had the effect he had wanted. Even Mrs Ofrey looked satisfactorily stunned. Then Captain Clodiak broke the silence. 'I don't get it,' she said. 'There's us and this Wilt guy in there, nobody else. Right?' Glaushof said nothing. 'So you bring up the stormtroopers and have us pinned against the wall as soon as we walk out and now you tell us it's an infiltration situation. I don't believe you, Major, I just don't believe you. The only infiltration I know of is what that bastard sexist lieutenant did up my ass and I intend to formalize a complaint against Lieutenant Harah and you can pull as many phoney agents out of your pinhead imagination as you like, you still aren't going to stop me.'

Glaushof gulped. He could see he'd been right to describe the Captain as a feisty woman and entirely wrong to have allowed Lieutenant Harah to act on his own. He'd also been fairly wrong in his estimation of the Lieutenant's antipathy for women though even Glaushof had to admit that Captain Clodiak was a remarkably attractive woman. In an attempt to save the situation he tried a sympathetic smile. It came out lopsided. 'I'm sure Lieutenant Harah had no intention of –' he began.

'So what's with the hand?' snapped the Captain. 'You think I don't know intentions when I feel them? Is that what you think?'

'Perhaps he was doing a weapon check,' said Glaushof, who knew now he would have to do something really astonishing to regain control of the situation. He was saved by the sound of breaking glass. Lieutenant Harah had waited exactly five minutes before taking action.

It had taken Wilt rather more than five minutes to unravel the bandage and slide it down his trouser leg and reassemble the box in a position where it would afford him some measure of protection from the spasmodic antics of his penis. In the end he had succeeded and had just tied the entire contraption together rather uncomfortably when there was a knock on the door.

'You okay, Mr Wilt?' asked the engineer.

'Yes, thank you,' said Wilt as politely as his irritation allowed. It was always the same with nice idiots. The sods offered to help in precisely the wrong way. All Wilt wanted now was to get the hell out of the base without any further embarrassment. But the engineer didn't understand the situation. 'I was just telling Pete how I had an uncle in Idaho had the same support problem,' said the engineer through the door.

'Really?' said Wilt, feigning interest while actually struggling to pull his zip up. A thread of bandage had evidently got caught in the thing. Wilt tried pulling it down.

'Yea. He went around for years with this bulky thing on until my Auntie Annie heard of this surgeon in Kansas City and she took my Uncle Rolf down there and of course he didn't want to go but he never did regret it. I can give you his name if you like.'

'Fuck,' said Wilt. A stitch on the bottom of his zip sounded as though it had torn.

'Did you say something, Mr Wilt?' asked the engineer.

'No,' said Wilt.

There was a moment's silence while the engineer evidently considered his next move and Wilt tried holding the bottom of the zip to his trousers while wrenching the tag at the same time. 'As I see it, and you've got to understand I'm not a medical man myself I'm an engineer so I know about structural failure, there's muscle deterioration in the lower –'

'Listen,' said Wilt. 'Right now where I've got a structural failure is in the zip on my trousers. Something's got caught in it and it's stuck.'

580

'Which side?' asked the engineer.

'Which side is what?' demanded Wilt.

'The ... er ... thing that's stuck in it?'

Wilt peered down at the zip. In the confines of the toilet it was difficult to see which side anything was. 'How the hell would I know?'

'You pulling it up or down?' continued the engineer.

'Up,' said Wilt.

'Sometimes helps to pull it down first.'

'It's already bloody down,' said Wilt allowing his irritation to get the better of him. 'I wouldn't be trying to pull the fucking thing up if it wasn't down, would I?'

'I guess not,' said the engineer with a degree of bland patience that was even more irritating than his desire to be helpful. 'Just the same if it isn't right down it could be the thing ...' He paused. 'Mr Wilt, just what is it you've got in the zip?'

Inside the toilet Wilt stared dementedly at a notice which not only instructed him to wash his hands but seemed to suppose he needed telling how to. 'Count to ten,' he muttered to himself and was surprised to find that the zip had freed itself. He'd also been freed from the unwanted helpfulness of the engineer. A crash of breaking glass had evidently disturbed the man's blandness. 'Jesus, what's going on?' he yelled.

It was not a question Wilt could answer. And by the sound of things outside he didn't want to. Somewhere a door burst open and running feet in the corridor were interspersed with muffled orders to freeze. Inside the toilet Wilt froze. Accustomed as he had recently become to the hazards seemingly inherent in going to the lavatory anywhere outside his own house, the experience of being locked in a cubicle with a hit squad of Anti Perimeter Penetration men bursting into the building was new to him.

It was fairly new to the engineer. As the canisters of Agent Incapacitating hit the floor and masked men armed with automatic weapons broke through the door he lost all interest in the problems of Wilt's zip and headed back into the lecture hall only to collide with the navigator and the PX clerk who were dashing the other way. In the confusion that followed Agent Incapacitating lived up to its name. The PX clerk tried to disentangle himself from the engineer who was doing his best to avoid him and the navigator embraced them both under the illusion he was moving in the other direction.

As they fell to the ground Lieutenant Harah loomed over them large and quite extraordinarily sinister in his gas mask.

'Which of you is Wilt?' he yelled. His voice, distorted both by the mask and by the effects of the gas on their nervous systems, reached them slowly. Not even the voluble engineer was able to help him. 'Take them all out,' he ordered and the three men were dragged from the building gurgling sentences that sounded as if a portable recorder with faulty batteries was being played under water.

In his cubicle Wilt listened to the awful noises with growing apprehension. Breaking glass, strangely muffled shouts and the clump of boots had played no part in his previous visits to the airbase and he couldn't for the life of him imagine what they portended. Whatever it was he'd had enough trouble for one evening without wishing to invite any more. It seemed safest to stay where he was and wait until whatever was happening had stopped. Wilt switched off the light and sat down on the seat.

Outside, Lieutenant Harah's men reported thickly that the hall was clear. In spite of the eddies of gas the Lieutenant could see that. Peering through the eyepiece of his gas mask he surveyed the empty seats with a sense of anti-climax. He had rather hoped the infiltrator would put up a show of resistance, and the ease with which the bastard had been taken had disappointed him. On the other hand he could also see that it had been a mistake to bring in the assault dogs without equipping them with gas masks. Agent Incapacitating evidently affected them too. One of them was slithering about the floor snarling in slow motion while another, in an attempt to scratch its right ear, was waving a hindfoot about in a most disturbing manner.

'Okay, that's it,' he said and marched out to question his three prisoners. Like the assault dogs they had been totally incapacitated and he had no idea which was the foreign agent he was supposed to be detaining. They were all dressed in civilian clothes and in no state to say who or what they were. Lieutenant Harah reported to Glaushof. 'I think you better check them out, sir. I don't know which son of a bitch is which.'

'Wilt,' said Glaushof, glaring at the gas mask, 'his name is Wilt. He's a foreign employee. Shouldn't be any difficulty recognizing the bastard.'

'All Limeys look the same to me,' said the Lieutenant, and was promptly rewarded with a chop across his throat and a knee in his groin by Captain Clodiak who had just recognized her sexist assailant through his gas mask. As the Lieutenant doubled up she grabbed his arm and Glaushof was surprised to see how easily his second-in-command was swept off his feet by a woman.

'Remarkable,' he said. 'It's a genuine privilege to witness –'

'Cut the crap,' said Captain Clodiak, dusting her hands and looking as though she would like to demonstrate her expertise in karate on another man. 'That creep said a sexist remark and you said Wilt. Am I right?' Glaushof looked puzzled. He hadn't recognized 'son of a bitch' as being sexist and he didn't want to discuss Wilt in front of the other women. On the other hand he didn't have any idea what Wilt looked like and someone had to identify him. 'Maybe we'd better step outside to discuss this, Captain,' he said and went out the door.

Captain Clodiak followed him warily. 'What do we have to discuss?' she asked.

'Like Wilt,' said Glaushof.

'You're crazy. I heard you just now. Wilt an agent?'

'Incontrovertible,' said Glaushof, pulling brevity.

'How so?' said Clodiak, responding in kind.

'Infiltrated the perimeter with enough radio transmitting equipment hidden in his car to signal our position to Moscow or the moon. I mean it, Captain. What's more it's not civilian equipment you can buy in a store. It's official.' said Glaushof and was relieved to notice the disbelief fade from her face. 'And right now, I'm going to need help identifying him.'

They went round the corner and were confronted by the sight of three men lying face down on the ground in front of Lecture Hall 9 guarded by two incapacitated assault dogs and the APP team.

'Okay, men, the Captain here is going to identify him,' said Glaushof and prodded the PX clerk with his foot. 'Turn over, you.' The clerk tried to turn over but succeeded only in crawling sideways on top of the engineer, who promptly went into convulsions. Glaushof looked at the two contorted figures with disgust before having his attention distracted even more disturbingly by an assault dog that had urinated on his shoe without lifting its leg.

'Get that filthy beast off me,' he shouted and was joined in his protests by the engineer who objected just as strongly though less comprehensibly to the apparent attempts the PX clerk was making to bugger him. By the time the dog had been removed, a process that required the efforts of three men on the end of its chain, and some sort of order was restored on the ground Captain Clodiak's expression had changed again. 'I thought you said you wanted Wilt identified,' she said, 'Well, he's not here.'

'Not here? You mean ...' Glaushof looked suspiciously at the broken door of the lecture hall.

'They're the men the Lieutenant told us to grab,' said one of the hit-squad. 'There wasn't anyone else in the hall I saw.'

'There's gotta be,' yelled Glaushof. 'Where's Harah?'

'In there where you –'

'I know where he is. Just get him and fast.'

'Yessir,' said the man and disappeared.

'You seem to have got yourself a problem,' said Captain Clodiak.

Glaushof tried to shrug it off. 'He can't have broken through the cordon and even if he has he's going to burn on the fence or get himself arrested at the gate.' he said. 'I'm not worried.'

All the same he found himself glancing round at the familiar dull buildings and the roadways between them with a new sense of suspicion as though somehow they had changed character and had become accomplices to the absent Wilt. With an insight that was alarmingly strange to him he realized how much Baconheath meant to him; it was home, his own little fortress in a foreign land with its comfortable jet noises linking him to his own hometown, Eiderburg, Michigan, and the

584

abattoir down the road where the hogs were killed. As a boy he had woken to the sound of their squeals and an F111 screaming for take-off had the same comforting effect on him. But more than anything else Baconheath with its perimeter fence and guarded gates had been America for him, his own country, powerful, independent and freed from danger by his constant vigilance and the sheer enormity of its arsenal. Squatting there behind the wire and isolated by the flat reaches of the Fens from the old crumbling villages and market towns with their idle, inefficient shopkeepers and their dirty pubs where strange people drank warm, unhygienic beer, Baconheath had been an oasis of brisk efficiency and modernity, and proof that the great US of A was still the New World and would remain so.

But now Glaushof's vision had shifted and for a moment he felt somehow disassociated from the place. These buildings were hiding this Wilt from him and until he found the bastard Baconheath would be infected. Glaushof forced himself out of this nightmare and was confronted by another. Lieutenant Harah came round the corner. He was clearly still paying for his sexist attitude to Captain Clodiak and had to be supported by two APPS men. Glaushof had almost been prepared for that. The garbled noises the Lieutenant was making were something else again and could hardly be explained by a kick in the groin.

'It's the AI, sir,' one of the men explained, 'I guess he must have loosed off a canister in the lobby.'

'Loosed off a canister? In the lobby?' Glaushof squawked, appalled at the terrible consequences to his career such a lunatic action seemed certain to provoke. 'Not with those women –'

'Affirmative,' ejaculated Lieutenant Harah without warning. Glaushof turned on him.

'What do you mean, affirmative?'

'Absolute,' Harah's voice hit a new high. And stuck there. 'Absolute absolute absolute absolute ...'

'Gag that bastard,' shouted Glaushof and shot round the corner of the building to see what he could do to rescue the situation. It was beyond hope. For whatever insane reason Lieutenant Harah, perhaps in an attempt to defend himself against a second strike from Captain Clodiak, had wrenched the pin from a gas grenade before realizing that his gas mask had come off in his fall. Gazing through the glass doors at the bizarre scenes in the lobby, Glaushof was no longer worried about Mrs Ofrey's interference. Draped over the back of a chair with her hair touching the floor and happily obscuring her face, the wife of the Chief Administrative Executive resembled nothing so much as a large and incontinent highland ewe which had been put rather prematurely through a Fair Isle knitting machine. The rest of the class were in no better shape. The astro-navigation officer lay on her back, evidently re-enacting a peculiarly passive sexual experience, while several other students of British Culture and Institutions looked as though they were extras in some film depicting the end of the world. Once again Glaushof experienced the ghastly sensation of being at odds with his environment and it was only by calling up reserves of approximate sanity that he took control of himself.

'Get them out of there,' he shouted, 'and call the medics. We got a maniac on the loose.'

'Got something,' said Captain Clodiak. 'That Lieutenant Harah's going to have a lot to answer for. I can't see General Ofrey being too pleased with a dead wife. He'll just have to play three-handed bridge with the Commander.'

But Glaushof had had enough of the Captain's objective standpoint. 'You're responsible for this,' he said with a new menace in his voice. 'You talk about questions you're going to have to answer some yourself. Like you deliberately assaulted Lieutenant Harah in the execution of his duty and –'

'Like the execution of his duty includes getting his hand up my . . .' interrupted the Captain furiously and then stopped and stared. 'Oh my God,' she said and Glaushof, who had been preparing for another demonstration of karate, followed her gaze.

In the broken doorway of Lecture Hall 9 a hapless figure was trying to stand up. As they watched, it failed.

Chapter 15

Fifteen miles away Wilt's Escort beeped its erratic way towards Ipford. Since no one had thought to provide the Corporal with adequate directions and he had distrusted Glaushof's assurances that he would be well protected by the Major and the men in the truck behind him, he had taken his own precautions before and after leaving the base. He had provided himself with a heavy automatic and had computed a route which would cause maximum confusion to anyone trying to cross-reference his position on their receivers. He had achieved his object. In short, he had travelled twenty quite extraordinarily complicated miles in no time at all. Half an hour after leaving Baconheath he was still only five miles from the base. After that he had shot off towards Ipford and had spent twenty minutes pretending to change a tyre in a tunnel under the motorway before emerging on a minor road which ran for several miles very conveniently next to a line of high-tension electricity pylons. Two more tunnels and fifteen miles on a road that wound along below the bank of a dyked river, and Inspector Hodge and the men in the other listening van were desperately transmitting messages to one another in an attempt to make out where the hell he had got to. More awkwardly still, they couldn't be entirely sure where they were either.

The Major shared their dilemma. He hadn't expected the Corporal to take evasive action or to drive – when he wasn't lurking in tunnels – at excessive speed along winding roads that had presumably been designed for single-file horse traffic and had been dangerous even then. But the Major didn't care. If the Corporal wanted to take off like a scalded cat that was his problem. 'He wants an armed escort he better stay with us,' he told his driver as they skidded round a muddy ninety-degree bend and nearly landed in a deep water-filled drain. 'I'm not ending my life in a ditch so slow down for Chrissake.'

'So how do we keep up with him?' asked the driver, who had been thoroughly enjoying himself.

'We don't. If he's going any place outside hell it's Ipford. I've got the address here. Take the motorway first chance you get and we'll wait for him where he's supposed to be going.'

'Yes sir,' said the driver reluctantly and switched back to the main road at the next turn-off.

Sergeant Runk would have done the same had he been given the chance but the Corporal's tactics had confirmed all Inspector Hodge's wildest dreams. 'He's trying to lose us,' he shouted shortly after the Corporal left the airbase and began to dice with death. 'That must mean he's carrying dope.'

'That or he's practising for the Monte Carlo Rally,' said Runk.

Hodge wasn't amused. 'Rubbish. The little bastard goes into Baconheath, spends an hour and a half and comes out doing eighty along mud roads no one in their right minds would do forty on in daylight and backtracks five times the way he's done – he must have something he values in that car.'

'Can't be his life, and that's for certain,' said Runk who was struggling to keep his seat. 'Why don't we just call up a patrol car and pull him for speeding? That way we can have him searched for whatever he's carrying.'

'Good idea,' said Hodge and had been about to send out instructions when the Corporal had taken radio refuge in the motorway tunnel and they'd lost him for twenty minutes. Hodge had spent the time blaming Runk for failing to have an accurate fix on his last position and calling for help from the second van. The Corporal's subsequent route near the power lines and below the river bank had made matters still more awkward. By then the Inspector had no idea what to do, but his conviction that he was dealing with a master-criminal had been confirmed beyond doubt.

'He's obviously passed the stuff on to a third party and if we go for a search he'll plead innocence,' he muttered.

Even Runk had to agree that all the evidence pointed that way. 'He also happens to know his car's been wired for sound,' he said. 'The route he's following he's got to know. So where do we go from here?'

588

Hodge hesitated. For a moment he considered applying for a warrant and conducting so thorough a search of the Wilts' house that even the minutest trace of heroin or Embalming Fluid would come to light. But if it didn't ... 'There's always the tape recorder,' he said finally. 'He may have missed that in which case we'll get the conversations he had with the pick-up artist.'

Sergeant Runk doubted it. 'If you ask me,' he said, 'the only way you're going to get solid evidence on this bugger is by sending Forensic in to do a search with vacuum-cleaners that'd suck an elephant through a drain pipe. He may be as canny as they come but those lab blokes know their onions. I reckon that's the sane way of going about it.'

But Hodge wasn't to be persuaded. He had no intention of handing the case over to someone else when it was patently obvious he was on the right track. 'We'll see what's on that tape first,' he said as they headed back towards Ipford. 'We'll give him an hour to get to sleep and then you can move in and get it.'

'And have the rest of the bloody day off,' said Runk. 'You may be one of Nature's insomniacs but if I don't get my eight hours I won't be fit for –'

'I am not an insomniac,' snapped the Inspector. They drove on in silence broken only by the bleeps coming from Wilt's car. They were louder now. Ten minutes later the van was parked at the bottom of Perry Road and Wilt's car was announcing its presence from Oakhurst Avenue.

'You've got to hand it to the little sod,' said Hodge. 'I mean you'd never dream to look at him he could drive like that. Just shows you can never tell.'

An hour later Sergeant Runk stumbled out of his van and walked up Perry Road. 'It's not there,' he said when he got back.

'Not there? It's bloody well got to be,' said the Inspector, 'it's still coming over loud and clear.'

'That's as may be,' said Runk. 'For all I care the little shit's tucked up in bed with the fucking transmitters but what I do know is that it's not outside his house.'

'What about the garage?' Runk snorted.

'The garage? Have you ever had a dekko in that garage? It's a ruddy furniture depository, that garage is. Stuffed to the roof with junk when I saw it and if you're telling me he's spent the last two days shifting it all out into the back garden so as he could get his car in there ...'

'We'll soon see about that,' said Hodge and presently the van was driving slowly past 45 Oakhurst Avenue and the Sergeant had been proved right.

'What did I tell you?' he said. 'I said he hadn't put it in the garage.'

'What you didn't say was he'd parked the thing there,' said Hodge, pointing through the windscreen at the mud-stained Escort which the Corporal, who hadn't been prepared to waste time checking house numbers in the middle of the night, had left outside Number 65.

'Well I'm buggered,' said Runk. 'Why'd he want to do a thing like that?'

'We'll see if that tape has anything to tell us,' said the Inspector. 'You hop out here and we'll go on round the corner.'

But for once Sergeant Runk wasn't to be budged. 'If you want that bloody tape you go and get it,' he said. 'A bloke like this Wilt doesn't leave his car down the road without a good reason and I'm not learning too bleeding late what that reason is, and that's final.'

In the end it was Hodge who approached the car warily and had just started to grope under the front seat when Mrs Willoughby's Great Dane gave tongue inside the house.

'What did I tell you?' said Runk as the Inspector clambered in beside him puffing frantically. 'I knew there was a trap there somewhere but you wouldn't listen.'

Inspector Hodge was too preoccupied to listen to him even now. In his mind's ear he could still hear the baying of that dreadful dog and the sound of its terrible paws on the front door of the Willoughbys' house.

He was still shaken by the experience when they arrived back at the station. 'I'll get him, I'll get him,' he muttered as he made his way wearily up the steps. But the threat lacked substance. He had been outwitted yet again and for the first time he appreciated Sergeant Runk's need for sleep. Perhaps

590

after a few hours his mind would come up with a new plan.

In Wilt's case the need for sleep was paramount too. The effects of Agent Incapacitating on a body already weakened by the administration of Dr Kores' sexual cordial had reduced him to a state in which he hardly knew who he was and was quite incapable of answering questions. He vaguely remembered escaping from a cubicle, or rather of being locked in one, but for the rest his mind was a jumble of images, the sum total of which made no sense at all. Men with masks, guns, being dragged, thrown into a jeep, driven, more dragging, lights in a bare room and a man shouting dementedly at him, all formed kaleidoscopic patterns which constantly rearranged themselves in his mind and made no sense at all. They just happened or were happening or even, because the man shouting at him still seemed somehow remote, had happened to him in some previous existence and one he would prefer not to relive. And even when Wilt tried to explain that things, whatever they were, were not what they seemed, the shouting man wasn't prepared to listen.

It was hardly surprising. The strange noises Wilt was in fact making hardly came into the category of utterances and certainly weren't explanations.

'Scrambled,' said the doctor Glaushof had summoned to try and inject some sense into Wilt's communications system. 'That's what you get with AI Two. You'll be lucky if he ever talks sense again.'

'AI Two? We used standard issue Agent Incapaciting,' said Glaushof. 'Nobody's been throwing AI Two around. That's reserved for Soviet suicide squads.'

'Sure,' said the doctor, 'I'm just telling you what I diagnose. You'd better check the canisters out.'

'I'll check that lunatic Harah out too,' said Glaushof and hurried from the room. When he returned Wilt had assumed a foetal position and was fast asleep.

'AI Two,' Glaushof admitted lugubriously. 'What do we do now?'

'I've done what I can,' said the doctor, 'dispensing with two hypodermics. 'Loaded him with enough Antidote AI to keep him out of the official brain-death category ...'

'Brain-death category? But I've got to interrogate the bastard. I can't have him cabbaging on me. He's some sort of infiltrating fucking agent and I got to find out where he's from.'

'Major Glaushof,' said the doctor wearily, 'it is now like zero three hundred hours and there's eight women, three men, one lieutenant and this ...' he pointed at Wilt 'and all of them suffering from nerve-gas toxicity and you think I can save any of them from chemically induced psychosis I'll do it but I'm not putting a suspected terrorist wearing a scrotal guard at the head of my list of priorities. If you want to interrogate him you'll have to wait. And pray. Oh yes, and if he doesn't come out of coma in eight hours let me know, maybe we can use him for spare-part surgery.'

'Hold it there, doctor,' he said. 'One word out of any of these people about there being –'

'Gassed?' said the doctor incredulously. 'I don't think you realize what you've done, Major. They're not going to re-member a thing.'

'There being an agent here,' shouted Glaushof. 'Of course they've been gassed. Lieutenant Harah did that.'

'If you say so,' said the doctor. 'My business is physical welfare not base security and I guess you'll be able to explain Mrs Ofrey's condition to the General. Just don't call on me to say she and seven other women are naturally psychotic.'

Glaushof considered the implications of this request and found them decidedly awkward. On the other hand there was always Lieutenant Harah ... 'Tell me, doc,' he said, 'just how sick is Harah?'

'About as sick as a man who's been kicked in the groin and inhaled AI Two can be,' said the doctor. 'And that's not taking his mental condition beforehand into account either. He should have been wearing one of these.' He held up the box.

Glaushof looked at it speculatively and then glanced at Wilt. 'What would a terrorist want with one of those things?' he asked.

'Could be he expected what Lieutenant Harah got,' said the doctor, and left the room.

Glaushof followed him into the next office and sent for

Captain Clodiak. 'Take a seat, Captain,' he said. 'Now I want a breakdown of exactly what happened in there tonight.'

'What happened in there? You think I know? There's this maniac Harah ...'

Glaushof held up a hand. 'I think you should know that Lieutenant Harah is an extremely sick man right now.'

'What's with the now?' said Clodiak. 'He always was. Sick in the head.'

'It's not his head I'm thinking about.'

Captain Clodiak chewed gum. 'So he's got balls where his brain should be. Do I care?'

'I'd advise you to,' said Glaushof. 'Assaulting a junior officer carries a very heavy penalty.'

'Yea, well the same goes for sexually assaulting a senior one.'

'Could be,' said Glaushof, 'but I think you're going to have a hard time proving it.'

'Are you telling me I'm a liar?' demanded the Captain.

'No. Definitely not. I believe you but what I'm asking is, will anyone else?'

'I've got witnesses.'

'Had,' said Glaushof. 'From what the doctors tell me they're not going to be very reliable. In fact I'd go so far as to say they don't even come into the category of witnesses any longer. Agent Incapacitating does things to the memory. I think you ought to know that. And Lieutenant Harah's injuries have been medically documented. I don't think you're going to be in a position to dispute them. Doesn't mean you have to, but I'd advise you to co-operate with this department.'

Captain Clodiak studied his face. It wasn't a pleasant face but there was no disputing the fact that her situation wasn't one which allowed her too many options. 'What do you want me to do?' she asked.

'I want to hear what this Wilt said and all. In his lectures. Did he give any indications he was a communist?'

'Not that I knew,' said the Captain. 'I'd have reported it if he had.'

'So what did he say?'

'Mostly talked about things like parliament and voting patterns and how people in England see things.'

'See things?' said Glaushof, trying to think why an attractive woman like Ms Clodiak would want to go to lectures he'd have paid money to avoid. 'What sort of things?'

'Religion and marriage and ... just things.'

At the end of an hour, Glaushof had learnt nothing.

Chapter 16

Eva sat in the kitchen and looked at the clock again. It was five o'clock in the morning and she had been up since two indulging herself in the luxury of a great many emotions. Her first reaction when going to bed had been one of annoyance. 'He's been to the pub again and got drunk,' she had thought. 'Well, he won't get any sympathy from me if he has a hangover.' Then she had lain awake getting angrier by the minute until one o'clock when worry had taken over. It wasn't like Henry to stay out that late. Perhaps something had happened to him. She went over various possibilities, ranging from car crashes to his getting arrested for being drunk and disorderly, and finally worked herself up to the point where she knew that something terrible had been done to him at the prison. After all he was teaching that dreadful murderer McCullum and when he'd come home on Monday night he'd been looking very peculiar. Of course he'd been drinking but all the same she remembered saying . . . No, that hadn't been Monday night because she'd been asleep when he got back. It must have been Tuesday morning. Yes, that was it. She'd said he looked peculiar and come to think of it what she really thought was that he had looked scared. And he'd said he'd left the car in a car park and when he'd come home in the evening he'd kept looking out the front window in the strangest way. He'd had an accident with the car too and while at the time she had just put that down to his usual absent-mindedness now that she came to think about it . . . At that point Eva had turned the light on and got out of bed. Something terrible had been going on and she hadn't even known it.

Which brought her round to anger again. Henry should have told her but he never did tell her really important things. He thought she was too stupid and perhaps she wasn't very clever when it came to arguing about books and saying the right things at parties but at least she was practical and nobody

595

could say that the quads weren't getting a good education.

So the night passed. Eva sat in the kitchen and made cups of tea and worried and was angry and then blamed herself and wondered who to telephone and then decided it was best not to call anyone because they'd only be cross at being woken in the middle of the night and anyway there might be a perfectly natural explanation like the car had broken down or he'd gone to the Braintrees for a drink and had had to stay there because of the police and the breathalyser which would have been the sensible thing to do and so perhaps she ought to go back to bed and get some sleep ... And always beside this bustle of conflicting thoughts and feelings there was the sense of guilt and the knowledge that she had been stupid to have listened to Mavis or to have gone anywhere near Dr Kores. Anyway, what did Mavis know about sex? She'd never really said what went on between her and Patrick in bed – it wasn't one of those things Eva would have dreamt of asking and even if she had Mavis wouldn't have told her – and all she'd ever heard was that Patrick was having affairs with other women. There might be good reasons for that too. Perhaps Mavis was frigid or wanted to be too dominant or masculine or wasn't very clean or something. Whatever the reason it was quite wrong of her to give Patrick those horrid steroid things or hormones and turn him into a sleepy fat person – well, you could hardly call him a man any longer could you? – who sat in front of the telly every night and couldn't get on with his work properly. Besides, Henry wasn't a bad husband. It was just that he was absent-minded and was always thinking about something or other that had no connection at all with what he was supposed to be doing. Like the time he'd been peeling the potatoes for Sunday lunch and he'd suddenly said the Vicar made Polonius sound like a bloody genius and there's been no reason to say that because they hadn't been to church for two Sundays running and she'd wanted to know who Polonius was and he wasn't anyone at all, just some character in a play.

No, you couldn't expect Henry to be practical and she didn't. And of course they'd had their tiffs and disagreements, particularly about the quads. Why couldn't he see they were special? Well, he did, but not in the right way, and calling them 'clones' wasn't helpful. Eva could think of other things he'd said that weren't nice either. And then there was that dreadful business the other night with the cake icer. Goodness only knew what effect that had had on the girls' ideas about men. And that really was the trouble with Henry, he didn't know what romantic meant. Eva got up from the kitchen table and was presently calming her nerves by cleaning out the pantry. She was interrupted at six-thirty by Emmeline in her pyjamas.

'What are you doing?' she asked so unnecessarily that Eva rose to the bait.

'It's perfectly obvious,' she snapped. 'There's no need to ask stupid questions.'

'It wasn't obvious to Einstein,' said Emmeline, using the well-tried technique of luring Eva into a topic about which she knew nothing but which she had to approve.

'What wasn't?'

'That the shortest distance between two points is a straight line.'

'Well it is, isn't it?' said Eva, moving a tin of Epicure marmalade from the shelf with pilchards and tuna fish on it to the jam section where it looked out of place.

'Of course it isn't. Everyone knows that. It's a curve. Where's Daddy?'

'I don't see how ... What do you mean "Where's Daddy?"' said Eva, completely thrown by this leap from the inconceivable to the immediate.

'I was asking where he is,' said Emmeline. 'He's not in, is he?'

'No, he isn't,' said Eva, torn now between an inclination to give vent to her irritation and the need to keep calm. 'He's out.'

'Where's he gone?' asked Emmeline.

'He hasn't gone anywhere,' said Eva and moved the marmalade back to the pilchard shelf. Tins didn't look right among the jam-jars. 'He spent the night at the Braintrees.'

'I suppose he got drunk again,' said Emmeline. 'Do you think he's an alcoholic?'

Eva clutched a coffee jar dangerously. 'Don't you dare talk about your father like that!' she snapped. 'Of course he has a drink when he comes home at night. Nearly everyone does.

It's quite normal and I won't have you saying things about your father.'

'You say things about him,' said Emmeline, 'I heard you call him –'

'Never mind what I say,' said Eva. 'That's quite different.'

'It isn't different,' Emmeline persisted, 'not when you say he's an alcoholic and anyway I was only asking a question and you're always telling us to –'

'Go up to your room at once,' said Eva. 'You're not speaking to me in that fashion. I won't have it.'

Emmeline retreated and Eva slumped down at the kitchen table again. It was really too trying of Henry not to have instilled some sense of respect in the quads. It was always left to her to be the disciplinarian. He should have more authority. She went back into the larder and saw to it that the packets and jars and tins did exactly what she wanted. By the time she had finished she felt a little better. Finally she chased the quads into dressing quickly.

'We'll have to catch the bus this morning,' she announced when they came in to breakfast. 'Daddy has the car and –'

'He hasn't,' said Penelope, 'Mrs Willoughby has.'

Eva, who had been pouring tea, spilt it. 'What did you say?' Penelope looked smug. 'Mrs Willoughby has the car.'

'Mrs Willoughby? Yes, I know I've spilt some tea, Samantha. What do you mean, Penny? She can't have.'

'She has,' said Penelope looking smugger still. 'The milkman told me.'

'The milkman? He must have been mistaken,' said Eva.

'He isn't. He's scared stiff of the Hound of Oakhurst Avenue and he only delivers at the gate and that's where our car is. I went and saw it.'

'And was your father there?'

'No, it was empty.'

Eva put the teapot down unsteadily and tried to think what this meant. If Henry wasn't in the car ...

'Perhaps Daddy's been eaten by the Hound,' suggested Josephine.

'The Hound doesn't eat people. It just tears their throats out and leaves their bodies on the waste ground at the bottom of the garden,' said Emmeline.

'It doesn't. It only barks. It's quite nice if you give it lamb chops and things,' said Samantha, unintentionally dragging Eva's attention away from the frightful possibility that Henry might in his drunken state have mistaken the house and ended up mauled to death by a Great Dane. And then again with Dr Kores' potion still coursing through his veins ...

Penelope put the idea into words. 'He's more likely to have been eaten by Mrs Willoughby,' she said. 'Mr Gamer says she's sex-mad. I heard him tell Mrs Gamer that when she said she wanted it.'

'Wanted what?' demanded Eva, too stunned by this latest revelation to be concerned about the chops missing from the deep-freeze. She could deal with that matter later.

'The usual thing,' said Penelope with a look of distaste. 'She's always going on about it and Mr Gamer said she was getting just like Mrs Willoughby after Mr Willoughby died on the job and he wasn't going the same way.'

'That's not true,' said Eva in spite of herself.

'It is too,' said Penelope. 'Sammy heard him, didn't you?'

Samantha nodded.

'He was in the garage playing with himself like Paul in 3B does and we could hear ever so easily,' she said. 'And he's got lots of *Playboys* in there and books and she came in and said ...'

'I don't want to hear,' said Eva, finally dragging her attention away from this fascinating topic. 'It's time to get your things on. I'll go and fetch the car ...' She stopped. It was clearly one thing to say she was going to fetch the car from a neighbour's front garden, but just as clearly there were snags. If Henry was in Mrs Willoughby's house she'd never be able to live the scandal down. All the same something had to be done and it was a scandal enough already for the neighbours to see the Escort there. With the same determination with which Eva always dealt with embarrassing situations she put on her coat and marched out of the front door. Presently she was sitting in the Escort trying to start it. As usual when she was in a hurry the starter motor churned over and nothing happened. To be exact, something did but not what she had hoped. The front door opened and the Great Dane loped out followed by Mrs Willoughby in a dressing-gown. It was, in Eva's opinion, just the sort of dressing-gown a sex-mad widow would wear. Eva wound down the window to explain that she was just collecting the car and promptly wound it up again. Whatever Samantha's finer feelings might persuade her about the dog, Eva mistrusted it.

'I'm just going to take the girls to school,' she said by way of rather inadequate explanation.

Outside the Great Dane barked and Mrs Willoughby mouthed something that Eva couldn't hear. She wound the window down two inches. 'I said I'm just going to . . .' she began.

Ten minutes later, after an exceedingly acrimonious exchange in which Mrs Willoughby had challenged Eva's right to park in other people's drives and Eva had only been prevented by the presence of the Hound from demanding the right to search the house for her Henry and had been forced to confine herself to a moral critique of the dressing-gown, she drove the quads furiously to school. Only when they had left was Eva thrown back on her own worries. If Henry hadn't left the car at that awful woman's – and she really couldn't see him braving the Great Dane unless he'd been blind drunk and then he wouldn't have held much interest for Mrs Willoughby – someone else must have. Eva drove to the Braintrees and came away even more worried. Betty was sure Peter had said he hadn't seen Henry nearly all week. It was the same at the Tech. Wilt's office was empty and Mrs Bristol was adamant that he hadn't been in since Wednesday. Which left only the prison.

With a terrible sense of foreboding Eva used the phone in Wilt's office. By the time she put it down again panic had set in. Henry not at the prison since Monday? But he taught that murderer every Friday . . . He didn't. He never had. And he wasn't going to teach him on Mondays either now because Mac wasn't a burden on the state, as you might say. But he had given McCullum lessons on Friday. Oh no, he hadn't. Prisoners in that category couldn't have cosy little chats every night of the week, now could they? Yes, he was quite sure. Mr Wilt never came to the prison on Fridays.

Sitting alone in the office, Eva's reactions swung from panic to anger and back again. Henry had been deceiving her. He'd lied. Mavis was right, he had had another woman all the time.

600

But he couldn't have. She'd have known. He couldn't keep a thing like that to himself. He wasn't practical or cunning enough. There'd have been something to tell her like hairs on his coat or lipstick or powder or something. And why? But before she could consider that question Mrs Bristol had poked her head round the door to ask if she'd like a cup of coffee. Eva braced herself to face reality. No one was going to have the satisfaction of seeing her break down.

'No thank you,' she said, 'it's very kind of you but I must be off.' And without allowing Mrs Bristol the opportunity to ask anything more Eva marched out and walked down the stairs with an air of deliberate fortitude. It had almost cracked by the time she had reached the car but she hung on until she had driven back to Oakhurst Avenue. Even then, with all the evidence of treachery around her in the shape of Henry's raincoat and the shoes he'd put out to polish and hadn't and his briefcase in the hall, she refused to give way to self-pity. Something was wrong. Something that proved Henry hadn't walked out on her. If only she could think.

It had something to do with the car. Henry would never have left it in Mrs Willoughby's drive. No, that wasn't it. It was ... She dropped the car keys on the kitchen table and recognized their importance. They'd been in the car when she'd gone to fetch it and among them on the ring was the key to 45 Oakhurst Avenue. Henry had left her without any warning and without leaving a message but he had left the key to the house? Eva didn't believe it. Not for one moment. In that case her instinct had been right and something dreadful had happened to him. Eva put the kettle on and tried to think what to do.

'Listen, Ted,' said Flint. 'You play it the way you want. If you scratch my back I'll scratch yours. No problems. All I'm saying is –'
'If I scratch your back,' said Lingon, 'I won't have a fucking back to be scratched. Not one you'd want to scratch anyway, even if you could find it under some bloody motorway. Now would you mind just getting out of here?'
Inspector Flint settled himself in a chair and looked round the tiny office in the corner of the scruffy garage. Apart from

a filing cabinet, the usual nudey calendar, a telephone and the desk, the only thing it contained of any interest to him was Mr Lingon. And in Flint's view Mr Lingon was a thing, a rather nasty thing, a squat, seedy and corrupt thing. 'Business good?' he asked with as little interest as possible. Outside the glass cubicle a mechanic was hosing down a Lingon Coach which claimed to be de luxe.

Mr Lingon grunted and lit a cigarette from the stub of his last one. 'It was till you turned up,' he said. 'Now do me a favour and leave me alone. I don't know what you're on about.'

'Smack,' said Flint.

'Smack? What's that supposed to mean?'

Flint ignored the question. 'How many years did you do last time?' he enquired.

'Oh Jesus,' said Lingon. 'I've been inside. Years ago. But you sods never let up, do you? Not you. A little bit of break-ing and entering, someone gets done over two miles away. You name it, who do you come and see? Who's on record? Ted Lingon. Go and put the pressure on him. That's all you buggers can ever think of. No imagination.'

Flint shifted his attention from the mechanic and looked at Mr Lingon. 'Who needs imagination?' he said. 'A nice signed statement, witnessed and everything clean and above-board and no trade. Much better than imagination. Stands up in court.'

'Statement? What statement?' Mr Lingon was looking un-easy now.

'Don't you want to know who from first?'

'All right. Who?'

'Clive Swannell.'

'That old poove? You've got to be joking. He wouldn't –' He stopped suddenly. 'You're trying it on.'

Flint smiled confidently. 'How about the Rocker then?'

Lingon stubbed his cigarette out and said nothing.

'I've got it down in black and white. From the Rocker too. Adds up, doesn't it? Want me to go on?'

'I don't know what you're talking about, Inspector,' said Lingon. 'And now if you don't mind ...'

'Next on the list,' said Flint, savouring the pressure, 'there's a nice little piece down Chingford called Annie Mosgrave. Fond of Pakis, she is. And Chinese threesomes. Sort of cosmopolitan, isn't she? But she writes a nice clean hand and she doesn't want some bloke with a meat cleaver coming round one night.'

'You're fucking lying. That's what you're doing,' said Lingon, shifting in his seat and fumbling with the cigarette packet.

Flint shrugged. 'Of course I am. I mean I would be. Stupid old copper like me's bound to lie. Specially when he's got signed statements locked away. And don't think I'm going to do you the favour of locking you away too, Teddie boy. No, I don't like drug buggers. Not one little bit.' He leant forward and smiled. 'No, I'm just going to attend the inquest. Your inquest, Teddie dear. I might even try to identify you. Difficult of course. It will be, won't it? No feet, no hands, teeth all wrenched out ... that is if there is a head and they haven't burnt it after they've done the rest of what was you over. And they do take their time over it. Nasty really. Remember Chris down in Thurrock. Must have been a terrible way to die, bleeding like that. Tore his –'

'Shut up,' shouted Lingon, now ashen and shaking.

Flint got up. 'For now,' he said. 'But only for now. You don't want to do business: that's fine with me. I'll walk out of here and you won't be seeing me again. No, it'll be some bloke you don't even know comes in. Wants to hire a coach to take a party to Buxton. Money on the table, no hassle and the next fucking thing you know is you'll be wishing it had been me instead of one of Mac's mates with a pair of secateurs.'

'Mac's dead,' said Lingon almost in a whisper.

'So they tell me,' said Flint. 'But Roddie Eaton's still out and about and running things. Funny bloke, Roddie. Likes hurting people, according to my sources, specially when they've got enough knowledge to put him away for life and he can't be certain they won't talk.'

'That's not me,' said Lingon. 'I'm no squealer.'

'Want to bet on it? You'll be screaming your rotten little heart out before they've even begun,' said Flint and opened the door.

But Lingon signalled him back. 'I need guarantees,' he said. 'I got to have them.'

Flint shook his head. 'I told you. I'm a stupid old copper. I'm not selling the Queen's pardon. If you want to come and see me and tell me all about it, I'll be there. Till one o'clock.' He looked at his watch. 'You've got exactly one hour twelve minutes. After that you'd better shut up shop and buy yourself a shotgun. And it won't do you any good picking up that phone because I'll know. And the same if you leave here to use a call-box. And by five past one Roddie will know too.'

Flint walked out past the coach. The rotten little bastard would come. He was sure of that and everything was fitting nicely, or nastily, into place. And Hodge was screwed too. It was all very satisfactory and only went to prove what he had always said, that there was nothing like years of experience. It helped to have a son in prison for drug smuggling too, but Inspector Flint had no intention of mentioning his sources of information to the Superintendent when he made his report.

Chapter 17

'An infiltrating agent?' boomed the Airforce General commanding Baconheath. 'Why wasn't I informed immediately?'

'Yes sir, that's a good question, sir,' said Glaushof.

'It is not, Major, it's a lousy question. It isn't even a question I should have to ask. I shouldn't have to ask any questions. In fact I'm not here to ask questions. I run a tight ship and I expect my men to answer their own questions.'

'And that's the way I took it, sir,' said Glaushof.

'Took what?'

'Took the situation, sir, faced with an infiltrating agent. I said to myself –'

'I am not interested in what you said to yourself, Major. I am only interested in results,' shouted the General. 'And I want to know what results you've achieved. By my count the results you've achieved amount to the gassing of ten Airforce personnel or their dependants.'

'Eleven, sir,' said Glaushof.

'Eleven? That's even worse.'

'Twelve with the agent Wilt, sir.'

'Then how come you just told me eleven?' demanded the General, toying with the model of a B52.

'Lieutenant Harah, sir, was gassed in the course of the action, sir, and I am proud to report that without his courage in the face of determined resistance by the enemy we could have encountered heavy casualties and possibly a hostage situation. Sir.'

General Belmonte put the B52 down and reached for a bottle of Scotch before remembering he was supposed to be in command of the situation. 'Nobody told me about a resistance situation,' he said rather more amicably.

'No, sir. It didn't seem advisable to issue a press release in the light of current opinion, sir,' said Glaushof. Having managed to avoid the General's questions he was prepared to apply more direct pressure. If there was one thing the Commander hated it was any mention of publicity. Glaushof mentioned it. 'As I see it, sir, the publicity –'

'Jesus, Glaushof,' shouted the General, 'how many times have I got to remind you there is to be no publicity? That is Directive Number One and comes from the highest authority. No publicity, dammit. You think we can defend the Free World against the enemy if we have publicity? I want that clearly understood. No publicity for Chrissake.'

'Understood, General,' said Glaushof. 'Which is why I've ordered a security blackout, a total no-traffic command to all information services. I mean if it got out we'd had an infiltration problem ...'

He paused to allow the General to get his strength back for a further assault on publicity. It came in waves. When the bombardment had finished Glaushof produced his real target. 'If you'll permit me to say so, sir, I think we're going to be faced with an informational problem on the Intelligence side.'

'You do, do you? Well, let me tell you something, Major, and this is an order, a top priority directive order, that there is to be a security blackout, a total no-traffic command to all information services. That is my order, you understand.'

'Yes, sir,' said Glaushof, 'I'll institute it immediately to the Intelligence Command. I mean if we had a leak to the press there ...'

'Major Glaushof, that is an order I have given you. I want it instituted pre-immediate to all services.'

'Including Intelligence, sir?'

'Of course including Intelligence ,' bawled the General. 'Our Intelligence services are the best in the world and I'm not jeopardizing standards of excellence by exposing them to media harassment. Is that clear?'

'Yessir,' said Glaushof and promptly left the office to order an armed guard to be placed on Intelligence HQ and to instruct all personnel to initiate a total no-traffic command. Since no one knew at all precisely what a no-traffic command was the various interpretations put on it ranged from a ban on all vehicles entering or leaving civilian quarters to a full alert on the airfield, the latter having been intermittently in force throughout the night thanks to wafts of Agent Incapacitating Two sounding off the toxic-weapon-detection sensors. By mid-morning the diverse rumours circulating were so manifestly at odds with one another that Glaushof felt safe enough to bawl his wife out over Lieutenant Harah's sexual insubordination before catching up on his sleep. He wanted to be in good shape to interrogate Wilt.

But when, two hours later, he arrived at the guarded room in the hospital Wilt was evidently in no mood to answer questions. 'Why don't you just go away and let me get some sleep?' he said blearily and turned on his side.

Glaushof glared at his back.

'Give him another shot,' he told the doctor.

'Give him another shot of what?'

'Whatever you gave him last night.'

'I wasn't on duty last night,' said the doctor. 'And anyhow who are you to tell me what to give him?'

Glaushof turned his attention away from Wilt's back and glared instead at the doctor. 'I'm Glaushof. Major Glaushof, doctor, just in case you haven't heard of me. And I'm ordering you to give this commie bastard something that'll jerk him out of that bed so I can question him.'

The doctor shrugged. 'If you say so, Major,' he said and studied Wilt's chart. 'What would you recommend?'

'Me?' said Glaushof. 'How the hell would I know? I'm not a goddam doctor.'

'So happens I am,' said the doctor, 'and I'm telling you I am not administering any further medication to this patient right now. The guy's been exposed to a toxic agent –'

He got no further. With a nasty grunt Glaushof shoved him through the doorway into the corridor. 'Now you just listen to me,' he snarled, 'I don't want to hear no crap about medical ethics. What we've got in there is a dangerous enemy agent and he doesn't even come into the category of a patient. Do you read me?'

'Sure,' said the doctor nervously. 'Sure, I read you. Loud and clear. So now will you take your hands off me?'

Glaushof let go of his coat. 'You just get something'll make

607

the bastard talk and fast,' he said. 'We've got a security problem on our hands.'

'I'll say we have,' said the doctor and hurried away from it. Twenty minutes later a thoroughly confused Wilt was bundled out of the hospital building under a blanket and driven at high speed to Glaushof's office where he was placed on a chair. Glaushof had switched on the tape recorder. 'Okay, now you're going to tell us,' he said.

'Tell you what?' asked Wilt.

'Who sent you?' said Glaushof.

Wilt considered the question. As far as he could tell it didn't have much bearing on what was happening to him except that it had nothing whatsoever to do with reality. 'Sent me?' he said. 'Is that what you said?'

'That's what I said.'

'I thought it was,' said Wilt and relapsed into a meditative silence.

'So?' said Glaushof.

'So what?' asked Wilt, in an attempt to restore his morale slightly by combining insult with enquiry.

'So who sent you?'

Wilt sought inspiration in a portrait of President Eisenhower behind Glaushof's head and found a void. 'Sent me?' he said, and regretted it. Glaushof's expression contrasted unpleasantly with that of the late President. 'Nobody sent me.'

'Listen,' said Glaushof, 'this far you've had it easy. Doesn't mean it's going to stay that way. It could get very nasty. Now, are you going to talk or not?'

'I'm perfectly prepared to talk,' said Wilt, 'though I must say your definition of easy isn't mine. I mean being gassed and –'

'You want to hear my definition of nasty?' asked Glaushof.

'No,' said Wilt hastily, 'Certainly not.'

'So talk.'

Wilt swallowed. 'Any particular subject you're interested in?' he enquired.

'Like who your contacts are,' said Glaushof.

'Contacts?' said Wilt.

'Who you're working for. And I don't want to hear any

608

crap about teaching at the Fenland College Of Arts and Technology. I want to know who set this operation up.'

'Yes,' said Wilt, once more entering a mental maze and losing himself. 'Now when you say "this operation" I wonder if you'd mind . . .' He stopped. Glaushof was staring at him even more awfully than before. 'I mean I don't know what you're talking about.'

'You don't, huh?'

'I'm afraid not. I mean if I did –'

Glaushof shook a finger under Wilt's nose. 'A guy could die in here and nobody would know,' he said. 'If you want to go that way you've only to say so.'

'I don't,' said Wilt, trying to focus on the finger as a means of avoiding the prospect of his going any way. 'If you'd just ask me some questions I could answer . . .'

Glaushof backed off. 'Let's start with where you got the transmitters,' he said.

'Transmitters?' said Wilt. 'Did you say transmitters? What transmitters?'

'The ones in your car.'

'The ones in my car?' said Wilt. 'Are you sure?'

Glaushof gripped the edge of the desk behind him and thought wistfully about killing people. 'You think you can come in here, into United States territory and –'

'England,' said Wilt stolidly. 'To be precise the United Kingdom of England, Scotland –'

'Jesus,' said Glaushof, 'You little commie bastard, you have the nerve to talk about the Royal Family . . .'

'My own country,' said Wilt, finding strength in the assuredness that he was British. It was something he had never really thought much about before. 'And for your information, I am not a communist. Possibly a bastard, though I like to think otherwise. You'd have to ask my mother about that and she's been dead ten years. But definitely not a communist.'

'So what's with the radio transmitters in your car?'

'You said that before and I've no idea what you're talking about. Are you sure you're not mistaking me for someone else.'

'You're named Wilt, aren't you?' shouted Glaushof.

'Yes.'

'And you drive a beat-up Ford, registration plates HPR 791 N, right?'

Wilt nodded. 'I suppose you could put it like that,' he said. 'Though frankly my wife –'

'You saying your wife put those transmitters in your car?'

'Good Lord no. She hasn't a clue about things like that. Anyway, what on earth would she want to do that for?'

'That's what you're here to tell me, boy,' said Glaushof. 'You ain't leaving till you do, you better believe it.'

Wilt looked at him and shook his head. 'I must say I find that difficult,' he muttered. 'I come here to give a lecture on British Culture, such as it is, and the next thing I know I'm in the middle of some sort of raid and there's gas all over the place and I wake up in a bed with doctors sticking needles into me and ...'

He stopped. Glaushof had taken a revolver out of the desk drawer and was loading it. Wilt watched him apprehensively. 'Excuse me,' he said, 'but I'd be grateful if you'd put that ... er ... thing away. I don't know what you've got in mind but I can assure you I am not the person you should be talking to.'

'No? So who should that be, your controller?'

'Controller?' said Wilt.

'Controller,' said Glaushof.

'That's what I thought you said, though to be perfectly honest I still don't see that it helps very much. I don't even know what a controller is.'

'Then you better start inventing one. Like the guy in Moscow who tells you what to do.'

'Look,' said Wilt, desperately trying to get back to some sort of reality which didn't include controllers in Moscow who told him what to do, 'there's obviously been some terrible mistake.'

'Yea, and you made it coming in here with that equipment. I'm going to give you one last chance,' said Glaushof, looking along the barrel of the gun with a significance Wilt found deeply alarming. 'Either you spell it out like it is or ...'

'Quite,' said Wilt. 'Point taken, to use a ghastly expression. What do you want me to tell you?'

610

'The whole deal. How you were recruited, who you contact and where, what information you've given ...'

Wilt stared miserably out the window as the list rolled on. He had never supposed the world to be a particularly sensible place and airbases were particularly nonsensical, but to be taken for a Soviet spy by a lunatic American who played with revolvers was to enter a new realm of insanity. Perhaps that's what had happened. He'd gone clean out of his tiny. No, he hadn't. The gun was proof of some kind of reality, one that was taken for granted by millions of people all over the world but which had somehow never come anywhere near Oakhurst Avenue or the Tech or Ipford. In a sense his own little world with its fundamental beliefs in education and books and, for want of a better word, sensibility, was the unreal one, a dream which no one could ever hope to live in for long. Or at all, if this madman with his cliché talk of guys dying in here and nobody knowing had his way. Wilt turned back and made one last attempt to regain the world he knew.

'All right,' he said, 'if you want the facts I'll give them to you but only with men from MI5 present. As a British subject I demand that right.'

Glaushof snorted. 'Your rights ended the moment you passed that guardhouse,' he said. 'You're telling me what you know. I'm not playing footsy with a lot of suspect faggots from British Intelligence. No way. Now talk.'

'If it's all the same to you I think it would be better written down,' said Wilt, playing for time and trying frantically to think what he could possibly confess. 'I mean, all I need is a pen and some sheets of paper.'

For a moment Glaushof hesitated before deciding that there was something to be said for a confession written out in Wilt's own hand. That way no one could say he'd beaten it out of the little bastard. 'Okay,' he said. 'You can use that table.'

Three hours later Wilt had finished and six pages were covered with his neat and practically illegible handwriting. Glaushof took them and tried to read. 'What you trying to do? Didn't anybody ever teach you to write properly?'

Wilt shook his head wearily. 'If you can't read, take it to someone who can. I've had it,' he said and put his head on his arms on the table. Glaushof looked at his white face and had to agree. He wasn't feeling too good himself. But at least Colonel Urwin and the idiots in Intelligence were going to feel worse. With a fresh surge of energy he went into the office next door, made photocopies of the pages and was presently marching past the guards outside Communications. 'I want transcripts made of these,' he told the head of the typists' pool. 'And absolute security.' Then he sat down and waited.

Chapter 18

'A warrant? A search warrant for 45 Oakhurst Avenue? You want to apply for a search warrant?' said the Superintendent.

'Yes, sir,' said Inspector Hodge, wondering why it was that what seemed like a perfectly reasonable request to him should need querying quite so repetitively. 'All the evidence indicates the Wilts to be carriers.'

'I'm not sure the magistrate is going to agree,' said the Superintendent. 'Circumstantial evidence is all it amounts to.'

'Nothing circumstantial about Wilt going out to that airbase and giving us the run-around, and I wouldn't say her going to that herb farm was circumstantial either. It's all there in my report.'

'Yes,' said the Superintendent, managing to imbue the word with doubt. 'What's not there is one shred of hard evidence.'

'That's why we need the search, sir,' said Hodge. 'There've got to be traces of the stuff in the house. Stands to reason.'

'If he's what you say he is,' said the Superintendent.

'Look,' said Hodge, 'he knew he was being tailed when he went out to Baconheath. He had to know. Drives around in circles for half an hour when he comes out and gives us the slip –'

'And that's another thing,' interrupted the Superintendent, 'your bugging the blighter's car without authorization. I consider that highly reprehensible. I want that understood clearly right now. Anyway, he may have been drunk.'

'Drunk?' said Hodge, finding it difficult to make the transition between unauthorized bugging being reprehensible, which in his opinion it wasn't, and Wilt being drunk.

'When he came out of Baconheath. Didn't know whether he was coming or going and went round in circles. Those Yanks drink rye. Sickly muck but it goes down so easily you don't notice.'

Inspector Hodge considered the suggestion and rejected it.

'I don't see how a drunk could drive that fast, not on those roads without killing himself. And choosing a route that'd take him out of radio contact.'

The Superintendent studied the report again. It didn't make comfortable reading. On the other hand there was something in what Hodge had said. 'If he wasn't pissed why leave the car outside someone else's house?' he asked but Hodge had already concocted an answer to that one.

'Shows how clever the little bastard is,' he said. 'Not giving anything away, that bloke. He knows we're onto him and he needs an explanation for all that run-around he's given us so he plays pissed.'

'If he's that bloody clever you're not going to find anything in his house and that's for sure,' said the Superintendent and shook his head. 'No, he'd never have the stuff on his own doorstep. He'd have it stored somewhere miles away.'

'He's still got to move it,' said Hodge, 'and that means the car. Look, sir, Wilt's the one who goes to the airbase, he collects the stuff there and on the way home he hands it over to a third party who distributes it. That explains why he took such pains to lose us. There was a whole twenty minutes when we weren't picking up any signals. That could have been when he was offloading.'

'Could have been,' said the Superintendent, impressed in spite of himself. 'Still, that only goes to prove my point. You go for a search warrant for his house you're going to end up with egg all over your face. More important, so am I. So that's out. You'll have to think of some other way.'

Hodge returned to his office and took it out on Sergeant Runk. 'The way they carry on it's a bloody wonder we ever nick any bugger. And you had to go and sign for those fucking transmitters ...'

'You don't think they give them out without being signed for,' said Runk.

'You didn't have to land me in the shit by putting "Authorized by Superintendent Wilkinson for covert surveillance." He loved that.'

'Well, wasn't it? I mean I thought you'd got permission ...'

'Oh no, you didn't. We pulled that stroke in the middle

of the night and he'd been home since five. And now we've got to retrieve the bloody things. That's something you can do tonight.'

And having, as he hoped, ensured that the Sergeant would spend the day regretting his indiscretion, the Inspector got up and stared out of the window for inspiration. If he couldn't get a search warrant ... He was still pondering the question when his attention was distracted by a car parked down below. It looked hideously familiar.

The Wilts' Escort. What the hell was it doing outside the police station?

Eva sat in Flint's office and held back the tears. 'I didn't know who else to come to,' she said. 'I've been to the Tech and phoned the prison and Mrs Braintree hasn't seen him and he usually goes there if he's ... well, if he wants a change. But he hasn't been there or the hospital or anywhere else I can think of and I know you don't like him or anything but you are a policeman and you have been ... helpful in the past. And you do know Henry.' She stopped and looked appealingly at the Inspector.

It wasn't a look that held much appeal for Flint and he certainly didn't like the notion that he knew Wilt. He'd tried to understand the blighter, but even at his most optimistic he'd never supposed for one moment that he'd got anywhere near fathoming the horrible depths of Wilt's extraordinary character. The sod came into the category of an enigma made all the more impossible to understand by his choice of Eva as a wife. It was a relationship Flint had always preferred not to think about, but here she was sitting foursquare on a chair in his office telling him, evidently without the slightest regard for his feelings, even as though it were some sort of compliment, that he knew her Henry. 'Has he ever gone off like this before?' he asked, with the private thought that in Wilt's shoes he'd have been off like a flash – before the wedding.

'No, never,' said Eva, 'that's what's so worrying. I know you think he's ... peculiar, but he's really been a good husband.'

'I'm sure he has,' said Flint for want of anything more reassuring to say. 'You don't think he's suffering from amnesia.'

'Amnesia?'

615

'Loss of memory,' said Flint. 'It hits people who've been under strain. Has anything been happening lately that might have caused him to flip ... to have a nervous breakdown?'

'I can't think of anything in particular,' said Eva, determined to keep any mention of Dr Kores and that dreadful tonic out of the conversation. 'Of course the children get on his nerves sometimes and there was that horrible business at the Tech the other day with that girl dying. Henry was ever so upset. And he's been teaching at the prison ...' She stopped again as she remembered what had been really worrying her. 'He's been teaching a dreadful man called McCullum on Monday evenings and Fridays. That's what he told me anyway, only when I phoned the prison they said he never had.'

'Had what?' asked Flint.

'Never been there on Fridays,' said Eva, tears welling up in her eyes at this proof that Henry, her Henry, had lied to her.

'But he went out every Friday and that's where he told you he was going?'

Eva nodded dumbly and for a moment Flint almost felt sorry for her. A fat middle-aged woman with four bloody tearaway kids who turned the house into a blooming bearpit and she hadn't known what Wilt was up to? Talk about being as thick as two short planks. Well, it was about time she learnt. 'Look, Mrs Wilt, I know this isn't easy to ...' he began but to his amazement Eva was there before him.

'I know what you're going to say,' she interrupted, 'but it isn't true. If it had been another woman why did he leave the car in Mrs Willoughby's?'

'Leave the car in Mrs Willoughby's? Who's Mrs Willoughby?'

'She lives at Number 65, and that's where the car was this morning. I had to go and get it. Why would he want to do that?'

It was on the tip of Flint's tongue to say that's what he'd have done in Wilt's place, dump the car down the road and run like hell, when something else occurred to him.

'You wait here,' he said and left the room. In the corridor he hesitated for a moment and tried to think who to ask. He certainly wasn't approaching Hodge but there was always Ser-

616

geant Runk. And Yates could find out for him. He turned into the open-plan office where the Sergeant was sitting at a typewriter.

'Got an enquiry for you, Yates,' he said. 'Have a word with your mate Runk and find out where they tailed Wilt last night. I've got his missus in my office. And don't let him know I'm interested, understand? Just a casual enquiry on your part.' He sat on the edge of the desk while Yates was gone five minutes.

'Right balls-up,' said the Sergeant when he returned. 'They followed the little bugger out to Baconheath airbase with a radio tail. He's in there an hour and a half and comes out driving like a maniac. Runkie reckons Wilt knew they were on to him, the way he drove. Anyway they lost him, and when they did find the car it was outside some house down the road from the Wilts' with a fucking big dog trying to tear the front door down to get at Hodge. That's about the strength of it.'

Flint nodded, and kept his excitement to himself. He'd already done enough to make Hodge look the fucking idiot he was; he'd broken the Bull and Clive Swannell and that little shit Lingon, signed statements and all; and all the time Hodge had been harrying Wilt. So why drop him in it any further?

Why not? The deeper the bugger sank the less he'd be likely to surface. And not only Hodge but Wilt too. The bastard had been the original cause of all Flint's misfortunes and to be able to drag him through the mire together with Hodge was justice at its most perfect. Besides, Flint still had to make the catch with Lingon, so a diversion was just what he needed. And if ever there was a diversion ready to hand it was sitting in his office in the shape of Mrs Eva Wilt. The only problem was how to point her in Hodge's direction without anyone learning what he had done. It was a risk he had to take. He'd better check first, though. Flint went to a phone and looked up the Baconheath number.

'Inspector Hodge speaking,' he said, slurring the name so that it might well have been Squash or Hedge, 'I'm calling from Ipford Police Station in connection with a Mr Wilt ... A Mr Henry Wilt of 45 Oakhurst Avenue, Ipford. I understand he visited you last night.' He waited while someone said he'd check.

It took a long time and another American came on the line. 'You enquiring about someone called Wilt?' he asked.

'That's correct,' said Flint.

'And you say you're police?'

'Yes,' said Flint, noting the hesitancy in the questioner with intense interest.

'If you'll give me your name and the number to call I'll get back to you,' said the American. Flint put the phone down quietly. He'd learnt what he needed and he wasn't having any Yank check his credentials.

He went back to his office and sat down with a calculated sigh. 'I'm afraid you're not going to like what I'm going to tell you, Mrs Wilt,' he said.

Eva didn't. She left the police station white-faced with fury. Not only had Henry lied to her but he'd been cheating her for months and she hadn't had an inkling.

Behind her Flint sat on in his office staring almost ecstatically at a wall-map of Ipford. Henry Wilt, Henry Bloody Wilt, was going to get his comeuppance this time. And he was out there somewhere, somewhere in one of those little streets, holed up with a dolly bird who must have money or he would be back at his job at the Tech.

No, he wouldn't. Not with Eva in pursuit. No wonder the bugger had left the car down the road. If he'd any sense he'd have left town by now. The bloody woman would murder him. Flint smiled at the thought. Now that *would* be poetic justice, no mistake.

'It's more than my life's worth. I mean I'd do it, I'd happily do it but what if it gets out?' said Mr Gamer.

'It won't,' said Hodge, 'I can give you a solemn assurance on that. You won't even know they're there.'

Mr Gamer looked mournfully round the restaurant. He usually had sandwiches and a cup of coffee for lunch and he wasn't sure how well Boneless Chicken Curry washed down with a bottle of Blue Nun was going to agree with him. Still, the Inspector was paying and he could always get some Solvol on the way back to the shop. 'It's not just me either, it's the wife. If you knew what that woman has been through these last twelve months you wouldn't believe me. You really wouldn't.'

'I would,' said Hodge. If it was anything like what he'd been through in the last four days, Mrs Gamer must be a woman with an iron constitution.

'It's even worse in the school holidays,' Mr Gamer continued. 'Those fucking girls ... I don't usually swear but there's a point where you've got to ... I mean you can't begin to know how awful they are.' He stopped and looked closely into Hodge's face. 'One of these days they're going to kill someone,' he whispered. 'They bloody near did for me on Tuesday. I'd have been as dead as a dodo if I hadn't been wearing rubber-soled shoes. Stole my statue from the garden and when I went round to get it ...'

Hodge listened sympathetically. 'Criminal,' he said. 'You should have reported it to us straight away. Even now if you made a formal complaint ...'

'You think I'd dare? Never. If it meant having them all carted off to prison straightaway I might but it doesn't work like that. They'd come home from court and ... it doesn't bear thinking about. Take that poor sod down the road, Councillor Birkenshaw. He had his name up in lights on a french letter with a foreskin on it. Floated right down the street it did and then they went and accused him of showing his privates to them. He had a horrible time trying to prove he hadn't. And look where he is. In hospital. No, it's not worth the risk.'

'I can see what you mean,' said Hodge. 'But this way they wouldn't ever find out. All we need is your permission to –'

'I blame the bloody mother,' Mr Gamer went on, encouraged by the Blue Nun and the Inspector's apparent sympathy. 'If she didn't encourage the little bitches to be like boys and take an interest in mechanical things it'd help. But no, they've got to be inventors and geniuses. Mind you, it takes some sort of genius to do what they did to Dickens' lawnmower. Brand new, it was, and God knows what exactly they did to it. Supercharged it with a camping-gas cylinder and altered the gear ratio too so it went like the clappers. And it's not as though he's a well man. Anyway, he started the bloody thing up and before he could stop it was off down the lawn at about eighty and mowing their new carpet in the lounge. Smashed the piano too, come to think of it. They had to call the fire brigade to put it out.'

'Why didn't he sue the parents?' asked Hodge, fascinated in spite of himself.

Mr Gamer sighed. 'You don't understand,' he said. 'You have to live through it to understand. You don't think they admit what they've done? Of course they don't. And who's going to believe old Duckens when he says four ruddy girls that age could change the sprocket on the driveshaft and superglue the clutch? No one. Mind if I help myself.'

Hodge poured another glass. Clearly Mr Gamer was a broken man. 'All right,' he said. 'Now supposing you know nothing about it. Just suppose a man from the Gas Board comes to check the meter –'

'And that's another thing,' said Mr Gamer almost dementedly, 'gas. The bill! Four hundred and fifty fucking pounds for a summer quarter! You don't believe me, do you? I didn't believe it either. Had that meter changed and checked and it still came to the same. I still don't know how they did it. Must have been while we were on holiday. If only I could find out!'

'Look,' said Hodge, 'you let my man install the equipment and you've a very good chance of getting rid of the Wilts for ever. And I mean that. For ever.'

Mr Gamer gazed into his glass and considered this glorious prospect. 'For ever?'

'For ever.'

'Done,' said Mr Gamer.

Later that afternoon Sergeant Runk, feeling distinctly uncomfortable in a Gas Board uniform, and with Mrs Gamer asking pitifully what could possibly be wrong with the chimney because they'd had it lined when the central heating was put in, was up in the roof space. By the time he left he had managed to feed microphones through a gap in the bricks so that they lay hidden among the insulating chips above the Wilts' bedrooms. 45 Oakhurst Avenue had been wired for sound.

Chapter 19

'I think we've got one hell of a problem, sir,' said the Corporal. 'Major Glaushof ordered me to ditch the car back at the Wilt guy's house and I did. All I can say is those transmitters weren't civilian. I had a good look at them and they were hi-tech British.'

Colonel Urwin, Senior Intelligence Officer USAF Baconheath, pondered the problem by looking coolly at a sporting print on the wall. It wasn't a very good one but its depiction of a fox in the far distance, being chased by a motley crowd of thin, fat, pale, or red-faced Englishmen on horseback, always served to remind him that it was as well not to underestimate the British. Better still, it paid to seem to be one of them. To that end he played golf with an ancient set of clubs and spent his idler moments tracing his family tree in the archives of various universities and the graveyards of Lincolnshire churches. In short, he kept an almost subterranean profile and was proud of the fact that he had on several occasions been taken for a master from one of the better public schools. It was a rôle that suited him exactly and fitted in with his professional creed that discretion was the better part of valour.

'British?' he said thoughtfully. 'That could mean anything or nothing. And you say Major Glaushof has put down a security clamp?'

'General Belmonte's orders, sir.'

The Colonel said nothing. In his opinion the Base Commander's IQ was only slightly higher than that of the egregious Glaushof. Anyone who could call four no trumps without a diamond in his hand had to be a cretin. 'So the situation is that Glaushof has this man Wilt in custody and is presumably torturing him and no one is supposed to know he's here. The operative word being "supposed". Obviously whoever sent him knows he never returned to Ipford.'

'Yes, sir,' said the Corporal. 'And the Major's been trying to get a message on line to Washington.'

'See it's coded garbage,' said the Colonel, 'and get a copy to me.'

'Yes, sir,' said the Corporal and disappeared.

Colonel Urwin looked across at his deputy. 'Seems we could have a hornet's nest,' he said. 'What do you make of it?'

Captain Fortune shrugged. 'Could be any number of options,' he said. 'I don't like the sound of that hardware.'

'Kamikaze,' said the Colonel. 'No one would come in transmitting.'

'Libyans or Khomeini might.'

Colonel Urwin shook his head. 'No way. When they hit they don't signal their punches. They'd come in loaded with explosives first time. So who's scoring?'

'The Brits?'

'That's my line of thinking,' said the Colonel, and wandered across to take a closer look at the sporting print. 'The only question is who are they hunting, Mr Henry Wilt or us?'

'I've checked our records and there's nothing on Wilt. CND in the sixties, otherwise non-political.'

'University?'

'Yes,' said the Captain.

'Which one?'

The Captain consulted the computer file. 'Cambridge. Majored in English.'

'Otherwise, nothing?'

'Nothing we know of. British Intelligence would know.'

'And we're not asking,' said the Colonel, coming to a decision. 'If Glaushof wants to play Lone Ranger with the General's consent he's welcome to the fan-shit. We stay clear and come up with the real answer when it's needed.'

'I still don't like that hardware in the car,' said the Captain.

'And I don't like Glaushof,' said the Colonel. 'I have an idea the Ofreys don't either. Let him dig his own grave.' He paused. 'Is there anyone with any intelligence who knows what really happened, apart from that Corporal?'

'Captain Clodiak filed a complaint against Harah for sexual

622

harassment. And she's on the list of students attending Wilt's lectures.'

'Right, we'll start digging back into this fiasco there,' said the Colonel.

'Let's get back to this Radek,' said Glaushof, 'I want to know who he is.'

'I've told you, a Czech writer and he's been dead since God knows when so there is no way I could have met him,' said Wilt.

'If you're lying you will. Shortly,' said Glaushof. Having read the transcripts of Wilt's confession that he had been re-cruited by a KGB agent called Yuri Orlov and had a contact man called Karl Radek, Glaushof was now determined to find out exactly what information Wilt had passed to the Russians. Understandably it was proving decidedly harder than getting Wilt to admit he was an agent. Twice Glaushof had used the threat of instant death, but without any useful result. Wilt had asked for time to think and had then come up with H-bombs. 'H-bombs? You've been telling this bastard Radek we've got H-bombs stashed here?'

'Yes,' said Wilt.

'They know that already.'

'That's what Radek said. He said they wanted more than that.'

'So what did you give him, the BBs?'

'BBs?' said Wilt 'You mean airguns?'

'Binary bombs.'

'Never heard of them.'

'Safest nerve-gas bombs in the world,' said Glaushof proudly, 'We could kill every living fucking thing from Moscow to Peking with BBs and they wouldn't even know a thing.'

'Really?' said Wilt. 'I must say I find your definition of safe peculiar. What are the dangerous ones capable of?'

'Shit,' said Glaushof, wishing he was somewhere under-developed like El Salvador and could use more forceful methods. 'You don't talk you're going to regret you ever met me.'

Wilt studied the Major critically. With each unfulfilled threat he was gaining more confidence but it still seemed inadvisable to point out that he already regretted meeting the bloody man. Best to keep things cool. 'I'm only telling you what you want to know,' he said.

'And you didn't give them any other information?'

'I don't know any. Ask the students in my class. They'll tell you I wouldn't know a bomb from a banana.'

'So you say,' muttered Glaushof. He'd already questioned the students and, in the case of Mrs Ofrey, had learnt more about her opinion of him than about Wilt. And Captain Clodiak hadn't been helpful either. The only evidence she'd been able to produce that Wilt was a communist had been his insistence that the National Health Service was a good thing. And so by degrees of inconsequentiality they had come full circle back to this KGB man Radek whom Wilt had claimed was his contact and now said was a Czech writer and dead at that. And with each hour Glaushof's chances of promoting himself were slipping away. There had to be some way of getting the information he needed. He was just wondering if there wasn't some truth drug he could use when he caught sight of the scrotal guard on his desk. 'How come you were wearing this?' he asked.

Wilt looked at the cricket box bitterly. The events of the previous evening seemed strangely distant in these new and more frightening circumstances but there had been a moment when he had supposed the box to be in some way responsible for his predicament. If it hadn't come undone, he wouldn't have been in the loo and ...

'I was having trouble with a hernia,' he said. It seemed a safe explanation.

It wasn't. Glaushof's mind had turned grossly to sex.

Eva's was already there. Ever since she had left Flint she had been obsessed with it. Henry, her Henry, had left her for another woman and an American airbase slut at that. And there could be no doubt about it. Inspector Flint hadn't told her in any nasty way. He'd simply said that Henry had been out to Bacon-heath. He didn't have to say any more. Henry had been going out every Friday night telling her he was going to the prison and all the time ... No, she wasn't going to give way. With

624

a sense of terrible purpose Eva drove to Canton Street. Mavis had been right after all and Mavis had known how to deal with Patrick's infidelities. Best of all, as secretary of Mothers Against The Bomb she hated the Americans at Baconheath. Mavis would know what to do.

Mavis did. But first she had to have her gloat. 'You wouldn't listen to me, Eva,' she said. 'I've always said there was something seedy and deceitful about Henry but you would have it that he was a good, faithful husband. Though after what he tried to do to me the other morning I don't see how ...'

'I'm sorry,' said Eva, 'but I thought that was my fault for going to Dr Kores and giving him that ... Oh dear, you don't think that's what's made him do this?'

'No, I don't,' said Mavis, 'not for one moment. If he's been deceiving you for six months with this woman, Dr Kores' herbal mixture had nothing to do with it. Of course he'll try to use that as an excuse when it comes to the divorce.'

'But I don't want a divorce,' said Eva, 'I just want to lay my hands on that woman.'

'In that case, if you're going to be a sexual helot –'

'A what?' said Eva, appalled at the word.

'Slave, dear,' said Mavis, recognizing her mistake, 'a serf, a skivvy who's just there to do the cooking and cleaning.'

Eva subsided. All she wanted to be was a good wife and mother and bring the girls up to take their rightful place in the technological world. At the top. 'But I don't even know the beastly woman's name,' she said, getting back to practicalities.

Mavis applied her mind to the problem. 'Bill Paisley might know,' she said finally. 'He's been teaching out there and he's at the Open University with Patrick. I'll give him a ring.'

Eva sat on in the kitchen, sunk in apparent lethargy. But underneath she was tensing herself for the confrontation. No matter what Mavis said no one was going to take Henry away from her. The quads were going to have a father and a proper home and the best education Wilt's salary could provide, never mind what people said or how much her own pride was hurt. Pride was a sin and anyway Henry would pay for it.

She was going over in her mind what she would say to him when Mavis returned triumphantly. 'Bill Paisley knows all about it,' she said. 'Apparently Henry has been teaching a class of women British Culture and it doesn't take much imagination to see what's happened.' She looked at a scrap of paper. 'The Development of British Culture and Institutions, Lecture Hall 9. And the person to contact is the Education Officer. He's given me the number to call. If you want me to, I'll do it for you.'

Eva nodded gratefully. 'I'd only lose my temper and get agitated,' she said, 'and you're so good at organizing things.'

Mavis went back to the hall. For the next ten minutes Eva could hear her talking with increasing vehemence. Then the phone was slammed down.

'The nerve of the man,' Mavis said, storming back into the kitchen pale-faced with anger. 'First they wouldn't put me through to him and it was only when I said I was from the Library Service and wanted to speak to the Education Officer about the free supply of books that I got to him. And then it was "No comment, ma'am. I'm sorry but no comment."'

'But you did ask about Henry?' said Eva who couldn't see what the Library Service or the free supply of books could possibly have to do with her problem.

'Of course I did,' snapped Mavis. 'I said Mr Wilt had suggested I contact him about the Library Service supplying books on English Culture and that's when he clammed up.' She paused thoughtfully. 'You know I could almost swear he sounded scared.'

'Scared? Why should he be scared?'

'I don't know. It was when I mentioned the name "Wilt,"' said Mavis. 'But we're going to drive out there now and find out.'

Captain Clodiak sat in Colonel Urwin's office. Unlike the other buildings at Baconheath which had been inherited from the RAF or which resembled prefabricated and sub-economic housing estates, Intelligence Headquarters was strangely at odds with the military nature of the base. It was in fact a large red-brick mansion built at the turn of the century by a retired mining engineer with a taste for theatrical Tudor, an eye to the value of black fen soil and a dislike for the icy

626

winds that blew from Siberia. As a consequence the house had a mock baronial hall, oak-panelled walls and a highly efficient central-heating system and accorded perfectly with Colonel Urwin's sense of irony. It also set him apart from the rest of the base and lent weight to his conviction that military men were dangerous idiots and incapable of speaking E. B. White's English. What was needed was intelligence, brains as well as brawn. Captain Clodiak seemed endowed with both. Colonel Urwin listened to her account of Wilt's capture with very close interest. It was forcing him to reassess the situation. 'So you're saying that he definitely seemed uneasy right through the lexture?' he said.

'No question,' said Clodiak. 'He kept squirming behind the lecturn like he was in pain. And his lecture was all over the place. Incoherent. Usually he takes off on tangents but he comes back to the main theme. This time he rambled and then this bandage came down his leg and he went to pieces.'

The Colonel looked across at Captain Fortune. 'Do we know anything about the need for bandages?'

'I've checked with the medics and they don't know. The guy came in gassed and no other sign of injuries.'

'Let's go back from there to previous behaviour. Anything unusual?' Captain Clodiak shook her head.

'Nothing I noticed. He's hetero, got nice manners, doesn't make passes, he's probably got some hang-ups, like he's a depressive. Nothing I'd class as unusual in an Englishman.'

'And yet he was definitely uneasy? And there's no question about the bandage?'

'None,' said Clodiak.

'Thank you for your help,' said the Colonel. 'If anything else comes to mind come back to us.' And having seen her out into the passage he turned to look at the sporting print for inspiration. 'It begins to sound as though someone's been leaning on him,' he said finally.

'You can bet your life Glaushof has,' said Fortune. 'A guy who confesses that easy has to have had some treatment.'

'What's he confessed to? Nothing. Absolute zero.'

'He's admitted being recruited by this Orlov and having a contact man in a Karl Radek. I wouldn't say that was nothing.'

'The one being a dissident who's doing time in Siberia,' said

627

Urwin, 'and Karl Radek was a Czech writer who died in a Gulag in 1940. Not the easiest man to contact.'

'They could be cover names.'

'Could be. Just. I'd choose something less obviously phoney myself. And why Russians? If they're from the Embassy ... yes, I suppose so. Except that he met quote Orlov unquote in the bus station in Ipford which is outside Soviet embassy staff permitted radius. And where does he meet friend Radek? Every Wednesday afternoon by the bowling green on Midway Park. Every Wednesday same place same time? Out of the question. Our friends from the KGB may play dumb occasionally but not that dumb. Glaushof's been dealt the hand he asked for and that doesn't happen by accident.'

'Leaves Glaushof up shit creek,' said Fortune.

But Colonel Urwin wasn't satisfied. 'Leaves us all there if we don't take care,' he said. 'Let's go through the options again. Wilt's a genuine Russian probe? Out for the reasons given. Someone running a check on our security? Could be some goon in Washington came up with the idea. They've got Shi'ite suicide squads on the brain. Why use an Englishman? They don't tell him his car's being used to make the test more effective. If so why's he panicking during the lecture? That's what I get back to, his behaviour in that lecture hall. That's where I really begin to pick up the scent. Go from there to this "confession" which only an illiterate like Glaushof would believe and the state of Denmark really is beginning to stink to high heaven. And Glaushof's handling it? Not any more, Ed. I'm pulling rank.'

'How? He's got a security blanket from the General.'

'That's where I'm pulling rank,' said the Colonel. 'Old B52 may think he commands this base but I'm going to have to disillusion the old warrior. About a great many things.' He pressed a button on the phone. 'Get me Central Intelligence,' he said.

Chapter 20

'Orders are no one in,' said the guard on the gate, 'I'm sorry but that's how it is.'

'Look,' said Mavis, 'all we've come to do is speak to the officer in charge of Education. His name is Bluejohn and –'

'Still applies, no one in.'

Mavis took a deep breath and tried to keep calm. 'In that case I'd like to speak to him here,' she said. 'If we can't come in, perhaps he'd be good enough to come out.'

'I can check,' said the guard and went into the gatehouse.

'It's no use,' said Eva, looking at the barrier and the high barbed-wire fence. Behind the barrier a series of drums filled with concrete had been laid out on the roadway to form a zigzag through which vehicles could only wind their way very slowly. 'They're not going to tell us anything.'

'And I want to know why,' said Mavis.

'It might help if you weren't wearing that Mothers Against The Bomb badge,' said Eva.

Mavis took it off reluctantly. 'It's utterly disgusting,' she said. 'This is supposed to be a free country and –'

She was interrupted by the appearance of a lieutenant. He stood in the doorway of the gatehouse and looked at them for a moment before walking over. 'I'm sorry ladies,' he said, 'but we're running a security exercise. It's only temporary so if you come back tomorrow maybe ...'

'Tomorrow is no good,' said Mavis. 'We want to see Mr Bluejohn today. Now if you'll be good enough to telephone him or give him a message, we'd be most obliged.'

'Sure, I can do that,' said the Lieutenant. 'What do you want me to say?'

'Just that Mrs Wilt is here and would like to make some enquiries about her husband, Mr Henry Wilt. He's been teaching a class here on British Culture.'

'Oh him, Mr Wilt? I've heard of him from Captain Clodiak,'

said the Lieutenant, expansively. 'She's been attending his course and she says he's real good. No problem, I'll check with the EO.'

'What did I tell you?' said Mavis as he went back into the guardhouse. '*She* says he's real good. I wonder what your Henry's being so good at now.'

Eva hardly heard. Any lingering doubt that Henry had been deceiving her had gone and she was staring through the wire at the drab houses and prefabricated buildings with the feeling that she was looking ahead into the drabness and barren years of her future life. Henry had run off with some woman, perhaps this same Captain Clodiak, and she was going to be left to bring up the quads on her own and be poor and known as a ... A one-parent family? But there was no family without a father and where was she going to get the money to keep the girls at school? She'd have to go on Social Security and queue up with all those other women ... She wouldn't. She'd go out to work. She'd do anything to make up for ... The images in her mind, images of emptiness and of her own fortitude, were interrupted by the return of the Lieutenant.

His manner had changed. 'I'm sorry,' he said abruptly, 'there's been a mistake. I've got to tell you that. Now if you'll move off. We've got this security exercise on.'

'Mistake? What mistake?' said Mavis, reacting to his brusqueness with all her own pent-up hatred. 'You said Mrs Wilt's husband ...'

'I didn't say anything,' said the Lieutenant and, turning on his heel, ordered the barrier to be lifted to allow a truck to come through.

'Well!' said Mavis furiously. 'Of all the nerve! I've never heard such a bare-faced lie in my life. You heard what he said just a moment ago and now –'

But Eva was moving forward with a new determination. Henry was in the camp. She knew that now. She'd seen the look on the Lieutenant's face, the changed look, the blankness that had been in such contrast to his previous manner, and she'd known. Without thinking she moved into the drabness of life without Henry, into that desert beyond the barrier. She was going to find him and have it out with him. A figure got in her way and tried to stop her. There was a flurry of arms

630

and he fell. Three more men, only figures in her mind, and she was being held and dragged back. From somewhere seemingly distant she heard Mavis shout, 'Go limp. Go limp.' Eva went limp and the next moment she was lying on the ground with two men beside her and a third dragging on an arm.

Three minutes later, covered with dust and with the heels of her shoes scuffed and her tights torn, she was dragged beneath the barrier and dumped on the road. And during that time she had uttered no sound other than to pant with exertion. She sat there for a moment and then got to her knees and looked back into the camp with an intensity that was more dangerous in its implications than her brief battle with the guards.

'Lady, you got no right to come in here. You're just asking for trouble,' said the Lieutenant. Eva said nothing. She helped herself up from the kneeling position and walked back to the car.

'Eva dear, are you all right?' asked Mavis.

Eva nodded. 'Just take me home,' she said. For once Mavis had nothing to say. Eva's strength of purpose needed no words.

Wilt's did. With time running out on him, Glaushof had resorted to a new form of interrogation. Unable to use more forceful methods he had decided on what he considered to be the subtle approach. Since it involved the collaboration of Mrs Glaushof clad in garments Glaushof and possibly even Lieutenant Harah had found so alluring – jackboots, suspender belts and teatless bras figured high in Glaushof's compendium of erotica – Wilt, who had been hustled yet again into a car and driven to the Glaushof's house, found himself suddenly lying on a heart-shaped bed clad in the hospital gown and confronted by an apparition in black, red and several shades of pink. The boots were black, the suspender belt and panties were red and the bra was black fringed with pink. The rest of Mrs Glaushof was, thanks to her frequent use of a sun lamp, mostly brown and definitely drunk. Ever since Glausie, as she had once called him, had bawled her out for sharing her mixed charms with those of Lieutenant Harah she had been hitting the Scotch. She had also hit a bottle of Chanel

No 5 or had lathered herself with the stuff. Wilt couldn't decide which. And didn't want to. It was enough to be cloistered (the word seemed singularly inappropriate in the circumstances) in a room with an alcoholic prostitute who told him to call her Mona.

'What?' said Wilt.

'Mona, baby,' said Mrs Glaushof, breathing whisky into his face and fondling his cheek.

'I am not your baby,' said Wilt.

'Oh, but you are, honey. You're just what momma needed.'

'And you're not my mother,' said Wilt, wishing the hell the woman was. She'd have been dead ten years. Mrs Glaushof's hand strayed down his body. 'Shit,' said Wilt. That damned poison was beginning to work again.

'That's better, baby,' Mrs Glaushof whispered as Wilt stiffened. 'You and me's going to have the best of times.'

'You and I,' said Wilt, frantically trying to find some relief in correct syntax, 'and you may consider – Ouch!'

'Is baby going to be good to momma now?' asked Mrs Glaushof, sliding her tongue between his lips. Wilt tried to focus on her eyes and found it impossible. He also found it impossible to reply without unclenching his teeth and Mrs Glaushof's reptilian tongue, tasting as it did of alcohol and tobacco, was so busily exploring his gums that any move that might allow it to go any further seemed inadvisable. For one insane moment it crossed his mind to bite the filthy thing but considering what she had in her hand the consequences didn't bear thinking about. Instead he tried to concentrate on less tangible things. What the hell was he doing lying on a quilted bed with a sex-mad woman clutching his balls when only half an hour ago a homicidal maniac had been threatening to plaster his brains on the ceiling with a .38 unless he talked about binary bombs? It didn't make even the vaguest sense but before he could arrive at any sane conclusion Mrs Glaushof had relinquished her probe.

'Baby's steaming me up,' she moaned and promptly bit his neck.

'That's as maybe,' said Wilt, making a mental note to brush his teeth as soon as possible. 'The fact of the matter is that I ...'

Mrs Glaushof pinched his cheeks. 'Rosebud,' she whimpered.

'Wosebud?' said Wilt with difficulty.

'Your mouth's like a wosebud,' said Mrs Glaushof, digging her nails still further into his cheeks, 'a lovely wosebud.'

'It doethn't tathte like one,' said Wilt and instantly regretted it. Mrs Glaushof had hoisted herself up him and he was facing a nipple fringed with pink lace.

'Suck momma,' said Mrs Glaushof.

'Thod off,' said Wilt. Further comment was stifled by the nipple and Mrs Glaushof's breast which was worming around on his face. As Mrs Glaushof pressed down on him Wilt fought for breath.

In the bathroom next door Glaushof was having the same problem. Staring through the two-way mirror he'd installed to watch Mrs Glaushof putting on the regalia of his fantasies while he bathed, he had begun to regret his new tactics. Subtle they weren't. The bloody woman had clearly gone clean over the top. Glaushof's own patriotism had led him to suppose that his wife would do her duty by cosying up to a Russian spy, but he hadn't expected her to screw the bastard. What was even worse was that she was so obviously enjoying the process.

Glaushof wasn't. Gritting his teeth he stared lividly through the mirror and tried not to think about Lieutenant Harah. It didn't help. In the end, driven by the thought that the Lieutenant had lain on that same bed while Mona gave him the works he was now witnessing, Glaushof charged out of the bathroom. 'For Chrissake,' he yelled from the landing, 'I told you to soften the son of a bitch up, not turn him on.'

'So what's wrong?' said Mrs Glaushof, in the process of changing nipples. 'You think I don't know what I'm doing?'

'I'm buggered if I do,' squawked Wilt, taking the opportunity to get some air. Mrs Glaushof scrambled off him and headed for the door.

'No, I don't,' said Glaushof, 'I think you're –'

'Screw off,' screamed Mrs Glaushof. 'This guy's got a hard-on for me.'

'I can see that,' said Glaushof morosely, 'and if you think that's softening him up you're fucking crazy.'

Mrs Glaushof divested herself of a boot. 'Crazy, am I?' she bawled and hurled the boot at his head with surprising accuracy. 'So what's an old man like you know about crazy? You couldn't get it up if I didn't wear fucking Nazi jackboots.' The second boot hurtled through the door. 'I got to dress up like I'm fucking Hitler in drag before you're anywhere near a man and that ain't saying much. Like this guy's got a prick like the Washington Monument compared to yours.'

'Listen,' shouted Glaushof, 'lay off my prick. That's a commie agent you got in there. He's dangerous!'

'I'll say,' said Mrs Glaushof now liberating herself from the bra. 'Is he ever.'

'No, I'm not,' said Wilt, lurching away from the bed. Mrs Glaushof staggered out of the suspender belt.

'I'm telling you you could get yourself deep in trouble,' Glaushof called. He'd taken refuge from any further missiles round the corner.

'Deep in it is,' Mrs Glaushof shouted back and slammed the door and locked it. Before Wilt could move she had tossed the key out of the window and was heading for him. 'Red Square here I come.'

'I'm not Red Square. I don't know why everyone keeps thinking –' Wilt began, but Mrs Glaushof wasn't into thought. With an agility that took him by complete surprise she threw him back on to the bed and knelt over him.

'Choo choo, baby,' she moaned and this time there was no mistaking her meaning. Faced with this horrible prospect Wilt lived up to Glaushof's warning that he was a dangerous man and sank his teeth into her thigh. In the bathroom Glaushof almost cheered.

'Countermand my orders? Countermand my orders? You're telling me to countermand my orders?' said General Belmonte dropping several decibels in his disbelief. 'We have an enemy agent infiltration situation with possible bombing implications and you're telling me to countermand my orders?'

'Asking, General,' said the Colonel gently. 'I am simply saying that the political consequences could be disastrous.'

'Having my base blown apart by a fucking fanatic is disastrous too and I'm not standing for it,' said the General.

'No, sir, I am not having a body count of thousands of innocent American service personnel and their dependants on my conscience. Major Glaushof's handling of the situation has been absolutely correct. No one knows we've got this bastard and he can beat the shit out of him for all I care. I am not –'

'Correction, sir,' interrupted the Colonel, 'a number of people know we're holding this man. The British police called in enquiring about him. And a woman claiming to be his wife has already had to be ejected at the main gate. Now if you want the media to get hold –'

'The media?' bellowed the General. 'Don't mention that fucking word in my presence. I have given Glaushof a Directive Number One, Toppest Priority, there's to be no media intervention and I am not countermanding that order.'

'I am not suggesting you do. What I am saying is that the way Glaushof is handling the situation we could find ourselves in the middle of a media onslaught that would get world coverage.'

'Shit,' said the General, cringing at the prospect. In his mind's eye he could already see the television cameras mounted on trucks outside the base. There might even be women. He pulled his mind back from this vision of hell. 'What's wrong with the way Glaushof's handling it?'

'Too heavy,' said the Colonel. 'The security clamp-down's drawing attention to the fact that we do have a problem. That's one. We should cool it all off by acting normal. Two is we are presently holding a British subject and if you've given the Major permission to beat the shit out of him I imagine that's just what –'

'I didn't give him permission to do anything like that, I gave him . . . well, I guess I said he could interrogate him and . . .' He paused and tried the comradely approach. 'Hell, Joe, Glaushof may be a shitass but he has got him to confess he's a commie agent. You've got to hand it to him.'

'That confession's a dummy. I've checked it out and had negative affirmation,' said the Colonel, lapsing into the General's jargon to soften the blow.

'Negative affirmation,' said the General, evidently impressed. 'That's serious. I had no idea.'

'Exactly, sir. That's why I'm asking for an immediate de-escalation of the security directive intelligencewise. I also want this man Wilt handed over to my authority for proper questioning.'

General Belmonte considered the request almost rationally. 'If he isn't Moscow-based, what is he?'

'That's what Central Intelligence intend to find out,' said the Colonel.

Ten minutes later Colonel Urwin left the Airbase Control Centre well satisfied. The General had ordered a security stand-down and Glaushof had been relieved of his custody right to the prisoner.

Theoretically.

In practice getting Wilt out of the Glaushof's house proved rather more awkward. Having visited the Security building and learnt that Wilt had been taken off, still apparently unharmed, to be interrogated at Glaushof's house, the Colonel had driven there with two Sergeants only to realize that 'unharmed' no longer applied. Ghastly noises were emanating from upstairs.

'Sounds like someone's having themselves a whole heap of fun,' said one of the Sergeants as Mrs Glaushof threatened to castrate some horny bastard just as soon as she stopped bleeding to death and why didn't some other cocksucker open the fucking door so she could get out. In the background Glaushof could be heard telling her plaintively to keep her cool, he'd get the door undone, she didn't have to shoot the lock off and would she stop loading that fucking revolver.

Mrs Glaushof replied she didn't intend shooting the fucking lock off, she had other fucking objects in fucking mind, like him and that fucking commie agent who'd bit her and they weren't going to live to tell the tale, not once she'd got that magazine fucking loaded and why didn't shells go in the way they were fucking supposed to? For an instant Wilt's face appeared at the window, only to vanish as a bedside lamp complete with a huge lampshade smashed through the glass and hung upside-down from its cord.

Colonel Urwin studied the thing with horror. Mrs Glaushof's language was foul enough but the shade, covered with a collage of sado-masochistic images cut from magazines,

636

pictures of kittens in baskets and puppy dogs, not to mention several crimson hearts and flowers, was aesthetically so disgusting that it almost unnerved him.

The action had the opposite effect on Glaushof. Less concerned about the likelihood of his drunken wife murdering a Russian spy with a .38 she had been trying to load with what he hoped was 9 mm. ammunition than with the prospect of having his entire house torn apart and its peculiar contents revealed to the neighbours he left the comparative safety of the bathroom and charged the bedroom door. His timing was bad. Having foiled any hope Wilt might have held of escaping by the window Mrs Glaushof had finally loaded the revolver and pulled the trigger. The shot passed through the door, Glaushof's shoulder, and one of the tubes in the hamster's complicated plastic burrow on the staircase wall before embedding in the tufted carpet.

'Jesus Christ,' screamed Glaushof, 'you meant it! You really meant it.'

'What's that?' said Mrs Glaushof, almost as surprised by the consequences of simply pulling the trigger, though definitely less concerned. 'What you say?'

'Oh God,' moaned Glaushof, now slumped to the floor.

'You think I can't shoot the fucking lock off?' Mrs Glaushof enquired. 'You think that? You think I can't?'

'No,' yelled Glaushof. 'No, I don't think that. Jesus, I'm dying.'

'Hypochondriac,' Mrs Glaushof shouted back, evidently paying off an old domestic score. 'Stand back, I'm coming out.'

'For fuck's sake,' squealed Glaushof, eyeing the hole she'd already made in the door near one of the hinges, 'don't aim at the lock.'

'Why not?' Mrs Glaushof demanded.

It wasn't a question Glaushof was prepared to answer. In one final attempt to escape the consequences of her next fusillade he rolled sideways and hit the stairs. By the time he'd crashed to the bottom even Mrs Glaushof was concerned.

'Are you OK, Glausie?' she asked and simultaneously pulled the trigger. As the second shot punched a hole in a Liberace-style bean bag, Wilt acted. In the knowledge that her next shot might possibly do to him what it had already done to

Glaushof and the bag, he picked up a pink furbelowed stool and slammed it down on her head.

'Macho man,' grunted Mrs Glaushof, inappropriate to the end, and slid to the floor. For a moment Wilt hesitated. If Glaushof were still alive, and by the sound of breaking glass downstairs it seemed as though he was, there was no point in trying to break the door down. Wilt crossed to the window.

'Freeze!' shouted a man down below. Wilt froze. He was staring down at five uniformed men crouched behind hand-guns. And this time there was no question what they were aiming at.

Chapter 21

'Logic dictates,' said Mr Gosdyke, 'that we should look at this problem rationally. Now I know that's difficult but until we have definite proof that your husband is being held at Bacon-heath against his will there really isn't any legal action we can take. You do see that?'

Eva gazed into the solicitor's face and saw only that she was wasting time. It had been Mavis' idea that she should consult Mr Gosdyke before she did anything hasty. Eva knew what 'hasty' meant. It meant being afraid of taking real risks and doing something effective.

'After all,' Mavis had said, as they drove back, 'you may be able to apply for a court order or habeas corpus or something. It's best to find out.'

But she didn't need to find out. She'd known all along that Mr Gosdyke wouldn't believe her and would talk about proof and logic. As if life was logical. Eva didn't even know what the word meant, except that it always produced in her mind the image of a railway line with a train running along it with no way of getting off it and going across fields and open countryside like a horse. And anyway when you did reach a station you still had to walk to wherever you really wanted to go. That wasn't the way life worked or people behaved when things were really desperate. It wasn't even the way the Law worked with people being sent to prison when they were old and absent-minded like Mrs Reeman who had walked out of the supermarket without paying for a jar of pickled onions and she never ate pickles. Eva knew that because she'd helped with Meals on Wheels and the old lady had said she never touched vinegar. No, the real reason had been that she'd had a pekinese called Pickles and he'd died a month before. But the Law hadn't seen that, any more than Mr Gosdyke could understand that she already had the proof that Henry was in the airbase because he hadn't been there when the officer's manner had changed so suddenly.

'So there's nothing you can do?' she said and got up.

'Not unless we can obtain proof that your husband really is being held against ...' But Eva was already through the door and had cut out the sounds of those ineffectual words. She went down the stairs and out into the street and found Mavis waiting for her in the Mombasa Coffee House.

'Well, did he have any advice?' asked Mavis.

'No,' said Eva, 'he just said there was nothing he could do without proof.'

'Perhaps Henry'll telephone you tonight. Now that he knows you've been out there and they must have told him ...'

Eva shook her head. 'Why should they have told him?'

'Look, Eva, I've been thinking,' said Mavis, 'Henry's been deceiving you for six months. Now I know what you're going to say but you can't get away from it.'

'He hasn't been deceiving me the way you mean,' said Eva. 'I know that.'

Mavis sighed. It was so difficult to make Eva understand that men were all the same, even a sexually subnormal one like Wilt. 'He's been going out to Baconheath every Friday evening and all that time he's been telling you he's got this prison job. You've got to admit that, haven't you?'

'I suppose so,' said Eva, and ordered tea. She wasn't in the mood for anything foreign like coffee. Americans drank coffee.

'The question you have to ask yourself is why didn't he tell you where he was going?'

'Because he didn't want me to know,' said Eva.

'And why didn't he want you to know?'

Eva said nothing.

'Because he was doing something you wouldn't like. And we all know what men don't think their wives would like to know, don't we?'

'I know Henry,' said Eva.

'Of course you do but we none of us know what even those closest to us are really like.'

'You knew all about Patrick's chasing other women,' said Eva, fighting back. 'You were always going on about his being

640

unfaithful. That's why you got those steroid pills from that beastly Dr Kores and now all he does is sit in front of the telly.'

'Yes,' said Mavis, cursing herself for ever mentioning the fact. 'All right, but you said Henry was undersexed. Anyway that only goes to prove my point. I don't know what Dr Kores put in the mixture she gave you ...'

'Flies,' said Eva.

'Flies?'

'Spanish flies. That's what Henry called them. He said they could have killed him.'

'But they didn't,' said Mavis. 'What I'm trying to get across is that the reason he wasn't performing adequately may have been –'

'He's not a dog, you know,' said Eva.

'What's that got to do with it?'

'Perfo ming. You talk as though he were something in a circus.'

'You know perfectly well what I meant.'

They were interrupted by the arrival of the tea. 'All I'm saying,' Mavis continued when the waitress had left, 'is that what you took for Henry's being undersexed –'

'I said he wasn't very active. That's what I said,' said Eva.

Mavis stirred her coffee and tried to keep calm. 'He may not have wanted you, dear,' she said finally, 'because for the last six months he has been spending every Friday night in bed with some American servicewoman at that airbase. That's what I've been trying to tell you.'

'If that had been the case,' said Eva, bridling, 'I don't see how he could have come home at ten thirty, not if he was teaching as well. He never left the house until nearly seven and it takes at least three-quarters of an hour to drive out there. Two three-quarters make ...'

'One and a half hours,' snapped Mavis. 'That doesn't prove anything. He could have had a class of one.'

'Of one?'

'One person, Eva dear.'

'They're not allowed to have only one person in a class,' said Eva. 'Not at the Tech. If they don't have ten ...'

'Well, Baconheath may be different,' said Mavis, 'and

anyway they fiddle these things. My bet is that Henry's teaching consisted of taking off his clothes and –'

'Which just shows how much you know about him,' interrupted Eva. 'Henry taking his clothes off in front of another woman! That'll be the day. He's too shy.'

'Shy?' said Mavis, and was about to say that he hadn't been so shy with her the other morning. But the dangerous look had come back on to Eva's face and she thought better of it. It was still there ten minutes later when they went out to car park to fetch the quads from school.

'Okay, let's take it from there,' said Colonel Urwin. 'You say you didn't shoot Major Glaushof.'

'Of course I didn't,' said Wilt. 'What would I do a thing like that for? She was trying to blow the lock off the door.'

'That's not the version I've got here,' said the Colonel, referring to a file on the desk in front of him, 'according to which you attempted to rape Mrs Glaushof orally and when she refused to co-operate you bit her leg. Major Glaushof tried to intervene by breaking the door down and you shot him through it.'

'Rape her orally?' said Wilt, 'what the hell does that mean?'

'I prefer not to think,' said the Colonel with a shudder.

'Listen,' said Wilt, 'if anyone was being raped orally I was. I don't know if you've ever been in close proximity to that woman's muff but I have and I can tell you the only way out was to bite the bitch.'

Colonel Urwin tried to erase this awful image. His security classification rated him 'highly heterosexual' but there were limits and Mrs Glaushof's muff was unquestionably off them. 'That doesn't exactly gel with your statement that she was attempting to escape from the room by blowing the lock off with a .38, does it? Would you mind explaining what she was doing that for?'

'I told you she was trying ... well, I've told you what she was trying to do and as a way out I bit her. That's when she got mad and went for the gun.'

'It still doesn't explain why the door was locked and she

had to blow the lock. Are you saying Major Glaushof had locked you in?'

'She'd thrown the fucking key out of the window,' said Wilt wearily, 'and if you don't believe me go and look for the thing outside.'

'Because she found you so sexually desirable she wanted to rape you ... orally?' said the Colonel.

'Because she was drunk.'

Colonel Urwin got up and consulted the sporting print for inspiration. It wasn't easy to find. About the only thing that rang true was that Glaushof's ghastly wife had been drunk. 'What I still don't understand is why you were there in the first place.'

'You think I do?' said Wilt. 'I came out here on Friday night to give a lecture and the next thing I know I've been gassed, injected, dressed up like something that's going to be operated on, driven all over the place with a fucking blanket over my head and asked insane questions about radio trans-formers in my car –'

'Transmitters,' said the Colonel.

'Whatever,' said Wilt. 'And told if I don't confess to being a Russian spy or a fanatical raving Shi'ite Muslim I'm going to have my brains plastered all over the ceiling. And that's just for starters. After that I'm in a horrible bedroom with a woman dressed up like a prostitute who hurls keys out of the window and shoves her dugs in my mouth and then threatens to suffocate me with her cunt. And you're asking me for an explanation?' He sank back in his chair and sighed hope-lessly.

'That still doesn't –'

'Oh, for God's sake,' said Wilt. 'If you want insanity ex-plained go and ask that homicidal maniac Major. I've had a bellyful.'

The Colonel got up and went out the door. 'What do you make of him?' he asked Captain Fortune who had been sitting with a technician recording the interview.

'I've got to say he convinces me,' said Fortune. 'That Mona Glaushof would screw a fucking skunk if there weren't nothing better to hand.'

'I'll say,' said the technician. 'She's been humping Lieutenant

Harah like he's a human vibrator. The guy's been taking mega-vitamins to keep up.'

'Dear God,' said the Colonel, 'and Glaushof's in charge of security. What's he doing letting Mona Messalina loose on this one for?'

'Got a two-way mirror in the bathroom,' said the Captain. 'Could be he gets his thrills through it.'

'A two-way mirror in the bathroom? The bastard's got to be sick watching his wife screwing a guy he thinks is a Russian agent.'

'Maybe he thought the Russkies have got a different technique. Something he could learn,' said the technician.

'I want a check run on that key outside the house,' said the Colonel and went out into the passage.

'Well?' he asked.

'Nothing fits,' said the Captain. 'That corporal in Electronics is no fool. He's certain the equipment he saw in the car was British classified. Definitely non-Russian. No record of it ever being used by anyone else.'

'Are you suggesting he was under surveillance by British Security?'

'It's a possibility.'

'It would be if he hadn't demanded MI5 attendance the moment Glaushof started putting the heat on,' said Urwin. 'Have you ever heard of a Moscow agent calling for British Intelligence when he's been blown? I haven't.'

'So we go back to your theory that the Brits were running an exercise on base security systems. About the only thing that adds up.'

'Nothing adds up for me. If it had been a routine check they'd have come to his rescue by now. And why has he clammed? No point in sweating it out. Against that we've got those transmitters and the fact that Clodiak says he was nervous and agitated all through the lecture. That indicates he's no expert and I don't believe he ever knew his car was tagged. Where's the sense?'

'You want me to question him?' asked the Captain.

'No, I'll go on. Just keep the tape running. We're going to need some help in this.'

He went back into his office and found Wilt lying on the

couch fast asleep. 'Just a few more questions, Mr Wilt,' he said. Wilt stared blearily up at him and sat up.

'What questions?'

The Colonel took a bottle from a cupboard. 'Care for a Scotch?'

'I'd care to go home,' said Wilt.

Chapter 22

In Ipford Police Station Inspector Flint was savouring his triumph. 'It's all there, sir,' he told the Superintendent, indicating a pile of folders on the desk. 'And it's local. Swannell made the contact on a skiing trip to Switzerland. Nice clean place, Switzerland, and of course he says he was the one who was approached by this Italian. Threatened him, he says, and of course our Clive's a nervous bloke as you know.'

'Could have fooled me,' said the Superintendent. 'We nearly did the bugger for attempted murder three years ago. Got away because the bloke he scarred wouldn't press charges.'

'I was being ironical, sir,' said Flint. 'Just saying his story for him.'

'Go on. How did it work?'

'Simple really,' continued Flint, 'nothing too complicated. First they had to have a courier who didn't know what he was doing. So they put the frighteners on Ted Lingon. Threaten him with a nitric acid facial if he doesn't co-operate with his coach tours to the continent. Or so he claims. Anyway he's got a regular run to the Black Forest with overnight stops. The stuff's loaded aboard at Heidelberg without the driver knowing, comes through to Ostend and the night ferry to Dover and halfway across one of the crew dumps the muck over the side. Always on the night run so no one sees. Picked up by a friend of Annie Mosgrave's who happens to be in his floating gin palace nearby and ...'

'Hang on a minute,' said the Superintendent. 'How the hell would anyone find a package of heroin in mid-Channel at night?'

'The same way Hodge has been keeping tabs on Wilt. The muck's in a bloody great suitcase with buoyancy and a radio signal that comes on the moment it hits the water. Bloke beams in on it, hauls it aboard and brings it round to a marker buoy in the Estuary and leaves it there for a frogman to pick up when the gin palace is back in the marina.'

'Seems a risky way of going about things,' said the Superintendent, 'I wouldn't trust tides and currents with that amount of money involved.'

'Oh, they did enough practice runs to feel safe and tying it to the chain of the marker buoy made that part easy,' said Flint. 'And after that it was split three ways with the Hong Kong Charlies handling the London end and Roddie Eaton fixing this area and Edinburgh.'

The Superintendent studied his fingernails and considered the implications of Flint's discoveries. On the whole they seemed entirely satisfactory, but he had a nasty feeling that the Inspector's methods might not look too good in court. In fact it was best not to dwell on them. Defending counsel could be relied on to spell them out in detail to the jury. Threats to prisoners in gaol, murder charges that were never brought ... On the other hand if Flint had succeeded, that idiot Hodge would be scuppered. That was worth a great many risks.

'Are you quite certain Swannell and the rest haven't been spinning you a yarn?' he asked. 'I mean I'm not doubting you or anything but if we go ahead now and they retract those statements in court, which they will do –'

'I'm not relying on their statements,' said Flint. 'There's hard evidence. I think when the search warrants are issued we'll find enough heroin and Embalming Fluid on their premises and clothing to satisfy Forensic. They've got to have spilt some when they were splitting the packages, haven't they?'

The Superintendent didn't answer. There were some things he preferred not to know and Flint's actions were too dubious for comfort. Still if the Inspector had broken a drug ring the Chief Constable and the Home Secretary would be well satisfied, and with crime organized the way it was nowadays there was no point in being too scrupulous. 'All right,' he said finally, 'I'll apply for the warrants.'

'Thank you, sir,' said Flint and turned to go. But the Superintendent stopped him.

'About Inspector Hodge,' he said. 'I take it he's been following a different line of investigation.'

'American airbases,' said Flint. 'He's got it into his head that's where the stuff's been coming in.'

'In that case we'd better call him off.'

But Flint had other plans in mind. 'If I might make a suggestion, sir,' he said, 'the fact that the Drug Squad is pointing in the wrong direction has its advantages. I mean Hodge has drawn attention away from our investigations and it would be a pity to put up a warning signal until we've made our arrests. In fact it might help to encourage him a bit.'

The Superintendent looked at him doubtfully. The last thing the Head of the Drug Squad needed was encouraging. He was demented enough already. On the other hand ...

'And how exactly is he to be encouraged?' he asked.

'I suppose you could say the Chief Constable was looking for an early arrest,' said Flint. 'It's the truth after all.'

'I suppose there's that to it,' said the Superintendent wearily. 'All right, but you'd better be right with your own cases.'

'I will be, sir,' said Flint and left the room. He went down to the car pool where Sergeant Yates was waiting.

'The warrants are all settled,' he said. 'Have you got the stuff?'

Sergeant Yates nodded and indicated a plastic packet on the back seat. 'Couldn't get a lot,' he said, 'Runkie reckoned we'd no right to it. I had to tell him it was needed for a lab check.'

'Which it will be,' said Flint. 'And it's all the same batch?'

'It's that all right.'

'No problem then,' said Flint as they drove out, 'we'll look at Lingon's coach first and then Swannell's boat and the back garden and leave enough for Forensic to pick up.'

'What about Roddie Eaton?'

Flint took a pair of cotton gloves from his pocket. 'I thought we'd leave these in his dustbin,' he said. 'We'll use them on the coach first. No need to bother going to Annie's. There will be something there anyway, and besides, the rest of them will try to get lighter sentences by pointing the finger at her. All we need is three of them as guilty as sin and facing twenty years and they'll drop everyone else in the shit with them.'

648

'Bloody awful way of going about police work,' said Yates after a pause. 'Planting evidence and all.'

'Oh, I don't know,' said Flint. 'We know they're traffickers, they know it, and all we're doing is giving them a bit of their own medicine. Homeopathic, I call it.'

That wasn't the way Inspector Hodge would have described his work. His obsessive interest in the Wilts' extraordinary domestic activities had been alarmingly aggravated by the noises coming from the listening devices installed in the roof space. The quads were to blame. Driven up to their rooms by Eva who wanted them out of the way so that she could think what to do about Henry, they had taken revenge by playing long-playing records of Heavy Metal at one hundred watts per channel. From where Hodge and Runk sat in the van it sounded as though 45 Oakhurst Avenue was being blown apart by an endless series of rythmic explosions.

'What the fuck's wrong with those bugs?' Hodge squealed, dragging the earphones from his head.

'Nothing,' shouted the operator. 'They're highly sensitive ...'

'So am I,' yelled Hodge, stubbing his little finger into his ear in an attempt to get his hearing back, 'and something's definitely wrong.'

'They're just picking up one hell of a lot of interference. Could be any number of things produce that effect.'

'Like a fifty-megaton rock concert,' said Runk. 'Bloody woman must be stone deaf.'

'Like hell,' said Hodge. 'This is deliberate. They must have scanned the place and spotted they were being bugged. And turn that damned thing off. I can't hear myself think.'

'Never known anyone who could,' said Runk. 'Thinking doesn't make a sound. It's an –'

'Shut up,' yelled Hodge, who didn't need a lecture on the workings of the brain. For the next twenty minutes he sat in comparative silence trying to figure out his next move. At every stage of his campaign he had been outmanoeuvred and all because he hadn't been given the authority and back-up he needed. And now the Superintendent had sent a message demanding an immediate arrest. Hodge had countered with

649

a request for a search warrant and had been answered with a vague remark that the matter would be considered. Which meant, of course, that he'd never get that warrant. He was on the point of returning to the station and demanding the right to raid the house when Sergeant Runk interrupted his train of thought.

'That jam session's stopped,' he said. 'Coming through nice and quiet.'

Hodge grabbed the earphones and listened. Apart from a rattling sound he couldn't identify (but which came in fact from Emmeline's hamster Percival getting some exercise in her wheel) the house in Oakhurst Avenue was silent. Odd. The place hadn't ever been silent before when the Wilts were at home. 'The car still outside?' he asked the technician.

The man turned to the car monitor. 'Nothing coming through,' he muttered and swung the aerial. 'They must have been using that din to dismantle the transmitters.'

Behind him Inspector Hodge verged on apoplexy. 'Jesus, you moron,' he yelled, 'you mean you haven't been checking that fucking car all this time?'

'What do you think I am? A bleeding octopus with ears?' the radio man shouted back. 'First I have to cope with all those stupid bugs you laced the house with and at the same time I've got two direction indicators to listen in to. And what's more I'm not a moron.'

But before Hodge could get into a real fight Sergeant Runk had intervened. 'I'm getting a faint signal from the car,' he said. 'Must be ten miles away.'

'Where?' yelled Hodge.

'East, as before,' said Runk. 'They're heading back to Bacon-heath.'

'Then get after them,' Hodge shouted, 'this time the shit isn't going to get back home before I've nabbed him. I'll seal that fucking base off if it's the last thing I do.'

Oblivious of the ill-feeling building up behind her Eva drove steadily towards the airbase. She had no conscious plan, only the determination to force the truth, and Wilt, out of somebody even if that meant setting fire to the car or lying naked in the roadway outside the gates. Anything to gain publicity.

650

And for once Mavis had agreed with her and been helpful too. She had organized a group of Mothers Against The Bomb, some of whom were in fact grandmothers, had hired a coach and had telephoned all the London papers and BBC and Fenland Television to ensure maximum coverage for the demonstration.

'It gives us an opportunity to focus the world's attention on the seductive nature of capitalist military-industrial world domination,' she had said, leaving Eva with only the vaguest idea what she meant but with the distinct feeling that Wilt was the 'It' at the beginning of the sentence. Not that Eva cared what anyone said; it was what they did that counted. And Mavis's demonstration would help divert attention away from her own efforts to get into the camp. Or, if she failed to do that, she would see to it that the name Henry Wilt reached the millions of viewers who watched the news that night.

'Now I want you all to behave nicely,' she told the quads as they drove up to the camp gates. 'Just do what Mummy tells you and everything is going to be all right.'

'It isn't going to be all right if Daddy's been staying with an American lady,' said Josephine.

'Fucking,' said Penelope, 'not staying with.'

Eva braked sharply. 'Who said that?' she demanded, turning a livid face on the quads in the back seat.

'Mavis Motty did,' said Penelope. 'She's always going on about fucking.'

Eva took a deep breath. There were times when the quads' language, so carefully nurtured towards mature self-expression at the School for the Mentally Gifted, seemed appallingly inappropriate. And this was one of those times. 'I don't care what Mavis said,' she declared, 'and anyway it isn't like that. Your father has simply been stupid again. We don't know what's happened to him. That's why we've come here. Now you behave yourselves and –'

'If we don't know what's happened to him how do you know he's been stupid?' asked Samantha, who had always been hot on logic.

'Shut up,' said Eva and started the car again.

Behind her the quads silently assumed the guise of four nice little girls. It was misleading. As usual they had prepared themselves for the expedition with alarming ingenuity. Emmeline had armed herself with several hatpins that had once belonged to Grandma Wilt; Penelope had filled two bicycle pumps with ammonia and sealed the ends with chewing-gum; Samantha had broken into all their piggy banks and had then bought every tin of pepper she could from a perplexed greengrocer; while Josephine had taken several of Eva's largest and most pointed Sabatier knives from the magnet board in the kitchen. In short, the quads were happily looking forward to disabling as many airbase guards as they could and were only afraid that the affair would pass off peacefully. In the event their fears were almost realized.

As they stopped at the gatehouse and were approached by a sentry there were none of those signs of preparedness that had been so obvious the day before. In an effort to maintain that everything was normal and in a 'No Panic Situation' Colonel Urwin had ordered the removal of the concrete blocks in the roadway and had instilled a fresh sense of politeness in the officer in charge of entry to civilian quarters. A large Englishwoman with permed hair and a carload of small girls didn't seem to pose any threat to USAAF security.

'If you'll just pull over there I'll call up the Education Office for you,' he told Eva who had decided not to mention Captain Clodiak this time. Eva drove past the barrier and parked. This was proving much easier than she had expected. In fact for a moment she doubted her judgement. Perhaps Henry wasn't there after all and she had made some terrible mistake. The notion didn't last long. Once again the Wilts' Escort had signalled its presence and Eva was just telling the quads that everything was going to be all right when the Lieutenant appeared from the guardhouse with two armed sentries. 'Pardon me, ma'am,' he said, 'but I'd be glad if you'd step over to the office.'

'What for?' asked Eva.

'Just a routine matter.'

For a moment Eva gazed blankly up at his face and tried to think. She had steeled herself for a confrontation and words like 'stepping over to the office' and 'a routine matter' were somehow threateningly bland. All the same she opened the door and got out.

'And the children too,' said the Lieutenant. 'Everybody out of there.'

'Don't you touch my daughters,' said Eva, now thoroughly alarmed. It was obvious she had been tricked into the base. But this was the opportunity the quads had been waiting for. As the Lieutenant reached for the door handle Penelope poked the end of the bicycle pump through the window and Josephine pointed a carving knife. It was Eva's action that saved him from the knife. She wrenched at his arm and at the same time the ammonia hit him. As the stuff wafted up from his soaked jacket and the two sentries hurled themselves on Eva, the Lieutenant gasped for air and dashed for the guardhouse vaguely aware of the sound of girlish laughter behind him. It sounded demonic to him. Half suffocated he stumbled into the office and pressed the Alert button.

'It rather sounds as if we have another problem,' said Colonel Urwin as sirens wailed over the base.

'Don't include me,' said Wilt. 'I've got problems of my own like trying to explain to my wife what the hell's been happening to me the last God knows how many days.'

But the Colonel was on the phone to the guardhouse. For a moment he listened and then turned to Wilt. 'Your wife a fat woman with four daughters?'

'You could put it like that, I suppose,' said Wilt, 'though frankly I'd leave the "fat" bit out if you meet her. Why?'

'Because that's what just hit the main gate,' said the Colonel and went back to the phone. 'Hold everything ... What do you mean you can't? She's not ... Jesus ... Okay, okay. And cut those fucking sirens.' There was a pause and the Colonel held the phone away from his ear and stared at Wilt. Eva's shouted demands were clearly audible now that the sirens had stopped.

'Give me back my husband,' she yelled, 'and take your filthy paws off me ... If you go anywhere near those children ...' The Colonel put the phone down.

'Very determined woman, is Eva,' said Wilt by way of explanation.

'So I've gathered,' said the Colonel, 'and what I want to know is what she's doing here.'

'By the sounds of things, looking for me.'

'Only you told us she didn't know you were here. So how come she's out there fighting mad and ...' He stopped. Captain Fortune had entered the room.

'I think you ought to know the General's on the line,' he announced. 'Wants to know what's going on.'

'And he thinks *I* know?' said the Colonel.

'Well, someone has to.'

'Like him,' said the Colonel, indicating Wilt, 'and he's not saying.'

'Only because I haven't a clue,' said Wilt with increasing confidence, 'and without wishing to be unnecessarily didactic I'd say no one in the whole wide world knows what the hell's going on anywhere. Half the world's population is starving and the overfed half have a fucking death-wish, and –'

'Oh for Chrissake,' said the Colonel, and came to a sudden decision. 'We're taking this bastard out. Now.'

But Wilt was on his feet. He had watched too many American movies not to have ambivalent feelings about being 'taken out'. 'Oh, no you're not,' he said backing up against the wall. 'And you can cut the bastard abuse too. I didn't do anything to start this fucking madhouse and I've got my family to think about.'

Colonel Urwin looked at the sporting print hopelessly. He'd been right to suspect the British of having hidden depths he would never understand. No wonder the French spoke of 'perfidious Albion'. The bastards would always behave in ways one least expected. In the meantime he had to produce some explanation that would satisfy the General. 'Just say we've got a purely domestic problem on our hands,' he told the Captain, 'and rout Glaushof out. Base security is his baby.'

But before the Captain could leave the room Wilt had reacted again. 'You let that maniac anywhere near my kids and someone's going to get hurt,' he shouted, 'I'm not having them gassed like I was.'

'In that case you better exercise some parental control yourself,' said the Colonel grimly, and headed for the door.

Chapter 23

By the time they reached the parking lot by the gates it was clear that the situation had deteriorated. In an entirely unnecessary effort to rescue their mother from the sentries – Eva had already felled one of the men with a knee-jerk to the groin she had learnt at a Rape Resistance Evening Class – the quads had abandoned the Wilts' car and, by dusting the second sentry with pepper, had put him out of action. After that they had occupied the gatehouse itself and were now holding the Lieutenant hostage inside. Since he had torn off his uniform to escape the ammonia fumes and the quads had armed themselves with his revolver and that of the sentry writhing on the ground outside, they had been able to isolate the guardhouse even more effectively by threatening the driver of an oil tanker which had made the mistake of arriving at the barrier and forcing him to offload several hundred gallons of fuel oil on to the roadway before driving tentatively into the base.

Even Eva had been appalled at the result. As the stuff swilled across the tarmac Lieutenant Harah had driven up rather too hurriedly in a jeep and had tried to brake. The jeep was now enmeshed in the perimeter fence and Lieutenant Harah, having crawled from it, was calling for reinforcements. 'We have a real penetration situation here,' he bawled into his walkie-talkie. 'A bunch of leftist terrorists have taken over the guardhouse.'

'They're not terrorists, they're just little girls,' Eva shouted from inside, only to have her words drowned by the Alert siren which Samantha had activated.

Outside in the roadway Mavis Mottram's busload of Mothers Against The Bomb had gathered in a line and had handcuffed themselves together before padlocking the ends of the line to the fence on either side of the gateway and were dancing something approximate to the can-can and chanting 'End the arms race, save the human' in full view of three TV cameras and a dozen photographers. Above their heads an enormous and remarkable balloon, shaped and veined like an erect penis, swung slowly in the breeze exposing the rather confusing messages, 'Wombs Not Tombs' and 'Screw Cruise Not Us' painted on opposite sides. As Wilt and Colonel Urwin watched, the balloon, evidently force-fed by a hydrogen cylinder, shed its few human pretensions in the shape of an enormous plastic foreskin and turned itself into a gigantic rocket.

'This is going to kill old B52,' muttered the Colonel who had until then been enjoying the spectacle of Lieutenant Harah covered in oil and trying to get to his feet. 'And I can't see the President liking it too much either. That fucking phallus has got to hit prime time with all those cameras.'

A fire truck shot round the corner past them and in a jeep behind it came Major Glaushof, his right arm in a sling and his face the colour of putty.

'Jesus,' said Captain Fortune, 'if that fire truck hits the oil were going to have a body count of thirty of the Mothers.'

But the truck had stopped and men were deploying hoses. Behind them and the human chain Inspector Hodge and Sergeant Runk had driven up and were staring wildly about them. In front the women still kicked up their legs and chanted, the firemen had begun to spray foam on to the oil and Lieutenant Harah, and Glaushof was gesticulating with one hand to a troop of Anti Perimeter Penetration Squad men who had formed up as near the Mothers Against The Bomb as they could get and were preparing to discharge canisters of Agent Incapacitating at them.

'For fuck's sake hold it,' yelled Glaushof but his words were drowned out by the Alert Siren. As the canisters dropped into the roadway at the feet of the human chain Colonel Urwin shut his eyes. He knew now that Glaushof was a doomed man, but his own career was in jeopardy. 'We've got to get those fucking kids out of there before the cameras start playing on them,' he bawled at Captain Fortune. 'Go in and get them.'

The Captain looked at the foam, the oil and the drifting gas. Already a number of MABs had dropped to the ground and Samantha had added to the hazards of approaching the guardhouse by accidentally-on-purpose firing a revolver

656

through one of the windows, an action which had drawn answering fire from Glaushof's APP Squad.

'You think I'm risking my life ...' the Captain began but it was Wilt who took the initiative. Wading through the oil and foam he made it to the guardhouse and presently four small girls and a large woman came out with him. Hodge didn't see them. Like the cameramen his attention was elsewhere, but unlike them he was no longer interested in the disaster taking place at the gates. A canister of AI had persuaded him to leave the scene as quickly as possible. It had also made it difficult to drive. As the police van backed into the bus and then shot forward and ricocheted off a cameraman's car before sliding off the road and onto its side, he had a moment of understanding. Inspector Flint hadn't been such an old fool after all. Anyone who tangled with the Wilt family had to come off worst.

Colonel Urwin shared his feelings. 'We're going to get you out of here in a chopper,' he told Wilt as more women slumped across the gateway.

'And what about my car?' said Wilt. 'If you think I'm leaving ...'

But his protest was shouted down by the quads. And Eva.

'We want to go up in a helicopter,' they squealed in unison.

'Just take me away from all this,' said Eva.

Ten minutes later Wilt looked down from a thousand feet at the pattern of runways and roads, buildings and bunkers and at the tiny group of women being carried from the gate to waiting ambulances. For the first time he felt some sympathy for Mavis Mottram. For all her faults she had been right to pit herself against the banal enormity of the airbase. The place had all the characteristics of a potential extermination camp. True, nobody was being herded into gas chambers and there was no smoke rising from crematoria. But the blind obedience to orders was there, instilled in Glaushof and even in Colonel Urwin. Everyone in fact, except Mavis Mottram and the human chain of women at the gate. The others would all obey orders if the time came and the real holocaust would begin. And this time there would be no liberators, no successive generations to erect memorials to the dead or learn lessons from past horrors. There would be only silence. The wind and the sea the only voices left. And it was the same in Russia and the occupied countries of the Eastern Europe. Worse. There Mavis Mottram was already silenced, confined to a prison or a psychiatric ward because she was idiosyncratically sane. No TV cameras or photographers depicted the new death camps. And twenty million Russians had died to make their country safe from genocide, only to have Stalin's successors too afraid of their own people to allow them to discuss the alternatives to building more machines to wipe life off the face of the earth.

It was all insane, childish and bestial. But above all it was banal. As banal as the Tech and Dr Mayfield's empire-building and the Principal's concern to keep his own job and avoid unfavourable publicity, never mind what the staff thought or the students would have preferred to learn. Which was what he was going back to. In fact nothing had changed. Eva would go on with her wild enthusiasms; the quads might even grow up to be civilized human beings. Wilt rather doubted it. Civilized human beings were a myth, legendary creatures who existed only in writers' imaginations, their foibles and faults expurgated and their occasional self-sacrifices magnified. With the quads that was impossible. The best that could be hoped was that they would remain as independent and uncomfortably non-conforming as they were now. And at least they were enjoying the flight.

Five miles outside the base the helicopter set down beside an empty road.

'You can drop off here,' said the Colonel, 'I'll try and get a car out to you.'

'But we want to go all the way home by helicopter,' shouted Samantha above the roar of the rotors, and was joined by Penelope who insisted she wanted to parachute on to Oakhurst Avenue. It was too much for Eva. Grabbing the quads in turn she bundled them out on to the beaten grass and jumped down beside them. Wilt followed. For a moment the air around him was thick with the downblast and then the helicopter had lifted off and was swinging away. By the time it had disappeared Eva had found her voice.

'Now look what you've been and done,' she said. Wilt stared

658

round at the empty landscape. After the interrogation he had been through he was in no mood for Eva's whingeing.

'Let's start walking,' he said. 'Nobody's coming out to pick us up and we'd better find a bus stop.'

He climbed the bank onto the road and set off along it. In the distance there was a sudden flash and a small ball of flame. Major Glaushof had fired a tracer round into Mavis Mottram's inflated penis. The fireball and the little mushroom cloud of smoke above it would be on the evening TV news in full colour. Perhaps something had been achieved after all.

Chapter 24

It was the end of term at the Tech and the staff were seated in the auditorium, as evidently bored as the students they themselves had previously lectured there. Now it was the Principal's turn. He had spent ten excruciating minutes doing his best to disguise his true feelings for Mr Spirey of the Building Department who was finally retiring, and another twenty trying to explain why financial cuts had ended any hope of rebuilding the engineering block at the very time when the College had been granted the staggering sum of a quarter of a million pounds by an anonymous donor for the purchase of textbooks. In the front row Wilt sat poker-faced among the other Heads of Departments and feigned indifference. Only he and the Principal knew the source of the donation and neither of them could ever tell. The Official Secrets Act had seen to that. The money was the price of Wilt's silence. The deal had been negotiated by two nervous officials from the United States Embassy and in the presence of two rather more menacing individuals ostensibly from the legal division of the Home Office. Not that Wilt had been worried by their attitude. Throughout the discussion he had basked in the sense of his own innocence and even Eva had been overawed and then impressed by the offer of a new car. But Wilt had turned that down. It was enough to know that the Principal, while never understanding why, would always be unhappily aware that the Fenland College of Arts and Technology was once again indebted to a man he would have liked to fire. Now he was lumbered with Wilt until he retired himself.

Only the quads had been difficult to silence. They had enjoyed pumping ammonia over the Lieutenant and disabling sentries with pepper too much not to want to make their exploits known.

'We were only rescuing Daddy from that sexy woman,' said

Samantha when Eva rather unwisely asked them to promise never to talk about what had happened.

'And you'll have to rescue your Mother and me from Dartmoor if you don't keep your damned traps shut,' Wilt had snapped. 'And you know what that means.'

'What?' asked Emmeline, who seemed to be looking forward to the prospect of a prison break.

'It means you'll be taken into care by horrible foster parents and not as a bloody group either. You'll be split up and you won't be allowed to visit one another and . . .' Wilt had launched into a positively Dickensian description of foster homes and the horrors of child abuse. By the time he'd finished the quads were cowed and Eva had been in tears. Which was the first time that had happened and was another minor triumph. It wouldn't last, of course, but by the time they spilled the beans the immediate dangers would be over and nobody would believe them anyway.

But the argument had aroused Eva's suspicions again. 'I still want to know why you lied to me all those months about teaching at the prison,' she said as they undressed that night.

Wilt had an answer for that one too. 'You heard what those men from MI5 said about the Official Secrets Act.'

'MI5?' said Eva. 'They were from the Home Office. What's MI5 got to do with it?'

'Home Office, my foot, Military Intelligence,' said Wilt. 'And if you choose to send the quads to the most expensive school for pseudo-prodigies and expect us not to starve . . .'

The argument had rumbled on into the night but Eva hadn't needed much convincing. The officials from the Embassy had impressed her too much with their apologies and there had been no talk of women. Besides, she had her Henry home again and it was obviously best to forget that anything had happened at Baconheath.

And so Wilt sat on beside Dr Board with a slight sense of accomplishment. If he was fated to fall foul of other people's stupidity and misunderstanding he had the satisfaction of knowing that he was no one's victim. Or only temporarily. In the end he beat them and circumstances. It was better than being a successful bore like Dr Mayfield – or worse still, a resentful failure.

'Wonders never cease,' said Dr Board when the Principal finally sat down and they began to file out of the auditorium, 'A quarter of a million in actual textbooks? It must be a unique event in British education. Millionaires who give donations usually provide better buildings for worse students. This one seems to be a genius.'

Wilt said nothing. Perhaps having some commonsense was a form of genius.

At Ipford Police Station ex-Inspector Hodge, now merely Sergeant Hodge, sat at a computer terminal in Traffic Control and tried to confine his thoughts to problems connected with flow-patterns and off-peak parking systems. It wasn't easy. He still hadn't recovered from the effects of Agent Incapacitating or, worse still, from the enquiry into his actions the Superintendent had started and the Chief Constable had headed.

And Sergeant Runk hadn't been exactly helpful. 'Inspector Hodge gave me to understand the Superintendent had authorized the bugging of Mr Wilt's car,' he said in evidence. 'I was acting on his orders. It was the same with their house.'

'Their house? You mean to say their house was bugged too?'

'Yes, sir. It still is for all I know,' said Runk, 'we had the collaboration of the neighbours, Mr Gamer and his wife.'

'Dear God,' muttered the Chief Constable, 'if this ever gets to the gutter press ...'

'I don't think it will, sir,' said Runk, 'Mr Gamer has moved out and his missus has put the house up for sale.'

'Then get those bloody devices out of there before someone has the place surveyed,' snarled the Chief Constable before dealing with Hodge. By the time he had finished the Inspector was on the verge of a breakdown himself and had been demoted to Sergeant in the Traffic Section with the threat of being transferred to the police dog training school as a target if he put his foot wrong just once again.

To add insult to injury he had seen Flint promoted to Head of the Drug Squad.

'The chap seems to have a natural talent for that kind of work,' said the Chief Constable. 'He's done a remarkable job.'

662

The Superintendent had his reservations but he kept them to himself. 'I think it runs in the family,' he said judiciously.

And for a fortnight during the trial Flint's name had appeared almost daily in the *Ipford Chronicle* and even in some of the national dailies. The police canteen too had buzzed with his praises. Flint the Drug Buster. Almost Flint the Terror of the Courtroom. In spite of all the efforts the defence counsel had made, with every justification, to question the legality of his methods, Flint had countered with facts and figures, times, dates, places and with exhibits, all of which were authentic. He had stepped down from the witness box still retaining the image of the old-fashioned copper with his integrity actually enhanced by the innuendoes. It was enough for the public to look from him to the row of sleazy defendants in the dock to see where the interests of justice lay. Certainly the Judge and jury had been convinced. The accused had gone down with sentences that ranged from nine years to twelve and Flint had gone up to Superintendent.

But Flint's achievement led beyond the courtroom to areas where discretion still prevailed.

'She brought the stuff back from her cousins in California?' spluttered Lord Lynchknowle when the Chief Constable visited him. 'I don't believe a word of it. Downright lie.'

'Afraid not, old chap. Absolutely definite. Smuggled the muck back in a bottle of duty-free whisky.'

'Good God. I thought she'd got it at that rotten Tech. Never did agree with her going there. All her mother's fault.' He paused and stared vacuously out across the rolling meadows. 'What did you say the stuff was called?'

'Embalming Fluid,' said the Chief Constable. 'Or Angel Dust. They usually smoke it.'

'Don't see how you can smoke embalming fluid,' said Lord Lynchknowle. 'Mind you, there's no understanding women, is there?'

'None at all,' said the Chief Constable and with the assurance that the coroner's verdict would be one of accidental death he left to deal with other women whose behaviour was beyond his comprehension.

In fact it was at Baconheath that the results of Hodge's

663

obsession with the Wilt family were being felt most keenly. Outside the airbase Mavis Mottram's group of Mothers Against The Bomb had been joined by women from all over the country and had turned into a much bigger demonstration. A camp of makeshift huts and tents was strung out along the perimeter fence, and relations between the Americans and the Fenland Constabulary had not been improved by scenes on TV of middle-aged and largely respectable British women being gassed and dragged in handcuffs to camouflaged ambulances.

To make matters even more awkward Mavis' tactics of blockading the civilian quarters had led to several violent incidents between US women who wanted to escape the boredom of the base to go souvenir-hunting in Ipford or Norwich and MABs who refused to let them out or, more infuriatingly, allowed them to leave only to stop them going back. These fracas were seen on TV with a regularity that had brought the Home Secretary and the Secretary of State for Defence into conflict, each insisting that the other was responsible for maintaining law and order.

Only Patrick Mottram had benefited. In Mavis' absence he had come off Dr Kores' hormones and had resumed his normal habits with Open University students.

Inside the airbase, too, everything had changed. General Belmonte, still suffering from the effect of seeing a giant penis circumcise itself and then turn into a rocket and explode, had been retired to a home for demented veterans in Arizona where he was kept comfortably sedated and could sit in the sun dreaming of happy days when his B52 had blasted the empty jungle in Vietnam. Colonel Urwin had returned to Washington and a cat-run garden in which he grew scented narcissi to perfection and employed his considerable intelligence to the problem of improving Anglo-American relations.

It was Glaushof who had suffered the most. He had been flown to the most isolated and radioactive testing ground in Nevada and consigned to duties in which his own personal security was in constant danger and his sole responsibility. And sole was the word. Mona Glaushof with Lieutenant Harah in tow had hit Reno for a divorce and was living comfortably in Texas on the alimony. It was a change from the dank Fenlands and the sun never ceased to shine.

It shone too on Eva and 45 Oakhurst Avenue as she bustled about the house and wondered what to have for supper. It was nice to have Henry home and somehow more assertive than he had been before. 'Perhaps,' she thought as she Hoovered the stairs, 'we ought to get away by ourselves for a week or two this summer.' And her thoughts turned to the Costa Brava.

But it was a problem Wilt had already solved. Sitting in The Pig In A Poke with Peter Braintree he ordered two more pints.

'After all I've been through this term I'm not having my summer made hellish in some foul camp site by the quads,' he said cheerfully. 'I've made other arrangements. There's an adventure school in Wales where they do rock-climbing and pony-trekking. They can work their energy off on that and the instructors. I've rented a cottage in Dorset and I'm going down there to read *Jude The Obscure* again.'

'Seems a bit of a gloomy book to take on holiday,' said Braintree.

'Salutary,' said Wilt, 'a nice reminder that the world's always been a crazy place and that we don't have such a bad time of it teaching at the Tech. Besides, it's an antidote to the notion that intellectual aspirations get you anywhere.'

'Talking about aspirations,' said Braintree, 'what on earth are you going to do with the thirty thousand quid this lunatic philanthropist has allotted your department for textbooks?'

Wilt smiled into his pint of best bitter. 'Lunatic philanthropists' was just about right for the Americans with their airbases and nuclear weapons, and the educated idiots in the State Department who assumed that even the most ineffectual liberal do-gooder must be a homicidal Stalinist and a member of the KGB – and who then shelled out billions of dollars trying to undo the damage they'd done.

'Well, for one thing I'm going to donate two hundred copies of *Lord of the Flies* to Inspector Flint,' he said finally.

665

'To Flint? Why him of all people? What's he want with the damned things?'

'He's the one who told Eva I was out at ...' Wilt stopped. There was no point in breaking the Official Secrets Act. 'It's a prize,' he went on, 'for the first copper to arrest the Phantom Flasher. It seems an appropriate title.'

'I daresay it does,' said Braintree. 'Still, two hundred copies is a bit disproportionate. I can't imagine even the most literate policeman wanting to read two hundred copies of the same book.'

'He can always hand them out to the poor sods at the airbase. Must be hell trying to cope with Mavis Mottram. Not that I disagree with her views but the bloody woman is definitely demented.'

'Still leaves you with a hell of a lot of new books to buy,' said Braintree. 'I mean, it's all right for me because the English Department needs books but I shouldn't have thought Communication and –'

'Don't use those words. I'm going back to Liberal Studies and to hell with all that bloody jargon. And if Mayfield and the rest of the social-economic structure merchants don't like it, they can lump it. I'm having it my way from now on.'

'You sound very confident,' said Braintree.

'Yes,' said Wilt with a smile.

And he was.